P9-DXE-459

The Great War: American Front

BOOKS BY HARRY TURTLEDOVE

The Guns of the South

THE WORLDWAR SAGA

Worldwar: In the Balance
Worldwar: Tilting the Balance
Worldwar: Upsetting the Balance
Worldwar: Striking the Balance

THE TIME OF TROUBLES SERIES

The Stolen Throne
Hammer and Anvil
The Thousand Cities

THE VIDESSOS CYCLE

The Misplaced Legion
An Emperor for the Legion
The Legion of Videssos
Sword of the Legion
Videssos Besieged (forthcoming)

THE TALE OF KRISPOS

Krispos Rising
Krispos of Videssos
Krispos the Emperor

Noninterference
Kaleidoscope
A World of Difference
Earthgrip
Departures

How Few Remain

HARRY TURTLEDOVE

THE GREAT WAR: AMERICAN FRONT

THE BALLANTINE PUBLISHING GROUP
NEW YORK

A Del Rey ® Book
Published by The Ballantine Publishing Group

Published in the United States by The Ballantine Publishing Group, a division of Random House, Inc., New York, and simultaneously in Canada by Random House of Canada Limited, Toronto.

Map by Mapping Specialists, Ltd.

http://www.randomhouse.com

ISBN 0-345-40615-X

Chapter art reprinted from *No Man's Land: a postwar sketchbook*, written and illustrated by George Pratt, Tundra Publishing Ltd., 1992
George Pratt is represented by Allen Spiegel Fine Arts
221 Lobos Avenue, Pacific Grove, CA 93950
Fax: (408) 372-4672

Text design by Ann Gold

Manufactured in the United States of America

For Steve and Peter,
who made it better.

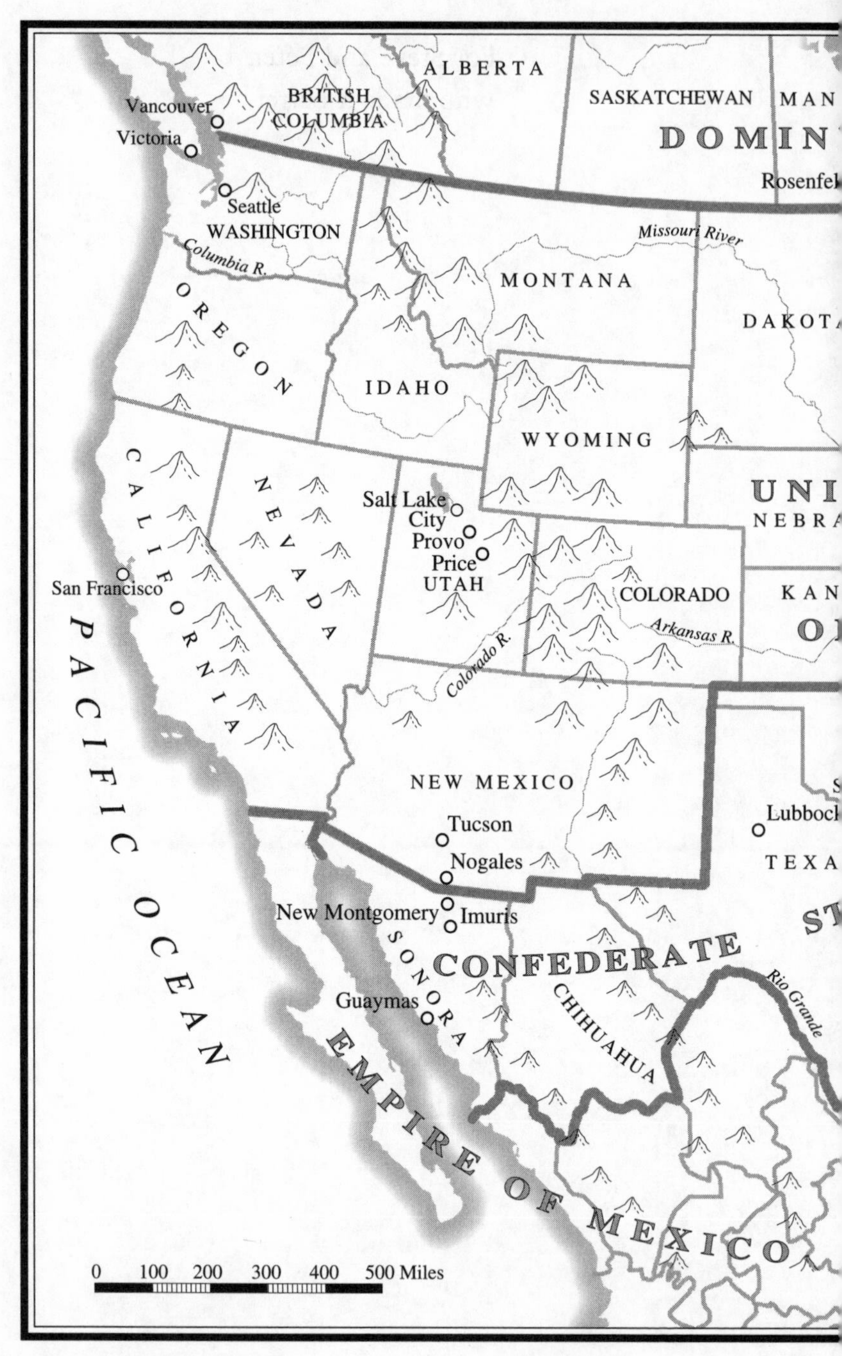

ALBERTA
BRITISH COLUMBIA
SASKATCHEWAN
MAN
DOMIN
Vancouver
Victoria
Rosenfel
Seattle
WASHINGTON
Missouri River
Columbia R.
OREGON
MONTANA
DAKOT
IDAHO
WYOMING
CALIFORNIA
NEVADA
Salt Lake City
Provo
Price
UTAH
UNI
NEBRA
San Francisco
COLORADO
KAN
Arkansas R.
Colorado R.
PACIFIC OCEAN
NEW MEXICO
Tucson
Lubbock
Nogales
TEXA
New Montgomery
Imuris
SONORA
CONFEDERATE
ST
Rio Grande
CHIHUAHUA
Guaymas
EMPIRE OF MEXICO
0 100 200 300 400 500 Miles

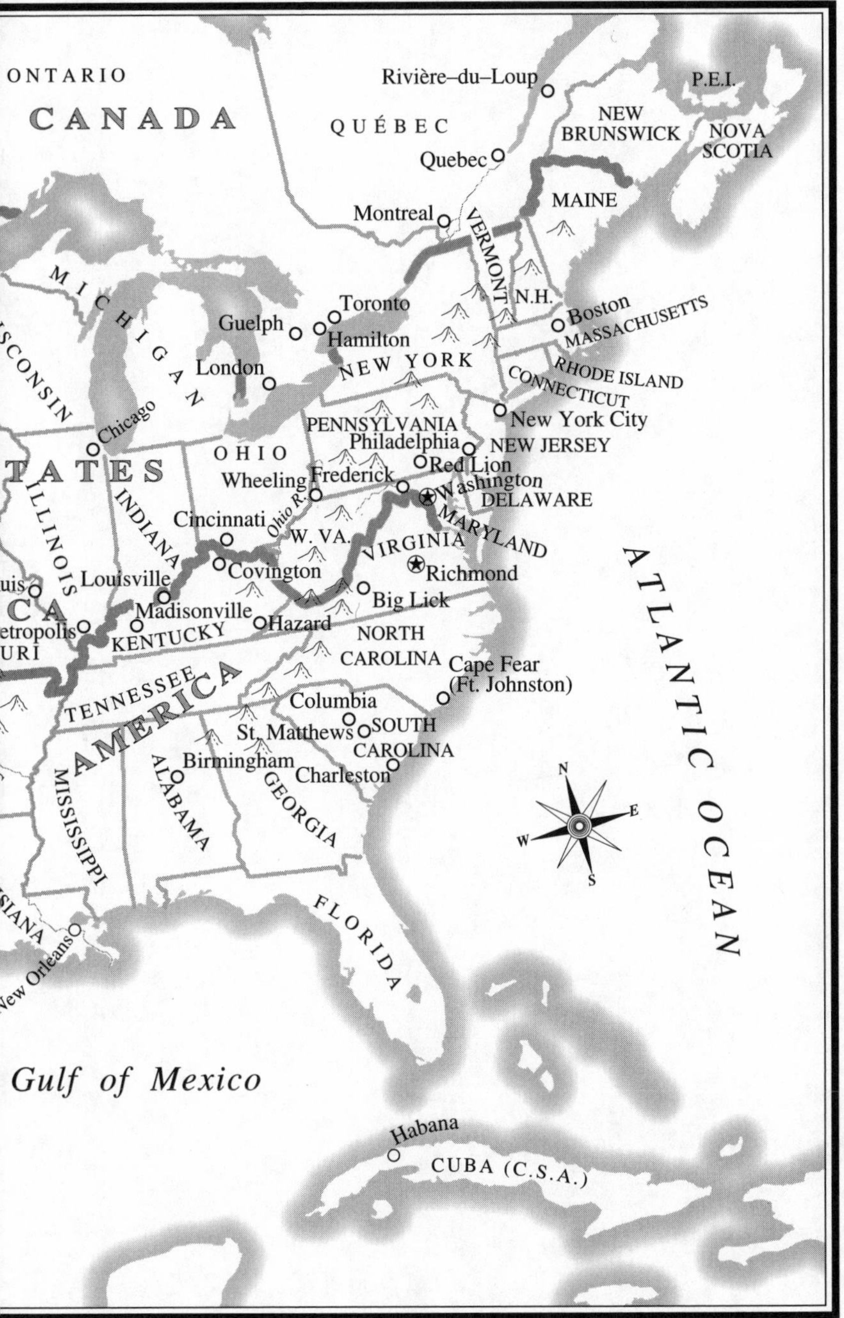

ONTARIO
CANADA
QUÉBEC
Rivière-du-Loup
P.E.I.
NEW BRUNSWICK
NOVA SCOTIA
Quebec
MAINE
Montreal
VERMONT
N.H.
MICHIGAN
Toronto
Guelph
Hamilton
Boston
MASSACHUSETTS
London
NEW YORK
RHODE ISLAND
CONNECTICUT
New York City
Chicago
PENNSYLVANIA
Philadelphia
NEW JERSEY
OHIO
Red Lion
TATES
Wheeling
Frederick
Washington
DELAWARE
ILLINOIS
INDIANA
Cincinnati
Ohio R.
W. VA.
MARYLAND
VIRGINIA
Covington
Richmond
Louisville
Big Lick
Madisonville
Hazard
KENTUCKY
NORTH CAROLINA
Cape Fear (Ft. Johnston)
TENNESSEE
AMERICA
Columbia
St. Matthews
SOUTH CAROLINA
Birmingham
Charleston
ALABAMA
GEORGIA
MISSISSIPPI
FLORIDA
New Orleans
ATLANTIC OCEAN
N
E
W
S
Gulf of Mexico
Habana
CUBA (C.S.A.)

The Great War: American Front

Prelude

1862

1 October—Outside Camp Hill, Pennsylvania

The leaves on the trees were beginning to go from green to red, as if swiped by a painter's brush. A lot of the grass near the banks of the Susquehanna, down by New Cumberland, had been painted red, too, red with blood.

A courier came galloping back to Robert E. Lee's headquarters, his face smudged with black-powder smoke but glowing with excitement beneath the minstrel-show markings. "We have 'em, sir!" he cried to Lee as he reined in his blowing horse. "We have 'em! General Jackson says for me to tell you D. H. Hill's division is around McClellan's left and rolling 'em up. 'God has delivered them into our hands,' he says."

"That is very fine," Lee murmured. He peered through the thick smoke, but piercing it was impossible, even with the polished brass spyglass that lay on the folding table in front of him. He had to rely on reports from couriers like this eager young man, but all the reports, from just after the rising of the sun when the battle was joined till now with it sinking in blood—*more blood,* he thought—behind him, had been what he'd prayed to hear.

Colonel Robert Chilton, his assistant adjutant general, was no more able than the courier to contain his excitement. "Very fine, sir?" he burst out. "It's better than that. With Longstreet holding the Yankees in the center, McLaws outflanking them on the left, and now Stonewall on the right, they're in a sack Napoleon couldn't have got out of. And if there's one soldier in the world who's no Napoleon, it's the 'Young Napoleon' the Federals have."

"General McClellan, whatever his virtues, is not a hasty man," Lee observed, smiling at Chilton's derisive use of the grandiloquent nickname the Northern papers had given the commander of the Army of the Potomac. "Those people"—his own habitual name for the foe—"were also perhaps ill-advised to accept battle in front of a river with only one bridge offering a line of retreat should their plans miscarry."

"I should say they've miscarried," the courier said. "Some of General Jackson's artillery is far enough forward, it's shelling that bridge right now."

"We do have them, sir," Colonel Chilton said. He stiffened to attention and saluted General Lee.

Lee glanced back over his shoulder. "Perhaps an hour's worth of light remaining," he said, then turned to the courier once more. "Tell General Jackson he is to exploit his advantage with all means at his disposal, preventing, as best he can, the enemy's retreat to the eastern bank of the Susquehanna." Better than any other man alive, Jackson knew how to turn a vague order like that into the specific steps needed to destroy the foe before him.

"Yes, sir," the lieutenant said, and repeated the order back to make sure he had it straight. Wheeling his bay gelding, he galloped off towards General Jackson's position.

"The Army of the Potomac cannot hope to resist us, not after this," Colonel Chilton said. "Philadelphia lies open to our men, and Baltimore, and Washington itself."

"I'd not relish attacking the works those people have placed around Washington City," Lee replied, "but you are of course correct, Colonel: that possibility is available to us. Another consideration we cannot dismiss is the probable effect of our victory here upon England and France, both of whom have, President Davis tells me, been debating whether they should extend recognition to our new nation."

"They'll have the devil's own time not doing it now," Chilton declared. "Either we are our own nation or we belong to the United States: those are the only two choices." He laughed and pointed toward the smoke-befogged battlefield. "Abe Lincoln can't say we're under his tyrant's thumb, not after this."

"Diplomacy is too arcane a subject for a poor simple soldier to vex his head over its niceties and peculiarities," Lee said, "but on this occasion, Colonel Chilton, I find it impossible to disagree with you."

4 November—The White House, Washington, D.C.

Both horses that brought Lord Lyons' carriage to the White House were black. So was the carriage itself, and the cloth canopy stretched over it to protect the British minister from the rain. *All very fitting,* Lord Lyons thought, *for what is in effect a funeral.*

"Whoa!" the driver said quietly, and pulled back on the reins. The horses, well-trained animals both, halted in a couple of short, neat strides just in front of the entrance of the American presidential mansion. The driver handed Lord Lyons an umbrella to protect himself against the rain for the few steps he'd need to get under cover.

"Thank you, Miller," Lord Lyons said, unfurling the umbrella. "I expect they will make you and the animals comfortable, and then bring you back out here to drive me off to the ministry upon the conclusion of my appointment with President Lincoln."

"Yes, sir," the driver said.

Lord Lyons got down from the carriage. His feet splashed in the water on the walkway as he hurried toward the White House entrance. A few raindrops hit him in the face in spite of the umbrella. Miller chirruped to the horses and drove off toward the stable.

In the front hall, a colored servant took Lord Lyons' hat and overcoat and umbrella and hung them up. John Nicolay stood waiting patiently while the servant tended to the British minister. Then Lincoln's personal secretary—Lincoln's *de facto* chief of staff—said, "The president is waiting for you, sir."

"Thank you, Mr. Nicolay." Lord Lyons hesitated, but then, as Nicolay turned away to lead him to Lincoln's office, decided to go on: "I would like the president to understand that what I do today, I do as the servant and representative of Her Majesty's government, and that in my own person I deeply regret the necessity for this meeting."

"I'll tell him that, Your Excellency." Nicolay sounded bitter. He was a young man—he could hardly have had more than thirty years—and had not yet learned altogether to subsume his own feelings in the needs of diplomacy. "When you get right down to it, though, what difference does that make?"

When you got right down to it (*American idiom,* Lord Lyons thought), it made very little difference. He was silent as he followed Nicolay upstairs. But for the personal secretary and the one servant, he had seen no one in the White House. It was as if the rest of the staff at the presidential mansion feared he bore some deadly, contagious disease. And so, in a way, he did.

John Nicolay seated him in an antechamber outside Lincoln's office. "Let me announce you, Your Excellency. I'll be back directly." He ducked into the office, closing the door after himself; Lord Lyons hoped he was delivering the personal message with which he had been entrusted. He emerged almost as quickly as he had promised. "President Lincoln will see you now, sir."

"Thank you, Mr. Nicolay," Lord Lyons repeated, striding past the secretary into the office of the president of the United States.

Abraham Lincoln got up from behind his desk and extended his hand. "Good day to you, sir," he said in his rustic accent. Outwardly, he was as calm as if he reckoned the occasion no more than an ordinary social call.

"Good day, Mr. President," Lord Lyons replied, clasping Lincoln's big hand in his. The American chief executive was so tall and lean and angular that, merely by existing, he reminded Lord Lyons of how short, pudgy, and round-faced he was.

"Sit yourself down, Your Excellency." Lincoln pointed to a chair upholstered in blue plush. "I know what you're here for. Let's get on with it, shall we? It's like going to the dentist—waiting won't make it any better."

"Er—no," Lord Lyons said. Lincoln had a gift for unexpected, apt, and vivid similes; one of the British minister's molars gave him a twinge at the mere idea of visiting the dentist. "As Mr. Nicolay may have told you—"

"Yes, yes," Lincoln interrupted. "He did tell me. It's not that I'm not grateful, either, but how you feel about it hasn't got anything to do with the price of whiskey." He'd aged ten years in the little more than a year and a half since he'd taken office; harsh lines scored his face into a mask of grief that begged to be carved into eternal marble. "Just say what you've come to say."

"Very well, Mr. President." Lord Lyons took a deep breath. He really didn't want to go on; he loathed slavery and everything it stood for. But his instructions from London were explicit, and admitted of no compromise. "I am directed by Lord Palmerston, prime minister for Her Majesty, Queen Victoria, who is, I am to inform you, operating with the full approbation and concord of the government of His Majesty Napoleon III, Emperor of France, to propose mediation between the governments of the United States and Confederate States, with a view to resolving the differences between those two governments. Earl Russell, our foreign secretary, generously offers himself as mediator between the two sides."

There. It was said. On the surface, it sounded conciliatory enough. Below that surface— Lincoln was astute enough to see what lay below. "I do thank Lord Palmerston for his good offices," he said, "but, as we deny there is any such thing as the government of the Confederate States, Earl Russell can't very well mediate between them and us."

Lord Lyons sighed. "You say this, Mr. President, with the Army of Northern Virginia encamped in Philadelphia?"

"I would say it, sir, if that Army were encamped on the front lawn of the White House," Lincoln replied.

"Mr. President, let me outline the steps Her Majesty's government and the government of France are prepared to take if you decline mediation," Lord Lyons said, again unwillingly—but Lincoln had to know what he was getting into. "First, the governments of Great Britain and France will immediately extend diplomatic recognition to the Confederate States of America."

"You'll do that anyhow." Like John Nicolay, Lincoln was bitter—and with reason.

"We shall do more than that, at need," the British minister said. "We are prepared to use our naval forces to break the blockade you have imposed against the Confederate States and permit unimpeded commerce to resume between those states and the nations of the world."

"That would mean war between England and France on the one hand and the United States on the other," Lincoln warned.

"Indeed it would, Mr. President—and, as the United States have shown themselves unequal to the task of restoring the Confederate States to their allegiance, I must say I find myself surprised to find you willing to engage in simultaneous conflict with those Confederate States and with the two greatest powers in the world today. I admire your spirit, I admire your courage, very much—but can you not see there are times when, for the good of the nation, spirit and courage must yield to common sense?"

"Let's dicker, Lord Lyons," Lincoln said; the British minister needed a moment to understand he meant *bargain*. Lincoln gave him that moment, reaching into a desk drawer and drawing out a folded sheet of paper that he set on top of the desk. "I have here, sir, a proclamation declaring all Negroes held in bondage in those areas now in rebellion against the lawful government of the United States to be freed as of next January first. I had been saving this proclamation against a Union victory, but, circumstances being as they are—"

Lord Lyons spread his hands with genuine regret. "Had you won such a victory, Mr. President, I should not be visiting you today with the melancholy message I bear from my government. You know, sir, that I personally despise the institution of chattel slavery and everything associated with it." He waited for Lincoln to nod before continuing, "That said, however, I must tell you that an emancipation proclamation issued after the series of defeats Federal forces have suffered would be perceived as a *cri de coeur*, a call for servile insurrection to aid your flagging cause, and as such would not be favorably received in either London or Paris, to say nothing of its probable effect in Richmond. I am truly sorry, Mr. President, but this is not the way out of your dilemma."

Lincoln unfolded the paper on which he'd written the decree abolishing slavery in the seceding states, put on a pair of spectacles to read it, sighed, folded it again, and returned it to its drawer without offering to show it to Lord Lyons. "If that doesn't help us, sir, I don't know what will," he said. His long, narrow face twisted, as if he were in physical pain. "Of course, what you're telling me is that nothing helps us, nothing at all."

"Accept the good offices of Her Majesty's government in mediating between your government and that of the Confederate States," the British minister urged him. "Truly, I believe that to be your best course, perhaps your only course. As Gladstone said last month, the Confederate States have made an army, a navy, and now a nation for themselves."

With slow, deliberate motions, Lincoln took off his spectacles and put them back in their leather case. His deep-set eyes filled with a bitterness beside which that of John Nicolay seemed merely the petulance of a small boy deprived of a cherished sweet. "Take what England deigns to give us at the conference table, or else end up with less. That's what you mean, in plain talk."

"That is what the situation dictates," Lord Lyons said uncomfortably.

"Yes, the situation dictates," Lincoln said, "and England and France dictate, too." He sighed again. "Very well, sir. Go ahead and inform your prime minister that we accept mediation, having no better choice."

"Truly you will go down in history as a great statesman because of this, Mr. President," Lord Lyons replied, almost limp with relief that Lincoln had chosen to see reason—with Americans, you never could tell ahead of time. "And in time, the United States and the Confederate States, still having between them a common language and much common history, shall take their full and rightful places in the world, a pair of sturdy brothers."

Lincoln shook his head. "Your Excellency, with all due respect to you, I have to doubt that. The citizens of the United States *want* the Federal Union preserved. No matter what the Rebels did to us, we would fight on against them—if England and France weren't sticking their oar in."

"My government seeks only to bring about a just peace, recognizing the rights of both sides in this dispute," the British minister answered.

"Yes, you would say that, wouldn't you, *Lord* Lyons?" Lincoln said, freighting the title with a stinging load of contempt. "All the lords and sirs and dukes and earls in London and Paris must be cheering the Rebels on, laughing themselves sick to see our great democracy ground into the dirt."

"That strikes me as unfair, Mr. President," Lord Lyons said, though it wasn't altogether unfair: a large number of British aristocrats were doing exactly as Lincoln had described, seeing in the defeat of the United States a salutary warning to the lower classes in the British Isles. But he put the case as best he could: "The Duke of Argyll, for instance, sir, is among the warmest friends the United States have in England today, and many other leaders by right of birth concur in his opinions."

"Isn't that nice of 'em?" Lincoln said, his back-country accent growing stronger with his agitation. "Fact of the matter is, though, that most of your high and mighty want us cut down to size, and they're glad to see the Rebels do it. They reckon a slaveocracy's better'n no ocracy at all, isn't that right?"

"As I have just stated, sir, no, I do not believe that to be the case," Lord Lyons replied stiffly.

"Oh, yes, you said it. You just didn't make me believe it, is all," Lincoln told him. "Well, you Englishmen and the French on your coattails are guardian angels for the Rebels, are you? What with them and you together, you're too strong for us. You're right about that, I do admit."

"The ability to see what is, sir, is essential for the leader of a great nation," the British minister said. He wanted to let Lincoln down easy if he could.

"I see what is, all right. I surely do," the president said. "I see that you European powers are taking advantage of this rebellion to meddle in America, the way you used to before the Monroe Doctrine warned you to keep your hands off. Napoleon props up a tin-pot emperor in Mexico, and now France and England are in cahoots"—another phrase that briefly baffled Lord Lyons—"to help the Rebels and pull us down. All right, sir." He breathed heavily. "If that's the way the game's going to be played, we aren't strong enough to prevent it now. But I warn you, Mr. Minister, we can play, too."

"You are indeed a free and independent nation. No one disputes that, nor will anyone," Lord Lyons agreed. "You may pursue diplomacy to the full extent of your interests and abilities."

"Mighty generous of you," Lincoln said with cutting irony. "And one fine day, I reckon, we'll have friends in Europe, too, friends who'll help us get back what's rightfully ours and what you've taken away."

"A European power—to help you against England *and* France?" For the first time, Lord Lyons was undiplomatic enough to laugh. American bluster was bad enough most times, but this lunacy— "Good luck to you, Mr. President. Good luck."

1914

George Enos was gutting haddock on the noisome deck of the steam trawler *Ripple* when Fred Butcher, the first mate, sang out, "Smoke off the starboard bow!" That gave George an excuse to pull the latest fish off the deck, gut it, toss it down into the icy, brine-smelling hold, and then straighten up and see what sort of ship was approaching.

His back made little popping noises as he came out of this stoop. *I'm getting too old for this line of work,* he thought, though he was only twenty-eight. He rubbed at his brown mustache with a leather-gloved hand. A fish scale scratched his cheek. The sweat running down his face in the late June heat made the little cut sting.

He followed Butcher's pointing finger with his eyes. "A lot of smoke," he said, whistling low. "That's not just another Georges Bank fishing boat, or a tramp freighter, either." His Boston accent swallowed the r's in the final syllables of the last two words. "Liner, I'd guess, or maybe a warship."

"I think you're right," Butcher said. He was little and skinny and quick and clever, his face seamed by wind and sun and spray till he looked to have ten more years than the forty-five or so he really carried. His mustache was salt and pepper, about evenly mixed. Like Enos, he grew it thick and waxed the ends so they pointed toward his eyes. Half the men in the United States who wore mustaches modeled them after the one gracing Kaiser Wilhelm's upper lip.

Captain Patrick O'Donnell came out of the cabin and pressed a spyglass to his right eye. "Warship, sure enough," he said, his Boston mixed with a trace of a brogue. "Four-stacker—German armored cruiser, unless I'm wrong."

"If you say it, Captain, we'll take it to the bank," Fred Butcher answered. That wasn't apple-polishing. O'Donnell had spent years in the U.S. Navy, rising to chief petty officer, before he retired and went into business for himself. He'd seen German warships at a lot closer than spyglass range; he'd exercised alongside them, out in the middle of the Atlantic, and maybe in the Pacific, too.

"She's going to pass close to us," Enos said. He could see the great gray hull of the ship now, almost bow-on to the *Ripple*. The plume of black coal smoke trailed away behind.

Captain O'Donnell still had the telescope aimed at the approaching ship. "Imperial German Navy, sure enough," he said. "I can make out the ensign. Now—is that the *Roon* or the *Yorck*?" He kept looking, and finally grunted in satisfaction. "The *Yorck*, and no mistaking her. See how her cranes are pierced? If she were the *Roon*, they'd be solid."

"If you say so, Captain. You're the one with the spyglass, after all." Enos' chuckle suited his wry sense of humor. He took another naked-eye look at the oncoming *Yorck*. The cruiser *was* nearly bow-on. When he spoke again, he sounded anxious: "We see her, Captain, but does she see us?"

The question was anything but idle. As the *Yorck* drew near, she seemed more and more like an armored cliff bearing down on the steam trawler. The *Ripple* was 114 feet long and displaced 244 gross tons. That made her one of the bigger fishing boats operating out of Boston harbor. All at once, though, Enos felt as if he were in a rowboat, and a pint-sized rowboat at that.

"How big *is* she, Captain?" Fred Butcher asked. The huge hull and great gun turrets gave him pause, too.

"At the waterline, 403 feet, 3 inches," O'Donnell answered with the automatic accuracy of the longtime Navy man he was. "She displaces 9,050 tons. Four 8.2-inch guns, ten 6-inchers, crew of 557. Four-inch armor amidships, two-inch belts at the ends. She'll make twenty-one knots in a sprint."

"If she runs us down, she won't even notice, in other words," Enos said.

"That's about right, George," O'Donnell answered easily. He took pride in the strength and speed of naval vessels, as if having served on them somehow magically gave him strength and speed as well. Even so, though, his glance flicked to the American flag rippling atop the foremast. The sight of the thirty-four-star banner rippling in the brisk breeze must have reassured him. "They'll see us just fine. Here, if you're still worried, I'll send up a flare, that I will." He dug a cigar out of his jacket pocket, scraped a match against the sole of his boot, and puffed out a cloud almost as malodorous as the coal smoke issuing from the *Yorck*'s stacks.

As if his cigar *had* been a message to the German cruiser, signal flags sprouted from her yards. O'Donnell raised the telescope to his eye once more. The cigar in his mouth jerked sharply upward, a sure sign of good humor. "By

Jesus, they want to know if we have fish to sell!" he burst out. He turned to Butcher. "Tell 'em yes, and don't waste a second doing it."

The affirmative pennant went up almost as quickly as the order had been given. The *Yorck* slowed in the water, drifting to a stop about a quarter-mile from the *Ripple*. Then everyone aboard the steam trawler whooped with delight as the German cruiser let down a boat. "Hot damn!" yelled Lucas Phelps, one of the men minding the trawl the *Ripple* had been dragging along the shallow bottom of Georges Bank. "The Germans, they'll pay us better'n the Bay State Fishing Company ever would."

"And it all goes into our pockets, too," Fred Butcher said gleefully. On fish that made it back to Boston, the crew and the company that owned the boat split the take down the middle. Butcher went on, "We're light five hundred, a thousand pounds of haddock, that's not ever gonna get noticed."

The happy silence of conspiracy settled over the *Ripple*. Before long, the eight men in the *Yorck*'s lifeboat came alongside the trawler. "Permission to come aboard?" asked the petty officer who evidently headed up the little crew.

"Permission granted," Patrick O'Donnell answered, as formally as if he were still in the Navy. He turned to Enos. "Let down the rope ladder, George."

"Right." Enos hurried to obey. He liked extra money as well as anybody.

Dapper in their summer whites, alarmingly neat, alarmingly well shaved, the German sailors looked out of place on the untidy deck of the *Ripple*, where some of the haddock and hake and cusk and lemon sole that George hadn't yet gutted still flopped and writhed and tried to jump back into the ocean. Blood and fish guts threatened the cleanliness of the sailors' trousers.

"I will give you for six hundred kilos of fish forty pfennigs the kilo," the petty officer said to O'Donnell in pretty good English.

O'Donnell scowled in thought, then turned to Butcher. "Would you work that out, Fred? You'll do it faster 'n' straighter than I would."

The first mate got a faraway look in his eyes. His lips moved in silent calculation before he spoke. "Two hundred forty marks overall? That makes sixty bucks for . . . thirteen hundred pounds of fish, more or less. Nickel a pound, Captain, a hair under."

"*Herr Feldwebel,* we'll make that deal," O'Donnell said at once. Everybody on board did his best not to light up like candles on a Christmas tree. Back in Boston, they'd get two cents a pound, three if they were lucky. Then O'Donnell looked sly. "Or, since it ain't like it's your money you're playing with, why don't you give me fifty pfennigs a kilo—you can tell your officers what a damn Jew I am—and we'll throw in a bottle of rum for you and your boys." He turned and called into the galley: "Hey, Cookie! Bring out the quart of medicinal rum, will you?"

"I've got it right here, Captain," Charlie White said, coming out of the galley with the jug in his hand. He held it so the German sailors on the *Ripple* could see it but any officers watching from the *Yorck* with field glasses couldn't. The smile on his black face was broad and inviting, although George expected the rum to be plenty persuasive all by itself. He was fond of a nip himself every now and then.

The petty officer spoke in German to the seamen with him. The low-voice colloquy went on for a minute or two before he switched back to English: "Most times, I would do this thing. Now it is better if I do not. The bargain is as I first said it is."

"Have it your way, *Feldwebel*," O'Donnell answered. "I said I'd make that deal, and I will." His eyes narrowed. "You mind telling me why it's better if you don't take the rum now? Just askin' out of curiosity, you understand."

"Oh, yes—curiosity," the petty officer said, as if it were a disease he'd heard of but never caught. "You have on this boat, Captain, a wireless telegraph receiver and transmitter?"

"No," O'Donnell told him. "I'd like to, but the owners won't spring for it. One of these days, maybe. How come?"

"I should not anything say," the petty officer answered, and he didn't anything say, either. Instead, he gave O'Donnell the 240 marks he'd agreed to pay. O'Donnell handed the money to Butcher, who stuck it in his pocket.

The captain of the *Ripple* kept on trying to get more out of the German sailor, but he didn't have any luck. Finally, in frustration, he gave up and told George Enos, "Hell with it. Give 'em their fish and we'll all go on about our business."

"Right," Enos said again. Had he got the extra ten pfennigs a kilo, he would have worked extra hard to make sure the *Yorck* got the finest fish he had in the hold. Some of the haddock scrod down there, the little fellows just over a pound, would melt in your mouth. When Charlie fried 'em in butter and bread crumbs—he got hungry just thinking about it.

But the young fish would also bring better prices back at the docks. He gave the Germans the bigger haddock and sole the trawl had scooped up from the bottom of the sea. They'd be good enough, and then some.

The Germans didn't raise a fuss. They were sailors, but they weren't fishermen. Their boat rode appreciably lower in the water when they cast off from the *Ripple*'s rail and rowed back to the cruiser from which they'd come. The *Yorck*'s crane lifted them out of the water and back on deck.

More flags broke out on the signal lines as the *Yorck* began steaming toward Boston once more. "Thank you," Captain O'Donnell read through the spyglass. "Signal 'You're welcome,' Fred."

"Sure will, Captain," the mate said, and did.

George wished he had a good tall tumbler of Cookie's rum. Moving better than half a ton of fish out of the hold was hard work. With that on his mind, he asked Lucas Phelps, "Ever hear of a sailor turning down the jug?"

"Not when you stand to get away with it clean as a whistle, like them squareheads did," Phelps answered. "Wonder what the hell was chewin' on their tails. That's good rum Cookie's got, too."

"How do you know?" Enos asked him. Phelps laid a finger alongside his nose and winked. By the veins in that nose, he knew rum well enough to be a connoisseur. George Enos chuckled. Sure enough, he'd wheedled a shot or two out of Charlie himself. It helped compress the endless monotony of life aboard a fishing boat.

They hauled in the trawl full of flipping, twisting bottom fish. Once the load had gone into the hold, Captain O'Donnell peered down in there to see how high the fish were stacked. They could have piled in another couple of trawlfuls, but O'Donnell said, "I think we're going to head for port. We're up over twenty tons; the owners won't have anything to grouse about. And we'll have some extra money in our pockets once Fred turns those marks into dollars at the bank."

Nobody argued with him. Nobody would have argued with him if he'd decided to stay out another day or two and fill the hold right up to the hatches with haddock. He made his pay by having the answers.

Enos went into the galley for a mug of coffee. He found Fred Butcher in there, killing time with the Cookie. By the rich smell rising from Butcher's mug, he had more than coffee in there. Enos blew on his own mug, sipped, and then said, "Bet we'd be out longer if that petty officer hadn't got the captain nervous."

"Bet you're right," the mate said. "Captain O'Donnell, he doesn't like not knowing what's going on. He doesn't like that even a little bit." Cookie nodded solemnly. So did George. Butcher's comment fit in well with his earlier thought about the captain: if he didn't have the answers, he'd go after them.

The *Ripple* puffed back toward Boston. At nine knots, she was most of a day away from T Wharf and home. Supper, near sunset, was corned beef and sauerkraut, which made the sailors joke about Charlie White's being a German in disguise. "Hell of a disguise, ain't it?" the cook said, taking the ribbing in good part. He unbuttoned his shirt to show he was dark brown all over.

"You must be from the Black Forest, Charlie, and it rubbed off on you," Captain O'Donnell said, which set off fresh laughter. Enos hadn't heard of the Black Forest till then—he'd gone to work when he was a kid, and had little schooling—but from the way the captain talked about it, he figured it was a real place in Germany somewhere.

They rigged their running lamps and chugged on through the night. The next day, they passed between Deer Island Light and the Long Island Head

Light, and then between Governor's Island and Castle Island as they steamed toward T Wharf.

On the north side of the Charles River, over in Charlestown, lay the Boston Navy Yard. Enos looked that way as soon as he got the chance. So did Captain O'Donnell, with the spyglass. "There's the *Yorck*, all right, along with the rest of the western squadron of the High Seas Fleet," he said. "Doesn't *look* like anything's wrong aboard 'em, any more than it does on our ships. All quiet, seems like." He sounded annoyed, as if he blamed the Germans and the Americans—easily distinguishable because their hulls were a much lighter gray—for the quiet.

Fred Butcher had his eye on profit and loss: he was looking ahead to T Wharf. "Not many boats tied up," he said. "We ought to get a good price at the Fish Exchange."

They tied up to the wharf and came up onto it to get their land legs back after more than a week at sea. An old, white-bearded man awkwardly pushing a fish cart with one hand and a hook mounted on the stump of his other wrist folded his meat hand into a fist and shook it at Charlie White. "You go to hell, you damn nigger!" he shouted in a hoarse, raspy voice. "Wasn't for your kind, we wouldn't have fought that war and this here'd still be one country."

"*You* go to hell, Shaw!" Enos shouted back at him. He turned to the Cookie. "Don't pay him any mind, Charlie. Remember, his family were mucky-mucks before the damn Rebels broke loose. They lost everything after the war, and he blames colored folks for it."

"Lots of white folks do that," Charlie said, and then shut up. It was hard for the few Negroes in the United States to get away from the scapegoat role that had dogged them for more than fifty years now. Compared to their colored brethren south of the Mason-Dixon line, they had it easy, but that wasn't saying much. The Rebels didn't have nigger hunts through the streets, either—those were an American invention, like the telegraph and the telephone.

"You're jake with us, Charlie," Lucas Phelps said, and all the fishermen from the *Ripple* nodded. They'd proved that, in brawls on the wharf and in the saloons just off it. George Enos rubbed a scarred knuckle he'd picked up in one of those brawls.

T Wharf was chaos—horse-drawn wagons and gasoline trucks, pushcarts and cats and dealers and screeching gulls and arguments and, supreme above all else, fish—in the wagons, in the trucks, in the carts, in the air.

Shouting newsboys only added to the racket and confusion. George didn't pay them any mind till he noticed what they were shouting: "Archduke dies in Sarajevo! Bomb blast kills Franz Ferdinand and his wife! Austria threatens war on Serbia! Read all about it!"

He dug in the pocket of the overalls he wore under his oilskins for a couple of pennies and bought a *Globe*. His crewmen crowded round him to read along. A passage halfway down the column leaped out at the eye. He read it aloud: "President Roosevelt stated in Philadelphia yesterday that the United States, as a member of the Austro-German Alliance, will meet all commitments required by treaty, whatever the consequences, saying, 'A nation at war with one member of the Alliance is at war with every member.' " He whistled softly under his breath.

Lucas Phelps' finger stabbed out toward a paragraph farther down. "In Richmond, Confederate President Wilson spoke in opposition to the oppression of small nations by larger ones, and confirmed that the Confederate States are and shall remain part of the Quadruple Entente." Phelps spoke up on his own hook: "England and France'll lead 'em by the nose the way they always do, the bastards."

"They'll be sorry if they try anything, by jingo," Enos said. "I did my two years in the Army, and I wouldn't mind putting the old green-gray back on, if that's what it comes down to."

"Same with me," Phelps said.

Everybody else echoed him, sometimes with profane embellishments, except Charlie White. The Negro cook said, "They don't draft colored folks into the Army, but damned if I know why. They gave me a rifle, I'd shoot me a Confederate or three."

"Good old Charlie!" George declared. " 'Course you would." He turned to the rest of the crew. "Let's buy Charlie a beer or two." The motion carried by acclamation.

From the heights of Arlington, Sergeant Jake Featherston peered across the Potomac toward Washington, D.C. As he lowered the field glasses from his eyes, Captain Jeb Stuart III asked him, "See anything interesting over there in Yankeeland?"

"No, sir," Featherston answered. His glance slipped to one of the three-inch howitzers sited in an earthen pit not far away. "Time may come when, if we do see anything interesting, we'll blow it to hell and gone." He paused to shift the chaw of tobacco in his cheek and spit a stream of brown juice onto the red dirt. "I'd like that."

"So would I, Sergeant; so would I," Captain Stuart said. "My father got the chance to hit the damnyankees a good lick thirty years ago, back in the Second Mexican War." He pointed over the river. "They repaired the White House and the Capitol, but we can always hit them again."

He struck a pose intended to show Featherston he was not only a third-generation Confederate officer but also as handsome as either his famous father—hero of the Second Mexican War—or his even more famous grandfather—hero of the War of Secession and martyr during the Second Mexican War. That might even have been true, though the mustache and little tuft of chin beard he wore made him look more like a Frenchman than a dashing cavalry officer of the War of Secession.

Well, Featherston had nothing against handsome, though he didn't incline that way himself. Though he was a first-generation sergeant, he had nothing against third-generation officers . . . so long as they knew what they were doing. And he certainly had nothing against Frenchmen. The guns in his battery were copies of French 75s.

Pointing over to the one at which he'd looked before, he said, "Sir, all you got to do is tell me which windows you want knocked out of the White House and I'll take care of it for you. You can rely on that."

"Oh, I do, Sergeant, I do," Captain Stuart answered. A horsefly landed on the sleeve of his butternut tunic. The British called the same color khaki, but, being tradition-bound themselves, they didn't try to make the Confederacy change the name it used. Stuart jerked his arm. The fly buzzed away.

"If they'd had guns like this in your grandfather's day, sir, we'd have given Washington hell from the minute Virginia chose freedom," Featherston said. "Not much heavier than an old Napoleon, but four and a half miles' worth of range, and accurate out to the end of it—"

"That would have done the job, sure enough," Stuart agreed. "But God was on our side as things were, and the Yankee tyrants could no more stand against men who wanted to be free than King Canute could hold back the tide." He took off his visored cap—with piping in artillery red—and fanned himself with it. "Hot and sticky," he complained, as if that were surprising in Virginia in July. He raised his voice: "Pompey!" When the servant did not appear at once, he muttered under his breath: "Shiftless, worthless, lazy nigger! *Pompey!*"

"Here I is, suh!" the Negro said, hurrying up at a trot. Sweat beaded his cheeks and the bald crown of his head.

"Took you long enough," Stuart grumbled. "Fetch me a glass of something cold. While you're at it, bring one for the sergeant here, too."

"Somethin' col'. Yes, suh." Pompey hurried off.

Watching him go, Stuart shook his head. "I do wonder if we made a mistake, letting our British friends persuade us to manumit the niggers after the Second Mexican War." He sighed. "I don't suppose we had much choice, but even so, we may well have been wrong. They're an inferior race, Sergeant. Now that they are free, we still can't trust them to take a man's place. So what has freedom got them? A little money in their pockets to spend foolishly, not a great deal more."

Featherston had been a boy when the Confederacy amended the Constitution to require manumission. He remembered his father, an overseer, cussing about it fit to turn the air blue.

Captain Stuart sighed again. He might have been thinking along with Featherston, for he said, "The amendment never would have passed if we hadn't admitted Chihuahua and Sonora after we bought them from Maximilian II. They didn't understand things so well down there—they still don't, come to that. But we wouldn't have our own transcontinental railroad without them, so it may have been for the best after all. Better than having to ship through the United States, that's certain."

"Yes, sir," Featherston agreed. "The Yankees thought so, too, or they wouldn't have gone to war to keep us from having 'em."

"And look what it got them," Stuart said. "Their capital bombarded, a blockade on both coasts, all the naval losses they could stand, their cities up on the Great Lakes shelled. Stupid is what they were—no other word for it."

"Yes, sir," the sergeant repeated. Like any good Southerner, he took the stupidity of his benighted distant cousins north of the Potomac as an article of faith. "If Austria does go to war against Serbia—"

It wasn't changing the subject, and Captain Stuart understood as much. He picked up where Featherston left off: "If that happens, France and Russia side with Serbia. You can't blame 'em; the Serbian government didn't do anything wrong, even if it was crazy Serbs who murdered the Austrian crown prince. But then what does Germany do? If Germany goes to war, and especially if England comes in, we're in the scrap, no doubt about it."

"And so are they." Featherston looked across the river again. "And Washington goes up in smoke." His wave encompassed the heights. "Our battery of three-inchers here is a long way from the biggest guns we've got trained on 'em, either."

"Not hardly," Stuart said with a vigorous nod. "You think Cowboy Teddy Roosevelt doesn't know it?" He spoke the U.S. president's name with vast contempt. "Haven't seen him south of Philadelphia since this mess blew up, nor anybody from their Congress, either."

Featherston chuckled. "You don't see anybody much there when it gets hot." He wasn't talking about the weather. "The last thirty years, they find somewheres else to go when it looks like there's liable to be shooting between us and them."

"They were skedaddlers when we broke loose from 'em, and they're still skedaddlers today." Stuart spoke with conviction. Then his arrogant expression softened slightly. "One thing they always did have, though, was a godawful lot of guns."

Now he looked across the Potomac, not at the White House and Capitol so temptingly laid out before him but at the heights back of the low ground by the river on which Washington sat. In those heights were forts with guns manned by soldiers in uniforms not of butternut but of green so pale it was almost gray. The forts had been there to protect Washington since the War of Secession. They'd been earthworks then. Some, those with fieldpieces like the ones Captain Stuart commanded, still were. Those that held big guns, though, were concrete reinforced with steel, again like their Confederate opposite numbers.

"I don't care what they have," Featherston declared. "It won't stop us from blowing that nest of damnyankees right off the map."

"That's so." Captain Stuart's gaze swung from the United States back to his own side of the river and Arlington mansion, the Doric-columned ancestral estate of the Lee family. "That won't survive, either. They'd have wrecked it thirty years ago if their gunnery hadn't been so bad. They aren't as good as we are now"—again, he spoke of that as if it were an article of faith—"but they're better than they used to be, and they're plenty good enough for that."

" 'Fraid you're right, sir," Featherston agreed mournfully. "They hate Marse Robert and everything he stood for."

"Which only proves what kind of people *they* are," Stuart said. He turned his head. "Here's Pompey, back at last. Took you long enough."

"I's right sorry, Marse Jeb," said the Negro; he carried on a tray two sweating glasses in which ice cubes tinkled invitingly. "I's right sorry, yes I is. Here—I was makin' this here nice fresh lemonade fo' you and Marse Jake, is what took me so long. *Ju*-ly in Virginia ain't no fun for nobody. Here you go, suh."

Featherston took his glass of lemonade, which was indeed both cold and good. As he drank, though, he narrowly studied Pompey. He didn't think Stuart's servant was one bit sorry. When a Negro apologized too much, when he threw "Marse" around as if he were still a slave, odds were he was shamming and, behind his servile mask, either laughing at or hating the white men he thought he was deceiving. Thanks to what Jake's father had taught him, he knew nigger tricks.

What could you do about that kind of shamming, though? The depressing answer was, *not much*. If you insisted—rightly, Featherston was convinced—blacks show whites due deference, how could you punish them for showing more deference than was due? You couldn't, not unless they were openly insolent, which Pompey hadn't been.

In fact, his show of exaggerated servility had taken in his master. "Get on back to the tent now, Pompey," Stuart said, setting the empty glass on the Negro's tray. He smacked his lips. "That was mighty tasty, I will tell you."

"Glad you like it, suh," Pompey said. "How's yours, Marse Jake?"

"Fine," Featherston said shortly. He pressed the cold glass to his cheek, sighed with pleasure, and then put the glass beside the one Stuart had set on the tray. With a low bow, Pompey took them away.

"He's all right, even if I do have to get down on him," Stuart said, watching the Negro's retreat. "You just have to know how to handle niggers, is all."

"Yes, sir," Featherston said once more, this time with the toneless voice noncommissioned officers used to agree with their superiors when in fact they weren't agreeing at all. Stuart didn't notice that, any more than he'd noticed Pompey laying the dumb-black act on with a trowel. He was a pretty fair officer, no doubt about it, but he wasn't as smart as he thought he was.

Of course, when you got right down to it, who was?

Cincinnatus stepped on the brake as he pulled the Duryea truck up behind the warehouse near the Covington docks. He muttered a curse when a policeman—worse, by the peacock feather in his cap a Kentucky state trooper—happened to walk past the alleyway and spy him.

The trooper cursed, too, and loudly: he didn't have to hide what he thought. He yanked his hogleg out of its holster and approached the Negro at a swag-bellied trot. Pointing the revolver at Cincinnatus' face, he growled, "You better show me a pass, or you is one dead nigger."

"Got it right here, boss." Cincinnatus showed more respect than he felt. He pulled the precious paper out of his passbook and handed it to the state trooper.

The man's lips moved as he read: "Cincinnatus works for Kennedy Shipping and has my leave to drive the Kennedy Shipping truck in pursuit of his normal business needs. Thomas Kennedy, proprietor." He glowered at Cincinnatus. "I don't much hold with niggers drivin', any more'n I do with women." Then, grudgingly: "But it ain't against the law—if you're really Tom Kennedy's nigger. What do you say if I call him on the tellyphone, hey?"

"Go ahead, boss," Cincinnatus said. He was on safe ground there.

The trooper stuck the pistol back in its holster. "Ahh, the hell with it," he said. "But I tell you somethin', an' you better listen good." He pointed north toward the Ohio River. "Just across there it's the You-nited States, right?" He waited for Cincinnatus to nod before going on, "Any day now, all hell's gonna break loose between us and them. Some people, they see niggers like you down here by the docks or anywhere near, they ain't gonna ask to see your pass. They gonna figger you're a spy an' shoot first, then stop an' ask questions."

"I got you, boss," Cincinnatus assured him. The trooper nodded and went on his way. When his back was turned, Cincinnatus allowed himself the luxury of a long, silent sigh of relief. That hadn't turned out so bad as it might have, not anywhere near. He was resigned to playing the servant to every white man he saw; if you didn't want to end up swinging from a lamppost, you did what you had to do to get by. And the state trooper had even given him what the man meant as good advice. That didn't happen every day.

As far as Cincinnatus was concerned, the fellow was crazy, but that was another matter. Keep all the black folks away from the Covington docks?

"Good luck, Mr. Trooper, sir," Cincinnatus said with a scornful laugh. Every longshoreman and roustabout on the docks was colored. White men dirty their hands with such work? Cincinnatus laughed again.

Then, all at once, he sobered. Maybe the state trooper wasn't so crazy after all. If war came, no riverboats would come down the Ohio from the United States or up it from the Mississippi and the heart of the Confederacy. Both sides had guns up and down the river trained at each other. Without that trade, what would the dockworkers do? For that matter, what would Cincinnatus do?

He looked toward the Ohio himself. One thing he wouldn't do, he figured, was try to run off to the United States, no matter how the trooper worried about that. In the Confederacy, there were more Negroes around than whites wanted (except when dirty work needed doing), so the whites gave them a hard time. In the United States, which had only a relative handful of Negroes, the whites didn't want any more—so they gave them a hard time.

"Shit, even them big-nosed Jews got it better up there than we-uns do," Cincinnatus muttered. Somebody could doubt whether you were a Jew. Wasn't any doubting about whether he was black.

Wasn't any doubt he'd spent too long daydreaming in the truck, either. A big-bellied white man in overalls and a slouch hat came out of the warehouse office and shouted, "That you out there, Cincinnatus, or did Tom Kennedy get hisself a real for-true dummy for a driver this time?"

"Sorry, Mr. Goebel," Cincinnatus said as he descended. For once, he more or less meant it. He knew he had been sitting when he should have been working.

"Sorry, he says." Goebel mournfully shook his head. He pointed to a hand truck. "Come on, get those typewriters loaded. Last things I got in this warehouse." He sighed. "Liable to be the last Yankee goods we see for a long time. I ain't old enough to remember the War of Secession, but the Second Mexican War, that was just a little feller. This one here, it's liable to be bad."

Cincinnatus didn't remember the Second Mexican War, he was within a year either way of twenty-five. But the newspapers had been screaming war for the past week, troops in butternut had been moving through the streets, politicians were ranting on crates on every corner . . . "Don't sound good," Cincinnatus allowed.

"If I was you, I'd get out of town," Goebel said. "My cousin Morton, he called me from Lexington yesterday and said, Clem, he said, Clem, you shake your fanny down here where them cannons can't reach, and I reckon I'm gonna take him up on it, yes I do."

White folks take so much for granted, Cincinnatus thought as he stacked crated typewriters on the dolly and wheeled it out toward the Duryea. If Clem Goebel wanted to get out of Covington, he just upped and went. If Cincinnatus wanted to get out of town and take his wife with him, he had to get written permission from the local commissioner of colored affairs, get his passbook stamped, wait till acknowledgment came back from the state capital—which could and usually did take weeks—then actually move, re-register with his new commissioner, and get the passbook stamped again. Any white man could demand to see that book at any time. If it was out of order—well, you didn't want to think what could happen then. Jail, a fine he couldn't afford to pay, anything a judge—bound to be a mean judge—wanted.

The typewriters were heavy. The stout crates in which they came just added to the weight. Cincinnatus wasn't sure he'd be able to fit them all into the bed of the truck, but he managed. By the time he was done, the rear sagged lower on its springs. Sweat soaked through the collarless, unbleached cotton shirt he wore.

Clem Goebel had stood around without lifting a finger to help: he took it for granted that that sort of labor was nigger work. But he wasn't the worst white man around, either. When Cincinnatus was done, he said, "Here, wait a second," and disappeared into his little office. He came back with a bottle of Dr Pepper, dripping water from the bucket that kept it, if not cold, cooler than the air.

"Thank you, sir. That's right kind," Cincinnatus said when Goebel popped off the cap with a church key and handed him the bottle. He tilted back his head and gulped down the sweet, spicy soda water till bubbles went up his nose. When the bottle was empty, he handed it back to Goebel.

"Go on, keep it," the warehouseman said. Cincinnatus stowed it in the truck after thanking him again. For once, he felt only half a hypocrite: he'd gladly pocket the penny deposit. He cranked the engine to start it, got the truck in gear, and headed south down Greenup Street toward Kennedy's storerooms.

A policeman in gray uniform and one of the tall British-style hats that always reminded Cincinnatus of fireplugs held up a hand to stop him at the corner of Fourth and Greenup: a squadron of cavalry, big, well-mounted white men with carbines on their shoulders, revolvers on their hips, and sabers mounted on their saddles, was riding west along Fourth. *Probably going to camp in Devon Park,* Cincinnatus thought.

People—white people—cheered and waved as the cavalry went by. Some of them waved Maltese-cross battle flags like the one that flapped at the head of the squadron, others Stars and Bars like the sixteen-star banner above the post office across the street from Cincinnatus. The cavalrymen smiled at the pretty girls they saw; a couple of them doffed their plumed hats, which looked much like the one the Kentucky state trooper had worn but were decorated with the yellow cord marking the mounted service.

After the last horse had clopped past, the Covington policeman, reveling in his small authority, graciously allowed north-south traffic to flow once more. Cincinnatus stepped on the gas, hoping his boss wouldn't cuss him for dawdling.

He'd just pulled up in front of Tom Kennedy's establishment when a buzzing in the air made him look up. "God almighty, it's one o' them aeroplanes!" he said, craning his neck to follow it as it flew up toward the Ohio.

"What are you doing lollygagging around like that, goddamn it?" Kennedy shouted at him. But when he pointed up into the sky, his boss stared with him till the aeroplane was out of sight. The head of the shipping company whistled. "I ain't seen but one o' those before in all my born days—that barnstorming feller who came through town a couple years ago. Doesn't hardly seem natural, does it?"

"No, sir," said Cincinnatus, whose acquaintance with flying machines was similarly limited. "That wasn't no barnstormin' aeroplane, though—did y'all see the flag painted on the side of it?"

"Didn't even spy it," Kennedy confessed. "I was too busy just gawpin', and that's a fact." He was a big, heavyset fellow of about fifty, with a walrus mustache and ruddy, tender Irish skin that went into agonies of prickly heat every summer, especially where he shaved. Now he turned a speculative eye toward Cincinnatus. He was a long way from stupid, and noticed others who weren't. "You don't miss much, do you, boy?"

"Try not to, sir," Cincinnatus answered. "Never can tell when somethin' you see, it might come in handy."

"That's a fact," Kennedy said. "You're pretty damn sharp for a nigger, that's another fact. You aren't shiftless, you know what I mean? You act like you want to push yourself up, get things better for your wife, the way a white man would. Don't see that every day."

Cincinnatus just shrugged. Everything Kennedy said about him was true; he wished he hadn't made his ambition so obvious to his boss. It gave Kennedy one more handle by which to yank him, as if being born white weren't enough all by itself. Sometimes he wondered why he bothered with ambitions that would probably end up breaking his heart. Sure, he wanted to push himself up. But how far could you push when white folks held the lid on, right above your head? The wonder wasn't that so many Negroes gave up. The wonder was that a few kept trying.

Seeing he wasn't going to get anything more than that shrug, Kennedy said, "You pick up the whole load of typewriters all right?"

"Sure did, sir. They was the last things left in Goebel's warehouse, though. He ain't gonna be left much longer his own self—says he's headin' down to Lexington with his cousin. This war scare got everybody jumpy."

"Can't say as I blame Clem, neither," Kennedy said. "I may get out of town myself, matter of fact. Haven't made up my mind about that. Wait till it starts, I figure, and then see what the damnyankees do. But you, you got nowhere to run to, huh?"

"No, not hardly." Cincinnatus didn't like thinking about that. Kennedy had more in the way of brains than Clem Goebel. If he didn't think Covington was a safe place to stay, it probably wasn't. He understood Cincinnatus was stuck here, too. Sighing, the laborer said, "Let me unload them typing machines for you, boss."

That kept him busy till dinnertime. He lived down by the Licking River, south of Kennedy's place, close enough to walk back and forth at the noon hour if he gulped down his corn bread or salt pork and greens or whatever Elizabeth had left for him before she went off to clean white folks' houses.

A shape in the river—a cheese box on a raft was what it looked like—caught his eye. He whistled on the same note Tom Kennedy had used when he saw the aeroplane. By treaty, the United States and the Confederate States kept gunboats off the waters of the rivers they shared and the waters of tributaries within three miles of those jointly held rivers. If that gunboat—the Yankees called the type monitors, after their first one, but Southerners didn't and wouldn't—wasn't breaking the treaty, it sure was bending it.

Cincinnatus whistled again, a low, worried note. More people, higher-up people, than Goebel and Kennedy thought war was coming.

"Mobilize!" Flora Hamburger cried in a loud, clear voice. "We must mobilize for the inevitable struggle that lies before us!"

The word was on everyone's lips now, since President Roosevelt had ordered the United States Army to mobilize the day before. Newsboys on the corner of Hester and Chrystie, half a block from the soapbox—actually, it was a beer crate, filched from the Croton Brewery next door—shouted it in headlines from the *New York Times* and the early edition of the *Evening Sun*. All those headlines spoke of hundreds of thousands of men in green-gray uniforms filing onto hundreds of trains that would carry them to the threatened frontiers of the United States, to Maryland and Ohio and Indiana, to Kansas and New Mexico, to Maine and Dakota and Washington State.

Just by looking at the crowded streets of the Tenth Ward of New York City, Flora could tell how many men of military age the dragnet had scooped up. The men who hurried along Chrystie were most of them smooth-faced youths or their gray-bearded grandfathers. The newsboys weren't shouting that the reserves, the men of the previous few conscription classes who'd served their time, were being called up with the regulars—they wouldn't reveal the government's plan to the Rebels or to the British-lickspittle Canadians: their terms. But Flora had heard it was so, and she believed it.

The papers told of pretty girls rushing up and kissing soldiers as they boarded their trains, of men who hadn't been summoned to the colors pressing twenty-dollar goldpieces into the hands of those who had, of would-be warriors flocking to recruiting stations in such numbers that some factories had to close down. The Croton Brewery was draped in red-white-and-blue bunting. So was Public School Number Seven, across the street.

The entire country—the entire world—was going mad, Flora Hamburger thought. Up on her soapbox, she waved her arms and tried to bring back sanity.

"We must not allow the capitalist exploiters to make the workers of the world their victims," she declared, trying to fire with her own enthusiasm the small crowd that had gathered to listen to her. "We must continue our ceaseless agitation in the cause of peace, in the cause of workers' solidarity around the world. If we let the upper classes split us and set us one against another, we have but doomed ourselves to more decades of servility."

A cop in a fireplug hat stood at the back of the crowd, listening intently. The First Amendment remained on the books, but he'd run her in if she said anything that came close to being fighting words—or maybe even if she didn't. Hysteria was wild in the United States; if you said the emperor had no clothes, you took the risk of anyone who spoke too clearly.

But the cop didn't need to run her in; the crowd was less friendly than those before which she was used to speaking. Somebody called, "Are you Socialists going to vote for Teddy's war budget?"

"We are going to do everything we can to keep a war budget from becoming necessary," Flora cried. Even three days earlier, that answer to that question had brought a storm of applause. Now some people stood silent, their faces set in disapproving lines. A few booed. One or two hissed. Nobody clapped.

"If war comes," that same fellow called, "will you Socialists vote the money to fight it? You're the second biggest party in Congress; don't you know what you're doing?"

Why weren't you mobilized? Flora thought resentfully. The skinny man was about twenty-five, close to her own age—a good age for cannon fodder in a man. Few to match him were left in the neighborhood. Flora wondered if he was an *agent provacateur*. Roosevelt's Democrats had done that sort of thing often enough on the East Side, disrupting the meetings not only of Socialists but also of the Republicans who hadn't moved leftward when their party split in the acrimonious aftermath of the Second Mexican War.

But she had to answer him. She paused a moment to adjust her picture hat and pick her phrases, then said, "We will be caucusing in Philadelphia day after tomorrow to discuss that. As the majority votes, the party will act."

She never would have yielded so much a few days before. Here in New York City, sentiment against the war still ran strong—or stronger than most places, anyhow. But many of the Socialists' constituents—the miners of Pennsylvania and West Virginia, the farmers of Minnesota and Dakota and Montana—were near one border or another, and were bombarding their representatives with telegrams embracing, not the international brotherhood of labor, but rather the protection of the American frontier.

Almost pleadingly, Flora said, "Can we let the madness of nationalism destroy everything the workers not just here in the United States but also in Germany and Austria and in France and England and even in Canada and the Confederacy?—yes, I dare say that, for it is true," she went on over a chorus of boos, "have struggled shoulder to shoulder to achieve? I say we cannot. I say we must not. If you believe the sacred cause of labor is bound up in the idea of world politics without war, give generously to our cause." She pointed down to a washed-out peach tin, the label still on, that sat in front of her crate. "Give for the workers who harvested that fruit, the miners who by the sweat of their brow dug out the iron and tin from which the can is made, the steelworkers who made it into metal, the laborers in the cannery who packed the peaches, the draymen and drivers who brought them to market. Give now for a better tomorrow."

A few people stepped up and tossed coins into the peach tin. One or two of them tossed in banknotes. Flora had plenty of practice in gauging the take from the racket the money made. She would have done better today working in a sweatshop and donating her wages to the cause.

She thanked the small crowd less sincerely than she would have liked, picked up the can, and started down the street with it toward Socialist Party headquarters. She'd gone only a short way when a beer wagon full of barrels pulled by a team of eight straining horses rattled out of the Croton Brewery and down Chrystie Street. It got more applause than she had—seeing a load of barrels was supposed to be good luck—and would make far more money for its firm than Flora had for the Socialists.

The thought depressed her. The Party had been educating the proletariat all over the world, showing the workers how they could seize control of the means of production from the capitalists who exploited their labor for the sake of profit. They'd made progress, too. No civilized government these days would call out troops to shoot down strikers, as had been commonplace a generation before. Surely the revolution, whether peaceful or otherwise, could not be far away. What sort of weapon could the plutocrats devise to resist the united strength and numbers of the working classes?

Her lips thinned into a bitter line. How simple the answer had proved! Threaten to start a war! All at once, you estranged German workers from French, English from Austrian, American from Confederate (though the Rebels also called themselves Americans). Few Socialists had imagined the proletariat was so easily manipulated.

Tenth Ward party headquarters was on the second story of a brownstone on Centre Market Place, across the street from the raucous market itself. A kosher butcher shop occupied the first story. Flora paused for a moment in front of the butcher's plate-glass window before she went upstairs. Some of her dark, wavy hair had come loose from the bobby pins that were supposed to hold it in place. With quick, practiced motions, she repaired the damage. Inside the shop, the butcher, aptly named Max Fleischmann, waved to her. She nodded in reply.

Fleischmann came out and looked down into the peach tin. He shook his head. "You've made more," he said in Yiddish, then reached into his pocket and tossed a dime into the can.

"You didn't have to do that." Flora felt her face heat. Her eyes flicked to her reflection in the window. She couldn't tell if the flush showed. Probably not, not with her olive skin. "You're not even a Socialist."

"So I voted for Roosevelt? This means my money isn't good enough for you? *Feh!*" Fleischmann's wry grin showed three gold teeth. "If you people go bankrupt and have to move out from upstairs, who knows what kind of crazy maniacs I get right over my head?"

"When we moved in, you called us crazy maniacs—and worse than that," Flora reminded him. She stared down into the can of peaches. That charity dime made the day's take no less pathetic. Shaking her head, she said, "The whole world is going crazy now, though. We're the ones who are trying to stay sane, to do what needs doing."

"Crazy is right." Fleischmann clenched a work-roughened hand into a fist. "The Confederates, they're moving all sorts of troops to the border, trying to get the jump on us. And the Canadians, their Great Lakes battleships have left port, it says in the papers. What are we supposed to do, what with them provoking us from all sides like this?"

Flora gaped at the butcher in blank dismay. The bacillus of nationalism had infected him, too, and he didn't even notice it. She said, "If all the workers would stand together, there'd be no war, Mr. Fleischmann."

"Oh, yes. If we could trust the Rebels, this would be wonderful," Fleischmann said. "But how can we? We know they want to fight us, because they've fought us twice already. Am I right or am I wrong, Flora? We have to defend ourselves, don't we? Am I right or am I wrong?"

"But don't you see? The Confederate workers are saying the same thing about the United States."

"Fools!" Max Fleischmann snorted. Realizing the argument was hopeless, Flora started upstairs. The butcher's voice pursued her: "Am I right or am I wrong?" When she didn't answer, he snorted again and went back into his shop.

The Socialist Party offices were almost as crowded as the tenements all around: desks and tables and file cabinets jammed into every possible square inch of space, leaving a bare minimum of room for human beings. Two secretaries in smudged white shirtwaists tried without much luck to keep up with an endless stream of calls. They mixed English and Yiddish in every conversation—sometimes, it seemed, in every sentence.

Herman Bruck nodded to her. As usual, he seemed too elegant to make a proper Socialist, what with his two-button jacket of the latest cut and the silk ascot he wore in place of a tie. His straw boater hung on a hat rack near his desk. He looked so natty because he came from a long line of tailors. "How did it go?" he asked her. Though he'd been born in Poland, his English was almost without accent.

"Not so good," Flora answered, setting down the can with a clank. "Do we know what's what with the caucus?"

Bruck's sour expression did not sit well on his handsome features. "A telegram came in not half an hour ago," he answered. "They voted eighty-seven to fourteen to give Roosevelt whatever money he asks for."

"Oy!" Flora exclaimed. "Now the madness is swallowing us, too."

"On theoretical grounds, the vote does make some sense," Bruck said grudgingly. "After all, the Confederacy is still in large measure a feudal economy. Defeating it would advance progressive forces there and might lift the Negroes out of serfdom."

"Would. Might." Flora laced the words with scorn. "And have they declared Canada feudal and reactionary, too?"

"No," Bruck admitted. "They said nothing about Canada—putting the best face on things they could, I suppose."

"Putting the best face on things doesn't make them right," Flora said with the stern rectitude of a temperance crusader smashing a bottle of whiskey against a saloon wall.

Bruck frowned. A moment before, he'd been unhappy with the delegates of his party. Now, because it *was* his party and he a disciplined member of it, he defended the decision it had made: "Be reasonable, Flora. If they'd voted to oppose the war budget, that would have been the end of the Socialist Party in the United States. Everyone is wild for this war, upper class and lower class alike. We'd have lost half our members to the Republicans, maybe more."

"Whenever you throw away what's right for what's convenient, you end up losing both," Flora Hamburger said stubbornly. "Of course everyone is wild for the war now. The whole country is crazy. *Gottenyu,* the whole *world* is crazy. Does that mean we should say yes to the madness? How wild for war will people be when the trains start bringing home the bodies of the laborers and farmers the capitalists have murdered for the sake of greed and markets?"

Bruck raised a placating hand. "You're not on the soapbox now, Flora. Our congressmen, our senators, are going to vote unanimously—even the fourteen said they'd go along with the party. Will you stand alone?"

"No, I suppose not," Flora said with a weary sigh. Discipline told on her, too. "If we don't back the caucus, what kind of party are we? We might as well be Democrats in that case."

"That's right," Bruck said with an emphatic nod. "You're just worn out because you've been on the stump and nobody's listened to you. What do you say we walk across the street and get something to eat?"

"All right," she said. "Why not? It has to be better than this."

Bruck rescued his boater from the hat rack and set it on his head at a jaunty angle. "We'll be back soon," he told the secretaries, who nodded. With a flourish, he held the door open for Flora, saying, "If you will forgive the bourgeois courtesy."

"This once," she said, something more than half seriously. A lot of bourgeois courtesy was a way to sugar-coat oppression. Then, out in the hall, Bruck slipped an arm around her waist. He'd done that once before, and she hadn't liked it. She didn't like it now, either, and twisted away, glaring at him. "Be so kind as to keep your hands to yourself."

"You begrudge bourgeois courtesy, but you're trapped in bourgeois morality," Bruck said, frustration on his face.

"Socialists should be free to show affection where and how they choose," Flora answered. "On the other hand, they should also be free to keep from showing affection where there is none."

"Does that mean what I think it means?"

"It means exactly that," Flora said as they started down the stairs.

They walked across Centre Market Place toward the countless stalls selling food and drink in a silence that would have done for filling an icebox. From behind the butcher-shop counter, Max Fleischmann watched them and shook his head.

All of Richmond streamed toward Capitol Square. Reginald Bartlett was one more drop of water in the stream, one more straw hat and dark sack suit among thousands sweating in the early August sun. He turned to the man momentarily beside him and said, "I should be back behind the drugstore counter."

"Is that a fact?" the other replied, not a bit put out by such familiarity, not today. "I should be adding up great long columns of figures, myself. But how often do we have the chance to see history made?"

"Not very often," Bartlett said. He was a round-faced, smiling, freckled man of twenty-six, the kind of man who wins at poker because you trust him instinctively. "That's why I'm on my way. The pharmacist told me to keep things running while he went to hear President Wilson, but if he's not there, will he know I'm not there?"

"Not a chance of it," the accountant assured him. "Not even the slightest—Oof!" Someone dug an elbow into the pit of his stomach, quite by accident. He stumbled and staggered and almost fell; had he gone down, he probably would have been trampled. As things were, he fell back several yards, and was replaced beside Bartlett by a colored laborer in overalls and a cloth cap. Nobody would be asking the Negro for a pass, not today. If he got fired tomorrow for not being on the job . . . he took the same chance Bartlett did.

There weren't many Negroes in the crowd, far fewer in proportion to the mass than their numbers in Richmond as a whole. Part of the reason for that, probably, was that they had more trouble getting away from their jobs than white men did. And part of it, too, was that they had more trouble caring about the glorious destiny of the Confederate States than whites did.

The bell in the tower in the southwestern corner of Capitol Square rang the alarm, over and over again. *Clang, clang, clang . . . clang, clang, clang . . . clang, clang, clang.* Most often, those three chimes endlessly repeated meant fire in the city. Today the alarm was for the nation as a whole.

Bartlett nimbly dodged round carriages and automobiles—some Fords imported from Yankee country; a Rolls full of gentlemen in top hats, white tie, and cutaways; and several Manassas machines built in Birmingham—that could make no headway with men on foot packing the streets. Even bicycles were slower than shank's mare in this crush.

He rounded a last corner and caught sight of the great equestrian statue of George Washington in Capitol Square. Washington, in an inspiring gesture, pointed south—toward the state penitentiary, wags said whenever scandal rocked the Confederate Congress.

The bronze Washington also pointed toward an even larger, more imposing statue of Albert Sidney Johnston. He and the bronze warriors in forage caps who stood guard at the base of the pedestal he topped memorialized the brave men, prominent and humble alike, who had fallen for freedom in the War of Secession.

Just to one side of the Johnston Memorial, a team of carpenters had hastily run up a platform to set dignitaries above the level of the common throng. The pine boards of the platform were still bright and yellow and unweathered. The same could not be said for the men who sat in folding chairs upon it. A lot of the graybeards had seen service not merely in the Second Mexican War but also in the War of Secession. Nor were the beards all that was gray: there side by side sat Patrick Cleburne and Stephen Ramseur wearing identical uniforms of the obsolete color more like what the Yankees wore nowadays than modern Confederate military dress. Aging lions, though, could wear what they pleased.

As everyone else was doing, Bartlett wiggled as close to the platform as he could. If the crush on the street had been bad, that within Capitol Square was appalling. Not twenty feet from him, somebody shouted in outrage: he'd had his pocket picked. Sneak thieves were probably having a field day, for people were packed so tight, they couldn't help bumping up against one another, and accidental contact was hard to tell from that made with larcenous intent.

The few ladies in the crowd were bumped and jostled almost as much as their male counterparts—not intentionally, perhaps, but unavoidably. "Beg your pardon, ma'am," Bartlett said after being squeezed against a pretty young woman more intimately than would have been proper on a dance floor. He couldn't tip his hat; he hadn't room to raise his arm to his head.

She nodded, accepting his apology as she'd probably accepted a dozen others. The remembered feel of her body pressed to his made him smile as the motion of the crowd swept them apart. He'd been polite—that came automatically as breathing to a well-raised young man—but his thoughts were his own, to do with as he would.

By dint of stubbornness worthy of what folks said about New England Yankees, Bartlett slithered and squirmed up to within a few yards of the ring of butternut-clad soldiers who held the crush away from the platform with bayoneted rifles. "Don't you take a step back, Watkins, damn you," the officer in charge of them shouted. "Make them do the moving."

Bartlett wondered if the guards would have to stick someone to make the crowd stand clear. The pressure behind him was so strong, it seemed as if the people could crush everything between themselves and the platform.

A high mucky-muck—not a graybeard but a portly, dapper fellow with a sandy, pointed beard like that of the King of England—leaned down over the railing and spoke to that officer. After a moment, Bartlett recognized him from woodcuts he'd seen: that was Emmanuel Sellars, the secretary of war. Was he giving the command for a demonstration against the crowd? Bartlett couldn't hear his orders. If he was, it would be pandemonium. Bartlett got ready to flee, and hoped the stampede wouldn't run over him.

The officer—a captain by the three bars on either side of his collar—shouted to his men. Bartlett couldn't make out what he said, either, but fear ran through him when some of the guards raised the rifles to their shoulders. But they aimed up into the air, not at the people, and fired a volley. Bartlett hoped they were shooting blanks. If they weren't, the bullets were liable to hurt somebody as they fell.

Into the sudden, startled silence the gunshots brought, a fellow with a great voice shouted, "Hearken now to the words of the President of the Confederate States of America, the honorable Woodrow Wilson."

The president turned this way and that, surveying the great swarm of people all around him in the moment of silence the volley had brought. Then, swinging back to face the statue of George Washington—and, incidentally, Reginald Bartlett—he said, "The father of our country warned us against entangling alliances, a warning that served us well when we were yoked to the North, before its arrogance created in our Confederacy what had never existed before—a national consciousness. That was our salvation and our birth as a free and independent country."

Silence broke then, with a thunderous outpouring of applause. Wilson raised a bony right hand. Slowly, silence, or a semblance of it, returned. The president went on, "But our birth of national consciousness made the United States jealous, and they tried to beat us down. We found loyal friends in England and France. Can we now stand aside when the German tyrant threatens to grind them under his iron heel?"

"No!" Bartlett shouted himself hoarse, along with thousands of his countrymen. Stunned, deafened, he had trouble hearing what Wilson said next:

"Jealous still, the United States in their turn also developed a national consciousness, a dark and bitter one, as any so opposed to ours must be." He spoke not like a politician inflaming a crowd but like a professor setting out arguments—he had taken the one path before choosing the other. "The German spirit of arrogance and militarism has taken hold in the United States; they see only the gun as the proper arbiter between nations, and their president takes Wilhelm as his model. He struts and swaggers and acts the fool in all regards."

Now he sounded like a politician; he despised Theodore Roosevelt, and took pleasure in Roosevelt's dislike for him. "When war began between England and France on the one hand and the German Empire on the other, we came to our allies' aid, as they had for us in our hour of need. I have, as you know, asked the Congress to declare war upon Germany and Austria-Hungary.

"And now, as a result of our honoring our commitment to our gallant allies, that man Roosevelt has sought from the U.S. Congress a declaration of war not only against England and France but also against the Confederate States of America. His servile lackeys, misnamed Democrats, have given him what he wanted, and the telegraph informs me that fighting has begun along our border and on the high seas.

"Leading our great and peaceful people into war is a fearful thing, not least because, with the great advances of science and industry over the past half-century, this may prove the most disastrous and terrible of all wars, truly a war of the nations: indeed a war of the world. But right is more precious than peace, and we shall fight for those things we have always held dear in our hearts: for the rights of the Confederate States and of the white men who live in them; for the liberties of small nations everywhere from outside oppression; for our own freedom and independence from the vicious, bloody regime to our north. To such a task we can dedicate our lives and our fortunes, everything we are and all that we have, with the pride of those who know the day has come when the Confederacy is privileged to spend her blood and her strength for the principles that gave her birth and led to her present happiness. God helping us, we can do nothing else. Men of the Confederacy, is it your will that a state of war should exist henceforth between us and the United States of America?"

"Yes!" The answer roared from Reginald Bartlett's throat, as from those of the other tens of thousands of people jamming Capitol Square. Someone flung a straw hat in the air. In an instant, hundreds of them, Bartlett's included, were flying. A great chorus of "Dixie" rang out, loud enough, Bartlett thought, for the damnyankees to hear it in Washington.

Someone tapped him on the shoulder. He whirled around—and stared into the angry face of Milo Axelrod, his boss. "I told you to stay and mind the shop, dammit!" the druggist roared. "You're fired!"

Bartlett snapped his fingers under the older man's nose. "And this here is how much I care," he said. "You can't fire me, on account of I damn well quit. They haven't called up my regiment yet, but I'm joining the Army now, is what I'm doing. Go peddle your pills—us real men will save the country for you. A couple of months from now, after we've licked the Yankees, you can tell me you're sorry."

II

Nellie Semphroch huddled behind the counter in the ruins of her coffeehouse, wondering if she would die in the next instant. She'd been wondering that for hours, ever since the first Confederate shells began falling on Washington, D.C.

Beside her, her daughter Edna wailed, "When will it stop, Mother? Will it ever stop?"

"Lord help me, I don't know," the widow Semphroch answered. She had twice her daughter's twenty years; on her, bitter experience seamed the long, oval face they otherwise shared. "I just don't know. It wasn't like this when—"

A shell crashed down nearby. The ground quivered and jerked, as if in pain. Fragments sprayed through the blank square that had been the front window before it shattered early in the bombardment. Edna brushed dark blond curls—a brighter shade than Nellie's, which were streaked with gray—out of her eyes and repeated, despairingly, "Will it ever stop?"

"It wasn't like this when the Southerners shelled us before," Nellie said, at last able to get in another complete sentence. "When I was a girl, they bombarded Washington, yes, but after an hour or so they were done. I was scared then, but only for a little while. That's why we didn't leave when—"

Now, instead of a shell, Edna interrupted her: "We should have, Mama. We should have gotten out while we could, along with everybody else."

"Not everybody left," Nellie said, her daughter's bitterness making her defensive. A great host of people had, though, as crisis in some distant part of Europe became by the magic of far-flung alliances crisis in America, too. While Washington remained the nation's capital, Congress hadn't met there since the Second Mexican War: going about their business under Confederate guns had seemed intolerable. Before war was declared, an endless procession of wagons and buggies and motorcars jammed the roads leading north out of the capital, and every train bringing in soldiers had been full of civilians on its outbound journey.

But Nellie and Edna had sat tight, selling coffee to panicky bureaucrats and swaggering soldiers alike. They'd made a lot of money, and Nellie had been certain that, even if war broke out, the Rebels would not seek to destroy what had once been their capital, too. They hadn't back in 1881.

She'd been wrong. Sweet Jesus Christ, how wrong she'd been! She knew that now, to her everlasting sorrow. The Confederacy's bombardment of Washington a generation before had been more a demonstration that the South could be frightful if it so chose than actual frightfulness in and of itself. Having hit a few targets, the Confederates had gone on to fight the war elsewhere.

This time, they seemed intent on leaving no stone in the capital of the United States standing upon another. Once, just before sunrise, Nellie had gone to a well to draw a bucket of water—shelling had burst the pipes that carried water through the city. The Capitol's dome was smashed, the building itself burning. Not far away, the White House had also become a pile of rubble, and the needle of the Washington Monument no longer reached up to the sky—that despite the Rebels' claims to revere Washington as the father of their country, too.

More guns boomed, these not the Confederate cannon across the Potomac but American guns replying from the high ground north of Washington. Shells made freight-train noises overhead, then thudded to earth with roars like distant thunder.

"Kill all those Rebel bastards!" Edna shouted. "Blow Arlington to hell and gone so we don't have the God-damned Lees looking down on us like lords. Blow their balls off, every fucking one of them!"

Nellie stared at her daughter. "Where ever did you learn such language?" she gasped. Absurdly, at that moment, her first impulse was to wash Edna's mouth out with soap. After a moment's reflection, though, she wished she let the words out more readily herself. She knew them—oh, she knew them. And when hell came up here on earth, what did a few bad words matter?

"I'm sorry, Mama," Edna said, but then her chin came up. "No, I'm not sorry, not a bit of it. I wish I knew worse to call the Confederates. If I did, I would, and that's the truth."

"What you just said is pretty bad." Nellie had not led a sheltered life—far from it—but she'd seldom heard a lady curse as her daughter just had. Then again, she'd never been in a situation where tons of death fell randomly from the sky. As the judge said of the man who knifed a poker partner because he spotted an ace coming out of his sleeve, there were mitigating circumstances.

More freight-train noises filled the air, these from the east and south: Rebel artillery, striking back at U.S. guns. Because the Confederates were trying to hit the cannons, shells stopped falling on Washington itself and began smashing the hills that ringed the city.

Edna stood up. "Maybe we can get out of town now, Mama," she said hopefully.

"Maybe." Nellie rose, too. The air was thick with smoke and dust and a harsh odor she supposed came from explosives. Half the chairs and tables in the coffeehouse lay on their sides or upside down. The fine linen tablecloths that gave the establishment a touch of class—and that Nellie was still paying for—were rags now, torn rags.

A shell fragment had ripped into the fancy brass coffee grinder that gleamed out in front of the counter. Nellie wouldn't be grinding coffee with it again, not any time soon. She shivered and had to grasp the counter for a moment. If a fragment had done that to sturdy, machined brass, what would it have done to flesh? A few feet to one side and she would have found out. No, 1881 hadn't been like this.

She walked toward what had been her front window and was now a square opening with a few jagged shards round the edges. Out in the street—which had suddenly acquired deep pocks, like the face of a man who'd never been vaccinated—a shattered delivery wagon sat on its side, the horses that had drawn it gruesomely dead in the traces. Nellie gulped. She'd killed and plucked and gutted plenty of chickens, and even a few pigs, but artillery was a horrifyingly sloppy butcher. She hadn't imagined horses had that much blood in them, either. A scrawny stray dog came up and sniffed the pool. She shouted at it. It ran away. Behind the wagon, she could just see an outflung arm. No, the driver hadn't been luckier than his animals.

"Can we get out of town, do you think, Ma?" Edna repeated.

Nellie raised her eyes from the street to the high ground. For a moment, she did not understand what she was seeing, and thought a Midwestern dust storm had suddenly been transplanted to those low, rolling hills. Dust there was aplenty, but no wind to raise it. Instead, it came from the carpet of shells the Confederates were laying down. When she looked more closely, she spied the ugly red core of fire in each explosion. She wondered how anything could live under such bombardment, and if anything did.

Her question there was answered a moment later, for not all the flames came from landing shells. Some sprang from the muzzles of U.S. guns hurling death back at the enemy. To her amazement, she discovered she could briefly follow some of the big American shells as they rose into the sky.

She turned her head toward the Potomac. Smoke and buildings obscured most of her view there but, from what she could tell, the Virginia heights were taking as much of a pounding as those around Washington. *Good,* she thought savagely.

From behind her, Edna said, "Let's go, Ma."

Nellie waved her daughter up alongside her and pointed to the bombardment raining down outside of town. "I don't think we'd better," she said. "Looking at that, we're safer where we're at." Edna bit her lip but nodded.

Across the street, something moved inside a battered cobbler's shop. Nellie's heart jumped into her mouth until she recognized old Mr. Jacobs, who ran the place. He waved to her, calling, "You are still alive, Widow Semphroch?"

"I think so, yes," Nellie answered, which brought a twisted smile to the cobbler's wizened face.

Before she could say anything more, the sound of many booted men running made her turn her head. A stream of green-gray-clad American soldiers in matching forage caps pounded past the wrecked delivery van and dead horses. Sunlight glinted from the bayonets they'd fixed to the ends of their rifles.

"You civilians better get back under cover," one of them shouted. "The damn Rebs—beg your pardon, ma'am—they're liable to try comin' across the river. They do, we're gonna give 'em what for. Ain't that right, boys?"

The soldiers made harsh, eager grunts unlike any Nellie had heard before. Not all of them were fuzz-bearded boys; some had to be close to thirty. Mobilization had scooped up a lot of men who'd done their two years a long time ago, and put them back in the Army.

A couple of the soldiers were trundling a machine gun along on its little wheeled carriage. When they came to shell holes in the street, they either maneuvered it around them or manhandled it over. Its fat brass water jacket must have been newly polished, for it gleamed brighter than the bayonets.

One of the machine-gun handlers stared at Edna and ran his tongue over his lips as if he were a cat that had just finished a saucer of cream. Nellie glanced over to her daughter, who was filthy, bedraggled, exhausted . . . but young, unmistakably young.

Men, Nellie thought, a one-word indictment of half the human race. Not long ago, or so it seemed, they'd looked at her that way, and she'd looked back. She'd done more than look back, in fact. That was the start of how Edna came to be, and why her name had changed from Houlihan to Semphroch in such a tearing hurry.

She heard a fresh noise in the air, a sharp, quick *whizz!* A couple of soldiers looked up to see what that was. A couple of others, wiser or more experienced, threw themselves flat on the ground.

Only a couple of seconds after the *whizz!* first reached her ears, it was followed by a huge *bang!* at the head of the column. Men reeled away from the explosion, shrieking. There were more whizzes in the air now, too. The Confederates had spotted the moving infantrymen, and decided to open up on them.

Bang! Bang! Bang! Shells struck up and down the length of the battalion. Nellie didn't see all the slaughter they worked. "Get down!" she screamed to Edna, even before the second whizzing shell fell and burst. To make sure Edna listened and didn't stare back at the machine gunner bold in his uniform, she dragged her daughter to the floor.

More fragments whined past overhead. The shells that went *whizz-bang* weren't very big; the front wall of the coffeehouse stopped most of their fragments, though plenty screamed through what had been the window and scarred the plaster above the counter.

The barrage stopped as suddenly as it had begun. That didn't mean the street was silent; far from it. Cries and screams and moans and wails and sounds of pain for which Nellie had no descriptive words filled the air. She got to her feet and looked out. The street had been a sorry sight before. The slaughter now was worse than anything she'd ever imagined.

Men and pieces of men lay everywhere. The ones who were dead were less appalling than the ones who were wounded. A trooper tried to stuff spilled intestines back into his belly through a neat slit torn in his tunic. Another sat staring foolishly at his right arm, which he'd picked up off the pavement and was holding in his left hand. Quietly, without much fuss, he crumpled over and lay still.

"We have to help them, Ma," Edna said. "We have plenty of rags and things—"

Nellie hadn't noticed her daughter get up beside her. She nodded, though she knew what would happen if more shells caught them out in the open.

Stretcher bearers were taking charge of some of the wounded. They nodded gratefully, though, when they saw Nellie and Edna come out with old clothes in their hands.

The second man Nellie bandaged was the machine gunner who'd leered at Edna. Now his face was waxy pale instead of ruddy and alight with lust. Nellie had to force his hands—protectively cupped too late—away from the wound at the base of his belly before she could try to stanch the bleeding. If he lived, he wouldn't be doing much with the girls, not any more.

Off to the west, rifle fire rang out. You lived in the city, you heard guns every so often; you got to know what they sounded like. But, a moment later, Nellie heard a sound she'd never known before. It was something like gunfire, something like a giant ripping a piece of canvas the size of a football field. It made the hair stand up at the back of her neck.

Mangled and in agony though he was, the machine gunner smiled a little. He knew what the sound was, though Nellie didn't. Seeing his knowledge made her understand, too.

"So that's the noise a machine gun makes," Nellie murmured. The pale-faced soldier nodded, a single short jerk of his head. "Good," Nellie told him. "That means the Rebs are catching it hot." He nodded again.

* * *

The wheat was turning golden under the warm August sun. From the front porch of his farmhouse, Arthur McGregor surveyed the crop with dour satisfaction. The quick-ripening hybrid Marquis strain he'd put in the ground these past few years beat the old Red Fife all hollow. Here a quarter of the way from the U.S. border to Winnipeg, every day you could shave off the growing season was a good one, especially since half your ground lay fallow each year.

McGregor—a tall, lean man, his face weathered almost like a sailor's from endless exposure to sun and wind—watched the wheat bow and then straighten, politely acknowledging the breeze. The fields seemed to go on forever. He let out a sour snort. That was partly because he'd had the work of plowing and planting them. But the Manitoba prairie was flat as a sheet of newspaper, flat as if it had been pressed. And so, in a way, it had; from what the geologists said, great sheets of ice had lain here in ancient days, squashing down any irregularities that might once have existed.

For hundreds of miles, the only blemishes on the surface of the land were the belts of wire and the fortifications on either side of the border between the United States and the Dominion of Canada. McGregor sighed, thinking about that long, thin, porous border. Late rains or early frost could blight his crops. So could war.

His wife Maude came out of the house to stand beside him. They'd been married fifteen years, ever since he'd got out of the Army and gone into the militia: almost all his adult life, in other words, and all of hers. If they hadn't thought alike back in the days when they were courting—he wasn't quite sure about that, not after so long—they certainly did now.

And so it was Maude who said, "They've come over the border, eh?"

"They have." Arthur McGregor sighed. "After Winnipeg, I've no doubt." Only a slight difference in accent, an extra tincture of Scots that made the last word sound like "doat," told him from one of the Americans he despised and feared. "They take the town, they cut the country in half, they do."

Maude turned and looked southward, as if in fear of locusts, though soldiers from the United States were liable to prove even more destructive. Under her bonnet, she wore her red hair tightly pinned down against her head, but it was so fine, wisps kept escaping the pins and springing out in front of her face. She brushed them back from her gray eyes with work-roughened hands: like her husband, she'd never known an easy day in her life. "The devil's own lot of them down there," she said, her voice worried.

"Don't I know it? Don't we all know it?" McGregor sighed again. "Sixty, sixty-five million of them, maybe eight million up here." By the way he spoke, he expected everyone in the United States, young or old, man or woman, to parade past the farmhouse in the next few minutes.

"We're not alone, eh?" Maude said; maybe she was seeing sixty or sixty-five million angry Americans in her mind's eye, too. "We've England with us, and the Confederacy, and the Empire of Mexico."

"England's going to be busy close to home," her husband answered with the ingrained pessimism of a man who'd been wrestling with a stubborn Mother Nature for a living since before he needed to shave. "Mexico's nothing, maybe less, and the Yanks outweigh the Confederates two to one or more, too. They can fight them and have plenty to spare for us."

Maude peered south again, this time as if looking past the USA to the CSA. "I don't know I much care for having those people on our side, when you get down to it. The way they treat their colored people, they might as well be—"

"Russians?" Arthur McGregor suggested wryly. "The Czar's on our side, too. The Yanks are no bargain, either; we'd never have had conscription up here if they didn't start it first, and these days down there, from what the newspapers say, you fill out a form for this, you fill out a form for that, you fill out a form for the other thing, same as you would if the Kaiser was running things. Only free land on the continent is where we're standing, seems to me."

"Pa! Pa!" His son Alexander came running toward the house, his voice cracking in excitement as any fourteen-year-old's was apt to do. "There's soldiers coming, Pa!" He pointed to the north.

Arthur, his mind focused on the threat from the United States, hadn't looked back toward Winnipeg in a while. Now he did. Sure enough, as his son had said, here came a cavalry troop, small in the distance, down toward the border with Dakota. Alexander jumped up and down, waving frantically at the soldiers. Arthur McGregor waved, too, but in a more measured way. He had a much better idea than his son of what war actually entailed.

The troopers waved back. Then, to McGregor's surprise, one of them peeled off from the rest and guided his chestnut toward the farmhouse at a fast trot. He reined in just in front of the porch: a little sallow fellow with waxed mustache who lifted his cap to Maude before nodding gravely to Arthur and less gravely to Alexander, who was all but hopping out of his overalls.

"Good day, my friends," the cavalryman said with a French accent that explained his swarthiness. "I am Pierre Lapin, lieutenant"—his fingers brushed the single pip on his shoulder board—"of the horse. Is it that my men and I could use your well for the purpose of watering ourselves?"

"Yes, sir, go right ahead, all of you." McGregor had to make a conscious effort not to stiffen to attention. The couple of weeks he spent drilling every year made him give an officer automatic deference.

"You are gracious. *Merci,*" Lapin said, and waved to his men. They all followed the path he had taken.

"Dipper's in the bucket," Maude McGregor said, pointing to the well.

Lieutenant Lapin tipped his hat to her again, which made her flush and giggle like a schoolgirl.

Unlike Lapin, who carried a pistol on his officer's Sam Browne belt, his troopers wore carbines slung on their backs and had sabers fixed to the left side of their saddles. They queued up at the well, chattering in the odd mix of English and French McGregor remembered from his own days in the Army. Not so long ago, as such things went, Canadians who used French and those who spoke English had disliked and distrusted one another. But with both groups disliking and distrusting their giant neighbor to the south even more, the older rivalry was less remembered.

McGregor went up to Lapin, who was waiting for his men to finish before he drank himself. Quietly, so Maude wouldn't hear, the farmer asked, "Will they get this far?" When the cavalry lieutenant didn't answer, he went on, "I've got a rifle in the house—use it for hunting. I'll hunt things in green-gray if I have to."

Lapin's shoulders went up and down in a Gallic shrug. "Whether they will come so far I cannot say with certainty. I will say, though, if they do come so far and you have not been called to the colors to resist them, be cautious with that rifle. The Americans, they take their lessons from the *Boches*"—his curled lip said what he thought of that—"and the *Boches*, in the war with France in the last century, were harsh against *francs-tireurs*."

"Thank you, sir. I'll bear that in mind," McGregor said. "But if they invade your country and you're defending your home, shouldn't matter whether you're in uniform or not."

"What should matter and what does matter, *monsieur,* are not one and the same thing, I regret to say," Lapin answered with another shrug.

A muttering in the distance, almost too deep, almost too soft, almost too far to hear. *Thunder, a long ways off,* McGregor thought. But it wasn't thunder, not on this fine, bright day—he realized that with the thought hardly formed. "That's artillery," he said, his voice flat and harsh.

"*Vous avez raison,*" Lieutenant Lapin agreed. "I could wish you were wrong, but—" Yet another shrug. "And so perhaps it grows more likely the Americans will reach this place. But if they do, they will have paid a stiff price."

"Good," McGregor said. "What price will you have paid, though?"

"That is of no consequence, not to my country," Lapin replied. His turn at the well came at last. He drained the dipper dry, refilled it, and drained it again. "It is the price I agreed to pay when I joined the Army." He touched the brim of his cap in half a salute. "I thank you for the water, and I wish you the best of fortune in the hard days that surely lie ahead." He swung up onto his horse, calling on his men to hurry and remount. They soon rode away.

More of what wasn't thunder came from the south. It didn't sound closer, but it was louder: more guns in action, or bigger guns. *Both, most likely,* McGregor judged. Now that the fight had started, the Americans, the Canadians, and the men of the mother country would throw everything they had into it.

With that growing rumble in the background, McGregor's satisfaction in his fields of amber grain evaporated. With his country and the United States harvesting the fruits of longtime enmity, any chance he'd have to bring in his own harvest seemed small and dim.

Instead of watching the waving wheat, he kept gazing southward, after the cavalrymen. Before long, he saw motion on the road coming up from the south. Without turning his head, he said, "Fetch me the rifle, Alexander."

"Yes, Pa," his son answered. The boy thundered up the stairs two at a time and returned a moment later holding the pump-action Winchester with the careful confidence of someone long used to guns. Arthur McGregor checked to make sure he had a cartridge in the chamber, then stood and waited to see what sort of onslaught was coming.

Before he could raise the rifle to his shoulder, he realized he wasn't seeing the imminent arrival of the Americans, only people fleeing from them. Fear had almost made him fire on his own countrymen. Thin across the wheatfields, their shouts reached him, urging him to join them.

He had a buggy in the barn. If he hitched up the horses to it and loaded Maude and Alexander and his two little daughters into it, he could be on the road to Winnipeg inside an hour, and there the day after tomorrow.

"Will we go, Pa?" Alexander asked. The sight of other folks fleeing seemed to have given him the idea that war was something more than a game. McGregor thanked God something this side of getting shot at—or maybe this side of getting shot—had done that.

He shook his head. "No, we won't go. We'll stick it out a bit longer, see what happens." Alexander looked proud.

More soldiers went down the road, a long column of marching infantry, some Canadian, some British, then trucks painted khaki, then more marching men. A plume of coal smoke rose from the stack of a distant southbound train. McGregor would have bet all the acres he had that every compartment on every car was full to overflowing with men in tunics and puttees. Some of them would be gay, some frightened. That wouldn't matter, and wouldn't say anything about what sort of soldiers they'd make once they got to the fighting.

The rumble of artillery went on and on. He went on, too: on about his chores. When you were forking hay or pulling weeds or shoveling manure, for long stretches of time you could forget about what your ears were telling you. Then, as you paused to wipe your face on your sleeve, you'd notice the noise again: in absurd surprise, almost as if it had snuck up behind you and tapped you on the shoulder to make you jump.

It was getting louder—and, unquestionably, getting closer.

He hadn't wanted to believe that at first. When you noticed the thunder only every so often, you didn't think to compare it from then till now, or think your hearing was telling you the enemy was drawing nearer, which meant your own men were falling back.

But that was true. By the time evening came—the sun didn't set quite so late as it had at the height of summer—there could be no doubt left. The family sat down to chicken stew with dumplings and carrots in a grim mood. No one, not even Julia and Mary, who usually prattled on in spite of *children should be seen but not heard*, said much. The girls helped their mother wash the dishes while Arthur McGregor smoked a pipe. He checked the tin from which he filled it: Virginia tobacco, an import from the Confederate States, not the USA. That made him feel better.

He woke several times in the night, not something he usually did—if God had invented anything more exhausting than farm labor, McGregor hadn't heard of it. But when he sat up in the blackness, he heard the crash of guns, not so steady as they had been during the day, but not stopping, either.

And whenever he sat up, the guns were closer.

He woke for good in the pale gray of false dawn. One arm flopped across the other side of the bed, which was empty. He sniffed, and smelled tea steeping. Maude was up before him, then.

He put on his overalls and boots and went downstairs. A couple of cups of strong tea heavy with milk and sugar gave back some of what he'd lost in sleep. "A lot of work to do today," he said, as if that were the only thing on his mind. Maude nodded, as if she believed him.

He was working when the sun came up, hammering a fresh board onto the side of the chicken coop. Something moving in the fields caught his eye. It was a man: a soldier, he saw after a moment, heading north without the slightest thought for road or anything else, trampling down the nearly ripe wheat and not caring at all.

McGregor opened his mouth for an angry shout. It died unspoken. That first soldier he'd seen was but one of many. Trotting through the wheat, their bodies hidden, only heads and shoulders showing, they looked like nothing so much as shipwreck survivors bobbing in the sea. Here, though, what might have been wrecked was Canada.

Before long, horsemen joined the retreat. They were in better order than the infantry, stopping every so often to fire shots in the direction of an enemy Arthur McGregor could not yet see. A cavalry officer leading a couple of packhorses and a squad of soldiers who seemed to be under his command rode up to McGregor.

"Lieutenant Lapin!" he said in surprise.

"*Oui, monsieur,* we meet again," the French-Canadian officer answered wearily. If he'd slept at all since riding south the previous day, he didn't show it. But he still had fight in him. Pointing to the packhorses, he went on, "I have here a pair of machine guns, ammunition, and soldiers who know how to use them. I desire to make strongpoints of your house and your barn. We have, as you see, been thrown back. We may yet damage the invader, though."

"Go ahead," McGregor said at once. He knew his permission was irrelevant. Lapin had disguised a firm statement of intent with politeness, but the intent remained. The farmer went on, "Can your men drive the livestock out of the barn first, and give me and mine a chance to get clear of the house?" Strongpoints drew fire; he knew that all too well. *I'd better hide the rifle,* he thought. Secrecy came easy to him, and fear made it come easier.

"That is but a matter of common decency, though I fear in war decency is anything but common." Lapin gave the orders. More men, seeing him not in headlong retreat, rallied around him. A firing line stretched across the wheatfield.

McGregor got Maude and Alexander, Julia and Mary, and took them off away from the house. They led the family cows and horses. No time to hitch the horses to the buggy, not now. McGregor didn't know where to go with his family and the animals. Toward the road was the only idea he had: to join the stream of refugees trudging toward Winnipeg.

He was about halfway to the dirt track when Alexander exclaimed, "Here come the Americans!"

You could tell them from the Canadian defenders by their green-gray uniforms, by the shouts of "Hurrah!" that burst from their throats every few paces, by the fact that they weren't looking back over their shoulders, and by how many of them there were. They came in a great wave, close together as far as the eye could see. Again McGregor had the horrible mental picture of everybody in the United States grabbing a gun and heading for Winnipeg. Now, though, the soldiers were heading for him.

Then the machine guns began to hammer, back in the buildings the neighbors had helped his father run up. Their hideous racket made his head snap back toward the house and barn. When he looked back in the direction of the American soldiers once more, it was as if his fields had had a thresher go over them: where the soldiers had been wheat, they were mowed into stubble. More of them came forward, and more of them went down as the machine guns spat fire through their ranks. They were too far away for McGregor to see how they died, only that they died. Not all of them died at once, of course; a great chorus of agony rose from the fields, even above the racket of machine guns and rifle.

Julia clamped her hands over her ears. "Make them stop it, Papa!" she screamed. "Make them stop!"

McGregor couldn't make them stop. If he could have, he wouldn't. He exulted to see the Americans fall and writhe and die. What business did they have, invading his country? Like their German allies, they seemed to specialize in attacking small, defenseless nations that had done them no harm. One way or another, he vowed to himself, he would make them pay.

They were paying now, but they were also still moving forward. A bullet kicked up dust, not far from McGregor's feet. He heard more bullets smacking into the timbers of the house and the barn, where Pierre Lapin was holed up. The machine guns kept working a fearful slaughter, but the skirmish line Lapin had set up was thin, and did not, could not, hold. To east and west, Yanks in green-gray bypassed the strongpoint, as if it were high ground still above water in the middle of a flood.

That didn't last long. The Americans swung round behind the buildings. Firing around them—firing inside them—grew to a crescendo before abruptly falling silent.

A couple of soldiers came up to the McGregors. They held their rifles at the ready. By the way they panted, by the way their eyes glittered, they would open fire at any excuse or none. Arthur McGregor was careful to keep his hands in plain sight and to make no sudden moves. He was glad he didn't have the rifle on his shoulder, too.

"That there your house?" asked one of the Yanks, a fellow with corporal's stripes on his sleeves. He and his companion smelled the way McGregor did before Maude heated up water for a Saturday night bath, only more so.

"It's mine," McGregor said shortly.

The American corporal gestured with his rifle. "Go on back to it. Put your critters in the barn again. We cleaned out your soldiers, and we ain't got nothin' against civilians. Go on back." He scratched his cheek. Maybe the upswept wings of the Kaiser Bill mustache tickled.

"Ever think maybe civilians have something against you?" Alexander said, his voice hot.

"You got a mouthy kid," the corporal said to Arthur. "He gets too mouthy, maybe the house and the barn catch on fire—just by accident, understand?"

"I understand," McGregor said. He didn't know whether, in the end, Canada could win the war. He did know he and his family had just lost it.

"Dowling!" The general's voice, cracking and full of phlegm, echoed through the St. Louis headquarters of the U.S. First Army. "God damn it to hell, Dowling, have you gone and died while I wasn't looking? Get yourself in here this instant, or you'll be sorry you were ever born!"

"Yes, sir. Coming, sir." Major Abner Dowling hastily finished buttoning his fly. At the moment, he was sorry he'd ever been born. Of all the men to whom he could have been adjutant—

"Dowling!" Wheezing thunder—the general hadn't heard him. The general was hard of hearing: not surprising, since he was heading toward seventy-five. Even when he did hear, he was confounded hard of listening.

"Here, sir." Dowling rushed into the office. He wanted to wipe off his face; he was built like a rolltop desk, and moving quickly in hot, muggy weather made sweat pour down his ruddy cheeks. But that would have been a violation of military decorum, and his commander—the First Army's commander—made men pay for such trifling lapses.

"About time, Major," the general grumbled, but let it go at that. Dowling knew some relief; the old fool was just as likely to have kept riding him all day. "Get me a cup of coffee, man, and put something in it to open my eyes up. You know what I mean."

"Yes, sir," Dowling said. The coffeepot sat on top of an alcohol lamp to keep what was inside hot. More alcohol rested in the sideboard drawer—brandy of a finer grade than the Army used for medicinal purposes. The general liked his medicine, though. His adjutant poured a hefty nip into the coffee cup, then handed it to him.

"Thank you very much." Now that he'd got exactly what he wanted, the general was gracious. Absurdly, he preened, as well as a fat old man shoehorned into a uniform three sizes too small could preen. Peroxided locks spilled out from under the hat he wore indoors and out to hide the bald crown of his head. He'd dyed his drooping mustachios, too—*the color of piss,* Dowling thought uncharitably. When the general sipped the coffee, his rheumy blue eyes did open wider. "That is the straight goods, Major."

"Glad you like it, General Custer," Dowling said. "With your permission—" He waited for Custer's nod before filling his own cup. Not without regret, he substituted cream and sugar for the commanding general's brandy.

Custer drank his coffee almost as fast as he would have had the cup contained nothing bur firewater. He held it out in an imperious, liver-spotted hand for a refill. Dowling didn't lace it with as much brandy this time: if the commander fell asleep over his maps, the First Army would do even less than it had up till now, and it hadn't done much.

"I'm not satisfied with the reports the cavalry is bringing us from western Kentucky," Custer declared, "not satisfied at all. By God, Major, they call that scouting? They call that gathering intelligence? Why, when I was in a blue uniform instead of this moss-colored monstrosity—"

Dowling inserted a couple of mental earplugs as his commander ranted on. Most of the men who'd fought in the War of Secession were dead, and just about all the ones who weren't dead had long since been put out to pasture. Custer should have been, as far as Dowling was concerned, but he hadn't. He'd flourished, albeit more on account of persistence and luck than any military virtue past blind aggressiveness.

He'd been on the plains when the Second Mexican War broke out, and spent that conflict, the graveyard of so many U.S. military reputations, using Gatling guns on the Kiowas and then on a division of Canadians led over the border by a British general even more blindly aggressive than he was. Having made himself a hero in two wars conspicuously lacking such—and having made sure the newspapers let the world know just what a hero he was—he'd assured his rise to lieutenant general's rank and his tenure in the Army for as long as his bloated body would endure. It hadn't given out yet.

The real problem was that he'd had only a couple of new thoughts since the 1860s, and none since the 1880s. Gently, Dowling tried to bring him up toward modern times: "Much harder for cavalry to move now, sir, than it used to be. Machine guns have been hard on horses, you know. Our aeroplanes have brought back excellent sketches of Confederate defenses, though, and with them—"

"Machine guns are all very well for mowing down savages, but properly trained and disciplined troops shouldn't be so leery of them," Custer said. "Our troops are shying from them like so many virgins at the touch of a man. And as for aeroplanes—" He snapped his fingers. "They're all very fine for impressing yahoos at county fairs, but you can't take them seriously as weapons of war. Mark my words, Major: in five years' time the newfangled contraptions will be as forgotten as Ozymandias."

"Yes, sir," Dowling said, that seeming a safer course than asking who Ozymandias was and having to sit through a lecture that had nothing to do with the war. Still trying valiantly to remind Custer that they had reached the twentieth century, he went on, "The couple of armored automobiles we've been able to deploy have also given good service."

"Newfangled contraptions," Custer repeated, as if scoring a point. "I know what we need to do, Major. I merely need to ensure the Navy's cooperation before we undertake it. If we can throw a strong force of infantry into Kentucky, they'll beat down the Confederates' defenses there, allowing our cavalry to get into the enemy's rear and complete his destruction as he flees. If the sailors can hold off the Rebel river monitors—"

"Yes, sir—if," Dowling said. If, on the other hand, one of those heavily armed, heavily armored craft got loose among the barges and such shipping Americans across the river, the slaughter would be horrendous. And, since the monitors were so heavily armored, holding them away from the landing force would be anything but easy—no wonder the Navy was shillyshallying about that.

"I shall go to the front," Custer said suddenly, catching Dowling off guard. "Yes, that's what I'll do. My presence there will surely inspire the men to give the utmost effort. And," he added with an angry snort, "I am sick to death of being bombarded with telegrams demanding that I move faster.

Roosevelt delights in having the War Department nag me. He has delighted in making my life difficult for more than thirty years." The general commanding First Army and the president had fought the British together during the Second Mexican War. By all the signs, neither had enjoyed the experience. Custer went on, "We are punching into Canada, I hear—but that is all Roosevelt will let me do: hear about it, I mean."

"Yes, sir," Dowling said in his most placating tones.

That did no good. Custer was off to the races: "Damn it to hell and gone, *I* should be the one punching into Canada. Roosevelt knows what I owe the goddamn Canucks. They murdered my brother—shot him down like a dog in front of my eyes. I *deserve* that command, and the chance to take revenge at last. But do I get it? Have I any chance of getting it? No, by jingo! Roosevelt has had it in for me since 1881, and he will not give it to me—not till my dying day, I wager. The one thing I want more than any other in all the world, and I cannot have it. Do you know—have you got any idea—how maddening that is?"

"I'm sure it must be, sir," Dowling said with some sympathy—some, but not much, for he'd been listening to Custer on the same subject for longer than he wanted to. Custer would not let it go. He clung like a bulldog, or, considering the bare natural state of his gums, perhaps more like a leech.

He took a couple of deep breaths, then went on, "We are fighting hard all across the plains. We have invaded western Virginia—so why, the brass hats in Philadelphia demand, don't I move? Idiots! Cretins! Imbeciles! Because Teddy Roosevelt has it in for me, they do, too. To them, Dowling, the Ohio and the Mississippi are little squiggly blue lines on a map, nothing more. I am the one who has to find the way across. Make arrangements at once to transfer headquarters to Vienna, Illinois, as soon as is practicable. Why are you still standing there gaping?"

"I'll attend to it immediately, sir," Dowling promised. Custer had a point—throwing an army into Confederate territory wasn't going to be easy here. But if he thought his presence at the front would help things along, he was probably fooling himself. Whether he understood it or not, war had changed over the past fifty years. Most of the soldiers wouldn't know he arrived, and most of the ones who did know wouldn't care.

"And one more thing," Custer ordered. "Keep it secret. Half these Missourians and more than half the downstate Illinoisans wish they were Rebs. Our scouts may have trouble in Kentucky, but theirs, I have no doubt, enjoy a fine old time here."

"I'll take care of that, too, sir," Dowling said. "If the Germans can keep their plans secret from the damned Frenchmen they rule in Alsace-Lorraine, I expect we can keep the would-be Southerners from getting word of ours."

"We'd better." Custer bared his teeth in what was meant for a fearsome grimace. Since those teeth were far too white and even and perfect to have stayed in his own mouth for three-quarters of a century, the effect was more nearly ludicrous than frightening. Dowling quickly turned his back so the commanding general wouldn't see him giggle, then hurried off to do Custer's bidding.

Baking in the late summer sun, the plains of Kansas didn't look much different from the plains of Sequoyah just to the south. "Hellfire," Corporal Stephen Ramsay said, "once we got past the barbed wire, we ain't had any trouble a-tall."

"Good," Sergeant Bobby Brock answered. "We want to do this quick and get the hell out." He looked around at the two companies of cavalry. "We ain't got the men to stand up to any big bunch o' Yankee soldiers."

Both men—Ramsay little and lithe, Brock taller, thicker through the shoulders, and slower-moving—rode just behind the standard bearer. The Stars and Bars flapped lazily. Pointing to it, Ramsay said, "Maybe the damnyankees up in Kingman'll think that's the United States flag till we're right up on top of 'em. They look enough alike, now don't they?"

"Sure enough do," Brock agreed.

Ramsay liked to talk. "Anything that makes our job easier is all right by me," he said. "I don't expect any trouble here. Not even the Yankees got enough men to cover all the barbed wire on all the frontier. Our boys shoot off some cannon a ways east of us, they all go runnin' over there to find out what we're doin', an' we slip across easy as you please."

"Yeah." Brock let his horse, a big sorrel gelding, trot on for another few paces, then went on, "I wonder how many soldiers the Yanks got into our country the same kind o' way."

"However many there was, only way they'll come out is feet first," Ramsay said confidently. "They're only Yankees, after all. We licked 'em twice running, an' we'll do it again. Hellfire, war'll be over by winter, on account of they'll have done given up."

"That'd be good," Brock said, and let it go, from which Ramsay concluded his sergeant had some doubts. He shrugged. Bobby Brock could be a bit of an old lady sometimes, but you didn't want anybody else along when the fighting got serious.

They rode past a farmhouse. The farmer was out in his fields. He knew right off they were from the Confederate States, and started running like hell back to his farmhouse. "Shall we get rid of him, sir?" Ramsay asked the captain in charge of the raiders.

Captain Hiram Lincoln often made himself out to be the toughest bird around, maybe because he had such an unfortunate last name. But now he shook his head. "Can't waste the time," he said. "Fellow doesn't have any telephone wires goin' into his house, so he's not going to get word to anybody. We keep riding. We'll hit the railroad track pretty soon."

"Remind me again, sir," Ramsay said, bowing to the appeal to military necessity. "We going in west of Kingman or east?"

"West," Captain Lincoln answered. "The blockhouse they built to protect the railroad is on the east side of town. We don't want to tangle with that. Them damn machine guns, they're liable to take all the fun out of war."

The standard-bearer, a kid named Gibbons, pointed ahead to a smudge on the horizon. "Reckon that's Kingman, sir."

"Swing left," Lincoln told him. "We'll want to set ourselves on the track a couple miles away from town."

Up ahead, a church bell began ringing as if announcing the end of the world. A machine gun in the blockhouse began to chatter, but the bullets fell far short of the Confederates. Ramsay nodded to himself. Captain Lincoln had known what he was talking about, all right.

He glanced over to Brock. The sergeant nodded back at him. It was nice to have an officer who knew which end was up.

"There's the track," Lincoln said. "Let's go!"

They knew what to do. Some of them had grandfathers who'd done the same thing in the War of Secession. They had better tools for mischief than their grandfathers had used, though. Under Captain Lincoln's direction, the troopers fanned out to cover the demolition crew. The specialists got to work with their dynamite. One of them hit the plunger on the detonator.

Ramsay's horse shied under him at the flat, harsh bark of the explosion. Clods of dirt came raining down on him and the animal both; he hadn't moved back quite far enough. You could make a hell of a hole with dynamite, a hole that would take a long time to fill by pick-and-shovel work. The explosive also did a good job of twisting rails out of shape. Till the Yanks brought in some fresh iron, they weren't going to be using this line to ship things from one coast to the other.

Dismounting, Ramsay gave the reins to a cavalryman who was already holding two other horses. Then he went over to the pack animals and started pulling crowbars off the panniers they carried to either side. "Come on, boys!" he shouted. "Let's tear up some more track."

The Confederates fell to work with a will, laughing and joking and whooping as they separated the iron rails from the wooden ties that bound them. The demolition men used gasoline to start a fire on the prairie. They didn't worry about its spreading, as they would have back in their own country. If it got out of hand, that was the Yankees' problem.

"Come on!" Ramsay said again. He lugged a cross tie over to the fire and threw it in. The rest of the troopers followed his example. Then, several men to a rail, they hauled the lengths of track over and threw them in, too. They'd slump in the heat and have to be taken to an ironworks to be straightened.

They had one rail left to cast into the fire when gunshots rang out in the east, over toward Kingman: not just rifle shots, but the hard, quick chatter of a machine gun. "Mount and form skirmish line!" Captain Lincoln yelled. "No more horseplay, not a bit—we've got some real work to do now."

Ramsay reclaimed his horse and sprang into the saddle. He checked to make sure he had a round in the chamber of his Tredegar carbine, then made sure his front pockets were full of fresh five-round clips. He had a cavalry saber, a copy of the British pattern of 1908, strapped to the left side of his saddle, but who could guess whether he'd get a chance to use it against a machine gun?

Captain Lincoln was holding a pair of field glasses up to his eyes. "Looks like they've got maybe half a company of horse," he said. "Half a company of horse and—uh-oh. They got one of those newfangled armored automobiles with 'em, too. That's where the machine gun is at." A predatory grin stretched across his face. "Well, let's go see what the contraption is worth. *Move 'em out!*" His voice rose to a shout again.

Before long, Ramsay could pick out the armored car without any help from field glasses. As it bounced over the prairie, it kicked up more dust than half a dozen horses would have. The Confederate pickets fell back before it; the Yankee horsemen, encouraged by the mechanical monster's presence, pursued a lot more aggressively than they would have otherwise, considering how outnumbered they were.

The armored car didn't move much faster than a trotting horse. The machine gun it mounted sat in a steel box on top of the superstructure; the gunner swung it back and forth through a slit in the metal, giving him about a ninety-degree field of fire. Ramsay waved toward the vehicle. "We get around to the side and it can't hurt us," he called to the squadmates who rode with him.

He rapidly discovered that wasn't quite true. Not only did the gun traverse in its mounting, but the driver, by swinging the front end of the armored car this way and that, could bring it to bear on targets it wouldn't have been able to reach otherwise. And the Yankee troopers were doing their best to make sure the Confederates couldn't outflank the ugly, noisy thing, anyhow.

A bullet cracked past Ramsay's head. The noise—and the fright it gave him—made him realize this wasn't practice any more. The U.S. soldiers were doing their damnedest to kill him, and their damnedest, by the way his comrades and their horses were crashing to the ground, was better than he'd expected. He'd never seen combat before, not even fighting Mexican bandits along the frontier with the Empire. His cherry was gone now, by Jesus.

He raised his carbine to his shoulder and fired at a green-gray-clad Yankee. The fellow did not pitch from the saddle, so he had to have missed. He worked the bolt to get rid of the casing and chamber a fresh round, then fired again. Another bullet zipped past him, and another. Now he didn't bother looking after he fired, to see what effect each round had. The more he put in the air, the better his chance of hitting something.

A lot of bullets were hitting the armored car. The sound of them rattling off its side put Ramsay in mind of hail hitting a tin roof. But the car kept on coming, like an ironclad smashing its way through a navy of wooden ships. The comparison was apt, for it was doing more damage to the Confederates all by its lonesome than all the troopers who came with it.

Bobby Brock made a noise somewhere between a groan and a scream. There was a neat hole in the front of his uniform tunic. As he slumped down over his horse's neck, Ramsay got a look at the hole the bullet had made going out through his back. That wasn't neat at all. It looked more as if somebody had set off half a stick of dynamite in his chest.

The trooper right alongside of Brock went down as his horse took three bullets—neck, barrel, and hock—from that damned machine gun in the space of a second and a half. The cavalryman pulled himself free, but he didn't bounce to his feet. Having a horse fall on your leg wasn't the best thing that could ever happen to it.

For a couple of dreadful minutes, Ramsay was afraid the armored car would win the little battle all by its lonesome, even though the Confederate troopers were mopping the floor with the damnyankees whenever they could engage them away from the car with its machine gun. But then the vehicle, all of its tires shot out, slowed to walking pace and, when it went into a hole, couldn't pull itself out no matter how the engine growled and roared and sent up clouds of stinking exhaust.

Ramsay threw back his head and let out the catamount wail of a Rebel yell. "Damn thing is stuck, boys!" he shouted. "Now we can get around behind it and settle the rest of these bastards."

The Confederates went wide to right and left around the bogged-down armored car, getting away from the deadly arc of fire its machine gun could command. Once that gauntlet was run, chasing the Yankee cavalry back toward Kingman proved the work of only a few minutes.

"And now we settle with this goddamn thing," Captain Lincoln said, riding toward the armored car from the rear. The machine gunner proved to have a firing port in the back of the steel box that enclosed him. He banged away with a pistol. The range was still long for a handgun, and he missed. Captain Lincoln yelled, "Parley, dammit!" The U.S. soldier held his fire. Lincoln said, "You come out of that damned iron turtle of yours, or we'll chuck a couple of sticks of dynamite under it and blow y'all to kingdom come."

With a squeal of metal against metal, a hinged roof on top of the armored car and a door in its side came open. The machine gunner stood up with his hands in the air and the driver stepped out. "All right, you've got us," the gunner said with a grin, sounding and looking a lot more jaunty than he should have, considering how much damage he'd done to good Southern men and horses. "Take us and—"

He never got any farther than that. Somebody's carbine barked at almost point-blank range. The back of his head blew off in a spray of blood and brain and bone. He collapsed, dead before he knew what hit him. With a cry of horror, the armored-car driver tried to dive back into his machine. Several more shots stretched him lifeless beside it.

"Chew our people up and make like it's a game you can just walk away from, will you?" Ramsay said. He hadn't fired at the men who'd surrendered, but he didn't miss them a bit, either.

"You want to fight us, get on a horse and fight fair," somebody else added, which made troopers' heads bob up and down in agreement.

Captain Lincoln set his hands on his hips and snarled in exasperation. "God damn it to hell, now we got to blow up that machine," he said. "Otherwise the Yankees'll find the bodies like that and start shootin' our prisoners, too."

The armored car went up in a ball of flame as a stick of dynamite set off the gasoline in the fuel tank. Machine-gun bullets, ignited by the fire, added brisk popping sounds as they cooked off one after another.

"All right, we did what we came to do," Lincoln said, looking from the funeral pyre of the armored car to the wrecked stretch of track. "Let's get back home."

Ramsay was happy to obey. Yes, they'd done what they'd come to do, but the cost— Of every three men who'd left Sequoyah, only two were going back, and one of them was wounded. And all that, or almost all of it, from one armored car that bogged down pretty fast.

He spurred his horse up close to Captain Lincoln's. "Sir, what's cavalry supposed to do when we run into four or five of those machine gun-totin' machines, not just the one like we fought today?"

Lincoln didn't answer for so long, Ramsay started to wonder if he'd heard. The captain looked back over his depleted command. "I don't know, Corporal. I just don't know."

"Come on! Come on! Come on!" Captain Irving Morrell urged his men forward. Dust spurted up under his boots as, with every stride, he penetrated deeper into Confederate Sonora. "The faster we move, the less chance they have of setting up lines against us."

One of his soldiers, sweat soaking through his uniform as he slogged through the desert under the weight of a heavy pack, pointed up into the sky. "They already got their lines set, sir," he said.

Morrell hadn't heard the buzz of a spying Confederate aeroplane, but looked up anyhow. He burst out laughing. No aeroplane up there, just half a dozen vultures, all of them circling hopefully. "*They* won't get us, Altrock," he said. "They're waiting for us to feed 'em some Rebs."

"That must be how it is, sir," the infantryman agreed. He stepped up his pace to match that of his commander.

"You bet that's how it is," Morrell said, kicking at the light brown sandy dirt. "Didn't we give 'em a blue-plate special when we crossed from Nogales into New Montgomery?"

Several men nodded enthusiastically in response to that. The bombardment of the Confederate town had done everything it was supposed to do, silencing the enemy's guns and sending civilians streaming away in panic—white Confederates, their black servants and laborers, and the brown folk who'd lived there since the days before the Rebels bought Sonora from a Mexico strapped for cash to pay England and France what it owed. The garrison had fought, but they'd been outnumbered as well as outgunned. The way into Sonora, toward Guaymas and the Pacific end of the Confederate railway net, lay open.

Morrell meant to do everything he could to make sure that line got cut. He was a lean man in his mid-twenties, with a long face, light eyes, and sandy hair he wore cropped close to his skull. He gulped a salt tablet and washed it down with a swig of warm water from his canteen. Other than that, he ignored the sweat gushing from every pore. He ignored everything not directly concerned with the mission, and pursued everything that was with a driving energy that brought his men along, too.

"Come on!" he called again, stepping up the pace. "We've cracked the shell. Now we get to suck the meat out."

One of his first lieutenants, a big, gangly fellow named Jake Hoyland, moved up alongside him, map in hand. "Next town ahead is Imuris," he said, pointing. "There's some mines around there, too: copper mines. Cocospera." He read the name off the map with the sublime disregard for Spanish pronunciation growing up in Michigan gave him.

"The division will secure those, and the United States will exploit them," Morrell said. "We have an advantage over our German allies here, Jake."

"Sir?" Hoyland wasn't much given to strategic thought. He'd make captain one day, but he probably wouldn't rise much further than that.

Patiently, Morrell explained: "Germany is attacking France on a narrow front, and the French and the damned English can be strong against them all along it. We have about the population of Germany, and the Confederacy and Canada together close to the population of France, but we have thousands and thousands of miles of frontier with our enemies, not a few hundred. Except in a few places, defense in depth becomes impossible."

"Oh. I see what you mean." Maybe Hoyland even did. He pointed to the map again. "How will we exploit these Cocospera mines?"

"Probably with the niggers the Rebels brought in to work them," Morrell answered, shrugging. "That's not our worry. Our worry is to take them."

"Yes, sir." Now Hoyland wiped his face with his sleeve, leaving a smear of dust on his cheek. "Even hotter here than it was up in the USA, you ask me."

"We've only come twenty miles, for God's sake," Morrell said in some exasperation. "We've got a long haul before we get to Guaymas."

He looked back over his shoulder. Dust clogged the horizon to the north, hiding the men and horses and cannon and horse-drawn wagons and motor trucks that had stirred it up. He knew they were there, though, intent on sealing the western part of the Confederacy from the rest of the country: not only was Guaymas a railhead, it was the only real Pacific port the Rebels had. Shut it down and this part of the South withered on the vine.

The Rebels knew as much, too. Their frontier force had been smashed in the opening U.S. attack, but they were still doing what they could to resist. Off to the northeast of Imuris, the desert rose up into low, rolling hills. They'd mounted some three-inch field guns up on the high ground, and were banging away at the advancing U.S. column.

More dust rising from the U.S. left showed cavalry—or, more likely, mounted infantry—peeling off to deal with the Confederates. Those nuisance field guns had accomplished their objective: to distract some of the American force from its primary mission.

Morrell refused to be distracted. He scrambled between strands of barbed wire that marked the outer bounds of some ranch's property. He could see the ranch house and its outbuildings a couple of miles ahead, shimmering in the heat haze. As on the U.S. side of the border, ranches were big here; because water was scarce and precious and the ground scrubby as a result, you needed a lot of acreage for your stock.

He didn't see any of that stock. The owner, whoever he was (*an old-time Mexican or a Southern Johnny-come-lately?* Morrell wondered), had run it off to keep the U.S. forces from getting their hands on it. They'd probably run off themselves, too—with luck, so fast they hadn't had a chance to take everything out of the ranch house. Whatever they hadn't taken, the U.S. Army would.

A rifle barked, up ahead. A bullet kicked up dirt, maybe fifty yards from Morrell's feet. As if that first one had been a test, a fusillade of rifle shots rang out. Morrell threw himself flat on his belly. Somewhere behind him, a wounded man let out a breathless, angry curse.

From the volume of fire, the Confederates were there in about platoon strength. Morrell didn't hear the deadly chatter of a machine gun, for which he thanked God. Even after the bombardment of New Montgomery, machine guns in the ruins had chewed holes in the U.S. forces.

"We'll flank 'em out!" he shouted. "Hoyland, your platoon to the left; Koenig, yours to the right. Foulkes, I'll stay with your boys here in the center. We'll advance by squads. Let's go."

The Confederates had had time to dig themselves holes, and their dun-colored uniforms weren't easy to spot against the gray-brown dirt: here, at least, they matched the terrain better than the U.S. troops did. They could not let themselves be taken from the sides, though, and began falling back toward the ranch house and other buildings as their foes moved forward. Here and there, a brave man or two would stay in a hole and die in place, buying his comrades time to retreat.

One of those diehards popped up not ten feet from Morrell. The U.S. captain shot first. With a cry of pain, the Confederate fell back. He wasn't through, though; he tried to bring his rifle to bear once more. Morrell sprang down into the hole and finished him with the bayonet.

He got out and resumed the advance. "We can't let 'em get set," he said. "Press 'em hard, every one of you."

A U.S. soldier was already sprawled behind a woodpile near the house, firing at the Rebels inside. A body sprawled out through a window and poured blood down onto the flowers below.

With better cover, though, the Confederates were taking a heavy toll on the U.S. troopers. Firing came not only from the ranch house but also from the barn, the chicken coop, and what looked like a little separate smithy. Then three of Morrell's men rushed into the smithy. After a sharp, short volley, it became a U.S. strongpoint rather than a Confederate one.

But heavy firing still came from both the ranch house and the barn. Several men in butternut burst out of the barn and ran toward the house, which was closer to the advancing U.S. soldiers.

"Come on!" Morrell shouted to his own men. He burst from the cover of a scraggly bush and sprinted toward the Confederates, firing as he ran. They fired, too; a couple of bullets cracked past him.

He didn't have time to be afraid. He fired again, saw one man fall, worked the bolt on his Springfield, and pulled the trigger. His only reward was a dry click; he'd just spent the last round in the magazine. No chance to fumble for a fresh one. The Rebels couldn't have been more than twenty or thirty feet away. He'd always been pretty good with the bayonet. If he stuck one Confederate, maybe the rest would run. Shouting once more for his men to follow him, he rushed at the enemy.

The bullet caught him in the right thigh. The rifle flew out of his hands and crashed to the ground. So did he. Looking down at himself, he saw in mild surprise that a chunk of meat about the size of a clenched fist was missing from the side of his leg. Blood spilled out onto the hot, dry, thirsty ground.

He didn't hurt—and then he did. His groans were lost in the racket of gunfire. Nobody could come to retrieve him, not when he lay right between the two battling forces. Nobody fired at him to finish him off, either. He was not altogether sure that was a mercy. The fierce sun beat down on him.

Next thing he remembered, the sun was in a different part of the sky. Somebody was rolling him over onto his back. Did they think him dead? The very idea made him indignant. But no—Private Altrock was wrapping something around his leg.

"Get that belt good and tight," Lieutenant Hoyland said. "He's already lost a hell of a lot of blood."

"Yes, sir," Altrock said, and grunted as he pulled the makeshift tourniquet tighter.

"Did we—take the position?" Morrell asked, each word a separate effort.

"Yes, sir," Hoyland told him. "You take it easy now. We'll get you out of here." Off to one side, a couple of men were improvising a stretcher from two poles and a shelter half. When they were done, Altrock and Hoyland got Morrell onto it, lifting him like a sack of grain. He remembered the stretcher coming off the ground, but blacked out again after that.

He woke up out of the direct sun, looking up at green-gray cloth. *A hospital tent,* he thought dimly. A man in a gauze mask bent over him with an ether-soaked rag. "Wait," Morrell croaked. "If you go into close combat, make sure you've got the last bullet." The rag came down, and with it blackness.

The *Dakota* slowed to a crawl to let the fuel ship *Vulcan* come alongside. Sailors cursed and grunted as they wrestled with the hose from the *Vulcan* and started pumping heavy fuel oil into the battleship.

Seaman First Class Sam Carsten looked on the refueling process with something less than approval: he was swabbing the deck nearby, and saw more work piling up for him every moment. "Can't you lugs be careful?" he demanded. "Bunch of filthy slobs, is what you are."

"Sorry, mother dearest," one of the men on the refueling party said in a high, scratchy falsetto. His comrades laughed. So did Carsten, who leaned on his mop to watch the work go on. He laughed easily, even at himself. He was a big, slow-moving blue-eyed blond, his skin ever more sunburned these days.

"Wish we were back in San Francisco," he said wistfully. "It was right nice there—good weather for a paleface like me. Another couple days of this and you can spread me with butter and marmalade, because I'll be a piece of toast."

"It's hot, sure as hell," the other sailor agreed. Black oil stains spotted his dungarees. "It ain't near as hot as we're gonna make it for the goddamn limeys, though."

"That's right," another hose-handler agreed. He eyed Carsten. "You're gonna be toast, are you? Maybe we'll use you for the Sandwich Islands, then." He snickered at his own wit.

"Pretty funny," Carsten said amiably. He swabbed a few strokes to satisfy any watching petty officer, then took it easy again. He'd been in the Navy five years, and was used to its rhythms and routines. Things had sped up on account of the war, sure, but not that much: on a ship you had to do things by the numbers even in peacetime, which wasn't so true in the Army. He paused to roll himself a cigarette, lighted it with a match he scraped to life on the sole of his shoe, and sucked in a breath of smoke before going on, "Any luck at all, we'll cornhole the limeys but good."

"Cornhole 'em, hey?" one of the hose jockeys said. "I like that, damned if I don't. We're sure comin' up at 'em the wrong way."

"Yeah." Carsten plied the mop again. If you looked busy, people would figure you were. If you didn't, they'd find something for you to do, probably something you'd like less than what you were doing now.

As he worked, he thought again about cornholing the Royal Navy. The more he thought about it, the better he liked it. The U.S. Pacific Fleet had put to sea days before war was declared, sailing out of San Francisco Bay and Los Angeles and San Diego. The Seattle squadron was still up there, to face the British and Canadian ships based in Vancouver and Victoria. But the main fleet had swung west and south in a long loop around the western end of the Sandwich Island chain, and now—

"Wish we'd have beaten the British to annexing those damned islands," said the sailor with the oil-spotted dungarees. "Then we could have sailed from there 'stead of the West Coast, and we'd be steaming for Singapore."

"Or maybe for the Philippines," Carsten said. "The Japs, they're England's good pals. One of these days, we kick them in the slats, too."

He tried to think like Admiral Dewey. If they could boot the British out of the Sandwich Islands, they booted them all the way across the Pacific, to Singapore and Australia. They'd have only the one chance, though; if things went wrong here, British battleships would be steaming up and down the west coast of the United States for the rest of the war, and there'd be damn all anybody would be able to do about it.

"So—we roll the dice," he muttered. If the Pacific Fleet took the Sandwich Islands away from England, the USA would have an easier time resupplying them than the British did now. They'd run around the chain so the limeys wouldn't spot them on the way in, and now they were picking up fuel for the last run on Pearl Harbor. One good surprise and the islands would be theirs.

One good surprise— Alarms began to ring. "Battle stations! Battle stations!" came the cry. "Aeroplane spotted. Not known whether hostile."

The fleet had launched a pair of aeroplanes a couple of hours before, to scout out what lay ahead. But were these American aeroplanes returning, or British machines doing some scouting of their own? If they were British, the fleet had to knock them out of the sky before they could report back to the Royal Navy and to the land-based guns defending Pearl Harbor.

Carsten's battle station was at the starboard bow, loading five-inch shells into one of the guns of the *Dakota*'s secondary armament. He threw his cigarette over the side as he ran to the sponson. Bringing it in would have been his own funeral, except that the gunner's mate, a bruiser named Hiram Kidde, would have taken care of that for him.

Behind him, the hose went back aboard the *Vulcan*, as if an elephant had owned a retractable trunk. They had enough fuel on board for the attack, and they could worry about everything else later.

"You ready, Sam?" Kidde asked.

Carsten would have bet any money you cared to name that the gunner's mate would have beaten him there, no matter where he was on the ship when the call for battle stations rang out. He sometimes thought Kidde could just wish himself to the sponson from anywhere on board.

"Aye aye, 'Cap'n,' " Carsten answered, with a salute more extravagant than he would have given Dewey. "Cap'n" Kidde chuckled; he'd had the inevitable nickname for as long as he'd been in the Navy.

The sponson was tiny and cramped, with plenty of sharp metal corners to gouge your legs or your arms if you weren't careful. Bare electric bulbs in wire cages on the ceiling shed a harsh, yellow light. The place stank of paint and brass and nitrocellulose and old sweat, odors no amount of swabbing could ever wash away.

Kidde patted the breech of the gun—affectionately, as if it were a trollop's backside in some Barbary Coast dive in San Francisco. "Wish we had some high-explosive shells for this baby along with armor piercing. She'd make a hell of an antiaircraft gun, wouldn't she?"

"Damned if she wouldn't," Carsten said. "Have to fuse 'em just right, to burst around the aeroplane, but damned if she wouldn't. You ought to talk to somebody about that one, Mate, you really should."

"Ahh, it's just stack gas," Kidde said with a shrug. By then, the other loader and the gun layer were in their places. Luke Hoskins, the number-two shell jerker, was slower than he should have been. Kidde reamed him up one side and down the other with a tongue sharp enough to chip paint.

"Have a heart, 'Cap'n' Kidde," Hoskins said. "First decent shit I've had in three days, and the goddamn battle stations sounds when I got my pants around my ankles in the aft head."

"Tough," Kidde said flatly. "Next time, don't waste time wipin' your ass. It won't matter what you smell like—we get into a real scrap and we'll all be shittin' ourselves any which way."

Carsten laughed till he incautiously jerked around and barked his shin on the edge of an ammunition rack. He swore, but kept on laughing. Part of that was good nature, part of it nerves. He didn't try to figure out which part was which.

A runner came by with word that the aeroplane spotted had been one of the ones they'd launched. "He's floatin' on the water now an' the *New York*, it's fishin' him out of the drink with a crane," he reported. "Old Man says to stay at battle stations, though." He hurried away.

The gun crew looked at one another. If they were staying at battle stations, that meant they'd be heading toward Pearl Harbor for the attack. And, sure enough, the rumble of the big steam engines got louder as they picked up steam. The *Vulcan* and the rest of the support ships would be dropping behind now—this was a job for the warships and the transports that carried a regiment of Marines and a whole division of Army men toward Oahu.

Another man stuck his head inside the blazing-hot metal box where Carsten and his comrades waited for orders. Voice cracking with excitement, the sailor said, "Word is, the limeys ain't done much with their fleet, an' a lot of it's still in the harbor. We caught 'em with their pants down."

"You think it's really true?" Hoskins breathed.

"Why not?" Sam Carsten said. "Battle stations got you that way, didn't it?" The other seaman glared at him, but he wasn't easy to get angry at.

"If it's so," Kidde said, "you can serve those Englishmen up with tea and crumpets, because they're dinner. They hit us a low blow back in granddad's day, comin' in on the side of the Rebels. Now we give it back. Sweet suffering Jesus, do we ever! All those ships sittin' inside Pearl Harbor, waiting for us to smash 'em . . ." His smile was beatific.

Carsten peered through one of the narrow vision slits the sponson afforded. Torpedo-boat destroyers sprinted ahead of the battleships, their creamy wakes vivid against the deep blue of the tropical Pacific. The *Dakota* and her fellow capital ships were still picking up speed, too; the steel deck hummed and shuddered against his feet as the engines reached full power. They had to be making better than twenty knots. At that rate, it wouldn't be long until—

"There it is!" he exclaimed excitedly. "Land on the horizon! We'll give 'em what-for any minute now. Well— Holy Jesus!"

"What?" The rest of the gun crew, the ones who weren't looking out themselves, all shouted the question together.

"Harbor defense guns just opened up on us. They may not have known we were here, but they sure as hell do now."

He didn't see the shell splash into the sea. Almost a minute later, though, the sound of the great cannon reached him: a thunder that cut through not only the roar of the *Dakota*'s engines but also the hardened steel armor of the sponson.

And then, bare seconds after that, the battleship's main armament cut loose, the two fourteen-inch guns in the forward superfiring turret and then the three from the A turret just below and ahead of it. He'd heard the noise from the distant British cannon; the roar of the guns from his own ship enveloped him, so that he felt it with his whole body more than with his ears. When the guns went off, the *Dakota* seemed to buck for a moment before resuming its advance.

Sailors crowded up to see what they could see. The shore and the harbor wouldn't be in range of their secondary armament for some time to come. It was like having a moving picture unreel right before your eyes, Carsten thought, except this had sound—all the sound in the world, not some piano-pounding accompanist—and bright colors.

More thunderclaps came from the guns of the other battleships in the fleet. The shore defenses sent up answering gouts of smoke and flame. This time, Carsten spied the splashes from a couple of shells. If you took a Ford, loaded it with explosives, and dropped it into the sea from a great height, you'd get a plume of water like that. Some of the splashes were close enough to the destroyers for the upthrown seawater to drench the men aboard.

"Christ!" Altogether involuntarily, Carsten turned away from his viewing slit. One shell from the salvo hadn't landed by a destroyer, but on it. The ship might suddenly have rammed headlong into a brick wall. In an instant, it went from a yappy little terrier leading the fleet into action to a pile of floating—or rather, rapidly sinking—wreckage.

"A lot of good men there," Hiram Kidde said, as if carving an epitaph on a headstone. So, in a way, he was.

The *Dakota* began to zigzag violently at what seemed like random intervals. Armored against such shells, it could take far more punishment than a thin-skinned destroyer. That didn't mean you wanted to be punished—anything but. "Cap'n" Kidde summed that up in one short phrase: "Hate to be zigging when we should have zagged."

"Wish you hadn't said that," Hoskins told him. The grin the gunner's mate gave him in return looked like a death's head.

Sam Carsten made himself look some more. A few men in life jackets bobbed in the water near the stricken destroyer. He hoped they'd get picked up before the sharks found them.

He raised his gaze to Oahu ahead. Shells slammed down around the forts holding the coast-defense guns. Smoke and dust rose in great clouds. But the guns kept pounding back in answer. And more smoke rose from within the sheltered waters of Pearl Harbor, smoke that did not spring from shells. Carsten said, "I think they're gonna come out and fight."

"They're in a bad way," Kidde said, relishing the prospect. "They can't just sit there and take it, but if they come out, we're going to cross the T on 'em."

Sure enough, one of the *Dakota*'s zigs to port became a full turn, so that she presented her whole ten-gun broadside to the emerging British warships, which could reply only with their forward-facing cannon.

"Hit!" everybody screamed at once as gouts of smoke spurted from a stricken British vessel, and then again, a moment later, "Hit!"

The ships of the Royal Navy were firing back; across blue water, orange flame and black smoke belched from the muzzles of their guns. And their gunnery was good. With a noise like a freight train roaring past when you were standing much too close to the tracks, a salvo of three shells smashed into the ocean a couple of hundred yards short of the *Dakota*. The battleship heeled to port as the captain took evasive action.

"Wish I could see what was happening on the port beam," Carsten said. "Have they bracketed us?"

"Sam, is that somethin' you really want to know?" Kidde asked him. After a moment, Carsten shook his head. If they put one salvo in front of you and one behind, the next one came down right on top of you.

"We in range for our piece yet, 'Cap'n'?" Hoskins asked.

"Not quite, but we're gettin' there," the gunner's mate replied. But then the *Dakota* turned so the gun didn't bear on the enemy. Carsten pictured the turrets that housed the main armament swinging back into position to carry on the fight. You fought your ship to bring them to bear on the most important targets the enemy had. If a torpedo boat or destroyer made a run at you, the five-inchers like the one Carsten manned were supposed to settle its hash. They were good for giving shore batteries hell, too: batteries that weren't main harbor defenses, anyhow.

Now, though, all Carsten could do was stare out to sea and wait for his turn. It bothered him less than he'd thought it would. Out there were the transports with the soldiers and Marines. If they all landed safely, the Sandwich Islands would fly the Stars and Stripes. The odds looked good.

"Hell of a start," he muttered.

The dandy up from Charleston studied the painting with a curious and critical eye. His pose was so languid and exquisite, Anne Colleton thought, that he should have been wearing knee breeches and frock coat and sneezing after a pinch of snuff, not in a dinner jacket and smoking a fragrant Habana. His Low Country drawl only strengthened the impression of aristocratic effeteness: "Upon my word, Miss Colleton, we surely have here an extraordinary series of contrasts, do we not?"

She brushed back a lock of pale gold hair that was tickling her cheek. "I can think of several," she said. *Starting with, why are you here at Marshlands while both my brothers have gone to serve their country?* But to say that out loud would have been impolite and, however often she flouted the code of a Confederate gentlewoman, she still adhered to some of it. And so, not a hint of worry showed in her voice as she went on, "Which ones cross your mind, Mr. Forbes?"

Alfred Forbes pointed to the canvas he had been examining. "First and foremost, hanging that sense-stretching cubist portrait and all these other pieces from Picasso and Duchamp and Gauguin and Braque and the other moderns here in this hall strikes me as making contrast enough all by itself." He examined the painting once more, then grinned impishly. "Are you sure it's right side up?"

"Quite sure," Anne replied, with less frost in her voice than she would have liked. Duchamp's *Nude Descending a Staircase* had been upside down for a day before anyone noticed. It hadn't been the fault of her Negro servants, either; a curator who'd accompanied the exhibition from Paris had made the mistake. They couldn't even ship him home in disgrace, not with Yankee and German warships prowling the Atlantic. She went on, "I'll have you know Marshlands was avant-garde in its day, too."

"No doubt, no doubt," Forbes said. Now his smile was somewhere between speculative and predatory. "But even should I have been so ungallant as to doubt, I could point out that yesterday's avant-garde is tomorrow's—" He checked himself.

"Yes?" Anne Colleton said sweetly. "You were about to say?"

"Tomorrow's treasured tradition, I was about to say," he replied. He'd probably been about to say something like *tomorrow's crashing bore*, but he'd managed to find something better. His blue eyes were so wide and innocent, Anne smiled in spite of herself.

She said, "Supposing that to be a contrast"—it was one that had amused her ever since she'd arranged to bring the sampler of the best of modern painting from Paris to the Confederacy—"what other odd juxtapositions do you find?"

"That you chose to hold the show *here*, among others," Alfred Forbes answered. "Worthy though St. Matthews is, it hardly ranks with Richmond or Charleston or New Orleans or even Columbia"—that, a Low Country man's dig at the decidedly Up Country capital of South Carolina—"as a center of cultural advancement."

"It does now," Anne said. "These works would never have been seen in the Confederate States if I hadn't made the effort"—*and spent the money,* she thought, although saying that would have been vulgar—"to bring them here. This is my home, sir. Where would you have me exhibit them? The New York Armory, perhaps?"

Forbes laughed out loud, showing off even white teeth. "Not likely! The next progressive Yankee I know of will be the first. When the USA ships in art from abroad, it's fat German singers in brass unmentionables bellowing about the Rhine while the orchestra does its level best to drown them out—presumably not in the said river."

Anne smiled again. "They deserve each other, the Yankees and the Germans." The smile slipped. "But we don't deserve either of them, and we have the Yankees on our border and the Germans helping to harry the coast."

"Which brings me to yet another contrast," Forbes said: "how long the exhibition was supposed to stay on these shores and how long it may actually be here. Wouldn't want these paintings sunk."

"No, though a Yankee ship captain would likely boast of having rid the world of them." Anne Colleton dismissed the USA with that sentence and a curl of her lip. But the USA was not so easily dismissed. "A pity the Royal Navy took such a beating in the Sandwich Islands last week."

"A date which will live in infamy for the British fleet," Forbes agreed sadly.

The butler approached with a silver tray. He wore white tie but, as if his dark brown skin were not enough to mark his status, his vest had stripes and the buttons on his cutaway were shiny brass, just as they would have been in London. "Something to drink, madam, sir?" he asked, his voice the bass pipe of an organ.

"Thank you, Scipio," Anne said, and took a crystal champagne flute.

Forbes took one, too. Scipio headed into the drawing room to serve some of the other art aficionados. "He's well spoken," Forbes remarked. "Can't say that for most of the niggers hereabouts—I can scarcely fathom their jargon."

"We had him specially trained in elocution," Anne said. "A butler, after all, reflects the standards of the house."

"Very true." Alfred Forbes raised his glass. "And here's to culture on the Congaree! Let New York keep the rancid Rhine; the wave of the future is here!"

Anne drank to that, quite happily. Forbes hung around and tried to draw her out, tried to make her interested in his admittedly handsome, well-groomed person. She could all but read his thoughts—*a woman who is a patroness of cubist art is surely a woman with other modern ideas, and a woman with modern ideas is surely a loose woman.* She pretended not to notice his hints. When he stepped forward to try to set his hand on her arm, she moved to one side: not in any offensive way, for he had not been offensive, but not permitting the contact, either. After a while, he gave up and went off to look at other paintings.

A couple in their fifties came up to scrutinize the Picasso. "Isn't it exciting?" the woman said. "You can see her back and her, er, bosom both together there. It's a whole new way of looking at the world."

"Maybe it takes special eyesight," the man replied with a dubious chuckle. The left sleeve of his jacket hung limp. Anne wondered whether he'd lost the arm during the Second Mexican War or, less romantically, in a railroading accident.

"Oh, Joseph, you are such a philistine," his wife—the wedding band sparkled on her ring finger—said in mock despair. They both laughed, comfortable as old shoes together, and, with a nod to Anne, went on to the next painting.

The salt of the earth, she thought with mingled admiration and scorn. Joseph and his wife, obviously, would never do anything scandalous, but they'd never do anything interesting, either.

Life should be interesting, she thought. *If it's not, what point to living it?* She felt like Eleanor of Aquitaine, free beyond the common limits of the world in which she lived. Royal birth had given Eleanor that freedom. Modern times were simpler: money did the job for Anne Colleton. The useless swamp along the Congaree aside, most of the land between St. Matthews and Columbia was Colleton cotton country.

She tapped a finger against the gleaming mahogany banister. Brains hadn't hurt Eleanor of Aquitaine, and they didn't hurt her, either. She'd doubled profits from the land in the five years since her father died, and they hadn't been low before. After a couple of protests more for form's sake than because they really wanted the job, her brothers had let her run the plantation as suited her. Why not? She let them have allowance enough to get into all the mischief they liked, and they liked quite a lot.

She'd grown used to patronizing Tom and Jacob in her mind. What they were getting into these days was worse than mischief. The casualty lists in the newspapers were hideously long, and the battles not going so well as everyone had been sure they would. *Too many damnyankees,* she thought bitterly.

And who would remember the Marshlands Exhibition of Modern Art now, except as the show that was going on when war raced around the world? She knew to the penny what the show had cost to set up and publicize. She'd made that back—she couldn't remember the last investment where she'd failed to turn a profit—and the artists had sold a good many works, but much of the fame that should have come to both the Marshlands mansion and to herself was gone forever now, lost in the cannon's roar. *One more reason to hate the United States.*

But, even if not quite so notorious as she'd hoped (in this modern age, what difference between notoriety and fame?), she was still free, and still reveling in that freedom. As she sometimes had before, she wondered how best to enjoy it.

Work for the vote for women? That thought had crossed her mind before, too. As she had when it last did, she shook her head. For one thing, advocates of suffrage were earnest to the point of boredom, and she did not want to be bored: life was too short for that. The cause, while worthy, reeked of bourgeois respectability. And, for another, South Carolina had only recently come to grant the vote to all white men, and its districts were so arranged that half of those white men or more might as well not have had it. Making headway against such resolute conservatism struck her as a long, slow job.

What then? She didn't know. She had time to find something. She was only twenty-eight, with the whole world stretched out before her.

That thought had hardly passed her mind when some sort of commotion broke out at the front of the mansion. She hurried forward to see what was going on. Looking out the window, she spied a new automobile near the mansion: a dusty Manassas, probably hired in St. Matthews. But getting out of it was . . .

She threw open the door and hurried forward, stopping to curtsy as her grandmother might have done before the War of Secession. "Mr. President!" she exclaimed. "I had no idea you would honor me with a visit here." Part of that was, *Why didn't you telegraph ahead, dammit?* But another part, a gloating part, said, *Now people* will *remember this exhibition, by God!*

Woodrow Wilson tipped his hat to her. "This is entirely impromptu, Miss Colleton. I'm due in Charleston tomorrow to christen a new submersible as she goes off the shipway there. When I remembered your showing was on the way down from Richmond, or at least not too far out of the way, I decided to stop and see the paintings that have the world so intrigued." His smile soured. "Frankly, this is more congenial to me than blessing another instrument of war."

"You are very welcome," Anne told him.

"I am glad to hear you say it," Wilson replied. "Your support for the Whig Party has been generous, and I certainly hope it may continue."

"I don't think you need to worry on that score," Anne said with a slow, thoughtful nod. She wondered just how impromptu the president's visit really was. Maybe Wilson himself didn't know. Politicians, in her experience, inevitably and inextricably mixed politics with every other facet of their lives—and her support for the Whigs had always been anything but ungenerous. She went on, "Please come in, Your Excellency. Don't stand there in the sun. If you had a heatstroke, they'd probably shoot me for treason."

Wilson smiled back. From everything she'd heard, he'd never been averse to smiling at a pretty woman. Anne knew her own good looks were about as useful to her as her money. Fanning himself with his straw hat, Wilson said, "I'm delighted to accept that invitation. Your climate here makes Richmond feel temperate by comparison, something many people would reckon impossible."

Servants—all save Scipio, who remained gravely impassive—gaped as the president of the Confederate States came into the Marshlands mansion, Anne Colleton on his arm. He let her guide him through the exhibition. He also let her shield him from people who might have pestered him. This time, she smiled inside, where it didn't show. Wilson knew who was important and who wasn't—and she was.

After gravely studying several of the paintings, the president turned to her and said, "This is why we fight, you know. To me, it is even more important than ties of blood and sentiment. Nothing so . . . so progressive as these works could possibly come into being in the United States or the German Empire. We truly are preserving civilization."

"Not just preserving it," Anne said. "Helping it grow."

"Of course." He accepted the correction with good grace, accepted it and took it as his own. But then the creases in his long, thin face got deeper. "The price, though, the price is dreadfully high. You have a brother in the service, don't you?"

"Two brothers," she answered proudly. The worry she couldn't help feeling she kept to herself.

"I hope, I pray, they will come through safely," Wilson said. "I do the same for every man in the Army and Navy. Too often—far too often already—my prayers have gone unanswered."

Before Anne could decide how to answer that, Scipio came back with his silver tray. "Would you like a glass of champagne, Your Excellency?" she asked the president.

"Thank you," Wilson said, and took one. So did Anne. He lifted his crystal flute to her. "To civilization, to victory, and to the safe return of your brothers."

"I'll gladly drink to that," Anne said, and did. She turned to Scipio. "You may go."

"Yes, madam." He bowed and went on his way, back straight, wide shoulders braced almost as if he were on parade.

"A fine-looking fellow," Wilson remarked. "Well-mannered, too."

"Yes, I'm lucky to have him here." Anne watched Scipio go. He did make an impressive servant, no two ways about it.

As butler, Scipio was of course a house servant, with quarters within Marshlands for himself. But, not least because he'd been chief cook before becoming butler, he kept up a closer relation with the outside Negroes than most servants of similar station would have done. He knew how much the larder depended on their ingenuity and goodwill: if they said hunting and fishing weren't going well, how could he prove they were lying? But the outside food bill would go up, and he'd catch the devil for that from the mistress.

Lightning bugs flashed on and off as he made his way out to the rows of Negro cottages behind Marshlands. He had every right to make the trip, but glanced back over his shoulder anyhow. It wasn't the mistress he thought was staring at him: it was Marshlands itself. The three-story Georgian mansion had been sitting here for more than a hundred years, and seemed to have a life of its own, an awareness of what went on inside and around it. The mistress would have called that superstitious nonsense. Scipio didn't care what she called it. He knew what he knew.

Perhaps, today, he also still felt the presence of Woodrow Wilson, though the president had gone back to St. Matthews to reboard his train and continue on down to Charleston. His mistress associated with any number of prominent people—which meant he did, too, not that they paid him much attention. He was, after all, only a Negro.

A groom coming out of the barn stared at him through deepening twilight. "Evenin'," he said, nodding. "Almos' didn't rec'nize you—gettin' dark earlier nowadays."

"I is still me," Scipio answered. Wherever white folks could hear him, he talked like an educated white man. That was what the mistress wanted, and what she wanted, she got. Among his own people, he spoke as he had since the day he first began forming words. He hadn't made a mistake switching back and forth between his two dialects in more than ten years.

Candles and kerosene lamps lighted the Negro cottages. Marshlands had had electric lights for a long time now. The mistress had plenty of money for paintings, but for wires for the help? Scipio shook his head. If he held his breath waiting, he'd be blue under his black.

Some of the little brick cottages were already dark. If you worked in the fields sunup to sundown, you needed all the rest you could get sundown to sunup. But you needed a little time to live, too. From out of open windows and doors flung wide against the muggy heat came snatches of song, cries of joy or dismay as dice went one way or the other, and the racket of children. More children made more racket outside, running after one another and pretending to be soldiers. None of them ever admitted he'd been killed. Scipio shook his head again. Too bad the real war didn't work out that way.

Here and there, a mother or a father taught children to read, mostly from books and magazines and newspapers the white folks had thrown away. Scipio, who'd been in his teens when manumission came, remembered the days when teaching a Negro to read had been against the law. He'd managed to pick up the knowledge anyway, as had a good many of his friends—too many things were being printed to keep them all out of Negroes' hands. Black literacy was legal now, but South Carolina still had no school for Negroes.

Scipio walked past Jonah's cottage, and was surprised to find no light burning in there. Jonah and his woman Letitia were always ones for singing and playing and dancing and carrying on. When he got to Cassius' cabin, though, the door was open and light streamed out into the night.

"Is you in there?" he called: good manners, by the standards of the field hands. The mistress' standards were something else again. Scipio moved between two sets of etiquette as readily as he did between dialects. If he ever thought about how he did what he did, he probably wouldn't be able to do it any more.

"No, ain't nobody to home here," Cassius answered. That drew raucous laughter from whoever else wasn't in there with him.

Snorting, Scipio went inside. If you took Cassius seriously, you were in trouble. He'd pull your leg till it came off in his hands, then walk off and leave you to hop home without it. But he was also the best hunter on the plantation, and that had been so for a long time. If you wanted something special for the larder, as Scipio did tonight, he was the man to talk to, even if you had to take your chances on everything else.

Now Cassius threw a hand up before his eyes. "Lord, Kip, you gwine blind we, the light shinin' off them brass buttons that way." Again, his crew of rascals and easy women laughed with him. The only thing that surprised Scipio about the inside of the cottage was that he didn't see any quart whiskey bottles on the mantel or sitting atop one of the rickety tables—or clamped in somebody's fist.

Cassius and the rest of the male field hands wore unbleached cotton shirts and trousers with no shape to them, nothing like Scipio's fancy suit of clothes—though better suited to this breathless heat. A couple of them had bright bandannas on their heads or wrapped around their necks to give themselves a spot of color. The women, by contrast, were in eye-searing calicoes and plaids and paisleys, with no shade of red too hot, no green too vibrant.

"You done been talking wid de president," Cassius said. "You don' reckon you too good to talk wid de likes of we now?"

"I talks wid de president," Scipio agreed with a weary sigh. "De president, he don't talk wid me. You hear what I say?"

Cassius nodded. That was how things worked for blacks in a white man's world. "So—what kin I do fo' you this day, Kip?" he asked. "You come here, you always want somethin'." It could have been an accusation, but it came out like a good-natured joke, which relieved Scipio, for it happened to be true.

In spite of that invitation, coming straight out with what you wanted was rude. "Where Jonah?" Scipio asked. "I see he cabin dark, an' he usually carry on damn near much as you do."

"Jonah?" Cassius shook his head. "He ain't here no more, not he. He leff this afternoon. Gone fo' good, I reckon."

"He *leff*? What you mean, Cass, he leff? That nigger pick cotton here since he big enough to do it, an' Letty, too."

"Not no mo'," Cassius said. "He say he light out fo' Columbia, he work in one o' them factories makin' shells and things."

Scipio stared. "They don' let no niggers work in they factories. Those is jobs fo' white folks, nobody else."

"Whole powerful lot o' white folks is gone to be sojers," Cassius pointed out. "But they still got to have they shells to shoot, o' the damnyankees kick they butts. Nigger kin do the job, nigger gonna get the job. They don' pay he like he was white folks, so the factory bosses, they happy, an' Jonah, he happy, too, 'cause they do pay more'n he make here. An' Letty, she gwine try an' fin' work at one of they tex-tile plants takin' care o' the cotton *after* it picked 'stead o' befo'."

"Mought do that my own self," said one of Cassius' friends, a big man called Island for no reason Scipio had ever been able to learn. "Mo' money fo' less work sound right good."

"Mo' money, yeah," Cassius said. "Less work?" He snorted. "When you ever know white folks give mo' money 'cep' fo' mo' work, an' heaps o' times not then, neither."

Island thought about that, then nodded. But he said, "Hard to think o' anything bein' mo' work'n growin' cotton."

Scipio, who knew how lucky he was to have escaped the fields, also nodded. Plenty of field hands would think the same way; he was sure of that. Jonah and Letitia wouldn't be the only ones to head off the plantation for the factory. He was sure of that, too. And how would the mistress like it? Not much, he figured. Could she do anything about it? He wasn't sure about that. She was a power, but not the only one in the state, not by a long shot.

Marshlands, though, wasn't the state. Here, for those who remained here, her word was still law. Scipio said, "Mistress want a couple gobblers for she dinner party tomorrow night. Kin you get 'em, Cass?"

"Reckon I kin," the hunter answered. His eyes, cool and confident, flicked to the shotgun above the mantel. "Yeah, reckon I kin."

Scipio's eyes also went to the gun and the mantel. On the length of pine wood sat a pamphlet or little book, upside down and open. "What this?" Scipio asked, and reached for it, expecting to find a religious tract. And sure enough, the bright blue paper cover said, DR. GILRAY'S COLLECTION OF CHRISTIAN HYMNS, PRINTED IN RICHMOND, CSA, IN THE YEAR OF OUR LORD 1912.

Idly, he picked it up, wondering what hymn Cassius, who'd never struck him as pious, was learning. At that same moment, Island slammed the door to the cottage shut. Scipio hardly noticed. He was staring down at the page to which the pamphlet had been opened. The printing was as bad and smudgy as he'd expected. The words were anything but what he'd expected: *Of all the classes that stand face to face with the bourgeoisie today, the proletariat alone is a really revolutionary class. The other classes decay and finally disappear in the . . .*

He noticed how quiet it had grown inside the cottage. He looked up from the page and saw Cassius and Island and the rest of the people who'd been in there with him, and how they were all staring at him. He didn't like what he saw in their eyes. Those intent looks frightened him even more than the book he held in his hands, and that wasn't easy.

"Do Jesus!" he said softly. "The mistress find out you got this, she not gwine whip you. She gwine *hang* you. Ain't gonna bother with no law, ain't gonna bother with no cou't. Niggers what spread revolutionary propaganda"—he brought out those two words in his educated voice, as he'd never imagined saying them in the dialect he'd been born speaking—"they gots to die."

"We knows," Cassius said, just as softly. "So they kills we fast 'stead of slow. So what? White folks, they in this big war. They ain't got time to pay no attention to we, we who is doin' they work fo' they. One fine day, they ain't 'spectin' it nohow, the revolution come. It a whole new world then."

"Come the revolution," one of the women—Cherry, her name was—said with a longing croon in her voice, the way a lot of women sounded in the clapboard Baptist church of a Sunday morning, praying for Jesus' second coming. "Come the revolution, this here gwine be a *different* country, it sho' will."

Something glittered in Island's hand—a knife. Scipio watched it with horrified fascination. He gathered himself to fight, knowing how bad his chances were. Island glanced over at Cassius. "We got to shut he up. He a *house* nigger, tell everything he know to the mistress."

Somehow—perhaps by magic—Cassius had produced a knife, too. Almost meditatively, he said, "Kip here, he have the chance to do me wrong plenty times. He never do it oncet, not even. He even take the blame hisself when huntin' go bad. Maybe he keep a secret here, too. Kip, what you think o' that book you holdin'?"

"I think niggers rise up against white folks, we get licked," Scipio answered truthfully. "I think I wish I wasn't so curious." How long had Karl Marx been here at Marshlands? The mistress didn't have the first notion Red revolution was simmering under her nose. Scipio hadn't the first notion, either. What was that white poet's line? *Ignorance is bliss,* that was it. That white folks had known what he was talking about.

Cassius said, "Mos' times, sho', we get licked. Ain't so many guns away from the border, now. Ain't so many white folks to tote 'em, neither. We rise up, they gonna use they army 'gainst we? Damnyankees tromp they into the mud, they try that." He wasn't arguing; he'd already made up his mind, and might have been a preacher talking about the Gospel. His gaze sharpened. "Now, tell me true, Kip—you gwine say about this to the mistress?"

"Not a word," Scipio declared. He thought about adding some strong oath to that, but in the end held his tongue. It was likelier to make Cassius and the others think he was lying than to make them believe him.

"I still say we stick he," Island said.

But Cassius shook his head. "I don' think he talk. He pay if he do, on account of we ain't the onliest ones here, an' he don' know who all we is. An' mistress, she don' know 'bout, she don' care 'bout no revolution. All she care about them crazy paintings, look like 'splosion in a shingle factory. She don' sniff roun', way some masters do. She start changin' she mind 'bout that, Kip, he tell us. Ain't that so, Kip?"

"That so," Scipio agreed through dry lips. Too much had happened too fast today. Having President Wilson come to Marshlands was a surprise. Knowing Karl Marx had come to Marshlands was a shock. Finding out Marx had come to Marshlands had almost proved deadly.

But he would live. His legs swayed under him in reaction and relief. Then he realized how he would be living from here on out. *Playing both ends against the middle* didn't begin to describe it. A phrase a preacher had used a few weeks before fit better. *Caught between the devil and the deep blue sea:* that was how he felt, all right.

Corporal Chester Martin paused behind an oak to spy out the ground ahead. Somewhere not far ahead was the Confederate strongpoint his squad had been sent out to find. In this miserable country, they were liable to find it by blundering onto it, in which case none of them would be able to bring the news back to the artillery so the boys with the red piping on their hats could give it a good walloping.

"I think God had His mind on something else when He was making this part of Virginia," he muttered under his breath.

One of his privates sprawled beneath a bush close enough to let him hear that mutter. Roger Hodges chuckled, almost inaudibly. "You ought to know better'n that," he answered in an upcountry twang that said he'd been born not far away. "God ain't had nothin' to do with it. This here part of the world is the Devil's business, and no mistake."

"Won't get any arguments from me," Martin answered. "Nothin' but up-and-down mountains and trees and brush and little creeks that don't go anywhere. The couple-three farms we found, they look like they're right out of Daniel Boone. And the people talk even funnier than you do, Roger. Hell of a place to try and fight a war, that's all I got to say."

"Captain said do it, so we do it." Hodges sighed.

With a chuckle, Chester slapped him on the back. "You've got the right attitude, that's for damn sure." He wasn't supposed to let a soldier know he liked him—that was bad for discipline. But he had a hard time hiding it when he was around Roger Hodges. The West Virginian took to the business of war the way a duck took to water. He was always ready, always resourceful, and groused as if he'd been in the Army for thirty years: when he complained, it was about things that mattered, not the little stuff that couldn't be helped or didn't count anyhow.

Smiling still, Martin grunted and slid forward another few feet toward the top of Catawba Mountain. He wasn't a mountain man himself—he'd been working in a steel mill in Toledo when his regiment was mobilized—but even these early days of the war had impressed on him the need to be careful with every move you made. The Confederates didn't have anywhere near the numbers of the U.S. force that had entered enemy territory from West Virginia, but the men they did have in the Alleghenies might all have been born there by the way they used the rough country to bushwhack one unit after another, then fell back to the next high ground and did it all over again.

"This here's the last piece of high ground they got to play with for a while, though," he muttered to himself, wiping his face with a sleeve. He wasn't altogether sorry so much of the fighting had been under the trees. He had the pale, freckled skin that went with green eyes and sandy hair, and sunburned easy as you please.

His wasn't the only squad looking for Rebel positions on Catawba Mountain. When the U.S. forces found those positions, they found them all at once. A rifle shot or two rang out, and then the deadly hammering of machine guns. Martin threw himself flat as bullets stitched through the trees, clipping leaves and twigs and men. The smell of mud and mold was thick in his nostrils. Better that, he thought, than the latrine stink of somebody with a belly wound. He'd been watching friends die ever since the Army crossed the border. He didn't want to do it again. He didn't want anybody watching him die, either. He didn't want that at all.

"See any of the bastards?" he called to Hodges.

"Nope," the West Virginian answered. Martin smacked a fist into the ground in frustration. Hodges lived in country like this. If he couldn't tell what was going on, how was a city boy supposed to manage? Hodges went on, "Reckon they dug themselves holes to hide in, make it harder for we-uns to find 'em."

"You're probably right," Martin said, scowling. "They probably had niggers up here, too, diggin' those holes for 'em. Probably took 'em out of the iron mines around Big Lick, brought 'em to work while we were fighting our way up this far, then took 'em back down again."

"I expect that's how it went, all right," Hodges agreed. "They don't give niggers guns, but they're worth almost as much as soldiers, way they free up white men to fight."

Messengers from the squad that had first developed the Confederate position must have got back to the artillery, because shells began whistling down on the enemy line. Some of them fell short; one burst only a dozen yards or so from Martin, showering him with clods of dirt and sending shrapnel balls whistling malignantly above his head.

"Sons of bitches!" Hodges shouted through the din. "They're more dangerous to us than they are to the damned Rebels!"

The barrage went on for half an hour. More shells fell short. Not far away, somebody screamed like a lost soul. You got hurt just as bad if your own side nailed you as you did from an enemy shell.

When the bombardment abruptly ended, whistles blew up and down the American line, piping like insistent sparrows. Martin scrambled to his feet, ignoring the pack that weighed him down like a mule. "Come on, you lugs!" he shouted to his men. "Let's go get 'em!"

Fear made his feet light as he rushed toward the Confederate line. That hadn't been a very long pounding, and the little mountain howitzers that were the only guns able to move up through this godawful country hardly threw any kind of shell at all. Plenty of Rebels would be left to draw beads on the oncoming men in green-gray. Maybe one of them was drawing a bead on his brisket right now.

Roger Hodges, light on his feet as a gandy dancer, sped past Martin. Then he tripped and staggered and started to fall, but was arrested by something just above waist high. "Wire!" he wailed in despair.

That was the last thing he ever said. As he hung there writhing, trying to twist free of the iron barbs that snagged him, two bullets smacked home in quick succession. They sounded like fists. He still hung after that, but no longer writhed.

Martin cautiously approached the area where his squadmate had found the wire the hard way. The Confederates hadn't made a real belt of it, just two or three strands to slow up their attackers. That had been all they needed to pot poor Roger Hodges.

If you knew the wire was there, a few snips with a cutter and you were through it. Martin ran on. Now he could see the Rebels' firing pits, and the flames that spurted from the muzzles of their rifles whenever they pulled trigger. All those flashes seemed aimed right at him. The Confederates were much more readily visible than his own comrades, who took advantage of every bit of cover they could find.

For the last few yards, there was no cover. Yelling like fiends, U.S. troopers were crossing those yards and routing out the Confederates with rifle fire and with bayonet. Chester Martin yelled, too. It helped, not much but a little. He sprinted toward the nearest hole he saw. He was almost there when a big fellow in butternut popped up in it and started to bring his rifle to his shoulder.

Martin shot from the hip. Drill sergeants said you never hit anything that way. He proved them right, because he missed. But he didn't miss by much, and he did rattle the Rebel enough to make him miss, too. The man never got a chance for a second shot; Martin's bayonet punched into his throat while he was still working the bolt to his rifle.

Blood sprayed into Martin's face. The Confederate made a horrible gobbling noise and clutched both hands to his neck. He swayed, tottered, and fell. In dozens of little fights like that one, the U.S. soldiers cleared the Rebels from their line. The Confederate machine guns fell silent. The men who fought under the Stars and Bars were brave enough and to spare; most of them died rather than retreating. A few plunged back into the trees and made for their next line, up closer to the crest of Catawba Mountain.

Martin looked around for his squad, trying to keep some order as the Americans advanced. Roger Hodges he didn't need to worry about; he already knew that. He was jolted, though, to find he had only five men with him. Another soldier was dead besides Hodges, he heard, and three more wounded.

As they formed up, one of his privates, a tall blond kid named Andersen, said, "If we lose half our guys every time we attack, how long till nobody's left any more?"

He'd probably meant it for a joke, the kind of graveyard humor that came naturally in the middle of a battle. But Chester Martin had the sort of mind that figured things out. Lose half the squad in the next attack and you'd have three left. Do it again and you'd have one and a half—say two, if you were lucky. Do it one more time after that and you'd be down to your last guy. No law said that guy had to be Corporal Martin, either.

By the looks on the soldiers' faces, they were working through the same calculation, and not liking what they came up with any more than he did. He paused to roll himself a cigarette and then, after he'd lighted it, to go through the pockets and pack of the Rebel he'd killed for whatever tobacco he had on him. The little cloth sack in which the fellow had carried his fixings had blood on it, but there was nothing wrong with the fine Virginia weed inside. Martin stuck it in his own pocket.

Handling the enemy's corpse gave him the answer, or part of it. He pointed to the body, and then to all the other sprawled corpses in the defense line the American troops had stormed. "Cost us a good bit to get here, yeah," he said, "but it cost them plenty, too, trying to hold us back. And we did what we were supposed to, and the Rebels didn't. Besides"—he pointed back the way he'd come—"we've got replacements moving up behind us, to help on the next push. Won't be us right on the shit end of the stick all the damn time."

That seemed to satisfy his men. And, sure enough, reinforcements were coming up, soldiers whose green-gray uniforms were less draggled than his own and who stared, mouths and eyes open wide, at bodies and pieces of bodies lying on blood-soaked grass and dirt. The sight of a few glum Confederate prisoners, some of them wounded, being hustled off to the rear did not seem an adequately glorious compensation.

"Come on, you birds," Martin called; the second-line soldiers' sergeants looked to be as stunned as any of the men they were supposed to be leading. "This is what it looks like; this is what they pay us for. Ain't you glad you was drafted?"

"That's telling them, Corporal," said Captain Orville Wyatt, the company commander.

Martin hadn't seen him since the attack started. "Glad you're okay, sir," he said.

"Now that you mention it, so am I," Wyatt said offhandedly. He was about thirty-five, with a little thin mustache instead of the more common Kaiser Bill. It suited his long, thin, pale face better than a Kaiser Bill would have; Martin had to admit as much. He didn't know how the devil the captain would get through the war with a pair of steel-framed spectacles riding his nose, but that was Wyatt's problem, not his. The company commander knew his business, which was what counted most.

Some of the Rebs who'd run off into the woods hadn't run all the way back to their next line after all. Instead, they started sniping at the U.S. troops who'd taken away their firing pits and trenches. A couple of groups of cursing Americans turned the captured machine guns around and fired long bursts at the trees upslope. That reduced the enemy fire but didn't stop it.

Somewhere—probably on the reverse slope of the mountain—the Confederates had a battery of their quick-firing three-inch howitzers. Martin had already come under fire from them, and didn't like them worth a damn. Now shells started landing in and around the captured line—not a lot of shells, and not very accurately delivered, but not the sort of greeting he wanted, either. As with fire from your own guns, you were just as dead from a lucky hit as you were if somebody drew a bead on you and drilled you through the chest.

Captain Wyatt, as if annoyed at untimely rain, remarked, "We're not going back, and I don't much fancy staying here. Only thing left to do is advance."

Martin tossed the tiny butt of his cigarette into the dirt and ground it out with his heel. "You heard the man," he told his squad—or what was left of it. "Into the woods we go, off to Grandmother's house. Keep your eyes open and watch where you set your feet. We already know there's wolves in there."

His men chuckled. If you laughed, you could let on that you weren't scared. Your buddies would believe it, or make like they did. If you got lucky, you might even believe it yourself.

They'd gone a couple of hundred yards farther up the mountain, trading shots with Confederates they couldn't see and who—God willing—had trouble seeing them, too, when they came to a clearing, an oval meadow maybe two hundred yards wide and a hundred across. It would have been the most inviting place in the world, except for the machine gun hammering away from the far side of it.

"Can't just charge that," Martin said, almost as if someone had asked him to do it. "We'd have dead piled up higher out there than they did at Camp Hill." His grandfather had been wounded in that fight. He'd worn a peg leg ever afterwards, and counted himself lucky to come out alive.

"We'll have to flank it out," Captain Wyatt agreed, and the corporal let out a silent sigh of relief. In spite of knowing what he was doing, Wyatt was a West Point man, and sometimes they got funny ideas about being duty-bound to die for their country. Chester Martin was more in favor of living for his country.

Captain Wyatt sent him and his squad around to the left of the clearing and another one off to the right. Martin and his men never made it to the machine gun. A couple of Rebels in the woods held them up and wounded one of them before they finally got flushed out and killed. Private Andersen didn't say anything, but his gloomy features had *I told you so* written all over them.

A fusillade of rifle fire put an end to the machine gun's deadly chatter. "Wonder what that cost," Andersen said glumly.

"Ahh, shut up, Paul," Martin told him. "If you aren't demoralizing the rest of the guys, you're sure as hell demoralizing me."

They swarmed on up toward the top of Catawba Mountain. The forest was full of men in green-gray now, with just enough Rebels in butternut lurking and shooting from concealment to make everybody jumpy and trigger-happy and to make sure that, every so often, a U.S. soldier got shot by his own buddies instead of the Confederates. Martin would have sworn that a couple of near misses came from behind him, not ahead, but what could you do except hope you didn't draw the short straw?

This time, he and his men found the Confederate barbed wire before it found them. Cutters clicked; the wire went *twangg!* as the tension on it was released. As before, the Rebs had run up only a couple of strands, not enough to impede troops who were alert for it—and a lot of men who hadn't been alert before were dead now.

Martin crawled and snaked forward till he could see the earth the Confederates—or rather, their Negro laborers—had thrown up in front of their firing pits. More and more U.S. soldiers joined him in the bushes, blazing away at the Southerners in the firing pits. Whistles sounded, up and down the line. Screaming like fiends, Martin and his comrades sprang to their feet and rushed the Confederate position.

As before, the fight was sharp but short; the U.S. forces had brought enough men forward that the advantage fighting from cover gave their foes wasn't enough to check them. "Come on!" Captain Wyatt shouted, even before the last Rebels in the line had been slain. "We're almost at the top of the mountain."

Still yelling, their blood up, the soldiers followed him and other officers on past the wrecked Confederate line. And, sure enough, another couple of hundred yards took them to the crest. Martin looked east toward the Roanoke River, toward the iron town of Big Lick on this side of it, toward the smokes rising from it and from the mines close by, toward the other stream of smoke from the train chugging out of the station: Big Lick was a major railroad junction. Once the U.S. Army fought its way down the mountain and to the river, it would badly hurt the Confederacy here.

A shot rang out, seemingly from nowhere. Not twenty feet from Martin, a private clutched at his throat and fell. "They've got snipers in the trees, the sneaky bastards!" somebody shouted.

"We'll get 'em out," Martin said grimly. Only a few miles separated him from Big Lick. He wondered how long it would take to get there.

Lucien Galtier clucked to his horse and flicked the reins. The horse snorted reproachfully, twitching its ears in annoyance. "I mean it, you old fraud," Galtier told it in his Quebecois French. "Do you want me to get out the whip and show you I mean it?"

The horse snorted again and got the wagon moving a little faster. Galtier chuckled under his breath. He and the horse had been playing this game for the past ten years. He hadn't used the whip since summer before last. He didn't expect to need it for another year or two more. They understood each other, the horse and he.

Drizzle slid down out of a leaden sky. He pulled his hat lower over his face—dark heavy eyebrows, swarthy skin, deep-set brown eyes, a goodly nose above a mouth that was almost a rosebud, dimpled chin in need of shaving—and wished he'd put on oilskins like the sailors wore. His shrug might have come from Paris. Not even a farmer could guess right about the weather all the time. *Not even a saint can do that,* he thought.

He couldn't see far through the rain. He didn't need to see far, though. He knew where he was—a couple of miles outside Rivière-du-Loup on the St. Lawrence River. The countryside was the same here as everywhere else in the neighborhood—farmland with wooden houses painted white, with the beams of the red-painted roofs projecting forward to create a veranda. Because of the drizzle, he couldn't see the tin spires of the churches in St.-Modeste and St.-Antonin, but he knew they were there. To look at things, all was as it might have been 250 years before.

And then, as he drew nearer to Rivière-du-Loup, things changed. The land grew pocked with shells, and the neat farmhouses and outbuildings were neat no more, but many of them charred ruins. The Canadians and British had made a stand, trying to keep the damned Americans from reaching the St. Lawrence. They'd failed.

"It is a terrible thing, war," Galtier told his horse. He and his ancestors hadn't seen the thing close up in a century and a half, not since the days when the British took Quebec away from France. It was here now, though. His nostrils twitched. Even through the rain, he could smell the sickly sweet odor of dead horses—and maybe dead men, too.

His horse also knew the odor for what it was, and made a nervous, snuffling noise. "Go on," Lucien told it. "Go on, my old. It cannot be helped and must be endured." How many times had his father said that to him and his brothers and sisters? How many times had he said it to his two sons and four daughters?

Boom! With a snort of fright, the horse stopped dead. Galtier wondered if he'd have to use the whip after all. *Boom! Boom!* Having reached the St. Lawrence, the Americans had put a battery of field guns with their wheels right on the edge of the bank. Now they were shooting at merchant ships on their way down to Montreal, ships whose captains hadn't got the word that the southern bank was in enemy hands. *Boom! Boom!*

Just when Lucien was reaching for the whip, the horse let out a human-sounding sigh and went on. Before long, the church spires of Rivière-du-Loup loomed out of the mist ahead. The town, which sat on a spur of rock that projected out into the St. Lawrence, was bigger than St.-Modeste and St.-Antonin put together, big enough to boast several churches, not just one. When Father Pascal had had perhaps a glass of wine too many, he talked about Rivière-du-Loup's being a bishopric one day. Like everyone else, Lucien listened and smiled and nodded and didn't hold his breath.

Boom! Boom! Now the sound of the artillery mingled with the plashing roar of the waterfall that plunged off the rock of Rivière-du-Loup and down ninety feet into the great river below. *Boom!* Like every other man his age, Galtier had done his time in the Army. He'd been an infantryman, like most conscripts, but he knew a little something about artillery. He wondered how the devil the fool of an American could find a target, let alone hit it, in this wretched weather.

Houses grew closer together as he came into town. Artillery had wrecked some of them. Once, a whole block was nothing but burnt-out wreckage. The stench of death lingered here, too. Some of the telegraph poles that had connected Rivière-du-Loup to the outside world were down, some leaning drunkenly, some standing but with the wires tangled at their bases.

Posters, now turning soggy in the drizzle, had been nailed or pasted to a lot of the telegraph poles. FREE AT LAST FROM BRITISH TYRANNY, some of them said in French, and showed Quebec's fleur-de-lis banner side by side with the

Stars and Stripes. "I, for one, did not feel myself tyrannized," Lucien Galtier said—softly, for he was not alone on the road now. He leaned forward and asked his horse, "Did you feel yourself tyrannized?" The horse did not answer, which he took for agreement.

The poles that did not have the FREE AT LAST poster mostly bore another, this one printed in red and in both French and English: CURFEW: 8 P.M. TO 6 A.M. VIOLATORS WILL BE SHOT ON SIGHT. "Ah, this is what freedom means," Galtier murmured. "I am so glad the Americans educate us in it."

A newsboy stood on a corner with a box of papers covered by a paint-smeared chunk of canvas tarpaulin. "Read *Ce-Soir*!" he called to Lucien. "Hear of the great victories of the Americans over the Confederates and of Germany over Russia and the English."

"No, thank you," Galtier answered, and rode on toward the market. *Ce-Soir* had experienced a remarkable change in content since the Americans came to Rivière-du-Loup. Before then, it had trumpeted of Confederate, Russian, and French triumphs against the USA, Austria, and Germany.

It all depends on how you look at things, Galtier thought. To hear the newspaper talk now, you would never know that Germany had invaded France, or that the Englishmen there were defending their ally from the *Boches*. That wasn't bad propaganda, but it would have been better had the townsfolk not enjoyed the memories God gave to normal, intelligent human beings.

FREE AT LAST, another poster shouted. Several American soldiers, bayonets fixed on their Springfields, stood on a street corner keeping an eye on people. They were almost invisible in the mist till Lucien got right up close to them. Their green-gray was even better than khaki at blending into the background here.

But Lucien had known they were there long before he saw them. The harsh sounds of English filled his ears. He'd learned some of the language in the Army, but not used it much since: some fishermen who came into town from the Maritimes spoke it, but he had little to do with them beyond passing the time of day in a tavern. Now, like the Americans, it had invaded Rivière-du-Loup. And they spoke of freeing the area from British tyranny! English-speaking Canadians for the most part had had the courtesy to stay away.

The hens in the back of the wagon clucked. That drew the American soldiers' eyes to Lucien Galtier. "Hey, buddy!" one of them called. "You want to sell me one of them birds?"

"Hell with that, Pete," another soldier said. "Just take one—take a couple—from the damn Frenchy, and if he don't like it, give him some .30 caliber persuading." The fellow laughed, showing bad teeth.

Galtier licked his lips. If they wanted to rob him, they could. What would he do afterwards? Complain to their officer? He did not think he would get far. He hadn't heard that the Americans were looting. Had he heard that, he would have stayed on his farm instead of venturing into town.

But the soldier who'd spoken first—Pete—shook his head. "Can't get away with that kind of stuff here in town—too many people watching. We'd wind up in Dutch, and I got some money in my pocket." He turned to Lucien. "How much for a chicken, hey? *Combien?*"

That he'd tried a word of French made Galtier dislike him a little less. He answered with a high price, as he would have in the marketplace, haggling with a housewife. "Fifty cent', *monsieur*." He knew how rusty his English was, and hoped the American soldier would understand.

To his amazement, the American, instead of offering half that or less, reached into his pocket, pulled out a silver coin, and tossed it to him. It was a half-dollar: a U.S. half-dollar, of course, with President Reed's plump profile on one side and the American eagle in front of crossed swords on the other. But fifty cents was fifty cents; Canada, the USA, and the CSA all coined to the same standard. Carefully keeping his face blank, Galtier stuck the coin in his own trouser pocket and pulled a chicken out of the latticework traveling coop for Pete.

"Obliged," the soldier said, holding the chicken by the feet with its head down toward the ground. He'd come off the farm, then, odds were.

"Here, lemme buy one, too," said the soldier who'd proposed robbing Lucien.

He sold five birds in the space of a couple of minutes, at half a dollar apiece. He was delighted. So were the soldiers. One of them said, "Pal, if you'd been eating hardtack and canned beast ever since the damn war started, you'd know how much we crave real grub for a change."

Was he supposed to sympathize with them? If they hadn't come over the border into his country, they could have been eating whatever they pleased back in New York. His only answer, though, was a shrug. He had his wife to think of, and his children. He could not take chances, not when he was one farmer with nothing more dangerous than a folding knife in his pocket and they soldiers with rifles and bayonets. He reminded himself of that, a couple of times.

When it became clear none of the rest of them wanted more chickens, he went on to the town market square, where he did not get nearly the price the Americans had given him for the birds. Another U.S. soldier walked by, but he was not interested in poultry. He had his arm around the waist of one of the girls who served drinks at the Loup-du-Nord, the best tavern in town—Angelique, her name was. The respectable wives of Rivière-du-Loup saw that, too, and clucked like the chickens Lucien was trying to sell.

And here came Father Pascal, almost as close to a heavyset American major (Galtier knew what the gold oak leaves on the officer's shoulder boards meant) as Angelique was to her soldier. The major was speaking French—clear Parisian French, which stood out almost as much as English did from the Quebecois dialect. English-speaking Canadian soldiers said Quebecois French sounded like ducks making love, a claim always good for starting a fight when you were bored.

Galtier couldn't make out much of what the major was saying. Whatever it was, Father Pascal was listening hard. That worried the farmer a little. Father Pascal was a good man, but ambitious—witness his desire for Rivière-du-Loup's becoming a bishopric. If the Americans fed his ambitions, he was liable to go further with them than he should.

Well, one Lucien Galtier couldn't do much about that. Having sold his chickens—and made more for them than he'd expected, thanks to Americans too stupid to bargain—he got into his wagon and started for home. *Boom! Boom! Boom!* The American field guns south of town, which had fallen silent, opened up on another ship out in the St. Lawrence. Galtier looked back over his shoulder. Yes, there was a dim shape moving on the river.

And then, to his surprised delight, that dim shape answered with booms of its own, booms attenuated by traveling over some miles of water but plainly of much larger caliber than the three-inch popguns that had fired at them. Explosions followed almost instantly thereafter, in the place from which the field guns had been firing. Some of the housewives jumped up and crossed themselves. Galtier waited to hear if the field guns could reply to what had to be at least a cruiser out there. They remained silent. He drove home, a contented man.

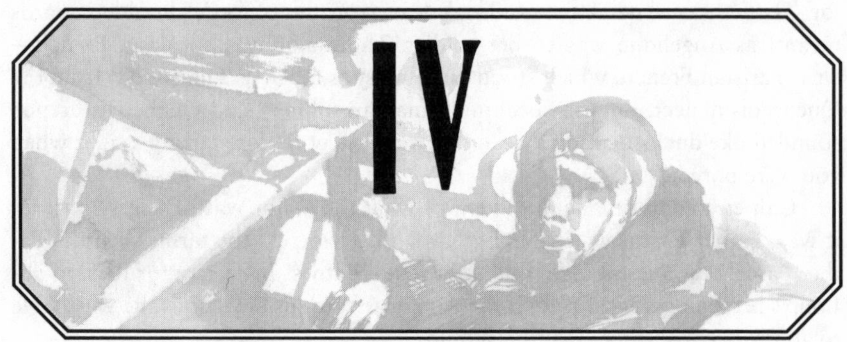

Paul Mantarakis wished he had a chaplain of his own faith with whom he could pray. He'd heard there were a few Orthodox priests in uniform, but he'd never seen one. Protestant ministers, yes. Catholic priests, yes. Rabbis, even—yes. But none of his own.

He fingered his amber worry beads and murmured, *"Kyrie eleison. Christe eleison."* Lord, have mercy. Christ, have mercy.

"Leave off your Latin and your rosary," declared Gordon McSweeney, a dour Scotsman in his platoon. "They are the road to hell."

"It's not Latin," Mantarakis said wearily, for about the hundredth time. McSweeney just glared at him with pale, angry eyes. If you prayed in a language that wasn't English, it was Latin to him. He even thought Jews prayed in Latin. Mantarakis would have liked to give him a good kick, but McSweeney made two of the little Greek, both of the two armored in cement-hard muscle.

"Shut up, both of you," Sergeant Peterquist said. "Come on, get moving onto the damn barge."

Onto the damn barge they moved, each man weighed down with pack and ammunition and rifle. If you went into the Ohio before you made it ashore on the Kentucky side, you'd surely drown. *Theou thelontos*—God willing—that wouldn't happen.

A couple of shells went by overhead and crashed down behind the small town badly misnamed Metropolis, Illinois. The Rebs were still shooting, but U.S. artillery had beaten down their guns to the point where General Custer thought the invasion of the Confederacy could begin. Mantarakis wasn't nearly sure he agreed with that, but he was just a private, so who cared what he thought?

Metropolis had already given him a taste of the South, with its rolling lawns and its magnolias. The South Philadelphia neighborhood where he'd cooked *dolmades* and cheese steaks hadn't been anything like this, not even close. But the little town had its own slums, down by the bridge the Rebs had dynamited when the war broke out: Brickbat Ridge, they called it.

"Come on, pack in tight, you birds!" Peterquist yelled in his raspy-foghorn voice. "Come on, come on, come on!" All over the barge, noncoms and officers said the same thing in a lot of different ways.

Mantarakis already felt like one anchovy in a whole tin. Anchovies and sardines, you packed the fish in tight as you could, because the oil that went in with 'em was worth more than they were. Finding out stuff like that was the only bad part of being a cook, as far as he was concerned: sometimes, because you were in the business, you learned things you'd rather not know.

Well, now he was in the business of killing people, and he had the feeling he was going to learn all kinds of things he'd rather not know. At the moment, what he was trying to learn was how to breathe without moving his chest.

"We're tight enough now, don't you think?" Paddy O'Rourke said in his musical brogue. "If I was jammed up against the pretty girls, now—but faith! It's all you ugly bastards."

The men around him laughed. When everyone exhaled at once, it did seem to give more room. Mantarakis said, "You're pretty ugly your own self, Paddy."

"Ah, but I can't see me," the Irishman answered.

What seemed like all the artillery shells in the world opened up then, on the Illinois side of the river. The roar of the guns, large and small, was music to Mantarakis' ears. The more shells that came down on the Rebels' heads, the fewer of the sons of bitches would be left to try and shoot him. He stood on tiptoe, trying to get a look at just what kind of hell the Kentucky side of the river was catching, but he couldn't see over the shoulders of his bigger comrades.

The steam engine that powered the barge started up, making the timbers tremble under his feet. "Cast off!" somebody yelled; Mantarakis heard the order through the thunder of the artillery. Somebody must have obeyed because, ever so slowly, the barge crawled away from the landing and out into the Ohio.

If he turned his head to one side, Mantarakis could see the river and catch glimpses of other barges wallowing across the current toward Kentucky. Something came down with a splash between his barge and the one closest to it. Cold water fountained up and splashed down on him.

"That came too damn close to hitting us," somebody behind him said. Only then did Paul realize the something had been a Confederate shell. If a shell did hit a barge packed with soldiers— He dug in his pocket and started working the worry beads again. If that happened, it would be like an explosion in a slaughterhouse, with young men playing the role of raw meat.

More shells landed in the river. Mantarakis got splashed again, and then again. Somewhere off to his left, he heard a shell hit a barge, and then heard a clamor of anguish from it. When you headed for battle this way, you were as helpless as a cow being driven along the chute to the fellow with the sledgehammer. You couldn't even fire back, the way you could when you got to solid ground.

How long to cross the river? It seemed like forever, though it couldn't have taken above fifteen minutes, twenty at the most. The soldiers in the front rows, who could see where they were going, passed word back that they were nearing the enemy side of the Ohio. One of them said, "Hope the Rebs don't have no machine guns down by the bank, or we ain't ever gonna make it onto dry land."

"You don't shut up, Smitty," somebody else said fiercely, "I'm gonna shove you in the river and *you* sure as hell won't make it to dry land."

Paul fingered the worry beads harder than ever. His sympathies were with the soldier who'd threatened to push Smitty overboard. The very idea of machine-gun bullets stitching through men who couldn't even duck was enough to make his testicles try to crawl up into his belly.

A big shell landed in the river, all too close to the barge. Mantarakis, who'd already been wet, was now soaked to the skin. Most of the shell fragments and shrapnel balls, fortunately, went into the water, though a couple of unlucky soldiers howled as they were wounded. The barge itself dipped and then recovered, almost as if it were a buggy jouncing over a pothole in the road.

Mixed in with the racket of artillery came the sharper discharges of rifles and, off in the distance, sure enough, the endless death-rattle bark of machine guns. A couple of men at the front of the barge started shooting, too. Mantarakis didn't know whether he liked that or not. It was liable to draw Confederate fire onto men who couldn't shoot back—him, for instance.

The barge lurched again. Paul didn't hear any explosions especially close by; no more upthrown water drenched him. Before he had time to think about what that might mean, whistles started squealing at the front of the barge and men screamed, "Out, you bastards! *Move!* Run! We've gone aground!"

All at once, Paul could move. Along with his squadmates, he ran forward and jumped off the bow of the barge. He got splashed then; the water into which he'd leaped came up past his knees. The mud on the bottom of the Ohio tried to pull his boots off his feet.

The water got shallower fast. Ahead of him, soldiers were running up onto dry land and then fanning out as they moved away from the bank. Now he saw what the artillery had done to the local landscape. It had probably been pleasant before the war started. It wasn't pleasant any more. Whatever grass and bushes had grown here were churned out of existence. He could tell that there had been trees down along the riverbank, but they were stumps and toothpicks now.

Beyond the trees—beyond what had been trees—the ground looked as if a chunk of hell had decided to take up residence in the Confederate States. He hadn't imagined anything could be so appalling as that cratered landscape. The U.S. guns had done their work well. Surely nothing could have survived the bombardment they'd laid down.

He made it up to the riverbank himself. His feet squelched dankly in his boots as he pounded inland. He reminded himself to put on dry socks if he ever got the chance. You let your feet stay soaked, all sorts of nasty things happened to them. He had cousins who worked on the wharfs in Philadelphia who'd made that mistake. Demetrios was still trying to get cured.

Up ahead, something moved, or Paul thought it did. Then, for a split second, he thought he'd made a mistake. And then, as flame spat from a rifle muzzle, he realized he hadn't; it was just that the Confederates' uniforms made them almost impossible to spot when they were in the dirt.

The rifle spat fire again. Ten or fifteen feet to Mantarakis' left, a man went down clutching at his leg. Paul went down, too, landing heavily enough to jolt half the wind from him. He brought his Springfield to his shoulder and drew a bead on the shell hole where he'd spotted the Reb. Was that movement? He fired, then crawled away on his belly. His own uniform, especially smeared with mud and dirt, gave pretty good concealment, too.

He found out how good the concealment was a moment later, when an American soldier he hadn't even seen got up, peering into the hole at which he'd shot, and waved everyone on. Paul got up and started to run before realizing he'd just killed a man. *I should be feeling something,* he thought. The only thing he felt was fear.

He stumbled in a hole in the ground and fell, counting himself lucky he didn't twist an ankle. When he got back to his feet, he looked behind him. He'd intended to see how the men on the barge were doing and whether it was all unloaded, but he kept staring, heedless of the occasional bullets still flying, at the grand spectacle of the Ohio River.

The river was full of barges and ferries of every size and age, with all the vessels laden to the wallowing point, almost to the capsizing point, with men in green-gray. Smoke billowed from scores, hundreds, of stacks, a deep black smoke different from the kind artillery explosions kicked up. Paul cheered like a madman at the display of the might the United States were putting forth. With that great armada, with the stunning artillery the gunners were laying down to ease the way for the Americans, how could the Confederate States hope to resist?

The plain answer, Paul thought, was that they couldn't. He cheered again, seized for a moment by war's grandeur instead of its terror.

And then, without warning, most of the barrage still descending on the Confederates ahead ended. "What the hell?" Paul said when the shelling eased up. He'd been in combat half an hour at most, but he'd already learned a basic rule: if anything strange happens, hit the dirt.

But he kept looking back over his shoulder—and, to his horror, he spotted a gunboat flying the Stars and Bars steaming west toward the lumbering vessels struggling across the Ohio. The engineers were supposed to have put mines in the river to keep Rebel craft away from the defenseless barges, but something had gone wrong somewhere and here this one was, a tiger loose among rabbits.

The river monitor—Mantarakis knew the Rebs didn't call them that, but he did—carried a turret like those aboard armored cruisers out on the ocean. Shooting up barges at point-blank range with six-inch guns was like killing roaches by dropping an anvil on them: much more than the job required. But the job got done, either way.

When a six-inch shell hit a barge, it abruptly ceased to be. You could, if you were so inclined, watch men and pieces of men fly through the air. They flew amazingly high. Then the monitor's turret would revolve a little, pick another target, and blow it out of the water. If that kept on for very long, it wouldn't have any targets left to pick.

Shells rained down around the gunboat, too, and on it—that was why the U.S. artillery had stopped its covering fire for the landing. If the guns didn't knock it out in a tearing hurry, there wouldn't be a landing, or not one with any chance of success. All at once, Paul realized he was in enemy country. Behind him, the Ohio looked uncrossably wide. He wondered if he'd ever see the other side of it again if the gunboat wasn't destroyed. Then he wondered if he'd ever see the other side of it if the gunboat *was* destroyed.

A shell slammed into the armored turret holding the monitor's big guns—slammed into it and bounced off. Those turrets were armored to keep out projectiles from naval guns; shells from field pieces they hardly noticed. But the rest of the Confederate riverboat was more vulnerable. The stacks were shot away; so was the conning tower. Rifle and machine-gun fire from the shore and from the barges kept the Rebels from putting anyone on deck to make repairs. Then the rudder went. The monitor slewed sideways. At last, a shell penetrated to the boiler. The monitor blew up even more spectacularly than the barges it had wrecked.

The barges it hadn't wrecked kept on coming across the Ohio. More loaded up and left the U.S. side of the river. The United States had a lot more manpower than did the Confederacy. Paul Mantarakis wondered if they had enough manpower to compensate for the mistakes their generals were bound to make.

He rose, grunting under the weight of his pack, and moved forward, deeper into Kentucky. One way or another, he'd find out.

Jefferson Pinkard always got the feeling he'd died and gone to hell on the job. Flame and sparks were everywhere. You couldn't shout over the triphammer din; no point in even trying. If you got accustomed to it, you could hear people talking in their ordinary voices under it. You could even hear a whisper, sometimes.

Steel poured from a crucible into a cast-iron mold. The blast of heat sent Pinkard reeling. "Godalmightydamn," he said in the harsh-soft accent of a man who'd grown up on an Alabama farm, bringing up a gloved hand to shield his face. "I don't care how long you work iron, you don't never get used to that. And doin' it in summertime just makes it worse."

"You think I'm gonna argue with you, Jeff, you're even crazier than I know you are," Bedford Cunningham answered. They'd worked side by side at the Sloss Furnaces for going on ten years now, and were like as two peas in a pod: broad-shouldered, fair-haired men with pale skins that turned red from any sun and even redder from the furnace atmosphere in which they labored.

The big crucible from which the molten metal had come swung away, not so smoothly as Pinkard would have liked. "New kid handlin' that thing don't know what the hell he's doin'," he observed.

Cunningham nodded. "He's gonna kill somebody 'fore they take him off—and it ain't likely it'll be hisself. God don't usually work things out that neat." He spat into the new pig of steel, as if quenching it. His spittle exploded into steam the instant it touched the metal. Meditatively, he added, "Wish ol' Herb hadn't got hisself called to the colors."

"Yeah." Pinkard spat, too, in disgust with the world. "How the hell they gonna fight a war, Bedford, if they take all the men who know how to make things and stick 'em in the Army? If they don't turn out guns and shells, what the hell they gonna shoot at the damnyankees?"

"You don't need to go preachin' to the choir," Cunningham said. "I already believe, I surely do. Bunch o' damn fools runnin' things up in Richmond, dogged if they ain't." Then he paused again. He was more given to contemplation than his friend. " 'Course, the other thing is, if they ain't got enough soldiers, they can't fight the war, neither."

"They want more soldiers, they should oughta pull 'em off clerkin' jobs and such like that, not the ones we do here," Jefferson Pinkard said stubbornly. "Folks like us, we should be the last ones chose, not the first."

"Reckon there's somethin' to that," Cunningham admitted. "I think maybe—" Jeff never did find out what he thought maybe, because a steam whistle blew then, the shrill screech cutting through even the insensate racket of the foundry. Cunningham grinned. "I think maybe I'm goin' home."

When Pinkard turned around, he found his replacement and Bedford Cunningham's waiting to take over for them. After a couple of minutes of the usual chatter—half Sloss Furnace gossip, half war news—the two men going off work grabbed their dinner pails and let the evening shift have the job. Another steelworker, Sid Williamson, joined them from the next big mold over. He could have been cousin to either one of them, though he was several years younger and hadn't been at the furnace as long. "Tired," he said, and then fell silent. He never could rub more than a couple of words together.

Along with a lot of other tired, dirty, sweaty men in overalls and cloth caps, they all trudged out toward the gate. Some of the workers—the sweepers, the furnace stokers, men with jobs like that—were black. They kept a little bit apart from the white men who did more highly skilled work and made more money.

Coming in with the evening shift was a white-mustached white man who wore a black suit and a plug hat instead of overalls. He dressed like a country preacher, but Jeff Pinkard had never set eyes on any preacher who looked so low-down mean.

He strode up to Pinkard and Cunningham as if he owned the walkway, then stopped right in front of them, so they either had to stop or run into him. "Do somethin' for you?" Pinkard asked, not much deference in his voice: by his clothes and bearing, the stranger had more money than he was ever likely to see, but so what? One white man was as good as another—that was what the Confederate States were all about.

The stranger said, "Where's your hiring office?"

"Back over yonder." Pinkard pointed to a long, low clapboard building that got whitewashed about once a week in a never-ending battle against the soot Sloss Foundry and the rest of the Birmingham steel mills poured into the air. To get a little of his own back for the fellow's arrogant attitude, Pinkard added, "Lookin' for work, are you?"

"You ain't as cute as you think you are." By the way a cigar twitched in the stranger's mouth, he was about ready to bite it in two. "I got me seven prime buck niggers done run off my plantation this past two weeks, lookin' for city jobs, and I aim to get 'em back, every damn one."

"Good luck, friend," Pinkard said as the man stomped past him. He and Bedford Cunningham exchanged glances. As soon as the irascible stranger was out of earshot, Pinkard said, "He ain't ever gonna see them niggers again."

"Bet your ass he ain't," Cunningham agreed. "Hiring office, they don't care what a nigger's passbook says, not these days. They just want to know if he's got the muscle to do the job. If he's a prime cotton-pickin' nigger, strong like that, they'll fix his passbook so it looks the way it ought to."

"Yeah." Pinkard walked on another couple of steps, then said, "That ain't the right way to do things, you know. Not even close."

"I know," Cunningham said. "But what are you gonna do, Jeff? This place has been jumpin' out of its tree ever since it looked like the war was comin'. When we went to three shifts, we had to get the bodies from somewheres, you know what I mean? Hell, we was runnin' tight for two, way things was. Night shift, I hear tell they got niggers doin' white man's work, on account of they just can't get enough whites."

"I heard that, too," Pinkard said, "an' I seen it when we come on shift in the mornin'. An' that ain't right, neither."

"What are you gonna do?" Cunningham repeated, shrugging. "They don't pay 'em like they was white, but even so, if you're chopping cotton for seventy-five cents a day, a dollar an' a half in the foundry looks like big money."

"Yeah, an' when they get enough niggers trained, you know what's gonna happen next?" Pinkard said. "They're gonna turn around and tell us, 'We'll pay you a dollar an' a half a day, too, an' if you don't like it, Julius Caesar here'll take your job.' Mark my words, that day's comin'."

"It's the damn war," Cunningham said mournfully. "Plant's gotta make the steel, no matter what. You complain about it even a little bit, they say you ain't a patriot and somebody else has your job, even if it ain't a nigger. What the hell can we do? We're stuck, is all."

The conversation had carried them out of the Sloss Furnace grounds and into the company housing that surrounded them. The Negro workers lived to the right of the railroad tracks, in cabins painted oxide red. The paint, like the cabins, was cheap.

Pinkard and Cunningham lived side by side in identical yellow cottages on the white men's side of the tracks. Cunningham's was closer to the foundry. He waved to Pinkard as he went up the walk toward his veranda. "See you in the mornin'," he called.

Nodding, Pinkard headed for his own house. The windows were open and so was the front door, to let some air into the place. A delicious aroma floated out. Pinkard tossed his cap onto a chair and fetched his dinner pail into the kitchen. "Lord, that smells good," he said, slipping an arm around the waist of his wife, Emily.

She turned and kissed him on the tip of the nose. The motion made her blue cotton skirt swirl away from the floor so he got a glimpse of her trim ankles. "Chicken and dumplings and okra," she said. "Cornbread biscuits already baked."

Spit flooded into his mouth. He thumped himself in the belly. "And it wasn't even your cooking I married you for," he exclaimed.

"Oh?" Something that looked like ignorant innocence, but wasn't, sparkled in her blue eyes. "What did you marry me for, then?"

Instead of answering with words, he gave her a long, deep kiss. Even though she wasn't wearing a corset, he could almost have spanned her waist with his two hands. She wore her strawberry-blond hair—almost the color of flames, really—in a braid that hung halfway down her back. She even smelled and tasted sweet to him.

When they broke apart, she said, "You still haven't answered my question."

He poked her in the ribs, which made her squeak. "On account of you were the prettiest gal I ever saw, an' you look better to me now than you did five years ago. How's that?" They didn't have any children yet. He wondered how that was, too. Not from lack of trying, that was for certain.

Emily smiled at him. "You always were a sweet-talkin' man. Probably why I fell for you. Why don't you get a couple of bottles of beer out of the icebox? Supper should be ready in about two shakes."

The beer was homebrew; Alabama had gone dry a couple of years before, which meant they didn't ship Jax up from New Orleans any more. As he yanked the corks out of the bottles, Pinkard supposed going dry was a good thing for a lot of people. But a beer every now and then didn't seem to him like drinking—and it went awful well with chicken and dumplings.

He handed one bottle to Emily, then cautiously swigged from the other. With homebrew, you never could tell what you'd get till you got it. He nodded in satisfaction and took a longer pull. "Old Homer, he did this batch pretty good."

Emily drank, too. "He's done worse, I'll tell you that," she agreed. "Why don't you go sit down, and I'll bring out supper."

The chicken was falling-off-the-bone tender. He used the cornmeal biscuits to sop up the gravy on his plate. As he ate, he told Emily about the planter who'd come to the foundry looking for his field hands. "We got more work to do now than we got people to do it, a lot more," he said, and mentioned how Negroes were doing white men's work on the night shift.

She paused before answering. It wasn't a full-mouth pause; she was thinking something over. At last, she said, "I went into town today to get some groceries—so much cheaper than the company commissary, when we've got the cash money to pay for things right there—and they were talkin' about that same kind of thing, about how there's so much work and not enough hands. It's not just the foundry. It's all over the place. Grocer Edwards, he was grumbling how he'd had to raise his clerk's pay twice since the war started to keep him from goin' off and workin' in one o' them ammunition plants."

"Wish somebody'd go an' raise my pay," Jeff said. "Way things look, they're liable to end up cuttin' it instead." Once more, he summarized part of what he and Bedford Cunningham had said.

"They aren't hiring niggers to work at the ammunition plants hereabouts—I know that for a fact," Emily said. She paused again, so long that Jeff wondered if something was really wrong. Then, instead of going on, she got up, carried the plates to the sink, and lighted the kerosene lamp that hung not far from the table. Only after that did she continue, in a rush: "I hear tell they are hiring women, though. Dotty Lanchester—I ran into her at the grocer's—she says she's gonna start next week. She says they really *want* women: what with sewin' and everything, we're good with little parts an' stuff, an' shells have 'em, I guess, even if you wouldn't think it to look at 'em."

"Milo's letting Dotty go to work at a factory?" Pinkard said, surprised. If your wife had to work, that meant you couldn't support her the way you should. *Shiftless* wasn't a name you wanted to wear.

"She said it was her patriotic duty to do it," Emily answered. "She said our boys in butternut need everything we can give 'em to beat the damnyankees, and if she could help 'em, she would."

How were you supposed to argue with that? Jefferson Pinkard turned it over in his mind. Far as he could see, you couldn't argue with it, not very well.

And then, after yet another hesitation, Emily said, "You know, honey, I wouldn't mind goin' to work there my own self. They got lots of ladies, like I said, so it wouldn't be like I was the only one, and with an extra two dollars a day, we could really set some money aside for when we do have young'uns." She looked at him sidelong. "Might be any day. You never can tell."

Two dollars a day was a little more than half what the ammunition factory paid the men who worked there: better than nigger wages, but not a whole lot. That was probably one reason the bosses were hiring women. But women were dexterous, too; Pinkard wouldn't have argued with that. He'd struggled a couple of times to thread a needle with his clumsy, work-roughened hands. Watching Emily do it easy as pie made him swear off trying to sew for good.

But wages weren't what made him hesitate. "Any other time, I'd say no straight out," he said.

"I know you would, honey," Emily answered. "But I'd be able to keep things goin' here, too; I know I would. It ain't like I'm thinkin' about it just on account of gettin' out of housework or that I don't love you or that I don't think you're workin' hard enough to make us all the money we need. It's nothin' like that, I swear to God it's not. You know I'm speakin' the truth, now don't you?"

"Yeah, I do," he admitted. He knew she was wheedling, too, but he didn't know what to do about it. What with the war, all of a sudden nothing was simple.

No sooner had that thought crossed his mind than Emily said, "If the damnyankees lick us, it don't hardly matter that we stuck by what was right and proper beforehand, now does it?"

He threw his hands in the air in defeat. "All right, Emily. That's what you want to do, you go do it. Like you say, the war's makin' everything all topsy-turvy. We'll put it back to rights oncet we done licked the United States again. Shouldn't take long, I reckon."

"Thank you, honey!" Emily got up, threw herself down into his lap, and flung her arms around his neck. The dining-room chair creaked; it wasn't used to holding two people's worth of weight. They didn't stay there long, though. Pretty soon, they got up and went into the bedroom.

From a mile in the air, the world looked like a map spread out below you. Not many people had been lucky enough to see the world that way, but Lieutenant Jonathan Moss was one of them.

He had a speck of something on the inside of one lens of his goggles. It wasn't enough to interfere with his vision, but it was annoying. Speck or no speck, though, he knew he could keep a close eye on the U.S. Army troops pushing from New York into Ontario, and on the struggles of the Canadians and British to stop them.

Shells pounded the enemy line south of Hamilton. "That's the way to go, boys!" Moss shouted, slamming a fist down on his thigh. The U.S. eagle and crossed swords were painted big and bold and bright on the fuselage, wings and tail of his Curtiss Super Hudson pusher biplane. He liked the pusher configuration; it gave him a better view of the ground than he could have got from a tractor machine, and also let him mount a machine gun in front of him to shoot at any aeroplanes that rose up to challenge his aircraft. If you mounted a forward-facing machine gun on a tractor aeroplane, you'd chew your own prop to bits when you opened fire.

Somebody ought to do something about that, Moss thought. The idea vanished from his head a moment later, though, for a Canadian battery started returning fire on the advancing—or rather, the stalled—Americans. Scribbling awkwardly in a notebook he held between his knees, Moss noted the position of the guns. When he landed, he'd pass the sketch on to Artillery. The enemy guns would get a wake-up call in short order.

"They've had too damn many wake-up calls already," he muttered. The wind in his face blew the words away.

The words were gone, but not the fact. For all the big talk in the United States about mopping the floor with the Dominion of Canada, reality, as reality has a way of doing, was proving harder. The damned Canucks and limeys had spent years fortifying the Niagara Peninsula, the part that ran west from Niagara Falls; every time they were blasted and bayoneted out of one position, they fell back to the next, just as tough as the one before. Forcing the crossing of the Welland Canal alone had put women by the thousands into mourning black.

But the canal had been crossed. Now the Canadians and British were moving back toward their last line, the one that ran from Hamilton on Lake Ontario through Caledonia to Port Dover on Lake Erie. When the United States broke through there, the country would widen out and numbers would count for more than they had yet.

As yet, the breakthrough hadn't happened. And, indeed, though the enemy had been thrown back on Hamilton in the north, they were still holding part of the line of the Grand River south of Caledonia. Farther west, the assault from Michigan hadn't been the walkover everyone—everyone south of the border, anyhow—had figured it would be. The line centered on London, Ontario, hadn't cracked yet, either, and when it would was anybody's guess.

Moss sighed. "We put too much money into Great Lakes battleships," he told the unheeding sky. He'd told everybody the same, since the day the war started. A fat lot of good it did, too. Great Lakes battleships weren't really battleships to rank with the great vessels in the Atlantic and Pacific Fleets: they were smaller and slower and didn't mount so many guns. In navies like Holland's or Sweden's, they would have been called coast-defense battleships.

What people in the USA had called them was victory. Each Great Lake had its own flotilla of them, and the Canadians didn't—couldn't—build ships to match, in quality or numbers. When war came, they'd bombard enemy towns and positions with a weight of metal you couldn't move by land.

The only problem being, it hadn't worked out that way. The first thing the Canadians had done when war broke out was to sow the Great Lakes with mines as thickly as potato soup was sown with potatoes. The *Perry* and the *Farragut*, both steaming full tilt toward Toronto, had blown up and sunk within a couple of hours of each other, as had the *John Paul Jones* over on Lake Huron. Losing millions of dollars' worth of ships and a couple of thousand trained sailors had made the flotillas less intrepid in a hurry.

As if that weren't bad enough, the Canadians had submersibles, too. Nobody—nobody American, anyhow—knew how many, but they'd picked off a Great Lakes battleship and a couple of light cruisers, too, before scuttling back to their home ports. Put it all together and it meant the Army was advancing through the toughest part of the enemy's defenses without a good bit of the fire support it had expected to have. And so the going was tough.

Jonathan Moss peered down at the Canadian and British guns. From a mile in the air, they looked like tiny lead toys, and the bare-chested men who served them like pink ants. He scribbled some more on the makeshift map. The enemy lines really did look like *lines* from up here: a zigzagging series of entrenchments that cut across the land. Even the entrenchments that ran back from the front-line positions zigzagged, to make a shell landing in one of them do as little damage as possible.

"Those bastards have been thinking about this for a long time," Moss said, penciling squiggles over the page to represent the zigzag entrenchments.

The American positions facing the foe were less neat. For one thing, the U.S. forces had to form their lines in territory they'd taken away from the Canadians, and every inch of that territory had been fought over till it was nothing but a crumpled, battered landscape that reminded Moss of nothing so much as telescopic photographs of the craters of the moon. For another, the Americans hadn't planned to conduct such a grinding campaign of attrition, and hadn't yet worked out the doctrine for fighting in those conditions.

Even getting supplies forward to the troops at the sharp end of the wedge was anywhere from hard to impossible. The railroads had been chewed up along with everything else in the territory over which the Americans had advanced. Food and ammunition had to come forward by wagon or else on people's backs.

By contrast, the rail network the defenders used was all but intact: Moss watched several trains chugging along toward the front, each one full of troops or munitions or food and fodder. He made a sour face. You could move more faster by train than with horses or people. That was what the second half of the nineteenth century had been about, if you looked at it the right way. It gave the defenders what struck him as an unfair advantage.

He was so busy noting the arriving trains, he didn't spot the other aeroplane till it started shooting at him. The sound of Lewis-gun bullets drumming through the fabric of his wings—and whipcracking past his head—got his attention in a hurry. He was banking to the left before he even looked up.

The Avro 504 ahead of him tried to turn with him, but his aircraft was more agile than the tractor machine. He swung away from the area the observer in the front cockpit could cover with his machine gun. The pilot in the rear cockpit blazed away at him with a pistol, but only fool luck would let you hit anything with a pistol when both you and your target were moving crazily and at high speed in different directions.

At high speed— The Avro was faster on the level than his Super Hudson, and could climb faster, too. That would nullify his ability to turn inside it if he didn't do something in a hurry. He lined up the nose of his aircraft on the Canadian biplane's tail and squeezed the triggers of his Maxim gun.

Brass cartridge cases streamed out of the breech, glittering in the sun as they fell away. In the Avro, the pilot threw up his hands and slumped forward against the fairing that helped deflect the slipstream. The Canadian aeroplane's nose went down; it began to dive, and then to spin.

Maybe the observer hadn't properly fastened his safety belt; maybe it gave way under the strain. However that was, the luckless fellow was thrown out of the Avro. As he plunged toward the earth, he looked like a man treading water. But the thin, thin air would not bear his weight. He fell, the fringed end of his red wool muffler flapping above him.

"Jesus!" Jonathan Moss shook like a man with the grippe. He'd never fired the Maxim gun in anger before. He'd never expected to have to fire it, despite reports of other aerial combats. He hadn't even wanted it mounted on his aeroplane. But it had just saved his life.

The Avro 504 smashed into the ground and burst into flame a few hundred yards inside the enemy's lines. Dutifully, Moss noted the position on his sketch map. The observer had undoubtedly smashed into the ground, too, but Moss could not see him.

"Jesus!" he said again, and licked his lips. With the wind blasting in his face, they would have been dry anyhow; some pilots smeared petroleum jelly on them before taking off. Moss' lips were drier now. His stomach turned loops that had nothing to do with the acrobatic abilities of the Super Hudson.

He'd thought one of the nice things about being an aerial observer was not having to kill anybody personally. War down on the ground was a filthy, nasty business, filthier and nastier than anyone had expected when it broke out. Watching the slow advance across the Niagara Peninsula had shown Moss that. And he'd seen it from high in the air, as if he were looking down on a chess match where both players could move at the same time. An awful lot of poor damned pawns had been captured and removed from the board.

"I was above all that," he muttered, meaning it both literally and metaphorically. Like a knight, he could jump over intervening space and appear where he was needed on the board. Now, abruptly, he realized that, like a knight, he also faced danger. He too could be sacrificed.

He'd killed, yes, but it was a fair fight. So he told himself, over and over. The fellows in the Avro had had just as much chance to send his aeroplane spinning down in ruins as he'd had to shoot down theirs. He wasn't some conscript rifleman, reduced to a corpse by a machine gunner who wasn't aiming at him or by an artilleryman back of the line who'd never seen him at all, merely pulled a lanyard and hoped for the best. Thousands of randomly killed men lay down there; sometimes the stink of them made him wish the Super Hudson would fly higher, to let him escape it.

A fair fight, single combat . . . Maybe that did make him a knight, not one from a chess set but a noble warrior from the days of chivalry, going forth into single combat as if into a joust. That was a better way to look at things, he decided: it shielded him from the blunt reality of having killed two men to keep them from killing him.

"A knight," he said, and touched the Maxim gun as if it were the lance a knight in shining armor carried into battle with him. "A knight of the air."

He carefully scanned the sky to make sure the Canadian aeroplane had been as alone up here as his own machine. He spied no other aircraft with red maple leaf inside white circle inside blue. Yes, it had been true single combat. If you were going to fight, that was the way to do it.

He had a sudden mental image of Teddy Roosevelt going into the gladiatorial arena against—would he fight Robert Borden or the Duke of Connaught, prime minister or governor general? Either way, Moss figured TR would quickly dispose of his foe. Then he could take on Woodrow Wilson. And, after he'd slain both enemy leaders, the United States would be declared winner of the war and could take whatever spoils it wanted from Canada and the Confederacy.

"That would be the easy way, the cheap way, to go about it," he said. It was also a pipe dream, as he knew full well. Statesmen didn't go out to fight for themselves; that had fallen out of fashion after the Crusades, he didn't know exactly when. Statesmen sent young men out to do the killing—and the dying—for them.

"If you have to do it," Moss muttered, feeling on the shaky side still as he turned back toward his aerodrome, "I suppose being a knight of the air is the way to go about it."

The only trouble was, nobody had seen fit to issue him a suit of shining armor.

Jake Featherston yanked the lanyard of his three-inch field gun and hoped for the best. The piece belched flames. The other five men on the gun crew, working like steam-powered machinery even though two of them were raw replacements, reloaded the gun. Five seconds after the first round, another was on its way.

"*Hell* of a gun!" Featherston shouted appreciatively. "Them Frenchies, they knew what they were doin' when they made the model." He pulled the lanyard yet again. *Boom!* Another shell went on its way toward the Yankee positions just outside of Glen Rock, Pennsylvania. Thanks to the muzzle brake on the French-designed howitzer, its recoil was a lot less than that of U.S. guns of similar caliber, which meant corrections between rounds were also less, which meant a good gun crew could get off a dozen rounds a minute. Featherston had a damn good gun crew.

A horse-drawn wagon full of wooden crates stenciled with the Confederate battle flag came rattling up. Jake Featherston and his crew let out a cheer. " 'Bout time we got more rounds," shouted Jethro Bixler, the loader. "You didn't show up soon, they was gonna give us Tredegars an' stick us in the damn infantry."

"Can't have that," the driver said, his grin exposing a missing front tooth. He glanced over to the colored servants who were standing by the team of horses that would move the field gun ahead as the Confederacy continued its conquest of southeastern Pennsylvania and Maryland. "*Git* your asses over here, you lazy damnfool niggers. Unload this bastard so's I can go fill 'er up agin."

Nero and Perseus came—at a faster clip than they'd used when the war first broke out. Then, they might have been picking cotton for a plantation owner they despised. They'd come to realize, though, that keeping their crew in shells was liable to mean keeping themselves alive. As with the soldiers they served, survival was a powerful incentive toward good performance.

Each crate held twelve shells. Counting the weight of the wood in the crate itself, the weight the blacks were hauling was up close to a couple of hundred pounds each go. Grunting with effort, they unloaded crates as the driver and the gun crew watched. Then, sweat running down their faces, they went back to the animals they'd been watching.

"Lazy," the driver repeated. He flicked the reins. The horses strained in harness. The driver tipped his hat to the artillerymen and headed southwest down the dirt track called School Road toward the division supply dump.

Jethro Bixler attacked the tops of the ammunition crates with a pry bar. Nails squealed as the tops came up. Bixler flung each aside in turn. He would have made two of either Nero or Perseus: a big blond broad-shouldered fellow with the look of a blacksmith to him. When one of the ammunition crates wasn't close enough to the howitzer to suit him, he picked it up singlehanded and set it where he wanted it. Then he struck a circus strongman pose, as if to proclaim to the world that that had been a deliberate demonstration of prowess, not a white man stooping to do nigger work.

Other wagons turned off from School Road for the rest of the guns in the battery. The Negroes attached to the artillery unit stopped what they were doing to unload the shells. Through the roar of guns that kept firing, Featherston listened to the artillerymen screaming at the blacks to hurry.

"Flip those lids over, Jethro," Featherston said when Bixler was through opening up the new crates. "Don't want anybody stepping on a nail. He'd miss all the fun." He let out a wry chuckle.

"Right y'are, Sergeant," Bixler said. "I tell you, I done had just about all the fun I can stand, thank you kindly. 'Fore we started, wasn't nobody said it'd be like this here. The damnyankees, they're tougher'n Paw an' Granddad made 'em out to be."

Several of the other men nodded agreement to that, Jake Featherston among them—it was hardly something you could deny. Featherston said, "If everything went the way it was supposed to, we'd be over the Susquehanna by now, drivin' for the Delaware River."

"Yeah." Jethro Bixler slammed a meaty fist into an equally meaty thigh in his enthusiasm. "My family, we had kin in Baltimore, back before the War of Secession. Hellfire, for all I know, we still do, but nobody on our side o' the border's heard from 'em in fifty years. We should have taken Maryland away from the damnyankees after we made peace with 'em the first time."

"And Delaware," added Pete Howard, one of the shell carriers. "All that country is ours by rights, by Jesus."

"Before it's ours, we got to take it," Featherston said, which drew more nods from the rest of the crew. "We ain't even in Baltimore yet."

"Ain't supposed to be *in* it," answered Bixler, who fancied himself a strategist. "Supposed to wheel around and cut it off so it damn well falls."

"Yeah, but we ain't done that yet, is the problem," Featherston retorted. "The damnyankees still got that railroad goin' through down alongside Chesapeake Bay. We can't wheel round an' cut that line, they're liable to do some cuttin' of their own and leave us stranded up here."

The wheel was supposed to have taken them to the west bank of the Delaware by Wilmington, and to have cut off the area south of the front from any possible support by the United States. It might still do that; Jake hoped to God it would still do that. But every day they fell farther behind their planned advance line, and that was another day the U.S. forces could ship more men and munitions down from Philadelphia. The Confederate army still had to cross the Susquehanna. Lee had done it, after hammering McClellan outside of Camp Hill. But Lee hadn't had to face machine guns that could melt a regiment down to platoon size in a matter of minutes if you tried attacking them head on—and how else were you going to attack them if you were forcing a river line?

Featherston looked back over his shoulder, down School Road. It hadn't been much of a road to begin with. It was even less now, after Yankee artillery had chewed it up—and Confederate artillery, too, before the men in butternut advanced so far. Half a mile back from the battery, mechanics worked on a couple of motor trucks that had broken down trying to bring supplies forward. The front demanded a flood of matériel. Thanks to the miserable roads, it got a trickle.

"No wonder the Yanks are givin' us such a hard time," Jake muttered.

Captain Jeb Stuart III trotted up to Featherston's gun. "Get the team hitched to your piece," the battery commander called. "We're moving forward, maybe a mile." He pointed northeast. "The damnyankees are holed up in a couple of stone farmhouses out that way, and they've got a whole regiment stalled on its track—haven't been able to clear 'em out with rifles and machine guns, so they want us to knock the houses down."

"You hear that, Nero, Perseus?" Featherston called as Stuart went off to give the order to the rest of the battery. The two Negroes nodded and brought the horses over. Hitching the animals to the gun trail was a matter of a few minutes, for they were already in harness. Hitching the other team to the supply wagon that followed the gun was also quickly done. Then, swearing and sweating, Nero and Perseus lifted the crates of shells they'd just unloaded from one wagon up onto another.

"Move 'em out!" Captain Stuart was shouting, and waving his cap in his hand to urge the men on. Pompey brought him a glass of something cool to drink. He upended it, gave it back to the servant, and went on shouting to the gun crew and to the laborers without whom they wouldn't have been nearly so efficient.

It hadn't rained for several days, so the road—or rather, track—to the new position wasn't muddy. When a howitzer bogged down hub-deep in muck, everybody, blacks and whites together, put shoulders to it to keep it moving. Leaves on some of the trees were beginning to go from green to gold and red. They wouldn't have started turning this early in September back in the CSA.

Since the dirt track was dry, they got dust instead of mud. By the time they reached the new position, everyone was the same shade of grayish brown, Featherston no less than Nero. The artillery sergeant peered through the field glasses at the farmhouses Captain Stuart wanted the battery to destroy.

"Range about thirty-five hundred yards, I'd make it," he said, and worked the elevation screw to lower the field gun's barrel to accommodate the shorter range. Stuart had been right; the Confederates had advanced past the farmhouses to either side, but were halted in front of them. Even through field glasses, corpses were tiny at two miles, but Featherston saw a lot of them.

He studied the gunsight again, then traversed the barrel slightly to the left. "Load it and we'll fire for effect," he said.

Jethro Bixler set a shell in the breech, then closed it with a scrape of metal against metal. He bowed to Featherston as if they were a couple of fancy gentlemen—say, Jeb Stuart III and one of the Sloss brothers—at an inaugural ball in Richmond. "Would you care to do the honors?"

"Hell yes," Jake said with a laugh, and pulled the lanyard. The field gun barked. He got the field glasses up to his eyes just as the shell hit three or four seconds later. "Miss," he said, and clucked to himself in annoyance. "Long and still off to the right."

He lowered the barrel a little more and brought it over another few minutes of arc to the left. The second round fired for effect was straight, but still long. The third fell a few yards short. By then, the other guns in the battery had gone into action, too, so he had to hesitate before he could be sure the round he had seen really came from his gun. He turned the elevation screw counterclockwise, about a quarter of a revolution, waited a couple of seconds for a fresh load, and fired again at the farmhouse.

"Hit!" The whole gun crew shouted it together. Smoke and dust shot up from the building; through the field glasses, Featherston saw a hole in the roof.

"Now we give it to 'em!" he said, and shell after shell rained down on and around the farmhouse. Its stone walls might have been thick enough to keep out small-arms fire, but they weren't proof against artillery. The building fell to pieces even faster than it would have under assault from a steam crane and wrecking ball.

He swung his field glasses to the other farmhouse. Half the guns in the battery had chosen that one, and it was in no better shape than the one his howitzer crew had helped to destroy. Confederate troops swarmed up out of the shallow trenches they'd dug to protect themselves from the fire coming out of those two buildings and rushed toward them. To his dismay and anger, he saw the barrage, though it had wrecked the farmhouses, hadn't killed or driven off all the enemy soldiers in them. Men in butternut fell, not quite in the horrific numbers Featherston had seen in some assaults, but far too many all the same.

"We gotta keep hitting 'em!" he shouted to the gun crew. More shells went out, fast as the artillerymen could serve the howitzer.

Featherston kept watching the assault on the farmhouses. The Confederate infantrymen surged toward them, still taking casualties but advancing now. Featherston held fire when they reached the buildings, not wanting to hit the soldiers on his own side. When he saw tiny figures in butternut waving their comrades forward past the farmhouses, he knew the position had been carried.

"Good job, boys," he said. It wasn't every day you could actually see what your firing had accomplished. A lot of the time, your shells were just part of a massive bombardment aimed at targets too far away for you to tell whether you'd done any good against them or not.

Perseus pointed up into the sky. "Lookit that—it's one o' them aeroplane contraptions," the Negro shouted. "Wonder whose side it's on."

"Reckon it's a Yankee machine," Featherston said, also looking up. "If it was one of ours, it wouldn't be hangin' up there over our lines—it'd be spyin' on the enemy instead."

What he wished was that he had a gun able to knock that snooping U.S. aeroplane right out of the sky. Wishing, though, didn't magically provide him with one. As the machine passed nearly overhead, something fell out of it and sped toward the ground. For a moment, Jake hoped that meant the pilot had gone overboard, or whatever the aeronautical equivalent was.

He realized the shape was wrong. He also realized two or three somethings were falling, not just one. And, with that, he realized what the somethings were. "He's dropping bombs on us!" he shouted indignantly.

Boom! Boom! Boom! There were three of them. They fell a couple of hundred yards behind the battery of field guns. The noise from the explosions smote Featherston like a thunderclap. Clouds of smoke and dust rose, but the bombs didn't seem to have done any damage.

Jethro Bixler looked back at where they'd blown up, then shook his fist at the aeroplane, which was now flying away toward the Yankee lines. But then he grinned and shrugged. "That wasn't so much of a much," he said. "By the sound of those things, they weren't a whole lot bigger'n what our three-inchers throw. An' we can put 'em just where we want 'em, and put a whole bunch of 'em there, 'stead o' droppin' a couple an' runnin' for home."

"They can put 'em back of our lines farther than artillery can reach," Featherston said, giving such credit as he could: the Confederacy had bombing aeroplanes of its own, after all, and he didn't want to think they were useless. But he also took pride in what he did: "Reckon you're right, though. Set alongside these here guns, I don't figure aerial bombs'll ever amount to much."

As George Enos came into his house, his wife Sylvia greeted him with bad news: "They're going to cut the coal ration this month, and it looks like it's going to stay cut."

"That's not good," he said, an understatement if ever there was one. He took off his cap and set it on the head of four-year-old George, Jr. Naturally, it fell down over his son's eyes. The boy squealed with glee. The fisherman went on, "Hard enough cooking if they cut the ration any further. But winter's coming, and this is Boston. How will we keep warm if we can't get as much coal as we need?"

"Mr. Peterson at the Coal Board office, he didn't say anything about that, and you can bet there were a lot of people asking him, too." Sylvia Enos' thin face was angry and tired and frustrated. She often looked that way when she got home from a couple of hours of fighting Coal Board paperwork, but more so today than usual. "All he said was, the factories have to have coal if they're going to make all the things we need to fight the war, and everybody else gets what's left over. The surtax is going up another penny a hundredweight, too."

"I already knew that much," George Enos said. "Some company bigwig was grousing about it when we coaled up *Ripple* before we went out last Monday."

"Well, sit down and rest a bit," Sylvia told him. "I haven't seen you since then, you know, and little George and Mary Jane haven't, either. It's hard for them, their father gone days at a time. Supper'll be about twenty minutes more."

"All right," Enos said. The pleasant smells of clam chowder and potatoes fried in lard wafted into the living room from the kitchen.

Sylvia started to head back into the kitchen, then turned with hands on her hips. "I swear to goodness, the forms they give you to fill out before you can even get a speck of coal now are worse than they ever used to be."

"Maybe we should burn all the forms," Enos said. "Then we wouldn't need so much coal."

"You think you're making a joke," Sylvia said. "It's not funny. When Mrs. Coneval's mother came over yesterday, she was complaining about them, too. She remembers back before the Second Mexican War, and she says there didn't hardly used to be any forms like there are now."

"That was a long time ago," George answered, which got him a dirty look from Sylvia. After a moment, he realized he'd pretty much called her friend's mother an old woman. Defensively, he went on, "Well, it was. From what people say, things haven't been the same since."

His wife nodded sadly. "Always the war scares. I don't know how many from then till now, but a lot of them. And all the factories busy all the time, making guns and shells and ships and I don't know what all else to use if the war came. And now it's come. But we'd have had so much more for ourselves if we hadn't been worrying about the war all the time."

"But we'd probably have lost it, too, because the Rebs have been building every bit as hard as we have," he said. "Harder, maybe; if they use their niggers in their factories, they don't have to pay 'em anything to speak of. Same with the Canadians, except they don't have niggers."

Talking about niggers made him think of Charlie White. But the Cookie was somebody he worked with, a friend, who just happened to have dark brown skin and hair that grew in tight curls. It wasn't the same, though he couldn't have put his finger on why it wasn't.

Sylvia said, "The Canadians, they have Frenchies instead of niggers." She sniffed loudly, but not on account of French Canadians. "I have to turn those potatoes, or they'll burn. And I'll start frying the fish with them in a couple of minutes, too."

"All right." George Enos sat down and lighted a cigar. He wondered how long he'd be able to keep doing that. Most tobacco came from the Confederate States, and they weren't going to be shipping any up north, not while they and the United States were shooting at each other.

George, Jr., came over and hugged one of his legs. Seeing that, Mary Jane toddled up and hugged the other one. She tried to imitate everything her older brother did, which often made her the most absurd creature George had ever seen. "Dadadada!" she said enthusiastically. She was a year and a half old now, and sometimes said "Daddy," but when she got excited—as she always did when her father first came home from the sea—she went back to baby talk.

Fresh sizzling noises from the kitchen said the fish had gone into the frying pan. The Enoses, like any other fisherfolk, ate a lot of fish: nobody begrudged George's bringing home enough to feed his family. He didn't have to fill out any forms to get it, either. Through the sizzle, Sylvia called, "When do you think you'll be going out again?"

"Don't know exactly," he answered. "Soon as Captain O'Donnell or somebody from the company can lay hold of more coal, I expect. Business is good, prices are up, and so they're sending us out as often as they can. Might be the day after tomorrow, might be—"

Somebody knocked on the front door, hard.

"Might be tomorrow morning," Enos said, heaving himself up out of his chair. In the kitchen, Sylvia groaned, but softly. He understood what she was feeling, because he was feeling all the same things himself. Getting to see his family once in a while mattered a lot. But he'd brought home a lot of money in the weeks since the war started. Prices were up, too, but as long as he stayed busy, he stayed ahead of them.

He opened the door. Sure enough, there stood Fred Butcher. "Hate to do this to you, George," the mate said, "but we've swung a deal for some fuel. We sail at half past five tomorrow morning."

"I'll be there," Enos said—what else could he say?

Butcher nodded. "I know you will. You and Cookie, we can always count on the two of you. Some of the others, I'm going to have to pry 'em out of the saloons and sober 'em up—if I can find 'em." He touched a finger to the bill of his cap. "See you on the wharf. Tell your missus I'm sorry." He hurried off, a busy man with more work ahead of him.

George Enos shut the door. "Supper's on the table," Sylvia called at the same moment. As he walked into the kitchen, she went on, "I can guess what that was all about. Nice I get to give you one meal before Charlie White gets his hands on you again. You eat more of his cooking than you do of mine, seems like."

"Maybe I do," Enos said, "but I like yours better." That made Sylvia smile; for a moment, she didn't look so tired. George wasn't sure he'd told her the truth, but he'd made her happy, which counted, too.

Sylvia cut up bits of fish and potato for the children. George, Jr., handled his fork pretty well; one day soon, he'd start using a knife. With Mary Jane, Sylvia had to make sure she ate more than she threw from the high chair onto the floor. It was about an even-money bet.

"Have to get them to bed early tonight," George remarked. "If we can."

"I don't want to go to bed early," his son declared indignantly. Mary Jane wasn't old enough yet to know what he was talking about.

"You'll do as you're told, though," Enos said.

George, Jr., knew that tone brooked little argument. He changed his tack, asking, "Why do I have to go to bed early? Mama? Daddy? Why?"

"Just because you do," Sylvia answered, glancing at her husband with an expression half amused, half harassed. When you had only occasional nights together, you needed to make the most of them.

And there were reasons sailors coming home from the sea had a salty reputation. "*Again,* George?" Sylvia whispered in the darkness of their bedroom, feeling him rise against her flank for the fourth time. "You might as well be a bridegroom. Shouldn't you sleep instead?"

"I can sleep on the *Ripple*," he said as he climbed back on top of her. "I can't do this." She laughed and clasped her arms around his sweaty back.

When the alarm clock jangled at four in the morning, he wished he'd slept more and done other things less. He made the clock shut up, then found a match, scratched it, and used the flame to find and light the gas lamp. Staggering around like a half-dead thing, he fumbled his way into his clothes.

By the time he was dressed, Sylvia, who'd thrown a quilted robe over her white cotton nightdress, pressed a cup of coffee into his hands. He gulped it down, hot and sweet and strong. "You should go back to bed," he told her. She shook her head, as she did whenever he said that in the small hours of the morning. She puckered her lips. He set down the cup and kissed her good-bye.

Some of the streets on the way down to T Wharf had gaslights, some new, brighter electric lamps. The lamps weren't bright enough to keep him from seeing stars in the sky. The air was crisp and cool. Fall wasn't just coming—fall was here. They might get a couple of weeks of Indian summer, and then again they might not.

T Wharf didn't care about day or night; it was busy all the time. And sure enough, there ahead of him strode Charlie White, a knitted wool cap on his head. "Hey, Cookie!" George called. The Negro turned and waved.

For a wonder, the whole crew got to the *Ripple* on time. "Wouldn't even expect that in the Navy," Patrick O'Donnell said: his highest praise. A few minutes later, coal smoke spurted from the steam trawler's stack. Along with Lucas Phelps, George cast off the mooring lines. The *Ripple* chugged out toward Georges Bank.

The Cookie served out more coffee, and then more still; a lot of the fishermen were short on sleep. And if any of them were hung over, well, coffee was good for that, too.

The day dawned bright and clear. Gulls screeched overhead. They knew fishing boats were a good place to cadge a meal, but they weren't smart enough to tell outbound boats from inbound. Off in the distance floated a plume of smoke from a warship outbound ahead of the *Ripple*. Enos liked seeing that; it made trouble from Confederate cruisers and submarines less likely. The warship, intent on its own concerns, soon left the *Ripple* behind; the smoke vanished over the eastern horizon.

Though the *Ripple* was a trawler, everyone fished with long lines on the way out to Georges Bank: no point wasting travel time. The cod and mackerel they caught went into the hold. So did a couple of tilefish. "Shallower water'n you'll usually see 'em in," Lucas Phelps remarked, pulling in a flopping three-foot fish. "More of 'em now than there have been, too, since they almost disappeared thirty years back."

"My pa used to talk about that," George Enos said. "Cold currents shifting almost killed 'em off, or something like that." He headed up to the galley for yet another mug of coffee.

When they reached the Georges Bank that night, the trawl splashed into the sea. The *Ripple* crawled along, dragging it over the ocean bottom. To keep from drawing raiders, Captain O'Donnell left the running lights off; he posted a double watch to listen for approaching vessels and avoid collisions.

But they might have been alone on the ocean. Another clear dawn followed, with water around them stretching, as far as the eye could tell, all the way to the end of the world. No smoke told of other fishing boats or warships anywhere nearby.

Enos was gutting fish when the captain spotted a smoke plume approaching from the east. "Freighter heading in toward Boston," he judged after a spyglass examination. He looked some more. "Carrying something under tarps on the bow, something else at the stern."

The freighter must have spotted the *Ripple*, too, for she swung toward the trawler. O'Donnell kept watching her every couple of minutes. Enos thought he was worrying too much, but, on the other hand, he got paid to worry.

And then the captain shouted, "Cut the trawl free! We've got to run for it. Those are guns under there!"

Too late. One of the guns roared, a sound harsh even across a couple of miles of water. A shell splashed into the sea a hundred yards in front of the *Ripple*'s bow. Then the other gun, the one at the armed freighter's stern, belched smoke and fire. That shell landed about as far behind the steam trawler.

Signal flags fluttered up the freighter's lines. Captain O'Donnell read them through the telescope. " 'Surrender or be sunk,' they tell us," he said. Like the rest of the fishermen, George Enos stood numb, unbelieving. You never thought it could happen to you, not so close to home. But that freighter, while no match for the cruiser that hadn't seen it, could do with the *Ripple* as it would. One of those shells would have smashed the steam trawler to kindling.

"What do we do, Captain?" Enos asked. O'Donnell was an old Navy man. Surely he'd have a trick to discomfit the approaching ship, which, George could see, now flew the Stars and Bars above the signal flags.

But O'Donnell, after kicking once at the deck, folded the telescope and put it in his pocket. "What can we do?" he said, and then answered his own question by turning to Fred Butcher and saying, "Run up a white flag, Mate. They've got us."

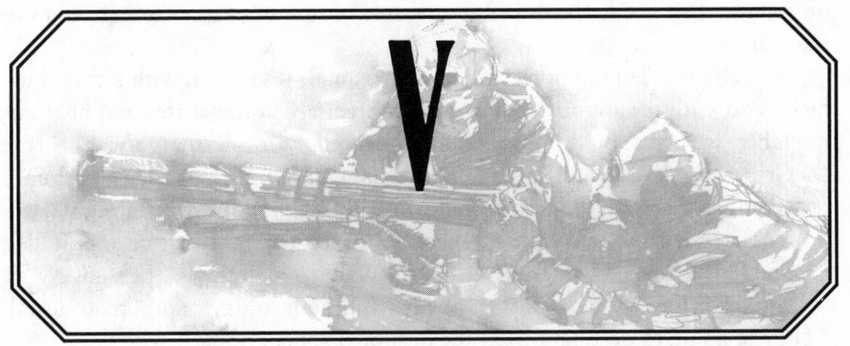

V

Rain with sleet in it blew into Arthur McGregor's face as he rode his wagon into Rosenfeld, the hamlet on the Manitoba prairie nearest his farm. At the edge of town, a sentry in a green-gray U.S. Army rain slicker stepped out into the roadway, his boots making wet sucking noises as they went into and came out of the mud. "Let's see your pass, Canuck," he said in a harsh big-city accent.

Wordlessly, McGregor took it out of an inside pocket and handed it to him. The farmer had wrapped the pass in waxed paper before setting out for Rosenfeld, knowing he'd need it: the Americans were sticklers for every bit of punctilio they'd set up in the territory they occupied, and people who didn't go along disappeared into jail or sometimes just disappeared, period.

After carefully inspecting the document, the sentry handed it back. "Awright, go ahead," he said grudgingly, as if disappointed he didn't have an excuse for giving McGregor more trouble. He gestured with his Springfield. Water beaded on the bayonet; he'd done a good job of greasing it to keep it from rusting.

Rosenfeld's only reason for being was that it lay where an east-west railway line and one that ran north-south merged into a single line heading northeast: in the direction of Winnipeg. Along with the train station, it boasted a general store, a bank, a couple of churches, a livery stable run by the blacksmith (who also did his best to fix motorcars, not that he saw many), a doctor who doubled as a dentist, a weekly newspaper, and a post office. McGregor hitched the horses in front of that last.

"Shut the door behind you," called Wilfred Rokeby, the postmaster, when McGregor came in. The farmer obeyed, not blaming him a bit: the coal stove made the interior of the post office deliciously warm. McGregor stood dripping on the mat just inside the door for a couple of minutes before going on up to the counter.

Rokeby nodded in approval. He was a small, fussy man with a thin mustache and with mouse-brown hair parted precisely in the center and held immovably in place by some cinnamon-scented hair oil that always made McGregor think of baked apples. "And what can I do for you today, Arthur?" he asked, as if certain the farmer had something new and exotic in mind.

McGregor took out another sheet of waxed paper. This one was folded around half a dozen ordinary envelopes. "Want to mail these," he said.

Rokeby looked pained. He always did, but today more than usual. "They're going to destinations in the occupied zone, I hope?"

"Can't send 'em anyplace else from here, now can I?" McGregor answered sourly. "Any mail wagon goes from one side of the line to the other, first the Yanks shoot it up and then we do."

"That is unfortunately correct." The postmaster made it sound as if it were McGregor's fault. He pointed to the envelopes lying on the counter between them. "Those'll have to go through the American military censor before I can send 'em out, you know."

"Yeah, I'd heard about that." McGregor's expression said what he thought of it, too. "It's all right." He spread the envelopes out fan-fashion so Rokeby could read the addresses on them. "Two to my brothers, two to my sisters and brothers-in-law, two to my cousins, just to let 'em know I'm alive and well, and so is the rest of the family. Censors can read 'em till their eyes cross, far as I'm concerned."

"All right, Arthur. Wanted to make sure you remembered, is all." Wilfred Rokeby lowered his voice. "The Yanks have arrested more'n a couple of people on account of they were careless about what they put in the mail. Wouldn't want anything like that to happen to you."

"Thanks," McGregor said gruffly. He dug in his pocket and came out with a handful of change. Setting a dime and two pennies on the counter beside the envelopes, he went on, "Why don't you let me have the stamps for them, then?"

"I'll do that." The postmaster scooped up the coins and dropped them into the cash box. Then he pulled out a sheet of fifty carmine stamps, tore off a strip of six, and handed them to McGregor. "Here you go."

"Thanks. I'll—" McGregor took a closer look at the stamps Rokeby had given him. The color wasn't quite right—that was what had first drawn his eye. When he took that closer look, he saw they didn't bear the familiar portrait of King George V, either. They were U.S. stamps, with a picture of Benjamin Franklin on them. On Franklin's plump face, the phrase MANITOBA MIL. DIST. was overprinted in black ink. "What the devil are these?"

"The stamps we have to use from now on," Rokeby answered. "Ugly, aren't they? But I don't have a choice about what I sell you: military governor says no mail with the old stamps goes out any more. Penalty for disobeying is . . . more than you want to think about."

One after another, mechanically, McGregor separated the stamps from the strip the postmaster had given him, licked them, and stuck them on envelopes. Even the glue tasted wrong, or he thought it did—more bitter than that to which he was accustomed. *The taste of occupation,* he thought. The U.S. stamps, specially made up for the occupied area hereabouts, brought home to him that the Americans expected to be here a long time in a way nothing else, not even the soldier outside of town, had done.

He shoved the letters at Rokeby, then turned on his heels and stomped out of the post office without another word. Suddenly the warmth in there felt treacherous, deceptive, as if by being comfortable Rokeby was somehow collaborating with the United States. He knew the idea was absurd, but it wouldn't go away once it occurred to him. The cold, nasty rain that beat in his face when he went outside was a part of his native land, and so seemed oddly cleansing.

The general store was a couple of doors down. His feet thumped on the boards of the sidewalk. A bell jingled when he went in. Henry Gibbon looked up from a copy of the Rosenfeld *Register*. He took a pipe out of his mouth, knocked it against an ashtray, and said, "Morning to you, Arthur. Haven't seen you in a while. Everything all right out at your place?"

"Right enough, anyhow," McGregor answered: a measure of life in wartime. "We didn't get hurt, thank God, and we didn't lose our buildings or too much of the livestock. I've heard of plenty of people who came through worse."

"That's a fact," the storekeeper said. Henry Gibbon looked like a storekeeper: bald and plump and genial, with a big gray mustache hiding most of his upper lip. He wore a white apron, none too clean, over a collarless shirt, a considerable expanse of belly, and black wool trousers. "You got your family, you got your house, you can go on."

McGregor nodded. He didn't tell Gibbon about how his wife had tried endlessly to get rid of the bloodstains on the floors and walls, or about the chunks of board he'd nailed over dozens of bullet holes to keep out the cold. The farmhouse looked as if it had broken out in pimples.

"So what can I sell you today?" Gibbon asked. Unlike some storekeepers McGregor had known, he made no bones about being in a business where he gave customers goods in exchange for money.

"Thing I need most is ten gallons of kerosene," the farmer answered. "Nights are starting to get longer, and they'll be really long pretty soon. I've got plenty of coal laid in for the winter, but lamp oil, now—" He spread his hands.

Henry Gibbon clicked his tongue between his teeth. "I can give you two gallons, no problem. Anything more than that at one time, or you buyin' more than two gallons a month, and you got to get permission from the Americans in writing." He reached down under the counter and pulled out a set of forms, which he waved in McGregor's face. "I got to account for every drop I sell: when and to who and how much at a time. They're fussy about checkin' on it, too. You don't want to run foul of 'em."

It was warm inside the store, as it had been in the post office. Again, McGregor had the sense of warmth betraying him. "Two gallons a month, that's not much."

"It's what I can sell you," Gibbon said. "Arthur, I'd do more if I could, but I got a family. You get in trouble with the Americans, you get in bad trouble." He waved the copy of the *Register*, much as he had the U.S. forms. Then he pointed to an item and read aloud: " 'The U.S. military governor in the town of Morden announces that ten hostages have been taken because of the shooting death of an American soldier. If the perpetrator of this vile and dastardly act of cowardice does not surrender himself to the duly constituted authorities within seventy-two hours of this announcement, the hostages will be executed by firing squad.' "

"Let me see that!" McGregor said. He'd paid little attention to the town weekly since the American tide rolled over this part of Manitoba. Now he got a good look at how things had changed since the occupation.

Oh, not everything was different from what it had been. Local stores still advertised on the front page of the *Register*, as they had for as long as Malachi Stubing had been publishing it—and through the tenures of two other publishers before him. He still announced local births and marriages. Farmers still plunked down money to tout the service of their stallions and jackasses, with the invariable ten-dollar fee and the phrase "Colt to stand and walk." If the foal was stillborn, the fee was waived. McGregor had put a good many such notices in the paper over the years.

Some of the death notices were as they'd always been: Mary Lancaster, age 71, beloved mother, grandmother; Georgi Pasternak, age 9 months, at home with the angels. But a good many bore familiar names gone at unexpected ages: Burton Wheeler, 19 years old; Paul Fletcher, age 20; Joe Teague, 18. None of those gave the least hint how the young men had died.

Another story listed men known to be prisoners of war, and gave their kin instructions on how to send them packages. "All parcels are subject to search," it warned. "Any found containing contraband of any description will result in the addressee's forfeiting all rights to receive future parcels."

That blunt warning took McGregor to the columns of small print that covered the broader world. And there, most of all, that world might have turned upside down with the arrival of the Americans. Suddenly Germany became the trusted ally, England and France the hated foes. The German failure in front of Paris was glossed over as a small setback, and much made of the victory the Kaiser's forces had won over Russians poking their noses into eastern Prussia.

As far as the *Register* was concerned, the United States could do no wrong, though each story did bear the disclaimer, *furnished by the American Military Information Bureau*. If you believed what you read, the Yanks were in Winnipeg, in Toronto, and bombarding Montreal and Quebec City, to say nothing of the triumphs they'd won against the Confederacy and the victories their Atlantic Fleet and the German High Seas Fleet had gained over the Royal Navy and its French and Confederate allies.

McGregor set the *Register* back on the counter. "What do you think of all this?" he asked Henry Gibbon.

The storekeeper paused before he spoke. "Well, the paper it's on is pretty thin now," he said at last. "That makes it better for wipin' your ass than it used to be."

McGregor stared at him, then chuckled, down deep in his throat. "I don't expect the American Military Information Board'd like that answer, Henry."

"Give me a penny and I'll care a cent's worth," Gibbon answered. This time, both men laughed.

"Come on, you damn nigger, shake a leg!" the lieutenant shouted, a silver bar gleaming on each shoulder strap. "You think we've got all day to unload this stuff? Get your lazy, stinking black ass in gear, or you'll be sorry you were ever born, and you can take that to the bank."

"I'm comin', sir, fast as I can," Cincinnatus answered. He walked onto the barge, threw a hundred-pound sack of corn onto his shoulder, and carried it to the waiting motor truck. The truck rocked on its springs as he tossed the sack on top of the others already in the cargo bed.

"Faster, dammit!" the lieutenant screamed, setting a hand on the grip of his pistol. He clapped the other hand to his forehead, and almost knocked the green-gray cap off his head. "Jesus Christ, no wonder the stinking Rebs go on about niggers the way they do."

Cincinnatus would have liked to see the lieutenant haul as much as he was hauling, or even half as much. The noisy little peckerwood ofay'd fall over dead. But he had the gun, and he had the rest of the U.S. Army behind him, and so Cincinnatus didn't see that he had much choice about doing what he was told.

He had no great love for the whites for whom he'd labored here in Covington. They'd told the truth about one thing, though: he didn't get better treatment now that the United States was running the town than he had when the Stars and Bars flew here. Some ways, things were worse. The whites who lived in Covington—Tom Kennedy came to mind—dealt with Negroes every day and were used to them. A lot of the soldiers from the United States—this buckra lieutenant surely among them—had never set eyes on a black man before they invaded the Confederacy. They treated Negroes like mules, or maybe like steam engines.

Another grunt, another sack of grain on his shoulder, another walk to the truck. The lieutenant shouted at him every inch of the way. No, you didn't cuss a steam engine the way that fellow cussed Cincinnatus. The Negro couldn't figure out whether the U.S. soldier blamed him for being black or for being the reason the South had broken away from the United States. He didn't think the lieutenant knew, or cared. The man could abuse him with impunity, and he did.

"Once we win here, we'll ship all you nigger bastards back to Africa," he said, sounding ready, willing, and able to pilot the boat himself.

Sensibly, Cincinnatus kept his mouth shut. Even if he hadn't had a lot of schooling, though, he could do arithmetic better than that damnfool lieutenant. There were something like ten million Negroes in the Confederate States. That made for a lot of boat trips back and forth across the ocean. For that matter, the USA hadn't shipped its own Negroes back to Africa. If they weren't there any more, whom would the white folks have left to despise?

At last, the back of the truck was full. Cincinnatus picked up a galvanized bucket, drank some water, and poured the rest over his head. The lieutenant glowered at him, but let him do it. Maybe he'd convinced the fellow he really was working.

A white man, a U.S. soldier, drove away in the truck. "I could do that, suh," Cincinnatus told the lieutenant. "You could use your boys for nothin' but fightin' then."

"No," the lieutenant barked, and Cincinnatus shut up again. If the damnyankee wanted to be stupid, that was his lookout.

But the damnyankees weren't stupid, not in everything, and you were in trouble if you didn't remember that. The railroad bridge and the highway bridge over the Ohio had crashed into the water as soon as the war started, blown up by Confederate sappers to keep U.S. troops from using them. The Yankee bombardment had done a lot of damage to the Covington docks and, when invasion looked imminent, the Confederates had done a lot more, again to keep the United States from gaining a military advantage. When Cincinnatus came out of the storm cellar of his house after the Confederate army retreated southward and the artillery fire tapered off, he was horrified at the devastation all around.

Things still looked like hell. The fires were out, yes, but every third building, or so it seemed, was either wrecked or had a hole bitten out of it. You didn't want to walk down the street without shoes; you'd slice your feet to ribbons on the knife-sharp shards of glass that sparkled like diamonds in the sun and were sometimes drifted inches deep.

None of that had kept U.S. forces from exploiting Covington once they'd seized it. Not one but two railroad bridges and one for wagons and trucks came down from Ohio now; they were pontoon bridges that blocked the river to water traffic, but the damnyankees didn't seem to care about that. And the docks had got back in working order faster than Cincinnatus had imagined possible. Barges and ferries—anything that would float—worked alongside the bridges in moving men and matériel down toward the fighting. The U.S. Army engineers knew what they were doing, no two ways about that.

Cincinnatus sighed. If the damnyankees had done as well dealing with the people of Covington as they had with transportation into and out of the place, everybody would have been better off. Nobody, though, had taught them the first thing about how to engineer human beings, and they weren't good at it. This damn lieutenant was a case in point.

He screamed at Cincinnatus and the rest of the Negroes doing stevedore work on the docks from the minute they got there to the minute they left. And he didn't just hate Negroes; whenever he had to deal with the white Southerner, he was every bit as bad.

When the owner of a livery stable complained about having had some horses requisitioned without getting paid for them, the lieutenant told him, "What you need isn't money or horses; it's the horsewhip, nothing else but. You damned traitor, you're dealing with the United States of America now, not your Rebel government. You'd better walk small or you'll be sorry. We're back now, and we're going to stay, and if you don't like it, you can jump in the river for all I care."

The livery stable man walked off. If looks could have killed, the lieutenant would have been the one in the Ohio, floating face down. Cincinnatus whispered to another black man working alongside him: "My mama always did say you catch mo' flies with honey than with vinegar."

"My mama say the same thing," the other Negro answered, also in a low voice. "That buckra there, though, I bet he don't have no mama." He dropped his voice even further. "An' he sure don't know who his papa was."

Cincinnatus laughed at that, loud enough to make the lieutenant glare at him. But he was working, and working hard, so the little man in the green-gray uniform went off to shout at somebody else.

When sunset came, the men on the docks lined up to get their pay. Armed guards stood around the paymaster to make sure nobody tried redistributing the wealth on his own. "Name," said the paymaster, a middle-aged white man with sergeant's stripes on his sleeves.

"Agamemnon," said the Negro in front of Cincinnatus.

The paymaster handed him a green-gray U.S. dollar bill. Covington was a border town, so some of those bills, along with U.S. coins, circulated here all the time. Now, though, the brown Confederate banknotes were no longer legal tender in areas the United States controlled. Till that moment, Cincinnatus hadn't noticed how each side's paper money matched its army uniform.

"Name?" the paymaster asked him.

"Cincinnatus," he answered.

"No." Shaking his head, the paymaster pointed across the Ohio River. "Cincinnati's over there." He chuckled. Cincinnatus smiled back. It wasn't the worst joke in the world, even if he heard it at least once a week. And the white sergeant didn't seem to have a chip on his shoulder, the way most damnyankees did. The fellow checked his name off on the list in front of him, then handed him a dollar and a fifty-cent piece. "Lieutenant Kennan says you get a hard-work bonus."

"He *does*?" Cincinnatus said, amazed.

"Believe it or else, buddy," the paymaster said with an eyebrow raised in amusement—maybe he knew about Lieutenant Kennan. Instead of waving Cincinnatus on, he said, "Ask you somethin'?"

"Yes, sir, go ahead," Cincinnatus said. The fellow seemed friendly enough—and having a white man ask him permission for anything before going ahead and doing it was a novelty in and of itself.

"All right." The sergeant leaned back in his chair and put his hands behind his head, fingers interlaced. "What I want to know is, how come all you niggers down here carry such highfalutin names?"

"Never hardly studied it," Cincinnatus said. He did, for a couple of seconds, then answered, "Reckon it's on account of the law don't allow us no last names—maybe they figure we'd be good as white folks if we had 'em, I don't know. So we only have the one, and we got to make the most of it."

"Makes as much sense as any other guess I've heard," the paymaster allowed. Now he did wave Cincinnatus on, asking the next man in line, "Name?"

"Rehoboam," the stevedore answered. The paymaster chuckled and gave him his money.

With an extra four bits in his pocket, Cincinnatus spent a nickel of it for a ride home on the trolley, which had been running for only a couple of days. He went to the back of the car and stood there, hanging onto a leather strap, as it clattered along. Some seats in the forward, white, section were vacant, but the U.S. officials hadn't changed the rules, and the U.S. soldiers in the forward section were liable to beat up a black man who tried to sit among them. He'd heard that had already happened more than once.

The trolley rolled past the city hall. The Stars and Stripes flew in front of it and on top of its dome. To Cincinnatus, the U.S. flag looked crowded and busy, with too many stars and too many stripes. *The Bleeding Zebra,* Southerners called it, and he could see why.

Plump, prosperous-looking white gentlemen wearing homburgs and somber suits, carrying fancy leather briefcases, and smoking cigars strode in and out of the city hall, as they had before the United States occupied Covington. Some were U.S. administrators, some Covington politicians licking the Yankees' boots.

And some, maybe, really did want to work with the USA. Kentucky was the only Confederate state that hadn't left the Union at the start of the War of Secession; Braxton Bragg had conquered it for Richmond when Lincoln pulled soldiers eastward to try to repair the disaster at Camp Hill. Up till the time of the Second Mexican War, when U.S. forces wrecked Louisville, a lot of Kentuckians had had sympathy for the United States, and, sympathy or not, Kentucky had always done a hell of a lot of business with the USA.

Along with the prosperous gentlemen, a good many U.S. soldiers held positions around the Covington city hall. Machine guns protected by sandbags stood at either side of the entrance. Not everybody in Covington sympathized with the damnyankees, not by a long shot.

Cincinnatus got out of the trolley not far from Tom Kennedy's warehouse. The lines did not run through the colored section of town. Standing still for the journey let him know how tired he was; he walked south to his house with the stoop-shouldered, stiff-jointed gait of an old man.

Motion by the Licking River caught his eye. A bunch of Yankee sailors in dark blue were swarming over the grounded, burned-out hulk of the river monitor he'd seen on the water that day just before the war broke out. The monitor had taken a licking, all right; Yankee shells had set it ablaze before it could do much damage. Now whatever bits of it that could be salvaged would be used against the Confederacy.

The smell of fried chicken floating out through the windows made Cincinnatus' mouth water and straightened his back. Just thinking about biting into a hot, juicy leg sent spit spurting into his mouth. "That better be done," he called as he walked inside, " 'cause I'm gonna eat it whether it is or whether it ain't. Smells as good as my mama makes."

"Be five, ten minutes," his wife Elizabeth answered. She waved to him from the kitchen. Then, to his surprise, his mother did, too. A heavyset woman of about fifty, she beamed at him and Elizabeth both. "My boy Cincinnatus, he has a *good* nose," she declared.

"That he does, Mother Livia," Elizabeth said. "You were right—he could tell. Must be the spices."

"What are you doin' here, Mama?" Cincinnatus asked. "Not that I ain't glad to see you, but—"

"I came to help my daughter-in-law," his mother said.

Cincinnatus scratched his head. His wife was as capable as she needed to be and then some, and his mother had said as much ever since they were married. Elizabeth had got out of her black-and-white housekeeper's clothes and put on a shirtwaist too old and spotted to wear in public any more and a bright red cotton skirt that set off her light brown skin—she was two, maybe three shades paler than Cincinnatus. "You're home sooner than I reckoned on," she said.

"Took the trolley," he answered. She frowned at the extravagance till he showed her not only the day's usual greenback but the forty-five cents he had left from his bonus. "That damnyankee strawboss lieutenant, he sure hates niggers, but he knows work when he sees it."

"All right," Elizabeth said, more grudgingly than he'd expect. "I wish you'd saved every penny, but—all right."

"What's the matter?" he asked. "We ain't broke." One reason he loved Elizabeth was that she was as dedicated to getting ahead—or as far ahead as Negroes in the Confederate States could get—as he was. Even so, worrying about a nickel's worth of bonus seemed excessive.

Then she set both hands on her belly, about where the shirtwaist tucked into the skirt. "Reckon we gonna have us a little one some time next spring."

"A little one?" Cincinnatus stared. All at once, he understood why his mother had come. He hurried forward to embrace Elizabeth. "That's wonderful!" And it was wonderful, even if the timing could have been better. But now he wished he hadn't spent that nickel.

The troop train rattled through Lynchburg and west toward the Blue Ridge Mountains. "If I'd known they were going to pack us into these cars like canned sardines," Reginald Bartlett said, feeling not just canned but cooked in his uniform and heavy kit, "I never would have volunteered."

"Ahh, quit whinin'," said Robert E. McCorkle. Since McCorkle was a corporal, his opinion carried considerable weight. So did he; his uniform could have held a couple of men of ordinary girth. He went on, "You don't like it, write your congressman."

"I can't," Bartlett said. "Can't raise my arms to write."

That put a smile on McCorkle's face; even noncommissioned officers responded to Bartlett's charm, a sure proof of its effectiveness. The corporal said, "Well, you ain't as bad as some here, and that's the Gospel truth. Some o' these birds, they even grouse in their sleep."

"Birds? Grouse?" Reggie Bartlett laughed, but McCorkle failed to join him: he didn't notice he'd made a joke. What were you supposed to do with such people? Burying them struck Bartlett as a good idea, but only for a moment. A lot of young men were getting buried, off in the direction they were going.

McCorkle said, "Ahh, what the hell, anyway? You turn out a bunch of soldiers who can't even complain when they feel like it, they might as well come from the United States."

"Or Germany," somebody said from behind the corporal.

"Yeah, or Germany," McCorkle allowed. "But it's different with the Huns. If it's got buttons on its coat, they salute it. The soldiers in the United States, once upon a time they was Americans, same as you an' me. Not any more. It's all the damn foreign riffraff they let in, you ask me."

Ahead, the bulk of the Blue Ridge notched the skyline. The sun was going down in fire above the mountains. The troop train rolled over an iron bridge spanning the Otter River. Less than half an hour later, it went through Bedford Court House; in the twilight, Bartlett saw street lamps going up into the hills at whose feet the town lay.

Night fell. The troop train kept on traveling. Its pace slowed as it climbed. Some of the peaks of the Blue Ridge rose well over four thousand feet: not so much out West in the United States or the CSA, but more than respectable hereabouts. The tracks went through the passes, not over the peaks, of course, but still rose considerably in a short stretch of time.

Reginald Bartlett made himself as comfortable as he could. Considering all the gear with which he was festooned, that wasn't very comfortable, but at least he had a seat on a hard second-class bench. The aisles were full of men who'd been standing since they left Richmond and who were trying to squat or lie down so they could try to get a little sleep.

That didn't come easy, for them or for him. His pack dug into his spine. If he let his head flop backwards, it went over the back of the seat, and made him feel his neck was breaking. If he leaned forward, he hit himself in the forehead with the rifle he held between his knees. The men on either side of him kept poking him with their elbows, and neither of them, by all the evidence, had ever heard of soap and water—or maybe Bartlett was just smelling himself.

"This whole business of war is a lot more entertaining to read about than to be a part of," he complained. "All the writers who go on about the Revolution and the Secession and the Second Mexican War leave out the parts that have no glory in them."

"And when they do talk about glory, they're talking about the fellows who lived," Corporal McCorkle added. "The poor bastards who died, yeah, they wave good-bye to them, you might say, but that's all."

Bartlett didn't want to think about that, and wished he'd kept his mouth shut. The Confederacy was mowing down damnyankees the way a steam-powered threshing machine mowed down wheat at harvest time. All the papers said so, and so did every military briefing Bartlett had heard since he'd showed up at the recruiting office. But the papers also printed hideously long casualty lists every day, and the maps showed that most of the fighting was on

Confederate soil. Things weren't so easy as he'd thought they would be when he joined up.

Just when he finally managed to doze off, the troop transport started down the grade on the western slope of the Blue Ridge Mountains. Couplings bumped and jolted—the weight of the train had shifted from the back end to the front. Bartlett jerked bolt upright. His start woke the soldier next to him, who cursed foully. He'd heard more blasphemy and obscenity in a few weeks of soldiering than he had in all his civilian life—but he remembered that from a few years before, when his birth class had been conscripted.

Iron wheels screamed on iron rails as the train slowed to a stop. "This here must be Vinton," McCorkle said. "This is where we get out."

Bartlett peered through the window. He couldn't see anything. If they were at a station, it was news to him. The doors at either end of the railroad car opened, though, and his companions stumbled out into the night. When his turn came, he went, too.

"This way! This way! This way!" Captain Dudley Wilcox shouted, waving around an electric torch so his men could see which way *this way* was. Bartlett was glad to be reminded the company commander existed; he'd neither seen nor heard him since the troop train pulled out of Richmond.

Captain Wilcox led them down a path full of pungent horse manure to a field where campfires were already burning. "We'll bivouac here tonight," he declared. "Bedrolls only—no tents. Get what rest you can—tomorrow we go into action."

As Bartlett spread his blanket on the ground and wrapped himself in it, a mutter of distant thunder came from the west. He looked up into the sky. The stars of early autumn twinkled down on him. The trees would be changing color, though he couldn't see that in the darkness. The thunder came again—only it wasn't thunder, it was artillery. Somewhere over there, gunners were launching shells into the dark—and when those shells came down, they probably killed people. That didn't strike Bartlett as glorious. He was too tired to care. He fell asleep almost at once.

Corporal McCorkle woke him with a boot in the seat of the pants. It was still dark. He sat up, stiff from lying on the ground and feeling he needed another two or three or six hours of sleep to turn himself into a properly functioning human being. He rolled up the blanket and put it away. No more sleep today.

"Listen here, you birds!" Captain Wilcox sounded indecently alert and indecently cheerful for whatever the hour was. "The damnyankees want to take Big Lick away from us, take away the mines, take away the railroad junction. There's so damn many of 'em, they've made it over the Alleghenies and they're coming down toward the city. That's why we're here—to keep 'em from taking it. The company—the regiment—the division—we all go across the Roanoke at ten this morning and we drive the Yankees back into the mountains. Sooner or later, we drive 'em out of Virginia. Any questions? I know you'll fight hard. We'll get us some breakfast and then we'll get us some damnyankees."

Negro cooks passed out cornmeal muffins and bacon. Bartlett wolfed his down. He filled the screw-on cup that doubled as a canteen lid with chicory-laced coffee. It made him feel more nearly alive.

He was gulping a second cup when the artillery barrage opened up. The noise was brutal, appalling, overwhelming. He loved every second of it. "More of that racket there is," he shouted to anyone who would listen, "more damnyankees the Devil's dragging down to hell, the fewer of 'em there are left up here to shoot at me."

"Amen to that," said one of his squadmates, a skinny, bespectacled fellow named Clarence Randolph. He'd been a preacher before the war started, and could have joined the Army as a chaplain, but he hadn't wanted to be a noncombatant. If he wasn't the best shot in the company, Bartlett didn't know who was.

Captain Wilcox blew a whistle. Its shrill screech cut through the roar of the barrage and the occasional blasts from shells the U.S. gunners threw back in reply. "Let's go," Wilcox said, waving his arm. Along with the rest of the regiment, along with the rest of the division, the company moved forward.

Under cover of darkness, Confederate engineers and colored laborers had run pontoon bridges across the Roanoke. The planks they'd laid over the pontoons rumbled under Bartlett's feet. He wanted to get across before day broke enough to give the fellows who manned the Yankees' cannon a good shot at the improvised bridges.

Horses snorted in a field as he marched past. The shadows in that field were centaurlike. "We punch the hole in the Yankee lines," Corporal McCorkle said gladly, "then the cavalry rides through, gets into their rear, and chases 'em to hell and gone."

"Good place for 'em," Clarence Randolph said. "I am a man brimming over with Christian charity, but I don't believe in wasting it on damnyankees."

As light gained on darkness, Bartlett saw how barrages by both sides had chewed the land to ruins. The Confederacy still held about half the valley between the Alleghenies and the river; the Stars and Bars floated over Big Lick, a couple of miles to the south, but nobody was working the mines these days.

A shell fell short and landed among a knot of soldiers off to Bartlett's left. Some of the screams that rose from them were those of injured men, others of sheer fury at wounds inflicted by friend rather than foe.

"Come on up." A corporal in a grimy uniform waved Captain Wilcox's company into the firing pits and connecting trenches that made up the Confederate line. "Come on up, new fish, come on up."

The soldiers already in line greeted the newcomers with nasty grins and even nastier questions: "Does your mother know you're here?" "Ever see guts all over everywhere?" "How loud can you scream, new fish? No, don't bother answerin'—you'll find out."

Their looks shocked Bartlett. It wasn't just that their uniforms and persons were filthy, though that was what he noticed first. The look in their eyes said more. They'd seen things he hadn't. Some of them—the ones who took obvious delight in those questions—knew a malicious glee that he and his comrades were about to see those things, too.

Some gave good advice: "You go forward, stay low. Zigzag a lot—don't let 'em draw a bead on you. Get down on your belly and crawl like a snake."

Bartlett wanted to see what the bombardment was doing to the Yankee lines, but when somebody stuck his head over the front edge of a firing pit, he slumped down dead a moment later, a bullet in his forehead just above the right eye, the back of his head blown out. One of the men who'd been in the line for a while shoved the body out of the path the newcomers were taking, as if it were an inconvenient log. Gulping, Bartlett stepped past the corpse. He decided he wasn't curious any more.

Here and there among the firing pits, steps made of dirt and sandbags led up to the ground ahead. The company halted by some of those steps. "When the barrage stops, we go," Captain Wilcox said.

Maybe the barrage would go on forever. Maybe the artillery would kill all the damnyankees and leave nothing for the infantry to do. Maybe staying behind a pharmacy counter back in Richmond hadn't been such a bad thing. Maybe Bartlett should have waited for his old regiment to be called up instead of volunteering in a new one. Maybe—

As suddenly as it had begun, the barrage stopped. Captain Wilcox blew that damned whistle again. Bartlett wished he'd lose it or, better yet, swallow it.

Soldiers started surging up over the steps. Somebody gave Bartlett a shove. He stumbled forward. His feet hit the first step and climbed all by themselves, regardless of what his mind was telling them. Then he was up on level if battered ground. He ran toward the even more battered firing pits and trenches ahead.

He could hardly see them because of all the smoke and dust the barrage had kicked up. Men in butternut trotted ahead of him, alongside him, behind him. He was part of the thundering herd. As long as he did what everyone else did, he'd be all right. A little more than a quarter of a mile—surely less than half a mile—and what had been Yankee lines would belong to the Confederacy once more.

Through the smoke of dust—*the fog of war,* he thought with the small part of his mind that was thinking—evil yellow lights began winking and flashing. The bombardment hadn't killed all the U.S. soldiers, then. Men started falling. Some crawled ahead. Some thrashed and twisted and screamed. Some didn't move.

Bartlett leaned forward, as if into a gale. He wasn't the only one. Lots of the soldiers still on their feet had that forward lean, as if bracing against a bullet's anticipated impact. Then, rifles and machine guns (he turned to tell Clarence Randolph that machine guns were satanic tools, but Clarence wasn't there, wasn't anywhere nearby—had, in fact, taken only a few steps before a bullet tore out his throat, but Bartlett didn't know that) tearing at them, they struggled through the Yankee wire and, screeching, threw themselves at the men in green-gray who had invaded their nation.

There were too many Confederate soldiers and too few Yankees, and those too shaken by the barrage to fight as well as they might have. Bartlett leaped down into a firing pit and pointed his rifle at an enemy. The man dropped his weapon and threw his hands in the air. Bartlett almost shot him anyhow—his blood was up—but checked himself, gesturing brusquely with the bayoneted muzzle of his Tredegar: *over that way.* The U.S. soldier went, a grin of doglike submission on his face.

"Come on!" Captain Wilcox shouted. "Spread out and move forward. They'll counterattack as soon as they can. We want to take back as much ground as we're able, then hold it against anything they can do to us."

Maybe the damnyankees had had trenches leading up into their forward positions, as had been true in the Confederate lines. If they had, the Confederate bombardment had destroyed them. Going deeper into the U.S.-held territory was a matter of scrambling from one shell hole to the next. Enemy fire picked up all the time.

There next to Bartlett was Corporal McCorkle. Wide as he was, he'd kept up with the assault and hadn't stopped a bullet. Turning to him, Bartlett said, "Aren't you glad we've won this land back for our dear country?" He waved—cautiously, so as not to expose his arm to a bullet—at the shell-pocked desolation all around.

McCorkle stared, then started to laugh.

The postman came to the coffeehouse, delivered a couple of advertising circulars, and went on his way. Nellie Semphroch glanced at the circulars. She didn't throw them away, as she might have before the war. Crumpled up, the papers would make good kindling.

Edna Semphroch came to the doorway to stand beside her mother. She looked after the postman, who was going on down the street whistling some new ragtime tune Nellie didn't recognize. "Doesn't seem right to see old Henry coming around every day, same as he did before the Rebs jumped on us," Edna said.

"Well, he does only come once a day now, instead of twice," Nellie said, "but yes, I know what you mean. He's—normal—and everything else has gone straight to the devil, hasn't it?"

Nellie had only to look at her own shop to see the truth of that. The front window, blown out in the earliest Confederate bombardment of Washington, D.C., was covered over with boards, and she was glad she had those. You couldn't get glass for love nor money: literally. One glazier she'd talked to had said, "I had a lady offer me an indecent proposal if I'd get her windows repaired." The fellow had chuckled. "Had to turn her down—couldn't find the goods for her any which way."

Nellie didn't know whether to believe him or to think he was trying to trick her into making an indecent proposal in exchange for glass. Men were like that. If he was, it hadn't worked. So many places were boarded up these days, Nellie didn't feel either embarrassed or at a competitive disadvantage for being without glass.

She looked up and down the block. Not a shop, far as the eye could see, still kept its original glazing. Some buildings were rubble; they'd taken direct hits from shellfire. Some weren't boarded up, but looked out on the street with empty window frames like the eye sockets of a skull: their owners had fled Washington before the Rebs crossed the Potomac. Bums—and people who wouldn't have been bums had their homes and businesses not been wrecked—sheltered in them, and sometimes came out to beg or steal. Nellie thanked heaven she wasn't living like that.

Rubble had been pounded down into the holes Confederate shells had torn in the street. U.S. prisoners had done that, under the eyes and guns of laughing Rebel guards. It had rained several times since the bombardment, but some of the bloodstains, brown and faded now, were still all too plain to the eye.

"The Rebs are having themselves a fine old time here," Nellie said to Edna in a low voice. You had to use a low voice if you called them Rebs. They'd tolerate Rebels, but preferred Confederates or even—travesty!—Americans.

Her daughter nodded. "Far as they're concerned, it might as well be *their* capital." She bared her teeth in what someone who didn't know her might have taken for a friendly smile.

From behind the two women, a Southern voice called, "Another cup here, if y'all'd be so kind."

Nellie put a smile on her own face as she walked back into her coffeehouse. It was akin but not identical to the grimace Edna had worn a moment before: the smile any business person gives a customer, a smile aimed at the billfold rather than the person who was carrying it. "Yes, sir," she said. "You were drinking the blend from the Dutch East Indies, weren't you?"

"That's right." The Confederate major nodded. He wore the tight, high boots and yellow uniform trim of a cavalry officer. "Mighty fine it is, too, ma'am—smooth as I've ever drunk."

"I'm glad you like it." Nellie refilled the cup from one of the pots behind the counter. Not all the cups matched any more—she'd foraged from here and there and everywhere to replace the ones broken in the fighting. "Enjoy it while you can—when it's gone, heaven knows how I'll be able to get more."

"Life's going to be hard for a while, I reckon," the major agreed. He took the cup, then added cream and sugar and a splash from a little tin flask he wore on his belt. "*Right* smooth," he said with a smile as he drank. He looked from Nellie to Edna and back again. "Would you let me buy either of you charming ladies, or the two of you together, a cup while you still have it to enjoy?"

Edna looked as if she might have said yes to that. The cavalry major was personable enough: even handsome in a florid way. But Nellie answered before her daughter could: "No, thank you. We'd best save it for the customers: can't afford to drink up our own stock in trade."

"However you like," the officer said with a shrug. There were a lot of Confederate cavalrymen in Washington. When they went closer to the front, they had a way of getting killed in a hurry. Their own comrades in the infantry and artillery ragged them about it; the coffeehouse had seen a couple of fights. Confederate military police swung billy clubs with the same reckless abandon Washington city constables had used.

After draining his augmented cup of coffee, the cavalry major got up, took a wallet out of a hip pocket, and pulled out a dollar of Confederate scrip. "I don't need any change," he said, and walked out the door.

"Of course you don't," Nellie muttered when he was gone. "It's like play money to you." The scrip the Confederates had instituted for Washington and for the chunks of Maryland and Pennsylvania they'd taken from the United States—the dollar note the major had set down bore the picture of John C. Calhoun—was nominally at par with the U.S. and Confederate dollars. But Confederate soldiers could buy occupation scrip for twenty cents of real money on the dollar. They spent freely—who wouldn't, with a deal like that?—which drove down the value of the scrip. Prices were going up, anyway; so much scrip in circulation just made them go up faster.

Nellie walked out to the doorway. Across the street, Mr. Jacobs' cobbler's shop had a sign tacked to the boards covering what had been his window: DISCOUNT FOR SILVER. If the Rebs didn't make him take that sign down, it struck Nellie as a good idea. If you fixed the discount as you should, you'd make money whether you got scrip or cash.

And Jacobs was doing a terrific business. You could get leather locally; it wasn't like coffee. Marching wore down boots, too, so Confederate soldiers were always going into the shop. He'd even had a general make use of his services, said worthy having arrived in a motorcar driven by a colored chauffeur with a face of such perfect insolence, it seemed to be aching for a slap.

Quietly—for there were still a couple of Confederate cavalry lieutenants in the coffeehouse, hashing out on the table the breakthrough that hadn't yet come and, God willing, never would—Edna said, "Ma, I wish there was something we could do to give the Johnny Rebs a hard time."

"I'm not going to put rat poison in the coffee, though I've thought about it a couple of times," Nellie answered.

"Maybe we ought to send them to the sporting house around the corner," Edna said. "If they get a dose of the clap, they can't very well fight, can they?" Her smile was wide and unpleasant.

Nellie's ears got hot. "What is the younger generation coming to?" she exclaimed: the cry of the older generation throughout recorded history. "Radicalism and rebellion and free love—" She'd been seduced at the age of fifteen and knew more than she wanted of sporting houses, but conveniently chose not to remember that.

Smiling still, Edna said, "If they go to the sporting house, Ma, love wouldn't be free. They don't take scrip there, neither, I hear tell."

"*Where* do you hear tell such things?" Nellie demanded. Edna was with her almost all day almost every day, but you couldn't keep an eye on somebody all the time, not unless you were a jailer, you couldn't.

Before her daughter answered, Mr. Jacobs came out of his shop along with a Confederate soldier carrying a pair of cavalry boots. The cavalryman went on his way. Jacobs called, "Lovely day, isn't it, Widow Semphroch, Miss Semphroch?"

"Yes, it is," Edna said, in lieu of replying to her mother's question.

"No, it isn't," Nellie declared.

The cobbler laughed at their confusion.

"Dowling!" As usual, George Custer made too much noise. The shout would have drawn his adjutant from the next county, not just the next room.

"Coming, sir!" Abner Dowling said, also loudly, the better to overcome the commanding general's deafness—which, of course, the commanding general denied he had.

Custer stabbed a nicotine-stained forefinger down at the map on the table before which he stood. "Major, I am not satisfied with our progress, not satisfied at all."

"I'm sorry to hear that, General," Dowling said, taking a discreet half step backwards: Custer's breath alone was plenty to get you lit up. "I think we've made excellent progress, sir."

He wasn't lying there, not even a little bit. The crossing of the Ohio had gone better than he'd expected—much better than he'd expected, considering that Custer was in charge of it. Facing simultaneous thrusts aimed at Louisville and Covington, the Confederates hadn't been able to put enough men into Kentucky to defend all of it. That First Army headquarters was in Marion these days proved the point.

"Well, I don't, dammit," Custer bellowed, which made Dowling draw back another half a pace, both from volume and from fumes. "Look at the map, you overfed twit! Second and Third Armies are going to break into the bluegrass country long before we do."

"Our advance has hurt the Rebs a lot already," Dowling said stoutly, refusing to take offense at the general's gibe. "Why, we've deprived them of all the fluor spar mines here around Marion, and—"

"Fluor spar!" Custer sneered. "Fluor-stinking-spar! Teddy Roosevelt will be thrilled to get a telegram telling him we've captured a whole great pile of fluor-goddamn-spar, now won't he? He'll send me to command in Canada because of fluor spar, won't he? Oh, yes, he'll be delighted—no doubt about it." Even by Custer's standards, the sarcasm was venomous. "The greatest horse country in the world just ahead of us, and you're babbling about fluor-fucking-spar? God preserve me from idiots!"

"But—" Dowling gave up. If you were going to make steel by any modern process, you needed fluor spar, and you needed it in multiton lots. But Custer had been a cavalry general back in the days when cavalry was good for something more than getting mowed down by machine guns, and so horses were all he thought about. *That he's a horse's ass doesn't hurt, either,* Dowling thought. He usually tried to keep from thinking disloyal thoughts, but that wasn't easy when Custer rode him on account of his size.

The general said, "I want to put paid to the Confederate cavalry once and for all."

"Yes, sir, I understand that," Dowling said, doing his best to get across the idea that Custer might better use his men in another way without coming right out and screaming in the famous general's wrinkled, sagging face. He also understood that Custer wanted to accomplish something so spectacular, Teddy Roosevelt would have no choice but to give him the command he truly craved. If Custer held his breath waiting for that, he'd be even redder in the face than he was already.

"I should hope you do," Custer declared. "Cavalry's done a lot of good work in this war, especially on the far side of the Mississippi."

"Yes, sir," Dowling said again, now in resignation. Try as you would, sometimes you couldn't win. Custer was going to go after cavalry horses, and that was all there was to it. Never mind that the Rebs west of the Mississippi drew their mounts from local stock. Never mind that the reason cavalry could be dashing and bold out West was that there were miles and miles of miles and miles out there, and not enough soldiers, Yankee or Confederate, to keep raiders from breaking through every so often. Never mind that two other armies were already advancing on the bluegrass country. Never mind any of that. Custer wanted his glory, and by jingo he was going to get it.

He said, "We'll push east past Madisonville and break through there. The Confederates can't keep throwing up lines against us indefinitely. Sooner or later, the losses they're suffering will force them to recognize they've met their match and then some in me." He struck a triumphal pose that put his adjutant in mind of a plaster-of-paris statue made by a bad artist having a worse day.

"Our own losses have also been heavy, sir," said Dowling, whose job, after all, involved keeping some tenuous connection between Custer and military reality. "Defending prepared lines is cheaper than storming them."

That was especially true because Custer didn't—wouldn't—allow enough time for proper artillery bombardment before he sent the poor damned infantry forward. Kentucky wasn't like the country west of the Mississippi. Here, the Confederacy had plenty of Negroes to build works and plenty of white men in butternut to man them. That was one of the reasons cavalry here didn't count for much.

Also— "Sir, if we concentrate our main thrust along an east-west line, we can't take proper precautions against the Confederate buildup we've been watching between Hopkinsville and Cadiz, southeast of here. If they take us in flank, we'll be as embarrassed as our German friends were on the Marne a few weeks ago."

"Fiddlesticks," Custer retorted. "I don't believe the Rebs can muster the sort of force they'd need to shift us, nor anything close to it. They're too heavily committed here and on too many other fronts. We have the initiative, Major, and we shall retain it."

"But, sir—" Dowling had to protest. He went through the papers in Custer's in-basket. Sure enough, there were the reconnaissance reports he'd stamped URGENT in crimson ink, and sure enough, Custer hadn't looked at any of them. "These scouting reports from our aeroplane pilots clearly show—"

"That those pilots are a pack of nervous Nellies," General Custer broke in. He seemed pleased with the phrase, so he repeated it: "A pack of nervous Nellies, yes indeed. You ask me, Major, what they call reconnaissance is greatly overrated anyhow."

"But, sir—" Dowling repeated himself, too, before continuing, "back in St. Louis, you were complaining you weren't getting the reconnaissance you needed from Kentucky."

" 'A foolish consistency is the hobgoblin of little minds,' " Custer quoted grandly. "Now let me tell you what reconnaissance can be worth. Back more than forty years ago now, this damned ragged Indian scout looked at the ground and told me all the Indians in the world—or in Kansas, anyhow—were camped along the Ninnescah, down near the border with Sequoyah: Indian Territory, it was then. Do you know what I ordered, Major? Do you know?"

"The whole country knows, sir," Dowling answered unhappily.

"Yes, but do you?" Custer glowered at him. "I ordered the charge, Major, that's what I did. We sent a raft of redskins to the happy hunting grounds by suppertime, and hardly let a one get back to the Confederate side of the border." He struck his splendid pose once more. "And no one has missed them from that day to this. Now I am going to order the charge again. If the enemy is there, you must strike him."

"The Confederates are better soldiers than those red savages were, I'm afraid, sir," Dowling said.

"They're not good enough to withstand a stroke from the brave soldiers of the United States of America," Custer declared, "and I aim to give them one they'll never forget. Besides which, as I've told you before, aeroplanes are nothing but newfangled claptrap."

Abner Dowling had the feeling he'd wandered into quicksand. The more he tried to flail his way toward common sense, the more deeply he got mired in Custer's prejudices, which were as entrenched as any of the Confederate works against which the general insisted on banging his head. You couldn't just ignore a building flank attack . . . could you?

Then, without warning, bombs started falling on Marion: four or five sharp explosions. One of them blew in Custer's office window; Dowling yelped when a flying shard cut his hand. He couldn't hear the buzz of the aeroplane that had dropped the bomb. It must have been flying as high as it could.

Outside, soldiers opened up on the aeroplane with their Springfields and with a couple of machine guns. Their chances of bringing it down were about the same as those of taking on the steel trust in court and winning.

"You see?" Custer said triumphantly. "They're only a nuisance, and couldn't hurt a fly."

Clutching his injured hand, Dowling reflected that he was obviously worth less than a fly to his commander. Well, that wasn't anything he hadn't already known. Later, he found out one of the bombs had fallen in the midst of a knot of soldiers, killing five of them (as well as an unfortunate local Negro who was cooking for them) and maiming another three.

But that was later. At the moment, he said, "We do have an urgent request for reinforcements on the southeastern part of our line. Wouldn't it be prudent to—"

"No, and quit pestering me about it!" Custer shouted. His pouchy, sagging features turned quite red. "We didn't start to fight this war to stand on the defensive, Major, God damn it to hell. We came to do to the Rebs what they did to us fifty years ago: to knock 'em down, and to kick 'em in the balls when they are down. We attack!"

"Yes, sir," Dowling said miserably.

Flora Hamburger stepped out onto the fire escape to get away. She wasn't trying to escape the heat trapped inside the flat she shared with her parents, an older sister, a younger sister, and two younger brothers. Escaping the heat was what you did in summer, and here with October heading toward November you were likelier to throw on a sweater or a coat, although she hadn't bothered doing that.

She wasn't going out to escape the noise, either. Her father and mother seldom spoke to each other or to their children at anything less than a shout, and her brothers and sisters weren't the quietest people God ever made. Flora wasn't one of those people, either, and she knew it.

But going out onto the iron floor of the fire escape didn't make the noise disappear. What her family lost in volume, the rest of New York gained. It was getting dark outside, but boys still played and screeched in the street below. "I got you, you lousy Reb!" one of them yelled in Yiddish in a high, piercing voice. "You're dead, so fall over!"

"You missed me by a mile!" another boy called back, this one in English, even more shrilly. "Nyah-nyah-nyah! Couldn't hit a barn." The first boy imitated a machine gun, which set Flora's teeth on edge. However many imaginary bullets he spat, though, he couldn't kill one real child. In the real war, unfortunately, it didn't work like that.

Every day, the front page of the *New York Times* screamed of battles won and battles lost. Every day, bordered in black, ran long lists of names: men and boys who would never come home because of those battles won and lost. More than anything else, the black-bordered casualty lists were what had driven Flora outside, away from her family.

If the rest of New York cared, it didn't let on. Along with the children playing, babies howled from every second flat. Flora's parents weren't the only ones shouting. Folk of their generation yelled in Yiddish or Russian or Polish or Magyar or Romanian. Folk of Flora's generation answered back, when they answered back, in all those languages, and sometimes in English, too. Sometimes getting an answer in English made parents yell even more, because it seemed to mean their children were slipping away from them, becoming American. And, sure enough, their children were.

When Flora didn't come back into the flat after a few minutes, her older sister, Sophie, stepped out onto the fire escape with her. Sophie was calm and steady and accepting, all the things Flora wasn't. Instead of being a Socialist Party agitator, she sat in front of a sewing machine twelve hours a day six days a week, turning linen and cotton into shirtwaists and, lately, into uniform tunics.

"Come back," she urged now. "You're making Mama upset, you do this so often now. It's not normal."

"I'm upset," Flora said. "Does anyone care about that? Thousands of people are getting blown to bits every day. Does anyone care about *that*?" She pointed down to the street and across it, to another crowded brownstone just like the one in which she and her family lived. "It doesn't look like it to me."

"People don't want our soldiers to get killed in the war. Nobody wants that," Sophie said reasonably. "But we can't do anything about it. Life has to go on, the way it's supposed to."

"This isn't the way it's supposed to, and it won't be the way it's supposed to until we find a way to make the fighting stop," Flora insisted. "And all the capitalists are making money from the fighting, so it can go on forever as far as they're concerned. If anyone goes against it, it will have to be the members of the working class—like you, for instance." She stared defiantly at Sophie.

Sophie sighed. She was—not surprisingly, given the hours she worked—exhausted when she came home, and every bit of that weariness showed in her voice. "Flora, I don't need you to agitate for me here," she said. Had she been more like her sister, she would have grown furious. "I hear plenty from the Socialist recruiters every day at the shop."

"You hear, but you don't listen," Flora exclaimed.

"However you like," Sophie answered. "But I'll tell you this much: the agitation sounds a lot more foolish than it would if the Socialists hadn't voted for the war credits. It takes a lot of *chutzpah*"—she had been speaking English, but let the Yiddish word find a place—"to say yes to something out of one side of your mouth and no from the other."

Flora bit her lip. "You're right about that, and I wish we hadn't. But I think all the congressmen thought this would be a sharp, short war. Doesn't look that way any more, does it?" She stamped her foot, as much to listen to and to feel the clatter of the cast iron as for any other reason. "And once we've voted yes once, how can we vote no after that without looking like—without being—even worse hypocrites?"

Before Sophie could reply, her mother stuck her head out onto the fire escape and said, "Yossel is here to see you."

"Oh, good," Sophie said, and, smiling, went back inside.

Sarah Hamburger glanced over to her middle daughter. "Flora, you'll say hello to your sister's fiancé, I hope?"

"All right," Flora said resignedly. She did not dislike Yossel Reisen, even if he was a reactionary—or maybe just an anachronism. Here in New York in the twentieth century, as progressive an era and as progressive a city as had existed in the history of the world, he could find nothing better to do with his life than to study Torah and Talmud. He might make a rabbi one day, but even if he did, Sophie would likelier end up supporting him than the other way round. But Sophie was happy, so Flora, for the sake of family peace, kept her opinions there to herself.

When she stepped back into the flat, Sophie and Yossel were sitting side by side on the divan couch against the far wall of the front room. Yossel, a tall, pale, thin fellow whose rusty beard obscured half the high collar on his shirt, was saying, "I have some news I should tell you." He spoke Yiddish with a hissing Litvak accent; every *sh* sound turned into an *s*.

"What is it?" Sophie asked, a beat ahead of her younger sister, Esther, and her brothers, David and Isaac. Her mother and father didn't blurt out the question, but they plainly wanted to know, too.

Yossel took a deep breath. His fingers plucked at the green tufted plush upholstery of the divan. He knew such furniture well; he must have slept on a dozen lounges and couches and davenports, boarding now with this family, now with that one, while he pursued his studies. He never had much money to pay anyone, which was why he moved frequently.

He needed a second deep breath before he could come out with his news: "I have volunteered for the Army of the United States. I am going into the service in one week's time."

"Why did you do that?" Sophie exclaimed, her placid face suddenly full of harsh lines of pain. "Why, Yossel, why? When they didn't call you up as soon as the war started, I thought—" She didn't go on. What she meant to say was probably something like, *I thought we could be married and go on with our lives as if the world weren't coming to pieces around us.* But the world was always there, no matter how much you tried to pretend it wasn't if you didn't look at things from an economic perspective.

"Good luck," said David Hamburger, who was seventeen and was raising a downy mustache that made him look younger rather than older.

"Get lots of Rebs or Canucks—wherever they send you," said Isaac, who was two years younger. Neither of them was yet eligible for conscription. As with a lot of young men, too, they still thought of war as adventure. The black-bordered casualty lists meant nothing to them.

Yossel answered Sophie, not them: "I volunteered to help the United States get back what they lost: what they had taken away from them. I volunteered because the Confederates and the English and the French deserve to be put down for what they have done to us—and because they are all allies of the Russians." No Lithuanian Jew was likely to think kind thoughts of Czar Nicholas and his regime.

"You've fallen victim to the capitalists' propaganda," Flora exclaimed. Everyone turned to look at her. "Don't you see?" she said. "Workers get nothing from this war, nothing but suffering and death. The ones who make the money are the factory owners and the munitions merchants. Don't listen to their lies, Yossel."

"I am in the United States," Yossel said stiffly. "Now I can be *of* the United States, too. This is my country. I will fight for it. And now, even if I wanted to, I could not withdraw my enlistment. But I do not want to."

Sophie started to cry. So did her mother. After a moment, so did Esther. Isaac and David both shouted angrily at Flora. Her father, Benjamin Hamburger, stood silent, puffing on his pipe. He didn't usually vote Socialist, but he came closer than the rest of the family to sympathizing with the Party's goals.

Yossel went back to explaining why he'd enlisted, but no one, save possibly Flora's father, was listening to him. Flora, desperate to get away, wished she'd stayed out on the fire escape. No one heeded her warnings. No one would—till too late, she feared.

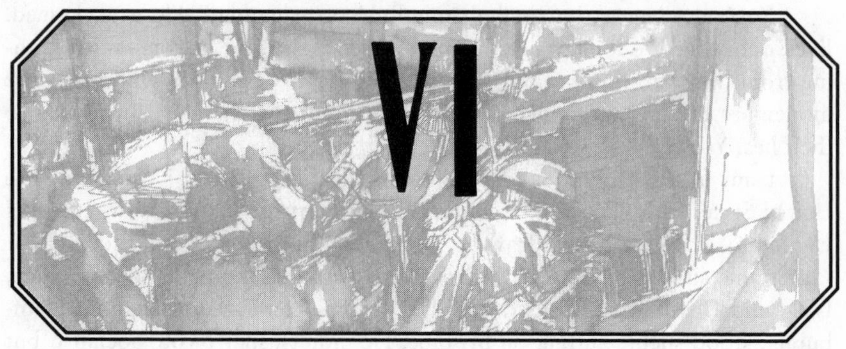

Along with the rest of Captain Lincoln's command, Corporal Stephen Ramsay rode out of Jennings, Sequoyah, on horseback to repel U.S. raiders. "Wouldn't think the damnyankees'd get the idea so quick," he said mournfully. It had rained the night before, and the horses were kicking up a lot of mud. Everybody would be filthy by the time the company got back into Jennings—everybody who was alive.

Lincoln said, "They're money-grubbing bastards, the Yankees. A chance to grab the oil south of the Cimarron'd look good to 'em. Then they can ship it over to the Huns, to burn Belgian babies with."

"Good luck to anybody shippin' anything on the Atlantic," Ramsay said. "Best I can tell, it's like a cavalry campaign a whole ocean wide."

Lincoln chuckled at that, though Ramsay had meant it seriously. Warships and liners and freighters and submarines from the CSA and the USA and England and France and Germany were scurrying all over the ocean, and shooting at one another whenever they knocked heads.

Ramsay added, "This here is better country for fightin' than the regular prairie or the ocean. If we can't hold the Yanks the far side of the river, we ain't gonna hold 'em anywheres."

"I'm not going to tell you you're wrong, Corporal," Captain Lincoln said. The territory between the Cimarron and the Arkansas, which came together about twenty miles east of Jennings, was rough and rugged: wooded hills and gullies took over for prairie. There were caves in the hills, if you knew where to find them. Outlaws and robbers had infested the area for years, because just about all the people who could find them after they'd fled from their crimes were either friends or relations.

"One other thing," Ramsay said. "They ain't gonna get one o' those armored automobiles through here. You try and run a motorcar in this kind of landscape and it'll fall to pieces before you've gone ten miles."

"Damn good thing, too," the company commander said, to which Ramsay could only nod. A lot of the men with them in the company were new recruits. Confederate raids into Kansas hadn't lasted long; the damnyankees had the initiative now, pushing down into Sequoyah and threatening the oil fields that gave the Confederacy so much of its petroleum.

The U.S. troopers were not better soldiers than their Confederate counterparts; anyone who claimed they were would have got himself pounded by any cavalryman in butternut who happened to hear. But what Ramsay and Lincoln had feared from the time of their first encounter was a reality: the U.S. cavalry usually advanced with armored cars bolstering the horsemen. Confederate armored automobiles, by contrast, were often promised, seldom seen. In open country, protected, mobile machine guns were deadly all out of proportion to their numbers.

Ramsay chuckled reminiscently as an exception to that rule came to mind. "Remember when we had that battery of field artillery with us, up near the border with the Yankees? We made 'em pay that day, by Jesus."

"Sure did," Captain Lincoln agreed. "Sure do. Pretty damn fine to have guns to outrange those damn cars—and to blow one of 'em to hell and gone when you hit it."

"Yes, sir," Ramsay said enthusiastically. The quick-firing three-inch field guns had hit two armored cars, setting them ablaze and making their fellows scuttle on back toward Kansas. They'd also started a grass fire that had slowed up the advance of the U.S. horsemen, who weren't nearly so eager to go forward without their mechanical buddies, anyhow.

But there weren't enough batteries of field artillery to go around, and the Yankees kept coming. Even if they weren't very good at what they did, enough mediocre soldiers were eventually liable to wear down a smaller force of good ones. And now parts of Sequoyah lay in U.S. hands.

Ramsay's horse stumbled. What passed for roads here in these badlands were pretty miserable even when they were dry. When they were wet, puddles disguised potholes deep enough to break an animal's leg—sometimes, it seemed, deep enough to drown an animal.

He sharply jerked the horse's head up. The beast let out an indignant squeal of complaint, but it didn't fall. Ramsay knew everything there was to know about complaining—he was a soldier, after all. He'd heard better, from men and horses.

The damp, muddy road wound round the edge of some bare-branched scrub oaks and opened out into a valley wider than most. A couple of farms took up most of the horizontal land and some that wasn't: the sheep grazing on a hillside would have done better if their right legs had been shorter than their left. Smoke curled up from the chimneys of both wooden farmhouses: cabins might have been a better word for them.

A woman wearing a kerchief, a man's flannel shirt, and a long calico dress was tossing corn to some scrawny chickens between one farmhouse and the barn. As the cavalry company drew nearer, Ramsay saw she was a half-breed, or maybe a full-blooded Indian. Sequoyah held more Indians than the rest of the Confederacy put together, and had even elected a couple of Indian congressmen and a senator.

Seeing soldiers approaching, the woman grabbed a shotgun that was leaning up against a stump. It wouldn't have done her much good, not against a cavalry company, but Ramsay admired her spirit. After a moment, the woman lowered the barrel of the shotgun, though she didn't let go of it. "You're Confederates, ain't you?" she said, her words not just uneducated but also flavored with an odd accent: she was Indian, sure enough.

"Yes, we're Confederates," Captain Lincoln answered gravely, brushing the brim of his hat with a forefinger. He pointed to the flag the standard bearer carried. "See for yourself, ma'am."

The woman peered at it, peered at him, and then nodded. She turned the barrel of the shotgun away from the troopers, using it to point north and west. "Yankees in them woods. Leastways, they was there last night. Seen their fires. Don't know how many—less'n you, reckon. Go over there and *kill* 'em."

Her vehemence made little chills run up Ramsay's back. One thing you could rely on: the Indians in the state of Sequoyah were loyal to Richmond. The government of the United States had made them pack up and leave their original homelands back east for this country. Since the War of Secession, though, the Confederacy had treated them with forbearance, and that was paying off now.

"Whereabouts exactly were they?" Captain Lincoln asked, getting down off his horse and standing beside the woman. A chicken walked over and pecked at the brass buckle of his boot—maybe the stupid bird thought it was a grain of corn.

The woman pointed again. "Halfway up this here side of that hill—you see it? Ain't seen 'em move out since. Maybe they still there."

Ramsay doubted that, but you never could tell. Maybe they'd decided to wait out the bad weather—even though it wasn't raining now—or maybe they were waiting for reinforcements to come up before they started pushing south again. Any which way, the company would have to ride on up there and find out what was going on.

Captain Lincoln touched his hat again. "Thank you, ma'am. Don't want to ride into trouble blind, you know."

"You just keep them damnyankees from tramplin' our garden and stealin' our critters," the woman said, as if such petty thievery were the only reason U.S. soldiers were in Sequoyah now. She probably thought that; Ramsay wondered if she'd been off this farm since she was married.

As if the thought had gone straight from his head to Captain Lincoln's, the company commander's voice suddenly got hard and suspicious as he demanded, "Where's your husband at?"

The farm woman spat, right between his feet. "Where the hell you think he's at?" she snapped. "He got drug into the Army, and I jus' hope to Jesus he come home again."

"Sorry, ma'am," Lincoln said, color rising in his face. A couple of the troopers snickered. One of them was in Ramsay's squad. He'd rake Parker over the coals later on; couldn't let discipline go to pot. The captain was saying, "Hope he comes home, too. Hope we all do, when this war is over." He swung back up into the saddle and waved to the company. "Let's go find those damnyankees."

They rode in loose order, with plenty of scouts forward and more out on either flank. This whole country was made for bushwhacking. And then, up ahead, they heard a brisk crackle of gunfire. "Somebody else done found 'em for us," Ramsay yelled. "Now we go in there and clean 'em out."

As the Confederates rode toward the shooting, a machine gun started hammering away. "That's Yankees, all right," Lincoln said. "God knows the outlaws have plenty of rifles, but they don't have any of those."

A winding little track led through the scrub oaks toward the fighting. Lincoln dismounted his men and sent them through the woods on foot, using them like dragoons rather than true cavalry. Ramsay heartily approved—galloping up that path was asking to be massacred.

Before long, the dismounted troopers ran into Yankee pickets. Whoever was commanding the U.S. forces was doing the same thing with them as Lincoln was with the Confederates: they might have ridden to get to the fight, but they were making it on foot.

They also seemed to be outnumbered, and had to give ground again and again to keep from being outflanked and cut off. What with the thick undergrowth, you couldn't see much. If anything moved, you took a shot at it. And when you moved, people you couldn't spot shot at you. Getting a taste of what infantry did for a living, Ramsay discovered he didn't much care for it.

Eventually, the crew for the company machine gun managed to lug both it and its mount through the woods and started spraying the Yankee positions with damn near as many bullets as the rest of the company put out all together. Ramsay waited for the U.S. troopers to move their own Maxim gun away from wherever they'd had it before and try to neutralize the Confederate weapon, but they didn't. Instead, here and there among the oaks, white flags started going up.

"Ease off, you Rebs!" somebody yelled. "You got us."

Firing slowly died away. "All right, Yanks, come out," Captain Lincoln called. The U.S. troopers obeyed, hands high over their heads. Nobody shot them down. This wasn't like the skirmish up in Kansas, the one by the railroad track. This one had been fair all the way—no armored automobiles to mess up the odds.

There were, all told, maybe twenty-five U.S. soldiers. Their leader, a fellow with a Kaiser Bill mustache that had lost a good deal of its waxed perfection, wore the single silver bars of a first lieutenant. "We have some wounded back there," he said, pointing in the direction from which he'd come.

"We'll take care of them," Captain Lincoln promised, and told off a detachment to lead the Yankee prisoners back toward the road.

"A good haul," Stephen Ramsay said, standing up and emerging from cover. "We'll pick up that machine gun and as much ammunition as they have left for it, and then somebody'll shoot it back at 'em till all the cartridges are gone."

Captain Lincoln gathered him up by eye. "Come on, Corporal," he said. "Let's go see who we rescued there."

Ramsay followed him through what had been the U.S. position. He was curious about that himself; he hadn't known any other Confederate cavalry was operating in this neck of the woods. He didn't know everything there was to know, though; he would have been the first—well, maybe the second—to admit as much.

From out of some woods that looked impenetrable, a voice called a sharp warning: "Don't come no further! We got you covered six different ways."

Captain Lincoln stopped. So did Ramsay, right behind him. "Who are you?" Lincoln asked; it hadn't sounded like a Yankee holdout.

A hoarse laugh answered him. "Ain't none of your damn business who we are and who we ain't," the unseen man said. "You jus' go on home, Captain; we ain't got a quarrel with you now, even if mebbe we used to."

"What's that supposed to mean?" Ramsay muttered.

He hadn't meant anyone, even Lincoln, to hear him, but his ears were ringing from the fire fight, and he spoke louder than he'd intended. "Means we wouldn't've mixed it up with them damnyankees if we hadn't thought they was you."

"Outlaws!" Captain Lincoln exclaimed.

"Yeah, and now we got a nice new Maxim gun to play with, too, you want to come in after us. You want to fight the USA, fine. Leave us the hell alone."

"What do we do, sir?" Ramsay asked.

"I think we leave them the hell alone, Corporal," Lincoln said loudly. "We're not the police and we're not the sheriffs. We owe these people one, too. They let us know where the Yankees were, and a machine gun's too heavy to lug around to robberies." He turned his back and started away. Nobody shot at him, or at Ramsay.

"Hell of a thing," Ramsay said when they were back among their comrades, and then, "We could take 'em."

"Oh, no doubt," Lincoln agreed. "But that's not our mission. We're having enough trouble with what is." Ramsay thought that over and decided the captain was right.

Sam Carsten wished he were someplace else. He'd had that feeling before, but never so bad. If he got noticed—

"This is what I get for volunteering," he muttered under his breath as the ugly freighter pulled away from Kapalama Basin, around Sand Island, and west over Keehi Lagoon toward the entrance to Pearl Harbor. "Cap'n" Kidde could have told him as much. Hell, Kidde *had* told him as much—after it was too late for him to do anything about it. But the gunner's mate hadn't been standing next to him when the captain of the *Dakota* asked for volunteers for a dangerous mission, and so his hand had shot up along with everybody else's. He hadn't particularly expected to be picked, but here he was.

Off to the west, the sound of big and medium-sized guns never let up. All of Oahu belonged to the United States Navy and Marines—all of it except one lump of rock and cement that made the U.S. hold on everything else a hell of a lot less secure than it should have been.

Smoke wreathed Fort William Rufus, the fort everybody, limey and Yank alike, called the Concrete Battleship. "Why the devil did the damned English have to go and build a fort right there?" Carsten said.

"Drive us crazy?" somebody next to him suggested.

It was as good an answer as any, and better than most. Anybody in his right mind would have thought batteries on the mainland were plenty to keep Pearl Harbor safe. The Royal Navy had to have been hearing voices when it built an artificial island to go with those mainland forts. But, since the mainland forts had fallen to the Marines and the Concrete Battleship was still very much a going concern, maybe the English hadn't been so stupid after all.

The twelve-inch guns in the fort's two turrets had sunk a cruiser and a couple of destroyers, and damaged two battleships to boot. Until it was reduced, the Pacific Fleet couldn't use Pearl Harbor for an anchorage. If the British sortied from Singapore, either alone or with the Japs from Manila, there was liable to be hell to pay.

But how were you supposed to take a fort you couldn't wreck? Pounding by naval guns had chipped and pitted the steel-reinforced concrete that made up so much of the superstructure, but no shells had been lucky enough to land right on top of a turret. Admiral Dewey had offered the fort's garrison full military honors if they surrendered; scuttlebutt was, he'd even offered them safe passage to anywhere they wanted to go in British or Confederate territory. Whatever he'd offered, they'd said no.

And so, brute force and sweet reason having failed, the Navy was trying something new: sneakiness. Carsten didn't know which bright boy in glasses had come up with this scheme. What he did know was that, if it went wrong, nobody would ever find enough pieces of him to bury.

The freighter rounded the headland and sped toward the stern of the Concrete Battleship. The only gun it had ever had that could be brought to bear in that direction was a three-inch antiaircraft cannon, which wasn't turret mounted. The limeys weren't going to use that one now; the bombardment had long since wrecked it.

It was the only one in the plans, anyhow; what was hidden away in the depths of the fort was anybody's guess, and one that made Carsten want to run to the head. But to keep the garrison too busy even to worry about what was sneaking up on them, the Navy was plastering the place again. Shells burst on it, sending up smoke with a core of fire, and all around it, sending up great columns of water. Watching all that made Carsten want to pucker, too. If one of those shells was badly aimed—

Most of the Navy ships were at extreme long range, for good and cogent reasons. The Concrete Battleship could still return fire—and did, with a salvo from one of its big-gun turrets. The noise of those two twelve-inchers going off was like the end of the world.

Closer and closer the freighter came. Carsten moved up to the bow, with the rest of the Navy files and Marines carrying rifles. At the bow was a boarding tower that looked like something out of Sir Walter Scott or other tales of medieval adventure. But, considering that the roof of Fort William Rufus was forty feet above the waterline, the boarding party was going to need help getting up there.

All at once, the Navy guns fell silent. Carsten approved of that; a couple of shells had come closer to the freighter than to the Concrete Battleship. The ship slid up to the stern or rear or whatever you wanted to call it of the fort, making contact with a decided thump.

"Well, if those bastards didn't know we were here, they do now," somebody close to Carsten said. That was undoubtedly true, and did nothing to make him feel better about the world.

A couple of Marines at the top of the boarding tower secured it to the broken concrete atop the fort. They waved. Sailors and Marines swarmed up the ladder, fast as they could. Sam was somewhere near the middle of the rush. His feet seemed to touch only every third rung. Then he was up on top himself, running through rubble to make sure no limeys came out of their starboard sally port to interfere with what the Americans were doing.

He got down behind a broken chunk of concrete and pointed his Springfield in the direction from which the British would come if they were trying something. He hoped to Jesus they wouldn't—after all, what harm could a few American sailors with rifles do on top of a fortress that had defied every big gun the U.S. Navy owned?

"Here come the guys with the hoses!" a Marine corporal yelled.

And, sure enough, here they came, up over the boarding tower with hoses just like the ones the *Vulcan* had used to fuel the *Dakota*. The Concrete Battleship had no fueling ports, of course. But it did have air vents, and the combat engineers knew where they were. They weren't badly covered with broken concrete, either; the Englishmen would have made sure of that.

Somebody fired up through one of the vents. An engineer howled and reeled backwards, clutching his shoulder. Carsten, seeing that plenty of people were covering the sally port, ran over to the vent and shot down into it a couple of times. He didn't know how much good he did; he heard the bullets ricocheting off the metal of the air ducts.

"Hell with that, sailor," an uninjured combat engineer barked at him. "Take Clem's place on the hose and hang on tight."

"All right," Sam said agreeably.

At the rear edge of the Concrete Battleship, somebody yelled "Let 'er rip!" down to the freighter. The hose jerked in Carsten's arms like a live thing. He did have to hang on tight, to keep it from getting away. A stream of thick, black liquid gushed from the nozzle and poured down the vent. Twenty feet away, another hose crew sent more of the stuff into the opening to a second ventilator shaft. Petroleum odors filled the air.

"What the hell is this stuff?" Carsten asked, doing his best to breathe through his mouth.

"Two parts heavy diesel oil, one part gasoline," the combat engineer answered. He let out a wry chuckle. "You don't want to go lookin' for a match for a cigar right about now, do you, buddy?"

"Now that you mention it, no," Sam said.

The engineer laughed again. "Good thinking. Real good thinking. We got ten thousand gallons of this stinking shit on that freighter. Take us maybe ten minutes to pour it all down on the limeys' heads."

"Good pumps," Sam observed. "*Damn* good pumps."

"It's not like we've got time to waste up here," the combat engineer said. He and Carsten held onto the hose till it suddenly went limp. Then he took a surprisingly small square box out of his pack and set it by the vent. In spite of his warning to Sam, he did light a match and touch it to the fuse. He looked up and grinned. "Now we get the hell out of here, is what we do."

"Yes, *sir*!" Carsten grabbed his rifle and ran for the boarding tower. Most of the boarding party was already off the Concrete Battleship. A couple of engineers were still busy lighting more demolition charges here and there on the roof.

Sam went down the boarding tower even faster than he'd gone up it. He wanted to get away from Fort William Rufus, far away, as fast as he could. "Everybody off?" somebody yelled. When no one denied it, that same voice shouted, "All astern full!" The freighter backed away from the Concrete Battleship.

"How long a delay did you put on those fuses?" Carsten asked the combat engineer, who'd come down right behind him.

"Ten minutes," the fellow answered cheerfully.

"Jesus!" Carsten said, and wished the freighter would go faster.

When they'd backed a few hundred yards, shore batteries opened up on the Concrete Battleship to discourage the Englishmen from heading up onto the roof. "If one of their shells fouls up our charges, I'll kill those sons of bitches with my own hands," the engineer promised.

Sam wasn't worrying about that. He was still hoping the freighter could make something better than its current slow progress away from the Concrete Battleship. How long had he taken to run across the battered but unpierced concrete roof? How long had he needed to get down the boarding tower? How much time had gone by since then? And what would happen when—?

That last thought had just gone through his mind when it happened. Fort William Rufus went up in a titanic blast of fire and smoke that obscured the whole artificial island. The shock wave from the explosion slapped the freighter like a barmaid's hand across your face when you got fresh and she didn't like it. Heat hit Sam as if he'd stuck his head in front of an oven.

He hardly noticed. He was watching an enormous slab of reinforced concrete fly high, high, high into the air—hundreds of feet up there, flung like the lid of a pot by a playful kid. But this lid weighed tons uncounted.

Beside him, the combat engineer clapped his hands with glee. "We did know where the main powder magazine was," he said happily.

"I guess you did," Carsten agreed. The ruined roof fell into the Pacific with a splash bigger than a hundred twelve-inch shells all hitting the same place at the same time. "I guess you did," Sam repeated. Fresh explosions tore at the Concrete Battleship. "We aren't going to have any trouble getting in and out of Pearl Harbor, not any more we're not."

Lucien Galtier chased bits of rabbit-and-prune stew around his plate with knife and fork. He ate some potato, too, then reached for a little glass of applejack that sat nearby. "Hard times coming," he said in a mournful voice.

"It will be all right," his wife, Marie, said. "Would you like more?" When he nodded, she picked up his plate and handed it to Nicole, their oldest daughter. "Get your father some more stew, please."

"Yes, Mama, certainly," Nicole said, rising from the table and heading back into the kitchen. Lucien smiled to watch her go. She reminded him of Marie when they'd been courting: small and dark and brisk and resolutely cheerful. No wonder half the young men in the neighborhood would come around on errands that didn't really need doing.

But he would not let Nicole distract him from his worries. "Hard times coming," he said again, and then went on before Marie could answer: "Wives, now, wives, they look at things and they say, 'It will be all right,' no matter what it is, no matter how unlikely things are to be right ever again. We face starvation, nothing less—starvation, I tell you."

"Yes, Lucien, of course," Marie said, full of calm acceptance, as Nicole brought back his plate, piled high with steaming stew and potatoes. The plums that made the prunes had come from his own little orchard. The potatoes were from his farm, too. So were the rabbits, who had paid the penalty for being uninvited guests. He knew how to make applejack, but old Marcel, two farms away, had a still going and did not charge outrageous prices, so what was the point in cooking up his own? He finished the glass, savoring the warmth it put in his middle.

After he'd methodically plowed through the second helping, he said, with the air of a man granting a great concession, "Of course, here on the farm it could be that times are not so hard as they are in the town. I do not say it is, mind you, but it could be."

"This I think is so," Marie replied. "In Rivière-du-Loup, in St.-Antonin, in St.-Modeste, people cannot get along with what they are able to make so easily as can we, who raise our own food and who can even make our own clothes at need." She glanced from Nicole to her other, younger, daughters, Susanne, Denise, and Jeanne. "In the attic, stored away, are a spinning wheel and the parts for a loom. I have not brought them down and shown you what to do with them because, till now, there has been no need; we have sewn with cloth bought from the store. But my mother taught me, as her mother taught her, and I can teach you if we are able to get no more cloth, as may happen."

The girls, who ranged in age from Jeanne's seven to Nicole's twenty, all clamored for Marie to bring down the old tools and teach them how to make cloth. Marie sent Lucien an amused glance. He returned it, saying, "See how bravely they take on new work. I remember my mother making cloth, too. I do not recall her being so eager to do it, though." He hid pride in his daughters behind gruffness.

"They want to find out something new, Lucien, or something so old, it seems new to them," Marie said. "That is not bad. When it is no longer new to them, it will no longer be exciting, either; no doubt you are right about that."

Lucien looked at his two sons: Charles, sixteen, compact like Marie, and Georges, a couple of years younger but already bigger than his brother. "Some people," he said pointedly, "have no interest in work even when it is of a new sort."

That was unfair, and he knew it; both boys worked on the farm like draft horses. Predictably, Charles got angry about it. Most times, Lucien would have been glad to see him turn eighteen, for the sake of the discipline with which he would have returned after two years' conscription. Most times, yes. With a war on—

Even more predictably, Georges turned it into a joke, asking, "*Eh bien,* Papa—this laziness, do you think we get it from you or from Mama?"

"You get it from the Devil, you little wretch," Lucien exclaimed, but then he had to cough a couple of times in lieu of laughing out loud. The next thing Georges took seriously—save, perhaps, a leather strap well applied to his backside, but he was getting too big for that—would be the first.

Outside, the dogs began to bark. A moment later came the sound of several men approaching the house, some of them mounted, others afoot. The Galtiers exchanged sudden glances of alarm. So many neighbors would never come together, not unannounced. That meant Americans, and Americans meant trouble.

Sure enough, in English rough as sandpaper, one of the men out there said, "Those hounds try and bite, you stick 'em or shoot 'em. The major, he ain't gonna give you no Purple Heart for a dog bite, boys."

Lucien realized he was the only one in the family who understood what the newcomers were saying. His sons would have learned their English in the Army when their time came; his wife and daughters would have had few occasions ever even to hear it.

"Shall we fight, Papa?" Charles demanded. He wanted to. At sixteen, you knew you could do the impossible.

At forty-three, you knew damn well you couldn't. "We have one rifle," Lucien said. "It is better for rabbits than for men. They have many guns out there, and can bring many soldiers here. No, we do not fight. We do as they tell us." When Charles and even Georges looked mutinous, he added, "Then we see what we can do afterwards." To his relief, that satisfied his sons. They were too young to be killed in a hopeless fight. It also had an element of truth that salved his own pride.

One of the Americans rapped on the door. The whole farmhouse shook. He had to be using his rifle butt, not a fist. Galtier opened the door. The American, a sergeant almost a head taller than he was, checked a piece of paper and said, "Galtier, Lucien." It was not a question, though the fellow mangled the pronunciation so badly that Lucien needed a moment to understand his own name.

"Yes, I am Lucien Galtier," he said when he did. He hated standing here with the door open; he could feel cold air sliding past him into the house. It wasn't as cold as it was going to be, but it was a lot colder than it had been, cold enough so you were glad of stove and fireplace.

"Good. You speak English," the U.S. sergeant said. Then his eyes, hard and pale, narrowed. "Round here, that means you been in the Army, ain't that right, Frenchy?"

"I have been in the Army, yes," Galtier said, shrugging. He paused to think of English words. "You find few men as old as I who are not in the Army, if they are not sick or—how do you say?" He mimed limping about.

"Crippled?" the American said. "Yeah, that's so, I guess. All right." He looked down at Lucien's stocking feet. "Get your shoes on, Frenchy. We're gonna have a look round your barn and your storehouses. You don't wanna waste time." He turned to a couple of his men and shouted, "Gosse, Hendrick, you go and start. Frenchy here'll be along."

"What is it you do here?" Galtier asked as he pulled on first one boot, then the other. He was glad they stood by the door, so he did not have to go away and let the sergeant—and maybe his followers—come in. To his family, he called in French, "Stay here. I am attending to this."

The sergeant nodded. "That's smart, pal. Don't want trouble." He understood French, then, even if he didn't deign to speak it. He went on, in ugly English, "Requisition of supplies, by order of the brigadier general commanding."

"Requisition?" Lucien got on his other boot and stepped out into the night, closing the door after him. "This means what?" He meant the question seriously; he was trying to remember what the word meant. Before the sergeant could answer, he did remember, and stopped in his tracks. "This means—you take?"

"You got it in one, buddy," the U.S. soldier said.

"You do not pay," Galtier went on.

"Well, yes and no," the sergeant said. "You'll see how it goes."

A couple of soldiers—presumably Gosse and Hendrick—were pawing over what Lucien had spent a lifetime maintaining and adding to, the farm having been in his family for generations. One of them said, "Sarge, he's got enough here to keep the battalion in food all winter long."

"Yeah?" the sergeant said. He turned around and shouted toward one of the mounted men who'd come up to the farm. "Blocksage! Ride back and tell the QM to send a truck out here. No, better make it two trucks. Plenty of goodies, yes indeed." The horse went trotting away.

Galtier did not like the sound of any of that. "How is it you have the right to—?" he began.

Before he could finish, the sergeant pointed his rifle at him. "*This* gives me the right, pal," he said. "We're the ones who won the war, remember? Now, we're supposed to treat you Frenchies nice, so you'll get some compensation, don't you worry about that. But don't you go telling us what we can do and what we can't, either. You'll be real sorry real fast, if you understand what I'm saying. You understand?"

"Oh, yes, *monsieur,*" Galtier said. "I understand."

Wherever the quartermaster had set up his headquarters, it wasn't far away. Within a few minutes, a couple of trucks came wheezing and rattling up the dirt road before turning and approaching the farmhouse. The looting began immediately thereafter.

They left Lucien his horse. They left him a cow and a few sheep and a pig. They left him a handful of hens and his rooster. They left him enough fodder to feed the animals he had left through the winter—if it wasn't too long or too hard and he didn't feed them too much. By the time they were done hauling away glass jars, they left his family in the same shape as the livestock: most of the food Marie had laboriously preserved was gone, along with lovingly smoked hams and flitches of bacon.

As food and fodder moved into the trucks, the sergeant kept meticulous notes on everything that was taken. When the sacking of the farm was complete, he handed Lucien a carbon copy of the list. "You want to take this in to Rivière-du-Loup"—from his mouth, it came out *rivy-air-doo-loop*—"to the commandant's office. They'll pay you off there."

"They will pay me off," Galtier echoed dully. He wished he had grabbed the little .22 Charles had wanted to get. That way, he could have died defending what was his instead of having to watch as he went from a prosperous farmer to a poor one in a couple of hours' time. He nodded to the sergeant. "You are sure this generosity will not cause them difficulties?"

He'd intended that for irony. The sergeant took it literally, which would have been funny in an absurd kind of way if he hadn't answered, "Don't worry about that, Frenchy. You ain't gonna get more than twenty cents on the dollar, and you'll have to yell and scream and cuss to get that much."

Galtier didn't yell or scream or swear, no matter how much he wanted to. He stood silent, holding the copy of the list of supplies requisitioned from him, as the big American soldiers finished their job, started the trucks' engines, and left. The infantry and horsemen went on to the next farm down the road. They were noisily arguing about whether it would yield more or less than they'd got from him.

When they were all gone, he went back into the house. His family crowded round him. "Thank God you are well," Marie said, taking his hand in a public display of affection unlike any she'd given him since they were newlyweds. "What have the *Boches américains* done?"

He told her and the children what they'd done. "Hard times are here, as I told you before," he said. Even in dismay, he recognized that he hadn't intended to be taken seriously before, but now he did.

"Hard times," Marie echoed somberly. He might have been wrong before, he might have been joking before, but no longer.

A string of the curses he hadn't aimed at the U.S. soldiers burst from him: "*C'est chrisse, maudit, calisse de tabernac.*" Like any Quebecois, he cursed by reviling the symbols of his church; English-speakers' ways of blowing off steam by talking about excrement and sex struck him as peculiar.

His family stared at him; he hardly ever said such things where even his sons, let alone his wife and daughters, could hear him. "It's all right," Marie said. "God will surely forgive you, so we must as well."

Lucien nodded gratefully to her. She always found a way to make things right. He said one thing more: "*Je me souviens*—I will remember."

Without hesitation, everyone nodded.

The train rolled westward toward New Orleans. As far as Anne Colleton could tell, she was the only unattached white female under the age of sixty on the whole train—certainly in her car. Not many women were traveling at all—soldiers in butternut and sailors in white took up most of the seats.

Not all her money, not all her influence, had been able to get her a Pullman berth for herself and her colored maidservant, Julia. When she boarded the train, she found out why: the Pullmans were full of military men, too, some of them with cots adding to their carrying capacity. When set against the needs of war, luxury was no longer practical.

Luxury no longer seemed fashionable, either. That distressed Anne: what point to living if you couldn't live graciously? With a cynicism older than her years but not older than her sex, she suspected the powers that be would soon grow bored with their egalitarian pose. These weren't the United States, after all: class mattered in the Confederacy, especially looking down from the top. Pretending that wasn't so struck at the heart of the nation's *raison d'être*.

Not that she wasn't the center of attention all the same. She coolly took that for granted, as much as she did Julia's presence beside her. Had the train been almost all women and only a handful of men instead of the other way round, she would have been as confident of drawing those men to her. Looks told. Even President Wilson responded to her smile. So did breeding. And, she thought, smoothing a pleat on the skirt of the cranberry-red silk dress she was wearing, so did money. She toyed with the lace at her throat, affecting not to notice that she was being watched.

Ordinary soldiers and sailors eyed her without approaching; they knew she was beyond them. Yes, breeding and money told. A couple of soldiers who stank of cheap whiskey tried to approach Julia, looking for nothing more than female flesh with which to slake their lusts. Anne Colleton sent them on their way with a few low-voiced words that left their ears red and tingling.

Officers, though, officers were drawn to Anne as moths were drawn to fires. And, like moths, they drew back with their wings singed. Attracting men was great sport. But most of the officers, especially those from the Navy and the cavalry and artillery, were aristocrats with all the virtues of their class—they were brave and loyal and randy—and also its vices—they were crashing bores, or so Anne found them.

When the porter announced that supper was being served, she and Julia went back to the dining car together. A couple of tables at the rear were reserved for Negroes, commonly servants. Just as Anne had not been able to get a Pullman berth, so she was not able to get a table for herself, either: the train was too full for that. Something like a football scrim developed among the officers in white and butternut to see who would get the other two seats at the corner table where she was sitting.

When the elbowing died away, a couple of Navy officers not far from her own age smiled down at her. "Mind if we join you, ma'am?" one of them asked. He might have been an officer, but he was no aristocrat, not with that rough accent. Anne shrugged and nodded permission.

They sat down. The crowd behind them thinned regretfully. The one who'd asked her leave was a lieutenant, senior grade, with wreathed stars on his shoulder straps and a stripe and a half of gold on each sleeve. He was growing a sandy beard; at the moment, he looked as if he'd forgotten to shave.

His companion, a lieutenant, junior grade, with plain stars and single sleeve stripes, was so blond and perfect, he might have stepped off a recruiting poster. Anne dismissed him at once. The other one, though, backwoods accent or not, was . . . interesting.

The colored waiter, resplendent in tailcoat livery like that which Scipio usually wore, poised pencil above notepad. "What can I bring you tonight, ma'am, gentlemen?"

"How are the ham and yams?" Anne asked.

"Very fine, ma'am," the waiter assured her.

"I'll have that, then, and a glass of rosé to go with it."

Pencil poised again, the waiter looked a question to the two officers. "Steak and potatoes here, and a bottle of bourbon for the two of us," the senior lieutenant said.

"Steak and potatoes for me, too," the junior lieutenant agreed.

"Of course," the waiter said. "How would you care to have those done?"

"Medium," the lieutenant, junior grade, said.

The other officer laughed. "How many times have I got to tell you, Ralph, you want to be able to taste the meat?" He looked up at the waiter. "I want that slab of meat just barely—and I mean *just* barely—dead. You tell the cook that if it doesn't go 'Ouch!' when I stick a fork in it, I'm going to tell his grandpappy's ghost to haunt him till the end of time." He made a curious gesture with one hand. Had the waiter been white, he would have turned pale. His eyes got big. He nodded and beat a hasty retreat.

"What was that?" the handsome junior lieutenant—Ralph—asked.

Anne surprised herself by speaking: "That was a hex sign. It means—it's supposed to mean, anyhow—your friend really can do things with, or to, the cook's grandfather's ghost."

The lieutenant, senior grade, raised a gingery eyebrow. "You're right, ma'am. Not many white folks—especially not many white women—know that one."

"I make it a point to know what goes on with my Negroes," Anne said. Smugly, she used a different sign. She was surprised again, because both naval officers recognized it, and she'd never yet run across a white man who did. "How did you know what that meant?" she asked quietly.

"We use that one for luck, ma'am, when we fire a torpedo," the senior lieutenant answered. "I didn't know anybody—anybody white, anyhow—outside of submarines knew about it."

"Submarines!" Now Anne looked at both of them with respect. They might not be gentlemen, but they had courage and to spare. You had to have courage—or be a little touched in the head—to go down under the ocean in what was basically a metal cigar.

"Submarines," the senior lieutenant repeated. "I'm Roger Kimball, off the *Whelk*, and this lug here is Ralph Briggs, off the *Scallop*. Heading for New Orleans, both of us, for reassignment."

"I'm on my way to New Orleans, too," Anne said, and gave her name.

Neither of them knew who she was. Even so, Ralph Briggs started slavering as if he were a dog and she that steak he'd ordered, not cooked medium but raw. Kimball, on the other hand, just shrugged and nodded.

Their meals did arrive then. If Roger Kimball's steak had been over the flames at all, you could hardly tell by looking. The waiter hovered anxiously all the same. When Kimball cut the meat, he let out a long "Mooo!" without moving his lips, which made the Negro jump. Only after he nodded did the fellow smile in relief and go on about the rest of his business.

Since she'd broken the ice herself, Anne expected the submariners to try whatever approach they thought would work. Briggs started to, a couple of times. But Kimball wanted to talk shop and, being senior to Briggs, got his way. It was almost as if the two men had started speaking some foreign tongue, one where words sounded as if they were English but meant obscure, indecipherable things. Anne listened, fascinated, to grumbles about fish that wouldn't swim straight, twelve-pounder and three-inch bricks, and eggs that would blow you to kingdom come if you couldn't keep away from them.

"We've laid ours, the damnyankees have laid theirs, and by the time both sides are done, won't be any room for boats left in the whole ocean, and I mean our boats and theirs both—ships, too," Kimball said.

"Don't know what to do about it," Briggs said, pouring whiskey from the bottle into his glass. He drank, then laughed, and said, "If we were still in those gasoline-engine boats, I'd be drunker'n this, just off the fumes."

"Diesel's the way to go there," Kimball agreed. "Gas-jag hangover is worse than anything you get from rotgut."

"Amen," Briggs said with what sounded like the voice of experience, though Anne wasn't quite sure what sort of experience. The lieutenant, junior grade, went on, "They're building heads in the new boats, too, thank God."

"Thank God is right," Kimball said, "even if they aren't everything they ought to be. You can't discharge 'em down deeper than about thirty feet, and you don't want to do it where the enemy can spot you."

"And when you do do it, you want to do it right," Briggs said.

"That's a fact." Kimball laughed out loud, a laugh that invited everyone who could to share the joke. "Ensign on my boat opened the wrong valve at the wrong time and got his own back—right between the eyes." He laughed again, and so did Ralph Briggs. Kimball finished, "After that, the poor miserable devil wouldn't even try unless he was crouched down in front of the pan."

When Anne Colleton discussed modern art, she and her fellow cognoscenti used terms that shut the uninitiated out of the conversation. Now she found herself shut out the same way. She didn't care for it. "What *are* you talking about?" she asked with some asperity.

Briggs and Kimball looked at each other. Briggs turned almost as red as the juice from Kimball's rare steak. Roger Kimball, though, laughed yet again. "What are we talking about?" he said. "You can't just flush the toilet when you're under the water in a submarine. You have to use compressed air and a complicated set of valves and levers. You have to use them in the right order, too, or else what you're trying to get rid of doesn't leave the boat. Instead, it comes back up and hits you in the face."

If Briggs had been red before, he was incandescent now. Kimball leaned back in his chair and waited to see how she'd take his blunt answer. She nodded to him. "Thank you. This happened to someone in your crew?"

"That's right. We were laughing about it for days afterwards," Kimball answered.

"Everyone but him, of course," Anne said.

Kimball shook his head. "Jim, too, after he got hold of a washrag."

Briggs poured his glass of bourbon full and gulped it down, maybe in an effort to drown his own embarrassment. Perhaps not surprisingly, he fell asleep in his chair about ten minutes later.

Kimball leaned him against the wall of the dining car. "There," he said in satisfaction. "Now he won't fall down and hurt himself." He got to his feet. "Thanks for sharing the table with us, Miss Colleton."

Not even *A pleasure to have met you* or *Hope to see you again sometime*, Anne noted, more than a little annoyed. She glanced back toward the table where Julia was eating and laughing and joking with other servants and some of the colored train crew. Her maid would be there for a while: she might stay there all night if she got the chance. Anne rose from her seat. "I'm going up to my car, I think."

Kimball made no effort to take up the unspoken invitation to walk with her. He didn't move so fast, though, as to leave her behind. They went through a couple of cars not quite together, not quite apart. Then he stopped in the hallway to a Pullman and said, "This is my compartment. Ralph's, too, matter of fact, but he found himself that berth in the diner. Not the one I'd take, but what can you do?" His eyes twinkled.

When he slid open the compartment door, Anne stepped in after him. She was a modern woman, after all, and did as she pleased in such things.

"What . . . ?" he said, both reddish eyebrows rising. Then she kissed him, and after that matters took their own course. The lower berth was cramped for one, let alone for two, or so Anne found it, but Kimball acted as if it had all the room in the world. Maybe, compared to arrangements aboard a submarine, it did. He didn't bang his head on the bottom of the upper berth or the front wall; he didn't bump his feet against the back wall. What he did do, with precision and dispatch, was satisfy both him and her. He even used his hand to help her along a little when her pace didn't quite match his.

Afterwards, just as efficient, he helped her dress again, those clever hands doing up hooks and buttons with accurate, unhurried haste. He stuck his head out into the hallway to make sure she could leave the compartment unnoticed. Now he did say, with a knowing smile, "A pleasure to have met you." As soon as she was on her way, he shut the door behind her.

She was almost back to her own seat when, ignoring her body's happy glow, she stopped so suddenly that the old man behind her stepped on the heel of her shoe. She listened to his apologies without really hearing them.

"That sneaky devil!" she exclaimed. "He planned the whole thing." And Kimball had done it so smoothly, she hadn't even noticed till now. She didn't know whether to be furious or to salute him. She, who'd manipulated so many people so successfully over the past few years, had been manipulated herself tonight. Then she shook her head. No, she hadn't just been manipulated. She'd been, in the most literal sense of the word, had.

* * *

Sergeant Chester Martin looked down at the three stripes on the sleeve of his green-gray tunic. He didn't delude himself that he'd done anything particularly heroic to deserve the promotion. What he'd done, and what a lot of people—an awful lot of people—hadn't, was stay alive.

He looked back toward Catawba Mountain. Coming down it had been almost as bad as fighting his way up it. The Rebs moved back from one line to another, and made you pay the butcher's bill every time you attacked.

"Dumb fool luck," he muttered. "That's the only reason I'm here, let alone a three-striper."

"You bet, Sarge," said Paul Andersen, who was using a wire-cutter to snip his way into a can of corned beef that let out an embalmed smell when he got it open. He wore a corporal's chevrons now himself, for the same reason that Chester was a sergeant. "A machine gun, it doesn't care how smart you are or how brave you are. You get in front of it, either you go down or you don't. All depends on how the dice roll."

"Yeah." Martin tore his eyes away from the scarred slopes of Catawba Mountain and looked east, toward the Roanoke River and Big Lick. He didn't stand up for a better look; you were asking for a sniper to blow your lamp out for good if you did anything that stupid. The lines were quiet right this minute, but what did that mean? Only that the Rebel snipers, who were used to shooting for the pot and reckoned men deliciously large targets, had plenty of time to get ready to take advantage of any chance you gave 'em.

He knew what he'd see, anyhow. Big Lick, or what was left of it after endless shelling, still lay in Confederate hands, though a lot of the iron mines nearby had the Stars and Stripes flying over them now. But the last big U.S. push had bogged down right on the outskirts of town, and after that the Rebs had counterattacked and regained a mile or two of ground. One of these days, he expected, the Army would try another push toward the river. He was willing to wait—forever, with luck.

He dug in his own mess kit and chose a hardtack biscuit. Hard was the word for it; it might have been baked during the War of Secession. And at that, troops were better supplied than they had been at the start of the campaign. Railroads were snaking out of West Virginia to the front, to bring in food and ammunition faster and in bigger lots than horses and mules and men could manage.

"Now if we could only put the Rebel trains out of action," he said. That was a big part of the reason the brass had attacked Big Lick in the first place. But the tracks remained in Confederate hands, though repeated bombardment meant the Rebs tried running trains through only at night.

"Good luck, Sarge," Andersen said. Now he pointed east. " 'Stead of earthworks, they got their niggers runnin' up new lines out of range of our guns, anyhow. Don't seem fair."

Chester Martin nodded gloomily. Captain Wyatt had been grousing about those lines, too. But the captain's grousing wasn't what worried Martin about the Confederate tracklaying. Sure as hell, the brass would want to push guns up close enough to pound the new lines. And who'd have to do the dirty work to make that happen? Nobody he could see but the infantry.

As if thinking of him had been enough to make him appear, Captain Orville Wyatt stepped into the firing pit Martin and Andersen were sharing. He tossed each of them a chocolate bar. "Courtesy of the cooks," he said. "They had so many, they didn't know what to do with 'em, so I liberated as many as I could. They'll probably eat the rest themselves."

"Yeah, who ever saw a skinny cook?" Martin said, peeling silver paper off the bar before he crammed it into his mouth. "Mm—thank you, sir. Beats the hell out of biscuits and corned beef." Wyatt was a damned good officer—he looked out for his men. If your captain took care of things like that, odds were good he'd also be an effective combat leader, and Wyatt was. He was also up for promotion to major, for most of the same reasons Martin and Andersen had seen their ranks go up.

Wyatt dug a much-folded newspaper out of his pocket. "This came up to the front on the last train—only four days old," he said; he believed in keeping minds full along with bellies. He gave the sergeant and corporal the gist of what was in the news: "Big fight out in the Atlantic. We torpedoed a French armored cruiser, and it went down. We sank some Confederate and Argentine freighters heading for England, too."

"Good," Martin said. "Hope the limeys starve."

Wyatt read on: "The Rebs torpedoed one of our cruisers, too, the cowardly sons of bitches, but we rescued almost the whole crew. And TR made a bully speech in New York City."

That got Martin's attention, and Andersen's, too. Nobody could make a speech like Teddy Roosevelt. "What does he say?" Martin asked eagerly.

Captain Wyatt knew nobody could make a speech like TR, too. He skimmed and summarized, saying, "He wants the world to know we're at war to support our allies and to restore what's ours by rights, what the English and the French and the Rebs took away from our grandfathers . . . Wait. Here's the best bit." He stood very straight and drew back his lips so you could see all his teeth, a pretty good TR imitation. " 'A great free people owes to itself and to all mankind not to sink into helplessness before the powers of evil. I ask that this people rise to the greatness of its opportunities. I do not ask that it seek the easiest path.' "

"That *is* good," Andersen said with a connoisseur's approval.

Chester Martin nodded, too. Roosevelt knew about the harder path.

Along with Custer, though on a slightly smaller scale because he'd been just a colonel of volunteers, he'd come out of the Second Mexican War a hero, and his stock had been rising ever since. No nation could have hoped for a better leader in time of war.

All the same, sitting in a firing pit that had started life as a shell hole, surrounded by the stench of death, the rattle of machine guns, the occasional roar of U.S. and Rebel artillery, lice in his hair, Martin couldn't help wondering whether Teddy Roosevelt had ever walked a path as hard as this one.

Scipio bowed and said in tones of grave regret, "I am sorry to have to inform you, sir, that we have no more champagne."

"No more champagne? *Merde!*" Marcel Duchamp clapped a dramatic hand to his forehead. Everything the modern artist did, as far as Scipio could tell, was deliberately dramatic. Duchamp was tall and thin and pale and in the habit of dressing in black, which made him look like a preacher—until you saw his eyes. He didn't behave like a preacher, either, not if half—not if a quarter—of the stories Scipio heard from the maids and kitchen girls were true. Now he went on, "How shall I endure this rural desolation without champagne to console me?"

Whiskey was the first thought that came to Scipio's mind. If it worked for him, if it worked for the Negroes who picked Marshlands' cotton, it ought to do the job for a dandified Frenchman. But he'd been trained to give the best service he could, and so he said, "The war has made importing difficult, sir, as it has disturbed outbound travel. But perhaps my mistress, Miss Colleton, would be able to procure some champagne in New Orleans and order it sent here for you. If you like, I will send her a telegram with your request."

"Disturbed outbound travel: yes, I should say so," Duchamp replied. "No one will put out to sea from Charleston, it seems, for fear of being torpedoed or cannonaded or otherwise discommoded." He rolled those disconcerting eyes. "Would you not agree, the risk of going to the bottom of the sea is only slightly less than the risk of staying here?"

By now, Scipio knew better than to try to match wits with Duchamp. The artist's conversation was as confusing as his paintings; he used words to reflect back on one another till common sense vanished from them. Stolidly, the butler repeated, "Would you like me to wire my mistress about the champagne, sir?"

"I give you the advice of Rabelais: do as you please," Duchamp said, which helped not at all. The Frenchman cocked his head to one side. "Your mistress, you say. In what sense is she yours?"

"I'm afraid I don't follow you, sir," Scipio said.

Marcel Duchamp stabbed out a long, pale forefinger. "You are her servant. You were, at one time, her slave, is it not so?" He waved a hand to encompass not just the dining room of the Marshlands mansion but the entire estate.

"I was a slave of the Colleton family, yes, sir, although I was manumitted not long before Miss Anne was born," Scipio said, nothing at all in his voice now. He didn't like being reminded of his former status, even if his present one represented no great advance upon it.

Duchamp sensed that. He didn't let it deter him; if anything, it spurred him on. "Very well. *You* are *her* servant. She may dismiss you, punish you, give you onerous duties, do as she likes with you. Is it not so?"

"It may be so in theory," Scipio said warily, "but Miss Colleton would never—"

Duchamp waggled that forefinger to interrupt him. "Never mind. It is in this sense of the word that you are her servant. Now, you say *she* is *your* mistress. How may you, in your turn, punish her if she fails of the requirements of a mistress?"

"What?" Even Scipio's politeness to a guest at Marshlands, and to a white man at that (not that the Marshlands estate was likely to entertain a colored guest), proved to have limits. "You ought to know I can't do that, sir."

"Oh, I do know it. I know it full well. Many have accused me of being mad, but few of being stupid." The artist winked, as if to say even here he did not expect to be taken altogether seriously. But he was, or at least he sounded, serious as he went on, "So how is the charming and wealthy Miss Colleton *yours*, eh, Scipio? You cannot punish her, you cannot control her, you cannot possess her, either in economic terms or in the perfumed privacy of her boudoir, you—"

Scipio abruptly turned on his heel and walked out of the dining room, out of the mansion altogether. That Frenchman was crazy, and the people who'd told him so knew what they were talking about. In the Confederate States of America, you had to be crazy if you talked about a Negro servant possessing a white woman in her bedroom—even if you called it a boudoir. Oh, such things happened now and again. Scipio knew that. They always ended badly, too, when they were discovered. He knew that, too. But whether they happened or not, you didn't go around *talking* about them. You sure as the devil didn't go around suggesting them to a Negro.

"Words," Scipio said in his educated voice. Then he repeated it in the slurred dialect of the Congaree: "Words." Marcel Duchamp played games with them nobody had any business playing.

The hell of it was, this time he did make a corrosive kind of sense. Anne Colleton wasn't *his* mistress in the same way he was *her* butler. The two sides of the relationship weren't heads and tails of the same coin, the way they looked to be if you didn't think about them. Few Negroes did think about them, instead taking them for granted . . . which was precisely what the white aristocracy of the Confederate States wanted them to do.

Scipio looked out toward the cotton fields from which Marshlands drew its wealth—from which Anne Colleton drew *her* wealth. The Negroes out in those fields were *her* workers, almost as they had been before manumission. But was she *theirs*? Hardly. In his own way, Duchamp was an influence as corrupting as *The Communist Manifesto*.

And Anne Colleton hadn't a clue that was so. There were a lot of things the mistress (*his* mistress?—he'd have to think about that) didn't have a clue about when it came to what really went on at Marshlands. Scipio hadn't had a clue about them, either, not until he discovered the forbidden book in Cassius' cottage.

He still wished he'd never seen it. But, to protect his own hide, he'd been reading a lot of Marx and Engels and Lincoln, and then talking things over with Cassius. The more you looked at things from an angle that wasn't the one white folks wanted you to use, the uglier the whole structure of the Confederacy looked.

And, as if deliberately sent by a malicious God to make his misgivings worse, here came Cassius, a shotgun over one shoulder, a stick with four possums tied by the tail to it on the other. The possums, presumably, were for his own larder: Scipio tried to imagine what Marcel Duchamp would say if presented with baked possum and greens. He'd learned a little about swearing in French. He figured that would teach him a good deal more.

Cassius couldn't wave, but did nod. "How you is?" he asked.

"I been better," Scipio answered, as usual in the dialect in which he was addressed.

Nobody else was in earshot, and it was normal for the hunter and the butler to stand around talking. With a sly grin on his face, Cassius said, "Come de revolution, all of we be better."

"You gwine get youself killed, is all, you talk like that," Scipio said. "The white folks, they shoot we, they hang we. The poor buckra, they look fo' the chance every day. You want to give it to they?"

"The poor buckra in the Army, fight the rich white folks' war," Cassius said. "Not enough leff to stop we, come de day."

They'd gone round and round on that one, pummeling each other like a couple of prizefighters. Scipio tried a new argument: "Awright. Suppose we beat the white folks, Cass. What happen then? Ain't just we the white folks is fightin', like you say. We rise up, we give the USA the fight. The USA, they don' love niggers hardly no better'n our own white folks."

He'd hoped he would at least rock Cassius back on his mental heels, but the hunter—the revolutionary, the Red—only shook his head and smiled, almost pityingly. "Kip, the revolution ain't jus' here. The USA, they gwine have they own revolution, right along with we."

Scipio stared at Cassius. Whatever else you could say about him, he didn't think small. At last, cautiously, Scipio said, "They ain't got enough niggers in the USA to rise up against they gov'ment."

"They got plenty white folks up no'th what's 'pressed," Cassius answered. "You get worked sunup to sundown, don't matter you is black or you is white. You 'pressed the same, either which way. You rise up the same, either which way. The damnyankees, they shoot they strikers same as they shoot niggers here. When the broom of revolution come out, it gwine sweep away the 'pressors in the USA the same as here."

He sounded like a preacher stirring up the congregation. That was what he was, though he would have been furious had Scipio said so. But a lot of workers on the plantation took *The Communist Manifesto* as Gospel. Gloomily, Scipio said, "You gwine get a lot o' niggers killed. They rise up in the USA, lots o' they poor buckra get killed. We don' rise up together. They white, we black. Things is like that, an' that's how things is."

"Come the revolution, black an' white be all the same," Cassius said.

For once, Scipio got the last word: "Yeah. All be *dead* the same."

VII

Captain Irving Morrell lay between starched white sheets in an airy Tucson hospital that smelled of carbolic acid and, below that, of pus. He was sick of hospitals. The words *sick to death of hospitals* ran through his mind, but he rejected them. He'd come too close to dying to make jokes, or even feeble plays on words, about it.

His leg still throbbed like a rotten tooth, and here it was December when he'd been hit in August. More than once, the sawbones had wanted to take it off at the hip, for fear infection would kill him. He'd managed to talk them out of it every time, and having a toothache down there was heaven compared to what he'd gone through for a while. He could even walk on the leg now, and with aspirin he hardly noticed the pain—on good days.

A doctor with captain's bars on the shoulders of his white coat approached the bed. Morrell had never seen him before. He didn't know whether he'd see him again. The doctors here—the doctors at every military hospital these days—were like factory workers, dealing with wounded men as if they were faulty mechanisms to be reassembled, often moving from one to the next without the slightest acknowledgment of their common humanity. Maybe that kept them from dwelling on what they had to do. Maybe they were just too swamped to invest the time. Maybe both—Morrell had learned things were seldom simple.

The doctor pulled back the top sheet. He peered down at the valley in the flesh of Morrell's thigh. "Not too red," he said, scribbling a note. The skin of his hands was red, too, and raw, cracked from the harsh disinfectant in which he scrubbed many times a day.

"It's the best I've ever seen," Morrell agreed. He didn't know whether that was true or not, but he did know how much he wanted to get out of here and return to the war that was passing him by.

The doctor prodded at the wound with a short-nailed forefinger, down at the bottom of the valley where a river would have run had it been a product of geology rather than mere war. "Does that hurt?"

"No." The lie came easily. Morrell's conscience, unlike his leg, hurt not at all. Compared to what he'd been through, the pain the doctor inflicted was nothing, maybe less. *I really am healing,* he thought in some amazement. For a long time, he'd thought he never would.

Another note, another prod. "How about that?"

"No, sir, not that, either." Another lie. *If I can convince everyone else it doesn't hurt, I can convince myself, too. If I can convince the quack, maybe he'll let me out of here. Worth trying for.* The judgment was as cool and precise as if Morrell were picking the weak spot in an enemy position. That was how he'd got shot in the first place, but he chose not to dwell on such inconvenient details.

Two orderlies came into the warm, airy room, one pushing a wheeled gurney, the other walking beside it. Bandages covered most of the head of the still figure lying on the gurney. Yellow serum stained the white cotton at a spot behind the left temple. Between them, the orderlies gently transferred what had been a man from the gurney to a bed. The axles creaked slightly as they turned the gurney in a tight circle and rolled it away.

In his time on his back, Morrell had seen a lot of wounds like that. "Poor bastard," he muttered.

The doctor nodded. Next to that breathing husk, Morrell *was* a human being to him. "The worst of it is," the doctor said, "he's liable to stay alive for a long time. If you put food in his mouth, he'll swallow it. If you give him water, he'll drink. But he'll never get up out of that bed again, and he'll never know he's in it, either."

Morrell shivered. "Better to be shot dead quick and clean. Then it's over. You're not just—lingering."

"That's a good word," the doctor said. "Head wounds are the dreadful ones. Either they do kill the man receiving them—and so many do, far out of proportion to the number received—or they leave him a vegetable, like that unfortunate soldier." He clicked his tongue between his teeth. "It's a problem where I wish we could do more."

"What's to be done?" Morrell said. "A service cap won't stop a bullet, any more than your tunic or your trousers would."

"Of course not," the doctor said. "Some of the elite regiments wear leather helmets like the ones the German army uses, don't they?"

"The *Pickelhaube,*" Morrell agreed. "That might help if you fell off a bicycle, but it won't stop a bullet, either. A steel helmet might, if it wasn't too heavy to wear. You probably couldn't make one that would keep everything out, but—"

He and the doctor looked at each other. Then, at the same moment, their eyes went to the bandaged soldier with half his brains blown out. The doctor said, "That might be an excellent notion, certainly in terms of wound reduction. I may take it up with my superiors and, upon your discharge, I suggest you do the same with yours. Knowing how slowly the Army does everything, we could hardly hope for immediate action even if we get approval, but the sooner we start seeking it—"

"The sooner something will get done," Morrell finished for him. He hated the way Army wheels got mired in bureaucratic mud. Maybe, with the war on, things would move faster. He hadn't had a chance to find out; he'd been flat on his back almost since fighting broke out. But the doctor had spoken a magic word. "Discharge?"

"You're not one hundred per cent sound," the doctor said, glancing down at the notes he'd written. "Odds are, you'll never be a hundred per cent sound, not with that wound. But you have function in the leg, the infection is controlled if not suppressed, and we may hope exercise will improve your overall condition now rather than setting it back. If not, of course, you will return to the hospital wherever you happen to be reassigned."

"Of course," Morrell said piously, not meaning a word of it. Inactivity had been a pain as bad as any from his wound. Once he got back in the field, he wouldn't report himself unfit for duty, not unless he got shot again—and not then, either, if he could get away with it. He'd buy a walking stick, he'd detail a sergeant to haul him around as necessary—but he'd stay in action. There had been times when he thought he'd go crazy, just from being cooped up in one place for weeks at a time.

"I am serious about that," the doctor said; Morrell had had better luck fooling some of the other quacks they'd sicced on him. "If the infection flares up again, or if it should reach the bone, amputation will offer the only hope of saving your life."

"I understand," Morrell said, which didn't mean he took the medical man seriously. If they hadn't chopped the leg off when it was swollen to twice its proper size and leaking pus the way an armored car with a punctured radiator leaked water, they weren't going to haul out the meat axe for it now.

"Very well." The doctor jotted one more note. "My orders are to put any men, especially experienced officers, who are at all capable of serving back on active-duty status as soon as possible. Therapeutically, this is less than ideal, but therapeutic needs must be weighed against those of the nation, and so you will be sent east for reassignment."

"I will be glad to get out of here," Morrell said, "but isn't there any chance of sending me back down to the campaign for Guaymas? Last I heard, we'd bogged down less than a hundred miles from the town."

"That's my understanding, too," the doctor said. "The reassignment center, however, has been established in St. Louis. You'll get your orders there, whatever they turn out to be."

Morrell nodded, accepting his fate. That sounded like the Army: set up one central center somewhere, and process everyone through it. If you went a thousand miles, then came back to somewhere only a hundred miles from where you'd started, that was just your tough luck. You chalked it up to the way the system worked and went on about your assigned business.

And, of course, there were no guarantees he'd get sent back to Sonora. He could as easily end up in Pennsylvania or Kansas or Quebec or British Columbia. War flamed all over the continent.

He started to ask the doctor when he could expect to head out of Tucson, but the fellow had moved on to the next bed and was examining a sergeant who'd taken a shell fragment that had shattered his arm. He had suffered an amputation, and was bitter about it. Now that the doctor was looking at him, Morrell might as well have ceased to exist.

Knowing he would soon be allowed to escape the confines of the military hospital, to see more of Tucson's notched, mountainous skyline than the window showed him, should have given him the patience to bear his remaining time in enforced captivity with good grace. So he told himself. Instead, he felt more trapped in his bed than ever. He fussed and fidgeted and made himself so unpleasant that the nurses, with whom he had for the most part got on well, started snapping back at him.

Three days later, though, an orderly brought him a new captain's uniform to replace the hospital robe he'd worn so long. In size, the new uniform was a perfect match for the blood-drenched, tattered one in which he'd been wounded. It hung on him like a tent. He could have concealed a football under his tunic without unduly stretching it, and he had to use the point of a knife to cut a new hole in his belt so his trousers would stay up. They flapped around his skinny legs like the baggy cotton bloomers women wore when they exercised.

He didn't care. Even with the stick, walking down the corridor to the buggy that would take him to the train station left him dizzy and light-headed. He didn't care about that, either. The driver was a gray-haired civilian who, by his bearing, had spent a good many years in the Army. "Glad to be getting back into it, sir?" he asked as Morrell struggled up into the seat behind him. After he spoke, he coughed several times. Morrell wondered if he'd come here to New Mexico in hopes of healing consumptive lungs.

That was however it was. The question had only one possible answer. "Hell, yes!" Morrell said. The driver chuckled and flicked the reins. The two-horse team started forward. Morrell leaned back in his seat. He could relax now. He was heading back toward the world where he belonged.

* * *

By the time Jonathan Moss pulled on woolen long johns, trousers, boots, tunic, heavy wool sweater, even heavier sheepskin coat, and leather flying helmet and goggles, he felt as if he'd doubled in weight. He'd certainly doubled in width. And, with so many layers of clothing swaddling him, he could hardly move. He waddled through the doorway of the battered barn by the airfield. Forcing each leg forward took a separate and distinct effort.

One of the mechanics looked up from a poker game in the corner and said, "Think you'll be warm enough, Lieutenant?" He laughed and, without waiting for an answer, turned his attention back to the dealer. "Gimme two, Byron, and make 'em good ones for a change, why don't you?"

Nettled, Moss snapped, "It's cold enough down here, Lefty. Go up five thousand feet and it's a hell of a lot colder."

"Yeah, I know, sir," the mechanic said, unabashed. He studied the cards Byron had dealt him. By his revolted expression, they hadn't even come out of the same deck as the other three in his hand. You took that expression seriously at your own peril. If Lefty wasn't a rich man by the time the war ended—if the war ever ended—it would only be because he'd invested his winnings in lousy stocks.

One thing about flying: going up in the air meant Moss wouldn't lose any money to the mechanic for a while. Bad weather had grounded the reconnaissance squadron the past few days. It wasn't exactly choice out there now, but they might be able to get up, look around, and come back in one piece.

Moss chuckled wryly to himself as he walked out into watery sunshine. When the fighting started—which seemed like a devil of a long time ago now—a lot of officers hadn't wanted to pay any attention to the reports the aeroplane pilots brought back. Now people were screaming blue murder because they'd been deprived of those reports for a few days. *Go on and fly,* the attitude seemed to be. *So what if you crash?—as long as we get the information.*

"Nice to be wanted," Moss said, and chuckled again. He climbed up into his Super Hudson. The first thing he did was check the action of the machine gun mounted in front of him. The next thing he did was check the belt of ammunition that fed the machine gun. He found a couple of cartridges he didn't like. He took off his mittens, extracted the bad rounds from the belt, and yelled for an armorer. He soon had new cartridges more to his satisfaction. If your machine gun jammed in an aerial duel, all you could do was run away. Since the Avros the Canadians flew were faster than the Curtiss machines, you didn't want to have to try to do that.

One by one, the other pilots of the four-aeroplane flight came out of the barn and got up into their aircraft. Baum and Nelson and McClintock were as heavily wrapped as he was, and distinguishable one from another mostly because McClintock was half a head taller than Nelson, who overtopped Baum by a like amount. They too started checking their machine guns and ammunition.

After what seemed like forever but couldn't have been more than a couple of minutes, the mechanics deigned to put down their cards long enough to help send the airmen on their way. Lefty sauntered out to Moss' aeroplane. He had an unlighted cigar clamped between his teeth; he wouldn't strike a match till he got back to the barn.

Around that cigar, he said, "You come back safe now, sir, you hear? You got money I ain't won yet."

"For which vote of confidence I thank you," Moss said, and Lefty laughed. The mechanic grabbed hold of one blade of the two-bladed wooden prop and spun it, hard. The engine sputtered but didn't catch. Lefty muttered something so hot, it should have lighted the cigar all by itself. He spun the prop again. The engine sputtered, stuttered, and began to roar.

Moss glanced over to his flightmates. Baum's engine was going, and so was McClintock's. Lefty trotted toward Nelson's aeroplane, as did a couple of other mechanics. Nelson spread his hands in frustration. You hated to break down, but what were you supposed to do sometimes?

Moss pounded a fist down onto his leg. He could hardly feel the blow through all the clothes he had on, but that didn't matter. The flight would be short a man, no help for it. If they got jumped, the Canucks and limeys would have an edge.

He shook his head. Lone wolves of the air didn't last long these days. The British and Canadians had started formation flying, and U.S. pilots had to match them or else come out on the short end whenever a single plane met up with a flight. The kind of scout mission he'd flown in September would have been suicidally risky nowadays; the air was a nastier place than it had been.

Down below, a couple of U.S. soldiers took shots at him; he spied the upward-pointing muzzle flashes. "God damn you, stop that!" he shouted—uselessly, of course, for they could not hear him, but he knew he was nowhere near the enemy lines. Only fool luck would let a rifleman down an aeroplane, but the troopers down there were surely fools for shooting at machines on their own side, and they might have got lucky.

He flew as leader, with Baum on his right and McClintock off to his left. He wished Nelson had been able to get his engine to turn over, then shrugged. He'd made a lot of wishes that hadn't come true. What was one more?

The flight buzzed along, inland from the northern shore of Lake Erie. After untold exertions and untold casualties, the U.S. Army had finally dislodged the limeys and Canucks from their grip on Port Dover. It did them a lot less good than it would have a couple of months before. For one thing, the Canadians had had plenty of time to build up new defensive lines behind the one that had fallen—the exhilarating hope of a charge to take the defenses at London in the rear remained just that, a hope.

And for another, the weather made movement so hard that the Canadians and British could probably have pulled half their men out of line without the Army's being able to do much about it. The closest big U.S. town to the fighting was Buffalo, and Buffalo was notorious for frightful winters. Moving up into Canada didn't do a thing to make the wind blow less or the snow not fall.

"The war was supposed to be over by now," Moss muttered. Troops weren't supposed to have to try to advance—hell, aeroplanes weren't supposed to have to try to fly—in weather like this. Canada was supposed to have fallen like a ripe fruit, at which point the United States could turn the whole weight of their military muscle against the Confederates.

Oh, parts of the plan had gone well. Farther east, the Army hadn't had any great trouble reaching the St. Lawrence. Crossing it, though, was turning out to be another question altogether, and the land on the other side was fortified to a fare-thee-well. They'd come ever so close to Winnipeg, too, though they probably wouldn't get there till spring, which in those parts meant May at the earliest.

But not quite reaching Winnipeg meant trains full of wheat and oats and barley kept heading east from the Canadian prairie—and there was talk that the Canucks, weather be damned, were pushing another railroad line through north of the city. The grain's getting through, in turn, meant the Canadian heartland, the country between Toronto and Quebec City, wouldn't starve. Of course, it hadn't been intended to starve Canada into submission, not at first—out-and-out conquest was the goal. But both the first plan and the alternative had failed, which left—what?

"Which leaves a whole lot of poor bastards down there dead in the mud," Moss said. When things didn't go the way the generals thought they would, soldiers were the ones who had to try to straighten them out—and who paid the price for doing it. The only thanks they got were mentions in TR's speeches. It didn't seem enough.

Clouds floated ahead, dark gray and lumpy. More of them were gathering, back toward the horizon: advance scouts for more bad weather ahead. Moss took his Super Hudson down below the bottom of the nearest clouds, wanting a good look at whatever the enemy had in the area.

His busy pencil traced trench lines, artillery positions, new railroad spurs. Some of the aeroplane squadrons were starting to get cameras, to let photographs take the place of sketches. Moss wasn't enthusiastic about the idea of wrestling with photographic plates in the cockpit of an aeroplane, but if he got orders to do that, he knew he would.

He and his wingmen were only a couple of thousand feet above the ground. The Canucks and Englishmen down there opened up on them with everything they had. *Thrum! Thrum!* The noise of bullets tearing through tight-stretched fabric was not one Moss wanted to hear. One of those accidental rounds—or maybe not so accidental, not flying this low—could just as easily tear through him.

Climbing a little helped, for it put ragged streamers of clouds between the aeroplanes and the men on the ground. But those ragged streamers also meant Moss couldn't see as much as he liked. After playing hide and seek for a minute or so, he came back down into plain sight so he could do his own job as it needed doing.

By then, he, Baum, and McClintock were past the front line. The fire from the ground was lighter here, and he descended another few hundred feet. Men down there swelled from ants to beetles.

And here came what looked like a procession of toy trucks and wagons, bringing supplies up from the railhead to the front. Jonathan Moss let out a whoop the slipstream blew away. He waved to catch his wingmen's attention, and pointed first down to the supply column and then to the machine gun mounted in front of him. The limeys and Canucks—and even the Americans—had been taking potshots at them the whole flight long. Now they could get some of their own back.

He swooped down on the column like a red-tailed hawk on a pullet in a farmyard. Safely back of the lines, the wagons and trucks had no armed escort whatever. He squeezed the triggers to the machine gun and sprayed bullets up and down the length of it. As he pulled up and went around, he yelled with glee at the chaos he, Baum, and McClintock had created. Some horses were down. So were some drivers. Two trucks were burning. Two more had run into each other when their drivers jumped out and dove into a ditch rather than staying to be machine-gunned. A cloud of steam in the chilly air said one of them had a broken radiator.

The three pilots shot up the column twice more, starting fresh fires and knocking over more horses, and then, at Moss' wave, flew eastward again, back toward the aerodrome. When he neared the front line this time, Moss was not ashamed to use the cover of clouds to avert antiaircraft fire. Getting information was important, but so was bringing it back to the people who could use it.

The bottom of the cloud deck was only a few hundred feet off the ground when the three Curtiss Super Hudsons landed. Moss had breathed a long sigh of relief on spotting the aerodrome; he'd worried that the clouds would turn into fog and force his comrades and him to set down wherever they could.

When his biplane bounced to a stop, he jumped out of it, an enormous grin on his face. Baum, a little skinny guy with a black beard, and McClintock, who, for reasons known only to himself, affected the waxed mustache and spikily pointed imperial of a Balkans nobleman, were also all teeth and excitement. "Wasn't that bully!" they shouted. "Wasn't it grand?"

"Just like the ducks in a shooting gallery," Moss agreed, and then, quite suddenly, he sobered. Not long before, he'd been sick because he had to shoot down a Canadian aeroplane to save his own life. Now here he was celebrating the deaths of a whole raft of men who, unlike the aeroplane pilot and observer, hadn't even been able to shoot back.

He'd always been glad he wasn't an infantryman: if you were a mudfoot, war, and the death and maiming that went with war, were random and impersonal. What had he just been doing but dealing out random, impersonal death? He'd thought of himself as a knight in shining armor. What sorts of filthy things had knights done that never got into the pages of Malory and *Ivanhoe*? He didn't know. He didn't want to find out, not really.

He looked down at himself. His imaginary suit of armor seemed to have a patch or two of rust on it. No matter who you were or what you did, you couldn't stay immaculate, not in this war.

"Close to quitting time," Jefferson Pinkard grunted as he and Bedford Cunningham secured a mold that would shape the steel just poured from the crucible into a metal pig a freight car could carry to whatever factory would turn it into weapons of war.

Before his friend could even begin to agree with him, that granddaddy of a steam whistle proclaimed to the whole Sloss Foundry that he'd been right. "Lived through another Monday," Cunningham said, not altogether facetiously.

Accidents were way up since the start of the war. Everybody was working flat out, with no slack time from the start of a shift to the end. A lot of the men were new because so many had gone into the Army, and the new fellows made more mistakes than the old hands they replaced. And, what with working like dogs every minute of every shift, new hands and old got drunk more often to ease the strain, which didn't help—especially on Mondays.

No sooner had that thought crossed Pinkard's mind than a horrible shriek rang out on the casting floor. "Oh, Christ!" he said, breaking into a run. "That damn fool up there poured when they weren't paying attention—probably talking about going off shift, just like we was."

There by the mold next to his lay Sid Williamson. He wasn't quiet now, as he usually was. He writhed and shrieked. The stink of hot iron was everywhere. So was the stink of burnt meat. Jeff looked at him and turned away, doing his best not to be sick to his stomach. He'd been burned plenty of times himself, but never like this—oh, God, never like this.

He shook his fist up at the kid handling the crucible, who was staring white-faced at what he'd done. Such things happened even with experienced men in that place, but that didn't keep him from blaming the son of a bitch who'd made this one happen. *It could've been me,* he thought. *Jesus God, it could've been me.*

"Burn ointment—" Bedford Cunningham began.

Another steelworker was already slathering it on Williamson. It wouldn't do any good. Jeff knew damn well it wouldn't do any good. So did everybody else on the floor, including, no doubt, the burned man. A couple of his pals got a stretcher under him, which brought out fresh cries, and hustled him away. He might live—he was young and strong. Pinkard wouldn't have bet on it, though. He'd never be back at the foundry again. Jeff would have bet anything he owned on that.

He wiped his sweaty, grimy face with a sweaty, grimy forearm. It was chilly and wet outside, but not in here. In here, it was always somewhere between August and hell, not that, in Birmingham, there was a whole lot of difference between one and the other. Even so, some of the sweat on his face was cold.

Still shaking, he and Cunningham turned together to let the fellows on the evening shift take over the work, which had to get done no matter what, no matter who. They both stopped with the turns a little more than half made. Pinkard watched Cunningham's jaw drop. He felt his own doing the same thing. He needed a couple of tries before he could say, "Where's Henry? Where's Silas?"

The two Negroes in collarless shirts looked nervous. They were big, strong bucks—they looked plenty strong enough to be steelworkers. But that didn't have anything to do with anything, and they knew it. So did Pinkard and Cunningham. One of the Negroes said, "They's in the Army, suh. We is their replacements."

"And who the hell are you?" Bedford Cunningham set his hands on his hips. Both black men were bigger than he was, and younger, too, but that didn't have anything to do with anything, either. A black man who fought back against a white—his goose was cooked, anywhere in the CSA.

"I'm Lorenzo," said the Negro who had answered before.

"My name's Justinian," the other one said.

"I don't care if you're Jesus Christ and the Holy Ghost," Jeff Pinkard exploded, which won him a startled chuckle from Cunningham. "What the hell they doin', puttin' Negroes on the evenin' shift? Nights was bad enough, but this here—"

"Suh, we been on nights since they let us," Lorenzo said, which was true; Pinkard had seen him around for a while. "When these white folks you was expectin', when they goed into the Army, the bosses, they look around, but they don't find no other whites kin do the job—no *'sperienced* whites, I should oughta say. And so here we is."

"World's goin' to hell in a handbasket, Jeff, no two ways about it," Bed Cunningham said mournfully. "We seen it comin', an' we was right. Next thing you know, a couple of coons'll be doin' *our* jobs, too."

"Yeah, well, if that's so, it's on account of they put a rifle in my hands instead," Pinkard answered. "And I'll tell you somethin' else, too: when I get out o' the Army, I'm *still* gonna have that rifle in my hands. Any nigger who tries to keep my job when I want it back, he's gonna be sorry. And any boss who tries to help him keep it, he's gonna be sorrier yet."

"Amen," Cunningham said, as if he'd been preaching in the Baptist church of a Sunday morning. "We had ourselves two revolutions in this here country to make it like we want it. Reckon we can have us a third one to keep it that way." He spat on the floor. "Shit, how do we even know these boys can do the work? Maybe we better watch and find out." He folded his arms across his chest.

"Ought to find out if they've got the balls to do it, too," Jeff said. He pointed over to the other mold. "You boys know what happened to Sid just now?"

"Yes, suh," Lorenzo answered quietly. "We seen that before, workin' nights. Hope he come through all right."

It was a soft answer, not one Pinkard particularly wanted to hear just then. He was edgy, looking for trouble. Since he couldn't find any, he scowled and said, "All right, get on with it, then." If they couldn't do the job, complaining to the foreman and maybe to the foundry manager would be worthwhile. Pinkard stepped aside. "We're gonna watch you."

And, for the next half hour, he and Cunningham did nothing but watch. To his dismay, the Negroes had no troubles. They weren't so smooth together as the two white men they were replacing, but they hadn't worked together for years, either. They did know enough of what they were doing to do just about all of it right.

At last, Jeff stuck an elbow in Cunningham's ribs. "Let's go home," he said. "Wives'll be worryin', thinkin' we got hurt or somethin'." He shivered. "Wasn't us, but it might have been."

"Yeah," his friend said with a strange kind of sigh: not quite defeat, but a long way from acceptance. As one, they turned their backs on the Negroes and left the Sloss Foundry building.

Walking home felt strange. Because they'd stayed past shift changeover, they were almost alone. A few men coming in late for evening shift rushed past them, worried expressions on their faces. They'd catch hell from the foremen and they'd see their pay docked. Would they get fired? An hour earlier, Pinkard would have thought no—who'd replace them with so many white men in the Army? Now that question had a possible new answer, one he didn't like.

Sure enough, when they got back to their side-by-side yellow cottages—

though they looked gray in the fast-fading evening twilight—Emily Pinkard and Fanny Cunningham were standing together on the grass of their front lawns, grass that was going brown from the cold December nights. "Where have you been?" the two women demanded as one.

"Stayed a little late at the foundry, is all," Jefferson Pinkard said.

Emily came up and stood close to him. After a moment, he realized she was smelling his breath to see if he'd been off somewhere drinking up some illegal whiskey. Fanny Cunningham was doing the same thing with Bedford. When Bedford figured out what was going on, he angrily shoved his wife away. Pinkard just shrugged. If he'd been Emily, he would have guessed the same thing.

"What were you doing at the foundry?" Emily asked, evidently satisfied he was telling the truth.

Then the tale came out, Jefferson and Bedford splitting it, their breath steaming as they spoke. Their wives exclaimed in indignation and fear, both because of what had happened to Sid Williamson and because of the news about the black men. Pinkard understood that plenty well. Henry and Silas had been replaced by Negroes after they went into the Army. Would Pinkard and Cunningham be replaced so they could go into the Army? Or would they be replaced for no better reason than that the foundry bosses could save some money?

"Come on inside," Bedford Cunningham said to his wife. "We got some things we better talk about, you an' me."

Pinkard had a pretty good notion what those things might be. Bedford had teased him when he'd let Emily go to work in the munitions factory, but all of a sudden he was pretty damn glad he had. Even if they did throw him out of work, he and Emily wouldn't go hungry. If his friend wasn't thinking about having Fanny look for some kind of work, he would have been surprised.

"I waited supper on you," Emily said. "I put that roast and the potatoes in the covered crock 'fore I left this mornin', and they'll still be fine now."

"All right." Pinkard let her lead him up the walk to their house. He hung his cap on the tree inside the door, right beside the flowered hat Emily had worn to her job today. Now that she was going out in public every day, she'd bought several new hats. Each one cost a day's pay for her, but she'd earned the money herself, so Pinkard didn't see how he had any business complaining.

In spite of her promises, the cottage wasn't so clean and tidy as it had been before Emily went to work. He'd said things once or twice, the first few weeks: after all, she had promised to keep up the housework. Before long, though, he'd stopped complaining. When you got right down to it, what difference did a little dust make? She was helping the CSA win the war. Didn't that count for more?

And supper, as she'd promised, was fine. She made a lot of meals like that these days: things she could fix up in a hurry, put over a low fire before she went out the door, and then just serve as soon as she and Jefferson were both home.

"That's mighty good," he said, patting his belly. "And since I wasn't off gettin' lit up like you thought I was, why don't you get me a bottle of beer?"

Even by the ruddy light of the kerosene lamp, he could see her face go red. "You knew, too?" she said over her shoulder as she went back into the kitchen. "You didn't let on like Bedford did."

"I think Fanny nags Bedford more'n you do me," he answered. "Makes him feel like he got to get his own back every so often. Ah, thanks." He took the illicit bottle she handed him, swigged, and made a sour face. "He's done a lot better'n that—tastes like he had a horse stand over the bottle." He swigged again. "A sick horse, you ask me."

Emily giggled, deliciously scandalized. She also drank. "It's not *that* bad," she said: faint praise. And, as usual, she was right. The beer was drinkable—or, if it wasn't, Jefferson's bottle emptied by magic.

He went into the kitchen with her and worked the pump at the sink while she washed the supper dishes. "How'd it go with you today?" he asked. He'd discovered, to his surprise, that he liked sharing work gossip with her. "You already heard my news for the day."

"Mine ain't much better," Emily said, scrubbing a greasy plate with harsh lye soap. "Clara Fuller, she hurt her hand on a drill press. They say she's liable to lose her little finger."

"That's no good," Pinkard said. "Accident like that, the whole shift is looking over its shoulder the next two days." Only after he'd said it did he realize how strange the idea of a woman at a machine would have struck him before the war started. About as strange as the idea of a Negro doing his job on the evening shift, as a matter of fact.

When the dishes were done and dried and put away, they went out to the living room and talked and read for a little while, till they were both yawning more than they were talking. After a few minutes of that, they gave up with sleepy laughs. They went out to the outhouse, first Emily, then Jeff. She was in bed by the time he came back to put on his pajamas. He slid under the cover and blew out the lamp.

Her back was to him. He reached over and closed a hand around her right breast. She didn't stir. She didn't say anything. She was already deep asleep. A moment later, so was he.

Somewhere up ahead along the muddy, miserable road lay the town of Morton's Gap, Kentucky. Somewhere beyond and maybe a little north of Morton's

Gap lay Madisonville. Somewhere beyond Madisonville—in a mythical land far, far away, as best as Paul Mantarakis could tell—lay the much-promised, seldom-seen glittering thing called Breakthrough.

Just at sunrise, Mantarakis walked slowly down the trench line. You couldn't walk any way but slowly; with every step you took, the mud grabbed your boot and made you fight to pull it out again. If you lay down in the mud, you were liable to drown. He'd heard of its happening, more than once, as the U.S. line congealed in the face of Confederate resistance and winter.

There stood Gordon McSweeney, his canvas shelter half wrapped around his shoulders as a cloak to hold the rain at bay, water dripping off the brim of his green-gray—now green-gray-brown—forage cap. His long, angular face was muddy, too, and set in its usual disapproving lines. McSweeney disapproved of everything on general principles, and of Mantarakis not just on general principles but also—and particularly—because he wasn't Presbyterian.

And then, to Mantarakis' amazement, those gloomy features rearranged themselves into a smile so bright, it was almost sweet. "Merry Christmas, Paul," McSweeney said. "God bless you on the day."

"Christmas?" Mantarakis stared blankly before nodding and smiling back. "Merry Christmas to you, too, Gordon. Doesn't seem like much of a spot for doing anything about it, though, does it?"

"If Christ is in your heart, where your body rests does not matter," McSweeney said. When he talked like that, he usually sounded angry. Today, though, the words came out as if he meant them, no more. He really must have had the Christmas spirit deep in his heart.

"Merry Christmas," Mantarakis repeated. He kept walking. It was Christmas for McSweeney, it was Christmas for everybody in his unit—and for the Rebs in their wet trenches a couple–three hundred yards away—but it wasn't Christmas for him. It wouldn't be Christmas for him till January 6. The Orthodox Church had never cottoned to the Gregorian calendar. *Maybe I should tell McSweeney it's Papist,* Mantarakis thought with a wry smile. That would give the Bible-thumper something new to get in a sweat about, not that you could sweat in this miserable weather.

He shook his head. For one thing, having McSweeney act like a human being for a change was too good to fool with. And, for another, he was too used to having the whole world celebrate Christmas almost two weeks ahead of him to try and change anybody's mind about it now.

"Hey, Paul!" Sergeant Peterquist called from a little way down the trench. "We got us a sheep here—Ben brought it up with the regular supplies. Don't know where he came by it, but I'm not asking questions, neither. You wanna see what you can turn it into?"

"Sure will, Sarge," Mantarakis said. He wasn't officially company cook, but he was better at the job than Ben Carlton, who was supposed to have it, and everybody knew as much. And what a Greek couldn't do with mutton couldn't be done. He added, "Merry Christmas," as he came up to the sergeant.

"Same to you, Paul," Dick Peterquist answered. He wasn't much bigger than Mantarakis, but towheaded instead of swarthy. Because he was so fair, he looked younger than the forty years Mantarakis knew he had. He might have carried a few gray hairs, but who could tell, in amongst the gold? He pointed down to the carcass at his feet. "Doesn't that look good?"

Paul whistled softly. It wasn't really a sheep, it was an almost-yearling lamb from this past spring's birth. "Ben outdid himself this time," he said. Carlton might not have been much of a cook, but he was a hell of a scrounger. "You said sheep, Sarge, and I figured something old and tough and gamy. This here, though—" His mouth watered just thinking about it. "Make stew with some and roast the rest, I guess. You can't beat roast lamb."

"You do it up the best way you know how, that's all," Peterquist said. "Make us a hell of a Christmas dinner."

Mantarakis nodded. He figured he'd save the tongue and the brains and the kidneys and sweetbreads for himself; nobody else was likely to want them, anyhow. To most soldiers, they were "guts," and not worth having. He wished he could get his hands on a little wine so he could sauté the kidneys in it. Of course, he wished he were back in Philadelphia, too, so what were wishes worth?

He unsheathed the bayonet he wore on his left hip: twenty inches of sharp steel. It wasn't a proper butcher knife, but it would do the job. He'd just squatted down over the lamb when a Southern voice, thin in the distance, called, "Hey, you Yanks! Wave a hankie an' stick a head up! We won't shoot y'all—it's Christmas!"

"What do we do?" Mantarakis asked Peterquist.

"Shit, they ain't gonna lie to us like that," the sergeant answered. He dug in his pocket and pulled out a handkerchief, then gave it a dubious look: it was more nearly brown than white. He waved it anyway, and stuck his head up above the front lip of the trench. Now he whistled. "I'll be damned."

That made Mantarakis look, too. The calls kept coming, from up and down the Confederate line. Some men in butternut were walking about in front of their trench line. Any other day of the year, they would have been asking to be shot dead. On Christmas, no. U.S. troops were coming up out of the trenches, too, and heading on over toward the drifts of barbed wire that separated one line from the other.

Without waiting on anybody's permission, Paul scrambled up onto the ground between the trench lines and headed toward the Confederate positions, too. He waited for Peterquist to yell at him or try to drag him back, but, a moment later, the sergeant was right up there beside him. "I'll be damned," he said again, and Mantarakis nodded.

Realizing he was still holding the bayonet he'd intended to use to cut up the lamb, he stuck it back in its leather sheath. He wasn't going to need it, not today. Rebs and U.S. soldiers were snipping through barbed wire not to kill one another but to get together, say "Merry Christmas," and shake hands. For a day, or at least a moment, fifty years and more of hatred vanished as if they'd never been.

Some of the Confederates had rifles slung on their shoulders, but they, like he, seemed to have forgotten about them. "Hey, you! Yank!" one of them called, and pointed at him. "Want some *see*-gars? Got anything you can swap me for 'em?"

This was tobacco country, but the fields had been fought over, not harvested. And cigars, with any luck, were going to be Habanas, anyhow. Kentucky tobacco couldn't come close to what they grew in Cuba. "I've got some garlic powder and some mint," Mantarakis answered. "Make your stews taste better, if you want 'em."

"Don't like garlic," the Rebel said, and made a face. "Stinks, if'n you ask me. But mint's right nice. What other kind o' tasty things y'all got?"

"Got some cinnamon, a little bit," Paul said. He hid the scorn he held for the Confederate: how could you dislike garlic? But the fellow's eyes lit up when he mentioned cinnamon, so maybe they had some hope of a deal after all. Mantarakis dug in his pack and displayed the little tins of spice, whereupon the Rebel held up four cigars. After some dickering, they settled on six.

By then, a couple of paths through the wire had been cleared. Paul went through one of them, toward the Confederate lines. He had the feeling of being partly in a dream, as if nothing could happen to him no matter what he did. It was the exact opposite of what he usually felt on a battlefield: that he was liable to end up dead or mangled in spite of everything he could do to prevent it.

He handed the tins over to his Confederate counterpart and received the cigars in return. The bands, printed on shiny, metallic paper, bore the picture of a fellow with a bushy gray beard, who, the gold letters underneath his face declared, was Confederate President Longstreet, who'd licked the United States in the Second Mexican War. Maybe the cigars were Habanas, then. He sniffed them. Wherever they came from, they smelled pretty good.

"Merry Christmas, Yankee," the Confederate said. He was a medium-sized, stocky fellow with muttonchops and light brown hair that stuck out from under his cap in all directions. As he stowed away the spices, he laughed a little. "Don't think I hardly ever said nothin' to a damnyankee before, 'cept maybe somethin' like 'Hands up 'fore I shoot you!' "

"Yeah, I'm the same way with you birds, pretty much," Mantarakis said.

Oh, maybe a Confederate sailor or two had come into one of the Philadelphia greasy spoons where he'd worked, but taking an order for a sandwich or a steak was damn near as impersonal as talking from one side of a rifle to the other. He gave his name, then said, "Who are you? What do you do?"

"I'm Colby Gilbert, Paul," the Rebel answered. He stuck out his hand. Mantarakis shook it. The Reb grinned. "Right glad to meet you, Paul, long as you don't ask me to say your last name. What do I do? I got me a farm, forty, maybe fifty miles outside o' Little Rock, Arkansas. How about your own self?"

"Cook in Philadelphia," Paul answered.

"No wonder you got them nice spices, then. You got a family?" Gilbert asked. Before Mantarakis could answer, the Reb pulled a photograph out of his breast pocket: himself, a plain blond woman, a little boy, and a baby of indeterminate sex, all in what had to be Sunday best. "This here's me and Betsy and Colby, Jr., and Lucy." The baby was a girl, then.

"I'm not married yet," Mantarakis said. "A couple of my brothers have children, so I'm an uncle." He trotted out a family joke: "One of my sisters is expecting, so I'll be an aunt pretty soon, too."

Colby Gilbert scratched his head, then laughed. "Didn't know you damnyankees could be funny. Never even thought you might. Ain't that queer?"

"Yeah, pretty much." Paul looked ahead to Morton's Gap, or what was left of it. What struck him as funny was being here in a foreign country, talking like an old friend with a real, live enemy.

Somebody, from one trench or another, had thrown out a football. Soldiers from both the USA and the CSA wanted a game, but before they could play, they argued over the rules—the United States' version let you advance the ball by throwing it forward, if you did it from five yards back of the scrim line, while by the Confederacy's rules no forward passes could be thrown, only laterals. The disagreement stayed good-natured, though, and, when the Rebs whooped and cheered to see how far one of the U.S. soldiers could heave the ball and how nimbly another one ran under it and caught it, they agreed to try the damnyankee style of play themselves.

Men in green-gray and men in butternut stood shoulder to shoulder and cheered the two teams of gladiators wrestling in the mud. Several flasks went through the crowd; Paul had a nip of brandy and another of raw, searing corn liquor. Probably because they understood the passing game better, the U.S. team won, 26–12. Everybody cheered both sides, anyway.

"Shitfire," a loud Southern voice declared, "if I'd knowed damnyankees was people just like us, damn me to hell if I'd've been so all-fired eager to grab me a gun an' shoot 'em."

"You Rebels, I think you may be Christians, too." That was Gordon McSweeney, sounding surprised. For once, Paul didn't blame him. If you lived in the USA, you figured everybody in the CSA grew horns and a pointy tail. From the way the Confederates talked, they seemed to think the same thing about Americans.

"What the hell we fightin' for, then?" somebody asked. Mantarakis didn't know whether the question had come from a soldier of the USA or the CSA. He decided it didn't matter, anyhow. And nobody tried to answer it.

The crowd from the football match dispersed slowly, reluctantly. A few U.S. soldiers followed new-made friends into the Confederate lines for supper; a few Rebs, Colby Gilbert among them, came back with the U.S. troops. "I'll show you what garlic is good for," Mantarakis said, going to work on the lamb carcass he'd been about to cut up before the impromptu Christmas truce broke out.

Gilbert showed his family photo again, and admired those of the U.S. soldiers who were married. He traded cigars for this and that, and did admit the meat Paul was cooking smelled mighty good. Mantarakis had just put a big chunk of roast leg on Gilbert's mess tin (shaped a little different from those the U.S. soldiers carried) when Lieutenant Norman Hinshaw, the platoon commander, came up to the fire, no doubt drawn by the rich cooking odors.

Hinshaw stared in dismay at Colby Gilbert. "They're raising hell about this back at regimental headquarters," he said. "If he doesn't get his ass back to his own side, we've got to take him prisoner."

"Aw, have a heart, Lieutenant," Mantarakis said. "At least let him finish eating. It's Christmas, right?" Even if it wasn't Christmas for him, he used the argument without qualm of conscience.

Lieutenant Hinshaw looked at the rest of his men. When he saw all of them, even Sergeant Peterquist, nodding, he threw up his hands. "All right, he can stay," he said. "But tomorrow, if we see him, we kill him."

"Same to you, Lieutenant," Colby Gilbert said. "Nothin' personal, of course."

He ate slowly, enjoying every bit, garlic or no. Mantarakis gave him another chunk of meat to take back to his own lines. A chorus of good-byes followed him when he left the U.S. trenches. As the sun set a couple of hours later, a new chorus rang out: Christmas carols, sung first by the U.S. soldiers, then by the Confederates, and at last by both armies together.

Not a shot disturbed the night. Paul rolled himself in his blanket, confident for once he'd wake up to see the dawn.

And when dawn came, a savage U.S. artillery bombardment tore at the Confederates' front-line positions. Mantarakis huddled in a little ball in the mud, for the Rebs were shelling the U.S. trenches, too. Maybe the brass on both sides was making sure the truce wouldn't last more than a day. If so, they got their wish. Rifles began to bark, and machine guns to hammer. The war had come back, and come back strong.

Later that day, it started to snow.

Church bells chimed in 1915 as if the new year were something worth celebrating. Sylvia Enos lay alone in her bed, listening to the bells, to the firecrackers, to the occasional gunshots, to the sound of happy—or at least drunk—people in the streets. Tomorrow was Saturday, a half day of work, and she knew she had to be up before six, but she could not relax her mind enough to sleep.

In the next room, George, Jr., whimpered. Most nights when he did that, Sylvia prayed he'd go right back to sleep. Now she wouldn't have minded his waking . . . too much.

She whimpered a little herself, and bit her lip to make herself stop. Not knowing was the hardest part. The *Ripple* hadn't come back from Georges Bank, and hadn't come back, and hadn't come back—and now, two months and more after it put out, no one, not even Sylvia, thought it would come back.

But what had happened to it? The weather had been good—not perfect, but good, so a storm couldn't have sunk the trawler. Had it collided with another vessel? Had a Confederate commerce raider sunk it? And if a raider had sunk it, had the crew had a chance to get off first?

"Please, God, do whatever You want with me, but let George be safe," Sylvia said quietly in the darkness. She hadn't been much given to prayer before the *Ripple* disappeared, but she'd found it made her feel she was doing something, however small a something, for her husband. Past prayer, she had nothing to do.

At last, she fell asleep, only to be wakened a few minutes later by a drunken brawl out in the hallway in front of her flat. The racket woke Mary Jane, too. She was wet, so Sylvia groggily changed her diaper and put her back to bed. The toddler sighed and went to sleep right away. Sylvia wished she'd be so lucky, but wasn't.

When the alarm clock went off beside her head, she thought at first it was the bells from the midnight just past. The clattering went on and on, though. Under her breath, she muttered something George had brought home from T Wharf. His hair would have curled to hear her say it, but there was no one to hear her say it, and so she did.

She struck a match and lighted the gas lamp by the bed, then quickly put on her corset, shirtwaist, and long, dark blue wool skirt over her winter underwear. She let out a silent thank-you to whatever gods of fashion had decreed bustles no longer mandatory. That saved time.

She stoked up the fire in the stove and set water to boil for oatmeal and for coffee. Breathing a sigh of relief that she'd managed to get through the month with a little coal left in the scuttle, she went into the other bedroom to get the children up and moving.

"I don't want to get up," George, Jr., moaned.

"I don't want to get up, either, but I have to, and so do you," Sylvia said. He grumbled some more, but got out of bed. If he'd dawdled, the flat of her hand on his backside would have got him moving in a hurry, and he knew it. Mary Jane, on the other hand, woke up sweetly, as she did most mornings.

She made the oatmeal, put on butter and salt, and fed alternate mouthfuls to herself and Mary Jane while George, Jr., ate. The children drank water; there had been a tainted milk scare the week before, and she'd been leery of buying it. She wished she had some for her coffee, too, but if her large wishes weren't being granted, she didn't expect to get her small ones.

"Come on—time to go to Mrs. Coneval's," she said. "It's Saturday today, so I'll be back in the afternoon, not at nighttime." George, Jr., nodded at that; Mary Jane was still too little to have it mean anything to her.

Brigid Coneval lived down at the end of the hall, near the bathroom. Her husband was off at the front: in New Mexico, if Sylvia's memory was straight. Instead of going off to work in a factory herself, Mrs. Coneval kept body and soul together by using the money he sent home and by caring for the children of other women who had to go out to work and who had no family to mind their own.

Sylvia knocked on her door. She had to knock loudly; the racket inside the flat was already frightful, and, when Brigid Coneval opened the door, Sylvia saw that only about half her usual mob had arrived. "Good mornin' to you, Mrs. Enos," Mrs. Coneval said in a musical brogue. "Have you had any word of that man o' yours, now?"

"No," Sylvia said bleakly. "Just—nothing." She urged her children into the flat, saying, as she did every day, "Do as Mrs. Coneval tells you, and play nicely with the other children." George, Jr., kissed her good-bye; Mary Jane nibbled the end of her nose, which amounted to the same thing.

Inside the flat, somebody sneezed. Sylvia sighed. Cooping her children up with so many others was asking for them to come down with colds or worse; diphtheria and measles, whooping cough and chicken pox (though George, Jr., had already had most of those) ran riot in wintertime, when people stayed tightly packed together so much of the time. But what else could she do? Unlike Brigid Coneval, she had no husband sending home even a little money. For all she knew, she had no husband at all.

Shaking her head, she went downstairs and out into the street. It was still dark outside; the sun wouldn't be up for most of another hour. Breath making a foggy cloud around her, she walked down to the corner and waited for the trolley. Up it came a few minutes later. She climbed in and dropped her nickel in the fare box. A fellow in a rain slicker who looked like a fisherman stood up to give her his seat. She took it with a murmur of thanks.

She changed trolleys, then got off and walked over to the canning plant, a square brick building that looked ancient though it wasn't and that smelled of fish even more powerfully than T Wharf. The workers coming in with her were a mixed lot, some white men who hadn't yet been called into the Army, some colored men who weren't likely to be called into the Army unless things got even worse than they were already, and a lot of women like her who needed to keep body and soul together and families running while their men were gone.

A couple of women were wearing black; they'd lost their husbands in the fighting that sprawled across North America. Sylvia wondered if she should be doing the same. Stubbornly, she refused to give up hope. She wouldn't don widow's weeds till she knew for a fact she was a widow.

Before she'd had to look for work, she'd never operated anything more complicated than a sewing machine. The machine that put labels on cans of mackerel as they came sliding along a conveyor belt wasn't much more complicated. You pulled a lever to shunt the can off the belt, another one to route it through the machine, and a third to send it on its way, now adorned with a fish that looked more like a tuna than a mackerel—but, since the housewife in Ohio or the bachelor in Nebraska had probably never seen either in the flopping flesh, what harm was done?

You did have to watch out that the labeling machine didn't run out of paste, and every once in a while the endless strip of labels would jam. When that happened, you had to shut down the line till you could clear and fix the feed mechanism. Most days, though, it was just pull this one, pull that one, pull the other one, then pull this one again, from the start of the shift right through to the end.

Sometimes time crawled by. Sometimes it sped; Sylvia had found herself almost mesmerized by what she was doing, and had an hour or two slip by almost without conscious thought. You could talk through the clatter of thousands of cans and of the machinery that moved them on their way, but often there wasn't a whole lot to say.

Saturday half-shift often passed more slowly, at least in mental terms, than a full day's work. Sylvia had expected that, especially after being off for the New Year's holiday. But it didn't happen. She came out into the bright winter sun with the feeling that she had a lot of time to do the rest of the day's chores. She went to the grocer's and the butcher's and the yard-goods store for cloth and patterns for the clothes her children would be wearing come spring.

"Good to see you, Mrs. Enos," the clerk there said as he took her money. "Business has been slow. A lot of people are buying ready-to-wear goods these days."

"Making them myself is cheaper—if I can find the time." Sylvia shook her head. She didn't have much money since George had disappeared, but she didn't have much time, either. How could you win?

When she got back to her apartment building, she checked the rank of mailboxes in the front hall. She found a couple of advertising circulars, a Christmas card from her cousin in New York (she muttered rude things about the post office), and an envelope with a stamp she did not recognize and a rubber-stamped notice saying it had been forwarded through the International Society of Red Cross Organizations.

The rubber stamp nearly obscured the address. When she got a look at that, she shivered and felt so light-headed, she had to lean against the iron bank of mailboxes for a moment before she could open the envelope: it was in her husband's handwriting.

Dear Sylvia, the note inside read, *I want you to know I am all right and not hurt. The* Ripple *was caught and sunk by the* (here someone had rendered a word or two illegible with black ink). *They took us to north Carolina, where I am now. They treat us well. The food is all right. You can write me in care of the Red Cross and it will get to me sooner or later. They may end up letting me go in a while because I wasn't in the Navy and they exchange civillans with the United States. I hope so. I love you. Give my love to the children to. I hope I see you before to long. Love again from your George.*

Sylvia leaned against the mailboxes again. Tears ran down her cheeks. "Oh, dear," Henrietta Collingwood, a neighbor, said as she came downstairs. She pointed to the letter Sylvia was still holding. "I hope it is not bad news." By her voice, she sounded certain it was.

But Sylvia shook her head. "No, Henrietta," she said. "The best news of all: he is alive."

"Come on, nigger-lovers, get movin'," the Confederate guard said. He gestured with the bayonet of his rifle as if he would have liked to use it on the crew of the *Ripple*.

George Enos and the rest of the captured fishermen obediently got up and headed across the barbed-wire enclosure of Fort Johnston for their daily louse inspection. Anybody discovered with the little pests got his hair washed with kerosene and his clothes and bedding baked in an oven. That killed the lice for a while, but in a week or two they'd be back again.

Enos shivered. The wind off the Atlantic here at the outlet of the Cape Fear River was bitingly cold, though he still had on the gear he'd been wearing when the commerce raider *Swamp Fox* captured the *Ripple*. "I thought North Carolina was supposed to be hot and sticky all the time," he said.

"Shut up, nigger-lover," the guard said, his voice flat and harsh. Enos would have been surprised if he was eighteen; his face was full of angry red blotches. But he had a gun and he had the rest of the Confederate Army behind him, so Enos shut up. The crew of the *Ripple* had that unlovely handle hung on them because they'd insisted on treating Charlie White like a human being even after the *Swamp Fox* plucked them off the steam trawler and then sank it.

Technically, they were detainees, not prisoners of war. U.S. commerce raiders had scooped up Confederate merchant seamen, too. They were being exchanged, one for one, in the order of capture, using the good offices of the Kingdom of Spain, one of the few nations neutral in the fight that roiled across the world. Enos figured he'd probably get back to Boston about a week before the war ended, if it ever did. He hadn't said that in his letter to Sylvia, but it remained at the back of his mind.

No matter what anybody called him, though, George felt like a prisoner of war. The worst of it was, he hadn't even been at war when the Confederates nabbed him. All he'd been doing was trying to make a living. The Rebels didn't give a damn about that. To them, capturing a fishing boat counted as a blow against the United States. It struck him as dreadfully unfair. War was about soldiers and sailors. It wasn't about fishermen, not as far as he was concerned. But nobody cared what he thought. Nobody cared how much he missed his wife, either. That was something else war was about: not caring.

Off to one side, chips flew as Charlie White chopped firewood. The cook worked with grim intensity, slamming the axe down again and again. It was his turn for the job; Enos had done it a couple of days before, and yesterday a sailor off a freighter the *Swamp Fox* had sent to the bottom. The Rebs didn't work Charlie any differently from the way they worked their other detainees. That would have been against international law, and they would have caught hell for it when word got back to the United States.

But they didn't treat him as they would have treated a white man, either, always jeering at him—and, to a lesser degree, at the crewmen of the *Ripple* for insisting he was their friend, not a servant or a pet. They had Negro servants here at Fort Johnston, men who acted like dogs around Southern whites. Enos wondered what they used for self-respect.

He didn't have much left himself. The medical orderly—the Rebs didn't waste a doctor on damnyankees, not unless they were dying—snapped, "Bend over, nigger-lover." When Enos obeyed, the fellow ran fingers through his hair, examining the nape of his neck and the short hairs behind his ears. Reluctantly, the orderly said, "All right, you're clean—go on."

Enos went. He suspected the Rebs of claiming the men from the *Ripple* were lousy even when they weren't, just so they could put them through the process of getting rid of the vermin. Afterwards, your head smelled for days as if you'd been soaking it in the well of a kerosene lantern.

To give him his due, the medical officer did try to keep from spreading lice from one man to another. Between inspections, he dipped his hands into a bowl from which rose the antiseptic smell of dilute carbolic acid, then dried them on a towel. He looked over Patrick O'Donnell, and let the captain of the *Ripple* pass inspection in the same grudging manner he had Enos.

O'Donnell went over to the barbed wire and stood around looking bored. Enos walked up and stood beside him. "Another exciting day, isn't it, Skipper?" he said.

"You might say that," O'Donnell allowed. Both men laughed. About the only excitement in these parts was finding out whether your day's ration of cornbread had mold or not, and whether the chunk of boiled sowbelly the Rebs gave you with it was all fat or whether it had a tiny bit of real meat attached.

Thinking of that made George Enos laugh again. "Remember that time when Fred got a whole strip of meat in his sowbelly? I bet they fired the cook who gave it to him the day after, because it sure hasn't happened again."

"Bet you're right," the skipper said. "Sure sounded like they were giving somebody holy hell that night, too. Might've been the cook."

Ever so casually, he turned and glanced toward the disappearing turrets that held Fort Johnston's three twelve-inch guns. Any ships that tried to ascend the Cape Fear River and bombard or mine Wilmington, North Carolina, would have to pass the guns here and in other forts farther up the river. Enos wouldn't have liked to try it. In their endless practices, the Rebs seemed very alert.

He'd never asked O'Donnell why he spent so much time by the wire. It wasn't really his concern, and confirming his suspicions wouldn't have done him or the captain of the *Ripple* any good. But he was pretty sure that, when they finally did get exchanged, O'Donnell would give the U.S. Navy a set of drawings for the interior grounds of Fort Johnston better than anything they had now.

Enos had other things on his mind. "You think they'll give us our jobs back when we get out of here?" he asked. "God only knows what Sylvia's doing to make ends meet."

"I hope you get your job back, George," O'Donnell answered. "With me, it doesn't matter so much." A skipper who lost his ship, even if it wasn't his fault, had trouble getting another one. But that wasn't what O'Donnell meant. If and when the Confederates shipped him back to the United States, he was going straight into the Navy. They'd be glad to have him again, what with his experience.

They'd probably be glad to have George Enos, too. He'd never served on a warship, but he was a sailor. He'd have an easier time figuring out what was going on than some landlubber from Dakota.

He didn't *want* to go into the Navy, the way O'Donnell did. Being kept away from Sylvia and his children had forcibly reminded him how much he missed them. You went aboard a cruiser, you were there for months at a time, and even when you got back to port, who could say where that port would be? If you were in San Diego, say, and got forty-eight hours' liberty, so what? You couldn't get back to Boston, let alone make the round trip, in that length of time.

He laughed. "What's funny?" O'Donnell asked.

"Thinking about getting liberty and what I'd do with it if I'm too far from home to go back and if I join the Navy and if I ever get out of here. Too damn many ifs." Enos laughed again. "Hell, liberty from the Navy is one thing. Liberty from here is a whole different one." To that, Patrick O'Donnell could only nod.

And liberty from Fort Johnston was a different thing for the two white men from what it was for Charlie White. A Confederate soldier walked up and stood watching the *Ripple*'s cook chop wood. "Hey, nigger," he said in an assumed tone of casual interest, "you think maybe back 'fore we manumitted you coons, my pa or granddad fucked your mother?"

Charlie stopped chopping. For a horrible second, George was afraid he'd try to use his hatchet against a rifle. But he just paused, then shook his head. "Nah. If that had happened, I'd be a whole lot uglier."

Every detainee who heard the answer howled and jeered at Charlie's comeback. The Reb who'd walked into it turned red as brick. He started to bring his rifle to bear on the cook. Now the detainees yelled even louder for a Confederate officer. Before anybody with bars or stars on his collar got to the barbed-wire enclosure, the soldier lowered the rifle, snarling, "Nigger gets uppity, he gets his sooner or later, wait an' see if he don't."

"You haven't got the balls to do that to anybody who could shoot back," Lucas Phelps told him.

"Fuck you, too, pal—fuck you special," the guard said. Phelps slowly and deliberately turned his back and walked away. The guard raised his voice: "Where you think you're goin', nigger-lover?"

"To the shithouse," the fisherman answered over his shoulder. "I'm gonna pretend the hole is your face."

"Watch it, Lucas," George Enos said softly. Then he and all the other fishermen cried out in alarm and horror, for the guard brought the rifle up to his shoulder, took aim—he could hardly have missed, not from a range of twenty feet at the most—and fired at the back of Lucas Phelps' head. Phelps took another half step and then crumpled, surely dead before he knew what hit him: George got a good look at the blasted ruin the bullet had made of his face as it exited. All the detainees screamed "Murder!" at the top of their lungs.

At the sound of the shot, an officer did come. He led the soldier away. Two days later, the fellow was back at his post, looking meaner than ever. Nobody said a word to him, not if he could help it.

Enos had another reason to hope exchange came soon. It was already too late for his comrade.

Dashing in spats and a double-breasted herringbone overcoat with a breast pocket slanted at the latest angle—or so he said—Herman Bruck came into the Socialist Party headquarters with a copy of the *New York Times* in one hand. He quickly hung his homburg on a tree and got out of the overcoat. It was icy outside, but very much the reverse with a couple of coal stoves and a steam radiator heating the office.

He went over to Flora Hamburger and set the newspaper on the desk in front of her. "Bully speech by Senator Debs," he said, pointing. The newsprint had smudged on the gray calfskin of his gloves.

Flora bent over it. "Let me see," she said. Debs had been the first Socialist elected to the Senate, coming out of Indiana when the Republicans broke up in disarray in the aftermath of the Second Mexican War. He'd been there ever since, and twice run unsuccessfully for president.

" 'Our losses in a few brief months have exceeded all those in the War of Secession, till now our bloodiest conflict,' " Flora read aloud. " 'Soon they will exceed those in all our previous wars combined. And for what? For what, I ask, Mr. President? When we fought to keep the Confederate States from abandoning our Union, we fought for a principle: that the covenant of the United States, once made, was indissoluble. Here, on what great principle do we stand? That the European alliances with which we have entangled ourselves be honored when even to be in them is to hold no honor? How splendid! How noble! What a fine principle for which to crucify mankind on a cross of blood and iron!' " She looked up in admiration. Several people who'd been listening to her broke into applause. "That *is* strong stuff," she said.

Bruck nodded, as proud as if he'd made the speech himself. "When Debs crosses swords with TR, sparks always fly."

Flora nodded. She read on down the column to the reply by Senator Lodge, who often spoke as Roosevelt's surrogate in the Senate. Halfway through the summary of his remarks, she winced and softly quoted one sentence: " 'The distinguished gentleman's remarks on the power of principle would seem more forceful had he not, in this very chamber, recently voted to support and finance the war he now so eloquently professes to despise.' " Her chin went up in defiance. "I knew that was a mistake, and I said so at the time."

"So you did," Bruck admitted. He saw the smudges on his gloves and took them off. His hands were winter pale. He spread them. "But what could we do? If we'd voted against the credits, we wouldn't have had five Socialists left in Congress after the November elections. As things are, we picked up half a dozen seats."

"What good does it do us to pick them up if we don't act like Socialists once we have them?" Flora said.

A secretary, an Italian woman named Maria Tresca, who, along with her sister Angelina, was one of the few gentiles in the Tenth Ward office, quoted from the New Testament: " 'What is a man profited, if he shall gain the whole world, and lose his own soul?' "

It was not language commonly heard in the Socialist Party office, but no less effective for that. Herman Bruck spread his hands again. "We've been talking about that ever since the Party decided to run for office and accept seats if we won. Does working within the government advance the cause of the proletariat or delay the revolution?"

The argument that spawned kept the office lively the rest of the day. While Bruck was putting on his hat and overcoat to leave for the evening, he asked Flora, "Would you like to go to the moving pictures with me? The Orpheum is showing the new play with Sarah Bernhardt in it."

"I can't, Herman," she answered, also buttoning her coat. "We're having cousins over for supper, and I promised my mother I wouldn't be late."

Herman Bruck made a sour face. Maybe he suspected the cousins were fictitious, as in fact they were. That, though, wasn't the sort of thing it was politic to say. "Another time, maybe," he mumbled, and hurried out the door.

Angelina Tresca sent Flora an amused look. She returned one of resolute innocence. The less you admitted to anyone, the less you had to worry about getting to the wrong ears. Flora waited a few moments so she wasn't likely to run into Bruck on the street, then went downstairs and walked home to her flat.

Cooking odors filled the hallway as she came up to her door. When she opened it, more came out. *Sweet-and-sour stuffed cabbage tonight,* she thought. Along with that savory scent came smoke from her father's pipe. It was harsher than it had been. He'd smoked Mail Pouch for years, but the

Virginia and Kentucky tobaccos that went into the blend weren't available any more. Now he fed the pipe with something called Corn Cake, which smelled, as far as Flora was concerned, like burning corn husks. She kept quiet about that, not wanting to hurt his feelings.

Esther was in the kitchen, helping their mother. David and Isaac bent over a chess board at the table from which they would soon be evicted so everyone could eat supper. Flora glanced at the game. Isaac was a couple of pawns up, which was unusual; his brother beat him more often than not. The two mental warriors said hello without looking up from their battlefield.

"And how are things with you today?" Benjamin Hamburger asked.

"All right," Flora answered. "I'm tired." The moment the words were out of her mouth, she felt ashamed of them. Sophie was the one who had the right to complain about being tired: she worked longer hours at a harder job for less pay than her younger sister. Especially since the start of the useless, stupid war, Sophie had been dragging herself home exhausted every night.

As if thinking about her were enough to bring her home, Sophie came in just then, worn out as usual. She sank down onto the divan couch with a soft sigh and a posture so limp, it said she didn't want to have to get up again for anything in the world.

Esther stuck her head out of the kitchen and said, "Oh, good, that was you. I thought I heard the door. Ready in a minute." Sophie nodded wearily. She'd even been too tired to eat lately, which alarmed her mother. Esther's eyes flicked to her brothers. Pointedly, she repeated, "Ready in a minute." When that didn't shift them, she started setting the table. They had to move the chess set in a hurry to keep from having a plate land on top of it.

Supper almost made Flora wish she'd gone out with Herman Bruck. Her family didn't really want to hear about Socialist Party doings, not even her father. All any of them seemed to care about was ways to rise into the bourgeoisie, not how to aid and radicalize the vast masses of the proletariat. She sadly shook her head. Her own flesh and blood, class enemies. They didn't even try to understand the goals toward which she worked.

After supper, she and Esther washed and dried dishes. Esther wanted to talk about how the war was going. Flora didn't. That it was going at all was bitter as wormwood to her.

As soon as she'd put the last fork in its drawer, she got her coat and went out onto the fire escape. Her mother's voice pursued her: "We're not good enough for you?" But that wasn't it, even if her family thought it was. It was just that she didn't fit in among them, and the harder they tried to drive her back into what had been her place, the less it suited her.

It was chilly out there, but not intolerable. The nip of January air on her cheeks made her feel as if she were in a sleigh gliding down some quiet country road, not in the middle of the most crowded part of the biggest city in the

United States, though she had to ignore the racket from her building and all the others to make the illusion complete.

A couple of minutes later, Sophie stepped out to join her. "Fresh air," her older sister said gratefully. "It's so stuffy in there."

Flora sent her a sympathetic look. "And you were cooped up in front of your sewing machine all day before that," she said. "No wonder you want to get all the air you can." She wouldn't have called New York City's air, full of smoke and soot and fumes, fresh, but if her sister wanted to, she wouldn't argue, either.

Sophie stepped down to the edge of the landing and looked over the iron rail. It was dark down there, with nothing worth mentioning to see. Not really to Flora—not really to anyone—Sophie said, "I should throw myself off."

Alarmed, Flora hurried over to her and put an arm around her shoulder, dragging her away from the rail. "What's wrong?" she demanded. "Is it something at work? I know they've been exploiting you without mercy, giving you much too much to try to do. The way you come home every night—"

Sophie shook her head. "It's nothing to do with work," she said, "and they aren't working me any harder than they were before. 'Exploiting'!" She laughed softly, though not in a way that said she thought anything was truly funny. "It's not anything—political."

"Then what is it?" Flora asked. "People don't talk about jumping off a building for nothing, you know."

Her sister's shiver had nothing to do with cold, no more than her laugh had had anything to do with mirth. "What is it, Flora? Do you really want to know?"

"Of course I do," Flora answered, indignant now. "I'm your sister. That counts for more than politics, even if we don't agree all the time."

"Yes, but it was politics you thought of first." Sophie sighed. "I suppose I may as well tell you. I have to tell someone—and if I don't, it'll be plain enough before long, anyway."

"What are you talking about?" Flora said. "Just come out and say it, if you're going to."

"All right, then." But Sophie needed to gather herself before she brought the words out, all in one low-voiced rush: "Flora, I'm going to have a baby."

Her sister stared. She felt as if she'd walked in front of a train without seeing or hearing it coming. "How did it happen?" she whispered.

Dimly lit by the lamps from the front room, Sophie's face twisted. "How did it happen? There's only one way I know of. Yossel was going into the Army, and I didn't know when I'd see him again or if I'd see him again, and I wanted to give him something special before he left. And so I . . . and so we—" She didn't go on, and then, after a moment, she did: "I gave him something special, didn't I?" All at once, without warning, she started to cry.

"Does mother know you're—expecting?" Flora asked. She put her arm around her sister, who clung to her like a survivor from a torpedoed liner.

Sophie shook her head violently against Flora's shoulder. "I couldn't tell her," she exclaimed. "I told you because—" She gulped and stopped.

Flora didn't have any trouble figuring out what her sister hadn't said. *Because you're the radical one, the one who believes in socialism and free love*—something like that, anyhow. Flora had had men approach her on that basis, some of them men in the Socialist Party. But being free to love didn't mean you had to, and didn't mean loving was free from consequences, either.

Well, Sophie surely knew that now, even if she hadn't thought it through before. And Sophie wasn't some man trying to entice her into something sordid; she was her sister. "You're going to have to tell her sooner or later," Flora said gently, at which Sophie cried harder. Flora found another question: "Does Yossel know?"

Sophie shook her head again. "Every time I write him, I mean to tell him, but I just—can't."

"He's going to be your husband," Flora said. *If he lives*—she fought that thought down. "That makes it a little better. If he weren't in the Army, I'm sure he'd marry you right now." Sophie nodded. But if Yossel hadn't been going into the Army, Sophie probably wouldn't have given herself to him till they were married, in which case they wouldn't have had this problem.

"What am I going to do?" Sophie wailed—but softly, not wanting anyone inside to hear her.

The obvious answer was, *You're going to have this baby.* What sprang from that— Flora thought. At last, as if she'd just come up with a good campaign plank for a Congressional candidate, she clapped her hands together, also softly. "We won't tell mother," she said. "Mother is too perfectly conventional for words. All she'll do is throw a fit, and we don't need that, not now."

Sophie nodded again, looking at her with a mixture of hope and dread. "We can't keep from telling her forever, though," she warned. Of itself, one hand went to her belly. "Pretty soon, she'll know regardless of what we say."

"I wasn't finished," Flora said. "She has to know before she finds out that way. No, we won't tell her. We'll tell Papa. He won't get excited, the way Mother would; he has some common sense. And then, after he and we figure out what to say, he can tell Mother for us. He can be a—what's the word I want?—a buffer, that's it."

"I don't know." Again, Sophie's shiver had nothing to do with the cold.

"It has to be done. It will be better afterwards," Flora insisted, as if to someone with a toothache whom she was trying to get to go to the dentist.

Dread drove hope from her sister's face once more. "It won't be better," Sophie said quietly. "It will never be better, not any more."

Flora feared she was right. Even so, she opened the window that gave access to the fire escape and said, "Papa, can you come out here for a moment, please?"

Benjamin Hamburger had been standing over the kitchen table, kibitzing that game of chess—or maybe a new one by now—between David and Isaac. A puff of smoke rose from his pipe when he exhaled in surprise. "All the plots hatched out there, and this is the first time I've been invited," he remarked as he walked over and stepped out onto the landing.

That mild irony encouraged Flora. She closed the window. Isaac, David, Esther, and her mother all peered out toward the fire escape. They were used to her going out there. They were used to Sophie's going out there every so often. But when the two of them invited their father out, that was new, so it had to be suspect. Flora hadn't thought of that. Keeping the secret wouldn't be easy.

But, having started, she couldn't very well draw back. Her father was looking from her to Sophie and back again. If he wasn't the picture of curiosity, he'd do till a better one came along. Flora hoped Sophie would say what needed saying. When she didn't, Flora sighed and said, "Papa, we have to tell you something." Then she stopped. It wasn't easy, not when you got down to it.

Her father looked back and forth again. "What you have to tell me, it isn't good news," he said after a moment.

Flora nodded. That was true. While she was trying to find the best way to break the news, Sophie blurted, "Oh, Papa, I'm going to have a baby!" and burst into tears all over again.

Flora waited for the sky to fall. Sophie looked as if she wanted to sink through the iron floor. Their father stood quiet for a moment. Then, slowly, he said, "I wondered. There's a look women have in that condition, and you have it. And you're tired all the time, the way your mother was when she carried you. So yes, I wondered." He sighed. "I hoped not, but—"

"Will you tell Mother?" Flora asked, breathing more easily on finding his reaction was what she'd hoped it would be.

"She already knows, or wonders, too," her father said, which made Flora and Sophie both stare. He coughed a couple of times before he went on, "Remember, Sophie, she does your laundry, and—" He stopped, most abruptly, and coughed some more. After a moment, Flora understood why. Her face heated. Of all the things her father had never expected to do, discussing intimate bodily functions with his daughters had to rank high on the list.

Again, though, without some other intimate bodily functions, the discussion would not have arisen. And if their mother had known, or at least suspected, and kept quiet about it, that said there was more to her than Flora had suspected.

"What am I going to do?" Sophie wailed. "What are we going to do?"

Benjamin Hamburger stood silent again. "The best we can," he answered.

"I don't know what else to say to you right now. The best we can." Flora had been worried a few minutes before, but now she began to hope that best might be good enough.

Abner Dowling escaped First Army headquarters with the air of a man leaving the scene of a crime. That was how he felt. Providence, Kentucky, was less than ten miles away from the front lines; the pounding of U.S. guns—and answering fire from Confederate artillery—was a never-ending rumble from the east, irksome like a low-grade headache.

Dowling pulled his cap lower over his face so the brim would keep the rain and occasional spatters of snow out of his eyes. General Custer liked being up as close to the front as he could get. In the stables, the grooms kept his saddle ready to be slapped onto his horse at a moment's notice, so he could lead the charge that would tear the Rebel position wide open.

"He doesn't understand," Dowling muttered, half to himself, half to the God who had so far paid remarkably little attention to any of his petitions. The major went on, still half prayerfully, "Even a blind man should be able to see that slamming forward in the middle of winter isn't going to get you anywhere."

One of the things serving under Custer had taught him was the difference between *should be able to* and *can*. The general kept feeding men and shells into the fight. Every furlong of bloody advance was hailed as the beginning of a breakthrough, every time the Confederates held seen as their last gasp.

"They've had more gasps than a brothel," Dowling said. His belly shook as he laughed at his own wit. Custer didn't laugh at anything. No, that wasn't true. When he heard about a squad of Rebs machine-gunned as they foolishly broke cover, he'd chortled till his upper plate fell out of his mouth.

A train chugged into Providence out of the west: another reason the little town was currently First Army headquarters was that the railroad tracks came under Confederate artillery fire when you got a little closer to the front line. Doors opened. Soldiers in green-gray, their uniforms clean and neat, their faces open and naive, spilled out of the cars and formed up into columns under the profane instructions of their noncoms.

Mud spattered their boots and puttees and breeches. The main streets of Providence had been paved with bricks, but the Confederates had fought for the town before finally retreating from it; the U.S. bombardment and, later, Confederate shellfire from the east had torn great gaps in the paving. The soldiers stared down anxiously at the dirt they were picking up, as if expecting the corporals and sergeants to start screaming about that.

Unblooded troops, Dowling thought with a sigh. They conscientiously marched in step as they tramped toward the front. They wouldn't worry about dirt there, not even a little bit. They'd be blooded, and bloodied, all too soon. "Meat for the meat grinder," Custer's adjutant said sadly.

Another engine got up steam and moved slowly along a side track till it switched onto the one down which the troop train had come. Then it backed up and coupled to the rear of that train. Meanwhile, as soon as the troops the train had disgorged marched off toward the front, other soldiers began refilling the long chain of cars.

They were meat on which the grinder had already done its work. Some of them, the ones with arms in slings or with bandages on their faces, climbed aboard under their own power, and some of those seemed pretty cheerful. Why not? They'd been wounded, yes, but they were probably going to get better, and they were going back to hospitals well away from the front. Nobody would be shooting at them, not for a while.

But after the ambulatory patients came the great many who had to be carried onto the train in litters. Some of them moaned as their bearers moved them. Some didn't, but lay very still. None of them—none of the walking wounded, either—wore fresh uniforms. Theirs were tattered and dirty, and their faces, even those of the men who seemed chipper, were a study in contrast to the way the raw troops looked. They'd seen the elephant, and he'd stepped on them.

Dowling wished Custer would come and take a look at what soldiers who had been through the grinder were like. But that didn't interest the general. He saw the glory he'd win with victory, not the price he was paying for advances that looked not the least bit victorious to anyone but him.

Down the street about a block and a half from First Army headquarters stood a nondescript brick building that hadn't been too badly shelled. Providence was supposed to be a dry town, but if you needed a drink you could find one. Dowling needed one now.

The Negro behind the bar poured whiskey over ice and pushed the glass across to him. "Here y'are, suh," he said.

"Thanks, uh—what's your name, anyhow? Haven't seen you here before."

"No, suh. I'm new hereabouts. Name's Aurelius, suh."

"You could do worse. You're named after a great man," Dowling said. By the bartender's smile, polite but meaningless, he didn't know anything about Marcus Aurelius. Dowling gulped down the whiskey and shoved the glass back for a refill. He didn't know why he'd expected a Southern Negro to know anything about the Roman Empire; from everything he'd seen, the Rebs did everything they could to keep their Negroes ignorant. He asked, "How do you like it in the United States?"

The bartender gave him a hooded look, of the sort he was used to getting from soldiers who'd been caught with dirty rifles. "Don't seem too bad so far, suh," the fellow answered. "Ain't easy nowheres, though, you don't mind me sayin' so."

And that was probably—no, certainly—nothing but the truth. Dowling thanked his rather deaf God he'd been born with a nice, pink skin. Niggers had it tough, USA, CSA, any old place. "Maybe you should go to Haiti," he remarked. "That's nigger heaven if ever there was one."

"No, suh." The bartender sounded very sure of himself. "Only difference 'tween Haiti and anywhere else is, in Haiti it's black folks doin' it to black folks, 'stead o' whites like it is here."

"You may be right," Dowling said, and sipped his drink. What he knew about Haiti was what a soldier of the United States needed to know: that the Confederates hated and despised the place because the Negroes there, no matter what they did to one another, were free and independent, and that Teddy Roosevelt had reaffirmed—loudly reaffirmed—President Reed's pledge to protect that independence.

One of the things he didn't know was how TR would go about making good on that pledge if the Confederates invaded Haiti. With Confederate Cuba so close by, with the long stretch of Southern coastline past which the U.S. Navy would have to steam, it wouldn't be easy. Or had TR intended to invade the CSA if the Rebs attacked Haiti? He shrugged. Trying to read Teddy's mind was always risky. Anyway, the USA had invaded the CSA without a Confederate attack on Haiti.

As he raised the whiskey glass to his lips, the rumble of artillery fire outside got louder. Dowling's head came up like a hunting dog's at a scent. The new roar of the big guns wasn't coming from the east, but from the south.

He slammed the glass down onto the bar. Whiskey sloshed over the side. He slammed down a couple of coins to pay for his drinks, and then, as an afterthought, an extra dime as well. "Here, buy yourself a drink," he told Aurelius. "It's the one I would have had in a minute." He rushed out of the bar and back toward First Army headquarters. The Rebel counterattack, the one between Hopkinsville and Cadiz—and the one Custer had insisted all along was impossible—had finally started. Dowling wondered how far the U.S. forces would have to retreat, and how fast.

A lieutenant clad in butternut spun on his heel and stomped away from the field telephone, muttering unsweet nothings under his breath. That meant it was Jake Featherston's turn to confront the marvel of the electrified age. To the corporal in charge of the care and feeding of the mechanical beast, he said, "Put me through to the main artillery dump, back toward Red Lion."

"I'll give it a shot," the corporal said, showing less than perfect faith in the gadget with which he'd been entrusted. He turned the crank and shouted into the mouthpiece: "Hello, Central?" When nobody shouted back at him, he muttered something that made what the lieutenant had said sound like an endearment. He cranked again. "Hello, Central, goddammit!"

Waiting for the connection—waiting to see if the corporal could make the connection—Featherston wished he'd sent a runner back to Red Lion. It was only a few miles southwest of Martinsville; the runner wouldn't have needed more than two hours—three at the outside—to make it there and back again.

But Captain Stuart was hellbent for leather about using the very latest thing. Sometimes, Featherston admitted to himself, that was because the very latest thing was better than what had gone before. His battery of French-inspired three-inch guns certainly fell into that class. But sometimes the very latest thing was just newfangled confusion replacing old-fashioned stupidity—or, worse, replacing something that worked well even if it had been around for a long time.

"Hello, Central!" the corporal screamed. Featherston was about to give it up as a bad job and walk off—he could tell the captain he'd tried to use the phone, but it hadn't wanted to work—when the operator said, in reverent tones, "I'll be a son of a bitch." He turned to Jake. "Who'd you say you wanted to talk to again? Been so long, I plumb forgot."

"The main artillery dump," Jake answered, and the corporal relayed his words to the central switchboard. Now, if the wire between there and the ammunition dump wasn't broken, he might be able to save some time after all. But even when, as they sometimes did, Negro laborers buried phone lines as they laid them, shell hits would dig them up and break them. And water soaked through insulation, and . . .

But, to his amazement, after a couple of minutes, the corporal handed him the earpiece and said, "Go ahead."

"Main ammo dump?" he bawled into the mouthpiece; he'd had botched connections before, too, even when everything was supposed to be working perfectly. Sometimes you were better off sending Morse over the line.

But, now, a thin, scratchy voice sounded in the earpiece: "That's right. Who're you and what d'you need?"

"Jake Featherston, First Richmond Howitzers." Jake didn't say he was just a lowly sergeant. If the fellow on the other end of the line wanted to assume he was the battery commander, that was all right with him. It was better than all right, in fact, because he was more likely to be taken seriously that way. "We're giving the damnyankees on the other side of the Susquehanna tarnation, or we would be, 'cept we're mighty low on shells."

"Whole army's mighty low on shells," that disembodied voice answered. "We can maybe get you a few up there, but not a whole lot. Sorry." The soldier back in safe, comfortable Red Lion didn't sound sorry. As best Jake could make out over this infernal apparatus, he sounded bored. Saying no was a lot easier over a wire than face to face.

"The Yankees get time to consolidate, they're gonna hit us back hard," Featherston said. These past few weeks, every mile forward had been gained only by wading through blood. The Confederates stood on the Susquehanna. Featherston wondered if they'd ever stand on the Delaware.

The telephone reproduced a sigh. "Featherstitch or whatever your name is, I can't give you what I ain't got. Some of the shells we were supposed to be gettin', they went to Kentucky instead, for the big push there."

"We don't got enough to do two things both at once?" Jake demanded. "Jesus Christ, is this an army or a man who's too stupid to fart while he walks?"

That got him a chuckle as tinny as the sigh had been. "Makes you feel any better, First Richmond, the Yanks are as bad off as we 'uns. You can shoot off shells faster'n you can make 'em, and that's a fact."

"Yeah, but if the Yanks are short in Kentucky and full-up here 'stead o' the other way round, that doesn't do us a hell of a lot of good," Featherston said.

"Send you all I can, promise," the fellow back at the dump said.

"You better, you expect us to keep fightin' the war," Featherston told him. He hung the earpiece back on its hook with a crash, muttering, "Son of a bitch acts like they're *his* goddamn shells." The corporal in charge of the telephone, who'd undoubtedly heard language a lot worse than that, snickered. Still fuming, Jake headed off toward the guns.

If the dump didn't send enough shells forward, as seemed highly likely, Captain Stuart would have to do the calling next time. What was the point of carrying a famous name if you couldn't exploit it every now and then?

When Featherston got back to his battery, he discovered his men gathered around a major he'd never seen before: a major of infantry, for the single stars showing his rank were mounted on blue-faced collar tabs. "What's up?" Jake asked, which really meant, *What the devil is the infantry doing sniffing around an artillery unit?*

The major turned to him. The fellow wasn't very big and his face wasn't very tough, but Featherston wouldn't have wanted any damnyankee with those hard, gray eyes staring at him over the sights of a Springfield. Almost without realizing he'd done it, he stiffened to attention and saluted.

Crisply, the major returned the salute. "Clarence Potter, Army of Northern Virginia Intelligence," he said. His voice was harsh and clipped and had a trace of a Yankee accent; Featherston wondered if he'd gone to college in the United States. Potter went on, "I am here to investigate a conspiracy threatening the security not only of this army but of the Confederate States of America."

"Jesus Christ!" Jake exclaimed, and then said, "Excuse me, sir, but I don't know anything about anything like that, and I'd be right surprised—I'd be more than right surprised—if anybody here does."

"That's what we were tellin' him, Sarge," Jethro Bixler said. The loader went on, "All we want to do—all any of us want to do—is tie a can to the damnyankees' tails and then get back to what we was doin' 'fore the damn war started."

"Sergeant, if your men are as good with their gunnery as they are at flapping their gums, the Confederate States are in good hands," Major Potter said. "If you'll listen, I'll tell you exactly why I'm here. What I want to know is, how far do you trust the niggers in this battery?"

"The niggers?" Featherston scratched his head. "Haven't hardly thought about the niggers. They do what we tell 'em, and that's that. You want to know the truth of it, most of the time I worry about the horses more. Something's wrong with a nigger, he can tell you what it is and where it hurts. With horses, you got to guess."

"That's how it is, all right," Bixler said, and the rest of the gun crew nodded agreement. Featherston relaxed. His best guess was that the intelligence unit had too much time on its hands and was running around making work for itself so it would look busy and important.

But Clarence Potter shook his head, as if reading Jake's mind. "That's what they want you to think," he said in a low voice. If he'd had long mustaches and twirled them, he would have looked as well as sounded like a stage villain. He went on, "We've broken up four cells of Red rebellion in the niggers of this army in the past two weeks. One of them was in another artillery battery. I won't name names, but we found out the niggers there were sabotaging shells so they wouldn't go off when they came down on the Yankees' heads."

"I be go to hell," Jake said softly. The rest of his men gaped at the major from Intelligence.

"It is a fact," Potter declared. "We shot four buck niggers yesterday—gave them blindfolds and cigars and tied them to posts and shot them dead. One thing this war has brought out is how deeply the rot has spread through the Confederate States. Half the niggers in government service and half the niggers back home, it seems, have been plotting against the white race and the Confederate government, and likely plotting against them for years. We will crush those plots if it means giving half our niggers blindfolds and cigars—if that is what we require, gentlemen, that is what we shall do, for the sake of our race and for the sake of our country."

"I have trouble imagining anything like that in this battery, sir," Featherston said. By the look in his eye, Major Clarence Potter had no trouble imagining almost any sort of trouble anywhere. Featherston continued, "Haven't had reports from the aeroplane pilots or the ground spotters that we're shootin' too many duds, anything like that. And besides"—he laughed ruefully—"it ain't like we got that many shells any which way, live or dud." He explained where he'd been, and why.

"We're investigating that particular scandal, too," Potter said in a tone of voice that did not bode well for whoever he and his cohorts decided was to blame. Featherston didn't know whether it was a scandal or not. The fellow back at the ammunition dump had a point, though Jake wouldn't have admitted it to him, not in a million years; you could shoot off shells a hell of a lot easier than you could make them.

"Red revolutionaries—in the Army?" Jethro Bixler sounded incredulous. "Those are the crazy people who throw bombs at senators, things like that."

"Not all of them are crazy, not even close," Potter said. "Life would be simpler if they were. A lot of them are as hard to spot as a rattler in dry leaves, and every bit as deadly. So, gentlemen—have you seen any Negroes acting in any way suspicious, any way at all?"

Jake glanced over toward the laborers and teamsters who were standing around watching the artillerymen chew the fat with this stranger. You couldn't tell anything from their faces, but then you never could. Jake's father had taught him that almost before he was out of short pants: overseers' lore, even though there weren't any overseers left, not in the old sense of the word, since manumission went through. He wouldn't have given long odds against the Negroes' knowing who Potter was: jungle telegraph, white men called it. He wondered what the blacks thought.

"Well?" the major snapped.

For close to half a minute, nobody said anything. Featherston understood that: even if the laborers and teamsters were imperfectly loyal, how was the battery supposed to function without them? If Major Potter arrested them, who, if anybody, would replace them? The saying about the devil you knew and the devil you didn't held true here.

Or it mostly held true. Jake said, "Captain Stuart's nigger, Pompey, he's . . . not uppity, but he thinks a good deal of himself, if you know what I mean."

"I do indeed know exactly what you mean, Sergeant," Potter said, his voice grim and predatory. Jake would not have liked to get in his way. But then even the iron-eyed intelligence officer hesitated. "Captain Stuart, you say? That would be Captain Jeb Stuart III, wouldn't it?"

"Yes, sir, sure would," Featherston agreed.

"Damnation," Major Potter muttered under his breath. "Well, we'll see what we can do about finding out what this buck Pompey knows, if he knows anything." He walked off, looking unhappy.

Jethro Bixler laughed softly. "Every time there's an election, everybody starts brayin' about how one white man, he's just as good as the next. Sounds mighty fine, don't it? Look what it's worth when you bump up against one of the big ones, though."

The crew of Featherston's gun nodded, all together. But then an ammunition wagon came doggedly forward over the muddy road. "This here First Richmond Howitzers?" called the driver, a white man. When the gun crew nodded again, the fellow said, "Why the devil didn't you say this here was Jeb Stuart's battery? Jeb Stuart III needs ammunition, by Jesus he gets it."

Featherston started to laugh. The rest of the gun crew joined in, uproariously. The driver first gaped and then started to get mad. For some reason, that only made Jake laugh harder. Every coin had two sides. If Pompey was plotting revolution, he'd be hard to get rid of, because Captain Stuart liked him and trusted him. But if the battery needed shells, shells the battery would have, because Captain Stuart commanded it.

"With a little luck," Jake said, "the good outweighs the bad."

Winter blew through Manitoba so that, when spring finally came, you wondered to find anything standing. Arthur McGregor thanked God that the Americans didn't come out to any of the farms very often. They were, from everything he'd seen and heard, holed up in towns and along railroad tracks. Not many of them had been ready for a winter like this one. He hoped they were a lot colder and more uncomfortable than he was.

"Serves 'em right," he said over supper one long early February night: salt pork from pigs he'd raised himself and bread baked from his own wheat. "They wanted to come up here and take away what's ours, did they? I wish they'd take our winter and ship it back to the USA with 'em, to some place that could use a hard one: Maryland, maybe, or—what was the name of that state of theirs?" Geography had never been his favorite subject in school, and he hadn't cracked a school book in more than half a lifetime.

His son Alexander was no great scholar, either, but his memory was fresher than Arthur's. "California?" he suggested.

"That's the one I meant," Arthur McGregor agreed.

"They say there are parts of that state where it doesn't snow for years and years at a time," Alexander said. "I can't hardly believe that."

"Well, Alexander, when did they tell you that you knew everything there was to know?" his mother asked, with just enough chuckle in her voice to take away the sting, the way medicine was sweetened to fight its bitter taste.

"Now, Maude," Arthur McGregor said, "I have trouble believing that, too." He'd lived in Manitoba since he was about ten years old, and in Ontario before that. Neither province went without snow for years at a time. From October through April, you counted yourself lucky if you went without snow for a week.

But, from the way the U.S. soldiers had trouble with the cold here, he thought it likely they were used to a much milder climate. If you started thinking the whole world was like the part of it where you lived, you were going to be wrong a lot of the time.

Maude got up and carried dishes to the kitchen. She was coming back for a second load when somebody knocked on the door. Maude froze; Arthur admired her for not dropping any of the dishes. Ice that had nothing to do with the weather ran up his back. The best he could hope for was that it was a neighbor in some kind of trouble. The worst . . . Sometimes, when the Americans ran short of supplies, they made up the lack by plundering the people whose land they'd invaded.

Alexander McGregor pointed to the cabinet where they'd hidden the rifle. Arthur McGregor shook his head. One gun against however many U.S. soldiers might have been out there wasn't betting odds.

The knock came again, louder, more insistent. Now Arthur thought about getting the gun. None of his neighbors would have knocked like that, which left American troops as the next best bet. But one against however many still looked grim. Slowly, he walked to the door. "Who's there?" he called without putting his hand on the latch.

Two words came through the timbers: "A friend."

McGregor scratched his head. Any neighbor would have said who he was, and probably would have been angry at him for not opening up right away, too. And the Americans would also have said who they were, loudly and rudely. Whom did that leave? Nobody likely to come to his door he could think of. "What kind of friend?" he demanded.

The answer came back at once: "A cold one, dammit."

He scowled, but threw the door wide. When he saw the uniformed rifleman outside in the snow, he thought the fellow was an American. Then he realized the greatcoat wasn't green-gray, but the khaki he'd once worn himself. Along with the greatcoat, the Canadian soldier wore a fur cap on his head and long, narrow boards on his feet. McGregor had snowshoes in his own closet, of course, but he wasn't good on skis. "Come in," he said now. "You're a friend indeed, and among friends."

The soldier bent down and undid the straps holding the skis to his feet. He set down the poles that had helped him travel over the snow and hurried into the house so McGregor could close the door behind him. "Thanks," he said with a theatrical shiver. "Have you got any tea or coffee? I've been going for a long time."

"Maude!" McGregor called. His wife hurried into the kitchen again. Her face bore an expression half proud, half worried. The American authorities had issued regulations against harboring Canadian or British (all of whom they described as "enemy") soldiers, with draconian punishments for disobedience spelled out in minute, loving detail. The Americans seemed very good at spelling things out in minute detail, without much caring what they were defining.

Alexander McGregor, on the other hand, looked as if he was going to bow down before the scruffy Canadian soldier the way the Israelites bowed down to the Golden Calf. Arthur's son was at the age where he was prone to hero worship, and anyone who could hit back at the United Sates was a hero in his eyes now.

A couple of minutes after the kettle started whistling, Maude came out with a steaming cup of tea. "Obliged, ma'am," the soldier said, and sipped. His eyebrows went up. "You even sugared it for me. I'm in your debt."

Maude glanced toward Arthur. Almost imperceptibly, he nodded back. He would have expected nothing less from her than giving a guest the best they had. Yes, sugar was in short supply in these days of occupation, but they wouldn't waste away and die for want of a couple of teaspoonsful.

The soldier drank the cup down while it was still steaming, the better to get all the warmth he could inside him. When it was empty, he sighed deeply. "God bless you," he said. "I may live. I may even want to. Long, cold trip down here, I tell you that." He blinked; his eyes were a startling blue. "Haven't given you my name, have I? I'm Sergeant Malcolm Lockerby, 90th Rifles."

"The Little Black Devils," Alexander breathed. His father nodded, too. The 90th Battalion had always had a good reputation and a fierce name. Alexander went on, "What are you down here for, sir?"

Arthur McGregor knew better than to call a sergeant *sir*, but didn't correct his son. Malcolm Lockerby grinned a lopsided grin. "For all the mischief I can bring our American cousins," he answered, shrugging out of his heavy pack and setting it and his rifle on the floor. He said nothing more than that, which made Arthur nod again, this time in somber approval. What you didn't know, American questioners couldn't sweat out of you if something went wrong.

"Can I help, sir?" Alexander exclaimed. Sure enough, if he thought he saw a way to give a yank to the Yank eagle's tail feathers, he'd grab it.

Much to Arthur's relief, Lockerby shook his head. "This operation was set up with one man in mind, and more would only complicate things," he said, letting Alexander down easy.

Maude disappeared into the kitchen yet again and came back with a plate of salt pork and bread and butter. She set it on the table, then said, "Eat," like a field marshal ordering an army corps to go over to the attack.

Lockerby obeyed the command with as much élan as any field marshal could have wanted. McGregor's wife refilled his teacup, and then filled it again. She brought a second helping of pork and more bread. Only when the sergeant leaned back in his chair with a sigh of contentment did she desist.

"Now I don't want to leave," Lockerby remarked, which brought a proud smile to Maude's face. The soldier went on, "But I have to, I know. Now—am I right in thinking the railroad is east of here?"

"No, it's to the west," McGregor said, pointing.

"I'll be—" Lockerby didn't say what he'd be, probably in deference to Maude's presence. He shook his head. "I must have skied right over the tracks without even knowing I'd done it. A lot of snow on the ground right now."

"So there is," McGregor agreed. "Tell us the news, or more of it than we get from the lying papers the Americans make people print. Is Winnipeg still holding out?"

"That it is," Lockerby said, "and likely to keep doing it, too, with the lines we've made south of the city. Nobody's moved much since the snows started, but we've done a lot of digging." His face clouded. "We haven't the men to dig like that along the whole length of railroad, though. When spring comes, we're liable to have the country cut in half."

"Aren't they building a new line north of the one that runs through Winnipeg?" Alexander asked. "Then we could keep shipping things east and west, even if—" He didn't go on. When you were still a youth, looking defeat in the face came hard.

"They're building it," Lockerby agreed. "They can't run it too far north, though, because of the lakes, and even if they did, the Americans might keep on pushing. We'll have to see. Have to see if England can spare us any more troops, too." He looked bleak and tired and older than his years.

After sitting for a few more minutes, he got up, donned pack and rifle once more, and went outside to put on his skis. As far as McGregor was concerned, they were outlandish contraptions, but when Lockerby went on his way, he glided across the surface of the snow amazingly fast, amazingly smooth. The farmer stared after him till he vanished into the night.

McGregor also watched the endless wind blowing away his trail. He looked north. Already, you could not tell Lockerby had come to the farm. That suited McGregor fine—better than fine. If mischief befell the Americans, he didn't want it traced back to him unless he'd had a part in it: no, not even then, he decided. Especially not then.

Lockerby's sudden appearance gave the family something to talk about till they went to bed. When Arthur McGregor got up the next morning, he hurried out to use the outhouse and feed the livestock he had left. The day was bright and clear. He peered west, toward the railroad tracks. He could see a train, and it wasn't moving. Wagons and men were gathered around it; he could make out no more because of the distance.

Whenever he went out for chores, he looked toward the stalled—sabotaged? bombed?—train. Toward evening, it got moving again. It went up the track for about half a mile. Then, all at once, it stopped. The engine and several of the cars left the tracks, or so McGregor thought, anyhow: with the sun in his face, it was hard to be sure.

Some seconds after he saw the train stop, a harsh, flat *bang!* reached his ears—without a doubt, the sound of an explosive going off. He wondered if another of those had come in the night to stop the train the first time. If one had, he'd slept right through it.

"That Lockerby, he did good work there," McGregor said to no one in particular, breath puffing out of his mouth in a frosty cloud as he spoke. He wondered how many other explosives the sergeant had planted along the track. The Americans would have to be wondering the same thing. How long would the line be out of service while they checked it? How many of them would get frostbite or pneumonia checking it?

Normally dour, he smiled from ear to ear as he went back inside.

Captain Wilcox stabbed a finger out at Reginald Bartlett. "How'd you like to lay some barbed wire tonight?" he said.

"Sir, if it's all the same to you, I'd rather lay one of those pretty little Red Cross nurses back at the aid station," Bartlett answered, deadpan.

The Confederate soldiers who heard him laughed and snorted and cheered. One or two of them sent up Rebel yells to show they agreed with the sentiment expressed. Captain Wilcox grinned. By now, he'd got used to the idea that expecting Bartlett to take anything, war included, seriously was asking too much.

"Only trouble is, Reggie, they wouldn't want to lay you," he said. "Your uniform is filthy, your face is grubby, you've got lice in your hair and nits in every seam of your clothes, and you smell like a polecat would if he didn't take a bath for about a year. Barbed wire, now, barbed wire doesn't care about any of that."

"That's all true, sir," Bartlett agreed, "but barbed wire can't foxtrot, either. Honestly, sir—"

It was a losing fight, and he knew it. It wasn't really even a fight at all, just a way to grumble about orders that was different from the profane complaints most men gave. When evening came, he *would* crawl out of the trench with a roll of barbed wire on his back, and he knew that, too. So did Captain Wilcox, who waved at him and went along the line to pick some more volunteers.

Down in the trenches, you were fairly safe unless you did something stupid like showing yourself to the damnyankees on the other side of the wire, or unless a shell landed right by you, or unless the U.S. soldiers decided to make another probe toward the Roanoke River and happened to pick your stretch of the line to raid.

Once you came out of the earthworks that protected you, though . . . once you came out of them, machine guns weren't nuisances any more. They were menaces only too likely to make your family get a "The government of the Confederate States of America deeply regrets to inform you . . ." telegram. Rifle bullets ran around loose up there, too.

And you were liable to run into damnyankees out between the lines doing the same sorts of things you were. Sometimes you'd work and they'd work and you'd pretend not to notice one another. And sometimes you'd go after them or they'd go after you with guns and bayonets and the short-handled shovels you used to dig holes in the ground. And then the rifles in both trench lines would open up, and the machine guns would start to hammer, and then oh Lord! how you wished you were back of the lines in bed with a nurse—or even down safe in your trench—instead of where you really were.

Captain Wilcox had called Reggie's face grubby. Before he climbed up out of the trench, he rubbed mud on himself till he looked like the end man in a minstrel show. The blacker you were, the harder it was for the Yankees to spot you.

"We ought to send niggers up to do this for us," he said. "They're already black."

"I hear tell they've tried that in Kentucky," Captain Wilcox said. "Didn't work. The Yankees shot at them like they were us, and they didn't have any guns to shoot back with. The ones who lived, you couldn't make 'em go up again."

"Too bad," Reggie said. "Better them than me. Better them than me for just about any job I don't want to do, matter of fact." But when the captain said go, you went. Bartlett nodded to his companions. "Let's get rolling."

The other half-dozen men nodded. He'd been fighting along the Roanoke longer than any of them, so they took his word as Gospel, even if he had no more rank than they did. He was that mystical, magical thing, a veteran. A lot of the men who'd come to the fight with him were dead now. That he wasn't was partly luck and partly being able to remember what he'd learned in his first few fights well enough not to repeat any of the stupid parts.

"Stay low and go slow," he said now. "The less racket we make spreading the wire, the less chance the damnyankees have of starting to shoot at us."

Some kind and thoughtful soul had made a stairway out of sandbags to help the heavily burdened wire men get out of the trench. Bartlett was grateful and angry at the same time: if he hadn't been able to get up onto the battered ground between the lines, he wouldn't have had to crawl forward toward the wire—and toward the enemy.

It was a dark and cloudy night. For once, Reggie wouldn't have minded rain or even snow: nothing better to keep the U.S. forces from knowing he and his chums were out there. But if a storm hid in those clouds, it refused to come out.

He set down his hands with great care every time he moved forward. Behind him, somebody let out a soft, disgusted oath, probably because he'd crawled over a soft, disgusting corpse or piece of corpse. The line had swung back and forth several times; a lot of the dead from both sides had gone without proper burial. And even those who had been thrown into hasty graves or holes in the ground might well have been disinterred by the endless, senseless plowing of the artillery. The smell was that of a meat market that had been out of ice for a month in the middle of a hot summer.

Up above his head, something went *fwoomp!* "Freeze!" he hissed frantically as the parachute flare spread harsh white light over the field. If you didn't move, sometimes they wouldn't spot you even when you were out there in plain sight. Some of the men in his company spoke of walking right past deer that had bounded away once they'd gone by.

Bartlett was no deer, but he knew he could be in some hunter's sights right now. His nose itched. His hand itched. His scalp and the hair under his arms always itched. He directed a few unkind thoughts to the cooties he carried around with him. But he didn't scratch. He didn't move. He did his best not to blink.

Some Yankee with a rifle started shooting, somewhere too close for comfort. Bartlett froze even colder. But whatever the U.S. soldier thought he saw, it wasn't the Confederate wiring party. Hissing and sputtering, the parachute flare sank ever so slowly, going from white toward red as it did. At last it died, plunging the debatable ground into darkness once more.

"Come on," Bartlett whispered. "Come on, but come quiet."

Like most things, that was easier said than done. When at last they got to the wire barrier they were to strengthen, the men couldn't just unroll the wire and scoot for home. To make it a proper obstruction, they had to mount it on poles and shove the poles in the ground. In some places, the ground was damp. Things were easy there. In some places, though, the ground was frozen. You had a choice then: either stab the supports into the dirt, knowing they wouldn't stay well, or hammer at them with a shovel or whatever you had, knowing the noise was liable to draw fire. Bartlett opted for quiet. "Hell," he muttered to himself, "it ain't like there's not enough wire out here already."

Somebody, though, somebody had to get intrepid. *Tap, tap tap.* In the middle of a quiet night, the noise might as well have been a shell going off. Along with everybody else in the wiring party, Bartlett made frantic shushing noises. The damnyankees would start tapping, too, the two-inch tap an experienced machine gunner used on the barrel of his weapon to traverse it through its deadly arc of fire.

And sure enough, the U.S. soldiers did open up, first rifles, then machine guns. When a bullet clipped the barbed wire, it sparked blue. There were a lot of blue sparks, as if lightning bugs had suddenly come to roost between the lines of the two armies.

"Out of here!" Bartlett said urgently. He'd just about finished unreeling his wire; he unhooked the roll from his back and, suddenly lighter, hurried back toward the Confederate front line. Never had a muddy, stinking hole in the ground seemed so welcome, so wonderful.

Bullets zipping all around him, he dove into a shell hole. There was a puddle at the bottom of it. A horrible stink rose when he roiled the water. Something—or more likely someone—had died in this hole, too long ago.

A series of two-inch taps sent the Yankees' stream of machine-gun bullets past him. He thought he could make it to the trench before the stream came back. Leaping up out of the shell hole, he ran for all he was worth. Somebody else, panting like a dog, sprinted stride for stride with him.

Slap! His comrade, whoever he was, went down: even with the machine gun busy elsewhere, plenty of rifle bullets were still in the air. Swearing, Bartlett grabbed the other man, slung him over his back in place of the roll of wire, and stumbled on.

He almost went into the trench headfirst. Soldiers caught him, steadied him. "Who have I got here?" he asked, easing the man on his back to the ground.

Somebody struck a match. "It's Jordan," he said, and then, a moment later, quite unnecessarily, "He's dead."

"Good job you picked him up even so," Captain Wilcox said out of the darkness. "You can't know, not for sure. How did the wiring go?"

Bartlett took a minute or so to stop gasping for breath and to let his heart slow as terror began to recede. "Routine, sir," he answered then. "Just routine."

"Routine," Sam Carsten said. "Just routine."

Hiram Kidde laughed out loud. "Ain't one damn thing about it that's routine," the gunner's mate said. "Wearin' summer whites in February, *sweatin'* in summer whites in February, bein' in the Sandwich Islands at all . . ." His grin was broad and delighted. "Still can't believe we caught the limeys with their drawers down."

"Might as well believe it," Carsten answered. "It's true."

He waved to show what he meant. The two off-duty sailors strolled along the grounds on the eastern side of the entranceway to Pearl Harbor. When the British ruled the Sandwich Islands, they'd built a parade ground there, so their Marines could get in the drill they needed. The parade ground was somewhat the worse for wear after the American invasion of the islands, but Marines still paraded on it: U.S. Marines in uniforms of forest green, several shades darker than Army men wore.

"Eyes—right!" the Marine drill sergeant shouted, marching along with his men. "Sing out—let me hear it, you birds!"

"One, two, three, four," the men sounded off. "Miss Maggie's why we'll win the war!"

Not even a Marine drill sergeant, as fearsome a creature as any ever born, could make the young men ignore the spectacular woman who came out to the parade grounds several days a week to watch them march—and to be watched. The sergeant, a man of sense, didn't even try. He stared at Maggie Stevenson, too. And so did Sam Carsten and "Cap'n" Kidde.

Maggie Stevenson had been in business for herself when the Union Jack flew over Honolulu, and the recent change of ownership hadn't fazed her a bit. Indeed, because there were more American sailors, soldiers, and Marines here now than there had been Englishmen before, her business was better than ever.

"There's one limey I'd like to catch with her drawers down," Carsten said reverently.

"Limey?" Kidde said. "I hear tell she's from Nebraska."

" 'Cap'n,' with Maggie it's not what you hear, it's what you see."

Kidde nodded reverently. There was a lot of Maggie to see. She was within an inch of Carsten's height, and was probably even fairer, but on her it looked good. She shielded her face from the sun with a broad-brimmed straw hat. Like a lot of women in Honolulu, she wore a *holoku*, a baggy, native-style dress that covered her from neck to ankles. Hers, though, wasn't cotton or linen. It was green silk, somewhere between translucent and transparent. When she stood between men and the sun, as she made a point of doing, you could see there was a hell of a lot of woman under there.

After thorough and judicious study, Hiram Kidde said, "Sam, I don't think she's *wearin'* drawers." He shook his head. "And you can get right there, too, just for the asking." He sighed. "Amazing."

"Not quite just for the asking," Carsten said. "For the paying. If she's not the richest gal in these islands, it ain't for lack of effort."

"Effort?" Kidde laughed. "There's coal-heavers down in the black gang don't work as hard as she does, I hear tell. You know about the setup dear Maggie's got?"

"Tell me," Carsten said. "Beats hell out of thinking about cleaning out a five-inch gun, that's for damn sure." He winked. " 'Course, you only got a five-inch gun, Miss Maggie ain't gonna want anything to do with you."

Kidde had been inhaling to say something, which meant he choked when he started to laugh. Sam Carsten pounded him on the back. "You got to watch that," he wheezed when he could talk again.

"I *was* watching that," Sam said, watching Maggie Stevenson, who was watching the Marines watch her.

"Shut up," Kidde said. "What the hell was I talkin' about? Oh, yeah—her place. They say she's got this big room with four, maybe five, Pullman-sized compartments in there, nothin' in any of 'em 'cept a red couch and a horny guy on it, and she just goes from couch to couch to couch, long as she can walk."

"No wonder she's rich," Carsten said, with the genuine respect a professional in one field gives a professional in another.

"Yup," Kidde agreed. "And she's got 'em lined up for every damn compartment, too, even if she does charge thirty bucks a throw." His hard, blunt face grew dreamy for a moment. "She must be a piece of ass and a half."

"Yeah, reckon so," Carsten said. "But most of a month's pay—hell, more than a month's pay if you're just an ordinary seaman—for five minutes, ten tops? That's a lot to spend just to get your ashes hauled."

"She's got a lot—" the gunner's mate started.

"Of satisfied customers," Sam said, beating him to the punch line. "Yeah." They both laughed. Carsten scratched the angle of his jaw. "I dunno. You can take yourself to just an ordinary everyday crib and lay one o' them Jap girls or a Filipino for a couple-three bucks. Maggie can't be that much better . . . can she?" But he was still watching the undisputed queen of Honolulu's ladies of the evening.

"You can get drunk on that *olikau* popskull the natives cook up here, too," Hiram Kidde observed. "If gettin' drunk is the only reason you're drinkin', fine. But every now and then, don't you hanker after some real sippin' whiskey?"

Carsten scratched his jaw without answering. Whiskers rasped under his fingers. He needed a shave. He had a razor back on the *Dakota*, but you could give a dime to one of the Chinese barbers in the little shops all around Pearl Harbor, and he'd shave you closer and smoother than you could do it for yourself. He got shaved a lot these days. His meals and his hammock were taken care of, so he didn't have a hell of a lot to spend his money on.

The drill sergeant led the marching Marines back toward the British barracks they were occupying. They were too well disciplined to go with really laggard step, but their footwork showed less mechanical precision than usual. A few sailors weren't enough of an audience for Maggie Stevenson to keep herself on display. She retreated to her carriage. The driver, a little, dark Oriental sweating in top hat and cutaway, flicked the reins. Two perfectly matched black horses bore her away. Carsten and Kidde both watched till the carriage was out of sight.

Sam went and bathed, then headed to one of the barbershops and paid a couple of cents extra for a splash of bay rum. The British had set up an electric trolley between Pearl Harbor and Honolulu, though the motormen who took your nickel were uniformly Japs. Carsten wasn't the only military man who got out at the Kapalama stop, east of downtown. Some of the men in white or green acted as if they knew exactly where they were going. He followed them.

The half-timbered house might have been transplanted from London, though it wouldn't have had palm trees around it there. From what "Cap'n" Kidde had said, Carsten had expected to see a line around the block. He didn't. Then the Oriental driver waved him and the rest of the newcomers around to the back. The line was there. *Discreet,* he thought.

In the Navy, you got used to lines. What was waiting at the end of this one was better than any of the other things for which he'd lined up. He shot the breeze with some of the other guys there. A couple of them seemed too embarrassed about being where they were to say much. Most, though, like him, took it for granted.

When he got up to the back door, another slanteye in formal wear took his money. The fellow wore a pistol, concealed not quite well enough in a shoulder holster. Carsten didn't blame him, not a bit. If Maggie Stevenson's place didn't keep as much cash around as your average bank, he'd eat his hat.

Still another Oriental, also armed, stood at the doorway to the big room Kidde had talked about. "You go Number Three," he said, pointing. Sure enough, the little compartments had brass numbers on the doors, as if they were hotel rooms. Carsten went into Number 3. Inside were a mirror on one wall, a red couch, a pitcher and basin and a cake of soap on a stool, and some hooks on which to hang his clothes.

Sam used the hooks, then lay back on the couch to wait. The noises coming from one of the other cubicles were highly entertaining. Maggie Stevenson worked her way through the other three—there were four in all, not five—and then opened a door on the far side of his compartment. She came in wearing nothing but a smile and a light sheen of sweat. Carsten stared and stared. "*Hell* of a woman," he muttered; what you could see through even the most diaphanous *holoku* barely gave you a clue.

"Hello, sailor," she said, her voice English, sure enough. She lathered up the soap and washed Sam's privates. "All part of the service," she said, smiling. Then she bent down and kissed him there, right on the tip, as if it were the end of his nose. "Now—what would you like?"

"You get on top," he said. "I want to see you, too."

"All right." And she did. Those perfect, pink-tipped breasts hung like ripe fruit, inches from his face. He squeezed them and kissed them and licked them. His hands clenched her meaty backside tight.

He wanted to make it last as long as he could. But he hadn't had any in a while, and Maggie made her money by having lots of customers on any one day, so she tried hard to hurry him along. She knew just what she was doing, too. Try as he would to hold back, he bucked and jerked and came, hard enough to leave him dizzy for a moment.

"Hope I see you again, sailor," Maggie said. She leaned over him for a second, just far enough that her nipples brushed against the hair and skin of his chest. Then she got off him and off the couch and headed for the next little cubicle.

Sam got dressed and left, too. One more Oriental in fancy dress showed him the way out. He was whistling as he walked back to the trolley stop. It had been a hell of a good time. Was it worth thirty bucks, worth coming back again? He didn't think so, not really, but he wasn't sorry he'd done it once.

Three or four guys in uniform were walking up the other side of the street toward Maggie Stevenson's place. One of them, he saw with amusement, was a spruced-up Hiram Kidde. He started to wave, then stopped. Later on, maybe, he'd find out if the "Cap'n" thought he'd got his money's worth.

Cincinnatus and his wife Elizabeth were getting ready for bed when someone knocked on the back door. It wasn't that late, but, ever since Elizabeth had found out she was going to have a baby, she'd been tired a lot of the time, even more tired than her domestic's work usually made her. "Who is that?" she said in some irritation. "I don't want visitors."

"You'd think visitors would come to the front of the house," Cincinnatus said as he headed out of the bedroom toward the kitchen. From the hall, he added over his shoulder, "One thing—it ain't U.S. soldiers. They don't just come to the front of the house, they go and break down the door, you don't let 'em in fast enough."

The knock came again. It wasn't very loud, as if whoever was out there didn't want the neighbors to notice. Cincinnatus frowned, wondering if it was a strong-arm man trying to trick him into opening the door. Crooks were having a field day. The Yankees didn't seem to care what people in Covington did to one another, so long as they left U.S. troops alone.

If it was a strong-arm man, Cincinnatus vowed to give him a hell of a surprise. He plucked a heavy iron spider out of the draining rack by the sink. Clout somebody upside the head with that and he'd forget about everything for a good long while.

Spider in his right hand, he opened the back door with his left. When he did, he almost dropped the frying pan. "Mistuh Kennedy!" he exclaimed. "What the devil you doin' here?"

Even in the dim light of the lamp from the kitchen, Tom Kennedy looked as if the devil had indeed brought him to his present state. He was haggard and skinny and dirty, and his eyes tried to move every which way at once, the way a fox's did when hounds were chasing it. "Can I come in?" Cincinnatus' former boss asked.

"I think maybe you better," Cincinnatus said. "What you doin' out, anyways? Curfew's eight o'clock, and I know it's past that."

"Sure is," Kennedy said, and said no more.

That made Cincinnatus ask the next question: "What are you doin' *here*, Mr. Kennedy? You don't mind me sayin' so, this ain't your part of town." If that wasn't the understatement of 1915, it would do till a better one came along. Why the devil would a white man come into the colored part of Covington after curfew? The only thing Cincinnatus was sure about was that it wasn't any simple, ordinary, innocent reason.

"Who is it?" Elizabeth called from the bedroom.

"It's Mr. Tom Kennedy, sweetheart," Cincinnatus answered, trying to sound as ordinary and innocent as he could, and knowing he wasn't having much luck.

Kennedy's hunted look got even worse. "Don't say my name so loud," he hissed urgently. "The fewer people who know I'm here, the better off everybody will be."

Elizabeth came into the kitchen. She'd put on a quilted cotton housecoat over her nightgown. Her eyes got wide. "It *is* Mr. Kennedy," she said, and then, determined to be a good hostess no matter what the irregular circumstances in which she found herself, "Shall I put on some coffee for you?"

Kennedy shook his head, a quick, jerky motion. "No, nothing, thanks. I've been running on nerves for so long, coffee would just make things worse."

"Mr. Kennedy," Cincinnatus said with a mixture of deference and annoyance that struck him odd even at the time, "what *are* you doing here after curfew?"

"Can you hide me for a couple of days?" Kennedy asked. "I won't tell you any lies—I'm on the dodge from the damnyankees. They catch up with me, it's a rope around my neck or a blindfold and a cigarette—except I don't think they'd bother with the cigarette."

"You're in real trouble," Cincinnatus said quietly. A moment later, he realized that meant he was in real trouble, too. The U.S. authorities didn't take kindly to people who harbored fugitives from what they called justice. Elizabeth's eyes widened again. She must have figured out the same thing at the same time. Cincinnatus clicked his tongue between his teeth. "Why'd you come here?" he asked, directing the question as much to the world at large as to Tom Kennedy.

"Yes, I'm in real trouble," Kennedy said. "My life is in your hands. You want to holler for the patrols, I'm a goner. They'll put money in your pocket, too. Up to you, Cincinnatus. All depends on how you like living under the

USA, because I'm doing everything I can to throw the damnyankees out of Kentucky. That's why they're after me, in case you haven't worked it out."

"Oh, I worked it out, Mr. Kennedy," Cincinnatus said, softly still. "I'm studyin' what I should oughta do about it, is all." He had no reason to love the CSA; what black man did? But the men from the United States hadn't shown him his lot was better with them in charge, not even close.

He glanced over to Elizabeth. Her belly hadn't started to swell, certainly not to the point where anyone could notice it when she was wearing clothes. He was acutely aware of her pregnancy all the same. It made him less willing to take chances than he would have been a few months before, and far less willing to take chances than he would have been before he got married.

And so he said, "What did you do, Mr. Kennedy? How come the damnyankees are after you so bad?"

"I don't want to tell you," Kennedy answered. "The more things you know, the more they can squeeze out of you if they ever take a mind to."

That made a certain amount of sense. Most times, Cincinnatus would have accepted it without argument. Now— He felt a curious sense of reversal. For what might well have been the first time in his life, he had the upper hand in a conversation with a white man. Even though he did, he used it cautiously, deferentially: "I don't know why they want you, suh, I don't know whether I should oughta help you or help them get you. You understand what I'm sayin'?"

"You won't buy a pig in a poke, not even from me," Kennedy said. Cincinnatus nodded—that was it, in a nutshell. Tom Kennedy sighed. He recognized the reversal, too. "All right, have it your way. I haven't broken any little old ladies' legs with a crowbar or stolen from the church poor box or anything like that. But I'm in the hauling and moving business, Cincinnatus, right? Some of the things I've hauled into Covington aren't the ones the U.S. Army's real happy to have here."

He meant guns. He had to mean guns, and maybe explosives, too. Under U.S. military law, the penalty for that kind of thing was death. Soldiers had nailed up placards saying as much, all over Covington. Warnings appeared in the newspapers about twice a week. And if you harbored a gun runner, you got the same thing he did. Those warnings were in the papers, too.

"You don't make it easy, Mr. Kennedy," Cincinnatus said. He came close to hating his former boss for putting him in a spot like this—not just his neck on the line now, but Elizabeth's and the coming baby's, too. If he turned him out into the street without saying anything to the authorities but Kennedy got caught later, he'd be in just as much trouble as if he'd concealed him. The only way not to be in trouble with the U.S. authorities was to hand Kennedy over to them now. He didn't have the stomach for that. As white men went,

Kennedy had been pretty decent to him—far better than that screaming U.S. lieutenant who bossed him nowadays.

He had just reached that conclusion when Elizabeth said, "Here, come on with me, Mistuh Kennedy. I got a good place to put you."

That relieved Cincinnatus, because he hadn't come up with any good place to hide Kennedy. He didn't want him under the bed, and the Yankees would be sure to look behind the couch and down in the storm cellar. He'd been wondering if he could take Kennedy over to his mother's or some other relative's, but he wasn't enthusiastic about involving them in the danger the white man had brought to him.

Elizabeth opened the door to the pantry by the stove. It was full of sacks of potatoes and beans and black-eyed peas. Cincinnatus didn't feel the least bit guilty about hoarding. No matter how bad things got, he and his wouldn't starve.

When Elizabeth started taking out the sacks, he quickly moved her aside and did it himself. That wasn't something he wanted his wife doing, not when she was in a family way. The sacks took up a surprising lot of room, all spread out on the kitchen floor.

Once he had them all out, he saw that several boards at the back of the pantry were rotten at the bottom. He hadn't noticed that before, but Elizabeth had. He stepped into the little cramped space and pulled at the boards. They came out with squeaks and squeals of nails, revealing a black opening behind them.

"God bless you both," Tom Kennedy said, and squeezed into the opening. Cincinnatus replaced the boards as well as he could by hand. He hoped Kennedy would be able to breathe with them back. One thing seemed pretty clear, though: if U.S. soldiers caught up with Kennedy, his former boss wouldn't be breathing much longer. Still muttering to himself, Cincinnatus put back the produce sacks; Elizabeth swept up a few beans that had escaped from one of them.

When she was done, she and Cincinnatus looked at each other. They both shook their heads. "Let's go to bed," Cincinnatus said, though he didn't think he was going to sleep much, no matter how tired he'd been.

"All right." By her tone, Elizabeth was thinking the same thing. If they didn't sleep like the dead tonight, they'd shamble like the living dead tomorrow. Nothing to be done about that, not now.

After he'd blown out the lamp in the bedroom, Cincinnatus said, "We can't keep him in there long. He go crazy, cooped up like that. An' we didn't even think to give him a thundermug or nothin'."

"I'll take care of that in the morning," Elizabeth answered around an enormous yawn. Cincinnatus felt himself fading, too. Now that he was horizontal, he suspected sleep might sneak up on him after all.

Sure enough, the *wham! wham! wham!* in the middle of the night woke him out of deep, sound slumber. At first, groggy and confused, he thought it was hail pounding on the roof. Then he realized that, while it certainly was pounding, it was all coming from one direction: that of the front door.

"Soldiers," he whispered to Elizabeth. She nodded. He felt the motion rather than seeing it. *Wham! Wham! Wham!* He groped for a match, found the box, struck a light, and lighted the lamp he'd blown out. Carrying it, he went out and opened the front door.

An electric torch blazed into his face, blinding him. "You just saved your door, nigger," a Northern voice said. "We were gonna break it down."

"What you want?" Cincinnatus asked. He didn't have to struggle very hard to sound stupid, not as tired as he was. Fright came easy, too.

The Yankee officer, hard to see past that powerful torch, said, "You know a white man name of Tom Kennedy, boy?"

"Yes, suh," Cincinnatus admitted. If they'd come here, they already knew he knew Kennedy. A lie would have got him in deeper trouble than the truth.

"You seen him any time lately?" the officer demanded.

Cincinnatus shook his head. "No, suh. Sure ain't, not since jus' a little while after de war start. He run out o' town, I hear tell, 'fore you Yankees come." He laid the Negro accent on with a trowel; it would help make the U.S. soldiers think he was stupid. He'd have done that for Confederates, too.

"Wish to Jesus he had," the officer said, so feelingly that Cincinnatus blinked; he hadn't thought any damnyankees took Jesus Christ seriously. The fellow went on, "He's been seen in Covington, and he's been seen not far from right here, so what we're gonna do is, we're gonna search this shack." He waved to the soldiers with him.

In they came. Cincinnatus got out of the way in a hurry. If he hadn't, they would have trampled him, or maybe bayoneted him. The U.S. troops turned his tidy little house—he bristled at hearing it called a shack—upside down and inside out looking for Tom Kennedy. They stabbed those bayonets into the sofa and into his mattress through the sheets. Had Kennedy been in there, he would have regretted it. As things were, Cincinnatus did the regretting, for his bed linen and the upholstery. Elizabeth, watching with round eyes, made distressed noises. The Yankees ignored her.

One of the soldiers got down on hands and knees to peer under the stove, though a midget would have had trouble hiding there. Another one flung open the pantry door. The officer—short, skinny, with gold-rimmed spectacles and a mean look—shone that torch in there. Cincinnatus' heart thumped—*had* he got those boards back well enough? He did his best not to show what he was thinking.

"Nothin' but a pile of beans," the officer said disgustedly, and slammed the pantry door. He turned to Cincinnatus. "All right, boy, looks like you were tellin' the truth." He dug into his pocket, pulled out a silver dollar, and tossed it to the Negro. "For the damage." He raised his voice. "Come on, men. We got other places to search."

Cincinnatus stared down at the coin he'd automatically caught. It wasn't enough, but it was a dollar more than he'd expected to get. He set it on the counter. When the U.S. soldiers were gone, he opened the pantry door and asked quietly, "You all right, Mr. Kennedy?"

The disembodied voice floated back from behind the wall: "Yes, thanks. God bless you."

"We take better care of you come mornin'," Cincinnatus promised, and went off to see if he could get some rest. He sighed. He wasn't even close to sure he'd done the right thing in hiding Kennedy. But that didn't matter now. Right or wrong, he was committed. He'd have to see what came of that.

Nellie Semphroch sighed wearily as she carried the big cloth grocery bag back toward the coffeehouse. The bag itself was lighter than she'd wished it would be; the grocers had trouble keeping things in stock. But she was tireder than she thought she should have been, and felt old beyond her years. Winter always wore at her, and this year it wasn't just winter, it was Rebel occupation, too.

She slipped, and had to flail her arms wildly to keep from falling: the sidewalk was icy in spots. Across the street, Mr. Jacobs came out of his shop with a Confederate soldier wearing one pair of boots and carrying another. The Reb strutted up the street as if he owned it, which, in effect, he did. As far as he was concerned, Nellie wasn't worth noticing.

Mr. Jacobs, being occupied rather than occupier, could see—and admit seeing—his fellow U.S. citizens. "You are all right, Widow Semphroch?" he called.

"Yes, I think so, thank you," Nellie answered. "One more thing on top of everything else." She bit her lip. What she wanted to say was, *I've been through so much. Why can't life be easy for a change?* The answer to that one was depressingly obvious, though: her life had never been easy, so why should it start now?

"I hope it will be better soon," the shoemaker said.

"So do I, Mr. Jacobs; so do I," Nellie said. A good Christian, she knew, would not resent another's honestly earned success, but she was jealous of Jacobs. His business flourished, while hers withered on the vine. Why not? Leather was easy to come by, coffee wasn't. The Confederate soldiers in Washington went through a lot of shoes and boots. They'd gone through a lot of coffee, too, but now only a tiny bit was left.

"Widow Semphroch, is there anything I can do to help you?" Mr. Jacobs asked.

Nellie shook her head. Things had come to a pretty pass, hadn't they, when even the shoemaker knew she was failing and pitied her? With stubborn pride, she picked up the grocery bag and went into the coffeehouse.

The little bell above the door didn't tinkle as she went in. After surviving the Confederate bombardment at the start of the war, it had fallen off its mounting a few weeks before, and she'd never bothered replacing it. Not much point to that, not when she or Edna was almost always there—and not when customers were few and far between, too.

But Edna wasn't behind the counter now. Frowning, Nellie set down the grocery bag. No customers were being slighted—all the tables in the front part of the shop were empty. But her daughter hadn't told her she was going anywhere—and, if Edna had decided to go out, she should have locked the front door. Nellie started down the hall, turned the corner—and there stood Edna, kissing a cavalryman in butternut, her arms tight around him, his big, hairy hands clutching at her posterior. Nellie gasped—not in dismay, but in fury. "Stop that this instant!" she snapped.

Intent on each other and nothing more, her daughter and the cavalry officer hadn't noticed her till she spoke. When she did, they sprang apart from each other as if they were a couple of the clever magnetic toys that had been all the go a couple of years before.

"Mother, it's all right—" Edna began.

Nellie ignored her. "Young man, what is your name?" she demanded of the Confederate soldier.

"Nicholas Henry Kincaid, ma'am," he answered, polite even though Nellie could still see the bulge in his trousers, the bulge he'd got from rubbing up against Edna.

"Well, Mr. Nicholas Henry Kincaid"—Nellie freighted the name with all the scorn it would bear—"your commanding officer will hear of this—this—this—" She couldn't find the word she wanted. But Edna wouldn't go the way she had gone. Edna *wouldn't*. Nellie shouted, "Get out!" and pointed to the front door.

Kincaid was more than a head taller than she was. He carried a knife and a large revolver on his belt. None of that mattered. Face red, expression mortified, he retreated: Nellie had accomplished more than the entire U.S. garrison of Washington, D.C. She tried to kick him in the shins as he went, but he was too fast for her, so she missed.

Still steaming, she rounded on Edna. "As for you, young lady—"

"Oh, Ma, leave it alone, will you, please?" her daughter said in a weary voice. "How's a girl supposed to have any fun these days, with the whole town turned into one big morgue?"

"Not like that," Nellie Semphroch said grimly. "Not like that, because—"

"Because you let some boy pull your knickers down a long time ago, and now you've decided I shouldn't." Edna tossed her head in disdain. "I'm grown up now, and you can't keep me from being alive myself, no matter how much you want to."

Nellie stared in dismay. Her cheeks got hot. The worst was, her daughter's shot was an understatement. Edna didn't know that, thank God. As parents will, though, Nellie rallied. "As long as you are living under my roof, you will—"

But Edna interrupted again: "Some roof." She tossed her head once more. "I could do better than this by lifting my little finger."

"By lifting your skirt, you mean," Nellie retorted. "No daughter of mine is going to make her way through the world by selling herself on street corners, I tell you that. I won't just report that cavalryman's name to the Rebel commandant, Edna—I'll give him yours, too."

They glared at each other, two sides of the same coin, though neither realized it. With what looked like a distinct effort, Edna made herself stop snarling. "It's not like that, Ma. I've never once prostituted myself, and I never will, neither. But I'm not going to sit cooped up in this damned shop all day long, either, watching the dust on the counter getting thicker and thicker and thicker. I'm going to be twenty-one in a couple months. Don't I deserve a life?"

"Not that kind," Nellie said, breathing hard. (She wished she could say everything Edna had.) "You want that kind, find yourself a man you're going to marry. *Then* you can have it." Only after she was done speaking did she realize how little Edna's language, which would have been shocking before the war began, shocked her now. Everything was coarsened, cheapened, turned to trash and vileness.

"And how am I supposed to meet anybody I might want to marry if I stay here all the time?" Edna shot back. "About the only people who come in are Confederate soldiers, and if you don't want me to have anything to do with them—"

"That man was not going to marry you," Nellie said positively. "All he wanted was to have his way with you." Edna did not have a snappy comeback to that, by which Nellie concluded she'd won a point. Trying to sound earnest rather than furious, Nellie went on, "You just can't trust men, Edna. They'll say whatever they have to to get what they want, and afterwards they'll leave you flat, go off whistling, and never care whether they've left you in a family way—"

"How do you know so much about it?" Edna said.

"Ask any woman. She'll tell you the same if you can get her to let her hair down." Automatically, Nellie's hand straightened the curls on her own head. She felt dizzy with anger at her daughter. Memories that hadn't come back to her in years—memories she'd thought, she'd hoped, long forgotten—came bubbling back up to the surface of her mind, memories of the harsh taste of rotgut whiskey and the deceptively sweet clink of silver dollars and the occasional quarter-eagle on the top of a pine nightstand.

"I'm not going to die an old maid, Ma," Edna insisted.

"I didn't ask you to," Nellie said. "But I—"

"Sure sounded to me like you did," her daughter interrupted. "Don't go out, don't meet nobody; if you do meet somebody, don't have any fun with him, on account of all he wants to do is lay you anyways. You maybe caught me this time, Ma, but you can't watch me every hour of every day. I'm not gonna wear your ball and chain, and you can't make me."

Edna stormed past Nellie and out of the coffeehouse. As Nellie had with Nicholas Kincaid, she tried to kick her daughter. As she had then, she missed. The door slammed. Nellie burst into tears.

At last, she dug in her handbag for a cheap cotton handkerchief. She wiped her eyes and blew her nose. Then, slowly, her steps dragging, she went to the door, too. She opened it, stepped outside, and looked up and down the street. She didn't see Edna. She started to cry again.

A Negro in fancy livery driving a high-ranking Confederate officer with a white mustache came down the street in a gleaming motorcar. Nellie wanted to scream the filthiest things she knew at him. After the automobile—a procession in and of itself—had passed, she crossed the street and went into Mr. Jacobs' cobbler's shop.

The little bell above his door worked. He looked up from the marching boot he was repairing. Behind magnifying lenses, his eyes looked enormous. The wrinkles on his round little face rearranged themselves into an expression of concern. "Widow Semphroch!" he exclaimed. "Whatever can be wrong?"

Nellie found herself telling him what was wrong. Everybody needed someone with whom to talk, and she'd known him for as long as she'd been in business across the street from his shop. He wasn't one to spread gossip around. He wouldn't blab of her troubles with Edna, either, or of how much she hated the Rebel soldiers and officers who kept sniffing round her daughter.

When she was finished, he pulled a handkerchief—a bright green silk—out of his trouser pocket, took off his spectacles, made a production out of polishing the lenses, and then set the glasses on the counter by his last. He studied Nellie for close to a minute without saying anything. Then, in a thoughtful tone of voice, he remarked, "You know, Widow Semphroch, I am sorry for you and for your poor daughter. I wish there were some way you could take revenge on these Confederates who have caused you so much grief."

"Oh, good Lord, so do I!" Nellie said fervently.

The shoemaker continued to study her. "When the Rebs came into your coffeehouse, they must have had all sorts of . . . interesting stories to tell.

Wouldn't you say that's so, Widow Semphroch? It is here, that I can tell you. The ones who come in to get their shoes repaired, they do run on at the mouth. And me, I just listen. I listen very carefully. You never can tell what you might hear."

Nellie started to answer Mr. Jacobs, then suddenly stopped before she'd said anything. Now she looked sharply at him. He'd just told her something, without ever once coming right out and saying it. If she hadn't been paying attention, she wouldn't have noticed—which, no doubt, was what he'd intended.

She said, "If I hear anything like that, Mr. Jacobs, maybe you'd like me to let you know about it. If you think that would be interesting, of course."

"It might," he answered. "Yes, it might." They nodded, having made a bargain neither of them had mentioned.

When she was in New Orleans, Anne Colleton had thought she would be glad to get home to South Carolina. Now that she was back in her beloved Marshlands, she often wished she'd stayed in Louisiana.

Even the trend-setting exhibition of modern art she'd arranged, the trend-setting artists who'd crossed the Atlantic to exhibit their works, now seemed more albatross than triumph. She set hands on hips and spoke to Marcel Duchamp in irritable, almost accent-free French: "*Monsieur,* you are not the only one who regrets that the outbreak of war has left you here rather than in Paris, where you would rather be. I agree: it is a great pity. But it is not something over which I have any say. Do you understand this?"

Before replying, Duchamp took a long drag at the skinny cigarillo in his hand; he used smoking as a sort of punctuation to his speech. He made everything he did, no matter how trivial, as dramatic as he could. Exhaling a long, thin plume of smoke the February sunlight—tolerably warm here—illuminated, he spoke in mournful tones: "I am confined here. Is that what you do not understand, *Mademoiselle* Colleton? This is the only word I can use—trapped like a beast in jaws of steel. Soon I shall have to gnaw off a limb to escape." He made as if to bite at his own wrist.

I haven't got the time to deal with this now, Anne thought. Aloud, she said, "You did not sound this way when you accepted my invitation—and my money—to come to the Confederate States last summer."

"I had not thought I would be here an eternity!" Duchamp burst out. "What is bearable—forgive me: what is pleasant—for a time in the end becomes unpleasant, imprisoning."

"Ships sail for England and France from Charleston every week, *Monsieur* Duchamp," Anne said in frigid tones. "You are not held here without bond, as if you were a Negro criminal. You have but to use the return fare I gave you when you came here. I would not have you stay where you feel unwelcome."

Duchamp paced back and forth, so swiftly that he almost appeared to be many places at once, as if he were the inspiration for his own *Nude Descending a Staircase*. Anne Colleton judged that much of his agitation was real. "Yes," he said. "Ships do sail. You have reason there. But it is also true that they reach their intended ports far less often than a prudent man would wish."

"Even prudence is not always prudent," Anne replied. "What did Danton say before the Legislative Assembly? *L'audace, encore l'audace, toujours l'audace*. If you wish so much to be gone, you will find the audacity to go."

The artist looked most unhappy. Anne smiled without moving her lips. He hadn't expected her to throw a quotation from the French Revolution in his face. Instead of answering her, he bowed and walked off, thin and dark and straight as his cigarillo.

Anne did smile then, but only for a moment. Duchamp would start being difficult again in another few days—unless, of course, he seduced a new serving wench, in which case he would imagine himself in love. But even if he did that, it wouldn't last long, either. The one constant about Marcel Duchamp was mutability.

In the Confederate States of America, mutability was not well thought of. The CSA tried to hold change to a minimum. If you shut your eyes just a little, the thought went, you could believe everything was as it had been before the War of Secession.

"We need to be reminded that isn't so," Anne murmured. "It just isn't." That was one of the reasons she'd arranged her exhibition: to make more people see what the twentieth century really meant. It was also one of the reasons the exhibition had been so deliciously scandalous.

But change had come to Marshlands in other ways, too, ways she didn't like so well. How was she supposed to raise a decent crop of cotton if her colored hands kept leaving the plantation to work in factories in Columbia and Spartanburg and even down in Charleston? *It's the war.* She'd heard that excuse so many times, she was sick of it.

And not even all her power, all her wealth, all her connections, had let her pull all her hands back to the fields. She'd had to raise what she paid to keep the drain from being worse than it was. That cut into her profits. And pay in the factories was going up, too. She scowled. She wasn't used to being in the position of wanting the good old days back again.

The front door opened and closed. Anne glanced at a clock. Half past eleven: time for the postman to come. She hurried toward the front hallway—and almost bumped into the butler, who was bringing the mail on a silver tray.

"Thank you, Scipio," she said, more warmly than she was in the habit of speaking to servants.

"My pleasure, madam," he replied, deep voice grave as usual.

She took the tray from him. His sober features were as familiar to her as anything else at Marshlands, and more comfortable than a lot of the furniture. She wondered for the briefest moment how she would run the plantation if Scipio took a position elsewhere. But no. It was inconceivable. Born and bred here, a fixture since the days when Negro slavery remained the law of the land, Scipio was as much a part of Marshlands as she was herself. *Nice to have something on which I can rely,* she thought.

After setting the tray on a stained mahogany table, she sorted rapidly through the mail. She discarded advertising circulars unread, as not deserving anything better. Invoices and correspondence pertaining to the business side of Marshlands she set aside for later consideration. That left half a dozen personal letters.

"Do you require anything else of me, madam?" Scipio asked.

He had already started to turn to go when Anne said, "Wait. As a matter of fact, I should like to discuss something with you in a few minutes." Obediently, the butler froze into immobility. He would stay frozen till she let him know he could move, however long that took.

To her disappointment, none of the letters was from her brothers. They were both in combat. Neither, so far, had been hurt, but she knew that was only by the grace of the God in Whom she believed so sporadically. Notes from friends and distant cousins were welcome, but could not take the place of news of her own flesh and blood.

And whom did she know in Guaymas? The grimy port and railroad town wasn't anyplace you'd want to go on holiday, especially not when the United States were still liable to cut the railroad line that linked it to the rest of the Confederacy. Making it back to civilization through the bandit-ridden hinterlands of the Empire of Mexico struck her as adventurous without being enjoyable.

Curious, she used a letter opener shaped like a miniature cavalry saber to slit the envelope. The letter inside was in the same firm, clear, unfamiliar hand as the outer address. *Dear Anne,* it read, *I hope this finds you as well as I found you on the train to New Orleans and in the town. As you will see, I remain there no longer, that not being a primary center for one of my training—not enough beasts to hunt. I can't say that here, having shot at several big ones and hit a few. Well, there's hunting and there's hunting, as the saying goes. I find I enjoy both kinds, and hope to pursue the other if I am ever out your way.* By contrast with the rest of the letter, the signature below was almost a scrawl: *Roger Kimball.*

Anne Colleton folded the letter again. The submariner had discretion; she gave him that much. No spy would be able to infer what he did from that letter. She could see why New Orleans was not a chief submarine base: the Gulf of Mexico being a Confederate lake, enemy ships were probably few and far between. Not so at Guaymas; the USA had a much longer Pacific coastline than the CSA.

No spy would be sure they'd been lovers, either. She worried about that less than most women might have, but it remained in her mind. She wondered whether to answer the letter or pretend she'd never got it. The latter choice was surely safer, but Anne had not got where she was by always playing safe. Either way, she didn't have to decide right now.

And, in fact, she didn't want to decide now. "Scipio," she said, and the butler began to move, seemingly began to breathe, for the first time since she'd started going through her mail. "Scipio," she repeated, gathering her thoughts, and then, "Do you know of anything special that's driving so many niggers out of the fields and into the factories? Besides money, I mean—I know what money does."

"I had not really thought about it, past endeavoring to see that we always have enough hands to perform the required labor," Scipio replied after a momentary hesitation: perhaps for thought, perhaps not.

Could she believe that? She did some fast thinking of her own, and decided she could. Scipio's duties centered on the mansion, and on keeping it and its staff in smooth working order. The field hands weren't his main concern. "Let me ask that another way," she said. "Have you noticed unusual unrest among any of the hands? I'm especially concerned about the new ones, you understand. I'm sure the bucks and wenches who've grown up on this plantation are contented with their lot: again, except possibly over money."

Scipio's dark, handsome features reflected nothing but meticulous attention to her words. So he had been trained, and no one could deny the training was a success. Not even Anne, who had caused that perfect mask to be made, could hope to lift up one edge, so to speak, and see what lay behind it. And his beautifully modulated voice revealed only a polite lack of curiosity as he replied, "Madam, I assure you I make every effort to weed out any undesirable influences before they find positions here. And, as you say, the loyalty of your longtime staff is of course unquestioning."

"Thank you, Scipio. You do relieve my mind," Anne said. With a gracious nod, she released him to pursue the rest of his duties. He'd told her exactly what she wanted to hear.

The Confederates had the U.S. soldiers exactly where they wanted them, or so they thought. Captain Irving Morrell wondered how—wondered if—he was going to prove them wrong. The war to which he'd returned two and a half months before bore only a faint resemblance to the one from which he'd been carried in Sonora back in August. For that matter, the heavily forested Kentucky hill country in which he was operating now wasn't anything like the dusty desert where he'd been wounded.

His leg throbbed. He ignored it, as he'd been ignoring it ever since he hiked out of Shelbiana. Somewhere ahead, a good many miles ahead, lay Jenkins right by the Virginia border. In between seemed to be nothing but mountains and valleys and tiny coal-mining towns and even tinier farming hamlets and enough Rebels with guns to make advancing slow, hard, painful work.

Atop the hill ahead and in the trenches at its base were enough Confederates not just to slow the U.S. advance but to bring it to a halt. With the lieutenants and sergeants under him, Morrell slipped from one tree to another, drawing as close to the Rebel line as he could.

The sergeants would have been doing that job anyhow, but both lieutenants—their names were Craddock and Buhl—looked notably unhappy. "See for yourself," Morrell said as they sheltered behind a gnarled oak. He spoke as if he were in the pulpit expounding on Holy Writ. "See for yourself. Without good reconnaissance, your force is only half as useful as it would be otherwise—sometimes less than half as useful."

They couldn't argue with him—he outranked them. But they didn't look convinced, either. It wasn't that they were cowards; he'd already seen them fighting with all the courage any superior officer could want from his men. What they lacked was imagination. The way the war was chewing up the officer corps, they'd make captain if they lived. He supposed they might even end up majors. He was damned, though, if he saw them going any further, not if the war lasted till they were ninety.

Bill Craddock pointed out to the cleared ground in front of the Confederate line. "How are we supposed to cross that, sir?" he said, clearly with the expectation that Morrell would have no answer. "Rebel machine guns'll chew us up like termites gnawing on an old house."

"We'll have to bring our own machine guns forward before we move," Morrell said. "We can bring them up within a hundred yards of their trenches, and concentrate our fire on the places where we want to break in. And . . . Lieutenant, have you ever gone down to the Empire of Mexico and watched a bullfight?"

"Uh—no, sir," Craddock answered. His broad, stolid face showed he hadn't the faintest idea what Morrell was driving at, either.

With a mental sigh, the captain explained: "The fellow in the bull ring has a sword. That doesn't sound like enough against an angry bull with sharp horns, does it? But he also has a cape. The cape can't hurt the bull, not in a million years. But it's bright and it's showy, and so the bull runs right at it—and the bullfighter sticks the sword in before the bull even notices."

Karl Buhl was marginally quicker than Craddock. "You want us to feint from one direction and hit them from the other, is that what you're saying, sir?"

Morrell glanced at his noncoms. They all understood what he was talking about without his having to draw them any pictures. Some of them were liable to end up with higher ranks than either of their present platoon commanders. But Buhl and Craddock were doing their best, so he answered, "That's right. We'll try going around the right flank, and then, as soon as they're all hot and bothered, the main force will come straight at 'em, with the machine guns delivering suppressive fire. We can assemble back there"—he pointed—"on the little reverse slope they've been kind enough to leave us."

Had he been commanding the Confederate defenders, he would have moved his line east from the base of the hill to the top of that reverse slope, so he'd have had men covering the ground Rebel bullets could not now reach. If the Rebs were going to be generous enough to give him a present like that, though, he wouldn't turn it down.

"Flanking party will attack at 0530 tomorrow morning," he said. "Buhl, you'll lead that one. We'll give you a couple of extra machine guns, too. If things go well, you won't be only a feint: your attack will turn into the real McCoy. You understand what you're to do?"

"Yes, sir," the lieutenant answered crisply. As long as you dotted all the i's and crossed all the t's for him, he did well enough.

"I'll lead the main force myself, starting at 0545," Morrell said. That left Craddock with no job but support. Morrell didn't care. For that matter, support mattered here, and could easily turn into something more. Crossing the open space toward the Confederate trenches was liable to get expensive in a hurry, and Craddock, however imperfectly qualified for company command, was liable to have it thrust upon him.

The reconnaissance party slid along the front for a while, then drifted back through the forest to where the rest of the company waited. An overeager sentry almost took a potshot at them before they would call out the password. When the soldier started to apologize, Morrell praised him for his alertness.

After darkness fell, Morrell guided the machine-gun crews forward to the positions he wanted them to take. That was nerve-wracking work; Confederate patrols were prowling the woods, too, and he had to freeze in place more than once to keep from giving away his preparations for the assault.

It was well past midnight when everything was arranged to his satisfaction. He returned to his soldiers, huddled without fire on that chilly reverse slope, and wrapped himself in his green wool blanket. Try as he would, sleep refused to come. Moving pictures kept running behind his eyes: all the different ways the attack might go, all the different things that could go wrong.

At 0500, his orderly, a scar-faced laconic fellow named Hanley, came to tap him on the shoulder. "I'm already awake," he whispered, and Hanley nodded and slipped away.

Just then, somebody fired a shot—a Tredegar by the sound of it, not a U.S. Springfield. The Rebel trenches came alive, with more gunfire ringing out. Morrell tensed, willing his men not to reply. They knew they shouldn't, but— After a couple of minutes, the Confederates stopped shooting. Somebody had seen a shadow he'd misliked, that was all.

Lieutenant Buhl got his half of the attack going at 0530 on the dot. He was, if uninspired, at least reliable. And, with a couple of machine guns yammering away for fire support, he sounded as if he had a hell of a lot more than a platoon's worth of men with him.

Morrell passed the word to the rest of his company: "All right, we move up now. No shooting unless the Rebs discover us, or until the time, whichever comes first. I'll skin the man who opens up too soon and gives us away."

Morning twilight was just beginning to seep through the branches of the trees. You could see a trunk a couple of paces before you'd walk into it, but not much farther than that.

The flank attack sounded as if it was going well, not only making progress but also, by the counterfire Morrell heard, drawing Rebels to their left, his right. He held his pocket watch up to his face. Another two minutes, another minute . . . He blew his whistle, a piercing blast easily audible through the racket of rifles and machine guns.

At the signal, the Maxims he'd sneaked up close to the Confederate lines started hammering at them. Morrell wouldn't have cared to be under machine-gun fire at what was as close to point-blank range as made little difference. Screams and cries of dismay said the Rebs didn't care for it, either.

"Narrow arc!" Morrell yelled. "Narrow arc!" The gunners were supposed to know that already; he'd told them their jobs the night before. If they made the Confederates stay under cover in the areas covered by those narrow arcs of fire, his men would have stretches of trench they could storm with minimal risk. If that didn't happen, his men would get slaughtered.

And so would he. He blew the whistle again, this time twice, burst from the cover of the woods, and ran, bad leg aching under him, toward the Confederate trenches. If you led like that, your soldiers had no excuse not to follow. Follow they did, yelling like so many madmen, firing their Springfields from the hip as they came. You weren't likely to hit anybody that way, but you made the fellows on the other team keep their heads down. That meant they couldn't do as much shooting at you.

A few bullets did crack past Morrell. He fired a couple of shots himself, but made sure he kept a round in the chamber for when he'd really need it. Faster than he imagined possible, he jumped down into the enemy trench.

Nobody waited there to bayonet him or fire at him while he was leaping. A Rebel with the top of his head neatly clipped off sprawled dead; another writhed and moaned, clutching a bleeding arm. But the only healthy Confederates were trying to get away, not fighting back.

One of his men hurled a grenade at the fleeing Rebs: a half-pound block of Triton explosive with sixteen-penny nails taped all around it, and with five seconds' worth of fuse hooked up to a blasting cap. Unlike guns, grenades could be used around corners and without showing yourself, which made them wonderfully handy for fighting in trenches. Talk was, the munitions factories would start making standardized models any day now. Till they did, improvised versions served well enough.

More grenades, more gunfire. A few Confederates kept fighting. More threw down their rifles and threw up their hands. And still more fled through the gulleys that ran east and south from their trench line.

"Shall we pursue, sir?" Lieutenant Craddock asked, panting. He had the look of a man who'd seen a rabbit pulled out of a hat he thought assuredly empty. Sounding happy but dazed, he went on, "We haven't lost but a man or two wounded, I don't think, and nobody killed."

"Good," Morrell said; it was, in fact, far better than he'd dared hope. After thinking for a moment, he shook his head. "No, Lieutenant, no pursuit, not in that terrain. The Rebs would rally and bushwhack us." He pointed ahead. "Where I want to be is the top of that hill. We control that, we control the countryside around it, too, and we can start flushing the Rebels out at our leisure."

Some of his men were already out of the Confederate trench lines and heading up the steep, rocky slopes. Around here, the elevation, which might have reached fifteen hundred feet, was reckoned a mountain; Morrell didn't like dignifying it with a name he didn't think it deserved. Whatever you called it, though, it was the high ground, and he intended to seize it. He scrambled out of the trench himself. He got to the top of the hill bare moments after the sun came out and let him see for miles. He pulled his watch out of his pocket and looked at it in some surprise: a few minutes past six. His part of the fight had taken only a bit more than twenty minutes. He put the watch back. He'd seen a couple of officers carrying pocket watches on leather straps round their wrists. That was more convenient than having to dig it out whenever you wanted to know the time. Maybe he'd do it himself one day soon.

"King of the mountain, sir," one of his soldiers said with a big grin.

"King of the mountain—such as it is," Morrell echoed, liking the sound of it. He would have liked it even better had the elevation been a more important conquest. But every little bit helped. Enough victories and you won the war. He rubbed his chin. "Now that we're up here, let's see what else we can do."

When Jefferson Pinkard and Bedford Cunningham came back to their side-by-side cottages after another day at the foundry, their wives were standing out in front, talking. The grass was still brown, but would be going green soon; spring wasn't that far away. That wasn't so unusual; Fanny and Emily were good friends, if not so tight together as their husbands, and Emily Pinkard had helped Fanny get a job at the munitions plant where she was already working.

What was unusual was the buff-colored envelope Fanny held in her left hand. Only one outfit used paper that color: the Confederate Conscription Bureau. Jeff recognized the envelope for what it was before his friend did, but kept his mouth shut. You didn't want to be the one who gave your buddy news like that.

Then Bed Cunningham spotted the CCB envelope. He stopped in his tracks. Pinkard walked on a couple of steps before he stopped, too. "Oh, hell," Cunningham said. He shook his head in profound disgust. "They went and called me up, the sons of bitches."

"It'll be me next," Pinkard said, offering what consolation he could.

"It's not that I'm afraid to go or anything like that," Cunningham said. "You know me, Jeff—I ain't yellow." Jefferson Pinkard nodded, for that was true. His friend went on, "Hell and damnation, though, ain't I worth more to the country here in Birmingham than I am somewhere on the front line totin' a rifle? Any damn fool can do that, but how many folks can make steel?"

"Not enough," Pinkard said. Like a lot of men, he'd picked up almost an attorney's knowledge of the way wartime conscription worked. "You could appeal it, Bed. If the local Bureau board won't listen to you, I bet the governor would."

But Cunningham gloomily shook his head. He'd kept his ear to the ground when it came to conscription, too. "Heard tell the other day how often the governor overrules the CCB when it comes to suckin' people into the Army. Three and a half percent of the time, that's it. Hell, three and a half percent don't even make good beer."

"I missed that one," Jeff Pinkard admitted.

"Three and a half percent," Cunningham repeated with morose satisfaction. "States' rights ain't like what it was in the War of Secession, when a governor could stand up and spit in Jeff Davis' eye and he'd have to take it. Don't dare do that no more, not with everybody so beholden to Richmond.

Sorry damn world we live in, when a governor ain't any better'n the president's nigger, but that's how it goes."

Slowly, they went on to Cunningham's walk and headed up it together. The expressions on their wives' faces took away any doubt about what might have been in the CCB envelope. Bedford Cunningham took it out of Fanny's hand, removed the paper inside, and read the typewritten note before crumpling it up and throwing it on the ground.

"When do you have to report?" Pinkard asked, that seeming the only question still open.

"Day after tomorrow," Cunningham answered. "They give a man a lot of time to get ready, now don't they?"

"It's not right," Fanny Cunningham said. "It's not fair, not even a little bit."

"Fair is for when you're rich," her husband answered. "All I could do is the best I could. We'll get by all right now that you're workin', honey. I didn't like the notion, I tell you that much, but it's turned out pretty good." He set a hand on Jefferson Pinkard's shoulder. "You're the one I feel sorry for, Jeff."

"Me?" Pinkard scratched his head. "I'm just goin' on doin' what I always did. They ain't messed with me, way they have with you."

"Not yet they ain't, but they're gonna, an' quicker'n you think." Cunningham sounded very certain, and proceeded to explain why: "All right, I take off my overalls an' they deck me out in butternut. Foundry work's got to go on, though—we all know that. *Who they gonna get to take my place?*"

Emily Pinkard saw what that meant before her husband did. "Oh, lordy," she said softly.

The light went on in Jeff's head a moment later. "They ain't gonna put no nigger on day shift," he exclaimed, but he didn't sound certain, even to himself.

"Hope you're right," Cunningham said. "I won't be around here to see it, one way or the other. You drop me a line, though, once I find out where my mail should head to, and you tell me whether I'm right or whether I'm wrong. Bet you a Stonewall I'm right." The Confederate five-dollar goldpiece bore Jackson's fierce, bearded image.

They shook hands on the bet, solemnly. Pinkard thought he was likelier to lose it than win, but made it anyhow. Five dollars wouldn't break him, and they'd come in handy to a private bringing in less than a dollar a day.

Muttering under his breath, Cunningham led Fanny into their house. The evening breeze picked up the conscription notice and skirled it away. Emily and Jeff walked across the lawn to their own cottage, up the steps, and inside. They were both very quiet over the chicken stew Emily served up for supper. Afterwards, when Jefferson got a pipe going, Emily said hesitantly, "Jeff, they wouldn't really put a nigger alongside you—would they?"

Pinkard savored a mouthful of honeyed tobacco before he answered, "You ask me that last year, before the war started, I'd've laughed till I ripped a seam in my britches—either that or I'd've grabbed me a shotgun and loaded it with double-aught buck. Nowadays, though, the war goin' like it is, suckin' up white men like a sponge sucks up water, who the devil knows what they'll do?"

"If they do . . . what'll you do?"

"Gotta make the steel. Gotta win the war," he said after some thought. "Don't win the damn war, nothin' else matters. Nigger don't get uppity, reckon I have to work with him—for now. Come the day the war's over, though, comes the day of payin' back debts. I got me a vote, an' I know what to do with it. Gets bad enough, I got me a gun, too, an' I know what to do with that."

Slowly, Emily nodded. "I like the way you got o' lookin' at things, honey."

"Wish there were some things I didn't have to look at," Pinkard said. "Maybe we're all wrong. Maybe I'll win that Stonewall from Bed after all. Never can tell."

Word of Cunningham's call to the colors spread fast. All the next day, people came by the foundry floor with flasks and bottles and jars of home-cooked whiskey. The foremen looked the other way, except when they swung by to grab a nip themselves. If any of them knew who was going to replace Cunningham, they kept their mouths shut.

The day after that, Pinkard walked to Sloss Foundry by himself, which seemed strange. His head pounded as if someone were pouring molten metal in there, then rolling and trip-hammering it into shape. He'd done more drinking after he and Bed got home. Hangovers made some men mean. He didn't feel mean, just drained, empty, as if part of his world had been taken away.

He got to the foundry on time, hangover or no hangover. There waiting for him stood Agrippa and Vespasian, the two Negroes who were his and Bedford Cunningham's night-shift counterparts. However wrong having them around had seemed at first, he'd grown used to it. Most days, he'd nod when he came on and even stand around shooting the breeze with them before they went home to get some sleep, almost as if they'd been white men.

He didn't nod this morning. His face went hard and tight, as if he were in a saloon and getting ready for a fight. Three black men stood waiting for him today, not just two. "Mornin', Mistuh Pinkard," Vespasian said. Agrippa echoed him a moment later. They knew what he had to be thinking.

"Mornin'," Pinkard said curtly. The moment had really come. He hadn't believed it. No, he hadn't wanted to believe it. It was here anyhow. What was he supposed to do about it? Before it turned true, telling your wife you'd stay was easy. Now— Should he stand up on his hind legs and go home? If he didn't do that, he'd have to stay here, and if he stayed here, he'd have to work side by side with this Negro.

"Mistuh Pinkard, this here's Pericles," Vespasian said, nodding at the black man Jeff hadn't seen before.

"Mornin', Mistuh Pinkard," Pericles offered. Like all the Negroes Sloss Foundry had hired since the war began, he was a big, strapping buck, with muscles hard and thick from years in the cotton fields. He couldn't have been more than twenty-one or twenty-two; he had open, friendly features and a thin little mustache you could hardly see against his dark skin.

Years in the cotton fields . . . Pinkard almost demanded to see his passbook. Odds were, Pericles had no legal right to be anywhere but on a plantation. But the same probably held true for Agrippa and Vespasian, and for most of the other newly hired Negroes at the foundry. If the inspectors ever started checking hard, they'd shut the Sloss works down—and the steel had to be made.

"He kin do the work, Mr. Pinkard," Vespasian said. "We been learnin' him on nights, so he be ready if the time come." He hesitated, then added, "He be my wife's cousin. I vouch for him, I surely do."

Fish or cut bait, Jeff thought. Damn it to hell, how could you walk out on your job when your country was in the middle of a war? You had to win first; then you figured out what was supposed to happen next—he'd had that much right, talking with Emily the night before. "Let's get to work," he said.

"Thank you, Mr. Pinkard," Vespasian breathed. Pinkard didn't answer. Vespasian and Agrippa didn't push him. Even if things were changing, they knew better than that. They nodded to Pericles and headed off the floor.

For the first couple of hours after his shift started, Pinkard didn't say word one to Pericles. When he wanted the Negro to go somewhere or do something, he pointed. Pericles did as he was directed, not with any great skill—a few nights' watching and pitching in couldn't give you that—but with willing enthusiasm.

When Pinkard finally did speak, it wasn't aimed at Pericles, but at the world at large, the same useless complaint Fanny Cunningham had made the night before: "It ain't fair."

"Mistuh Pinkard?" Pericles didn't know how to talk under the foundry floor racket; he bellowed to get permission to speak himself. When Jeff nodded, the Negro said, still loudly, "Fair is for when you're white folks. I can only do the best job I know how."

Pinkard chewed on that for a while. It sounded a hell of a lot like what his friend had said a couple of nights before. When you were down, everybody above you looked to have it easy. When you were a Negro, you were always down, and everybody was above you. He'd never really thought of it in those terms before. After a bit, he shoved the idea aside. It made him uncomfortable.

But he did start talking with Pericles after that. Some things you couldn't explain with just your hands, and some things Bedford Cunningham would have done without thinking were just the sort of things Pericles didn't know, any more than any other new hire would have. The Negro caught on fast enough to keep Pinkard from snarling at him.

A couple of times, Pericles tried to talk about things that weren't directly tied to the job. Pinkard stonily ignored those overtures. Answering back, he thought, would have been like a woman cooperating with her ravisher. After a while, Pericles gave up. But then, when the closing whistle blew, he said, "G'night, Mr. Pinkard. See you in the mornin'."

"Yeah," Pinkard said, his mouth out in front of his brain. *What the hell?* he thought as he walked home alone. *Didn't do any real harm. Maybe I'll even say "Mornin' " tomorrow—but nothin' after that, mind.*

Chester Martin knew the Roanoke River lay only a few hundred yards ahead, though he also knew better—much better—than to stick his head up and see just how close the river was. The latest U.S. push had moved the battle line in western Virginia forward into the suburbs of Big Lick again. A couple of more pushes and they'd be over the river at last so they could clean out the eastern side of the Roanoke valley.

"That's what Captain Wyatt says, anyhow," Martin remarked to Paul Andersen, summarizing the latest Army bulletins. "You believe it any more than I do?"

"Hell, no, Sarge," the corporal answered. "What's gonna happen next is, the Rebs'll put on a push of their own, knock us halfway back to Catawba Mountain again. You wait and see."

"*I'm* not gonna argue with you," Martin said. "We push them, they push us, we push them some more . . . These lines aren't going to move more than a couple of miles either way from now till doomsday, doesn't look like." He wished he hadn't said *doomsday*. Too many men with whom he'd started the war—too many replacements, too—had already found their doom here.

"I can see it in the fancy history some fool will write after the war," Andersen said: "you know, some educated fool, the kind who wears those spectacles that stick on your nose but don't have any side pieces to hook 'em to your ears. He'll talk about the thirty-seventh battle of the Roanoke, and that'll be us pushin' the Rebs back a ways, and then he'll talk about the thirty-eighth battle of the Roanoke two weeks later, and that'll be the Rebs kickin' us back to where we started from, and maybe another half a mile besides."

"That all sounds pretty likely," Martin agreed. "I just hope to Jesus we ain't any of the ones who get buried before that thirty-eighth battle." Most of the time, you didn't like to think about such things, not when the whole battlefield stank of death to the point where, if you weren't used to it and just fell here from, say, Philadelphia, you'd puke your guts up for a week. It wasn't cold enough to fight the stink, as it had been a few weeks before.

"Heads up." Andersen pointed down the trench. "Visiting fireman coming this way."

Sure enough, here came Captain Wyatt with a fellow Martin hadn't seen before, an older man wearing a major's uniform cleaner than those of most soldiers who actually made their living in the front lines. *Some sort of inspector, snooping around to see what he thinks we've done all wrong,* Martin thought. He hated people like that, hated them with the cold contempt a practical man gives a theoretician's high-flown, useless notions.

He started to laugh, and turned his face away so the new major, whoever he was, wouldn't see. The fellow had spectacles just like the ones to which Paul Andersen had slightingly referred, and a sandy mustache heavily streaked with gray, and a mouth full of big, square teeth . . .

Chester Martin's head whipped around. It couldn't be, but it was. Andersen was staring and staring. Captain Wyatt said, "Boys, here's the President of the United States, come to see the war for himself."

Martin hadn't come to attention in the front-line trenches in months. Now he stiffened to straightness so suddenly, his backbone cracked like knuckles. Beside him, Andersen also came to a stiff brace. "At ease," Teddy Roosevelt said. "As you were. I came here to see soldiers, not marionettes."

"Yes, *sir*!" Martin relaxed, though not all the way. If the battlefield stench bothered TR, he didn't let on. He acted like a soldier, though he hadn't led troops into battle in thirty years or so. But he really could have been an elderly major, not just some politician posturing for the newspapers.

As if picking that thought out of Martin's mind, Roosevelt said, "Reporters don't know I'm here. Far as they know—which isn't far, believe me, not with most of them—I'm still in Philadelphia. If the papers don't know, maybe the Rebs don't know. You think they wouldn't like to put one between my eyes?"

"Yes, sir, they sure would," Martin said. If the Confederates did know the president was here, they'd do everything they could to keep him from getting away again.

"This isn't what war was like out on the plains back before you were born," Roosevelt said. "There was glory in that, the sweep of horses rushing forward, movement, adventure. This . . . The most I can say for this, gentlemen, is that it's necessary, and what we gain from it will make certain that the United States of America take their proud and rightful place among the nations of the world once more."

When you listened to the president talking, you forgot the reek of unburied bodies, the mud, the lice, the barbed wire, the machine guns. You saw farther than your length of trench. You got a glimpse of the country that would come out the other side of this war. It was a place where you wanted to be, too.

Yeah, and what are the odds of that? asked the part of Martin that had been under fire for months. *Do you really think you're going to come through alive, or with all your arms and legs if you do live?*

Captain Wyatt said, "We hope, sir, that the next offensive will bring us up to the river, and from there we'll proceed toward the Blue Ridge Mountains."

"Bully," TR said. "Our German allies have offensives in the works, too. With God's help, they'll strike the French and the English a heavy blow on the continent." He shook his head. "I don't know what we would have done without Germany, boys. With England and France backing up the Rebels, we were fighting out of our weight when we tried to scrap with them. Not now, though, by jingo, not now."

"Yes, sir," Martin said. "We have friends in high places, eh?"

"The All-Highest place," TR answered with his famous chuckle, still boyish though he was in his mid-fifties. "Kaiser Wilhelm's done everything he could for us, and we've paid him back, thanks to soldiers like you men."

Martin didn't stand straighter now; Roosevelt had ordered him to be at his ease. But he felt tall and proud just the same. Again, TR made him believe the war had a point, a goal, beyond the miseries of the front. He wondered how long he'd go on believing that once the president left.

A few hundred yards off, a couple of U.S. machine guns started hammering away at some Confederate target or other. Rifle fire answered from the Rebel lines, and then their machine guns. After a few minutes, U.S. field guns started pounding the enemy's forward trenches.

Captain Wyatt frowned. "They shouldn't be doing that, not now. It's going to bring down—"

"Captain, I didn't come here to watch a Sunday-school debating society," President Roosevelt said. "This is war. I know what war is. I—"

Before he could finish, the Confederates' quick-firing three-inch guns started raining shells down, on and near the U.S. front lines. The Rebs seldom wasted time replying to an artillery bombardment.

Paul Andersen threw himself flat, Captain Wyatt threw himself flat. To Martin's horror, he saw TR start to stand up on a firing step so he could get a better look at what was going on. Without thinking, he knocked the president down with a block from behind that would have been illegal in a football match, then flopped over TR's squirming body. "Stay flat, dammit!" he shouted. He'd never expected to have the president's ear. Now that he did, this was what he got to tell him? It would have been funny if he hadn't worried about getting killed.

Shrapnel balls and jagged bits of shell casing whined through the air. Bigger U.S. guns started firing, trying to silence the Confederate field pieces. Bigger Rebel guns struck back at the bigger U.S. guns. Both sides forgot about the men at the front for a while.

Warily, Chester Martin sat up. That let TR get up, too. Martin gulped, wondering what the penalty was for leveling the president. But all Roosevelt said was, "Thank you, Sergeant. You know conditions here better than I."

"Uh, thank you, sir." Martin looked at Roosevelt, whose green-gray uniform was now as muddy as his own. "You look like a real, modern soldier now, sir." The president of the United States laughed like a man possessed.

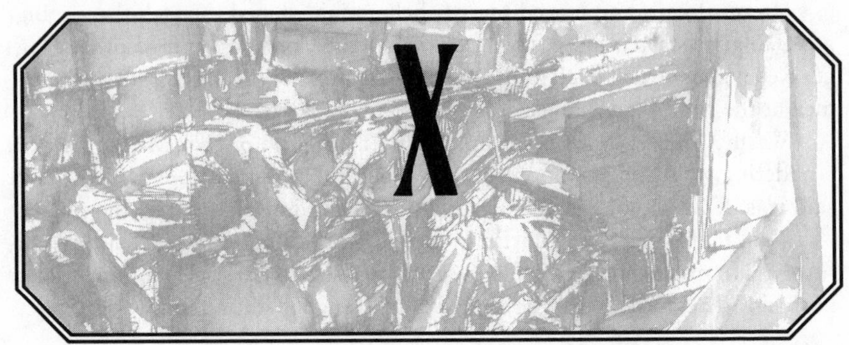

X

Lucien Galtier muttered unhappily to himself as he loaded the jug of kerosene into the back of his wagon. The ration the American soldiers allowed people was ridiculously small. Thank God, nights were shorter now than they had been in the middle of winter, but he still had to leave a lot of his lamps dry. The world, he was convinced, held no justice.

"No, it certainly is not fair," he told his horse, which, for once, forbore to argue with him. "When a man comes into a town, he cannot even buy for himself a drink of a sort he cannot get at home."

Strictly speaking, that wasn't true. None of the taverns in Rivière-du-Loup had signs up ordering—or even advising—townsmen and local farmers to stay out. Nor were the taverns out of liquor; a lot of their stock these days was shipped up from the United States, but that did not mean it would not burn in your boiler. Drinks, in fact, were actually cheaper these days than they had been before the war started, because the occupying authority taxed liquor at a lower rate than the provincial government had.

All of which was silver lining on a large, dark cloud. If you went into a tavern, you were almost certain to find it full of American soldiers, which was the reason the occupying authority held down liquor prices. And American soldiers, especially American soldiers with drink in them, did not take kindly to sharing what they thought of as their taverns with the locals.

"Oh, you might go in, have a whiskey, and get out again," Lucien said. His horse's ears twitched, perhaps in sympathy but more likely, knowing the beast, in mockery. "But if there should be a fight, what is one to do? There are always many soldiers, they are always all against you, and, even if your countrymen come to your aid, it leads merely to riot and then to punishment of the entire unfortunate town. All this for one little drink? It is not worth it!"

The horse snorted. Maybe that meant it agreed Maybe that meant it thought Galtier was complaining too much, too. If it did, too bad. He could complain to the horse without worrying his wife—and without making her angry, too, for she was less than delighted when he went into a tavern even for one whiskey, her fixed view of the matter being that no one ever went into a tavern for only one whiskey.

Galtier was just climbing up into the wagon when, from behind him, a cheery voice said, "God bless you, Lucien."

He turned. "Oh. Good day to you, Father Pascal. Pardon me, if you please. I did not hear you come up. I am desolate."

"There is no need to apologize, my son," Father Pascal said with an amiable wave of his hand. "You are full of your own concerns, as any busy man would of course be." He studied Galtier. His black eyes, though set rather close together, were clever and keen. "I pray your affairs march well?"

"They march well enough, thank you, Father." Lucien would complain to his horse. He would complain to his wife. He would not complain to Father Pascal. These past months, he had even taken to editing his confessions, which he knew imperiled his soul but which helped keep his mortal flesh secure. Father Pascal was too friendly to the Americans to suit him.

"I am glad to hear that." The priest salted his words with the lightest sprinkling of irony. Lucien sometimes thought he talked like a lawyer. Father Pascal went on, "I am glad to see you have survived a winter difficult in so many ways."

"Yes, I have survived," Galtier agreed. *I would have done better than that had the Americans whom you love so well not stolen everything that would have let me get through with something more than bare survival.*

"And your family, they are all thriving?" Father Pascal asked.

"We are well, thank you, yes." No one had starved, no one had come down with tuberculosis or rheumatic fever. Was that thriving? Lucien didn't know, not for certain. Whatever doubts he had, though, he would not admit to the priest.

Father Pascal raised his hands in a gesture of benediction. His palms were pink and plump and soft, with none of the calluses ridging Galtier's hands. His nails were clean, and not a one of them broken. Truly, he lived a different life from that of a farmer.

"God be praised they are well," he said, turning his clever eyes toward heaven for a moment. "And how do your prospects seem for the coming year?"

"Who can guess?" Lucien said with a shrug. "The course of our health, the course of the weather, the course of the war—all these things are in God's hands, not mine." *There. Now I have been pious for him. Maybe he will go away.*

But Father Pascal did not go away. "In God's hands. Yes. We are all in God's hands. The course of the war—who can guess the course of the war? But then, who would have guessed a year ago the Americans would be here?"

"You are right in that regard, Father," Galtier said. Some priests might have compared the coming of the Americans to the Ten Plagues God had visited upon the Egyptians. Father Pascal didn't. Every line on his chubby, well-fed face said he was content with the military government.

Maybe Lucien let some of that thought show on his own face: a mistake. Father Pascal said, "I am but a humble religious, a priest of God. Who the secular ruler over my parish may be is not my concern."

Father Pascal was a great many things, but humble was none of them. Was he lying, or did he think of himself so? Galtier couldn't tell. "Certainly, Father, I understand," he said, still seeking a polite way out of this meeting.

"I am so glad you do," the priest said heartily, laying one of those smooth, well-manicured hands on Lucien's arm. "For too many people, impartiality is often mistaken for its opposite. Do you believe it, I am often accused of favoring the Americans?"

Yes, I believe that. I have good reason to believe that. "What a pity," Galtier said, but he could not bring himself to shake off Father Pascal's hand, climb into the wagon, and get away as fast as he could. That might arouse suspicion, too.

"If you should hear this vicious lie, I beg of you, give it no credit," Father Pascal said, with such earnestness in his voice that for a moment Lucien wondered whether what everyone said was wrong. But then the priest continued, "Should you hear such calumnies, my son, I would be in your debt if you would be generous enough to inform me who has spoken them, that I may pray for the salvation of his soul."

"Of course, Father," Lucien said. Clocks in the church towers began chiming eleven, which gave him the excuse he needed. "Father, forgive me, but I have a long ride back to my farm, and the hour is later than I thought."

"I would not keep you. Go with God." Smiling, sleek, doing ever so well under the new regime, Father Pascal went on down the street with the determined strides of a man who has important places to go, important things to do. He nodded to two American soldiers and then to an old woman in mourning black.

"Does he think me a simpleton, a cretin?" Lucien asked his horse when they were well out of Rivière-du-Loup and the animal's ears were the only ones that could hear. "Tell me who is saying bad things about me and I will pray for him, he says. He will pray, by God: pray that the Americans catch the poor fellow. And he will tell the American commandant, to help make his prayers come true. What do you think of that, my old?"

The horse did not answer. The Lord had not chosen to do for it as He had once for Balaam's ass.

To Lucien's silent, patient audience of one, he went on, "A simpleton? A cretin? No, he thinks me worse than that. He thinks me a collaborator, as he is himself. And this, this is what I think of him." He leaned over the side of the wagon and spat in the dirt. The very idea offended him. Why would anyone collaborate with the Americans?

Whenever Scipio went to Cassius' cottage, he went with fear and trembling in his heart. The fear was not a simple one, which only made it tougher to deal with. Half the time, he was afraid the mistress had found out what he was doing and that white patrollers—or maybe white soldiers—with rifles and bayonets and dogs with long sharp teeth were on his trail. The other half, he was afraid Cassius and his fellow would-be revolutionaries had somehow divined he was not heart and soul with them in their Red fervor, and that they were going to get rid of him because of that.

Sometimes, too, he carried both fears at once. In odd moments, he tried to figure out which was deeper, more compelling. It was like trying to decide whether you'd rather be hanged or shot—*just like that,* he thought uncomfortably. When all your choices were bad, did worse matter?

Here was the cottage. He felt conspicuous coming out to the huts in his fancy butler's livery, though he'd been doing it for years. He'd been passing a good deal of time in Cassius' cottage for years, too. He kept telling himself no one should notice anything amiss. Making himself believe it was harder. Never till the previous fall had he done the kinds of things in this cottage he was doing now.

He knocked. "That you, Kip?" came the question from within: Cassius' voice.

"This me," Scipio agreed, swallowing the misery he dared not show.

The door opened. There stood Cassius. "Come in wid we," he said, smiling, slim, strong, dangerous as a water moccasin in the swamps. "Set a spell. We talk about things, you 'n' me."

"We do dat," Scipio said, and stepped into the cabin. He never saw anyone there but the people who had been reading *The Communist Manifesto* together the night he'd found out they weren't just laborers but Reds. That made sense; the less he knew, the less he could betray.

"Wet yo' whistle?" Cassius asked, and pointed to a jug of corn whiskey sitting up on the mantel.

Scipio started to shake his head, but found himself nodding instead. Cassius handed him the jug. He took a long pull. The raw, illegal whiskey ran down his throat like a river of fire and exploded in his belly.

The woman named Cherry said, “You he’p we learn dese prayers, Kip?” She handed him a paperbound book with an orange cover. The printing on that cover did indeed proclaim it a tract, just as the blue-covered book that had got him into this mess had said it was a hymnbook. You couldn’t tell a book by its cover, though, not in Cassius’ cottage you couldn’t.

Island and a couple of other people did start to sing hymns, in case anybody was snooping around outside. Under cover of their racket, Cassius sat down by Scipio at the rickety table in his cottage and bent over the book with the orange cover with him. The hunter’s finger pointed out a passage. “Read dat,” he said.

Obediently, Scipio’s eyes went back and forth. *Labor is prior to, and independent of, capital,* he read. *Capital is only the fruit of labor, and could never have existed if labor had not first existed. Labor is the superior of capital, and deserves much the higher consideration.*

“What you think o’ that there?” Cassius asked.

“All fit in wid everything else,” Scipio answered. “Sound like de trut’.” He almost slipped out of the dialect of the Congaree; the words he’d just read did not fit in with that ignorant speech.

Cassius’ finger—scarred, callused—found another place. “Now you read dat.”

We all declare for liberty; but in using the same word *we do not all mean the same* thing, Scipio read. *With some, the word means for each man to do as he pleases with himself, and with the product of his labor. With others, the same word means for some men to do as they please with other men, and the product of other men’s labor. The fullness of time, I am convinced, will prove to the world which is the true definition of the word, and my earnest hope remains that the United States of America shall yet lead the way in the proving.*

“Who write this?” Scipio asked. A lot of what he’d read here had the taste of being translated from a foreign language. Not this; it was simple and direct and powerful, English as it was meant to be written. One of the things he’d acquired serving Anne Colleton, and which he discovered he could not simply abandon, was a sense of style.

Cassius’ eyes gleamed with amusement. “Same fellow write the other.”

Scipio gave the hunter a dirty look. Cassius enjoyed leading him around by the nose, the same way he enjoyed all reversals and practical jokes. Cassius also enjoyed having an intellectual advantage on him. Scipio had never believed Cassius did much thinking at all. He hadn’t even known the hunter could read. He’d turned out to be wrong. Cassius’ thought was anything but wide-ranging, but in its track it ran deep.

Patiently, Scipio asked the next question. “And who that is? Not them Marx and Engels fellers, I bet.”

Everybody looked at him. When your thought ran in a narrow track, and ran deep in that track, climbing up and peering over the edge became suspicious. These Reds despised the way all the white folks in the Confederate States thought alike. But if any of their own number presumed to deviate from their doctrine, he got in just as much trouble, maybe more.

"Why for you say dat?" Cherry demanded. She looked as if she wanted to drop Scipio in the Congaree swamp right then and there.

He wished he'd kept his mouth shut. He'd wished that a lot of times around these people. But, since he hadn't, he had to answer the question: "It ain't wrote like t'other stuff I read."

Cassius laughed. "Got we a *per*fesser here. But is he *dat* smart?" He shook his head. "No, or he know who do dat work." Unlike a lot of jokers, he knew when to cut a joke short, as he did now. "These words wrote by Abraham Lincoln."

"Lincoln? Do Jesus!" Scipio thumped his forehead with the heel of his hand. "Should cipher that out my own self."

"He see the truth early on," Cassius said. "He say that first one while he president of the USA, an' de second one years after, in Montana Territory."

"Do Jesus!" Scipio said again, impressed. Lincoln had served only one term as president of the United States; he'd been unceremoniously booted out of office after the Confederacy broke away from the USA. But he hadn't left politics even then. He'd led most of the Republicans into union with the Socialist Party after the Second Mexican War. "No wonder he sound like one o' we."

Cassius nodded strong agreement. "Dat man be alive today, he *wid* we. He want ev'body equal. Only way to do dat, make de revolution. Cain't do it no ways else. Git de 'pressors off we, we do swell. Whole country do swell."

He and his revolutionary cohorts all nodded, like the preacher and the congregation in church on Sunday morning. Scipio made sure he nodded, too. If you didn't pay attention to the preacher, he gave you a hard time later. If you didn't pay attention to Cassius, he gave you a funeral.

Now he said, "Miss Anne, she talk wid any new strange white folks? They after our scent like hounds. We got to watch sharp."

"Nobody new I see," Scipio answered truthfully. Then he asked, "How they after we?" From the moment he'd first set eyes on the deadly words of *The Communist Manifesto*, he'd known what sort of game he was playing and what its likely outcome would be, but he didn't like Cassius reminding him of it.

The hunter—the Red—said, "They done cotched a few o' we: Army niggers get careless, talk too much where de white folks hear. Sometimes you catch one, he know de name o' 'nudder one, and *he* know *two* more names—"

That picture was clearer than any Marcel Duchamp had ever painted. Scipio wanted to get up and run somewhere far away from Marshlands. As Anne Colleton's butler, he had a passbook that gave him more legal freedom of movement than any other Negro on the plantation. He wasn't very much afraid of the patrollers' catching up to him. But if he tried to disappear, it was all too likely Cassius' revolutionaries would hunt him down and dispose of him. He imagined Red cells in every group of blacks in the Confederacy. What one knew, all would know; whom one wanted dead, all would work to kill . . .

Cassius said, "De day don' wait much longer. De revolution happen, an' de revolution happen *soon*. We rise up, we get what dey hol' back from we fo' so long. De white folks want de cotton, let de white folks grow de cotton an' grub it out o' de groun'. Dey don't 'sploit us no mo', never again."

Scipio did keep his mouth shut, though that meant biting down on the inside of his lip till he tasted blood. The white folks weren't going to sit around peaceable and quiet when the rebellion started. He'd tried saying that a few times, but nobody wanted to listen to him.

He wondered if he could get into the Empire of Mexico some kind of way, and never, ever come back.

Marching with a hangover was not Paul Mantarakis' idea of fun. It did, however, beat the stuffing out of going into a front-line trench to be shot at and shelled. He'd be doing that soon enough—much too soon to suit him. Any time between the current moment and forever would have been much too soon to suit him.

A couple of men away from Mantarakis, Gordon McSweeney tramped along singing "A Mighty Fortress Is Our God." McSweeney had a big bass voice and couldn't have carried a tune in a washtub. His booming false notes made Mantarakis' headache worse.

You couldn't just tell him to put a sock in it, though, however much you wanted to. If you did, you'd find yourself facing a couple of hundred pounds of angry, fanatical Scotsman. Guile was called for.

Even hung over, guile Mantarakis had. "That was a good leave, wasn't it, Gordon?" he said.

Addressed directly, McSweeney felt obliged to answer, which meant he stopped singing: the point to the exercise in guile. "Indeed, a good leave," he said seriously—he was always serious, except when he was furious. "I prayed harder, I think, than I ever have before."

"Dice weren't going your way, eh?" Mantarakis knew that was a mistake, but couldn't resist. The idea of praying in a town like Dixon, Kentucky, after it had become a U.S. Army leave center tickled his sense of the absurd.

"I do not gamble," McSweeney said indignantly. "I do not poison my body and my spirit with spirituous liquors, and I do not consort with loose, vile, immoral women."

Sergeant Peterquist was marching along a couple of men over on McSweeney's other side. Grinning, he said, "Sort of takes a lot of the point out of going on leave, doesn't it?"

"I will not be mocked," McSweeney said, about as close as he dared come to telling his sergeant to go to hell. He was bigger than Peterquist, and meaner, too, but Mantarakis would have bet on the noncom if they ever tangled. Peterquist was a sneaky bastard. He would have made a pretty fair Greek, Paul thought, meaning it as a compliment.

Ignoring McSweeney, the sergeant asked Mantarakis, "You go to a house with white girls or colored?"

"Colored," Mantarakis answered. "It was cheaper. And you go to any place like that, white or colored, you ain't lookin' for anything special, just to get the lead out of your pencil. Had a little more money to drink with."

McSweeney started singing his hymn again, louder than ever, so he wouldn't have to listen to his comrades' lewd conversation. Peterquist looked at Mantarakis. They both grinned ruefully. Maybe neither of them made a good Greek—they should have been able to figure out what the effect of talking about going to a whorehouse would have on the pious McSweeney. But when you were coming out of Dixon, what was on your mind (unless you were pious) was all the different ways you'd had a good time.

The countryside looked as if hell had been there, but had gone away on vacation. Like every inch of Kentucky in U.S. hands, it had been fought over, but that had been the fall and winter before. New grass was beginning to spring up, hiding the worst scars of the fighting.

Even the town of Beulah, Kentucky, eight or nine miles north of the front, didn't look too bad. It had also been in U.S. hands, and out of Confederate artillery range, most of that time, though the Rebel offensive coming up out of the south meant long-range guns bore on it again. Still, it seemed resigned to the prospect of flying the Stars and Stripes for the first time in a couple of generations, and a good many buildings damaged when it was captured had been repaired since.

South of Beulah, though, you were back in the war, no two ways about it. Mantarakis trudged past wagon parks city blocks on a side, and horse corrals alongside them full of animals chewing on hay and oats. Every so often, his regiment had to get off the dirt road onto the verge to let a convoy of trucks rumble past, carrying supplies up to the line, or to make way for an ambulance, red cross prominently displayed on a white background, transporting wounded men back toward Beulah.

There were munitions dumps scattered here and there across the landscape, too, shells standing on the ground as if they were the dragon's teeth

Cadmus had sown to raise a crop of soldiers. But they didn't raise men; they razed them. When the pun occurred to Mantarakis, he tried to explain it to the men marching with him, and got only blank looks for his trouble.

The Rebel offensive had been halted just south of Dawson Springs. There, hell hadn't gone on vacation. The Confederates might not have managed to take the town, but they'd shelled it into ruin. So many of the buildings were either burnt or wrecked, so many craters pocked the ground, it was hard to tell where exactly the roads had run before Dawson Springs made war's acquaintance.

Just past Dawson Springs, Mantarakis heard a buzzing in the air. His head swiveled rapidly till he spotted the aeroplane coming north. It skimmed along low to the ground, paralleling the road down which he was marching. For a moment, that made him think it was an American aeroplane returning from the front. Then he spied the Confederate battle flags painted on the fabric under each wing.

The pilot must have seen the regiment before Paul noticed him. He brought the aeroplane down even lower, right down to treetop height. That gave the observer a perfect chance to rake the column of U.S. soldiers with his machine gun.

Men screamed and fell and ran every which way. A few, cooler-headed than the rest, stood in place and fired back at the Rebel aeroplane with their Springfields. Mantarakis admired their sangfroid without trying to imitate it. He was utterly unashamed to dive into a muddy ditch by the side of the road. Bullets kicked up dirt not far away.

Ignoring the rifle fire, the aeroplane wheeled through a turn and came back south down the other side of the road, raking the regiment all over again. Then, pilot and observer no doubt laughing to each other about shooting fish in a barrel, it streaked away for home, going flat out now.

Mantarakis got out of the ditch. He was filthy and wet, as if he'd been in the trenches for a month instead of away from them. Muddy water dripped from the brim of his cap, his nose, his chin, his elbows, his belt buckle.

Gordon McSweeney stood like a rock in the middle of the roadway, still firing after the Confederate aeroplane although, by now, his chances of hitting it were slim indeed. Officers and noncoms shouted and blew whistles, trying to get the regiment back into marching order.

A familiar voice was missing. There lay Sergeant Peterquist, not moving. Blood soaked the damp, hard-packed dirt of the roadway. A bullet had torn through his neck and almost torn off his head. *"Kyrie eleison,"* Mantarakis murmured, and made the sign of the cross.

"Popery—damned popery," McSweeney said above him.

"Oh, shut up, Gordon," Mantarakis said, as if to a pushy five-year-old.

The really funny thing was that the Orthodox Church reckoned the pope every bit as much a heretic as any Scotch Presbyterian did.

"You'll do his soul no good with your mummeries," McSweeney insisted.

Paul paid no attention to him. If Peterquist was dead, somebody would have to do his job. Mantarakis looked around for Corporal Stankiewicz, and didn't see him. Maybe he'd been wounded and dragged off, maybe he was still hiding, maybe . . . Maybe none of that mattered. What did matter was that he wasn't here.

Even if he wasn't, the job, again, needed doing. Mantarakis shouted for his section to form up around him, and then, as an afterthought, to get the dead and wounded off to the side of the road. A lot of people were shouting, but not many of the shouts were as purposeful as his. Because he sounded like someone who knew what he was doing, men listened to him.

Lieutenant Hinshaw had his whole scattered platoon to reassemble. By the time he got around to the section Sergeant Peterquist had led, it was ready to get moving again, which was more than a lot of the column could say.

"Good work," Hinshaw said, looking over the assembled men and the casualties moved out of the line of march (Stankiewicz was among them: shot in the arm on the Rebel aeroplane's second pass). Then he noticed the absence of noncoms. "Who pulled you people together like this?"

Nobody said anything for half a minute or so. Mantarakis shuffled his feet and looked down at the bloodstained dirt; he didn't want to get a name for blowing his own horn. Then Gordon McSweeney said, "It was the little Greek, sir."

"Mantarakis?" Most of the time, Paul was in trouble when the lieutenant called his name. But Hinshaw nodded and said, "If you do the work, you should have the rank to go with it. You're a corporal, starting now."

Mantarakis saluted. "Thank you, sir." That meant more pay, not that you were ever going to get rich, not in this man's Army. It also meant more duties, but that was how things went. You got a little, you gave a little. Or, in the Army, you got a little and, odds were, you gave a lot.

The pillar of black, greasy smoke rose high into the sky northwest of Okmulgee, Sequoyah, maybe higher, for all Stephen Ramsay knew, than an aeroplane could fly. The fires at the base of that pillar didn't crackle, didn't hiss, didn't roar—they bellowed, like a herd of oxen in eternal agony. Even from miles away, as he was now, it was the biggest noise around. It was the biggest sight around, too: an ugly red carbuncle lighting up a whole corner of the horizon.

Captain Lincoln looked at the vast, leaping, hellish flames with somber satisfaction. "We've denied that oil field to the enemy," he said.

"Yes, sir," Ramsay said. "Anybody tries to put out those fires, he's gonna be a long time doin' it."

"Less than you'd think, Sergeant, less than you'd think," Lincoln said. "Put a charge of dynamite in the right place and *whump!*—out it goes. But even if the damnyankees do that, they won't be drawing any crude oil or gas from those wells for a long time, which was the point of the exercise."

"They sure won't, sir." Ramsay sighed and patted his horse's neck with a gloved hand. "Who would've thought the damnyankees could push us back like this? We don't do *some* fightin' back, they're gonna run us out of Sequoyah altogether, push us into Texas an' Arkansas."

"Too damn many of 'em." Lincoln spat down into the dirt. "We're liable to have to fall back through Okmulgee, and the chief of the Creek Nation will pitch a fit if we do."

"Yeah, well, if he doesn't like it, he's just going to have to go peddle his papers," Ramsay said. "Either that or pull some men out from under his war bonnet."

Lincoln sighed. The war had worn on him—not just the fighting, but the dickering, too. Ramsay hadn't figured dickering would be a part of war—if you had a gun, you could tell the other guy what to do, couldn't you?—but it was. The captain said, "We aren't like the USA. One of the reasons we fought the War of Secession was to keep the national government from telling the states what they had to do."

"Makes us a hell of a lot freer than the damnyankees," Ramsay said, it being an article of faith in the CSA that living in the USA was at most a short step better than living under the tyranny of the czars. These days, of course, Russia was an ally, so nobody said much about the czars, but the principle remained the same.

"Yeah, it does," Lincoln said with another sigh. "But it means sometimes we have to go through a whole lot of arguing to get through something the Yanks could deal with by giving a couple of orders. And here in Sequoyah, you may have noticed, it's even more complicated than it is anyplace else."

"Now that you mention it, sir, I have noticed that," Ramsay admitted, drawing a wan smile from the captain.

Sequoyah, by itself, was a Confederate state. But within its borders lay five separate nations, those of the Creeks, Cherokees, Choctaws, Chickasaws, and Seminoles, the Five Civilized Tribes. They kept their local autonomy and guarded it with zeal; the governor of Sequoyah sometimes had more trouble getting their chiefs to cooperate with him than President Wilson did with the governors of the Confederate states. And, since a lot of the state's petroleum and oil lay under land that belonged to the Indian nations, they had enough money on their own to keep the state government coming to them hat in hand.

They were enthusiastic about the government in Richmond, not resigned like most people in the Confederacy. They had reason to be, because it kept the state government off their backs. But they expected the national government—which now meant the Army—to come through for them, too, and justify faith by works.

Lincoln said, "If I have to tell Charlie Fixico I'm pulling out of Okmulgee without even trying to defend the town, you know what he's going to do? He's going to write his congressman, back in Richmond. And since his congressman just happens to be named Ben Fixico, that makes me toast without any marmalade. But what am I supposed to do?"

He wasn't really looking for an answer. Captains didn't get answers from sergeants. Lieutenants frequently did, but not captains. Captains had to come up with their own answers, no matter how unpleasant a prospect that was.

And come up with an answer Lincoln did. He got help from a Yankee field gun, which started landing shells in front of the cavalry company. The fountains of smoke and dirt were several hundred yards short, but the Confederates had no field guns of their own with which to reply. Before long, the U.S. forces would move that gun forward and bring up others alongside it.

"Back to Okmulgee!" Lincoln shouted. At his order, the company bugler sounded the retreat.

With the rest of the company, Ramsay rode southeast toward the capital of the Creek Nation. Okmulgee lay in a low, broad valley, with tree-covered hills on either side. As the Confederates came into the valley, Ramsay saw that the town was seething like an anthill to which somebody had just delivered a good swift kick. A train was pulling out, heading south. It had nothing but freight cars, but Ramsay would have bet those were packed with people; he'd even seen some with signs painted on their sides: 36 MEN OR 8 HORSES. The road south out of Okmulgee was certainly packed, with people, wagons, buggies, barrows, horses, and other livestock. Captain Lincoln might have intended retreating through Okmulgee rather than into it, but getting out the other side wouldn't be easy.

The Creek Nation Council House was a two-story brown stone building in the center of town. With the cupola rising above it, it was easily the most impressive structure in Okmulgee, and would have made a good fort till cannon started blowing it to bits. Outside the Council House waited a delegation of red-skinned men in somber black suits. They had gathered together a bunch of younger Indians who wore much more nondescript clothes—except for red bandannas tied to their left sleeves as armbands—and who carried a motley assortment of weapons: shotguns, squirrel guns, and what looked to be a couple of single-shot muzzle-loaders that went all the way back to the days of the War of Secession.

One of the Creek bigshots stepped out into the middle of the road as the cavalry drew near. He held up his right hand. Captain Lincoln had the choice of reining in or pretending he wasn't there. Swearing under his breath, the captain reined in.

"Save our city!" the Indian cried. "Save our nation! Do not abandon us to the merciless United States, whose soldiers we fought a hundred years ago, long before the South saw it had to escape the brutal oppression that came from Washington. As chief of the nation, I beg you. The delegations from the House of Kings and the House of Warriors beg you as well."

Charlie Fixico gestured to the Indians in fancy dress. They added their voices to his. It was, when you got down to it, a hell of an impressive performance.

He moved his hand, and the delegation—local senators and congressmen, Ramsay supposed they were—fell silent so he could talk some more. "We do not ask you to perform any duty we would not share," he said, now pointing to the young Indians with armbands. "We will help you defend our homes and our lands. We will fight whether you stay or go, but we beg you to stand by us now as we stood by you in the War of Secession and the Second Mexican War."

Captain Lincoln looked mad at first, and then helpless. Stephen Ramsay understood that. It was a hell of a speech. He wondered how many times Charlie Fixico had practiced it in front of a mirror so he could bring it out pat like that. If Captain Lincoln led the cavalry out of Okmulgee now, he'd feel like a skunk for the rest of his days—and a lot of the troopers who heard the speech would think he was a skunk, too.

Ramsay glanced over to the young Creek men. Were they really ready to do or die for the Creek Nation? Even if they were, would it make any difference? You ran amateur soldiers up against veterans, odds were the amateurs would come out looking as if they'd just been through a grinding mill.

He was glad the decision was not his to make. Captain Lincoln looked back toward the northwest, toward the burning oil wells his troopers had had to abandon. There were more oil wells in and around Okmulgee, and still more south of town. If he could save any of them for the Confederacy, that would be worth doing. If, on the other hand, he was just throwing his command away . . .

Charlie Fixico went down on his knees and held his hands up high in the air. At that, so did the men from the House of Kings and the House of Warriors. Ramsay had never seen anybody just get down and beg like that.

"God damn it," Captain Lincoln muttered under his breath, with luck not so loud the Creeks could hear it. Then, realizing he had to give an answer, he raised his voice: "All right, Chief, we'll make a stand in Okmulgee. Let's get some firing pits dug, and we'll see what we can do."

Charlie Fixico scrambled to his feet, spry for a fellow a long way from young. He clutched Lincoln's hand. "God bless you, Captain. You won't be sorry for this," he exclaimed.

By the look in his eye, Captain Lincoln was sorry already. In town here, the company would have to fight as infantry, sending their horses south with the retreating Creeks. Ramsay took charge of the young men—*am I supposed to call 'em braves?* he wondered—with armbands on their sleeves. They were ready as all get-out to shoot at the damnyankees, but when he sent them into a hardware store to commandeer shovels so they could start digging foxholes and trenches, they almost balked.

"Look," he said, more patiently than he'd expected, "the idea is to kill the other guy, not to get killed yourself. Shells start falling here, bullets start flying around, you're going to be damn glad to have a hole in the ground to hide in."

They weren't soldiers. It wasn't so much that they didn't believe him. They didn't have a clue as to what he was talking about. They worked like sulking Negroes till Charlie Fixico yelled something at them in their own language. After that, they sped up—a little.

Captain Lincoln sited one of the company machine guns so it fired up Sixth Street and the other so it fired up Fourth. When the Yankees came into town, those would give them something to think about. "Wait till you have a good target," Ramsay told the crew at Sixth and Morton, in front of the Creek Council House. "We want to make the bastards pay for everything they get."

U.S. troops were not long in coming. Field guns started landing three-inch shells on the town. The red-armbanded Creeks dove for the holes they hadn't wanted to dig. To Ramsay's amazement, one of them shouted an apology to him.

He waved back. He wondered how much ammunition each Indian had for his gun. With all those different calibers, no hope in hell the cavalry could resupply them when they ran dry. He also wondered what the Yankees would do with any Creeks they captured. Was a red armband uniform enough to let them count as prisoners of war? Or would the Yanks call them *francs-tireurs* and shoot them out of hand, the way the Huns had done in France and were doing in Belgium? For the Creeks' sake, Ramsay hoped they didn't find out.

He had his own foxhole nicely dug, sited under a tree that would give him cover if and when he had to pull back, as he probably would sooner or later. He peered north up Fifth Street, looking to see how close the Yanks were.

As he'd expected, here they came, green-gray waves of infantry trudging toward Okmulgee, leaning forward a little under the weight of their packs. "Hold fire till they're good and close," Captain Lincoln yelled. "We want the machine guns to be able to chew up a whole bunch of 'em when we open up."

His own men understood the reasoning behind the order. But the Creeks had never been in combat before. As soon as they saw U.S. soldiers, they started shooting at them. Sure as hell, one of them not far from Ramsay did have a rifle musket from his grandfather's day. A great cloud of black-powder smoke rose above the kid's firing pit.

The Yankees went to earth the minute they started taking fire. Ramsay swore under his breath. Now they'd advance in small groups instead of the one great wave the machine guns might have broken.

Well, the game didn't always go the way you wished it would. "Fire at will," Captain Lincoln shouted, sounding as disgusted as Ramsay felt. The machine guns started chattering. U.S. soldiers fell. Ramsay found a target and fired. The Yankee he'd aimed at went down.

But more U.S. soldiers kept coming. The Confederates fired steadily, taking a good toll. And the Creeks surprised Ramsay. They stayed in their places and kept shooting. You couldn't hope for anything more, not from raw troops. They might not have had discipline, but they were brave.

When their entry into Okmulgee stalled, the damnyankees gave the town another, bigger dose of artillery to make the defenders keep their heads down. Under cover of the bombardment, they got men into the northern fringes of the built-up area. The forwardmost Confederate troopers came running back toward the center of town. Ramsay didn't notice any Creeks coming back. He whistled softly. They *were* brave.

He felt cramped, fighting in amongst buildings rather than out on the plains. Unhorsed, he felt slow, too. *Could* he get away, if trouble got bad? He began to think he'd have to find out the hard way.

Then—and he laughed as the comparison occurred to him—like cavalry riding to the rescue, artillery fire began falling on the advancing Yankees just outside of Okmulgee. If that wasn't a whole battery of those quick-firing three-inchers, he'd go off and eat worms. Caught out in the open, the U.S. soldiers toppled as if scythed.

Ramsay whooped like an Indian—just like an Indian, because several Creeks not far away were letting out the same kind of happy yells. They probably figured the fight was as good as won. Ramsay wished he could believe the same thing. Unfortunately, he knew better. Whatever else you said about the Yankees, they were stubborn bastards.

Still, if there was artillery in the neighborhood, maybe there was infantry around, too. Put a regiment in here instead of a cavalry company and some ragtag civilians, and Okmulgee would hold against damn near anything the USA could throw at it. He looked back over his shoulder, then started laughing all over again.

"Hell of a war," he muttered, "when the cavalry's got to look to the infantry to come to the rescue."

Jonathan Moss looked with something less than joy untrammeled toward the new aeroplanes the squadron was receiving. The Wright 17s, usually nicknamed Wilburs, were very different machines from the Curtiss Super Hudsons they were replacing. He'd grown used to the Super Hudsons. He knew everything they could do, and he wasn't so stupid as to try to make them do things they couldn't. That was how you ended up dead.

Captain Elijah Franklin expounded on the Wilbur's virtues: "Now we have aeroplanes than can climb and dive with the Avros the damned Canucks and limeys are flying. We won't have to scurry for home if we get in trouble."

Moss caught Lyman Baum's eye. Both men shook their heads, just a little. They hadn't run for home when they faced Avros—very much the reverse. A Curtiss machine could turn inside the circle of which the British-made aeroplanes were capable, but the Wilbur was a bus as big as a bus itself, and—

"Sir?" Moss stuck up a hand.

"What is it?" Franklin asked, a bit testy at being interrupted before his spiel was done. He had a pinched, narrow face, and looked as if his stomach pained him all the time. It probably did. That didn't keep him from drinking like a fish when he wasn't flying.

"Sir, one of the biggest advantages we had in the Curtiss was a forward-facing machine gun," Moss said. "This is a tractor machine, with the prop in front. Now we're going to be limited to observer fire, just like the Canucks. If I see a target, I want to be able to aim at it and shoot it straight on, not wiggle around so the observer gets to fire off at an angle."

Everybody in the squadron spoke up, loudly agreeing with him. Franklin stood quiet, perhaps waiting to see if the hubbub would die away. When it didn't, he held up a hand. Little by little, he got quiet. Into it, he said, "They're working on that," and then clammed up again.

The terse announcement produced more hubbub. Through it, Jonathan Moss called, "You mean somebody has finally made a working interrupter gear, sir?"

If you could synchronize the speed at which your machine gun fired with that at which your prop revolved, you could mount a forward-facing gun on a tractor aeroplane and not shoot yourself down faster than the enemy. Moss had heard of a couple of people who'd shod their wooden propellor blades with steel to deflect ill-timed bullets, but sooner or later a ricochet was going to come straight back at you, so that wasn't the ideal solution. An interrupter gear, though—

Then Captain Franklin said, "No, they don't have one yet," and dashed his hopes. But the squadron commander went on, "They are getting close, though, or at least they think they are. And when they do get one, they promise the front-line squadrons will have it first thing."

"They promise Santa Claus brings you toys, too, and the Easter Bunny hides eggs," Stanley McClintock said. "They promised we'd be in Toronto before the snow fell, and Winnipeg, and Richmond, and Guaymas—though I don't know that it ever snows down there. But I believe that kind of story when it comes true, and not a minute before then."

"If you're a defeatist," Franklin said coldly, "you can take off your wings right now. I'll give you a white feather instead, the way the limey girls do when their boyfriends don't want to go off and fight."

McClintock stomped toward the squadron commander, of whom he made close to two. Franklin moved not an inch. It wasn't his rank armoring him, Jonathan Moss knew, just a stubborn determination not to back down to anybody. McClintock shouted, "God damn it, Captain, you know I'm no coward. But when I switch buses, I want to have a pretty good idea that I'm doing it for a reason, that the new bus"—he jerked a thumb toward a Wilbur—"is likelier to keep me in one piece than the old one was."

"You've flown it," Franklin said. "We've all flown it. It performs a damn sight better than a Curtiss. Is that so, or isn't it?"

"It doesn't turn as well," Moss said.

"That's true," Franklin admitted, "but it climbs better and it dives better and it accelerates better. One of the reasons the Super Hudson turned so tight was that it couldn't go fast enough to take up a lot of space in a turn. Is that so, or isn't it?"

Moss kept quiet. It was so. You didn't want the Canadians or British chasing you, because they'd damn well catch you. But he'd got comfortable with his old machine. It was, he supposed, like a marriage: you knew what your partner was going to do. Now he was going to a partner he didn't know nearly so well.

Franklin said, "Enough of this nonsense. We've got them and we're damn well going to use them till we get something better. They've shipped the Super Hudsons off to . . . Colorado, I think they said, or maybe Utah. Someplace where they can do reconnaissance and not have to go up against anybody's varsity, anyway. We do. That's another reason we get the Wilburs—you men can do your job as pilots, and the observers you'll have with you can observe. Life's getting too complicated for one man to do both jobs up there at the same time."

But for a sigh, Moss remained quiet. Again, the squadron commander was probably right. Again, Moss found the truth unpalatable.

Lyman Baum said, "Other thing is, sir, I don't like trusting my neck to the observer. I'd rather have my own gun now instead of waiting to get one in the great by-and-by. Observers—"

He let that hang there. Most observers who were just observers and not pilot-observers like the members of the squadron were guys who had been through flight school and hadn't made it as pilots. That made everybody suspect there was something second-rate about them. If you knew darn well you were first-rate and you'd got used to being your own gunner, how were you going to shout "Hurrah!" at the idea of turning over the shooting to somebody you didn't figure could match you?

As if Baum's question had been a cue, a truck chugged up to the aerodrome and started disgorging men in khaki with overladen duffel bags and with flight badges that had only one wing, not a pilot's two. Captain Franklin nodded; he'd expected them. "Gentlemen, your observers," he said while the newcomers were still getting out. "Does anyone care to express any further ill-founded opinions? . . . No? Good."

Moss kicked at the dirt. The captain had a point. You couldn't condemn out of hand a man you'd never met. But Baum had a point, too. If a fellow was liable to be a lemon, did you really want to meet him?

Whether you did or not, you were going to. From a breast pocket, Franklin pulled out a sheet of stationery folded in quarters. Before he unfolded it, he waved the observers over to him. They came, some with their bags slung over a shoulder, some carrying them in front, some dragging them along the ground. "We have the following pairings," Franklin announced, unfolding the paper: "Pilot Baum and Observer van Zandt; Pilot Henderson and Observer Mattigan . . ." On and on he went, till he said, "Pilot Moss and Observer Stone."

"Oh, for Christ's sake!" Moss burst out amid laughter. "You did that on purpose, Captain, and don't try to tell me different."

"Well, that tells me who you are," the newly teamed observer said, stepping forward. "I'm Percy Stone." He let his duffel bag fall from his shoulder to the ground and stuck out his right hand.

"Jonathan Moss," Moss said, shaking it, and studied Captain Franklin's idea of a joke. Stone was a couple of years younger than he, he guessed, with a long, ruddy face, a brown Kaiser Bill mustache, and a disarming grin underneath it. He didn't look like a loser or a washout. "What did you do before the war started?" Moss asked him.

"I had a little photography studio in Ohio," Stone answered. "You?"

"I was studying the law," Moss said. He waved that aside, as he would have any question both irrelevant and immaterial, and stared at Percy Stone. Maybe Captain Franklin's idea of a joke had given him something a good deal better than your average One-Wing Wonder. "A photographer, were you? No wonder they turned you into an observer."

"No wonder at all," Stone agreed. "I wanted to be a pilot. They told me if I kept squawking about it they'd stick me in the infantry, and I could see how I liked that. You know what, Lieutenant Moss? I believed 'em."

"Good thing you did," Moss said. "I don't have any doubt the powers that be meant every bit of it." He kicked Stone's duffel bag, then picked it up himself. "Come on; let's get you settled in. Tomorrow, if the weather's decent, we'll get up there and you can take some pretty pictures of the enemy line. How does that sound?"

"Better than a poke in the eye with a carrot," Stone said, and both young men grinned. The observer waved toward the tents. "Lead on, Macduff!" It was a misquotation, but Moss wasn't about to ruffle any feathers by saying so.

As if the arrival of the observers had changed the squadron's luck, the weather, which had been cold and foggy and drizzly, turned something close to springlike the next morning. Of course, by the calendar spring was only a week and a half away, but, up till now, Ontario had shown no signs of paying attention to the calendar. As far as Moss could see, blizzards were liable to keep coming all the way through July.

The next morning, Percy Stone exclaimed with pleasure when he saw the camera he was to use. "Ah, one of the new models," he said. "They're the next thing to foolproof. In fact, they're the next thing to moronproof." He exclaimed again when he discovered the Wright in which he was to fly had a conical recess in which the camera would fit built into the fuselage floor in the observer's cockpit. "Someone was awake during the design work here."

Moss shrugged as he climbed into the forward cockpit. A groundcrew man spun the prop. The engine started to roar, seemingly right in his lap. He didn't like that. The slipstream blew the noise to him now, not away from him as it had in a Curtiss pusher. No help for it, though. This was the bus he had, so this was the bus he'd fly.

Fly he did, north and west. Every so often, Percy Stone would shout something at him. He caught perhaps one word in five. One of these days, somebody would have to figure out how to let pilot and observer talk back and forth and understand each other. That could be as important as perfecting the interrupter gear.

Endless hammering had finally let the Americans break out of the Niagara Peninsula. Threatened from west and east at the same time, the foe had evacuated the town of London, which had held so long and cost so many American lives. One fairly short push along the northern shore of Lake Ontario and Toronto would fall. That would bring the war in the north a long step closer to being won.

Under his flying goggles, Moss made a sour face. The limeys and Canucks, damn them, hadn't been idle while the U.S. soldiers pounded at their front door. They'd built a whole new series of lines behind the ones they'd had to abandon. Smash one and you found the next just as tough.

Moss was supposed to get Percy over the town of Berlin, south and west of Guelph, so the observer could photograph Canadian railheads and other targets for the U.S. artillery. Berlin was the name the town bore on his map, anyhow; the Canadians were calling it Empire these days. The region had been settled by Germans, a lot of whom, after the war broke out, had been resettled to Baffin Island and other such tropic climes lest they prove gladder to see Germany's American allies than the forces of the British Empire.

Both the USA and Germany had trumpeted the Canadians' inhumanity to the skies. The Canadians and the British defended themselves on the grounds of the exigencies of war. (Moss suspected the argument sold newspapers down in South America. Past that, he didn't see much point to it.)

Because the weather was so clear and fine, the Canadian landscape—what had been farming country, now chewed to pieces by the war, torn and gouged and tied down with barbed wire—lay neatly spread out below the Wright 17. And, because it was so clear and fine, the biplane and its flightmates were all too easily visible to the enemy troops down below.

Black puffs of smoke started appearing in the sky, all around Moss and Stone. Moss started stunting the aeroplane, changing course and speed at random intervals to confuse the antiaircraft gunners and throw off their aim. The gunnery—the hate, everybody on the receiving end called it—was more a nuisance than anything else, but you didn't want to think you'd stay lucky all the time.

A shell burst a scant handful of yards below the Wilbur, which bounced in the air. Percy Stone picked that moment to shout "Now!" over and over till Moss waved to show he understood. For the photographic run, the aeroplane had to fly level and straight.

Back there, the observer would be yanking the loading handle to bring the first photographic plate into position, then pulling a string every few seconds. Every time he did, the camera would expose the plate then behind the lens. Sliding the loading handle forward and back again brought the exposed plate down into an empty changing box below and to the side of the camera body and slid a fresh one into place, ready for the next pull of the string. The camera held eighteen plates altogether.

Stone yelled something else. Moss couldn't make out the words, but he thought it was about time to go around and return to the aerodrome on a track parallel to the course they'd flown so far. When he did that, the observer stopped screaming, so he supposed he'd been right.

"Done!" Stone shouted at last, and Moss gave the Wright all the juice it had to get out of the antiaircraft fire and head for home.

The aeroplane rolled to a stop on the landing strip. Moss killed the engine. For a moment, silence seemed louder than the roar had. He needed a distinct effort of will not to shout as he said, "That wasn't so bad." After a reflective pause, he added, "Any run where they don't send their aeroplanes up after you is a pretty good one, as a matter of fact."

"Oh, I don't know," Percy Stone said. "I was sort of looking forward to the chance of shooting the tail right off my own bus." His grin was so disarming, it almost let Moss forget that that was one of the things that could happen when an observer got overeager.

Moss climbed out of the cockpit and jumped down to solid ground. Stone followed more slowly and more carefully; he had to remove the camera and the precious exposed plates from their mounting. Moss liked the precise way he did things. "This may work out pretty well," he said.

Percy Stone's grin got wider and more wicked. "Oh, darling," he breathed, "I didn't know you cared." Laughing, the two men headed off toward the photographic laboratory together.

Sylvia Enos stared at the new form the Coal Board clerk handed her. "Fill this out and bring it to Window C, over there, when you've finished it," the clerk droned, almost as mechanically as a gramophone record. Sylvia wondered how many times a day he said the exact same thing.

She wished Brigid Coneval weren't down with the grippe. But Mrs. Coneval was, which meant Sylvia had had to bring George, Jr., and Mary Jane with her to the Coal Board office of a Saturday afternoon. She was just glad the office stayed open on Saturday afternoons; if it hadn't, she would have had to try to get time off from work to fill out this new and hideous form.

She sat down in one of the hard chairs that filled the open area in front of the Coal Board office windows. George, Jr., sat down next to her. She plopped Mary Jane into the chair on the other side. "Be good, both of you, while I answer these questions," she said.

Every time she had to fill anything out, it was a race against the clock. The children *would* get into mischief; it was only a question of when. To delay the inevitable, she gave her son a lollipop and her daughter a bottle, then took out a fountain pen and bent over the sheet full of tiny type to find out what sort of information they wanted from her now.

COAL RATION ALLOTMENT REASSESSMENT EVALUATION SURVEY REPORT, the form said at the top. Sylvia sighed. It seemed to be a law—or perhaps a Coal Board policy—that every form had to be more complicated than the one it replaced. This one certainly lived up to the requirement.

She had no trouble filling out her own name or the address of the flat in which she and the children lived. Then the form asked for the names of all individuals residing at that address. That was all fine. But next it asked for the present status of each individual, and gave check-off boxes for MILITARY, CIVILIAN GAINFULLY EMPLOYED, CIVILIAN UNEMPLOYED OTHER THAN STUDENT, STUDENT, and CHILD BELOW AGE 12.

None of those boxes fit her husband, and there was no OTHER line on which to explain. Painful experience had taught her nothing caused more trouble than filling out a Coal Board form the wrong way. She glanced at her children. They both seemed occupied. "Wait here," she told them. "I have to go ask that man a question."

When she got to the front of the line again, the clerk who'd given her the form looked as delighted to see her as she was to see the landlord on the first of every month. "What seems to be your trouble?" he asked in a voice that said he knew she was bothering him on purpose.

She pointed to the check-off boxes. "What do I do about my husband here?" she asked. "He's a Confederate prisoner at—"

"Prisoners of war go under the Military heading," the clerk said, more exasperated than ever.

"But he's not a prisoner of war; he's a detainee," Sylvia said. "A commerce raider captured him when he was out on Georges Bank."

"Then he's a Civilian Gainfully—" The Coal Board clerk stopped. You couldn't say George Enos was gainfully employed, not when he was at a camp or wherever the Rebs kept their detainees down in North Carolina. But he wasn't unemployed, either. The clerk looked as if he hated Sylvia. He probably did, for breaking up the smooth monotony of his day. He turned and called, "Mr. Colfax, can you please come here for a moment?" Being his superior, Mr. Colfax rated politeness. Sylvia barely rated the time of day.

She turned to look back at her children. George, Jr., was teasing Mary Jane with the lollipop. She could have told him that was a mistake. Mary Jane grabbed the lollipop and stuffed it into her own mouth. George, Jr., started to scream.

"Excuse me," Sylvia said hastily. She took the lollipop away from Mary Jane, returned it to its rightful owner, swatted every available backside, and warned of measures yet more dire if the two of them didn't behave themselves. That done, she went back to the clerk. The next woman in line had come up to the window in the meanwhile, giving him an excuse to pretend she didn't exist. He seized on the excuse with alacrity.

But then Mr. Colfax, who wore not only pince-nez but a red vest to show he was someone above the common run of clerk, came out of whatever office he'd been given to prove he was above the common run of clerk. The window clerk proved willing to ignore the other woman at the window instead of Sylvia: as long as he was ignoring someone, he was happy.

Upon hearing of the ambiguity, Mr. Colfax chewed on his lower lip, which was red and meaty and made for such mastications. At last, he said, "Properly speaking, this man should not be included in the calculations, for no coal need be expended on cooking and heating water for him."

"It's not his fault he's not here," Sylvia protested. "He's a prisoner—"

"No, he is a detainee, as you yourself specified," the window clerk said, relishing his moment of petty triumph. "Fill out the form accordingly and take it to Window C. Thank you, Mr. Colfax." Mr. Colfax nodded and disappeared. Sylvia wished he were gone for good.

When she looked to her children again, Mary Jane was toddling over to take a good look at the brass cuspidor in one corner of the room. Its polished, gleaming surface was stained here and there—as was the floor around it—by the tobacco-brown spittle of men whose intentions were better than their aim. Sylvia let out a small shriek and, skirts flapping around her, managed to intercept Mary Jane just before her daughter got feet and hands in the disgusting stuff.

Gripping Mary Jane in one hand and the precious if annoying form in the other, she returned to the seat where George, Jr., waited placidly. "Why didn't you keep your sister from wandering off and getting into mischief?" she said. "You have to be my big boy till Papa gets home, you know."

"I'm sorry, Mama," he said, his face serious, his eyes big, looking so much like his father, Sylvia thought her heart would break. "I didn't see her go, I really didn't. I was looking at this bug I caught." He opened his hand. He was holding a cockroach. It jumped down and started to scurry across the floor toward any shelter it could find.

Sylvia lashed out with a foot. The cockroach crunched under the sole of her shoe. George, Jr., started to cry, but then discovered the remains of the cockroach were about as interesting as it had been alive. "Look at its guts sticking out!" he exclaimed, loudly and enthusiastically.

Heads turned, all through the Coal Board office. Sylvia felt herself flushing, and wished she could sink through the floor. "Don't play with them any more, do you hear me?" she told George, Jr. "They're dirty and nasty."

At last, she got the chance to finish filling out the form. It asked for things she didn't know, like the quality of the insulation in her flat, and for things she had a devil of a time figuring out, like the number of cubic feet the flat contained. Her education had stopped in the middle of the seventh grade, when it became obvious she needed a job more than schooling. She hadn't had to figure out the volume of anything since then, and hadn't expected to need to do it now.

At last, the dreadful task was done. By the time it was, Mary Jane was getting cranky. Sylvia carried her over to the line in front of Window C. "You stay here," she told George, Jr., "and no more bugs, not if you want to be able to sit down when we ride the trolley home." *If we ever get a chance to go home,* she thought wearily. But she'd got through to her son, who sat on both hands, as if to protect the area she'd threatened.

The line moved about as slowly as U.S. troops advancing on Big Lick, Virginia—Big Licking, the papers had taken to calling it. Some of the people must have made mistakes on their forms, because, faces set and angry, they had to go back to the previous window and get new copies to fill out. They had to stand in line again there, too.

When she finally reached him, the clerk who reigned supreme over Window C proved to be a fresh-faced young fellow who, for a miracle, seemed friendly and anxious to help. He smiled at Mary Jane, who stared back at him over the thumb she had in her mouth.

Then he glanced down at the coal ration form. "I don't see your husband listed here, ma'am," he said to Sylvia. "You're a widow?" He actually sounded sympathetic, which, from Sylvia's previous experience with Coal Board clerks, should have been more than enough to get him fired.

"No," she said, and explained what had happened to George.

"That doesn't matter," the clerk said. "If he's a captive of the Confederate States, you're entitled to the coal for him."

"Back there—" Sylvia pointed to the window from which she'd come. "Mister, uh, Colfax said I wasn't, because George is a detainee, not a prisoner of war."

"Doesn't matter," the clerk repeated, his voice firm. "Mr. Colfax doesn't know everything there is to know."

Sylvia shot a venomous look back at that window. But when she started to cross lines out and make changes on the form, the clerk said, "I'm sorry, ma'am, but these forms must be perfect the first time, to eliminate any suspicion that the changes originated in this office. I'm afraid you do have to go back and get a fresh copy to fill out."

She stared at him, at Mary Jane, at George, Jr. (would he catch a mouse instead of forbidden bugs?), and at the line to the window from which she'd thought she'd escaped. She needed the coal. Coal Board rations were stingy. Even with what she'd get for George, she'd have none too much. But standing in line again—in two lines again—and then having to fill out the requisition form once more, even if this time she could copy from what she'd done before . . . Another half hour? Another hour? Was it worth the time? When could she shop?

"Come on, lady," a gruff voice said behind her. "I ain't got all day."

Sylvia didn't have all day, either. But she did need the coal. Sighing, ignoring George, Jr.'s, stricken look, she walked across the room and got back into the line in which she'd stood before.

Sometimes you dished it out, sometimes you had to take it. Jake Featherston knew that was true, even if he didn't like it for beans. He was taking it now, and his whole battery with him.

"Fire!" he yelled, and the field gun blasted a shell back at the damnyankees on the far side of the Susquehanna. The whole battery was pounding the U.S. positions, as far back as it could reach.

Trouble was, the battery couldn't reach far enough. The Confederacy's three-inch field guns had been the most wonderful thing in the world when the war was new and positions changed not just from day to day but from hour to hour. They moved with the advancing columns of men in butternut and slaughtered the U.S. soldiers who opposed them: slaughtered by tens, by hundreds, by thousands.

Because they did that job so well, the CSA had a lot of them. What the Confederates didn't have, and what they were needing more and more now that the front wasn't going anywhere fast, was a lot of big guns, guns that could reach well behind the enemy line and do some damage when they did reach. Nobody had thought the Confederacy would need so many guns like that.

"Only goes to show," Featherston muttered. "People ain't as smart as they wish they was."

The USA had the big guns, or more of them than the CSA did. Now that the front had stabilized along the Susquehanna, the United States had brought up their heavy artillery, and their gunners were using the big, long-range shells to raise hell deep among the Confederates' secondary positions. If the Yankees decided to try to force the Susquehanna line, they could beat down the opposition with their artillery till the Confederate forces would have a tough time fighting back.

"Wish we could do more to those damned six- and eight-inch guns," Jethro Bixler said as he set another shell in the breech of the field piece.

"Yeah." Featherston adjusted the elevation screw for maximum range, then pulled the lanyard. The field gun bucked and roared, but the muzzle brake kept the recoil short. If they hadn't worn the rifling out of the barrel of the gun, it wasn't because they hadn't tried. As Bixler slammed yet another shell into the breech, Jake went on, "What I wish is, we weren't so damned far forward. We got to be, I know, but if they do start dropping stuff on us, they'll be awful damn accurate on account of it won't be way out at the end of their range, like we are when we try to reach where they're at."

Another shell screamed off. Featherston wondered if he'd have any hearing left by the time the war was done. No sooner had the thought crossed his mind than he realized it contained two possibly false assumptions: that his hearing was the most important thing he risked, and that the war would ever end.

Pompey came up to Featherston and waited to be noticed. When the sergeant gave him a curt nod, he said, "Cap'n Stuart's compliments, suh, and we gonna shift our fire to a new Yankee position, range 5,300 yards, bearing 043."

"Range 5,300, bearing 043," Featherston repeated; he had to work to keep from imitating Pompey's mincing accent. Captain Stuart's servant nodded and went off to give the word to the next howitzer in the battery.

Featherston sighed. He didn't know whether Major Potter had investigated Pompey or not. If the major had, nothing had come of it. Pompey remained Jeb Stuart III's trusted servant: too trusted, as far as Jake was concerned. He knew Captain Stuart had given the command. All the same, getting it from Pompey was too close to taking orders from a Negro to suit him.

He glanced over at Nero and Perseus, who were combing down the horses. They were all right. They knew white men gave the orders and they took them. Pompey, just because he worked for somebody important, thought his own station improved, too. *Thinks his shit don't stink, is what he does,* Jake thought.

And then he stopped worrying about things as trivial as the right status of the Negro in the Confederate States of America. At any other time, that would have been important. Not now, not when Yankee shells came whistling in straight toward where he was standing.

Big ones, he thought with a chill as the freight-train noises in the sky grew to a roar, a scream. The damnyankees' three-inchers fired more slowly than the Confederacy's guns, but their shells gave the same scant warning coming in. A little *whizz* before the bang, that was all you got.

Not these. Through the growing shriek of torn air, Jethro Bixler screamed something. If it wasn't "Get down!" it should have been. A split second before the shells went off, Featherston threw himself flat.

Back home outside of Richmond, he'd gone to church a lot of times to hear a preacher work himself up into a good sweat over hellfire and damnation and brimstone. You listened to a preacher who was good enough, who threw off his jacket and waved his white-shirtsleeved arms at the congregation, you could get the feeling hell wasn't more than half a mile off.

That's what he'd thought then. Since the war started, he'd begun to get the notion he had a more intimate personal acquaintance with hellfire than any preacher ever spawned—unless the preacher served a gun, too.

But now, with the war that had started in summer and should have ended before winter still going strong at the start of spring and heading into its second summer of what looked like a great many yet to come, he discovered he didn't know so much after all. The battery had been under fire before, plenty of times. That was why he wasn't working with all the same gun-crew men who'd started out with him bombarding Washington, D.C. You shot at the damnyankees, they shot at you. That was fair.

They weren't just shooting at the battery this time, though. They wanted to wipe it off the face of the earth. He frantically hugged the dirt as the big shells burst all around him. Black puffs of smoke with red flame at their hearts sprang into being everywhere. Shrapnel balls and fragments of shell casing hissed through the air. The ground jerked and bucked. Featherston had never felt an earthquake, and after this bombardment was convinced he didn't need to. If you were in a house when an earthquake hit, the worst that would happen was things falling on you. Things weren't just falling here. They were accelerated, viciously accelerated, by high explosive.

Worst was knowing that whether he lived or died was altogether out of his hands. If a shell came down so near the blast ripped his lungs to bits from the inside out, if an explosion blew him to smithereens, if a tiny steel splinter awled through his skull and into his brain . . . then that was what happened. He had no say, and whether he was a good soldier or a bad didn't matter. Luck, that was it.

Shells kept raining down on the battery. He heard someone screaming, and realized it was himself. He felt not the least bit ashamed. You had to let some of the terror loose, or it would eat you from the inside out. Besides, in the many times worse than thunderstorm all around, who could hear him?

He wondered what else the Yankees were bombarding. Front-line trenches? Ammunition dumps? It mattered in theory, but not in practice, not right now. He couldn't do anything about it any which way. All he could do was lie flat and scrabble at the ground with the knife he wore on his belt, trying to dig a shallow hole in which he could shelter from the storm of steel—the storm of hate, the infantry called it—raging all around.

Blast from a near miss picked him up and slammed him back down to the ground, the way you might throw a kitten you didn't want against a brick wall to get rid of it. "Oof!" he said, and then, as he got more air back into his lungs, several less printable remarks.

How long the bombardment went on, he never knew exactly. When at last it lifted, it went down into the trenches even nearer the river than the battery was. Dazedly, Jake Featherston sat up. His hands shook. He tried to make them steady, and discovered he couldn't.

His gun, for a miracle, was still upright. Nobody else from the crew was sitting up, though. A couple of people were down and moaning, a couple of others down and not moving. The rest of the battery's howitzers had been tossed every which way, as if they were jackstraws.

He looked toward the smoke and dirt rising from the front-line trenches. Through that haze, he saw Yankees coming out of their own trenches and rushing toward the Susquehanna. They were going to try to force a crossing right now.

He ran to the howitzer. His head swiveled wildly. He had a target artillerymen dreamed of—but if he had to handle the three-incher by himself, he couldn't possibly fire often enough to do the CSA any good. He spied motion. Somehow, Nero and Perseus had come through the bombardment with as little damage as he had.

"You niggers!" he shouted. "Get your black asses up here on the double!" The laborers obeyed. If they hadn't, he would have drawn his pistol and shot them both. As things were, he barked, "You've seen the crew serve this gun often enough. Reckon you know how to do it your own selves?"

The two Negroes looked at each other. "Mebbe we do, Marse Jake," Perseus said at last, "but—"

"No time for buts." Featherston pointed toward the Susquehanna. "Every damnyankee in the world is headin' straight this way. They get this far, they're gonna kill you the same as me. Only way to keep 'em from gettin' this far I can think of is to blow 'em up first. Now—you gonna serve the gun?"

He didn't know whether his logic or his hand on the butt of his pistol was the more convincing. But the Negroes, after glancing at each other again, both nodded. "I kin load, I reckon," Nero said, "an' Perseus, he kin tote the shells. You got to do the rest, Marse Jake. We don't know nothin' 'bout how to aim."

"I'll handle that," Featherston promised. He looked around for Jethro Bixler, then wished he hadn't. The loader was spread out over the ground like an anatomy lesson. He hoped Nero wasn't lying to him, the way blacks did sometimes when they wanted to impress a white man.

Nero wasn't. He waited while Jake frantically worked the elevation screw to lower the muzzle of the gun and shorten range, then opened the breech, slammed in a shell, and dogged it shut almost as fast as poor dead Jethro could have done.

With a whoop, Featherston yanked the firing lanyard. The howitzer bellowed. A couple of seconds later, the shell burst among the swarming Yankees. They were close enough for Jake to watch the ones near the burst going down like ninepins. He whooped again and traversed the piece a little to the left.

Nero worked the breech. Out came the old shell casing. In went the new round. Jake jerked the lanyard. More U.S. soldiers fell. Methodically, he kept pumping shells into them. Despite the Yankee bombardment, not all the Confederate machine gunners were blasted out of their positions. They too began scything the U.S. attackers with bullets. Some of the Yankees did manage to ford the river and get into the Confederate trenches. The only ones who went any farther than that came to the rear as prisoners.

Seeing the glum, bloodied men in green-gray, Nero howled like a wolf. "We done it!" he shouted. "Jesus God almighty, we done it!"

They hadn't done it all by themselves—some guns from other batteries had spread death through the Yankee ranks, too—but they had done it. The eastern bank of the Susquehanna was littered with corpses tossed at every possible angle, and at too many impossible ones. A few last U.S. soldiers were scuttling back to their own trenches, like dogs fleeing with tails between their legs.

"We really did do it." Featherston knew he sounded stunned and shaky. He didn't feel bad about it; he *was* stunned and shaky. He slapped Nero on the back, and then Perseus. "You boys can serve my gun any time you please, and that's a fact. For a while there, I figured we'd be fightin' off the damnyankees with pistols."

"Ain't got no pistol, Marse Jake," Nero pointed out. He looked in the direction of a dead artilleryman. "Them Yankees break through an' come this way, though, reckon I woulda had me one."

"Yeah," Jake said abstractedly. Except when Negroes were doing things like hunting for the pot, they weren't supposed to have firearms. You let black men get their hands on guns and you were sitting on a keg of powder with the fuse lighted and heading your way.

And Nero and Perseus hadn't just got their hands on a pistol, or even a Tredegar. They'd served an artillery piece, and they'd done a hell of a job at it, too. You couldn't make them forget how to do it, or that they'd done it. If there ever was a black rebellion, they could do it again, provided they got themselves a field piece.

But if Featherston hadn't put them on the gun, he almost certainly wouldn't have been alive to worry about things like that. If Major Potter ever found out he'd turned them into impromptu artillerymen, he was liable to order them dragged off somewhere and shot. Part of Jake said that was a good idea. Hell, part of him wanted to yank out his pistol and use it now, so nobody would know what he'd done.

He couldn't. They'd saved his neck along with their own. He would never have yelled for their help if he could have yelled for white men instead, but there hadn't been any white men to yell for. He'd done what he'd had to do, and he'd got away with it.

Now he said what he said to say: "It's over, boys. You got to go back to bein' niggers again. You know what I'm tellin' you?"

He wondered if they could obey, even if they wanted to. They'd just been soldiers, after all. One of the reasons you didn't let a Negro get a gun in his hands was that, if he did some fighting with it, he'd start feeling like a man, not like a servant. A Negro who felt like a man was liable to be a dangerous Negro.

But Nero and Perseus understood what Jake meant. Perseus said, 'Yes, suh, Marse Jake, we be your niggers again, till the next time y'all need us to be somethin' different." He sounded almost as if he was inviting Featherston to share a joke.

"All right," Jake answered, not knowing what else he could say. Eventually, the battery would get replacements: young white men, eager—or at least willing—to serve the guns. And, eventually, they'd get slaughtered, too. So would Jake, like as not. He carried on about his business with a grim fatalism; the Yanks could throw more metal at him than he could easily throw back.

And who would serve the guns in 1917, or 1919, or 1921, or however long the war lasted? Negroes? He shook his head. It couldn't happen, not really. He glanced over at Perseus and Nero. Could it?

"Breakthrough!" George Armstrong Custer pounded the desk. "That's what I want, nothing less!" In an old-fashioned dark blue uniform, the fringe on his epaulets would have shaken back and forth. Modern U.S. uniforms didn't have epaulets. He had to make do with shaking jowls instead. "I want to run riot through the Rebels, and by God that's what I'm going to do."

"Sir." Major Abner Dowling took a deep breath. Every time Custer started bellowing about breakthroughs, men died by thousands for gains best measured in yards. "Sir, with the machine gun and barbed wire and artillery, breakthroughs don't come easy these days."

That was not only true, it was the understatement of the year. But Custer shook his head. He didn't want to see it, so he wouldn't. If you imagined a dumpy, half-senile ostrich with its head in the sand, that was Custer, at least in Dowling's uncharitable imagination. But, though he wore no epaulets, he did have stars on his shoulders. "The Rebs have worn themselves out," he declared. "Holding us off has been hard enough on them, and then they tried an offensive of their own. What can they possibly have left?"

Dowling didn't answer, not right away. The Confederate counterthrust from the south had been easier to stop than he'd expected. Maybe that meant the Rebs couldn't force a breakthrough, either. Maybe it just meant their generals were as bad as Custer. The great man's adjutant wasn't sure which of those was the more depressing conclusion.

Direct argument having failed again and again, he tried analogy: "Sir, when Coronado came into the USA from Mexico, he was looking for the Seven Cities of Cibola, all of them stuffed with gold. What did he find? Nothing but a bunch of damn redskins living in mud huts."

"What the *hell* are you talking about, Major?" Custer demanded: so much for analogy.

"I just meant, sir, that we keep looking for breakthroughs and keep thinking the Rebs are back to their last ditch, but it never seems to be true. Maybe we ought to try some different way of going at 'em," Dowling said.

"Shall we settle the war with a game of football, the way some idiots tried doing Christmas Day?" Custer suggested with sardonic glee.

"Uh, no sir," Dowling said hastily. From what he'd heard, First Army and the Confederate Army of Kentucky hadn't been the only forces that made impromptu Christmas truces with one another. From what he'd heard, the war had damn near fallen apart on Christmas Day, from the Gulf of California all the way to the Susquehanna. But it hadn't. It ground on, and would for who could guess how long.

In a way, the generality of the truce was too bad. If it had happened here and nowhere else, TR would have had all the justification he needed for sacking Custer and replacing him with someone who had some notion of how the world had changed since 1881. But no, no such luck.

"What *do* you propose, then, Major?" Custer sarcastically courteous was worse than Custer almost any other way. His ruling assumption seemed to be that, since he had no brains, no one else could possibly have any, either.

The trouble was, Dowling had no good answer for him here. That embarrassed the adjutant, but not as much as it might have. Nobody on the U.S. General Staff—or the Confederate General Staff, either, come to that—had any good answer on how to force a breakthrough. West of the Mississippi, the war was still mobile, but that was because there were a lot fewer men and a lot more miles west of the Mississippi. Wherever there were enough soldiers to man a solid trench line, offense literally stopped dead.

But if Dowling didn't know what the answer was, he had a pretty clear notion of what it *wasn't*. "Sending men out by the division to charge into machine-gun fire wastes lives, sir," he said. "We'd be better off pounding the Rebs with artillery, using soldiers to create positions from which we could pound them from three sides at once, things like that."

"We have the advantage in manpower, Major," Custer said. "What good is it if we don't use it?"

If we keep using it your way, we won't have it much longer, Dowling thought. Saying that aloud was probably fatal to a career. He braced himself to speak up anyway; maybe they'd give him an actual combat battalion as punishment for his crime.

Before he could make himself say anything, though, someone knocked on the door to Custer's office. The commanding general snarled something profane, then barked at Dowling: "See who the devil that is."

"Yes, sir," Dowling said resignedly. You interrupted Custer's meetings at your own risk. Dowling opened the door. Standing there was a scared-looking lieutenant from Cryptography, holding an enciphered telegram and a sheet of typewritten paper that was, presumably, the same message decoded. The lieutenant handed Dowling the paper—actually, thrust it into his hand—and then retreated at a clip not far short of flight.

As soon as Dowling had read the first two lines of the decryption, he understood why. But he was the one who'd have to break the news to Custer. Compared to that, the prospect of leading a combat battalion straight at the Rebel trenches looked downright delightful.

"Well?" the general commanding First Army snapped. "Don't just stand there like an upright piano. Tell me what in tarnation this is all about."

Dowling stiffened to rigid attention. Doing his best to keep vengeful glee from his voice, he said, "Yes, sir. Sir, you are ordered to detach two divisions from your front for immediate transfer to another theater."

That had about the same effect on Custer as hitting him between the eyes with a two-by-four would have done. He went white, and then a red that rapidly deepened to a dusky purple. "Who's stealing my men?" he whispered hoarsely. "If it's Pershing, I'll kill the son of a bitch with my own hands if it's the last thing I ever do. That upstart whippersnapper wants to steal all the glory for the Kentucky campaign, and damn me to hell if I aim to let him. I'll defy the order, that's what I'll do, and I'll fight it out in the paper if TR sacks me for it. First Roosevelt keeps me from the northern command he knows I want—and he knows why I want it, too—and now, just when I'm beginning to make decent progress here, he robs me of my forces."

"They aren't being transferred to General Pershing, sir." Now Dowling concealed regret: Pershing had made far more progress against the Rebels than Custer had. He'd also had the sense to save lives by pinching off Louisville from the flanks instead of going straight into the city, as the U.S. Army had tried to do during the Second Mexican War. "The order comes directly from General Wood, at General Staff headquarters in Philadelphia."

Custer expressed an opinion of the relationship between Wood and Roosevelt that reflected poorly on the heterosexuality of either man. Like any underling with an ounce of sense, Dowling knew when to feign deafness. "Why the devil is Wood stealing my men, then?" Custer said, rather more pungently than that.

"Sir, a major Mormon uprising has broken out in Utah," Dowling said, waving the decipherment of the telegram to show the source of his news. "They're right on one of our cross-country rail lines; we have to bring them back under the flag as fast as we can."

"God damn them to hell, and may the U.S. Army send them there," Custer exclaimed. "We should have done it before the War of Secession, and we really should have done it during the Second Mexican War, when they tried to sneak out of our beloved Union. If anyone had listened to me then—" He shook his head. "But no. We had to clasp the viper to our bosom. I was there, by God. I wanted them to hang all the Mormons' leaders, not just a handful of them. I wanted them to hang Abe Lincoln, too, while they had the chance. But would anybody hear a word I said? No. Are we better off because no one would? No again."

"Sir, I wouldn't call what we did in Utah during the Second Mexican War clasping the Mormons to our bosom, or afterwards, either," Dowling said; Custer had a selective memory for facts. John Pope and later military governors in Utah had jumped on the Mormons with both feet then, to make sure they didn't try giving the USA any more hard times. He supposed he could see why they'd outlawed polygamy, but suppressing public worship along with all other public meetings had always struck him as far too heavy-handed. Even after Utah joined the Union, public worship by groups larger than ten remained illegal; since the Second Mexican War, the Supreme Court hadn't been much inclined to interfere with claims of military necessity. And so the Mormon Temple in Salt Lake City remained empty to this day. No wonder the Mormons didn't love the U.S. government.

Custer coughed rheumily. Still glowering at his adjutant, he asked, "Are the damned Mormons in bed with the Rebs or the Canucks or both at once?"

"That's—not immediately clear from the reports I have here, sir," Dowling answered, studying his boss with an emotion he wasn't used to feeling: respect. The sole piece of the military art with which Custer was familiar was the headlong smash, but his red-veined nose had a genuine gift for intrigue. "There are some foreign agitators in the state, but no details as to who they are."

"Could be either one," Custer judged. "The Mormons don't like niggers much better than the Rebels do, but the Canadians could be seducing them with lies about freedom of religion." He laughed unpleasantly. "If they were up in Canada, they'd have gotten the same short shrift the Germans who settled that town called Berlin did, and you can bet your bottom dollar on it."

"That's probably true, sir," Dowling said, and for once simple agreement was just that, nothing more. He went on, "Shall I draft orders implementing this command for your signature, sir?"

"Yes, go ahead," Custer said with a melodramatic sigh. "They must have timed their damned uprising with a view to spoiling my offensive and robbing me of the breakthrough I surely would have earned. They'll pay, the scum."

Dowling sighed as he bent over the situation map to figure out how he'd pull thirty thousand men or so out of the line. That let him turn away from Custer, which in turn let him snigger wickedly. If the Confederates and Canadians didn't have worse threats than First Army to worry about, the war was going better than he'd figured.

A sharp explosion close by made Reggie Bartlett jump and look around for the nearest hole in the ground in which to dive. People in civilian clothes on the streets of Richmond gave him odd looks: why on earth would a soldier be frightened of a backfiring motorcar? The Duryea, plainly having engine trouble, backfired a couple of more times before finally beginning to run a little better.

Another soldier coming his way, though, nodded in complete understanding. "Just back from the front, are you?" he said.

Bartlett nodded. "Sure am." His laugh was self-deprecating. "You can take the soldier out of the trenches, but it's not so easy taking the trenches out of the soldier. This is my hometown, and I feel like I'm a stranger here."

"Know what you mean, pal," the other soldier said. "You get away for a while and it doesn't seem like the real world's real, if you know what I mean." He stuck out a hand. "Name's Alexander Gribbin—Alec, they call me." He had swarthy, handsome features and a neat little chin beard that made him look like a Frenchman.

Giving his own name, Reggie shook hands with him. He said, "Alec, shall we find someplace where the only pops we're likely to hear come from corks going out of bottles?"

"Friend, I like the way you think," Gribbin said enthusiastically. "If this is your town, you ought to know about places like that, eh?"

"You just want a drink, we can do that anywhere," Bartlett said.

"I've seen that," Gribbin agreed. "Thank your lucky stars, Reggie my friend, the Drys haven't gotten their way here in Virginia. Down in Mississippi, where I come from, it's a desert, nothin' else but."

"That's hard. That's cruel hard," Bartlett said, and his newfound companion nodded, his mournful expression showing just how hard it was. Bartlett went on, "What we could do, though, if you want the chance of something livelier, is to go to the saloon over at Ford's Hotel, right across the street from Capitol Square. It's only a couple blocks from here. Never know who's liable to show up there—congressmen, foreigners, admirals, who can say?—but they don't turn common soldiers away."

"They'd better not," Gribbin said indignantly. "I'm a white man, by Jesus, and I'm as good as any other white man God ever made."

"Not only that," Reggie Bartlett said, "but I've got money in my pocket—some, anyhow—and it spends as good as any other money the mint ever made."

Alec Gribbin grinned widely. "I'm the same way, and so is my money. Let's go."

Ford's Hotel, on the corner of Broad and Eleventh Streets, was a four-story building of white marble, with a fancy colonnaded entrance. The Negro doorman, who wore a uniform with more gold buttons and ribbons and medals than a French field marshal could have displayed, tipped his hat in salute as the two Confederate soldiers in their plain butternut walked past him.

"*Hell* of a place," Gribbin said with a low whistle, gazing around at the rococo splendor of the lobby. He winked and lowered his voice: "Wouldn't it make the bulliest damn sporting house in the whole wide world?"

"Matter of fact, it would," Bartlett said, "but I wouldn't have the money to go into a sporting house tricked out this fancy." He walked down the hall. His boots sank into the thick pile of the Turkish carpets underfoot. That wasn't so bad; the rugs didn't try to pull the boots off his feet, the way the trench mud had in the Roanoke River valley.

The saloon was a saloon: long bar, brass rail, mirror behind it so the bottles of whiskey and gin and rum looked to be twice as many as they really were, free-lunch counter with a painting of a nude above it. But the place catered to a prosperous crowd. Not only was the free lunch more appetizing than the usual run of sardines and sausage and limp cheese, but the nude, a voluptuous redhead, was a lot more appetizing than the common saloon daub.

"Makes me wish I was an artist," Gribbin said, eyeing her with genuine respect. "Get to see girls like that, and in the altogether—I tell you for a fact, Reggie, it just beats the stuffing out of freezing your feet in a trench in Pennsylvania. That country's so cold in the wintertime, the Yanks are welcome to it, far as I can see."

They strode off to the bar, squeezing in alongside of a couple of portly, middle-aged men in expensive suits. "Beer," Bartlett said. Gribbin ordered a whiskey. Reggie put a quarter on the bar. It disappeared. No change came back.

"Not your five-cents-a-shot place," Gribbin observed. Then he knocked back the whiskey. His eyes got big. "I see why, too. That's the straight goods there. Those cheap joints, they put in red peppers and stuff, make you think you're getting better'n raw rotgut. You know, real whiskey's *good.*" He watched Bartlett drink half his schooner of beer, then said, "Come on, finish that so as I can buy you another one. We can hit the free lunch, too. We drink enough, they won't care how much we dent the profits with what we eat."

Bartlett drained the schooner. "Ahh," he said. His new friend slapped down a quarter. The barkeep, a Negro in a boiled shirt, fixed refills.

The two portly fellows were talking about pension plans for soldiers after the war was over: congressmen, or else lobbyists. Important people, yes, but Bartlett wasn't much interested in pension law. He wished he had more money now, sure, but he wasn't going to worry about fifty years down the line, especially not when his life expectancy once he got back to the front was more likely to be measured in weeks than in years.

Gribbin returned with salami and radishes on rye bread, a couple of deviled eggs, fried oysters, pickles, and pretzels. Reggie went and got some food for himself. The spread the Ford Hotel set out was another reason to come here, and the congressmen or lobbyists or whatever they were didn't have too much pride to keep them from raiding it, either.

A tough-looking fellow in a foreign naval uniform came up and stood at the bar next to Bartlett. He ordered scotch, which, with his accent, gave a pretty clear notion of his nationality. Nodding affably to Bartlett, he said, "Confusion to the Yankees, what?" and lifted his glass.

"I'll drink to that." Reggie proceeded to prove it.

The Englishman made his drink disappear so fast, he might have done it by magic or inhalation. He got another, then raised his glass again and proceeded to elaborate on his earlier toast: "To the Empire and the Confederacy, and to keeping the United States in their place."

"And out of ours," Bartlett added, which made Alec Gribbin laugh and the naval officer smile wide enough to show a pair of front teeth a rabbit would have been proud to claim. He drank his second shot of scotch as fast as he had the first. Emboldened by his friendly manner, Reggie asked, "How's it going, out on the ocean?"

Before replying, the Royal Navy man ordered a third scotch. Then he said, "Damned if I know how it will all turn out. Damned if anyone knows how it will all turn out. Honors about even thus far in the Atlantic. Argentina's coming in on our side, I'd say, outweighs Chile's joining the Americans and Germans, though none of the South American navies is important enough to swing the balance in any decisive way." Then, seeming to contradict himself, he went on, "I do wish the Empire of Brazil would come to a decision of one sort or the other."

"They damn well better come in on our side when they come," Reggie said angrily, to which Alec Gribbin gave an emphatic assent. Bartlett went on, "Hell, they held on to their slaves longer than we did."

He had thought that a convincing argument. He kept on thinking it a convincing argument. The Royal Navy man called for yet another drink and gulped it with the same alacrity he'd shown with the ones before. "Allies," he muttered, but it didn't sound like a toast. Mostly to himself he went on, "The South and the czars. God have mercy on a free country."

"And what the devil is that supposed to mean?" Alexander Gribbin demanded. He sounded a lot hotter with whiskey in him than he had without. "You saying we aren't free? Is that what you're saying? Go up to the USA and see how you like it there. The Confederacy is the freest country in the world, and that's a fact."

"Is it?" The Englishman had taken on whiskey, too. He pointed to the bartender. "Would you agree with that statement, sir? The statement that this great nation is the freest country in the world, I mean."

The bartender looked from the English officer to the two Confederate privates and back again. He didn't say anything, though his eyes were wide in his dark face. "Oh, hell, what are you asking him for, anyway?" Bartlett said with a dismissive wave of his hand. "He's just a nigger. He doesn't know anything."

"Something more than one man in three of your populace falls into that category," the Royal Navy man said. "In spite of that, you still call yourself the freest country in the world?"

"Of course we do," Reggie said. "We are."

He and the Englishman stared at each other in mutual incomprehension. "Enjoy it, then," the fellow said at last. He called for one last drink, drained it, and left after adding a tip for the bartender.

Bartlett shook his head. "Can't figure out what's chewin' on him. I'd say lice, but he's never seen the inside of a trench, not the likes of him."

"Don't worry about it, soldier," one of the prominent men in dark suits said. "There's a certain kind of Englishman who thinks that if you're not English, you're sort of halfway to being a nigger yourself."

"Is that a fact? Well, to hell with him, then," Gribbin said, and started after the naval officer. "Anybody who thinks I'm halfway to a nigger, he's halfway to the hospital."

Reggie grabbed him by the arm. "Ease off, Alec," he said urgently. "You beat on an ally, you get yourself in more trouble than you can shake a stick at."

"That, in essence, is correct," the man in the suit said. "It doesn't matter whether we love the limeys and they love us. What matters is that, no matter what else we do, we don't do anything to make them like us less than they like the USA. Should that misfortune ever strike us, boys, you can buy a coffin, on account of we are dead and buried."

"I don't want to buy me a coffin," Reggie said. "All I want is another schooner." He raised his voice to call to the Negro tending bar: "Boy, another beer!"

"Yes, sir," the bartender said, and brought him one.

After he paid for it, he turned to Gribbin and said, "You know what's nice about niggers? You don't have to waste time bein' polite with 'em."

"I'll drink to that," Alec said, and did.

The bartender picked up a rag and polished the gleaming surface of the bar, over and over again. He did not look up at the two soldiers.

Sam Carsten slept in the middle bunk on the *Dakota*, which made him feel like the meat in a sandwich. You had a guy on top of you and a guy underneath, to say nothing of a whole bunk room full of guys all around. Your skinny mattress creaked and groaned on the iron frame, as did those of your two bunkmates. Everybody snored. Everybody farted. Nobody washed his feet often enough.

And, half the time or more, you didn't even notice, not from lights-out to the klaxon that yanked you from your bunk as if it physically grabbed you and threw you down on the deck. If you weren't dead beat when you lay down, you'd figured out how to screw around so well, it looked as if you were working to some chief petty officers who'd long since seen every kind of screwing around known to man.

This particular morning, Sam really resented the klaxon. In his dream, Maggie Stevenson had just started doing something highly immoral and even more highly enjoyable. If she'd kept on for another few seconds—

His feet hit the iron deck before his eyes came open all the way. When they did, they saw not voluptuous Maggie but skinny, hairy, snaggle-toothed Vic Crosetti, who had the top bunk. "You ain't no beautiful blonde," Carsten said accusingly.

"Yeah, and if I was, I wouldn't want nothin' to do with the likes of you," Crosetti said, scrambling into his trousers.

Sam got dressed, too, and staggered down the hall to the galley for breakfast. After oatmeal, bacon, stewed prunes, and several mugs of scalding, snarling coffee, he decided he was going to live. He went up on deck for roll call and sick call.

The sky was brilliantly blue, the sea even bluer. The sun blazed down. He could feel his fair skin starting to sizzle, the same way the bacon had on the griddles down below. *No help for it,* he thought ruefully. He'd smeared every ointment under the tropic sun on his hide, and that tropic sun had defeated them all. He thought longingly of San Francisco, of mist, of fog, of damp. He'd been happy there; that was the country he was made for.

"Romantic," he muttered under his breath as he started chipping paint, stopping rust before it got started. "The South Pacific is supposed to be romantic. What the hell's so romantic about looking like an Easter ham all the goddamn time?"

Chip, chip, chip. Chip, chip, chip. The *Dakota* plowed through light chop, several hundred miles south and west of Honolulu. The only way to find out what the limeys and the Japs were up to—if they were up to anything—was to go out on patrol and look around.

With the *Dakota* steamed the *Nebraska* and the *Vermont*, as well as a pair of cruiser squadrons and a whole flotilla of speedy destroyers. The fleet could handle any probe the English and the Japanese tried, and could damage a full-scale assault against the Sandwich Islands, meanwhile warning Honolulu of impending danger. "We caught the limeys napping," Carsten said, chipping away so industriously, no one could give him a hard time about it. "They won't give us the same treatment."

As if to underscore his words, a high-pitched buzzing, as if from a gnat made suddenly bigger than any eagle, rose from the bow of the *Dakota*. Sam stopped what he was doing and looked that way. The buzz rose in volume, then steadied. It was followed by an enormous hiss that might have come from an outsized snake alarmed at the outsized gnat. A rattling and clattering unlike any found in nature accompanied the hiss.

The compressed-air catapult threw the aeroplane off the deck of the *Dakota*. Inside a space of fifty feet, it had accelerated the flying machine up past forty miles an hour, plenty fast enough for the aeroplane to keep on flying and not fall into the Pacific.

Carsten stood for a moment, watching the aeroplane gain altitude. He shook his head in bemusement. It was such a flimsy thing, wood and canvas and wire, a mere nothing when measured against the armor plate and great guns of a battleship. But if it spotted the enemy where the bulge of the earth still hid them from the *Dakota*, it made a formidable tool of war in its own right.

Up at the bow, the catapult crew were taking their toy apart and stowing it so it wouldn't be in the way if the guns of the *Dakota* had to go into action. That didn't take long. They had an interesting job up there, and people seemed to fuss more about aeroplanes with every passing month.

"People can fuss all they want," Sam said. "Let's see an aeroplane sink a ship. Then I'll sit up and take notice. In the meantime, guns are plenty good enough for me."

He worked away for a while. Then horns blared and voices started shouting through megaphones. Sam sprinted toward the forward starboard sponson, one running sailor among hundreds. "Battle stations!" officers and senior ratings shouted, over and over again. "Battle stations!"

When he was working out in the open, Carsten hadn't too much minded the warm, muggy air. He would have enjoyed it, had the sun not pounded down on him. Down below in the sponson, the sun wasn't baking him. In that hot, cramped place, though, he felt as if he were being steamed like a pot of beans in the galley.

"This the real thing?" he asked Hiram Kidde.

The gunner's mate shrugged. "Damned if I know," he answered. "Could be, though. That new wireless they've put on board the aeroplanes, it lets 'em pass on the news before they come back to us."

"Yeah," Carsten said. "Wish we would have had a set like that last year, when we were steaming for the Sandwich Islands. Would have come in mighty handy, spying out the harbor and everything."

Kidde nodded. "Sure would. But the new aeroplanes got bigger engines, so they can carry more'n the ones we brought with us last year, and the new wireless sets are lighter than the ones they had then, too."

"Things keep changing all the damn time." Carsten could not have said for sure whether that was praise or complaint. "Hell, one of these days, 'Cap'n,' maybe even battleships'll be obsolete."

"Not any time soon." Kidde set an affectionate hand on the breech of the five-inch gun whose master he was. But then he looked thoughtful. "Or maybe you're right. Who the devil can say for sure? You're just a pup; the way it looks to you, the Navy hasn't changed a whole hell of a lot since you've been in. Me, though, I joined in 1892. An armored cruiser nowadays'd run rings around what they called battleships back then, and blow 'em to hell and gone without breaking a sweat. You look back on things, they ain't the same as they used to be. Nobody ever heard of aeroplanes when I joined up, that's for damn sure. So who really does know what things'll look like twenty, thirty years from now?"

"I was thinking about aeroplanes when we launched ours," Carsten said.

"Probably thinking when you should have been working," Kidde said with a laugh—he'd been in the Navy a long time, all right.

"Who, me?" Sam answered, drolly innocent. Kidde laughed again. Carsten went on, "I was thinking how good they were for spotting, but that they couldn't really do anything to a ship. What you're saying, though, makes me wonder. If their engines keep getting bigger, maybe they'll be able to haul big bombs or even torpedoes one of these days."

"Yeah, maybe." Kidde frowned. "I wouldn't like to be on the receiving end of something like that, I tell you. Torpedoes from submersibles, they pack more punch than a twelve-inch shell, even if they don't have the range. But you can outrun a submersible. You can't outrun an aeroplane."

"You can shoot an aeroplane down, though, a lot easier than you can get at a submersible when it's under the water," said Luke Hoskins, sticking an oar into the conversation.

Before either Hiram Kidde or Sam could answer the other shell-heaver, the all-clear sounded. Carsten let out a sigh of relief. "Nothing but a drill," he said.

"Got to treat it like the real thing, though," Kidde replied. "You never can tell when it's gonna be."

Despite the all-clear, the gun crew stayed at their station till the starboard gunnery officer poked his head into the sponson and dismissed them. Carsten went back to the upper deck at about a quarter of the speed at which he'd run to his gun. When you'd just wondered whether you were about to go into battle, fighting rust didn't seem so important any more.

A couple of hours after the all-clear was given, the aeroplane splashed down into the water not far from the *Dakota*. Before long, the battleship's crane hauled it out of the Pacific, only a few feet away from where Sam was working. He waved to the pilot as the fellow came level with the upper deck of the ship.

The pilot waved back, a big grin on his face. "Always good to come home," he called. "Gets lonesome out there when all you can see is ocean."

"I believe it." As far as Carsten was concerned, you had to be crazy to go up there in one of those contraptions in the first place. If your engine quit when you were a hundred miles from anywhere, what did you do? Oh, maybe you could send a wireless message for help, and maybe they'd find you if you did, but did you want to count on that? Not so far as Sam could see, you didn't. The ocean was a hell of a big place; five years' sailing on it had taught him that. An aeroplane bobbing in the chop wasn't even a flyspeck on its immensity.

Not long after the aeroplane was hauled out of the ocean, one of the cruisers with the fleet, the *Avenger*, sent up a kite balloon. As always, the hydrogen-filled canvas bag put Sam in mind of an outsized frankfurter that had escaped its roll and floated up into the sky. From his distance, he couldn't see the cable that moored the balloon to its mother ship. He had a hard time making out the wicker basket that held the observer below the balloon and the wind cups that stabilized the gasbag as an ordinary kite's tail did for it.

Fleet orders were to have either an aeroplane or a kite balloon aloft as nearly continuously as possible. Balloons, of course, couldn't fly away from the U.S. ships the way aeroplanes could, but, floating four thousand feet above the fleet, could see a lot farther than lookouts on even the tallest observation masts.

The fellow up there had a telephone link to the *Avenger*. If he spotted anything, he'd pass on the news and they'd haul him down as fast as they could. A kite balloon would stay up fine at cruising speed. You couldn't keep it up, though, if you needed to go flat out, the way you did when you had a battle to fight.

Carsten was glad to watch the sausage floating up there. It felt like a life insurance policy to him. If the Royal Navy or the Japanese spotted the Americans before the U.S. fleet saw them, that meant trouble, big trouble. You wanted to be in position to do what you intended to do, and do it first. What had happened at Pearl Harbor would have taught that to anyone foolish enough to doubt it.

Sam waved to the balloonist, as he had to the aeroplane pilot. Unlike the pilot, the balloonist didn't see him. That was all right. The balloonist had more important things to look for than one friendly sailor.

"And you know what?" Carsten muttered to himself. "I hope to God he doesn't see any of them."

George Enos peered out over the rail of the *Mercy* at the broad Atlantic all around. The *Mercy* flew not only the Confederate flag but also that of the Red Cross. It also had the Red Cross prominently displayed on white squares to port and starboard. Any submarine that got a good look at it would, with luck, sheer off.

With luck. Those were the key words. With luck, the *Swamp Fox* never would have spotted the *Ripple* in the first place, and Enos' ordeal in Confederate prison camps wouldn't have started. He hoped his luck was better now than it had been then.

There, in the east—not a star, but a plume of smoke. He turned to Fred Butcher and said, "That's the Spanish ship—I hope."

"Yeah, I hope so, too," the *Ripple*'s mate answered. "If it's not a Spanish ship, then it belongs to . . . somebody else." In these waters, *somebody else* might be the USA or Germany or England or France or the Confederate States. Maybe whoever it was would let the *Mercy* go on its way anyhow—ships from other nations performed similar duties, and wanted to keep reciprocal good treatment—but maybe it wouldn't, too.

"They were saying, before we set out, that ships from Argentina don't go into the open waters of the North Atlantic any more," Enos said. "They scurry across to Dakar in Africa where the ocean's narrowest, and then hug the coast the rest of the way up to England."

"England would starve without that Argentine grain and beef," Butcher said. "I wish they would starve, but we can't get at those ships, not way the hell out there we can't."

Charlie White came over and stood with his crewmates. George leaned across Fred Butcher and slapped him on the shoulder. "Bet that smoke looks even better to you than it does to me," he said.

The Negro nodded. "I don't care if that's the neutral ship to take us home to the USA or a cruiser that's going to sink us," he said. "Either way, it's better off than being a colored fellow down in the CSA."

He was a lot skinnier than he had been when they were captured. Somehow, his rations had never come out quite right—and the Confederates had worked him harder than any white detainee. All that was supposed to be against the rules, which didn't keep it from happening.

In a musing voice, White went on, "Isn't a whole lot of fun being a Negro in the USA, either. But now I know the difference between bad and worse, I tell you that for a fact."

"I believe it," Enos said. He peered across the ocean again. Now he could see a ship out there, not just smoke. It looked slow and boxy, not like a steam-powered shark. "That's a freighter—and I think that means it's the Spanish ship."

Closer and closer came the ship to the *Mercy*. Not only did it fly a huge Spanish flag, it also had Spain's red-and-gold flag painted on its flanks, the same way the *Mercy* bore the Red Cross. It looked gaudy, but that was better than looking like a juicy target.

An officer in the dark gray of the Confederate Navy shouted, "Detainees, line up by the boats for exchange!"

Along with the other crewmen from the *Ripple* and several dozen more U.S. sailors captured by Confederate submersibles, commerce raiders, and warships, George Enos hurried to take his place by a lifeboat. The officer, who had a list on a clipboard, went down the line of men, checking off names. He had to ask George who he was, but needed to put no such question to Charlie White, who stood behind Enos. "All right, nigger," he said, drawing a thick, black line through White's name, "we're rid of you. Got rid of your great-granddaddy a while ago, and now we're rid of you. What do you think of that?"

"Sir," Charlie White said (even angry, he was polite), "since you ask, sir, I think that when my grandfather—that's who it was—ran away from Georgia, he knew what he was doing."

The Confederate officer stared at him. George Enos bit his lip. Half of him wanted to cheer Charlie; the other half feared the Negro's outspokenness would queer the exchange for everyone. The officer took a deep breath, as if to shout an order. But then, reluctantly, he shook his head. "If we weren't getting our own back for you, nigger, you'd pay plenty for that," he said, and wrote something next to the name through which he'd just lined. "And you'd better get down on your black knees and pray we don't ever catch you again, you understand me?"

"Oh, yes, sir," White answered. "I understand that real well." The officer gave him one last glare before continuing down the line.

"Good for you, Charlie," George whispered when the Rebel was out of earshot.

"Sometimes your mouth is smarter than your brains, that's all," the cook said.

At the officer's command, the detainees boarded the boats—all except for poor Lucas Phelps, who was buried down in North Carolina and would never see Boston again. *God damn the Rebels,* George thought, even as the sailors of the *Mercy* lowered them to the waters of the Atlantic.

Swinging down, ropes creaking as they ran through the pulley, Enos felt as if he were on a Ferris wheel. "One thing," he said as he and his fellow sailors started rowing toward the Spanish ship: "we all know how to handle a boat." A couple of men laughed; most just kept on rowing. A couple of Confederates sat, stolid and silent, at the stern: they would row back to the *Mercy.*

The Spanish ship—her name was *Padre Junipero Serra*—loomed up like a gaudily painted steel cliff. Her sailors had hung nets over the side, up which the detainees could scramble. A Spanish officer in a uniform fancy enough to have come out of a comic opera took the names of the sailors as they clambered up on deck and checked them off on a list he held on a clipboard exactly like the one his Confederate counterpart had used.

When everyone was accounted for, the Spaniard blew a whistle. A line of thin men in shabby clothes came up out of the hold and walked to the *Junipero Serra*'s lifeboats. *They look just like us,* George thought, and then shook his head—why should that surprise him? Only the sailors' drawls—an accent he heartily hoped never to hear again—said they came from the CSA, not the USA.

Their names got checked off as meticulously as those of Enos and his comrades had aboard the *Mercy.* Once the Spanish officer satisfied himself that the count was full, complete, and accurate, the Confederate sailors boarded the boats and were lowered to the sea. A couple of Spaniards sat in each boat, as a couple of Confederates had sat in the boat Enos had helped row here.

No doubt the Rebels on the *Mercy* scrutinized their returning detainees as closely as they had the men they were releasing. Some little while went by before they ran up signal flags: ALL PROPER. THANK YOU. Black smoke poured from the *Mercy*'s funnels. Picking up speed, she made a long, slow turn and started back toward her home port.

"We are going to take you to Nueva Iorque," the Spanish officer said, in English that would have been very good if Enos hadn't needed a couple of seconds to realize he meant New York. That hesitation made him miss a few words: ". . . have a pilot to take us through the minefields around the city. The minefields of the USA, I mean to say. If we meet a Confederate mine, it is as God wills." He made the sign of the cross. Several U.S. sailors, among them Patrick O'Donnell, the captain of the *Ripple*, imitated the gesture.

"I bet there's mines outside of Boston harbor, too, to keep the Rebs and the limeys from getting too close," Fred Butcher said. "World hasn't stood still while we were stuck in that camp."

George hadn't thought much about that, past getting back to Sylvia and his children. Now he said, "Bet some poor damned fishermen got blown to hell and gone, too, when they hit a mine that wasn't supposed to be where it was."

Everybody who heard him nodded somberly. That was the way things worked. Fishermen always ended up with the shitty end of the stick.

A Spanish sailor, working with a few words of English and a lot of dumb show, took the exchanged detainees belowdecks to their cabins. Enos' would have been small and cramped with two men in it, and it held four. He didn't much care. Except for sleeping, he didn't plan on spending much time there.

If Charlie White had turned out chow anything like what the *Junipero Serra*'s cooks served up, the *Ripple*'s crew would have lynched him and hung his body on T Wharf as a warning to others. Enos didn't care about that, either. He didn't think he'd starve to death before they got to New York.

The cigar a Spaniard gave him turned out to be nasty, too. He smoked it anyway, and went up on deck to look around. The Atlantic—what a surprise!—looked the same from the *Junipero Serra* as it had from the *Mercy*. In the west, the sun was going down toward the ocean. Most ships on most oceans these days showed no lights at night: people who noticed them were too likely to be enemies. But the *Junipero Serra* lit herself up like a Christmas tree. She wanted everyone on both sides of the war to know exactly what she was. The more obvious she made it, the less likely she'd become a target.

Enos looked around again. He changed his mind. The Atlantic did seem different after all. "I'm going home," he said.

Irving Morrell stared at the list Lieutenant Craddock had just handed him. "You know, Bill," he said mildly, "I don't have time for this." That made a pretty fair understatement. He'd been promoted to major after winkling the Rebs in southeastern Kentucky out of their tough hilltop position, and was now heading up the battalion where he'd commanded a company till a couple of weeks before.

"Sir, I compiled this list on orders direct from the War Department." Craddock could have spoken no more reverently of the Book of Genesis.

"I understand that," Morrell said, trying for patience. "I handed on the orders myself, if you'll remember. But don't you think getting ready for our next move against the Rebs is more important than a witch hunt?"

Craddock looked stubborn, sticking out his chin. It was firm as granite, and about as hard. The same, unfortunately, held for the rest of his cranium.

"Sir, since you asked my opinion, I think rooting out disloyal elements has a very high priority. If our next move against the enemy should fail, it might be on account of"—he lowered his voice to a dramatic whisper—"subversion."

"Oh, for Christ's sake!" Morrell exploded. "All right, you hunted through the pay records. We have in this battalion"—he glanced down at the list Craddock had given him—"four, count them, four Mormons. Has any one of them ever given the slightest sign of disloyalty?"

"No, sir," Craddock said. "But you never can tell, not with these people you can't. They looked loyal to the USA, too, till this Deseret rebellion kicked up. They might be laying low."

"Lying," Morrell corrected absently.

"Yes, sir, they might be lying, too," Craddock agreed with earnest ignorance. Morrell heaved a silent sigh. The lieutenant said, "But the orders require that they be identified and interrogated. As you see, sir, I've identified them."

He was trained in military subordination. That meant he didn't yell, *Now you've got to interrogate them*. But he couldn't have shouted it any louder than he didn't say it. And he did have the orders, if not common sense, on his side.

Morrell sighed again, this time loud and long. "All right, Bill. Bring the Mormons to me and I'll have a talk with them." He didn't think a Kentucky forest the ideal spot for this sort of procedure, but this was where he happened to be.

"Yes, sir!" Now Craddock sounded happier. Things were going as they were supposed to on paper, which warmed the cockles of his heart. "I'll go get them. One at a time, of course, so they can't overpower the two of us, escape through the woods, and warn the Rebs of our plans."

Beyond arguing by then, Morrell said, "However you want to do it." Craddock hurried away, intent on his mission. If he'd used that much ingenuity figuring out the trouble real enemies could cause, he would have been a better soldier for it.

He soon returned with a young, towheaded private who looked confused and worried. Morrell would have looked the same way if he'd suddenly been hauled up before his commanding officer. The soldier came to stiff attention. "Dinwiddie, Brigham," he said, rattling off his pay number.

"At ease, Dinwiddie," Morrell said. "You're not in trouble." Lieutenant Craddock's face set in stern, disapproving lines. Morrell ignored him. Dinwiddie was from the company he'd commanded. He'd always thought of the youngster as too good to be true. Dinwiddie didn't drink, he didn't smoke, he didn't gamble, he wasn't out to lay every woman he set eyes on, and he obeyed every order promptly, cheerfully, and bravely. What little Morrell knew about Mormonism made him think it was a pretty silly religion, but it had to have something going for it if it turned out people like Dinwiddie. Picking his words with care, Morrell asked, "What do you think of what's going on in Utah these days, son?"

He'd never seen Dinwiddie's bright-blue eyes anything but open and candid. He did now. Shutters might have slammed down on the private's face. He spoke like a machine: "Sir, I don't know much about it."

Lieutenant Craddock stirred. Morrell glared him into continued silence and tried again: "Have you heard from your family? Are they all right?"

"I got one letter not long ago," Dinwiddie answered. "It was censored pretty bad, but they're well, yes, sir."

"Glad to hear it," Morrell said, on the whole sincerely. "With things the way they are, how do you feel about being a soldier in the United States Army?"

That hooded look stayed on Dinwiddie's face. "Sir, it doesn't have anything to do with me right now, does it? Provo's a long way from here."

"So it is." Morrell cocked his head to one side and studied the young Mormon. "Rebel lines, though, they're only a few hundred yards off." He waved southwest. As if on cue, a rifle shot rang out, silencing the spring peepers for a moment.

Dinwiddie looked horrified. If he was an actor, he belonged on the stage. "Sir, what the Rebs do to Latter-Day Saints in the CSA— You hear stories about what the Russians do to Jews. It's like that, sir. They don't want any of us, and they don't make any bones about it."

Morrell wondered what things were going to be like for Mormons in the USA after the Army finished crushing the Deseret revolt. They hadn't been easy before; they'd get harder now. It had been more suppression than persecution. What it was going to be . . . Well, if Brigham Dinwiddie hadn't thought of that for himself, no point doing the job for him. "All right, Dinwiddie—dismissed," Morrell said. "Go on back to your unit."

The Mormon saluted and left. Lieutenant Craddock said, "Sir, forgive me, but I didn't think that was a very thorough interrogation."

"Neither did I," Morrell said. "The way I see it is, if I rake these people over the coals when they haven't done anything, I'll give them a reason to be disloyal even if they didn't have one before. Now go fetch me Corporal"—he checked the list—"Corporal Thomas."

Corporal Orson Gregory Thomas—who made a point of asking to be called Gregory—echoed Brigham Dinwiddie's comments almost word for word. Lieutenant Craddock found that suspicious. Morrell found it natural—put two men of the same beliefs in the same awkward situation and you could expect to get the same kind of answers out of them.

Homer Benson, another private, again gave almost the same set of responses. Lieutenant Craddock's granite jaw stuck out like the Rock of Gibraltar as he listened, his face even more disapproving than it had been at the start of the interrogations. He didn't say anything when Morrell dismissed Benson back to his unit, but his stiff posture and even stiffer manner spoke volumes.

Dick Francis, still another private, was the last man on the list Craddock had so laboriously compiled. He looked enough like Dinwiddie to have been his first cousin, and shared his diffident manner. But when Morrell asked him what he thought about the Mormon uprising in Utah, he said, "I hope they kick the Army out of there, sir. That's our land. All the United States ever did was give us grief."

Morrell pointed to the green-gray uniform Francis had on. "What are you doing wearing that, then?"

"Sir, I was rendering unto Caesar," the private answered. "When the Prophet and the Elders said that, since we were part of the United States, we should take part in this war, I obeyed: it was a teaching inspired by God. But now that they see things differently, I won't lie and say I'm sorry. I think Deseret should be free, so we can worship as we please."

"Want a whole houseful of wives, do you?" Lieutenant Craddock said, a nasty leer on his face.

"That will be enough, Lieutenant," Morrell said sharply.

But the damage was done. "You see what I mean, sir?" Francis said. "Why should I love a government that looks at us like that? The way we get treated, we're the niggers of the USA."

From what Morrell had heard, the Mormons didn't treat Negroes as if they were their brothers. That, though, was neither here nor there. Morrell rubbed his chin. "What the devil am I supposed to do with you, Francis?" he asked. He hadn't expected this problem, assuming all the Mormons in the battalion would stay loyal. Craddock looked vindicated.

Dick Francis shrugged. "Why are you asking me, sir? You're the United States Army officer." While sounding perfectly respectful, he somehow managed to turn Morrell's title into one of reproach.

Morrell thought hard about doing nothing whatever to him. When the Rebs started shooting his way, he'd have to shoot back if he wanted to go on living. But Morrell couldn't take the chance, not with somebody who'd openly admitted he was hoping for the ruination of the USA.

"I'm going to send you back to divisional headquarters," he said. "I don't want any man on the front line whose first loyalty isn't to his country and to the men on either side of him."

He didn't know what Division HQ did with people like Francis. The Mormon soldier did; he'd had more incentive to learn such things. "Detention camp for me, then," he said, sounding not a bit put out. "I'll pray for you, sir. For a gentile, you're a good man."

Not knowing what to do with such faint praise, Morrell turned to Craddock. "Take him back to Division," he said. "Tell them he doesn't feel in good conscience he can go on being a soldier." He tried not to think about what lay in store for Francis. He hadn't made a point of learning about detention camps, either, but they bore an evil reputation.

"Yes, sir," Craddock said enthusiastically. He turned to Francis. "Let's go, you."

Watching them tramp away from the front, Morrell shook his head. War would have been a much simpler, easier business with politics out of the mix.

XII

Emily Pinkard looked at the alarm clock, which, as she did every morning, she'd carried out from the bedroom to the kitchen. "Oh, goodness, I'm late," she said, and gulped down her coffee.

Jefferson Pinkard was still plowing his way through bacon and eggs. He got up, though, when his wife set her cup in the tin sink, and grabbed her. "Give me a kiss before you go," he said. When she did, he tightened his arms around her. Her lips and tongue were warm and sweet and promising. "Mm," he said, still holding her. "I don't think I want you to leave."

She twisted away from him. "I got to, Jeff," she said. "You can just walk on over to the foundry, but I got to catch the trolley if I'm gonna get where I'm going. They dock you every minute you're not there, too. I'll see you tonight, honey." Her eyes told what she meant by that. It was everything he could have hoped for and then some.

Reluctantly, he nodded, no matter how much he wanted to take her back to the bedroom now. By the time they got home tonight, they'd both be worn to nubs. "Miserable war," he growled, and sat back down to finish his breakfast.

Emily nodded from the front hall. "Sure enough is." She pointed to the stove. "I got supper goin' in there. Don't forget to soak your dishes 'fore you leave. Makes 'em a lot easier—and quicker—to wash." She blew him another kiss, then hurried out the door, closing it after herself.

Jeff did soak his breakfast dishes. The quicker Emily got them clean, the more time she'd have for other things. He'd been doing more chores around the house than he'd expected when she started working, just to keep her from being too tired to feel like making love. Life got crazy sometimes, no two ways about it.

He grabbed his dinner pail and headed out the door himself. Walking to work alone still felt unnatural, but Bedford Cunningham was toting a gun these days, not a sledgehammer or a crowbar or a long-handled slag rake. The Cunningham house looked sad and empty. Fanny was gone, too, on her way to work. Pinkard wondered if she and Emily were riding the same trolley car.

He had his own job to worry about, though, and trudged off to Sloss Foundry. You had to take care of your business first, and worry about the rest later. What he did didn't take a wagonload of brains, but his life had got a lot more complicated, these months since the shooting started.

He'd got used to greeting Vespasian and Agrippa when he came down onto the casting floor every morning. It wasn't the same as talking with the white men who'd been there before, but it wasn't so bad. Both of them were old enough to have been born before manumission, and they both understood their place in the scheme of things. You could work with a nigger like that, Pinkard thought. When the time came for them to go back to stoking the furnaces or whatever they'd done before the war, they'd do it, and keep whatever complaint they had to themselves.

Pericles, now . . . "Mornin', Pericles," Pinkard said. He talked to the young black man now, the same way he did with Agrippa and Vespasian. He'd decided life was too short to get yourself all in an uproar over little things, and working the day through without gabbing with the guy alongside reminded him of nothing so much as a fellow who'd had a fight with his wife trying to show her who was boss by clamming up. It didn't work at home, and it didn't work here, either.

"Mornin', Mistuh Pinkard," Pericles answered. There wasn't anything wrong with the way he acted, not so you could put your finger on it there wasn't, but his manner was somehow different from those of the older Negroes who worked the night shift. Pericles acted as deferential to Jefferson Pinkard as they did, but—

Maybe that was it, Pinkard thought as a huge crucible swung by over his head and positioned itself to pour a fresh load of molten steel into the big cast-iron mold that waited to receive it. Then he stopped thinking about such things for a while. You had to watch the pouring like a hawk. If anything went wrong, you needed to be ready to jump and run—either that or you got yourself burned to a crisp, dead or wishing you were. Sid Williamson had lingered a week before he finally died, poor bastard.

That was especially true since the new crucible operator still wasn't so smooth as Herb, who'd gone into the Army when the war was new and looked like being over in a hurry. But Herb wasn't coming back. Somewhere up in Kentucky, near a town nobody two towns over had ever heard of till the war started, he'd stopped a bullet or a shell. His widow worked with Emily, too, and wore somber black all the time.

This pour, though, went well. A great cloud of steam hissed out of the mold, steam heavy with the bloody smell of hot iron. Jeff and Pericles worked side by side, going right up to the pour and making sure it didn't escape the mold before it started solidifying. "Warm this mornin'," Pericles said with a grin. The heat of the foundry floor dried the sweat on his face as fast as it tried to spring forth.

Pinkard knew the same thing happened with him, but he turned fiercely red from working up by the pour. Pericles seemed unaffected, as if he were made of cold-forged iron himself. He handled his tools with nonchalant confidence; a little more experience and he'd be as good a steel man as Bedford Cunningham ever was.

"You are gettin' to know what you're doin'," Pinkard said, acknowledging that.

"Thank you, Mistuh Pinkard," Pericles answered. That was fine. So was his self-effacing tone of voice. But then he added, "Ain't so hard, is it? Once you get the hang of it, I mean."

Neither Agrippa nor Vespasian would have said anything like that. Even if they thought it, they wouldn't have said it. Every once in a while, though, Pericles came out with something like that, something that made the way he acted around Jefferson Pinkard seem just that: an act. You couldn't call him for being uppity; he never showed disrespect, nor anything close to it. But even a Negro with self-confidence was something new on Jeff's mental horizon.

After a while, Pericles said, "Mistuh Pinkard, you knew Herb, didn't you?"

"Sure did," Pinkard said. "That's funny: I was thinking about him not so long ago, when the kid up there was pouring. What about him?"

"Did you hear tell they gonna throw his widow and her children out o' their company house, on account o' he don' work here no mo' an' he ain't never comin' back? Agrippa, he tol' me that this mornin'. His wife, she go over there with some catfish fo' to give her las' night, an' she all cryin' an wailin' to beat the band. Don' hardly seem right, the bosses do that."

"It sure as hell don't," Pinkard agreed. He thought about it for a little while. "That grates so much, I don't know that I want to swallow it."

Pericles held up his right hand. The bottom of the pale patch on his palm showed below the edge of his leather glove. "I ain't makin' it up, swear to God I ain't," he said, now sounding completely serious.

"Emily will know," Jeff said. "I'll ask her when she gets home tonight. If it is so, it's a pretty low-down piece of dealing, that's all I've got to say."

" 'Fore I started workin' here, what I was thinkin' was that everybody white in this whole country had it easy, just on account o' he *was* white," Pericles said. "More I look, though, more I see it ain't like that. The white folks in the suits an' the collars an' the tall hats, they do things to the white factory hands, ain't so much different than happens to niggers every day."

"That there is a natural-born fact," Pinkard said, slamming one gloved fist into the palm of the other hand to emphasize his words. "Damn all we can do about it, though. They got the money, they got the factories, like you say. All we got is our hands, an' there's always plenty more hands around."

"You dead right, Mistuh Pinkard," Pericles said. "Same way in the fields—planter don't like what a nigger does, he gets hisself another nigger. Don' matter what the first one did. Don' matter he did anything. They don' like him, he gone. Didn't think it was like that fo' white folks."

"Shouldn't ought to be." Having his position in life compared to a Negro's made Pinkard sit up and take notice. "They shouldn't be able to throw us out like an asswipe with shit on it. Wasn't for the work we did, what would they have? Nothin'. Not one thing, I tell you."

"Hard row everybody hoes these days," Pericles said. "Shouldn't be harder'n it's got to. The men who work in the factory, they should have some kind o' say in how the factory runs. Got more right to it than the fat cats with the bulgin' money bags, you ask me." He paused, as if wondering whether he'd said too much.

But Jefferson Pinkard clapped his hands together. "Damn straight!" he said. "Things'd run a hell of a lot smoother if somebody who knew what he was doin'—if somebody who'd done the work himself—had charge of things, not a big wheel with a diamond ring on his pinky."

I'm talking politics with a nigger, he realized. And if that didn't beat all, when Pericles couldn't even vote. But the young black man had touched Pinkard's own dissatisfaction with the way things were, and had brought it out into the open so he could see all of it for himself.

After that, Pericles clammed up. Now it was Jeff who wanted to talk more, and the Negro who went about his job without wasted words. Pinkard started to get angry, but his temper cooled down after a bit. Pericles had walked dangerous ground, saying even as much as he'd said. But Pinkard was feeling damn near as trampled on as the black man. That was just what the bosses were doing, he thought: trying to turn white men into niggers.

When the closing whistle wailed, Pinkard almost ran home, he was so anxious to find out from Emily whether Pericles had the straight goods about Herb's widow. He got back to the yellow cottage before his wife did; she was probably still on the trolley. He busied himself by setting the table for the two of them, as he'd got into the habit of doing when he made it home first. Bedford Cunningham, had he known about that, would have given him a hard time over it. But Bed was worried about machine-gun bullets these days, not china and cheap iron flatware.

The door opened. In came Emily. "You'll never guess what they've done to Daisy Wallace," she said.

"Herb's widow? Thrown her out on the street like a dog, on account of her husband got hisself shot savin' the Sloss family's greedy behinds," Jeff answered.

Emily stared at him. "For heaven's sake, how did you know that?" He hadn't usually heard the gossip she brought home.

"I got ways," he answered, a little smugly. "Sure does stink, don't it?"

"Sure does," she agreed, hanging up her hat and taking off the apron that protected her skirt. "Makes me want to spit, is what it does." She walked past Jeff into the kitchen, slowly shifting gears from work to home. When she saw the table ready for supper, she paused and said, "Oh, thank you, honey," in a voice suggesting his thoughtfulness had surprised her. That made him feel better about helping than he would have if she'd taken it for granted.

Even over the stew of salt pork and hominy and green beans, both of them kept on fuming about the way the crucible man's widow had been treated. Borrowing Pericles' idea, Jeff said, "We'd all be better off, I reckon, if the workers had the say in how the factories got run."

He'd expected Emily to agree to that. Instead, she paused with a bit of meat halfway to her mouth. "That sounds like somethin' a Red would say," she told him, her voice serious, maybe even a little frightened. "They been warnin' us about Reds almost all the time lately, maybe 'cause makin' shells is such an important business. Never can tell who's a bomb-flingin' revolutionary in disguise, they say."

"You ain't talkin' about me," Jefferson Pinkard declared. "Don't want no revolution—nothin' like it. Just want what's right and what's fair. Lord knows we ain't been gettin' enough of that."

"Well, that's so," Emily said, nodding. She ate the bite that had hung suspended. Neither one of them said much more about politics afterwards, though.

Jeff worked the pump while Emily did the dishes. Afterwards, he slid his arm around her waist. He didn't need to do much talking about that to let her know what he had in mind. By the way she smiled at him, she was thinking the same thing. They went into the bedroom. He blew out the lamp. In the darkness, the iron frame of the bed creaked, slow at first, building to a rhythm almost frantic.

Afterward, Emily, spent and sweaty, fell asleep almost at once. Jeff stayed awake a little longer, his mind not on the feel of his wife's arms around him but on Red revolutionaries. As far as he could see, these days people feared Reds and anarchists the same way they'd feared slave uprisings back before manumission.

Pericles, a Red? The idea was ridiculous. He was just a poor damned nigger sick of getting stuck with the short straw every draw. In his shoes, Jefferson figured he would have felt the same way. Hell, he *did* feel that way, thanks to the dislocations the war was bringing. He'd thought having a white skin made him immune to such worry, but he'd turned out to be wrong.

"Maybe we need another revolution, after all," he muttered. He was glad Emily hadn't heard that; it would have made her fret. But saying it seemed to ease his mind. He rolled over, snuggled down into his pillow, and fell asleep.

A voice with a Southern twang: "Ma'am?" An arm encased in a butternut sleeve, holding up an empty coffee cup. "Fill me up again, if you please."

"Of course, sir," Nellie Semphroch said, taking the cup from the Rebel lieutenant colonel. "You were drinking the Dutch East Indian, weren't you?"

"That's right," the officer answered. "Sure is fine you have so many different kinds to choose from."

"We've been lucky," Nellie said. She carried the cup to the sink, then took a clean one and filled it with the spicy brew the Confederate evidently enjoyed. She brought it back to him. "Here you are, sir."

He thanked her, but absently. He and the other Rebs at the table were busy rehashing an engagement up along the Susquehanna that had happened a couple of weeks before. "Damnyankees would have crossed for sure," an artillery captain said, "if one of my sergeants hadn't fought his gun with niggers toting shells and loading: his own crew got knocked out in the bombardment."

"Heard tell about that," the lieutenant colonel said. "Damned—pardon me, ma'am," he added with a glance toward Nellie, "I say, damned if I know whether they ought to pin medals on those niggers or take 'em out somewhere quiet, have 'em kneel down in front of a hole, and then shoot 'em, cover 'em up, and try to make out the whole thing never happened." All the Rebs around the table nodded. The lieutenant colonel nodded to the artillery captain. "You're closest to the matter, Jeb. What do you think about it?"

"Me?" The captain—Jeb—was boyishly handsome, with a little tuft of beard under his lower lip that should have looked absurd but somehow seemed dashing instead. "I think I'd like another cup of our hostess' excellent coffee, too." He held out his cup to Nellie. As she hurried off to refill it, he lowered his voice—but not quite enough to keep her from overhearing—and said, "I wouldn't mind a go with our hostess' excellent daughter, either."

Hoarse male laughter rose. Nellie stiffened. If Edna judged by looks—if Edna judged by anything—she probably wouldn't have minded a go with this Jeb, either. Nellie thought hard about dosing his coffee with a potent purgative. In the end, she didn't. All men were like that. Some, at least, were honest about it.

When she got back to the table, the artillery captain was saying, ". . . niggers don't seem to be putting on airs on account of it. They're back to driving and fetching, same as they were before. You ask me, it's worth knowing niggers can fight if their necks are on the block. Way we're losing men, we may need black bodies one of these days."

One of the other officers—a major—got out a silvered flask and poured a hefty shot of something into his coffee. "That's not the most cheerful notion I've ever heard," he said, taking a big swig of the augmented brew. "Ahh! Don't like the idea of niggers' getting their hands on guns. Don't like 'em getting their hands on military discipline, either."

"I don't like it myself," the lieutenant colonel said. "We've got ourselves a white man's country. That's how it ought to be, and that's how it ought to stay."

"Well, gentlemen, you won't hear me disagreeing there," Jeb said, "but if it turns into a matter of winning the war with niggers or losing it without 'em, what do we do then?"

An uncomfortable silence followed that question. The major with the flask poured another shot into his cup. What he had in there was probably more hooch than coffee. That didn't keep him from gulping it down as if it were water. "Ahh!" he said again, and then, "What we do is, we pray to God to keep that cup from passing to us."

"Amen," Jeb said, and the rest of the officers nodded. But the artillery captain went on, "War's already gone on longer than we thought it would. The middle of April now, and no end in sight. Christ! We ought to be ready in case it goes on longer yet."

"Not up to you and me to decide that kind of thing, thank heaven," the lieutenant colonel said, which brought another round of nods. "The president and the secretary of war, they'll do whatever they choose to do, and we'll make the best of it. That's what the Army's for."

The major started telling a long, complicated story about a mule that had tried to kick an aeroplane to death. It would have been funnier if he hadn't had to go back and repeat and correct himself over and over again. *That's what the demon rum does to you,* Nellie thought; in her mind, all liquor got lumped together as rum. *It calcifies the brain, and serves you right.*

She had other tables on which to wait. The coffeehouse was jumping these days, business better than it had been since before the war, maybe better than it had ever been. Being able to get her hands on all the coffee she needed didn't hurt there. A lot of places in Washington had gone belly-up, just as she had been at the point of doing not so long before.

She'd wondered if anyone would ask how she managed to keep getting coffee beans in the middle of a tightly rationed town. But that hadn't happened. Even Edna hadn't been unduly curious. *She probably thinks I'm sleeping with someone,* Nellie thought sadly. It was, she feared, what her daughter would have done in her place. Or maybe Edna only noticed the beans were there and truly did think no more about it.

The next morning, Nellie and Edna were sweeping up the floor by the light of a couple of kerosene lamps—neither gas nor electricity had yet come back to this part of Washington. Outside, black night brightened toward dawn; a coffeehouse's customers started showing up early. As Nellie emptied the dustpan into a wastebasket, a light went on across the street.

A small pot of coffee was already on the coal stove, to give her and Edna an eye-opener before customers started coming in. Nellie poured a cup from the pot and set it in a saucer. "I see Mr. Jacobs is up and about, too," she said. "I'll take this over to him. It will be better than anything he's likely to make for himself."

"All right, Ma." Edna's laugh was not altogether kindly. "Beyond me what you see in a little wrinkled old shoemaker, though."

"Mr. Jacobs is a very nice man," Nellie said primly. Her daughter laughed again. Nellie took a haughty tone: "Your mind may be in the gutter, but that doesn't mean mine is."

"Now tell me another one, Ma," Edna said; her mind *was* in the gutter, sure enough. To keep from heating up one of their all too frequent fights, Nellie let the door she closed behind her serve in place of an angry response.

No sooner had she crossed the street than a long line of trucks rolled past, their acetylene lamps turning morning twilight to noon. She looked back at the growling monsters. Almost all of the drivers were Negroes. She had to tap twice to get Mr. Jacobs to hear her.

He peered through his magnifying glasses. His wizened face wrinkled in a new way when he smiled. "Widow Semphroch! Come in," he said. "And you have brought me coffee, too. Oh, this is wonderful. I was afraid you would be a Confederate soldier with boots that had to be repaired at once because he was going back to the front. I am glad to be wrong." He stood aside and bowed like an Old World gentleman as he welcomed her.

She set the coffee on his work counter, by the last. Closing the door after her, he came over, picked up the cup, and sipped. At his appreciative hum, Nellie said, "Thank you so much for helping to arrange to get the beans delivered to my shop in the first place."

"It is my pleasure," he said, and then, sipping again, "It *is* my pleasure. And it is so very kind of you to bring a cup to me every morning." He cocked his head to one side. "You hear all sorts of interesting news in a coffeehouse. What have you heard lately?"

Nellie told him what she'd heard lately, chief among the stories being the one about the Negroes who had served as artillerymen after the men for whom they labored went down, wounded or killed. She recounted the tale in as much detail as she could. "The commander of the battery was a captain named Jeb, though I don't know his last name," she finished.

"I do not know this, either, but I think I may have friends who will." Mr. Jacobs nodded thoughtfully. "Yes, thank you for bringing this to my notice,

Widow Semphroch. I think my friends may be most interested to hear it. I am very glad we were able to help you in your difficulty." He finished the coffee and set cup back in saucer. "Here you are. Your business grows busy before mine, and I would not keep you from it."

"Edna will take care of things till I get back," Nellie said. But she picked up the cup and saucer and hurried back to the coffeehouse even so. Leaving Edna alone in there with all those lecherous Confederates was asking for trouble.

And sure enough, when she walked inside, there sat the handsome artillery captain from the night before, with Edna pouring him a cup of coffee and looking, to Nellie's jaundiced eye, as if she was about to plop herself down in his lap. But the scene was outwardly decorous, so Nellie, in spite of what she was thinking, kept her mouth shut.

Edna didn't. Subscribing to the notion that the best defense was a good offense, she said, "Hello, Ma. Took you long enough to get back from the shoemaker's shop. What were you doing over there, anyhow?" Her tone was light; Jeb the Confederate gunner would have noticed nothing amiss. But Nellie knew she meant something like, *You went over there and tore one off with Mr. Jacobs, didn't you? And since you did, what are you doing meddling in* my *life?*

But Nellie had gone across the street for patriotic reasons, not vile ones. She said, "We were just talking—he's a good friend. Why don't you go back and scrub out the sinks?" *Why don't you wash out your mouth with soap while you're doing it, too?*

Edna went, with a walk that, Nellie thought, would have got her arrested for soliciting had she done it on the street—and had the Confederates bothered arresting streetwalkers. They mostly didn't; their basic attitude seemed to be that all U.S. women were whores, so what point to worrying about a few in particular?

Jeb followed Edna with his eyes till she disappeared. Then he seemed to remember the coffee growing cold in front of him. He gulped it down, set a coin on the table, and rose, setting his red-corded artilleryman's hat on his head. Touching the brim, he nodded to Nellie and said, "Obliged, ma'am."

Nellie nodded back. *Why not?* she thought. She was obliged to him, too, for running off at the mouth so freely the night before. And he hadn't got his hands on Edna: the moonstruck way he looked at her proved that. She knew all about the ways men looked at women. If he'd had her, his stare would have been more possessive, more knowing. He was still wondering what she was like, and all the more twitchingly lustful for that.

Keep right on wondering, you stinking Reb, Nellie thought.

Plowing the land had an ancient, timeless rhythm to it. Walking behind horses, guiding the plow, watching the rich, dark earth of Manitoba furrow up on either side of the blade made Arthur McGregor think of his grandfather, who had done the same thing back in Ontario; of his several-times-great-grandfather, who had done his best to scratch a living from the stony soil of Scotland; and, sometimes, of an ancestor far more distant than that, an ancestor who didn't speak English or Scots Gaelic, either, an ancestor who wore barely tanned skins and walked behind an ox scratching a furrow in the ground with a stick sharpened in the fire.

Like his ancestors, going back to that ancient, half-imaginary one, McGregor eyed the sky, worrying about the weather. If he hadn't, his son would have taken care of that for him. Here came Alexander, with a pitcher of cold water from the well. "Think it's safe, getting the seed in the ground so soon, Pa?" Alexander asked, as he already had more than once. "A late frost and we're in a lot of trouble."

Alexander was a good boy, Arthur McGregor thought, but he was getting to the age where he thought everything his father did was wrong, for no better reason than that it was the old man doing it. "This year, son, we're in a lot of trouble no matter what we do, I think," McGregor answered. "But I want to plow and plant as early as I can, before the Americans find a reason to come round and tell me I can't."

"They can't do that!" Alexander exclaimed. "We'd starve."

"And if the lot of us did, do you think they'd shed a single tear?" Arthur McGregor shook his head. "Not likely."

There, for once, his son had a hard time disagreeing with him. But Alexander found a different question to ask: "Even if we do get our crop in, will they let us keep enough of it to live on?"

His father sighed. "I don't know. But if we have no crop, I'm certain sure we'll not be able to live on that."

Arthur McGregor looked north. Like all his ancestors save a couple of lucky ones, he worried about war hardly less than weather. The front lay a good way off now—but who could guess where it would be when harvest time rolled around? Would the Yanks have overrun Winnipeg by then? Or would the Canadians and British have rallied and pushed the thieves in green-gray back south over the border where they belonged? If you read the newspapers, you figured Canada was in a state of collapse. But if you believed all the lies the Americans made the papers tell, Winnipeg had already fallen twice, Montreal three times, and Toronto once—maybe for luck.

Alexander persisted: "How do you feel about raising a crop when the Americans will end up eating most of it while they're fighting Canada?"

McGregor sighed. "How do I feel about that? Like the mother bird after the cuckoo laid the egg in her nest, son. But what am I supposed to do, I ask you that? What the Americans don't take, we'll eat ourselves."

His son kicked at the dirt. When you were young, you were sure everything had answers either black or white. Alexander was getting his nose rubbed in the reality of gray, and didn't much care for it. Trying to avoid it, he said, "Why not just plant enough for us, and leave the rest of the fields"—he waved at the broad, flat acreage—"to lie fallow for the year?"

"I could do that, I suppose, if I didn't need to make some cash to buy the things we can't raise on the farm," Arthur McGregor said. He eyed his son with genuine respect; the boy—no, the young man—could have come up with many worse notions. But— "If I try that, too, the other thing likely to happen to me is farming at the point of an American bayonet."

"If every farmer in Manitoba did the same thing, they couldn't put bayonets to all of our backs." Alexander's face flamed with excitement. In the course of a couple of sentences, he'd given himself a bold and patriotic movement to join. "A farmers' strike, that's what it would be!"

The only drawback to the movement was that it didn't exist. Arthur McGregor shook his head: no, it had more. "For one thing, son, with all the Yanks in Manitoba these days, they likely do have enough men to put a bayonet at every farm. And for another, the way they shoot hostages, they wouldn't wait more than a minute or two before they started shooting farmers. And once they shot a few, the rest would—"

"Rise up and throw the Yanks off our soil!" Alexander broke in.

"Not that easy," McGregor said with a sigh. "I wish it was, but it's not. They shoot a few, most of the rest will do just what they say and nothing else but. Other thing is, there's too many Americans up here for us to throw 'em out even if we did rise up. Oh, we could make nuisances of ourselves, that I don't deny, but no more. The Yanks are bastards, sure enough, but we've seen too much to have the notion that they are cowards and they are fools. They'd beat us down, and we'd spend our blood for nothing."

Alexander still looked mutinous. It was in the nature of youths his age to look mutinous: that is, to have their looks accurately reflect their thoughts. To quell the mutiny, McGregor didn't shout or bluster. Instead, he pointed to the roadway. Small in the distance but growing steadily larger as they approached, here came a battalion of U.S. soldiers marching north toward the front. In column of fours, they made a green-gray snake slithering across the land. The snake was having heavy going, the road still being muddy from melted winter snows.

After the troops came supply wagons topped with white canvas, lineal descendants of the Conestogas in which so many Americans—and not a few Canadians, too—had gone west to settle. Hooves and wagon wheels had even more trouble advancing through mud than did marching boots.

About half a mile behind that battalion came another, barely visible in the distance as yet but all too soon to approach in turn. "Do you see, son?" McGregor asked, his voice halfway between gentle and rough. "There are just too many of them, and us spread too thin on the ground to be much use fighting 'em. Either we find some other way to drive 'em mad, or we do as much of what they tell us as we have to and trust to God it'll all come out right in the end."

"That's a bitter pill, Father," Alexander said.

"I never told you it wasn't," McGregor agreed. "And trusting in God is hard, because He does what He wants, not what we want. I don't know what else to say, though. We get along, and we wait, and we see what happens."

He couldn't have given his son much harder advice, and he knew it. The advice was hard for him, too. He wanted nothing so much as to strike back at the Americans. Before the war began, he'd been starting to think about buying a gasoline-powered tractor. Now he counted himself lucky to have a team of horses. He flicked the reins; he'd been standing idle long enough. The horses snorted and strode forward.

As the sun sank toward the flat horizon that evening, he and the team headed back toward the farmhouse and the barn. He'd curry the animals and get them fed and watered, and then go in to see what Maude had done up for supper.

The horses stopped, snorting, their ears twitching. McGregor stopped, too. For a moment, he failed to sense anything out of the ordinary. Then he too caught the low rumble out of the north. Far-off thunder, he would have thought the year before. He knew better now, an education he would willingly have done without. That was artillery. He hadn't heard it for a while. The front was a long way off these days. A bombardment had to be big to be noticed across so many miles.

"And whose guns are they?" he wondered out loud. Spring was here, summer coming: fighting weather. He had the feeling he'd be hearing guns a lot in days to come. He hoped they'd get louder, not softer: that would mean the front was drawing closer, his countrymen and whatever soldiers the mother country could spare pushing back the invaders.

He and his family spoke of little else over supper: rabbit stew. All they could do, though, was guess and hope. The artillery barrage went on through the night; it was still roaring away when McGregor visited the outhouse in the wee small hours.

And it was still roaring away when he took the horses out to the fields at sunrise. A train no doubt full of troops roared up the track toward the front; the road was full of marching men. By afternoon, ambulances and trains showing the Red Cross rolled south. Were their wounded the residue of advance or retreat? The hell of it was, Arthur McGregor had no way of knowing.

* * *

For Remembrance Day, Flora Hamburger and the other Socialists, not only from the Tenth Ward and the rest of the Lower East Side but from all over New York, came to Broadway to watch the parade. Coming as it did just nine days before May Day, their own great holiday, it was a rival focus for the energy and allegiance of the American working class.

As always, the parade route was packed to commemorate the day of mourning. Flags fluttered from poles on top of every building, every one of them flown upside down, symbolizing the distress of the United States when they had had to yield to the forces of the Confederacy, England, and France, and to recognize the Confederate States' acquisition of Chihuahua and Sonora.

Burly policemen cordoned the Socialist Party delegation away from the rest of the crowd. Brawls broke out every year after the Remembrance Day parade. Now, with the war on, who could say what might happen?

Flora peered across Broadway, to the three-story brick building that housed Slosson's Café and Billiards. Men looked out through the plate-glass window of the pool hall, and men and women both watched from the cloth-awninged windows of the upper floors. She wondered what sort of bosses squeezed profit from their labor.

Beside her, Herman Bruck said, "Far more of the people are with us than the minions of the ruling class"—he pointed to the policemen—"would ever admit. They'll let the veterans' groups, with their fat bellies and their minds full of blood and iron, they'll let them know what they think." He looked like a boss himself, in his broadcloth suit and stovepipe hat: a younger son, maybe, or one just taking over the business. But, whether Flora cared for him or not, she had to admit he was Socialist to the core.

"So many have lost husbands and brothers and sons," she said, nodding, "and for what? How are we better? What have we gained? How many more young men will have to die on the altar of capitalism and nationalism before the war ends?"

"All that is true," Maria Tresca put in, "but some will say, 'We have come this far, so how can we stop halfway?' This is the biggest stumbling block we have to overcoming the support of the masses for the war." Her sister Angelina nodded.

"It is a problem," Flora admitted. "I have run into it many times myself."

"It should not be a problem." Bruck sounded angry. "We should be able to show clearly why this war is immoral, unnatural, and serves only the interests of the ruling class."

A few feet away, a policeman with a red Irish face heard that. He turned to Bruck and, smiling nastily, made motions as if of counting money. Then, with theatrical scorn, he turned his broad, blue-clad back.

"Do you see?" Flora said triumphantly. "We voted to finance the war along with everyone else, and now no one lets us forget it. I said at the time that was a mistake."

"So you did," Herman Bruck muttered. He was in a poor position to do anything but mutter, as he had supported paying for the war. He still did, sometimes, but not when policemen mocked him for it. And so it was with some relief that he pointed down Broadway and said, "Here comes the parade."

Leading it, as had hardened into ritual over the past generation, came an enormous soldier carrying the Stars and Stripes, once more upside down. A Marine band at slow march followed him; they played "The Star-Spangled Banner" with the tempo of a dirge. As the flag-bearer and the band went by, men uncovered and held their hats over their hearts.

Flora recognized the white-bearded bandmaster. "That's Sousa!" she exclaimed with the respect one can give an effective foe. The musician's stirring songs had done more to fire narrow national patriotism and make the proletariat forget its international ties than the work of most jingo politicians.

Here and there in the crowd beyond the police lines, men left their hats on: odds-on candidates to be Socialists. Fights had started over such things in years past. Now, beyond a couple of low-voiced calls of "Shame!", no one did anything. Almost no one in the Socialist Party delegation uncovered. The Marine musicians did not turn their heads, but sidelong glances said they took mental note.

Behind the band rolled a limousine that carried—Flora stiffened as she saw who the man standing in the back of the car was—Theodore Roosevelt. The president only showed himself; he did not wave to the crowd. His suit was as black and somber as Herman Bruck's, and almost as well cut. A few Socialists shouted catcalls at him. He ignored them.

Then came the veterans. After the limousine marched a contingent of men older than John Philip Sousa, survivors of the War of Secession. Some still strode straight and slim despite their years. Others shambled along as best they could, helped along by a stick or a cane. Some had one sleeve flapping empty or pinned to the front of their jackets. Some had one trouser leg pinned up, and propelled themselves with crutches. At the rear, attendants pushed a few legless men along in wheelchairs.

The old soldiers' faces, almost to a man, bore a grim sadness the passage of half a century had not erased. Flora sympathized with them; the USA had surely been more progressive than the feudal-minded Rebels. But, however sure the historical dialectic was, it did not always move straight ahead. The memory of failure still stung the veterans of the War of Secession.

Behind them marched another group of veterans, these middle-aged, many of them plump and prosperous: men who had fought in the Second Mexican War. Where their predecessors seemed proud of what they had done even in defeat, these ex-soldiers, some of them, had almost a hangdog air, as if they felt they should have done better but didn't quite know how.

Then came Count von Bernstorff, the German ambassador, fantastically bemedaled and riding in a limousine flanked by a color guard of German soldiers carrying the black-white-red banners of the German Empire. Those drew both cheers and jeers, many of the jeers either in German or in Yiddish, close enough to German for the spike-helmeted soldiers in field-gray to understand.

"Germany taught the USA to ignore the needs of the proletariat!" Herman Bruck shouted, shaking his fist.

"Germany taught the USA to fool the proletariat into thinking its needs are met," Flora cried a moment later, which gave her the double satisfaction of telling the truth and correcting the self-righteous Bruck.

The mixture of applause and catcalls went on after the German ambassador and his escort passed. Behind him came a troop of men hardly younger than the Second Mexican War veterans: Soldiers' Circle members of the first class, men who had served their two years in the Army after conscription was passed in the wake of two lost wars.

Flora and Bruck and Maria and Angelina Tresca and all the Socialist representatives joined with their Party members in the crowd in shouting abuse at the marching men of the Soldiers' Circle, each successive troop from the conscription class a year later than its predecessor. Men who stayed in the Soldiers' Circle after they served their time were apt to be of a reactionary cast of mind: men who gladly served as strikebreakers, scabs, goons, men to whom even Teddy Roosevelt was a dangerous radical for worrying about the untrammeled power of the bosses.

As the Soldiers' Circle troops passed by, as the men became of the age where their contemporaries were fighting, other jeers rang out alongside those of the Socialists. Chief among them was the swelling cry, "Why aren't you in the Army?"

While the youngish men who had done their time as conscripts but had not yet been dragged into the war ignored the mockery and marched stolidly down Broadway, mockery was all they got. But then, not far from the Socialist delegation, one of the men of the conscription class of 1901 lost his temper. He turned his head and shouted at an abuser, "Why ain't I in the Army now? Fuck you and fuck your mother too, why ain't you?"

With a roar of rage, the fellow he'd cursed rushed at him, pulled out a knife, and plunged it into his side. The Soldiers' Circle man went down with a groan, blood bright on his white shirt. Four of his comrades threw the man with the knife to the ground, kicked the blade away, and methodically began stomping the stabber.

A few people in the crowd cheered, but others ran out to try to rescue the man who'd used the knife. More Soldiers' Circle men set on them.

Somebody—in the rapidly swelling chaos, Flora had no idea who, or on which side—fired a pistol. An instant later, several guns were popping away, as if the war had decided to pay New York a visit.

"Jesus, Mary, and Joseph!" shouted the Irish policeman who'd made money-counting motions at Herman Bruck. Along with his fellows, he dashed toward what had gone in the space of half a minute from patriotic parade to riot.

Flora Hamburger turned her back on it. To her fellow Socialists, she cried, "Stay here! Don't join it! Don't let the reactionaries exploit us in the newspapers!"

Angelina and Maria Tresca loudly added their voices to Flora's. Flora looked around for support from Herman Bruck. To her dismay, she saw him, along with several other hot-blooded Socialists, running straight toward the men from the Soldiers' Circle. They had their own rallying cry: "Direct action!" The Socialist call to arms had rung out in mines and factories and lumber camps and fields across the USA for a generation, but now . . . ? Flora shook her head in dismay. The place and the timing could hardly have been worse.

Riot spread up the parade, toward the Marine marching band at the front. From that direction, Flora heard a couple of explosions louder and fiercer than pistol shots. "Bombs!" she exclaimed. "They're throwing bombs!"

She didn't know who *they* were, but she feared with sick horror the Socialists would get the blame. In the 1880s and 1890s, *direct action* had often meant more than words; the Party's past had blood in it.

Another bomb went off, this one frighteningly close. Injured men and women screamed. Above their cries rose a great voice bellowing, "Justice for Utah!"

Absurdly, relief flooded Flora: maybe the hard hand of the government would land on the Mormons, not on the Party. She was ashamed of herself a moment later. *Do it to them, not to us* was not the answer; the government, no matter how TR thundered about swinging a big club, had no right to oppress anyone.

Analyzing that in fullness, though, would have to wait. She grabbed Maria and Angelina. "We'd better get out of here," she said. The secretaries nodded vehemently.

It was easier said than done. A lot of the crowd was trying to flee the brawls and battles that roiled in the middle of Broadway, but almost as many people, women as well as men, were pressing forward, trying to get into the fray. Yet another pistol shot rang out, this one terribly close, terribly loud. Angelina Tresca shrieked. Blood, vividly, impossibly red, stained the white front of her shirtwaist. She stood staring in astonishment. When she opened her mouth to say something, only more blood came from it—not a word. Blood poured from her nose, too. She swayed, toppled, fell.

More *pop-pop-pop*s went off, incongruously cheerful. Maria's shriek was louder than her sister's. She couldn't even run to Angelina; the crowd, panicked by gunfire, swept them apart. When Maria tried to go against it, she was swept off her own feet. Flora dragged her up before she could get too badly trampled, then dragged her away.

Clinging to each other, weeping, the two of them struggled to get off Broadway and onto Twenty-third Street so they could escape the riot. "Oof!" A portly man ran into Flora. He acted as if he were trying to fend her off, but his hands slid up her body till they closed on her breasts, the crowd and turmoil offering concealment for what he did. She'd had such unwelcome attentions before. Snatching a pin from the floral hat she wore, she stuck him with it. He howled and whirled away. She stuck him again as he fled, this time where he sat down. He howled again, almost seeming to levitate. The pin was long and sharp and had blood on a good part of its length. Savagely pleased at that, she stuck it back amidst the artificial greenery on her hat.

Maria Tresca didn't react, staring numbly. Maybe she was too numb to think too much about Angelina yet.

"It would be better if they knew not to do such things," Flora said, not wanting to think about Angelina, either, "but we have to educate them if they don't."

She wished her sister had stuck a hat pin in Yossel Reisen. But no, that wasn't fair. He hadn't taken anything from Sophie she hadn't wanted to give. It was only what he'd given her in return . . .

A man stepped on her foot. He didn't try to feel her up; he just went on his way as if she didn't exist. That she didn't mind so much; it could have happened at any time in the streets of New York City, the biggest, most indifferent city in the USA. In a way, in fact, it almost comforted her, showing the world wasn't devoid of normality even in the midst of riot.

Off Broadway, things were quieter. Flora and Maria walked quickly down Twenty-third Street, to put some distance between themselves and the insanity that had swallowed the Soldiers' Circle parade.

"Trouble will come from this," Flora said grimly, and then amended that: "More trouble, I mean." Back behind them, Angelina was almost surely dead.

Even as Maria nodded, tears streaming down her face, a burly policeman grabbed a Jewish-looking fellow in a shabby suit and demanded, "You wouldn't be a Socialist, would you now?" When the man nodded, the policeman hit him in the head with his billy club. Blood streaming down his face, the fellow turned to run. The policeman kicked him in the seat of the pants, shouting, "Lucky I don't shoot you, you black-hearted traitor!"

"Shame!" Flora cried, and Maria added her voice an instant later. Flora went on, "You have no business beating a man for what he believes, only for what he does. Haven't you heard of the Constitution of the United States?" Yes, thinking of politics was easier than thinking of death unleashed on the streets of New York.

The policeman stamped toward her and Maria, nightstick still upraised. To Flora's relief, at the last moment he discovered he didn't quite have the crust to beat two women. Voice strangled with rage, he said, "Get out o' here this minute, or I'll run the both of you in."

"On what charge?" Flora asked, her chin jutting in defiance.

"Streetwalking." The policeman stripped her and Maria with his eyes.

"We're not the ones who sell ourselves to get our daily bread," Flora retorted.

"Get out!" the policeman screamed. His face was crimson, furious. He spat on the sidewalk. "And *that* for the God-damned Constitution of the United States. There's a war on now, and the gloves are off. *Get* out!"

He would have hit them had they stayed an instant longer. Flora was willing to suffer a beating for the cause, but now Maria dragged her away. "We can't," the secretary said. "Enough blood spilled already. *Please,* Flora—not after Angelina."

Later, Flora decided the secretary was right; the Socialists already had martyrs aplenty today, Maria Tresca's sister among them. The policeman's hate-filled words kept ringing in her ears. *The gloves are off.* She shivered. If TR felt the same way—and he probably would—what was the government going to do now?

A Negro maid lifted her feather duster from the windowsill—not that she'd been working hard anyhow, but an excuse to stop was always welcome—in one of the forward-facing rooms at Marshlands and said to Scipio, "Here come de man from de *Mercury* wid a paper for we."

"Thank you very much, Griselda," he answered gravely, and heard her snicker by way of reply. He ignored her amused scorn; so long as he was on duty in the mansion, he was obliged to sound like an educated white man, not a Negro of the Congaree.

He checked for himself before going to the front hall to open the door; the rest of the staff was not above playing small jokes. But, sure enough, here came Virgil Hobson on a mule, carrying with him a copy of the *Charleston Mercury*. Anne Colleton got the *Daily Courier*, too, and the *South Carolinian* and *Southern Guardian* from Columbia. Marshlands was a good way out of the way for all of them, but you declined to render its mistress a service at your peril.

Virgil was just climbing down off the mule as Scipio opened the door for him. "Good afternoon, sir," he said. Hobson was a poor buckra who spent half his time drinking and the other half hung over, but he was white folks—and the white folks who didn't deserve respect raised the most hell if they didn't get it.

"Afternoon," Virgil said. He walked straight, but very gently, as if touching the ground hurt. That meant he was after a binge, not in the middle of one. He thrust the *Mercury* at Scipio. "Here y'are." Without waiting for a reply, he turned and walked back toward his long-eared mount.

"Thank you, sir," Scipio said to his back. He waited till the delivery man rode away before shutting the door. As he set the newspaper on the tray to take it to Anne Colleton, he glanced down at the front page.

Big black headlines shouted up at him: SOCIALISTS AND MORMONS RAMPAGE IN NEW YORK CITY! REDS AND FANATICS RIOT, FORCE YANKS TO DECLARE MARTIAL LAW! UNREST IN U.S. ARMY REPORTED. He didn't know how the *Mercury* had got the story or how much truth was in it, but if it was even a quarter true, the USA was in a peck of trouble.

On reading past the headlines, the other thing he noted, less happily, was that the U.S. Army, despite the claims of unrest in its ranks, was going about the business of keeping a lid on New York City. The people they were putting a lid on might be Socialists, but they were white folks. If damnyankee soldiers would put down an uprising from white folks, what would Confederate troops do if—when—their Negro laborers rose up under the red flag?

He was afraid he knew the answer to that question. He'd tried telling it to the Reds among the field hands here. They kept laughing at him. He resolved to hang on to this newspaper and the others that came in over the next few days, to let Cassius and his fellow revolutionaries see what happened in the real world. How could you expect a band of Marxist fanatics to seize power in a country? They didn't seem to understand how big a place a country was.

Going on with that argument, fortunately, could wait. He carried the *Charleston Mercury* upstairs to Anne Colleton's office: of an afternoon, you could expect to find her there. She was on the telephone. He stood in the doorway, waiting to be noticed.

"No," she said crisply into the mouthpiece. "I told you to buy, not sell. You shall carry out my instructions as I give them, sir, or I will find another broker and you will find a lawsuit . . . What? . . . An oversight? I have no more tolerance for oversights than I have for deliberate errors. Whatever it was, this is your first, last, and only warning. Good day." She hung up, muttered something sulfurous under her breath, and then, anger expunged, smiled at Scipio. "I hope you have better news for me than that chucklehead did."

"I believe so, yes." Without another word, Scipio set the tray with the *Mercury* on the desk in front of Anne Colleton, turning it as he did so to make sure the headlines were right side up for her.

Her eyes widened. Her mouth twisted into something halfway between a smile and the expression a tiger wears on spotting a juicy sheep. Scipio was heartily glad that expression bore on the newspaper, not on him. The mistress of Marshlands rapidly read through the stories having to do with the troubles in the USA, pursuing them into the inner pages. When she finished, she looked up at Scipio and asked, "Did you take any notice of these?" She paused. "You must have. You told me the news was good."

"I did look at the headlines, yes, ma'am," Scipio answered. You didn't want to be in a position of having to lie to Anne Colleton. She was sharp as the edge of a straight razor, and even more dangerous.

Her finger stabbed down at one of those headlines. "*That's* why we'll win the war, Scipio. The United States are divided against themselves. They haven't the stomach for a fight to the finish. We have no Socialists here, by God!" That predatory expression grew even fiercer. "We have no Mormons here, either, but that doesn't keep us from using them against the USA. Our states are truly united, even if the Yankees have the name. And because of that, we'll dictate terms to them in the end, as we did two generations ago and then again in my parents' time."

"Yes, ma'am," Scipio repeated. Some of the sweat springing out on his face came from having to wear tailcoat, vest, and boiled shirt on a muggy spring day that threatened summer. Part, though, came from his own fear. Sharp as Anne Colleton was, she looked right at Negroes—at one person in three in the CSA—without even seeing them . . . or maybe seeing them only as laborers, not as people. An awful lot of white folks saw—or didn't see—blacks the same way. Anne Colleton was more clever than most of them, though. If she ever really looked instead of taking things for granted—

She looked . . . toward a clock on the wall. Her expression faded to one of discontent. "Probably too late for Cassius to bring in a couple of turkeys before nightfall. Go tell him to hunt tomorrow. I want to lay on a fancy supper then."

"Yes, ma'am." Scipio slid the tray out from under the *Charleston Mercury* and took it back to the table in the front hall where it rested. He was always delighted at escaping the mistress' attention—except when she sent him out to Cassius. Her eyes remained closed to the double game Scipio was playing. Whatever else you said about him, Cassius had his eyes wide, wide open.

He was sitting on the steps in front of his cottage, running a cleaning patch through the barrels of his shotgun, when Scipio came up. The hunter's weathered face cracked into a leathery grin. He jumped to his feet, limber as a man half his age. "Kip! What fo' you do me de favor o' yo' comp'ny?" Ignoring the irony, Scipio told him what Anne Colleton wanted. Cassius nodded vigorously. "I do that." He waved Scipio an invitation. "Come inside. You 'n' me, we talk."

Normally, Scipio dreaded that invitation, though he found it impossible to refuse. Today, though, he thought he would do more talking than usual. As soon as Cassius shut the door to give them privacy, he began, "You know what de Socialists do in New York City? They rise up, an' do Jesus! they make the USA—"

Cassius waved him to silence. "Kip, dat *ol'* news," he said scornfully. "Dat happen *las'* week. It over an' done with now, 'cep' fo' de 'pression. De 'pression, dat go on a long time. Always do." He sounded very cynical, very sure.

Scipio stared. "But de newspaper jus' say today—"

"White folks' paper." Cassius laced his voice with even more scorn than before. "Dey got to wait, dey got to decide what they want they good little boys an' girls to hear about. De buckra, you give bad news to they, they get res'less."

"How you know 'fo' de newspaper come?" Scipio asked.

"Somebody not so far, they got a wireless set," Cassius answered after a moment's hesitation. In lieu of staring, Scipio looked down at the weathered pine boards of the floor. That somebody—presumably a Negro—among the Red would-be revolutionaries had the knowledge to run a wireless set, that that somebody (and, unless Scipio was wrong, a lot of somebodies in the CSA) had acquired such knowledge under the nose of the Confederate authorities . . . put that together with the undoubted desperation of the rising that would come, and maybe, just maybe . . .

"Maybe, jus' maybe, come de revolution, we win," Scipio said softly.

"Do Jesus! Hell yes, we win," Cassius declared. "De dialectic say, when de whole of de proletariat rise up, de capitalists an' de bourgeoisie, they cain't no way put we down again."

Saying a thing didn't make it so. Scipio knew that. He'd even tried telling Cassius and Island and the other Reds as much. They didn't listen to him, any more than the preacher would have if he'd denied Jesus. If they had men on wireless sets—maybe, just maybe, they had reason not to listen.

Chester Martin ducked behind a stretch of brick wall that reached up to his belly button. It was a hard landing; more bricks lay all around what was left of the wall. Somewhere not far away were two whitewashed pieces of wood nailed together at right angles. Once upon a time, this had been a church on the outskirts of Big Lick, Virginia. Now it offered him a different kind of salvation.

A Confederate bullet smacked the other side of the bricks. Maybe it had been aimed at him, maybe fired at random. He had no way of knowing. What he did know was that the bricks were good and solid, and would keep rifle and machine-gun fire from him, as long as he stayed low. Anybody who hadn't learned to stay low by now was already dead or wounded.

Martin took advantage of the momentary respite to put a fresh, full clip on his Springfield. Never could tell when you'd have to try to kill somebody—or several somebodies—in a hurry. If one of the Rebs had more bullets in his rifle than you did in yours . . . "You'd be sorry," Martin muttered. "I don't want to be sorry. I want the other son of a bitch to be sorry."

Paul Andersen crawled up beside him. "Ain't this fun?" he said, also pausing to reload.

"Now that you mention it," Chester said, "no."

Andersen's grin was wry. "Let me ask it a different way. Ain't this fun, next to leave back in White Sulphur Springs?"

Martin considered that fine philosophical point. "Nobody's trying to kill you back there," he said at last. "Other than that, though, you got a point."

"Nobody's trying to kill you back there?" Andersen exclaimed. "You mean you didn't think they were trying to bore you to death?"

"Hmm," Martin said, and then, "Yeah, maybe they were. I mean, if you don't like lemonade and you don't like hot water that stinks like somebody cut the cheese in it, not a hell of a lot to do back there."

"I hear they got saloons—hell, I hear they got whorehouses—in leave towns on what used to be Confederate territory," Andersen said. "The Army has charge there, and the Army knows what soldiers want to do when they get away from the front for a while. But White Sulphur Springs, that's back in the USA, and it ain't the Army in charge. It's the damn preachers."

"No whiskey," Chester Martin agreed. "No women, except the Red Cross girls handing out the lemonade. A couple of them were pretty, but once I'm back there and cleaned up, I want to do more than look at a woman, you know what I'm saying?"

"You bet I do," Andersen answered. "Me, too. Hell, looking is harder, some ways, than not being around 'em at all."

"I think so, too," Martin said. "I—" He shut up then, and flattened himself out among the bricks, because the Rebs started throwing whizz-bangs into the neighborhood. The shells burst all around, throwing deadly fragments every which way.

The barrage—mostly those damned three-inchers that seemed to fire almost as fast as machine guns, but some bigger cannon, too—went on for about half an hour. Stretcher-bearers hauled groaning, thrashing U.S. soldiers back toward the doctors. Some men didn't need stretcher-bearers. If all that was left of you was your leg from the knee down, your foot still in your boot, doctors wouldn't do you any good.

As soon as the bombardment stopped, Martin and Andersen popped up like a couple of jack-in-the-boxes. Sure as hell, here came the Rebs, dashing forward through the ruins of Big Lick. They ran low and bent over, not wanting to expose themselves any more than they had to. *Veteran troops,* Martin thought; new fish had less sense.

He was a veteran, too. The more you let the other guys take advantage of a bombardment, the worse off you'd be. The time to smash them was as soon as they jumped out of their holes. If you could pot a couple then, the rest lost enthusiasm for the work they'd been assigned.

He squeezed the trigger. The Springfield slammed against his shoulder. A Reb pitched over on his face. Martin worked the bolt and fired again. Another Confederate soldier fell, this one grabbing at his arm. Martin seemed to have all the time in the world to swing his rifle toward a third figure clad in butternut, to squeeze the trigger, to watch the fellow topple.

Beside him, Paul Andersen was also banging away. Somewhere not far off, a machine gun started hammering. A lot of Rebels went down. But a lot of them kept coming, too. They pitched improvised grenades at the U.S. soldiers. Martin didn't like the idea of carrying those damn things around—if a bullet hit one, it would blow a hole in you they could throw a dog through. But he didn't like being on the receiving end of grenades, either. It was as if the infantry started having its own artillery.

Shouts of alarm from the left made him whip his head around. The Confederates were in among the U.S. trenches and foxholes, trying to drive the Americans back to White Sulphur Springs without benefit of leave.

Martin ran toward the battling, cursing men. In a fight like that, you used anything you had: rifle, bayonet, knife, the sawed-off spade you carried to dig yourself in. The question was brutally simple: would enough Rebs get past the U.S. rifle and machine-gun fire to overwhelm the defenders and make this wrecked stretch of suburb their own once more, or would the men who were in place and whatever reinforcements who could get forward blunt the attack and throw it back?

Butternut smeared with mud and grass stains didn't look much different from similarly dirty green-gray. Being sure of who was who was anything but easy. You didn't want to go after the wrong man by mistake, but you didn't want to hesitate and get yourself killed, either.

An unmistakable Rebel leaped out from behind a pile of rubble and swung one of those short-handled shovels at Chester Martin's head. He threw up his rifle just in time to fend off the blow. The force of it staggered him even so. The Confederate, intent on his work, drew back the shovel for another blow. Before he could deliver it, a bullet—from a U.S. soldier or a Rebel, Martin never knew—caught him in the shoulder. The spade spun from his hands. "Ahh, shit," he said loudly. "You got me now, Yank."

Martin dashed past him. If he'd stayed there an instant longer, he would have shot the wounded Rebel in the head. Accepting the surrender of a man who'd been doing his best to kill you till he got hurt himself felt fiercely unnatural. A lot of such attempted surrenders never got made. Machine gunners, in particular, had a way of dying heroically at their posts.

Yells from the rear told of fresh U.S. troops coming up. The Confederates still battling in among their foes weren't getting reinforcements; their barrage hadn't made the U.S. defenders say uncle. "Give up!" Martin shouted to the Rebs. "We got you outnumbered, and you ain't gonna make it back to your own lines. You want to keep breathin', throw down what you got."

For a few seconds, he thought that call would do no good. The Rebs were stubborn bastards; he'd seen them die in place before. But then a sergeant in butternut said, "Hell with it," and threw up his hands. His example was enough for his comrades, who dropped their rifles and whatever other lethal hardware they were holding.

The U.S. soldiers stripped their prisoners of ammunition, grenades, and knives, and of their pocket watches and cash, too. None of the Confederates said a word about that. Several of them had U.S. coins and bills in their pockets, which argued they'd stripped a prisoner or two themselves.

"Hammerschmitt, Peterson, take the Rebs back to where they can deal with 'em," Martin said. The rest of the U.S. soldiers looked enviously at the two men their sergeant had chosen: they'd get away from the front and the fighting, if only for a little while.

"Hear tell the food in Yankee prisoner camps ain't too bad," the Confederate sergeant who'd been first to throw down his Tredegar said hopefully.

As Specs Peterson and Joe Hammerschmitt gestured with their bayoneted rifles to get the prisoners of war moving, Chester Martin answered, "Listen, Rebs, I'll give you one warning: whatever you do, don't let 'em ship you to White Sulphur Springs."

The sergeant nodded, grateful for the advice, then looked puzzled when the U.S. soldiers started laughing. "Come on, you lugs," Peterson said, sounding as fierce as any man with glasses could. Hands still high, the Confederates shuffled off into captivity.

"You're a regular devil, Sarge, you are," Paul Andersen said as the U.S. soldiers shared out the weapons and other loot they'd got from the Rebels. Four men all wanted a knife with a brass handle made as a knuckle-duster; they had to go down on their knees and roll dice to decide who got to keep it.

"Who, me?" Martin said. "Listen, how much difference is there really between a prisoner camp and where they sent us? You can't do what you want either place, now can you?"

"Hadn't looked at it like that," the corporal admitted after a little thought.

"And I'll tell you another thing," Martin said, warming to his theme: "we can joke however goddamn much we want, but they're both better than being at the front." This time, Paul Andersen nodded at once.

XIII

Usually, Scipio or one of the lesser servants looked out from the front windows to see who was coming. This time, Anne Colleton did the job herself. It would not give the Negroes any wrong ideas about her place and theirs in the Marshlands scheme of things, not when the motorcar she was waiting for had her brother in it.

She wondered whether she ought to give Tom a sisterly hug and a kiss or box his foolish ears for him. The first clue she'd had that he was anywhere but up in Virginia was a telephone call from Columbia less than an hour before. He'd just got off the train, he'd said, and was on his way.

Scipio came up to her, tall, imposing, perfectly formal. "Have you any special suggestions on how we may make your brother's stay as comfortable and pleasant as possible?" he asked in his pipe-organ voice.

Anne waved him away. "I leave it in your hands, Scipio. I can't think now. Maybe I'll have some ideas later. If I do, I'll tell you." The butler bowed and withdrew. Since the start of the war, he'd pulled back even further than usual into the shell of service he wore around himself like armor. He'd always been a private person, even before his training for high service, but now it was as if he didn't want anyone having the slightest inkling of what he was thinking or feeling.

Stinking war—it oppresses everyone, she thought. *Sometimes I wish I were a simple field nigger, so I wouldn't have to think about it.* But even the plantation hands were thinking about the war, thinking how they could make money from it by going to work in the factories instead of staying here where they belonged and raising cotton. Anne sighed. Even for a field nigger, life wasn't simple any more.

She drew herself straighter. All right. Life wasn't simple. Up till now, she'd always reveled in complication, and profited from it, too. Nostalgia belonged to the last century. If you didn't look ahead, you were in trouble.

Then all such worries vanished from her head. Here came the motorcar, kicking up a cloud of dust from the red-dirt path that led up to the mansion. The Negro driver stopped the automobile, leaped out of it, and got out Tom Colleton's bags. Then he opened the door to the rear seat and let out Tom, who handed him a silver coin that sparkled in the sun. Tom picked up his own bags and carried them to Marshlands' front door.

He wouldn't have done that before the war started, Anne thought, and then, an instant later, with concern more maternal than sisterly, *He's gotten so thin.*

She hurried to the door. Scipio somehow got there ahead of her; he shared with cats the ability to leave later than you did but to arrive sooner anyhow, and without seeming to have crossed the intervening space. He opened the door, letting in the warm May air, and said, "Welcome home, Captain Colle—" He stopped, for a moment looking quite humanly surprised. Tom Colleton wore a single star on each collar tab. Scipio corrected himself: "Welcome home, *Major* Colleton."

Anne threw herself into her brother's arms. He dropped his bags and squeezed her tight. After the joyous hellos and I-love-yous and good-to-see-yous, Anne said indignantly, "You didn't tell me you've been promoted again."

Tom shrugged. "We've seen a lot of casualties. Somebody has to step up and do the work." When he'd joined the Army, bare days after war broke out, he'd put a fancy plume in his hat and gone off gaily, like a knight heading out on a Crusade. Now he sounded both tired and altogether matter-of-fact about his business, more like a cabinetmaker than a cavalier.

He looked tired, too. His forehead had lines that hadn't been there the year before—he was eighteen months younger than Anne—and he carried dark circles under his eyes. His cheeks were hollow; a long, pink scar seamed one of them. Hesitantly, Anne reached up to touch it. "You didn't tell me about this, either."

Her brother shrugged again. "Got kissed by a shell fragment. Battalion doctor's assistant sewed it up. I didn't lose any duty time, so I didn't think it was worth talking about."

"You've changed," Anne said, perhaps more wonderingly than she should have. The young man who'd gone off to war had been the little brother she'd always known: witty, easygoing, not too effectual—certainly not effectual enough to want to put in any work at operating Marshlands when his sister seemed happy enough doing it all. And that had suited Anne fine; she rejoiced in the power it gave her. But when she looked into the eyes of the lean near-stranger who was her own flesh and blood, she didn't know what she saw. It flustered her. Tom had always been so easy to read, so predictable.

Scipio scooped up the bags. "I shall put these in your room, sir," he said.

"My room," Tom echoed, as if the phrase were in a foreign language. Slowly, he nodded. "Yes, go ahead and do that, Scipio." The butler carried the bags into the mansion. Tom took one step to follow him, then stopped, still outside. "Very strange," he murmured. "Unbelievable."

"What is?" Anne asked. She wasn't used to being unable to follow his train of thought.

"That all this"—Tom waved at the Marshlands mansion—"and all this"—the next wave encompassed the many square miles of the Marshlands estate—"is mine—part mine; excuse me, dear sister. And excuse me for sounding not quite like my old self. For most of the past nine months, my horizons have been limited to a hole in the ground and whether there'd be enough beans in the pot for my men and me. Coming back to this is like falling asleep and dreaming you've gone to heaven."

"It should be like waking from a nightmare," Anne said. "This is where you live. This is where you belong." *At least for as long as you don't get in my hair while you're here. You never used to. Will you now? Harder to tell.*

Her brother's mouth set in a hard line: another expression she'd never seen on his face till now. "I'm going back to the front in three days' time," he said, his voice flat. "Till the war is done, this is the dream. And when the war is done, it's liable to disappear like a dream, too."

"What *are* you talking about?" Of all the people in the world, Anne should have been able to keep up with—to keep ahead of—her brother. Ever since they were tiny, she'd been the clever one, the dominant one, in the family. She'd taken that so much for granted, it had never occurred to her things might change.

"Never mind." Tom stepped past her, into the hallway. His grin was more like the one she'd known, though not quite the same. "Feels good to get out of the sun." He kept on walking, and looked up toward the second-floor galleries. Like the grin, his chuckle had something new in it—restraint, maybe. Pointing, he said, "Still got the funny pictures hanging on the walls, do you?"

"Some of them," Anne said; he'd teased her about the exhibition ever since she'd had the idea for it. "Marcel Duchamp is still here, too."

"Is he?" Tom's lips thinned again. "Do we have any liquor left, and how many yellow babies are due?" That wasn't teasing, it was cold contempt, one more thing she wasn't used to hearing from him. That it matched her own feelings about the Frenchman was, next to the unaccustomed harshness, a small thing.

She decided taking Tom literally might be the best way to defuse the situation: "There's enough whiskey left for you to have a drink, if you want one." When her brother nodded, she called for Scipio. As usual, he answered the call faster than should have been possible. "Two whiskeys over ice," she told him. He bowed and disappeared again.

"Ice," Tom said. "Saw plenty of that this past winter. Not in my drink, though." He shook himself, as if realizing at last he really was away from the trenches of the Roanoke valley. "I heard from Jacob not long before I hopped on the train down here. He's well, or was then."

"I got a letter from him just the other day," Anne answered. "He said it looks like the Yankees are up to something in Kentucky, but nobody seems to know what it is or when the storm breaks."

"Won't be long now," Tom said. "Roads should all be dry. They can build their supply dumps up to as big as they want them, put their reserves in place. As soon as they're ready, they'll hit us." He spoke again like someone discussing the ins and outs of a business he knew well. Musingly, he went on, "Show probably would have started there already if they hadn't had to pull men to deal with the revolt in Utah."

Anne nodded. "Between the Mormons and the Socialists, they have so much trouble inside their own borders, it hurts them when they try to fight us." She spoke with vindictive relish. Scipio returned then, two tumblers full of amber whiskey gleaming on a silver tray. Ice clinked gently. Anne took one drink, Tom the other. She said, "It's not like that here, thank God. We all stand behind the cause."

To her amazement, her brother threw back his head and laughed. "This is the dream, all right," he said, and knocked back his whiskey with a flick of the wrist. "You're not living in the real world, that's certain."

Being the object of her brother's scorn angered her. "Who in the Confederate States throws bombs and rises up against the government?" she demanded, and then answered her own question: "No one, that's who."

"No?" Tom set the tumbler down hard on the tray Scipio still held. "These past few months, they've executed a couple of dozen niggers in my division alone. Reds, every last one of 'em, out-and-out Reds. Worse than plain old Socialists and Mormons put together, if you ask me."

"That's not the same as—" Anne began.

Her brother cut her off, one more thing he wouldn't have done—wouldn't have dared do—before the war. "And that's just in my division alone. Others, it's been worse. And God only knows how deep the rot has spread, away from the front."

"I've heard that. I don't believe it," Anne said firmly. "It's not a problem here, I can tell you that much."

When she used that tone of voice, it was supposed to make Tom shut up and knuckle under. It always had in the past. It didn't any more. "Everybody says the same thing—till they get their noses rubbed in it," he told her. "A plantation this size, if there's not a Red cell somewhere on it, I'll eat my hat." He pointed to the brown felt he'd hung just inside the door, and turned a hard and thoughtful gaze on Scipio.

That was too much for Anne. "Tom, stop this at once, or you'll make me sorry you've come home," she said. "Scipio has raised both of us since we were babies. The idea that he could be a Red—it's disgusting. That's the only word I can find for it."

"Things change." Tom Colleton swung back toward her. He leaned forward a little. The implied threat of attack made Anne take half a step back before she realized what she'd done. And her brother did attack, though only with words: "You're the one who's always going on about change. It's not as much fun as you make it out to be, not all the time it isn't. And if you think it can't happen right here at Marshlands, you're deliberately blinding yourself."

Anne stared, first at him, then at Scipio. Her brother's face was grim and intent. Scipio showed nothing of what he thought, but then, he never did. Anne finished her whiskey, then, even harder than her brother had done, slammed the tumbler down onto the tray the butler was holding. A chunk of ice jumped out, leaving a little wet trail as it skidded across the polished silver surface.

"Get me another drink, Scipio." She kept her voice low, but it was brittle with fury even so. The butler hurried away. When he came back a moment later with the second whiskey, she drank it fast, too. She could feel the liquor building a transparent wall between her and the world, but even that numbing could not disguise the fact that her kid brother's homecoming, far from being the celebration she'd expected, looked more like a disaster.

Percy Stone was dressed in his flying togs and had his camera by his side, but that hadn't kept him from sitting in on a poker game while he waited for Jonathan Moss to finish getting ready to fly. By the expression on his face, it hadn't kept him from losing money to Lefty the mechanic, either. He was in good company there; almost everybody rash enough to sit down with Lefty ended up sadder, if not necessarily wiser.

"Oh, thank God—duty calls," Stone said when Moss came in. "I think I'd sooner go up there and get shot at than stay here and get skinned." Amid laughter, he studied his cards, then tossed a big silver coin into the pot. "Raise a dollar."

"And other one." The mechanic named Byron tossed in a folded bill.

Two other players threw in their hands with various noises of disgust. Lefty said, "I'll see those and bump it another three." He made his five dollars with a gold half-eagle.

"That's enough for me," Stone said, and folded. Byron looked harassed, but called—and promptly regretted it. Chuckling, Lefty scooped up the pot.

"I could have told you not to play cards with Lefty," Moss said as Stone picked up the camera and the two fliers walked out to their Wright 17. "As a matter of fact, I *have* told you not to play cards with Lefty."

"It's the Socialist in me," Stone answered. Moss let out a questioning grunt. The observer explained: "I make more money than Lefty does, but at the poker table we redistribute the wealth." He shook his head. "I wouldn't mind it so much if the redistribution went my way a little more often."

Moss blew air out through his lips with a snuffling noise, like a horse. "I'm a Democrat," he said. "Always have been, probably always will be. If I earn something, I figure it's mine, and I want to keep it. I don't much like riots, either, so Socialism was a hard sell for me even before the Remembrance Day horrors."

"That was pretty bad, if you believe what you read in the newspapers," Stone agreed. He lifted the camera into his cockpit, then climbed in after it. Once he'd set it in the mount, though, he added, "Of course, if you believe what you read in the newspapers, we've already won the war four or five times by now, which does make me wonder what the two of us are doing, going up in this contraption." He slapped the doped linen fabric covering the side of the fuselage. It was taut, and thumped like a drum.

He had such a disarming manner to him that even political arguments that could have turned hot and heavy in a hurry got defused. "Earning our salaries, so you can give yours to the groundcrew," Moss replied, scrambling into the forward cockpit.

"You have less faith in my card-playing than I do, and I didn't think that was possible," Stone said. He whacked the pilot on the shoulder with a length of rubber tubing to which a cheap tin funnel had been attached. "Stick this up to your ear and let's see how it does."

The rubber tubing was of the sort that ran from the speedometer to the pitot tube out at the far end of the wing. Moss undid the funnel and stuck it through one ear hole of his flying helmet, then fixed it to the tube again. Stone tossed him another length of rubber tubing with funnel. That one Moss left in his lap; his observer would have the other end pressed to one ear.

Stone's voice sounded metallically in his ear: "Can you hear me all right?"

Moss spoke into the funnel of the second tube: "Yeah, sure, down here when it's quiet. How we'll do at eight thousand feet with the engine going is liable to be a different ball of wax." He chuckled. "This isn't a whole hell of a lot fancier than tying a couple of tin cans to a string, the way we did when we were kids."

"Sure isn't," Stone agreed. "They don't pay off for looks, though, not in this man's army they don't. If we can make it work, somebody else'll make it pretty, sooner or later."

The groundcrew men came out to help them get the two-seater started. Lefty grinned through gibes about bulges in his trousers that had more to do with his financial endowments than his masculine ones. He spun the prop. The Wright's motor buzzed to life at once.

Tachometer, gasoline gauge, gasoline-flow indicator, gasoline feed system pressure indicator, oil gauge, oil-pressure gauge, radiator temperature indicator—all the instruments were good. Moss waved to the groundcrew men. Byron and another mechanic, a fellow named Edwin, pulled the chocks away from the wheels. Moss advanced the throttle. The Wright 17 bounced down the airstrip. After enough bounces, it didn't come back to earth.

Percy Stone's voice sounded in his ear: "Can you hear me?"

He shifted the other tube to his mouth. "I sure can. Can you hear me?" When the observer assured him he could, Moss went on, "Say, this is great. We can really talk to each other now." Percy Stone promptly started singing "America the Beautiful." Moss made a hasty amendment: "Maybe it's not so great after all."

Both young men laughed, pleased with their ingenuity. More seriously now, Stone said, "We have to spread the word about this. Biggest problem two-seaters have is that the pilot and observer can't talk back and forth."

"I've seen that with us working together," Moss agreed. "Now that we know pitot tubing makes a good speaking tube, we could come up with better earpieces and mouthpieces than these funnels, I bet. Playing with them makes me feel like I'm home from school on summer vacation."

"That's not bad," Stone said. "Better than thinking about this like it is school, anyway. If you flunk here, they don't make you take the class over. You get expelled—for good."

"Yeah," Moss said; it wasn't anything on which he cared to dwell. He peered ahead. "Front's coming up. Get ready for some hate."

Land over which the American and Canadian armies had already fought was barren, chewed to shreds, as if an insane giant had gnawed on it for a while and then, deciding it wasn't to his taste, spit it out again. Over the front itself, smoke and dust rose high into the air, a legacy of the shelling the two sides kept trading. Percy Stone said, "You'd think we'd have fired enough shells by now to kill all the Canadians there are, by hitting them over the head if no other way."

"Don't I wish we had," Moss said, "them and the Englishmen both." British reinforcements for the dominion hadn't come in any great numbers, but the ones who had come had stiffened the Canucks' will to keep fighting in spite of being outnumbered and outgunned by the USA. And, in spite of being outnumbered and outgunned, the Canadians were a long way from out for the count.

As soon as the Wilbur flew over the front, the Canucks proved that. They gave the American aeroplane all the hate anyone could want. Black puffs of smoke filled the sky all around the Wright machine. The ones that burst close sounded like big, mean dogs barking: *waugh! waugh! waugh!*

"Nice to know they love us," Stone said. Moss laughed. He sped up and slowed down and turned now off to the left of his course, now off to the right, all in an effort to keep the gunners down on the ground from putting a lucky shell right where the aeroplane would be. He had never been sure dodging and changing speed did that much to improve the odds, but they couldn't hurt.

"The front hasn't moved much for a while," he said sadly. He'd expected things to pick up with the coming of spring, but it hadn't happened yet. He knew, from seeing the mud back at the aerodrome, how thick and clinging it was. Trying to advance in it was anything but easy. The Canuck and British offensive south from Winnipeg had started off alarmingly well, but the enemy proved to have no easier time advancing through muddy, broken country than did the Americans.

Once he flew past the reach of American artillery, the towns and rich farmlands of southern Ontario gave him much more attractive things to view than he'd had till then. The farms glowed green with early growth: the Canucks not yet at the front were getting in what crops they could.

Even the farmlands, though, bore scars. Looking down and seeing the same thing, Percy Stone said, "They're digging in for a long fight." Digging in the Canadians and British certainly were. Trench lines drew dark brown furrows across green fields every mile or so, with zigzag communication trenches running back from one set to the next. Just as in the Niagara Peninsula, if the U.S. Army blasted them out of one position, they'd fall back to the next and keep on fighting.

"They fight hard, too," Moss said, giving the foe grudging respect. "I go to bed every night getting down on my knees and thanking God for not making me an infantryman."

"Ahh-men!" Percy Stone sang out, as if at the end of a hymn. Then, in an entirely different tone of voice, he said, "Jesus!" He amplified that: "Bandit on our tail, and diving on us!"

Moss swung the Wright's nose up till the aeroplane almost stalled, then rolled hard to the right, trying to slip away from the pursuer he hadn't seen. Fear and excitement ran through his body, a jolt stronger than 151-proof rum. The rum wouldn't kill you, even if, come the next morning, you wished it had. The enemy, though—

He thanked God for the speaking tube. Without it, Stone would have had the devil's own time warning him they had company in the sky. They weren't supposed to have had company; the enemy's aeroplane force was supposed to have been so beaten down, one-aeroplane missions were allowed again. Like a lot of things that were supposed to have happened, that one hadn't.

He gave the aeroplane full throttle, swinging through a quick circle in the sky to try and get on the foe's tail instead of the other way round. Acceleration and centrifugal force threw him around in the cockpit.

Halfway through the turn, he got his first glimpse of the enemy bus: an Avro, an aeroplane whose performance closely matched the Wilbur's. The Canadian pilot—or maybe, for all Moss knew, he was an Englishman—rolled through a maneuver like his own, so the two flying machines turned away from each other.

Behind him, Percy Stone squeezed off a burst with his machine gun. The Avro's observer fired back; Moss saw flame burst from the muzzle of the enemy machine gun. Tracers sparked across the open, empty air.

Thwump! Thwump! Thwump! Bullets punched through fuselage fabric, sounding like flung stones off a tightly stretched awning. Stone's fire abruptly ceased. "I'm hit!" sounded tinnily in Moss' ear.

He couldn't answer for a moment; he needed both hands to twist the aeroplane through a roll that had earth and sky twisting dizzily all around him. Where was the Avro? Were more enemy aeroplanes in the sky? With his observer wounded, he couldn't fight back. He wished again for the Super Hudson he wasn't flying any more. Of course, had he been in that bus, the bullets might have gone through him, not Stone.

His head swiveled wildly as he leveled off and scooted back toward the American lines. His altimeter was still unwinding; it hadn't been able to keep up with his dizzying dive. He didn't need it to tell him he'd shed several thousand feet. His ears ached dully. They'd popped several times in the descent, but, like the altimeter, hadn't caught up with the rest of him.

He didn't see any Canucks or limeys. Grabbing the speaking tube, he shouted into it: "Percy! You there? How bad are you?"

"One in the side, one ricocheted off the damn camera and nicked me in the leg," Stone answered. A moment later, another word dragged from him: "Hurts."

Moss flew straight and level, sacrificing everything for speed, till tracer bullets zipped past the Wright 17. Then he began dodging and swerving again. You couldn't outrun a bullet; your best hope was to evade one. Behind him, the observer's machine gun started chattering. He had no idea how accurately Percy Stone was firing. That he was firing at all seemed a good sign.

But tracers were coming from more than one direction, which, by unpleasant logic, meant he had more than one aeroplane on his tail. That *wasn't* a good sign. Anything you did to evade one was liable to bring you right under the gun of another.

And then, like angels with flaming swords, a flight of American aeroplanes dove on the Canucks or limeys, who went from pursuers to pursued in seconds. "They're breaking away," Stone said. Moss didn't like how quiet and tired he sounded. He should have been screaming for joy, leaning forward to pound his pilot on the back. Straight and level, that was the answer: get Stone to a sawbones on the double.

Enemy antiaircraft gunners sent up a storm of hate as Moss flew over the front line. He didn't waste time on evasive action, not now. Odds weren't so good as if he'd been dodging all over the landscape, but they were still on his side.

He got away with it. "Almost home, Percy," he said. Stone didn't answer. Moss looked back over his shoulder. The observer was slumped to one side, his eyes closed. Moss tried to fly even faster, but the Wilbur was already going flat out.

He landed at as high a speed as he could, using the whole airstrip and taxiing to a stop close to the barracks. He was waving for help before the aeroplane stopped rolling. As soon as it did, he scrambled back into the observer's cockpit.

Blood was everywhere back there: on the walls, on the seat, on the floor, on the camera—and on Percy Stone's flying togs. Moss yanked back the observer's sleeve and jabbed his finger down on the inside of Stone's wrist. He let out a whoop when he felt a pulse.

"Hurry up, dammit!" he shouted. "He's hurt bad!"

By then the groundcrew were already at the bus. They had a stretcher with them. Lefty helped Moss unbuckle Stone and get his limp weight out of the cockpit and down to the ground. "Can't let him die," the mechanic said. "I need his money." If he was kidding, he was kidding on the square.

He and Byron rushed Stone away. Jonathan Moss looked down at himself. His friend's blood was on his flight suit, on his boots, on his hands. Wearily, he trudged in to make his report to Captain Franklin. No pictures to develop, not today; Stone had got hit before he had the chance to take any—and the camera looked to be *hors de combat*, too.

Somebody brought him a whiskey. He gulped it down without tasting or feeling it. After what seemed a very long time, the telephone jangled. Lefty got it before Moss could even move from his chair. "Yeah?" the mechanic said, and again: "Yeah? All right. Good. Thanks." He hung up, then turned to Moss. "Collapsed lung and he's lost a lot of blood, but they think he's gonna pull through."

"Thank God," Moss said, and fell asleep where he sat.

* * *

Stephen Ramsay sipped coffee from a tin cup, then said, "Captain Lincoln, sir, ain't this a hell of a war? I've been a cavalryman a long time. When we got into Okmulgee here, I didn't mind fighting like a dragoon, on account of that's what you got to do when you fight in built-up country. But now they've dragooned us into the infantry—and it's not even the Confederate States infantry. Well, not exactly," he amended.

"You're the captain now, Ramsay," Lincoln said. "I'll have you remember I'm a colonel these days." His hand went to his collar. He didn't wear the three bars of a Confederate captain any more, or the three stars of a Confederate colonel, either. Instead, he had two red costume-jewelry jewels, the newly devised insigne for a colonel in the equally newly devised Creek Nation Army.

Ramsay had shed his sergeant's stripes, too. He wore one red costume-jewelry jewel on either side of his collar. Both he and Lincoln also had red armbands on the left sleeves of their tunics. Other than that, they, unlike the soldiers they were now commanding, retained ordinary Confederate uniform.

"Captain? Me?" Ramsay snorted. "Doesn't seem real." He drank some more coffee. It was hot and strong. Past that, he couldn't think of anything good to say about it. After swallowing, he went on, "Last time I got paid, though, it was a captain's money, so I can't kick about that."

"Same here—I got a colonel's money," Lincoln said. "And we're earning what they pay us, by God. Do you doubt it?"

"When you put it that way, no sir." Ramsay laughed a little. "Crazy how things work out, isn't it? We were the first white soldiers in town, we helped the Creeks throw back the damnyankees, so Chief Fixico figures we're the ones to turn his braves into real soldiers." Under his breath, he added, "Stupid damn rank badges, anyone wants to know."

"I told him the same thing." Lincoln's chuckle was wry. "They turned out to be his idea, so we're stuck with them as long as we do this job." He shrugged. "I hear tell English officers, when they get hired to bring an Indian maharajah's militia up to snuff—their kind of Indian, I mean, not ours—they have to wear the native-style uniform, too. It could be worse—they could have put us in war paint and feathers."

"Creeks don't seem to go in for that kind of thing much," Ramsay said. "You look around at this place—the way it was before the fighting started, anyway—and it could be anybody's town. You wouldn't know red—uh, Indians—had built it."

You had to be careful about saying *redskins* hereabouts. The Indians didn't like it for beans. Ramsay had the idea Negroes didn't like being called niggers, either, but he didn't let that stop him. It was different with the Creeks, though. They weren't just hewers of wood and drawers of water. By law and by treaty, they were every bit as much Confederate citizens as he was. Up till manumission, they'd kept slaves of their own.

"Captain Ramsay?" That was Moty Tiger, probably—no, certainly—the best sergeant Ramsay had. He was the young fellow who'd apologized to Ramsay when he suddenly got a lesson in what foxholes were worth. Now his broad bronze face was worried.

When Moty Tiger worried, Ramsay figured he ought to worry, too. "What's up, Moty?" he asked, getting to his feet.

"I've got a discipline problem, Captain," the Creek sergeant said carefully.

"Well, let's see what we can do about that," Ramsay said. The Indian with the picturesque name turned and led him down the trench, presumably toward whoever was involved in the discipline problem.

Ramsay kicked at the muddy dirt as he followed. The Creek Nation Army—both regiments of it—had an inordinate number of discipline problems. Part of that was because the men had been under military discipline for only a few weeks. They chafed under it, like barely broken horses. And part of it was that they were Indians, and maybe less used to taking orders from anybody than a like number of whites would have been.

They particularly didn't like taking orders from their own people. They accepted it better from their white officers. Ramsay didn't think that was because he was white, as he would have if he were dealing with Negroes. But the Creeks seemed to figure that, as a real live working soldier, he knew what he was doing, whereas to them their noncoms were the same kind of amateurs they were.

"Ten-shun!" Moty Tiger called as he came up to the knot of Indians gathered around a fire. The Creeks got to their feet, not with the alacrity Confederate regulars would have shown, but fast enough that Ramsay couldn't gig them about it. In lieu of uniforms, which hadn't arrived yet from back East, they wore denim pants, flannel shirts with red armbands like Ramsay's, and a variety of slouch hats.

"All right, what's going on here?" Ramsay asked with something close to genuine curiosity.

"He gave me the shit duty again!" one of the Creeks exclaimed.

"Somebody's got to have it, Perryman," Ramsay said. "We don't take the honey buckets to the pit and cover it up, we'd get even worse stinks than we have already, and we'd start getting sick before long, too. No way to keep clean or anything close to it, but we've got to do what we can."

"Those damn buckets are disgusting," Perryman said. "Hauling them is nigger work, not soldier work."

"Mike, we ain't got no niggers here," Moty Tiger said, more patiently than Ramsay would have expected. "All we got is us, and if we don't do it, nobody will. And it's your turn."

"*Is* it your turn?" Ramsay asked Mike Perryman; there was always the chance Moty Tiger was picking on his fellow Indian, which would have to be stopped if it was happening. But, reluctantly, Perryman nodded. "Then you've got to do the job," Ramsay told him. "I've done it myself, on maneuvers and out in the field. Take 'em to the pit, fling 'em in, cover everything up, and then you can pretend it never happened."

"You really did that?" Perryman asked, his black eyes scanning Ramsay's face, searching for a lie.

But it was the truth. Ramsay nodded with a clear conscience. "You're a soldier now," he said. "This isn't a lark and it isn't a game. It isn't pretty. It isn't a whole lot of fun. But it's what needs doing. So—are you going to be a soldier, or are you going to be an old soldier, somebody who's always complaining and carrying on when he's got no cause to? You said yourself your sergeant wasn't being unfair. If you don't do the job, somebody else will have to, and that wouldn't be fair to the rest of the men in your squad."

He waited to see what would happen. He didn't want to have to punish Mike Perryman. He'd already seen that punishment didn't work as well with the Creeks as it did with white soldiers. The Indians only resented you more.

Perryman muttered something Ramsay only half heard. He didn't think it was in English. That was liable to be just as well. If he didn't understand it, he didn't have to notice it. But then, slowly and with nothing like enthusiasm or even resignation, the Creek got to his feet and headed off to the latrine bay dug out from the main trench. Nobody watched him as he carried the buckets off to the disposal pit. Nobody watched him bring them back, either—more courtesy than white soldiers would have shown one of their comrades in the same fix.

"Thank you, Captain," Moty Tiger said quietly as the two of them walked back toward where Ramsay had been drinking his coffee.

"You're welcome," Ramsay answered. "You were right, so I backed you up. Before too long, everybody will have the idea, and you won't need me to back you up."

"I shouldn't have this time." The Creek sounded angry at himself.

As an old sergeant himself, Ramsay understood that. But things were different here from the way they were in the Confederate Army or any other long-established force. "Next time, or maybe the time after that, everything will go smooth," Ramsay said. "What you want to do is this—you want to make sure they do what you tell 'em before the damnyankees try another push into Okmulgee. That'll keep a lot more of 'em alive, whether they're smart enough to know it or not. They won't thank you for it, but they'll be here."

"I understand," the Creek sergeant said. He hesitated, then asked, "If the United States soldiers do attack here, can we hold them back?"

"We've got the Creek Nation Army, we've got some good Texas infantry, we've got artillery back of town and over in the hills," Ramsay said, and then, because honesty compelled him, "Damned if I know. Depends on how hard the Yankees push things. Attacking costs more than defending, but they've got more men than we do, too."

Moty Tiger nodded soberly. "This is not war, the way we Creeks talk of war. This is not warrior against warrior. It is a whole nation throwing itself at another nation. It does not bring men glory or fame. It uses them up, and it buries them, and then it reaches out and uses more."

"You're only wrong about one thing," Ramsay said. The Indian looked a question at him. He explained. "A lot of the time, this here war doesn't bother with buryin' the men it uses up."

Moty Tiger pondered that. He showed his teeth in a grimace of pain, but didn't argue with Ramsay. Instead, after a grave nod, he turned around and went back down the trench, back toward his squad. They and he—and Ramsay—hadn't been used up . . . yet.

The train shuddered to a stop. Paul Mantarakis, conscious that the two dark green stripes on the sleeve of his tunic meant he had more important work to do—and that he had to do it under more important eyes—than before, said, "My squad, get ready to pile on out."

Soldiers stirred on the floor of the boxcar. Not so long ago, it had been carrying horses. The strong smell lingered. Some of the farm boys found it soothing. As far as Paul was concerned, that was their problem, not his. They grabbed their rifles, made sure they had all their gear, and grunted as they slung their packs onto their backs.

Not far away, Gordon McSweeney, also sporting corporal's stripes, was telling his squad, "Properly speaking, these Mormons are not even Christians. They will go to hell regardless of whether we shoot them down or they die in bed. Spare not the rod, then, for not only are they heretics, they are rebels in arms against the United States of America."

Lieutenant Norman Hinshaw was talking to the whole platoon: "We have to root out these bandits and rebels and bring Utah back under the Stars and Stripes. Remember, most of the people we come across will be loyal Americans. Only a handful have sold themselves to the Canucks and the Rebs, and they're the ones causing all the trouble. Once we get rid of them, Utah should be a peaceable state, just like all the others." He paused to let that sink in, then went on, "When they first hatched their plot, these Mormon madmen blew up the railroad line right at the border and seized the weapons in every arsenal in the state. Now we've pushed more than halfway to Salt Lake City. The town ahead of us is called Price. We'll take it, repair the tracks, and move on." He didn't ask for questions. He worked the latch on the boxcar door and slid it open. "Let's go!"

After so long cooped up on the train, Mantarakis' eyes filled with tears when he stepped out into bright sunshine. The first breath of fresh air told him he wasn't in Kentucky any more, or in Philadelphia, either. It was hot and dry, with an alkaline tang to it. It wasn't summer yet, but it felt that way. Ahead—westward—and to the north, he saw forested mountains in the distance. A nearer line of green marked the Price River. But the land where he was standing had only scattered sagebrush and tumbleweeds and other desert plants on it. All it needed was the bleached skull of an ox to make it the perfect picture of an arid waste.

"This is the abomination of the desolation, as was spoken of in the Book of Daniel," McSweeney said, and Mantarakis, for once, was not inclined to disagree.

The boxcar from which they'd emerged was one of dozens, hundreds, carrying the two divisions pulled out of Kentucky to their new theater of operations. They unloaded men, horses, mules, wagons, trucks, guns—all the tools needed to wage war in the modern age, and to keep on waging it in country like this, where they would be hard pressed to draw supplies from the land.

Every officer of captain's rank or higher was running around with a list and a pencil, checking things off as fast as he could. In an amazingly short time, what had been two entrained divisions turned into two divisions ready for action. In spite of himself, Paul was impressed. Soldiers spent a lot of time groaning about officers, but every now and then they showed what they were worth.

Dust puffed up under Mantarakis' boots as he marched along. Dust hovered all around the thousands of marching men. It held a stronger dose of the alkaline tang he'd noticed before. How the devil were you supposed to raise crops on soil like this?

Plainly, the Mormons did it. He marched past a big farmhouse of a sort he'd never seen before: it looked to be made of rammed earth. In a country where it rained more often, a house like that would fall apart pretty damn quick. This one looked to have been standing for a generation, maybe two.

It stood open now. So did the barn alongside. Whoever had lived here didn't want to stick around and greet the United States Army with a big smile and an American flag. *They like the Rebels,* Mantarakis thought, not very happy with the idea. If only a handful of people were in revolt, why had the squad run across some of them so soon?

Then, ahead and off to the right, the familiar *pop-pop-pop* of gunfire rang out. "We will move to the firing, to support our soldiers under attack," Lieutenant Hinshaw proclaimed. The whole platoon—the whole company—did just that.

The Mormons were holed up in another farmhouse. It had a big flag flying above it, on what had to be a makeshift pole. Paul couldn't make out what the flag was, but it wasn't the Stars and Stripes. He saw muzzle flashes from several windows; the Mormons were putting a lot of lead in the air, doing their best to hold the U.S. troops at bay.

They hadn't built the place for defense, though. The barn offered one avenue blind to them for soldiers to approach. The well and the haystacks and the outhouse gave other approaches. Before long, Mantarakis' whole company was peppering the farmhouse from pretty short range. A machine gun came up and started rattling away. Dust flew from the adobe as bullets stitched back and forth. Its pole clipped, the flag fell in the dirt in front of the house. Mantarakis and his comrades cheered.

"Let's go!" Lieutenant Hinshaw shouted. Under cover of the machine gun, he rushed toward the farmhouse. Mantarakis and the rest of his squad followed. So did McSweeney and his men. If an officer had the guts to go out there, you couldn't let him go by himself.

A bullet whistled past Paul's head—not everybody in the farmhouse was down. The machine gun blasted away at the window from which the shot had come. Paul trampled on the fallen flag—it was, he saw, a beehive with the word DESERET beneath it—on the way to the front door. Along with several men, he hammered at it with the butt of his rifle. Someone inside fired through the door. A U.S. soldier fell with a groan.

Then the door went down. Soldiers were already clambering into the house through the windows. Mantarakis rushed in. Somebody shot at him from point-blank range—and missed. After a last fusillade of firing, silence fell: only U.S. soldiers were left alive in there.

Of the Mormon defenders, five had been men and two women. They had all had rifles, and had all known what to do with them. Mantarakis had seen plenty of death, but never till now a woman in a white shirtwaist with pearl buttons and a long black skirt—and with half her head blown away. He turned away, a little sickened. "They fought harder'n the Rebs ever did," he muttered.

"Fanatics," Lieutenant Hinshaw said. "This is what they warned us about, these nests of maniacs. But most of the people are loyal to the USA. We'll see that when we get into Price. Come on, men." He led his soldiers outside. Once out there, he picked up the Mormons' flag. "Spoil of war. Now—on with the advance."

If the people of Price, Utah, were loyal to the United States, nobody had bothered telling them about it. They had a trench line just east of town, and defended it ferociously till machine-gun and artillery fire drove them back in amongst the buildings. But when the U.S. soldiers tried to advance into Price, rifle fire and a couple of Mormon machine guns hurled them back with heavy losses.

"Looks like we're going to be in the next wave," Mantarakis told his squad unhappily. He'd become numbed to the prospect of charging straight ahead at the enemy's line: that was how First Army operated.

But the divisional commander showed a little more imagination than General Custer ever had. Instead of drowning Price in U.S. blood, he decided to shell it into ruins. Back of the U.S. line, more artillery unlimbered and started bellowing away. The Mormons had machine guns, but evidently no cannon of their own. A great cloud of smoke and dust rose above the Utah town.

In an abstract way, Mantarakis sympathized with the Mormons who'd been stupid enough to rise up against the might of the United States. He'd had artillery barrages come down on his position only too often; he knew what being under one of them was like. He hoped, though, that this one would be so stunning, so deadly, that the defenders would be either blown to bits or too battered to fight back. After the barrage let up, his neck would be on the line.

It went on for three hours. When it stopped, whistles blew, ordering the U.S. soldiers forward. Paul came up out of the foxhole in which he'd crouched and sprinted toward the outskirts of Price.

He hadn't gone fifty yards before a Mormon machine gun started stuttering out death. After that, he didn't run any more. He scrambled from one piece of cover to the next, firing as he went. So did the men with him. They'd learned in a hard school.

He didn't know where the Mormons had learned. Wherever it was, they'd earned high marks. They defended every ruined store and pile of rubble as if losing it meant losing the war. They wouldn't retreat. They wouldn't surrender. Sometimes they would hold their fire till a party of U.S. soldiers had gone by, then shoot at them from behind, blazing away with no hope of escape until they were either dead or too badly wounded to hold a rifle.

Men, women, children down to about the age of eight—every Mormon in Price—fought, and fought to the death. Every smashed house had to be combed through room by room, every cellar checked for lurkers with guns. It was a grimmer, bloodier, more expensive nightmare than Paul had ever imagined.

He crouched down behind tumbled boards that had probably once been a false front and lighted a cigarette. A moment later, Gordon McSweeney took cover with him. "Tobacco is a filthy weed," McSweeney said.

As far as Mantarakis could see, the big Scotsman disapproved of everything. "I'm not making you smoke it," he pointed out. He blew a stream of smoke toward the little patch of Price to which the Mormons still clung. "Still think this is just a few fanatics fighting us? If the rest of Utah is anything like this, the next Mormon who likes us will be the first."

"You may be right about that," McSweeney said. "But what if you are? I keep telling you, the Mormons will burn in hell regardless of what they do here on earth."

"Thanks a lot, Gordon," Mantarakis muttered. McSweeney didn't see it, but to him fighting a whole bunch of people who all hated you was different from fighting fanatics who hated you hidden among people who mostly didn't. If all the Mormons hated the U.S. government, what did that make them when they rose up against it? Patriots?

Whatever it made them, it made them dangerous. A couple of bullets snapped by, too close for comfort. Paul stubbed out his cigarette on a rock, made sure he had a full clip in his Springfield, and went back to clearing the Mormons out of Price.

Sylvia Enos looked at her husband in dismay. "Are you sure this is what you should do?" she asked, in lieu of screaming, *Are you out of your mind?* "You haven't been home long enough to be sure of anything."

"I'm sure of this," he answered, and she could hear he meant it.

But being sure wasn't the same as being right. "Can't you wait a little longer before you join the Navy?" Sylvia knew she was pleading. She didn't care.

"Would you rather I signed up on a fishing boat?" George asked. Sylvia flinched by way of answering. The Confederates, the Canadians, and the British had sown Georges Bank and the other fishing waters around Boston full of mines. Not a week went by when a boat didn't blow up. If another boat was nearby, it sometimes brought back survivors. More often than not, though, the only way you knew—or thought you knew—a fishing boat had hit a mine was when it didn't come back to T Wharf.

"I'd rather you didn't put to sea at all," Sylvia said. It was about the worst thing a fisherman's wife could tell her man. Sylvia knew that, and said it anyhow. She was listening to George, Jr., and Mary Jane snoring in their bedroom. They were both getting over colds, with their heads full of snot. They counted for something, too. She went on, "I'd rather you stayed ashore, is what I'd rather."

He didn't get angry, as she'd expected he would. He just shook his head in absolute rejection. "I had a lot of time to think about this, down in the camp in Rebel country. Nobody on land would hire me. Fishing is all I know."

"They'll take any bodies they can get," Sylvia shot back. "I didn't know anything to speak of, and they hired me."

"Yeah, but conscription won't drag you into the Army, like it will me," George answered. "I wouldn't last a month before the letter came. If I'm going to go fight, I'd rather do it on the water. I thought about that, too. I thought real hard."

Sylvia didn't have a good comeback. She'd already had a cousin wounded. The Army seized men and mangled them—that was the sense you got when you scanned the casualty lists every day, anyhow. She let out a sad, defeated sigh. "You were gone so long. You had to make friends with your children all over again after you got off the train. How long will you be away if you join the Navy? Years at a time, maybe. Stay here a while."

He shook his head again. "And live off the money you're making? That's not anything for a man to do. I know you had to get work while I was gone. You had to keep bread on the table. But I feel useless sitting around here. If I'm in the Navy, they'll send part of my pay home every month to help you and the kids out. That's a better bargain."

"Pride," she said bitterly, as if it were a dirty word. As far as she was concerned, it was. "Men's pride." Along with the children's snores, she heard the relentless ticking of the alarm clock from the bedroom she now shared once more with her husband. Shared now . . . but for how long? Every tick meant a second less. She did not have that many ticks to spare. "What good is it? If it weren't for men's pride, we wouldn't have this war."

"I don't know anything about that," George told her. "All I know is, I didn't like what the Rebs did to me—I sure as the devil didn't like them murdering poor Lucas Phelps—and I'm going to give some of it back to them when I get the chance."

That was men's pride, too, but what point to saying so? *He got me, so I'm going to get him back.* You heard it in the schoolyards, on the streets. You saw it in feuds between fishing captains, feuds that sometimes ended up fought out with broken bottles or with pistols. And here was a war, throwing half the world into the fire. *He got me, so I'm going to get him back.*

"I wish I were a heathen Chinese," Sylvia said. "They have better sense than to mix themselves up in such foolishness."

"No, they don't," her husband answered. "They're on the Rebs' side, same as the Japs are. I remember one of the guards gloating about it and about all the people China has. And Captain O'Donnell, he looked at that Confederate and he said, 'Yeah, and all of 'em put together ain't worth a regiment of United States Marines in a scrap.' That Reb, he was angry, but he didn't know what to say."

"Captain O'Donnell!" The light that went on in Sylvia's head was brighter than the gas lamps that lit their apartment; it blazed like an electric light. "You spent all that time down there in North Carolina listening to him. He's the reason you want to join the Navy so bad."

When George didn't answer right away, she knew she'd hit that one on the nose. At last, slowly, he said, "We talked about it, sure, but I wouldn't say I made up my mind just on account of him."

"You wouldn't say that? Does that mean it's not true?"

When she had him, he folded up. To his credit, he didn't usually bluff and bluster, the way so many men did. He took her by surprise by not folding up now. "It wasn't just the captain," he insisted. "Like I said, a lot of it was the way the Rebs treated us down there, like we were dirt because we came from the USA. They shot poor Lucas. And what they did to Charlie White . . . He's joining the Navy, too. For all I know, he may have signed up already—I haven't seen him, past couple of days."

That surprised Sylvia, too, in a different way. She said, "I didn't know they let colored people into the Navy."

"Not in the Army, no," George said, "but in the Navy they do. Even back in the War of Secession, they did. Coal-heavers, cooks, that kind of thing. The way Charlie is with a frying pan, he'd get himself whatever rank they give number one cooks in nothin' flat."

Sylvia had no great use for Negroes in general, but Charlie wasn't a Negro in general. He was a Negro in particular, and somebody who fed her husband at least as often as she did. She saw him more as a man and less as a colored man than anyone else of his race she'd ever known—not that that took in any great sample of Boston's Negro community.

"I can see why Charlie would want revenge, but—" she said, and then stopped in dismay at her own words. *He got me, so I'm going to get him back.* God in heaven, where did it end?

"Like I said, we all owe the Rebs," George said, sensing her hesitation. "And me joining the Navy is the best I can do. Safer than being a fisherman these days, safer than being in the Army by a long shot. If I sit idle or if I get a land job, the Army hooks me sure."

If you looked at things logically, what he said made good sense. Sylvia didn't want to look at things logically. What she wanted, now that George was home at last, was for him to stay home. He didn't want to stay home. Even if he had reasons for not wanting to stay home, it still hurt. She put her face in her hands and started to cry. She'd kept up a strong front for the children for so long that when the dam finally broke, it broke wide open.

"Honey, cut that out." George sounded nervous, almost alarmed. Sylvia didn't cry very often, and he didn't know how to cope when she did. Helplessly, he went on, "It doesn't do any good."

He was right, but Sylvia couldn't stop. "You just came back, and now you're—going away again," she sobbed. That was it, in a nub.

George slid closer on the sofa. He reached out awkwardly to stroke her wet cheek. His hand wasn't so hard and rough as it had been before the Rebs captured him. Whatever they'd had him doing down there in the prison camp, it was easier than fishing. "It'll be all right," he said, and put his arm around her.

They ended up in the bedroom not much later. Since he'd come home, they'd made love more than they had even when they were first married; Sylvia had joked about pausing to take an occasional look at the floor, because all she ever saw was the ceiling. This had more a feel of desperation to it. Even when she gasped and quivered as powerfully as she ever had in her life, fear as much as healthy excitement drove her to that height.

And afterwards, lying there spent in the darkness beside her husband, she realized making love didn't do any more good than crying did. When you were done, the world hadn't changed a bit.

"God damn the war," she whispered as she got up to put on her nightgown. George didn't hear her. He was already breathing the deep, regular breaths of sleep. She lay down beside him. She knew she had to go to the canning plant in the morning, but lay a long time awake even so.

Ugly as a drunk white man with a chunk of firewood in his hand looking for a Negro to beat on, the barge made its slow way up to the Covington wharf. Unlike a drunk white man, though, it was in full and complete control. The fellow piloting it was a master, in fact; Cincinnatus had never seen anybody do a better job of easing such an ungainly craft into place.

The Army men on board threw lines up to a couple of roustabouts on the wharf. Even before the barge was fully fast, they ran a gangplank up to the wharf, too. That was what Lieutenant Kennan had been waiting for. "All right, you lazy niggers," he shouted to the work gang of which Cincinnatus was a part, "you been lollygagging long enough. Now get your black asses down there and get to work. Two men to a crate. That's what my order says, and that's how we're gonna do it. Move, God damn you!"

"Lord have mercy," said a gray-haired Negro named Herodotus. "I been workin', doin' *hard* work, since slavery days, an' I didn't never have no overseer with as mean a mouth as that Yankee."

"Watch out he don't hear you," Cincinnatus warned, though the other Negro, being no one's fool, had kept his voice down. "Ain't just his mouth that's mean. He'd just as soon kick a black man as look at him."

Along with the rest of the work crew, he and Herodotus went down into the barge. The crates they were to unload were a funny shape, as long as a man, but only a foot or so high and wide. They were of more solid wood than the usual run of box, and bound with iron straps, too. Whatever was in there, the people back in the USA who'd packed it didn't want it coming out.

Each crate had, neatly stenciled on it, BATTERY F, and, below that, DISINFECTION. Cincinnatus scratched his head. You put those two together, they didn't make a whole lot of sense. But then, you could say that about a whole lot of things he'd seen since the war started.

He and Herodotus lifted a crate. It was heavy enough to need two men on it, sure enough. "You niggers want to watch out what you're doin'," Lieutenant Kennan said as they started up the gangplank. "Anybody who drops one of these here crates, he doesn't just get his ass fired. He gets himself blacklisted—no work at all for him. And you want to know what I think about that, I hope the fucker starves, and all the little pickaninnies he's spawned, too."

"Give that man a whip and put him in the cotton field, he get five hundred bales to the acre," Herodotus said.

"Yeah, till one fine mornin' they find him with his head broke in, and what a shame, nobody knows who done it," Cincinnatus said. "Wouldn't take long, neither." Herodotus nodded. That sort of thing happened, every so often.

But Lieutenant Kennan had more than a whip to back him up. He had the United States Army on his side. If anything happened to him, the Yankees would take hostages and shoot them. That had happened before, too.

Cincinnatus and Herodotus loaded the long, narrow crate into the back of a motor truck. Whatever it was, that said it had a certain amount of importance, because things that weren't of high priority got hauled to the front in horse-drawn wagons. More than the usual number of U.S. soldiers were standing around the trucks, too, keeping an eye on the loading but not, of course, deigning to help with what they, like whites in the CSA, called nigger work.

Back and forth, back and forth, back and forth. Cincinnatus was glad he was wearing leather gloves. His hands were hard, but the rough boards of the crates would have torn them up anyhow. He didn't want to stop for the dinner break. He'd got into a rhythm. Pausing to eat took him out of it. When you were working like a machine, that happened sometimes. But stop he did. If you didn't take whatever breaks the Yankees doled out to you, they were liable to figure you didn't need 'em and not dole out any; they were nasty in a more efficient, cold-blooded way than Confederate whites.

Sure enough, when he went back to work after his sowbelly and greens and his canteen full of cold coffee, he needed a while to get used to things again, and he never did quite find the trancelike state in which he'd been working before dinner. Thinking about what he was doing made the afternoon seem to last three times as long as the morning had.

About halfway through the afternoon, another big barge came across the river from Cincinnati. It too was loaded almost to the wallowing point with long, skinny crates stenciled BATTERY F and DISINFECTION. As the Negro laborers unloaded the crates, U.S. soldiers strung up electric lamps so another crew could eventually replace them and keep working through the night.

Herodotus raised an eyebrow. "Ain't never seen 'em do that before," he said. Cincinnatus nodded; he hadn't seen them do that before, either.

At last, Lieutenant Kennan shouted, "All right, nigs, knock off. Anybody back here even one minute later than seven o'clock tomorrow morning, he can kiss my ass, but he still won't get any work. Go on now, get the hell out, and we'll put some fresh mules on the job."

"That's how he thinks of us—mules," Cincinnatus said as he and Herodotus lined up to get their day's pay. Cincinnatus knew he'd busted his hump, but Kennan wasn't handing out fifty-cent bonuses to anybody, not today.

"Mus' be his time of the month," Herodotus said. "He's sure enough cranky like that."

Some of the work gang stood at the trolley stop and waited for a ride back to the Negro district of Covington. Others—men who saved every nickel—left them with waves and weary calls of, "See you in the mornin'," and started walking south, away from the Ohio. Cincinnatus was one of those. He hadn't ridden the trolley since he found out Elizabeth was in a family way.

A little south of downtown, he peeled off from the group of laborers. "Got to buy me some new laces for my shoes," he said. "Got so many knots holding these ones together, it's like puttin' rocks in my shoes."

"You could pick a better place," Herodotus said. "Conroy there"—he pointed to the name on the awning above the storefront—"he don't like black folks much. Feldman down the street, he's a better bet."

"I ain't never had no trouble with Conroy, an' he's cheaper to buy from than the Jew," Cincinnatus answered. Herodotus shrugged, waved, and kept on walking.

Conroy's general store was typical of the breed. The proprietor, a big, red-faced fellow with a formidable grizzled mustache and a wad of tobacco in one cheek, looked a lot more pregnant than Elizabeth did. He had dry goods at the right of the store, yard goods at the back, groceries to the left, with barrels of flour, sugar, and crackers in front of his counter. Cigars and candy reposed in glass jars on the counter.

A white man and a couple of white women were in the store. Cincinnatus took off his cap and waited till Conroy served them. Another white man came in after Cincinnatus but before the storekeeper was done taking care of the others. He got served ahead of Cincinnatus, too.

At last, the laborer's turn came. The storekeeper got him three pairs of shoelaces and gave back ninety cents change on the day's dollar Cincinnatus handed him. Some of the coins were Confederate, others U.S.

"Seen somethin' interesting," Cincinnatus remarked, making sure Conroy hadn't shortchanged him. Casually, as if it were no particular import—and, for all he knew, it wasn't—he described the unending loads of crates he'd hauled all day long, and the curious words on them.

Conroy tugged at one end of his mustache. "That a fact?" he said. "Well, you're right. Mebbe that is interesting." He spat, and fell a little short of the cuspidor. By the brown stains on the pale pine boards near the spittoon, he missed a good deal of the time.

With ninety cents in change clinking in his pocket, Cincinnatus irrationally felt richer than he had with a single silver cartwheel. He got out of the store as fast as he could; passing the time of day like that with a white man felt unnatural to him, and, by Conroy's attitude, to the storekeeper as well.

When he got home, Elizabeth had a stew of chicken and okra and rice waiting for him. "I was startin' to be worried about you," she said, and then yawned. She'd been tired all the time since she was expecting, but she hadn't worked any less. With everything more expensive because of war and occupation, she couldn't afford that.

"Put in some extra time," Cincinnatus explained. "Didn't get any extra money for it, but I didn't have no choice, neither. And afterwards, I stopped by Conroy's, bought me some shoelaces."

"Did you?" Elizabeth said, and let out a long sigh. "Dear God, I wish we didn't have to have nothin' to do with Conroy or any of the other people still spyin' for the CSA up here."

"Lord have mercy, so do I," Cincinnatus said, "but after we didn't give Tom Kennedy to the Yankees, they got themselves a hold on us."

"No good will come of it," Elizabeth predicted gloomily. "No good at all."

Cincinnatus couldn't argue, and didn't try. While Kennedy was in the house, he'd had the upper hand on the white man. Once Kennedy had left, though, despite whatever profuse thanks he gave, the upper hand was his again, because he could blackmail Cincinnatus and Elizabeth, threatening to let U.S. authorities know what they'd done. He hadn't ever made that threat, but when he asked Cincinnatus to let Conroy the storekeeper know about anything intriguing he picked up on the wharfs, his former driver didn't see how he could say no.

"Besides the shoelaces, why did you stop by Conroy's?" Elizabeth asked him. He explained. His wife nodded. "That's peculiar, it sure is. Did Conroy say anything about it when you told him?"

"Not a word," Cincinnatus answered. "But he wouldn't. If I don't know it, I can't blab it."

"That's so," Elizabeth said. "What do *you* suppose is in them crates?"

"No way to know," he replied, "but I expect we'll find out."

XIV

Lucien Galtier looked up in the sky with something like approval. Winters were long. Winters were hard. They wore at a man; it seemed he never saw the sun for weeks at a time. But spring, when it finally burgeoned, made up for that . . . at least until winter came again.

Fluffy white clouds drifted from west to east, their shadows sailing across the farmland like clipper ships across a smooth sea. The weather—he paused to thank God—had been very good this year. True, from time to time, there were Americans on the road, in trucks or on horseback or in long columns afoot, but God didn't take care of all the little details in your life. You had to do some of the work for yourself. If the farm survived the ravages of rabbits and rats and insects, it was likely to survive the ravages of Americans, too.

Here came Georges, running up the path that separated potatoes on the one side from rye on the other. "Papa!" he called, and waved when Lucien straightened up from weeding the potato plot. "Papa, Father Pascal is back at the house with an American officer, and they want to see you."

"*Calisse,*" Galtier said; he'd been so engrossed in his hoeing, he'd paid no attention to traffic on the road for a while. Now he put the hoe up on his shoulder, as if it were a rifle. "Well, if they want to see me, then see me they shall. It is an invitation I cannot refuse, not so?"

His younger son's eyes twinkled. "They want to see you, but they did not bother to ask if you wanted to see them," Georges said with Gallic precision.

"They do not care. They have no reason to care. They are the authorities, and I? I am but a farmer of the humblest sort." Lucien sounded too humble to be quite convincing, but that was what happened when you took on an unfamiliar role. And, as he had said, whether he wanted to see them was an irrelevance. He tramped back toward the farmhouse, Georges running ahead to let the important visitors know he was coming.

Father Pascal and the American officer, whoever he was, had come in the priest's buggy; the horse bent its head down to crop grass by the rail to which it was tethered. Seeing the buggy relieved Galtier's mind. He would have thought senility closing in on him had he missed the noisy arrival of a motorcar.

Inside, Marie and Nicole had already presented the priest and the officer—he was, Lucien saw, the heavyset major with whom Father Pascal had been talking when Galtier first went into Rivière-du-Loup not long after the Americans arrived—with coffee and cakes. He would have been astonished had his wife and eldest daughter done anything less. Even if your guests' going would have been more welcome than their coming, you had duties as a host—or hostess.

"Here he is," Father Pascal said, rising from the sofa with a wide smile on his smooth, plump face. "Allow me to present to you the truly excellent husbandman, Lucien Galtier. Lucien, I have brought here Major Jedediah Quigley."

"*Enchanté, Monsieur Galtier,*" Quigley said in the elegant Parisian French Lucien had heard him using up in town. "Father Pascal has been loud in singing your praises."

"He honors me far beyond my poor worth," Galtier replied, wishing the priest had chosen to throw himself into the St. Lawrence rather than praising him to the occupying authorities. The less notice he attracted from them, the happier he was.

"You are a modest man," Father Pascal said. "This is the mark of a godly man, a Christian man of solid virtue. I have also taken the liberty of passing on to Major Quigley your generous willingness to inform me of anyone who misunderstood my role in the situation as it is."

Galtier spread his hands. They were hard and rough, with callused palms and dirt under his nails and ground into the folds of skin at each knuckle. "I am desolate, Father, that I have had nothing of which to inform you. Spring is a busy season for a farmer, and I have had little to do with anyone of late."

"Galtier, Lucien." Major Quigley took a piece of paper from one of the many pockets with which his uniform was adorned. From another pocket he drew a pair of steel-rimmed spectacles, which he set on his nose. He unfolded the paper and studied it for a moment. "Ah, yes. I regret that the requisitions drawn from this farm were so heavy last winter. I should not be surprised if it turned out that the soldiers who carried out the program did so with an excess of zeal. As a result, you must think less than kind thoughts of the American military government for this district."

"Major, in a war, each side does what it can to win," Galtier answered with a shrug. "I am not a soldier now, but you must know I served my time. I know these things." He chose his words with great care. This American major who talked like a Parisian aristocrat was liable to be as dangerous as half a dozen of the likes of Father Pascal.

Quigley folded up the paper and put it in his pocket. He got out a pipe, a pouch of tobacco, and a match safe. After a glance toward Marie for permission, he lit the pipe. Once it was drawing well, he spoke in musing tones: "I am confident that, when requisition time comes round again, it will be easier to restrain the enthusiasm of the soldiers carrying out their duties."

Not, *it may be easier to restrain them*—if *you cooperate*. Most men, trying to establish such cooperation, would have spelled out the terms of the bargain to be struck. That was how Father Pascal operated, for instance. Not Major Quigley. He started at the point of assuming cooperation and went on from there. A man to reckon with, indeed.

And, of course, it would be impossible to keep the neighbors from learning he and Father Pascal had been here. Some of them would assume that alone meant Lucien was collaborating with the Americans: why else would the major and the priest have come? Keeping his good name was going to take Galtier some work.

He wanted to glance over at Marie, to see what she was thinking. A winter free of requisitions—or anything close to that—would all but guarantee a successful year. A full belly, peace of mind against what was in essence robbery at gunpoint—those were not small items on the balance sheet . . . provided he grew a beard so he did not have to look at himself in the mirror when he shaved every morning.

But looking at yourself in the mirror was not a small item, either. "As I say, Major, I am only a farmer, and spend most of my time here on my land. I am not a man who often hears things of any sort—certainly not scandal and slander spoken about the pious father here."

"No, eh? Father Pascal led me to believe it might be otherwise. What a pity," Major Quigley said. He didn't snarl and bluster at Lucien. He didn't turn and glower at Father Pascal, either. He just spread his hands. "Such is life." He got to his feet, which meant the priest also had to rise hastily. Major Quigley bowed to Marie. "Thank you, Madame Galtier, for your generous hospitality. We shall not take up any more of your time, or of your husband's—he is, as he says, a busy man."

He didn't even warn Galtier that the requisitions, instead of being extra gentle when harvest time came around, would be extra harsh. If Lucien couldn't figure that out for himself, he'd learn come fall.

But Lucien knew perfectly well what would happen come fall. He also knew he'd have to spend almost as much time working to make the farm seem poor as he would making sure it really wasn't. As the major with the strange Christian name had said, that was life.

Major Quigley climbed into the buggy. Father Pascal untied his horse, then joined the American soldier. The priest was expostulating violently and gesturing with such passion, he could hardly handle the reins. But the horse must have been used to his theatrics. It turned around and started back up the road toward Rivière-du-Loup.

Lucien Galtier sighed. Now he did turn to Marie, wondering if she was going to shout at him for guaranteeing the whole family a harder time when autumn rolled around. Instead, she ran to him and squeezed the breath out of him with the tightest embrace she'd given him outside the bedroom in years. A moment later, Nicole and Georges piled onto him, too, and after that his three younger daughters, who must have been listening somewhere out of sight. Only his son Charles, busy in the barn, didn't know to join and mob him, and Galtier knew perfectly well how Charles felt about the American occupiers.

"Oh, Papa, you were so brave!" Nicole exclaimed.

"I was?" Lucien said: that had not occurred to him. "What was I supposed to do, turn my coat? For a little more in the barn? It is not worth it."

"You were very brave, Lucien," Marie said; if she thought so, it was likely to be true. "We would have loved you whatever you told the American, but after what you did—we are proud of you."

"Well," Galtier said, "this is all very good, I am sure, and I am glad you are proud of me, but pride does nothing to weed the potato patch. I shall have to work harder today because of the *Boche américain* and the foolish priest. For that, I do not thank them. I work long enough as it is." He disentangled himself from the arms—the proud arms—of his family, went outside, picked up his hoe, shouldered it, and headed back toward the potatoes.

Not much was left of Slaughters, Kentucky, a few miles north of Madisonville. U.S. troops pushing east had managed to drive the Confederates out of it only a few days before, after fighting that fully lived up to the name of the place fought over. As far as Abner Dowling was concerned, the fight, like most of those General Custer planned, had been far more expensive than it was worth.

However much he wanted to, he couldn't say that to the war reporter walking through the ruined streets of Slaughters beside him. Custer's famous name was what had drawn Richard Harding Davis out to Kentucky to see the American troops in action.

Davis had seen a lot of wars, all around the world. His reports from

Manila as the Japanese were entering the city were classics in their way. So were his reports on what they'd done to the Spanish prisoners they'd taken, though those hadn't been filed till he was safely out of the Philippines.

And now here he was with Custer's First Army—and with the chance, even if he hadn't known it when he got here, to write stories about something new in warfare on the North American continent.

"You're sure the general will let me go right up to the front?" the reporter asked Dowling for about the fourth time. Davis was fifty or so, ruggedly handsome (though his color wasn't all it could have been, and he panted a little as he walked along beside Dowling), and wore a green-gray jacket halfway between a military style and one a big-game hunter might have used. It had more pockets than you could shake a stick at. Dowling wished he owned one like it.

"Mr. Davis," he answered, "General Custer is going up to the front. He wants to see this for himself. He has already told me repeatedly, you are welcome to accompany him and me." *Now that you're here, Mr. Davis, General Custer would strangle with his own liver-spotted hands anyone who had the gall to try to get between him and headlines, which is to say, between you and him.*

Custer had billeted himself in one of the few houses in Slaughters only lightly damaged: a two-story Victorian structure whose windows had only jagged shards of glass in them but whose walls and roof remained intact. A couple of sentries stood outside the front door. They'd dug foxholes nearby, into which they could dive in case the Rebs started shelling the town again. They saluted Dowling and eyed Richard Harding Davis with respectful curiosity. He wasn't just a reporter, but had a name as a novelist and playwright as well.

"Go on in," one of them said, opening the door. "The general should be finishing up his breakfast about now, and I know he'll be glad to see you."

As the sentry had said, Custer sat at the kitchen table. The view through the bay window had probably been lovely, back before it turned into a prospect of charred rubble and shell holes. The general was attacking his plate with knife, fork, and great gusto.

He turned when Dowling and Davis came into the room. Pointing down at his breakfast, he exclaimed, "Raw onions!" Such was his delight that, had he been writing, he probably would have used capital letters and four exclamation points.

Dowling did not share that delight. He coughed and did his best not to inhale, but his eyes started watering to beat the band in spite of the improved ventilation the shattered bay window gave the kitchen. He'd known about Custer's love for onions—anyone who had anything to do with Custer found out about that—but why had the general chosen today of all days for them?

Richard Harding Davis did his best to take the potent vegetables in stride. "A warmup for the rest of the day's show, eh?" he said, but could not help wiping his eyes with his sleeve.

"That's right, by jingo!" Custer said, shoveling another odorous forkful into his mouth. He went on till he was done. When he'd finished the whole plate, he spoke in meditative tones: "Those onions could have used some salt. Well, can't be helped. Shall we go disinfect some Rebels, gentlemen?"

Off they went. Custer's motorcar, despite having to veer off the road a couple of times to avoid craters, brought them past the artillery posts, where men without shirts stood waiting in the June sunshine for the order to rain death down on the Confederate lines. Custer talked gaily about Custer all the while. Davis scribbled an occasional note. Dowling wished the commanding general would shut up, not only because he'd heard all the stories before but also because, even with the wind streaming by in the open motorcar, Custer's breath was still hideously vile.

Once they came to the rear of the trench system, the motorcar could advance no farther. Dowling wondered if Custer would make it to the front under his own power. The commanding general was a long way from being the spry, dashing soldier of thirty-odd years gone by, though obviously he was convinced that time's wrinkled hand hadn't touched him at all.

He was spry enough to reach the trenches without undue difficulty, though. Richard Harding Davis proved to be the one who had trouble there. "Wind isn't what it used to be," he said apologetically, letting a hand rest on his chest for a moment, as if his heart pained him. He lighted a cigarette and went gamely on.

Here and there along the way, pieces of crates stenciled BATTERY F and DISINFECTION were used as corduroying on the floor of the trench or as pieces of lean-tos and other shelters cut into the earth of the trench wall. Custer had just started talking about them when a Confederate aeroplane came buzzing overhead.

"Shoot him down!" the general shouted, his sagging features twisting in alarm. "If the Rebs see what we're up to, there'll be hell to pay!"

For once, Dowling agreed completely with his commander. Yelling in the middle of the trench line, though, didn't strike him as the best way to get the antiaircraft gunners to go to work. Fortunately, they didn't need Custer's encouragement. They opened up on the Confederate scout with everything they had. The air around his aeroplane filled with black puffs, as intense a barrage as Dowling had ever seen. The Reb must have felt the same way. He turned around and scooted for his own lines. The antiaircraft fire followed him till he was out of range.

Moving forward grew difficult then, because the trenches were packed with men in green-gray, their gauze masks making them all look alike, waiting to storm forward when the order was given. It wouldn't be long now. Dowling's bulk and the magic of Custer's name cleared the path enough that the general, his adjutant, and Davis were able to reach the very forwardmost trenches in good time.

Resting at the front of those trenches, spaced several yards apart, were metal cylinders about as long as a man, each one painted dark blue. Alongside each cylinder stood a masked man with a wrench, ready to open the fitting and let its contents spew forth into the air.

"What is the hour, Major?" Custer demanded.

He had a pocket watch of his own, but asking Dowling the question was easier than taking it out and looking at it. "Sir, it's 0625," Dowling said resignedly after checking his own watch.

"Splendid!" Custer said. "Capital! Couldn't be better. We're scheduled to begin at 0630, provided the wind holds." He licked a finger and stuck it up in the air. He stuck it up high enough, as a matter of fact, that he was lucky not to get shot in the hand. "Holding very nicely—straight out of the west, just as we want."

"When the Germans used chlorine gas against the French and the English at Ypres, they made gains, but not a breakthrough," Davis said. "How will you make sure we do better than our allies?"

That was a good question. Dowling wondered how Custer would answer it. Dowling wondered if Custer *could* answer it. The truth was that the USA, like everyone else in the war, seized eagerly on anything that might yield a small edge in the murderous struggle. Every U.S. army in Kentucky was trying chlorine gas today. Making gains without losing men by the tens of thousands looked very good, even to Custer, who normally used up soldiers as if they were so many pieces of blotting paper.

But instead of replying, Custer shouted, "Release the gas!" It was, by Dowling's watch, still a minute early, but Custer's watch might have run faster—not that he checked to find out.

The men at the closest chlorine cylinders gave counterclockwise twists with their wrenches. Puffs, as of pale green smoke, spurted from the cylinders. Custer had been right about one thing; the wind was out of the west. It blew the puffs of smoke into a single dirty green cloud and sent that cloud rolling and billowing toward the Confederate trenches.

"That'll shift them!" Custer said jubilantly. He got up on the firing step to watch the progress of the gas. Davis got up beside him. If he didn't watch the progress of the gas, he didn't have much of a story. And Dowling got up there, too. As long as he was Custer's adjutant, this was as close to real combat as he was likely to come.

Every now and then, little bits of high ground between the U.S. and C.S.

lines would remain visible above the chlorine cloud, which, being heavier than air, stuck close to the ground except when the wind blew it up into little puffs and wisps. Despite that steady wind, the harsh, bleachlike odor of the gas made Dowling's throat raw, his nose sore, and his eyes even more watery than Custer's vicious onions had done.

As soon as the chlorine cloud rolled over and into the Confederate trenches, observers telephoned word back to the U.S. artillery emplacements. They opened up with a savage bombardment. Explosions sent dirt flying and made the gas jump and writhe like a plateful of gelatin.

Before long, the cylinders of chlorine gas were empty. The artillery stopped pounding the Confederates' forwardmost trenches and moved back to the support trenches to keep reinforcements from moving up. All along the U.S. line, officers' whistles blew. Cries of "Let's go!" and "Get moving!" rang out. One nearby officer added, "Come on, the closer we stay to the hind end of that gas cloud, the worse shape the Rebs'll be in when we hit 'em." Over the top the troops went.

That would have been plenty to inspire Abner Dowling to follow close behind the chlorine. Only in books by writers who'd never smelled powder (more to the point, who'd never smelled the shit from spilled guts) did soldiers want a fair fight. What soldiers wanted was a walkover, with none of them getting hurt. They didn't get what they wanted very often. Maybe today . . .

"Brave men," Richard Harding Davis said quietly, watching the soldiers in green-gray, their uniforms fading almost to invisibility when seen against the chlorine, swarming out of the U.S. trenches and toward those of the Confederates. "Very brave men."

Here and there, rifle and machine-gun fire greeted the Americans. Not all of the Rebels had been overcome by the poisonous gas. Men caught between the trench lines fell, sometimes one by one, sometimes in rows. But most of the U.S. soldiers moved forward. One after another, the weapons aimed at them fell silent.

"Do the Rebels know how to block the chlorine's effect?" Davis asked.

"I wouldn't be surprised," Dowling said, at the same time as General Custer was snapping, "I doubt it."

Custer glared at his adjutant. Dowling hung his head and muttered an apology. Reports from Europe, though, showed how chlorine could be countered. Even something as simple as pissing in a rag and holding it over your mouth and nose could keep most of the gas out of your lungs, though it would still burn your eyes. And the limeys and the frogs were supposed to be using the same sort of masks German and now U.S. troops had, too.

"I shan't give any details," Davis said, "though I doubt the Confederate States need to read my columns to garner military intelligence." That was sure to be true; where the USA had German reports on the effects of chlorine, the CSA would have got details from Paris and London.

Whatever the reports had said, though, the Rebs hadn't paid much attention to it. U.S. soldiers still flooded forward, and, now, Confederate prisoners, herded along by jubilant Americans—some wearing their masks, some with them hung around their necks—came stumbling back to the U.S. lines.

Some of the Rebs were ordinary captives, either men who'd surrendered in the fighting or were taken after being wounded. But others showed the effects of the poisonous gas. Some had blood running from their mouths or bubbling out of their noses. Others seemed to be doing their best not to breathe at all. From the tiny taste of chlorine Dowling had got, he tried to imagine what their throats and chests felt like. He was glad he failed. A couple of Confederates tried to scream at every breath they took, but emitted only little gasping sounds of agony.

"Not much glory here," Dowling observed, watching the wretched prisoners.

"Defeating the enemies of my country is glory aplenty for me," Custer declared. In his own way, he meant it, but his own way included seeing his name in the newspapers, preferably in letters several inches high.

And, by the way the attack was developing, he might get glory on his own terms. A big victory here, and Roosevelt would be hard pressed to keep from giving him the command in Canada he so desperately craved. A runner came up and said, in tones of high excitement, "Sir, we just captured a whole battery of those damn fast-firing three-inch guns the Rebs have. Not a man at 'em: most of the gunners ran, and the gas got the rest."

"That's first-rate," Custer said. "Positively first-rate. We have to keep throwing men at them till they crack. Pour it on, by God! Pour it on!"

"Have you got more chlorine ready, to make another breach in their lines after they manage to plug this gap?" Davis asked.

Dowling nodded. Again, the reporter had found the right question to ask. The right answer, unfortunately, was no. The USA didn't turn out—or hadn't turned out—chlorine in the quantity Germany, a chemical powerhouse, did. If the thought of not having more bothered Custer, he didn't let on. "We won't need more," he said grandly. "Now that we've got them on the run, we'll make sure they keep running. I'll send in the cavalry to complete their demoralization. The stalemate on this front, Mr. Davis, is over, and you can quote me."

Davis wrote the words down. He didn't ask any more questions. Maybe that meant Custer had convinced him. Maybe, on the other hand, it meant the reporter had seen enough war on his own to know the general commanding First Army was talking through his hat. Abner Dowling was glumly certain about which way he would have bet.

* * *

Retreat. It was an ugly word. Jake Featherston hated the sound of it. But he hated the sound of *annihilation* a lot more. If the First Richmond Howitzers hadn't pulled back from the Susquehanna when they did, they would have been in no position to do it later.

"I knew we were in trouble when we didn't make it to the Delaware," he muttered as he trudged along a dirt road that coated him, the horses, the guns, and everything else nearby with a red-brown haze of dust.

He hadn't expected to be overheard, not through the clopping of the horses' hooves and the rattle and squeak of the gun carriage. But the new loader for the piece, a youngster named Michael Scott, said, "Why's that, Sarge?"

Featherston scowled. He almost didn't answer. As far as he was concerned, Nero and Perseus had manned the gun better than the kind of replacements you got nowadays. What they'd learned when they were serving their time as conscripts, God only knew. Featherston wasn't convinced they'd learned anything. But he replied, as patiently as he could, "When we didn't finish the big wheel to the Delaware, that let the damnyankees keep shipping supplies into Baltimore. And that let the bastards break out of Baltimore, too. If they cut us off, we're still liable to be in a lot of trouble."

"Never happen," Scott declared. "Not in a million years. We'll whip 'em, same as we've done twice running."

"I figured the same thing when the fighting started," Featherston answered. "It's already gone on a hell of a lot longer than I figured it would. The Yankees this time, feels like they mean business, same as us."

They crossed Codorus Creek, the gun-carriage wheels rumbling over the planks of the bridge. On the southwestern side of the creek, Negro laborers and Confederate infantry were digging in, aiming to hold back the advancing U.S. troops, at least for a while, and to hold on to the town of Hanover, a couple of miles to the west.

Featherston was glumly certain they wouldn't keep Hanover long. With the chunk of land they'd carved out of Yankee territory being nibbled away at the base, they'd have to keep moving back toward Washington, and smartly, or the U.S. soldiers would cut them off. But they couldn't just skedaddle, not unless they wanted endless grief from the damnyankees who'd halted them at the Susquehanna.

Scott said, "If things had gone the way they were supposed to, we'd have been in Philadelphia a long time ago."

"Yeah, and if pigs had wings, we'd all carry umbrellas," Featherston replied with a snort. "When you've been through even a little more fighting, kid, you're going to see that things just *don't* go the way they're supposed to.

The Yanks, they've got their own set of supposed-to's, and what we get is what's left over when ours bump up against theirs."

The loader nodded respectfully. Not only was Featherston a sergeant, he was that even more exalted creature, a veteran. The combination gave his views an authority few mortals could claim.

More hoofbeats: here came Pompey, mounted on one of Captain Stuart's fine horses. "Captain's compliments, Sergeant," he said in his syrupy voice, "an' we gonna go into battery by that slate quarry over yonder." He pointed off to the west of the road.

"All right," Featherston said shortly. He still didn't care for the way Stuart used the Negro to relay orders, but however much authority he might seem to have to Michael Scott, to the battery commander he was just another noncom who did what he was told. Pompey rode on to give the rest of the guns in the battery the word.

Jake admitted to himself that Stuart had picked a good spot in which to deploy the howitzers. They were only a couple of miles back of Codorus Creek, in good position to pound the Yankees when they approached the line the Confederates were creating. Better yet, piles of spoil from the mine offered fine cover for the guns, and Negroes were already busy digging firing pits to protect them even better.

As Featherston supervised the emplacement of his own howitzer, Captain Stuart rode up himself. Featherston saluted. Stuart watched the black men in butternut tunics of simpler, baggier cut than soldiers wore. With a sly grin, he said, "Got yourself a whole ready-made gun crew this time, in case the one the government issued you goes down."

"Uh, yes, sir," Jake said, a little nervously. He still wasn't happy about having used Nero and Perseus as fighting men. Nobody else was happy about it, either, except possibly the two Negroes—and their opinion didn't count. What the reaction of the brass amounted to was that Featherston had done what he'd had to do, and it was too damn bad he'd had to do it. That was pretty much how he felt about it himself.

Stuart swung down off the horse and tied the reins to a sapling. "What really makes life difficult is that you put the niggers on the guns right after that Major Potter came sniffing around with all his crazy talk about every other nigger in the army being a damned Red. Would you believe it, he wanted to take Pompey away for questioning."

"Is that a fact, sir?" Featherston said, in tones he devoutly hoped were unrevealing. He, after all, had been the one who'd suggested Pompey could do with some investigating.

"It is indeed." Jeb Stuart III kicked at the ground to show his indignation. It wasn't aimed at Jake, from which he concluded Stuart didn't know who mistrusted his supercilious servant. "I had to get hold of my father back in the

War Department, and he had to do some pretty plain talking to the Army of Northern Virginia Intelligence before they turned Pompey loose. When those people question somebody, he's lucky if he comes out of it in one piece, especially if he's a nigger."

Ever since the days of Robert E. Lee, Confederates had used *those people*, spoken in a particular tone of voice, as a euphemism for *the enemy*. Featherston had never heard it used that way to mean part of the Confederate Army, not till now. He hoped he didn't hear it used that way again for another fifty or sixty years.

So Jeb Stuart, Jr., had saved Pompey from the tender mercies of Army Intelligence, had he? If Pompey wasn't any more than an ordinary black servant stuck up beyond his station because of whom he served, that was fine. If Pompey was a snake in the grass, it was anything but fine. But how were you supposed to know which if you didn't try to find out?

"Pompey's family has been with my family since my great-grandfather's day," the captain said. "He'd be loyal to the Stuarts before he'd join up with a pack of Red revolutionaries just because they have black skins."

Featherston didn't answer. Arguing with your superior had no future in it. Arguing with your superior when he was also in the third generation of a leading Confederate military family had less than no future.

And, in any case, he had enough other things to do. Making sure the gun was sited as well as it could be, making sure the wheel brakes were set and the spade on the end of the trail dug into the ground, making sure there was a good, thick earthen rampart between the ammunition and the crew so a lucky shell hit wouldn't—or might not—blow them all to Jesus . . . all that took time and work.

As he readied the position, he kept peering over the creek, looking for the caterpillar ripples on the distant ground that marked advancing Yankee infantry. Sure enough, here they came. Larger dots punctuating the ripples were horses. *Cavalry*, Featherston thought, with a mixture of respect for their courage and scorn for their uselessness.

Then the dots peeled off. *They know better than to get their precious horses—and their precious selves—too close to the machine guns,* Jake thought. *Poor dears might get hurt.* Cavalry would charge, though, when ordered. After staring a moment, he recognized the pattern the horses were forming.

"That's not cavalry!" he shouted. "That's field artillery."

Jeb Stuart III came trotting up beside him. He nodded as he stuck a brass telescope up to his eye. "Field artillery, sure as hell," he agreed. "I make the range about two and a half miles—say, four thousand yards for starters. Let's give them a hello, shall we?"

He started bawling for the whole battery. Featherston handled his gun. It was the second one of the battery to open up. The shell fell a couple of hundred yards short of the U.S. field gun. The next shell, a few seconds later, was long. After that, they started landing in the right general area. You put enough shells in the right general area, you did damage. The Yanks had probably figured they could get their battery into position and into action before the retreating Confederates were ready to reply. They'd made a mistake there, and they were going to pay for it.

The U.S. battery did get a few shots off, shells crashing down on the trench line behind Codorus Creek. But that kind of nuisance firing went on every day of the war. It was hardly worth noticing, even by the Negro laborers, who were more flighty than soldiers when it came to being on the receiving end of bullets. Since they couldn't shoot back, Jake found it hard to blame them for that.

He glanced over to Nero and Perseus. They stood by the horses, and were plainly ready to dive into the foxhole if the damnyankees started hurling shells at the battery. They'd shot back. Featherston hoped to high heaven they'd never have to do it again.

After a few minutes, the U.S. field guns couldn't stand the heat from deploying out in the open. They started moving again, this time against the tide of the advancing U.S. infantry. "So long!" Featherston shouted at them. "Tell your mama what it's like when you really have to work for a living." His gun crew yelled and waved their hats. At Captain Stuart's orders, they started pouring shells into the foot soldiers approaching the creek.

They worked a formidable slaughter among them, too, but a couple of hours later they had to abandon their position and pull back another mile or two: somewhere farther west, the Yankees had forced a crossing of the creek.

"Doesn't seem right," Michael Scott grumbled as Nero and Perseus hitched the horses up to the guns. "We were massacring the bastards."

"Wasn't so much what they did in front of us that made us start this retreat," Featherston answered. "It was what happened off to the flank and the rear. You can win your own part of the battle and still have the whole army lose."

"I wish you hadn't said that," the loader told him. After Jake thought about it for a while, he wished he hadn't said that, too.

When Flora Hamburger went downstairs from the Socialist Party offices to walk across Centre Market Place and buy a sandwich in the market, Max Fleischmann was arguing with two goons outside his butcher's shop.

"No, I don't got no ham," he said to them. "Don't got no pig's knuckles. Don't got no head cheese. Don't got no bacon. Don't got no time for no silliness, neither. I'm a Jew. You maybe may have noticed."

"Yeah, pop, we noticed," one of the goons said. His nasty grin showed a couple of broken teeth. "Maybe you noticed this." He raised the billy club he carried in his right hand. The armband wrapped around his left sleeve read, PEACE AND ORDER. He and his equally unpleasant friend looked like a couple of Soldiers' Circle men, and were helping to hold down the staunchly Socialist neighborhood by main force.

"Leave that man alone," Flora said crisply. Her English was precise and almost unaccented. The two volunteer policemen gaped at her as she went on, "Not only has he done nothing to you, but if you beat him, you will be beating one of the few Democrats in this part of New York."

"Ain't no Democrats here," said the goon with the club ready to use. "Just Jews and Socialists." He leered at her. "Which are you, lady?"

"Both," Flora answered. The thugs undoubtedly knew that; they hung around the Socialist Party office to harass the Party regulars, and, Maria Tresca aside, few gentiles came here. Angelina Tresca wouldn't, ever again. Flora's party affiliation, though, was a sword that cut both ways. "And if you beat me today—or if you beat Mr. Fleischmann—every Socialist paper in the country will carry the story tomorrow."

That was true. By the unhappy look on the goons' faces, they knew it, too. The one with the club raised lowered it. "Come on, Paddy," he said in disgust. "We'll find games to play somewheres else." They mooched off, looking for people more willing to be intimidated.

"Thank you," the butcher said to Flora in English before dropping back into Yiddish. "When you go home, you stop in here. I'll have something for you to take back to the flat. Not something big, maybe, but something."

"You don't need to do that," she said, also in Yiddish.

"Hush," Fleischmann told her, his voice stern. "You have a sister who can use good food right now. Take it for her, if not for you." His stiff-backed pose declared he would allow no disagreement.

Flora gave up. "I'll stop," she promised, wondering how Fleischmann knew about Sophie. Gossip on the crowded Lower East Side was an amazing thing. No doubt Fleischmann also knew the baby would be illegitimate. Flora sighed. Even if you disapproved of bourgeois conventions, you couldn't escape them.

More goons patrolled the Centre Market. The Remembrance Day riots had given the authorities the excuse they needed to clamp down on Socialist strongholds throughout New York City, though no one had proved or could prove a Socialist had started the disturbances.

Flora bought a smoked-tongue sandwich from a little stall in the market, a couple of pickled tomatoes from a man who carried his great vat of spiced brine on a pushcart, and coffee from another fellow with a pushcart, this one mounting a samovar. She ate quickly, then went back upstairs, where she spent the afternoon writing one letter after another, all of them aimed at getting Roosevelt's repressive restrictions lifted from New York City.

"If the president keeps up with them," said Herman Bruck, who was also writing, "he'll provoke a working-class uprising a hundred times worse than anything we saw in the Nineties. That will play hob with carrying on his foolish war."

His bruises had faded. Roentgen-ray photographs had shown his left hand wasn't broken after all. He wore as a badge of honor the gap in his smile that he'd got when somebody wearing a heavy Soldiers' Circle ring had punched him in the face during the riots, and loudly proclaimed to whoever would listen that he preferred it to going to the dentist for bridgework. Flora found that absurd, but didn't say so; whenever she argued with Bruck about anything, he thought it meant she was interested in him. Maria Tresca, in mourning black, was very quiet.

Flora finished her letter-writing, said her good-byes, and went downstairs. Max Fleischmann stood waiting for her, as if in ambush. He thrust a paper-wrapped package into her hands. Her eyebrows flew up at the weight of it. "This is too much!" she exclaimed.

"I'm sorry, I'm not hearing very well today," the butcher said, and went back into his shop. That left her the choice of pursuing him when he plainly did not want to be pursued and going home. Shaking her head, she went home.

"What do you have there?" her mother asked when she walked into the crowded apartment.

"I kept Mr. Fleischmann the butcher from having some trouble with TR's hooligans, so he gave me this," she answered, and opened it on the kitchen counter. "Marrow bones and stewing beef: there must be three or four pounds of it."

"That's very nice," her mother said. "We can use that—barley soup with onions and carrots, maybe, the way your father likes."

"Yes, Mama," Flora said; to her mother, utility made anything, even Socialism, worthwhile. "I'll put it in the icebox."

Her brothers came in then, bantering with her and their younger sister Esther as they hung up their jackets and caps. David lighted a cigarette, a habit he was just acquiring and one Flora wished he'd lose. The harsh smoke made the flat stink; it wasn't flavorful like the pipe tobacco their father used—even the cheaper grades he was using nowadays smelled better than this nasty weed.

When Benjamin Hamburger came in, he got the pipe going right away, perhaps in self-defense. Sophie dragged in last of all. The war had created relentless demands on seamstresses in New York City, all over the USA, and, no doubt, all over the world. The bosses didn't care if you were going to have a baby. You had to show up and you had to work no matter how tired, no matter how sick you were. If you didn't, somebody else was waiting to do your job.

Over small helpings of pot roast and big ones of potato kugel, Benjamin Hamburger remarked on that: "With so many jobs needing doing now, wages may be going up. *Alevai,*" he added, dragging superstition into a discussion of what should have been the most unsuperstitious study of economics.

Before Flora could turn the discussion into a more rational pattern, someone knocked on the door. Flora's mother bounced to her feet and strode to the door with a determined stride, saying, "A peddler who comes round at suppertime deserves a *choleryeh* he'll remember for a year, and I'll give him one, you see if I don't."

But when she threw open the door, it was not a peddler hawking knives or pens or stereoscope slides through the block of flats. Instead, it was an unfamiliar-looking man in a green-gray uniform. "Yossel!" Sophie exclaimed, recognizing him without his beard where Flora had not.

"May I come in?" Yossel Reisen asked when Sarah Hamburger showed no signs of getting out of his way.

"You may come in," Benjamin called over his wife's shoulder. When she whirled around to protest, he waved for her to calm down, continuing, "How long you stay depends on what you have to say for yourself once you are in here."

Thus appeased, Sarah grudgingly stepped out of the way. Yossel came past her and into the flat. Esther quickly got up. "Here, find a chair and eat something," she said, hurrying into the kitchen and returning with a plate piled high with potato kugel.

"Thank you." Reisen did sit down, and looked around nervously. The grimace with which he greeted Sophie was no doubt intended for a smile, but failed of its purpose. "Hello," he said, cautiously, as if she were an armed Rebel behind a wall. "How are you?"

"As well as I could be—considering," she answered. "You know how I am—the rest of it, though. You must have got my letters, even if I haven't heard from you." She stared at him as defiantly as a Confederate soldier in arms.

He had a mouth full of kugel, and used that respite to good advantage. "Yes, I know," he said, and then, "I'm sorry, Sophie. I didn't intend that to happen."

Didn't intend which to happen? Flora wondered. *Didn't intend to sleep with Sophie or didn't intend to get her with child?* But she held her tongue, to see what her older sister would do.

"People don't intend that to happen," Sophie said, taking him to mean he hadn't planned to impregnate her. "But it does, and then they have to decide what to do next."

"That's why I came here," Yossel answered. "I managed to get four days' leave. I spent most of one day coming up from Maryland, and I'll need most of another to get back. Between times"—he licked his lips—"we can get married."

Bourgeois respectability, Flora thought as Sophie clapped her hands together once and nodded. The idea should have carried more scorn than it did. Somehow, the feeling of contempt for bourgeois values was harder to come by when those values benefited her sister.

Benjamin Hamburger also nodded, as if he'd expected nothing less from Yossel. Maybe he had expected nothing less. But he raised an objection: "Even with the war, you'll have trouble finding a rabbi to perform the ceremony on such short notice."

Yossel Reisen shrugged. "Then we'll find a judge, and find a rabbi when I get a longer leave, or else after the war is over."

"*You* say that?" Flora exclaimed. "You, who wanted to do nothing but sit on your *tokhus* and study Talmud all day?"

"Flora!" Sophie said indignantly. Flora realized everyone else must have heard what she said as an insult. She hadn't meant it that way; what she'd been expressing was astonishment.

For a wonder, Yossel understood that. He held up a hand, which, after a moment, quieted the angry outcry from the rest of Flora's family. "Yes, I say that," he answered. "When you have been where I have been, when you have seen what I have seen, when you have done what I have done . . ." His voice trailed away. He was sitting across the table from Flora, and looking in her direction, but he wasn't looking at her. He looked through her, to some place he alone saw, some place maybe more real to him than the crowded apartment in which he sat. He needed a little while to realize he had stopped talking, and coughed a couple of times before he resumed: "When all that is true, you know, right down to the soles of your boots you know, how little time there is. And when you have a little of that little time, you do what you can with it, and what you cannot do now, you will do later, if God lets you."

No one spoke for a minute or so after that. Then, quietly, Benjamin Hamburger asked, "Sophie, is this all right with you?"

"Yes," Sophie answered, also quietly. Perhaps of its own accord, her left hand settled on her belly, which was beginning to bulge. "As Yossel said, we have only a little time. We'll do as much as we can with it."

Flora's father looked to her mother. Sarah Hamburger didn't say yes, but she didn't say no, either. "It is not a perfect arrangement," Benjamin said, "but what in life is perfect except God? If Sophie agrees, it will do."

Flora was temperamentally opposed to compromise of any kind: she was the one who'd wanted to fight to the end against voting to pay for Roosevelt's war. Here, though . . . when it was her own family, things didn't look the same. It wasn't her choice, anyhow; it was Sophie's.

"You'll sleep here on the divan tonight," her father told Yossel, "as if you were a boarder again." Everybody smiled at that. Benjamin Hamburger got up and went into the kitchen. He rummaged in the pantry and in a cabinet, and came back with a bottle of whiskey and enough glasses for everyone; Flora's brothers told how the old men at the *shul* had given each of them his first shot just before his bar mitzvah.

Amid toasts of *"L'chaym!"* everybody knocked back the drinks. Isaac might have been emboldened by the whiskey, for he asked Yossel Reisen, "What—is it like at the front?" Emboldened or not, he sounded hesitant.

Yossel looked into the depths of his glass as he had looked through Flora. At last, he answered, "Think of all the worst things you know in the world. Think of them all in one place. Think of them as ten times as bad as they really are. Then think of them ten times worse than that. What you are thinking about when you do that is one ten-thousandth of what the front is like."

Nobody asked him any more questions.

Somewhere in the Yankee lines in the ruins of Big Lick, Virginia, a rifle cracked. About fifty feet away from Reggie Bartlett, an incautious Confederate soldier toppled back into the trench, shot through the face. He wasn't dead, not yet; a scream bubbled through the blood flooding from his nose, his mouth, and the wound between them.

"God damn that fucking sniper to hell," somebody snarled as a couple of men hauled their wounded comrade back toward the doctors to see if they could do anything for him. "That's the fourth one of us he's got on this sector this week. We ever catch him, I'll gut-shoot him and watch him die."

Bartlett hardly looked up, either for the gunshot or for the screams and curses following it. He was hunting lice, a matter that could have taken up most of his waking day if duties demanded by his officers hadn't intervened. Every one of the little bastards you crunched between your thumbnails was one more that wouldn't bite you, one more that wouldn't leave sores and scabs in your hair, one more that wouldn't leave itchy welts on your body.

He tried to remember his leave in Richmond. He knew he'd been there, seen old friends, made new ones, got drunk, got laid at a soldiers' brothel full of bored-looking colored girls. It was a matter of a few weeks, not months or years, but seemed far more distant than that. When you were at the front, everything else was distant.

If you singed the seams of your tunic and trousers, you killed nits and drove lice out to where you could grab them and squash them. Reggie lighted a candle, shed his tunic, and ran the flame along one sleeve, pausing every so often to slaughter the vermin he'd flushed out.

A fat rat came strolling down the middle of the trench. It was light enough not to get stuck in the mud from the recent rains; Bartlett wished he could have said the same. The rat paused and stared at him with its beady black eyes. *I'll steal your rations, see if I don't,* it seemed to say. *And if I don't, one day soon a Yankee shell will turn you into rations—for me.*

Shells never seemed to kill rats—or maybe it was just that there were so many of them, every piece of artillery in the world couldn't have slaughtered them all. Well, if wholesale didn't work, there was always retail. Reggie snatched up the entrenching tool beside him and threw it at the rat. The rat was quick and alert, but he'd guessed right about which way it would jump, and it couldn't outrun the sharpened shovel blade, which cut it almost in two. Bartlett retrieved the tool and used it to smash in the twitching rat's head. The twitching ceased. He looked around to see if any more rats were close by. Spying none, he went back to delousing his tunic.

"You hammered that fat, ugly bastard," Corporal Robert E. McCorkle said.

"Sure did," Bartlett agreed. McCorkle was a fat, ugly bastard himself, but saying so struck Reggie as impolitic. "They're getting awfully bold these days, parading through the trenches like they've got stars in wreaths on their collars."

McCorkle laughed at that. Reggie relighted the candle, which had gone out, and went back to killing lice. He had just started on the other sleeve when first one man and then several began banging with entrenching tools on shell casings that had been hung like temple bells from tripods made of boards. With the unmusical banging, a warning cry raced up and down the trench line: "Gas! The Yanks are using gas!"

Being shot at, having artillery shells land all around, even going out between the trench lines to lay wire or to raid—Reggie was used to all that, almost to the same degree he'd been used to waiting at a Richmond corner for the streetcar to pick him up on his way between his apartment and the pharmacy where he'd worked. It wasn't that he was fearless; it was much more that anything, even the worst of horrors, becomes routine, and what is routine no longer terrifies.

But gas, gas was new. The U.S. soldiers hadn't used it on the Roanoke front, not till now. The masks—which looked like plump versions of the ones surgeons wore over their mouths and noses—and the hyposulfite solution in which to soak them had arrived days before. He snatched his mask out of the breast pocket in his tunic where he'd stowed it and sprinted, bare-chested, for the hyposulfite tin.

There, he discovered arrangements could have been better. Everybody else was as frightened of the poisonous stuff the damnyankees were spewing as he was, and the big tin stood at the center of a struggling knot of men.

"Form a line!" Corporal McCorkle shouted from behind him. "God damn you, form a line, and on the double!"

Discipline held; when a voice with command told the men what to do, they did it. Bartlett dipped his mask into the big, wide-mouthed tin and tied it over his face as the first yellow-green tendrils of chlorine gas came down into the trench like so many poisonous snakes slithering in the late spring sun.

His eyes burned. He passed the palm of his hand over the dripping mask and then over his eyes. That helped, a little. He had no idea whether the hyposulfite solution would hurt his eyes. He knew damn well the chlorine would, though.

His lungs burned, too. He could smell the harsh chlorine in his nose, taste it in his mouth. The mask he wore like a cold, clammy veil was anything but perfect. But men who hadn't donned masks, or who hadn't tied them tight, were coughing and choking, clutching at their throats and turning blue. Not perfect, no, but a hell of a lot better than nothing.

"If you can't get to the chemical, piss on your mask!" That was Captain Wilcox, his voice muffled by the mask he was wearing. "It's disgusting, but it may keep you alive."

As the chlorine spread from the front-line trenches toward those farther to the rear, U.S. artillery opened up, pounding the Confederates with a harsh bombardment. Reggie Bartlett huddled in the mud near the rat he had killed. Any one of those shells could lay him open the way his entrenching tool had gutted the rat. He held his hands over his face, both to protect it from splinters and to keep his mask on tight.

The bombardment was sharp, but it was also short: no more than fifteen minutes. "Up, dammit, up!" Captain Wilcox shouted. Farther along the trench, the battalion commander, Major Colleton, echoed the command: "Get up and fight like Americans! Here come the damnyankees!"

Bartlett's eyes burned worse than ever; tears streamed down his face. But he hadn't been killed, he hadn't been maimed. *Thank you, Jesus.* He scrambled to his feet and ran to the firing step. Sure enough, the Yankees were cutting their way through the wire. Most of them wore masks like his. The white cloth squares made good targets. He fired again and again and again. U.S. soldiers fell. More kept coming, though, their uniforms almost the color of chlorine.

Confederate machine guns opened up. The damnyankees started falling faster. But still they came, urgent shouts blurred under the hyposulfite-soaked gauze pads on their mouths. Some of them got close enough to throw grenades. One burst near Bartlett, leaving him stunned and half deafened. After a moment, he realized his left leg hurt. *Fragment or a nail or whatever must have kissed me,* he thought. When he put weight on the leg, it held. He could worry about the wound later, then.

A few Yankees leaped down into the Confederate trench, but none near him: those men were dead or wounded or running or crawling back to their own lines. A pistol barked, its sharp report like a terrier yapping amid retrievers. Probably Major Colleton, doing some of his own fighting. You couldn't fault him for guts.

"God damn," a man in butternut beside Reggie said reverently as the firing slowed. "We beat the sons of bitches back."

Bartlett needed a moment to recognize Jasper Jenkins with a mask on his face, even though the two of them had shared cornbread and jam and coffee for breakfast that morning. "Sure as hell did, Jasper," he answered, using his friend's name to cover his own embarrassment. "These masks do help. Nice to know we got something at least partway right."

Negro stretcher-bearers, Red Cross armbands on their left sleeves and masks on their faces, came forward to take the men who had been gassed and the other casualties back to where the doctors could work on them. Staring at the yellowish foam on the lips of one poor fellow who moaned with every breath he took, Reggie wondered what the quacks could do for him, and if they could do anything at all. He brought his hand up to his mask. If he'd been at the tail end of that line instead of near the front . . .

"I'd have pissed on my mask," he said. "Anything is better than nothing." He unbuttoned his fly and faced the wall of the trench. He noticed he was pissing on a dead rat. Nobody had smacked it with an entrenching tool: like the gassed soldier he'd seen, it had yellow foam on its whiskers.

As he walked along the trench, he saw more rats, either frozen in death or thrashing like soldiers who'd inhaled what wasn't an immediately fatal dose of chlorine. He kicked a couple of the corpses, and stamped the life out of a couple that were still breathing.

"Gas must bring the sons of bitches up out of their holes," Jasper Jenkins said.

"Reckon so," Reggie agreed. "They come up for fresh air, but there isn't any fresh air. Maybe we'll have a few days without them thieving and chewing on dead bodies." He picked up the tunic he'd thrown down when the gas attack started. "I wonder if that chlorine stuff kills lice, too. If it does, there may be something to it after all." He squatted down to examine the tunic and find out.

Nellie Semphroch went from table to table with a tray for empty plates and coffee cups and a damp rag to wipe the tables clean of spilled coffee and bits of bread from sandwiches. Thanks to Mr. Jacobs, she hadn't had any trouble getting good bread and meats, despite what her ration books said. No snoopy Confederate inspectors had walked in and started asking questions; Mr. Jacobs evidently knew a way to keep that from happening, too.

She looked around the coffeehouse. Business was good. Business, in fact, was booming. If she wasn't careful, she'd get rich. Confederate inspectors might not come into the coffeehouse, but Confederate officers did, and they told their friends, and— She stiffened. There sat Nicholas H. Kincaid, moodily sipping at a cup of coffee. He hadn't come in for food or drink. He'd come in to try to seduce Edna, having come so close once before.

Why, Nellie thought resentfully, *hasn't he gone and gotten himself killed?* She wished she could walk up to him and throw him out on his ear. Since he was an occupier and she one of the occupied, she couldn't do that. What she could do, and did, was thank heaven she had Edna in the back washing dishes and not here out front waiting tables. With a final scowl at Kincaid, she carried the tray back to her daughter.

"Hello, Ma," Edna said, looking up from the sink. "You got more presents for me? Why don't you bring me a diamond ring and a motorcar, instead of all these miserable, stinking, goddamn dishes?"

"You've got the soap right there." Nellie pointed to it. "Why don't you wash your mouth out with it?"

Mother and daughter glared at each other. Mother and daughter had been doing a lot of that lately. The more Nellie tried to keep an eye on Edna, the more Edna took to sneaking around. Nellie didn't know what to do about it. She had to sleep, she had to eat, she had to mind the customers—and Edna was so wild for life these days—that was what the young people called it, anyway; to Nellie, it was just another word for *loose*—that fifteen or twenty minutes unwatched might well have been all she needed.

"Why don't you let me be?" Edna said.

"Oh, no," Nellie answered. "I know you too well." *You're too much the way I was, more than half a lifetime ago.* Easing back never occurred to her, nor did the notion that part of Edna's wildness might have sprung from being watched too closely too often for too long.

With a martyred sigh, Edna took the cups and saucers and plates from the tray and set them in the soapy water in the sink. Nellie nodded—that was what her daughter was supposed to be doing. Leaving Edna to the scrubbing, Nellie went back out to see what her customers needed.

A couple of Rebels held up empty cups and asked for refills. One of them asked for another ham sandwich, too. It was a good thing she was getting those extra rations, thanks to Mr. Jacobs; if the Rebs fought half as well as they ate, the United States were in more trouble than they knew.

She had just served the sandwich when a civilian came into the coffeehouse. That did happen now and again; some Washingtonians came in arm-in-arm with Confederate officers, and a lot of those who didn't still had the slick, prosperous look of men who were getting along well by getting along well with the enemy. She'd passed a name or two to Mr. Jacobs, in the hope of helping a collaborator to an untimely demise.

This fellow didn't have that look. He was a middle-aged man with gray muttonchop whiskers, and hadn't shaved the rest of his face any time in the past couple of days. He wore a suit and tie, but he'd been wearing his collar for a while, and his jacket had shiny elbows and a couple of spots on the front.

Nellie prominently posted her prices. One look at them was plenty to send most customers not armed with either Confederate scrip or good connections fleeing out into the street. The stranger studied the list, sighed, shrugged, and sat down at a corner table. Nellie went over to him. "May I help you, sir?"

He looked up at her, sharply, almost disconcertingly. His eyes were tracked with red. He might have had a drink or two, but he didn't stink too badly of booze. "A turkey sandwich and a cup of coffee," he said.

"Yes, sir," Nellie answered. When a customer didn't say what kind of coffee he wanted, he got the cheapest she had. "That'll be a dollar even," she went on, in a tone of voice suggesting she wanted to see the dollar before she served him.

Getting the unspoken message, the fellow dug in his trouser pocket. A big silver cartwheel chimed sweetly on the tabletop. "There you are," he said, still studying her.

She ignored that. She was good at ignoring men when they looked at her more closely than they should have. She didn't ignore the dollar. That she scooped up. Maybe this fellow thought he could leave it sitting there till she gave him his order, then scoop it up and slide out the door. Washington had always been full of grifters, and all the more so since the Rebs occupied it.

Money in hand, she went back behind the counter, poured the coffee, and made the man his sandwich. Because he looked down on his luck, she piled the smoked turkey higher than she would have for a damned Reb, and stuck a couple of sweet pickles alongside even though she usually tacked on an extra nickel apiece for them.

She carried the turkey sandwich and the steaming coffee cup over to him. He smiled, which stretched his mouth out almost to the tips of his muttonchops. "That looks mighty good," he said, tucking the napkin into his collar to protect his shirtfront. "Thank you, Little Nell."

Nellie froze. No one had called her that since a couple of years before Edna was born. She'd hoped—she'd thought—no one would ever call her that again, as long as she lived. "Eat your sandwich, whoever you are," she said tonelessly. "Eat your sandwich, drink your coffee, get out, and never come back here again."

"Time was when you gave me something better for my dollar than meat and bread," the man said with a reminiscent leer. Yes, there was whiskey on his breath.

"Get out now," Nellie said, perhaps more quietly than she'd intended, because she felt a scream boiling up inside her that would shake the place down if she let it loose. "Get out now, or I'll have the Rebs here throw you out."

He assumed an injured expression. "Don't take it like that, Little Nell. Don't you remember Bill Reach of the *Evening Star*?"

And, for a wonder, she did. He'd been panting after stories in those days. He'd been panting after anything else he could get his hands on, too, and he'd got his hands on her once a week or so for months at a time. He'd been better than some, but that wasn't saying much, not with what she'd seen there for a couple of years. Men were brutes, men were beasts, no doubt about it.

"Your voice hasn't changed at all," he said, which explained how he'd recognized her. "You're not as blond as you used to be, though."

Her golden curls had come out of a bottle. They drew customers, so she'd kept them that color till she managed to escape the life she'd been leading. Bill Reach's looks weren't what they had been, not by a long shot. He looked to be about two steps up from a bum, too. *Serves him right,* she thought.

But, because he'd been better than some—only out for his own pleasure, not actively cruel—she said, "All right, eat before you go. But don't come back. Don't you ever come back here."

"Is that any way to talk to an old friend?" he demanded indignantly. Maybe that was how he thought of himself. As if she'd made friends with the men who set money on the nightstand! The idea made her want to laugh in his stubbly face. The only thing they'd ever done to make her happy was to get up, get dressed, and leave.

A large shape loomed up beside her: a Confederate officer. "Is this man bothering you, ma'am?" Nicholas H. Kincaid asked. The clear implication was that, if she said yes, Bill Reach would regret it for a long time.

She would have been happier with anyone but Kincaid coming to her aid. He wasn't helping her because he felt like helping her; he was helping because, if she approved of him, he'd have a better chance at laying Edna. She knew how men's minds worked, oh yes she did, all too well.

"It's all right," she said, surprising Reach and disappointing Kincaid. "He didn't mean any harm." She looked that eat-and-get-out warning at the ex-reporter. (What was he doing now? Nothing too well, by the look of him.) Reluctantly, Kincaid went back to his table and sat down again.

Nellie stayed out front till Reach had eaten and left. Then she gathered up his dirty dishes and those from several other tables and carried them in to Edna.

"What's the matter, Ma?" her daughter asked. "You look like you seen a ghost or something."

"Maybe I have," Nellie answered. Her daughter scratched her head.

XV

Major Irving Morrell was waiting for the stew pot full of odds and ends to come to a boil when a runner hurried up to him. "Sir," the fellow said, saluting, "I'm supposed to bring you back to division headquarters right away."

"Are you?" Morrell raised an eyebrow. "Well, you're going to have to wait a minute, anyhow." He raised his voice: "Schaefer!"

"Sir?" the senior captain in the battalion called.

"I'm ordered back to Division, Dutch," Morrell told him. "Try not to let the Rebs overrun us till I get back."

"I'll do my best," Captain Schaefer said, chuckling. "As long as you're going back there, see if they'll send another couple of machine guns forward. We can use the firepower."

"I'll do that," Morrell promised. He turned to the runner. "All right, lead the way."

He was sweating by the time he got out of the front-line trenches; the runner had taken him literally, and was setting a hard pace. His wounded leg had unhappy things to say about that. Sternly, he told it to be quiet. It didn't want to listen. He ignored the complaints and pushed on through the hot, muggy summer night.

Division staff was too exalted to try to survive under canvas. They'd taken over several houses in the little town of Smilax, Kentucky. The one to which the runner brought Morrell had sentries all around and a U.S. flag in front of it. He gave the fellow a startled look. "You didn't say General Foulke wanted to see me."

"Yes, sir, that's who," the runner said. He spoke to one of the sentries: "This here's Major Morrell." The soldier nodded and went inside. He emerged a moment later, and held the door open for Morrell to go in and see the divisional commander. As Morrell climbed the stairs, the runner trotted off down the street, perhaps on another mission, perhaps to escape one.

Major General William Dudley Foulke was sitting in the front room scribbling a note when Morrell came in. The general was a plump man in his mid-sixties, with a bald crown, a white fringe around it, and a bushy white mustache. He looked more like a French general than an American one; all he needed was a kepi and a little swagger stick to complete the impression.

"At ease, Major," Foulke said after they exchanged salutes. "Effective immediately, I am removing you from command of your battalion."

"Sir?" Morrell hadn't expected to be summoned before the divisional commander at all, and certainly not for that reason. "On what grounds, sir?"

"What grounds?" Foulke wheezed laughter, then held up a plump, pink hand. "On the grounds that Philadelphia asked me for a younger officer who could fill a staff position there, and that your name topped the list. Are those satisfactory grounds, Major?"

"Uh, yes, sir," Morrell said. "I can't imagine any better ones, and a whole slew that are worse." When General Foulke had told him he was being removed, he'd imagined that slew of worse grounds, though he didn't think he'd given reason for invoking any of them. Stubborn honesty, though, compelled him to add, "After I spent so long in the hospital, sir, I do regret being pulled away from active service again, if you don't mind my saying so."

"I don't mind at all," General Foulke said. "I'd be disappointed if you said anything else, as a matter of fact. A staff officer who likes being a staff officer because he has a soft billet far away from the line isn't a man of the sort the country needs. Men who want to go out and fight, they're the sort who do well for the general staff. You *will* be fighting, I promise you; the only difference will be, you'll do it with map and telegram, not with a rifle."

"Yes, sir." Morrell knew he should have been overjoyed; a tour on the General Staff would look very good on his record. But he reveled in the rugged outdoor life, whether in the Sonoran desert or the Kentucky mountains. Getting stuck behind a desk struck him as altogether too much like being stuck in a hospital bed.

William Dudley Foulke was thinking along with him, at least up to a point. Steepling his fingers, the general said, "Staff work can be the making of a promising young officer. If you see opportunity, by all means seize it. Here." He handed Morrell a book. "Something for you to read on the train: my translation of the Roman military writer Vegetius. Either it will engage your interest or help you sleep the miles away."

"Thank you very much, sir," Morrell said, wondering whether an ancient writer's precepts would have any bearing on the modern art of war.

"My pleasure." Foulke sighed. "When I was a boy, I thought I would be a lawyer or a scholar. But I was fourteen years old when the Rebs beat us the first time, and I knew then I wanted to spend the rest of my life in the military service of my country. That little volume there is a relic of what might have been, I'm afraid, nothing more." He grew brisk again. "Well, you don't want to hear an old man maundering on about himself. I certainly didn't when I was a young officer, at any rate."

Morrell flushed. That embarrassed him, which only made him flush more. "I'll treasure the book, sir," he said.

"Or perhaps you won't," Foulke said. "It's all right either way, Major. I've sent Philadelphia a wire, letting them know you're on your way. Now the trick will be getting you there. This part of Kentucky isn't what you'd call overburdened with railroads. We'll send you up the Hyden-Hazard road, and east from there to Hazard, where you can catch a train. You're ready to go now, I assume."

"Uh, two things, sir," Morrell said. "First, I promised I'd ask for a couple of more machine guns for my battalion."

"They'll have them," Foulke promised. "What else?"

Morrell looked down at himself. "If I'm going to Philadelphia, shouldn't I clean up a bit first?"

Foulke snuffled air out through his mustache. "Seeing what a real front-line soldier looks like would do Philadelphia good, but you may be right." He called for his adjutant—"Captain Rothbart!"—and said, "Get Major Morrell a hot bath, get him a fresh uniform, and get him on the road to Hazard so he can catch the train for Philadelphia."

"Yes, sir!" Rothbart said, and efficiently took care of Morrell. If he handled everything as smoothly for the divisional commander, General Foulke was well served.

Inside an hour's time, Morrell, clean and newly decked out, was jouncing along in a motorcar over dirt roads never intended for automobile traffic. The motorcar had three punctures before he got to Hazard, which, in the light of that experience, seemed well-named. Morrell stood guard with a rifle while the driver fixed the first two punctures; bushwhackers and Rebel guerrillas still roamed behind U.S. lines, looking like innocent civilians when they weren't out raiding. For the third puncture, Morrell pitched in and helped with the repair job. He thought about the state of his uniform only after his knees were already dirty.

No Rebs shot at the motorcar, but the train he boarded in Hazard took gunfire three different times before it got out of Kentucky, and once had to turn around on a siding when the Confederates blew up a bridge on the route north. Occupied, eastern Kentucky might have been; subdued it was not.

Under the white glare of the train's acetylene lights, Morrell pondered Vegetius. Some parts of the book, the ones that dealt with Roman military equipment, were as dry and dusty as he'd feared, and Vegetius' own proposed inventions didn't strike him as any great improvements. He started wondering why General Foulke had wasted his time translating such a useless work.

But when Vegetius started talking about principles of the military art, the book came to life. It was as if more than fifteen centuries had fallen away, leaving Morrell face-to-face with someone who worried about all the same things he did: ambushes, ways to deceive the enemy, the importance of intelligence, and other such concerns as vital in the twentieth century as they had been in the fourth.

And one sentence seized his attention and would not let it go: "Let him who desires peace prepare for war." Being ready to fight, he thought, instituting conscription and all the rest of it, had kept the United States from having to do more fighting after the defeat in the Second Mexican War.

When he finished the volume, he set it down not only with respect, but also with real regret. Not only was it interesting in and of itself, but General Foulke wrote gracefully, an attribute more common among officers of the War of Secession than their busy modern successors.

He changed trains in Wheeling, West Virginia. The new one pulled into the Pennsylvania Railroad station at Thirtieth and Market in the middle of the night. Waiting for him at the station was a spruce young captain who might have been Rothbart's cousin. His hat cords were intertwined black and gold; he wore black lace on his cuffs and a badge with the coat of arms of the United States superimposed on a five-pointed star—the marks of a General Staff officer.

His salute might have been machined. "Major Morrell?" he said, his voice as crisp as the creases on his trousers. At Morrell's nod, he went on, "I'm John Abell. As soon as we pick up your bags, I'll take you over to the War Department and we'll find quarters for your stay in the city."

"I haven't got any bags," Morrell told him. "When General Foulke let me know I'd been detached from my battalion, he gave me time to take a bath and put on a clean uniform, and then he stuck me in an automobile. My gear will catch up with me eventually, I expect."

"No doubt," Captain Abell said, looking at the mud on Morrell's knees. Well, if a General Staff officer didn't know motorcars got punctures on bad roads, that was his lookout. The captain shrugged, plainly deciding not to make an issue of it. "Let's go, then."

A couple of antiaircraft cannon stuck their snouts in the air outside the train station. "Philadelphia's been in the war," Morrell observed.

"That it has." Captain Abell waved. A driver in an open-topped Ford came up. He opened the door to the rear seat for the two officers, then used the hand throttle to give the automobile more power as he chugged east through the streets of Philadelphia toward the War Department headquarters. Abell went on, "When the Rebs came storming up out of Virginia, we were afraid we'd either have to fight for the town or declare it an open city and pull out. That would have been very bad."

"I'll say it would," Morrell agreed. Since the War of Secession, and especially since the Second Mexican War, Philadelphia had been the *de facto* capital of the United States: Washington was simply too vulnerable to Confederate guns in the hills on the south side of the Potomac. Could the United States have gone on with the war after losing both their *de jure* and *de facto* capitals? Maybe. Morrell was glad they hadn't had to find out.

Despite the hour, motor traffic kept rumbling through the city, probably interrupting bureaucrats' sleep. Philadelphia wasn't just an administrative center; it was also a key assembly point for southbound men and matériel. Here and there, Morrell saw houses and shops and buildings that had taken damage. "The Rebs never got into artillery range of you, did they?" he asked.

"No, sir," Abell answered. "They send bombing aeroplanes over us when they can, though. A lot of bombs have fallen around the War Department, but only a couple on it." His lip curled. "They can't aim for beans."

It wasn't as if the War Department were a small target, either. It covered a lot of space between the United States Mint and Franklin Square. Thinking of it as one building was a mistake, too; it was a whole great complex, some structures of marble, some of limestone, some of prosaic brick. The driver had to jam on the brake several times to keep from running down uniformed men hustling from one building to another.

When he finally stopped, it was in front of a building that looked more like a tycoon's house than anything the government maintained. "One way to keep from being noticed is to look poor and worthless," Captain Abell said, noting Morrell's expression. "Another way is to look rich and useless."

If the Confederates didn't know exactly where the U.S. Army General Staff made its headquarters, Morrell would have been astonished. He didn't say anything, though, but hopped out of the Ford and followed Captain Abell into the building. By the captain's reasoning, the sentries outside should have been decked out in servants' livery and carried trays for visitors' cards rather than rifles. Morrell was relieved to see they weren't and didn't.

Inside, the place was ablaze with electric lamps. Morrell blinked several times. The security officer to whom Captain Abell took him was brisk, thorough, efficient. After satisfying himself that Morrell really was Morrell, he gave him a temporary pass and said, "Good to have you with us, Major."

"Thanks," Morrell answered, still a long way from sure he was glad to be here. No matter what William Dudley Foulke had said, could you really fight a war in a fancy place like this?

Then Abell took him into the map room. Morrell had always had a fondness for maps; the more you studied them, the more you geared strategy and tactics to the terrain, the better off you were liable to be.

And here was the whole war, spread out before him in blue and red lines and arrows. Both Ontario fronts kept on being clogged, the enemy had the initiative in Manitoba, Kentucky still hadn't been knocked out of the fight. Guaymas remained in Rebel hands. (Morrell's leg twinged.) Utah was still in flames, too. But the Confederates were being driven from Pennsylvania, the USA had bitten off big chunks of Sequoyah, and the Rebs had been chased from New Mexico and well back into Texas. Other maps showed the confused fighting at sea.

His head swung back and forth, as if on a swivel. Seeing all the maps together, he felt like a general, not just a major worrying about his tiny part of the big picture. "I think I'm going to like this place," he said.

The motorcar carrying Jacob Colleton kicked up a plume of red-brown dust as it came up the path toward Marshlands. "Is everything ready?" Anne Colleton demanded of Scipio, her voice harsh.

"Yes, ma'am," he answered; she would have been astonished to hear him say anything else. "The room is waiting for him. Dr. Benveniste should be here momentarily, and we are prepared to do all we can."

"All we can," Anne echoed. There in the back seat of the motorcar sat her brother, stiff and pale as a mannequin. He'd be sitting or standing for a long time, maybe for the rest of his life. If he lay down, the telegram had warned her, the fluids in his gas-ravaged lungs were liable to choke him to death.

She opened the door as the motorcar jounced to a stop. Scipio rolled out the wheeled chair that had belonged to her great-grandfather after he started having strokes. But he'd been an old man. Jacob should have had a long, healthy life stretching ahead. It might still be long. The question was, did Jacob wish it would be short?

The Negro chauffeur (Anne wondered if he was the man who'd driven Tom down from Columbia, but who paid enough attention to Negroes to be sure?) opened the door so Jacob could get out of the motorcar. The effort of sliding over, getting out, and walking two steps to the chair set him coughing, and that set him groaning. He sighed when he sat in the chair, and that made him groan anew.

Anne gave the chauffeur two dollars. "Thank you, ma'am!" he exclaimed, tipping his cap. The grin was broad and white across his black face; she'd greatly overpaid him. She didn't care. Her brother was worth it. The Negro climbed back into the automobile, put it in reverse so he could turn away from the mansion and the people who had come out of it, and drove off.

Jacob Colleton looked up at his sister. "Not quite the homecoming I had in mind when I went off to war," he said. His voice was a rasping whisper, as if he were a hundred years old and had smoked a hundred cigars a day for every one of those years.

"You hush, Jacob. We'll make you as comfortable as we can," Anne replied. Her brother's voice, so far from the vibrant baritone she remembered, made her grind her teeth at the inadequacy of what she'd just said. So did the purple circles under his eyes, almost the only color in his corpse-pale face. "You're coming home a hero, the same way they did after the War of Secession."

"A hero?" His laugh was a coughing wheeze. "I'd had two cups of coffee and I was on my way to the latrine when the damnyankees gassed us. Only fool luck my men took me with 'em when they fell back. Otherwise I'd be in a prison camp or a Yankee hospital. Not a damn thing heroic about it."

Speaking so much gave him color, but not of a healthy sort: his whole face turned a leaden violet, as if he were being strangled. And so he was, from the inside out. He sounded much the way Tom had, too, utterly forgetful of the patriotism that had sent him rushing to join the fight against the USA.

"When we get you to your room, what can we bring you?" Anne asked.

"Whiskey," Jacob answered. "Morphia, if you can lay hold of it."

"Dr. Benveniste is on his way," she said. "He'll prescribe it." *If he doesn't, he'll be sorry.* She nodded to Scipio. "Take him upstairs. We'll discuss permanent service arrangements for him shortly."

"Yes, ma'am," the butler said, and then, to Jacob, "I'll be as careful as I can, sir."

Jacob let out a sound full of pain only once, when Scipio had trouble getting the chair smoothly over the threshold. Then, in the front hall, he had to stop, because Marcel Duchamp was standing there and would not move. The artist stared avidly at Jacob Colleton. "Modern man as defective part in the assembly line of war," he murmured. "Or is it man as perfect part?—the end product of what war is designed to produce."

He probably did not mean to be offensive; he must have seen Jacob not as Anne's injured brother but as an inspiration for art. At that moment, she did not care what he meant. "Get out," she said in a cold, deadly voice. "Pack your paintings and be gone from this house by tomorrow."

"But where shall I go?" Duchamp exclaimed in horror, sweat beading on his forehead.

"You can go to Columbia. You can go to Charleston. Or, for that matter, you can go to hell," Anne told him crisply. "I don't care. You are no longer welcome here." He tried to outstare her, to will her into changing her mind. Men had tried that with her before, and all of them had gone away defeated. So did Marcel Duchamp.

Then he tried for the last word: "You are not modern. You are only a rich atavism, playing with the new but belonging to the old."

That held enough truth to hurt. Looking down at poor Jacob, Anne saw how important things like the ties of family truly were to her. If those things had a smaller place in the world Duchamp inhabited, she would turn her back on that world, or on the parts of it she did not care for. She let the Frenchman see none of that. "I'll take my chances," she said. "And what I told you stands. Now get out of the way, or I'll throw you out this instant."

"Should have thrown him out before he got here," Jacob croaked; like Tom, he'd had no use for the exhibition of modern art. "But you don't need to throw him out now on account of me. Far as I can see, he was right. That's what war does: makes lots and lots of things just like me."

"Take him upstairs, Scipio." Anne didn't directly answer her brother, but she was never one to change her mind once she'd made it up. Duchamp would go, or she would throw him out.

Dr. Saul Benveniste arrived a few minutes later: a short, dark, clever man who looked, she thought, as Confederate founding father Judah P. Benjamin might have looked were he as thin as Alexander Stephens. The doctor went upstairs and came down a few minutes later. "I've given him morphia," he said. "I'll leave a supply here so you can give him more whenever the pain is very bad. Past that—" He spread his hands and shrugged.

"Is there any treatment you can give?" Anne asked. "Something that will make his lungs better, I mean, not just something to relieve the pain."

"I don't know of any," the doctor answered, his brown eyes mournful. "But then, nobody knows much about the business of poisonous gases, though I expect we'll all learn. You have to understand—the tissue in there is burned. I can't repair that from the outside. Breathing warm, moist air may help, and Marshlands has a good supply of that. He may heal some on his own, too. I can't really offer a long-term prognosis. I'm too ignorant."

"Thank you for being honest with me," she said.

"I'll do everything I can for him," Benveniste said. "I don't want you to get any exaggerated notions of how much that's likely to be, though."

"Thank you," Anne repeated. Then she said, "He wants whiskey. Will having it make him worse?"

"His lungs, you mean? I don't see why," Dr. Benveniste told her. "Most of the time, I don't have much good to say about drinking whiskey. Now, though—" He shrugged again. "If he hurts less drunk, is that so bad?"

"Not in the least," she said. "All right, Doctor. I'll call you as I need you."

Benveniste nodded and left. His Ford started up with a bang and a belch, then rattled away.

Anne went upstairs. Her brother was sitting up in bed, propped up by pillows. He had a bit more color than when he'd arrived at Marshlands. Nodding to Anne, he said, "Here I am, a relic of war," in his ruined voice.

"Dr. Benveniste said they might come up with new ways to make you better before too long," Anne told him. Dr. Benveniste hadn't quite said that, but he had said he didn't know much about treating poison-gas cases, so surely he and other medical men would be learning new things about them. And giving her brother hope counted a good deal, too.

"Best thing he could have done for me was shoot me through the head," Jacob said. "Morphia's the next best thing, though. I'm still on fire inside, but it's not as big a fire." He yawned; the drug was making him sleepy. Though his bedroom was rather dim, the pupils of his gray eyes were as small as if he'd been in bright sunshine.

He yawned again, then started to say something. The words turned into a soft snore. Without his seeming to realize it, his eyelids slid shut. The snore got deeper, raspier; Anne could hear the breath bubbling in and out of his tormented lungs, as if he had pneumonia.

She walked out into the hall and called one of the servants: "Julia!" When the Negro woman had come into Jacob's bedroom, she said, "I want you to sit here and make sure my brother does not lie down, no matter what. If he starts to slump away from the pillows that are supporting him, you are to straighten him up. Someone will have to be here all the time when he's asleep. I'll make arrangements with Scipio for that. Do you understand what I've told you?"

"Yes, ma'am," Julia said. "Don' let Mistuh Jacob lay hisself down, no matter what."

"That's right. You stay here till he wakes up or till someone takes your place." When Julia nodded again, Anne went out of the room, half closing the door behind her. Quite cold-bloodedly, she decided to arrange for Jacob's tenders to be chosen from among the younger, better-looking wenches of the household. She didn't know whether, injured as he was, he would be able to do anything with them or have them do anything for him. If he could, she would give him the chance.

In her office, a few doors down from Jacob's room, the telephone rang. She hurried down the hallway, the silk of her dress rustling around her ankles. Picking up the earpiece, she spoke into the mouthpiece: "Anne Colleton."

"How do, Miss Anne?" The voice on the other end of the line had a back-country rasp to it: not a Carolina accent at all, and certainly not the almost English phrasing of her broker, who was the likeliest person to call at this hour and who came from an old Charleston family. She couldn't immediately place who this caller was, though he did sound vaguely familiar. When she didn't say anything for a few seconds, he went on, "This here's Roger Kimball, Miss Anne. How are you?"

She needed a moment to place the name, even though he'd written to her more than once after their encounter on the train to New Orleans: the randy submersible skipper. "Hello, Lieutenant Kimball," she said. "I'm well, thank you. I didn't expect to hear from you. Where are you calling from?"

"Lieutenant Commander Kimball now," he told her proudly, "though I reckon you know me well enough to call me Roger." That was true in a biblical sense, but probably in no other. "Where am I at? I'm in Charleston, that's where. Fishing over on the other coast is so bad, they moved a good many of us back here."

"I wish you luck with your fishing," Anne said. That was true. After what the damnyankees had done to her brother, she wanted every ship flying their flag to go straight to the bottom of the sea. True or not, though, she wished she'd phrased it differently. Kimball would think . . .

Kimball did think. "Since I'm so close now, I was figurin' on gettin' me some liberty time, and then comin' up there and . . ." He let his voice fade, but she knew what he had in mind. Since she'd already given herself to him, he thought he could have her any time he wanted.

That she'd made a related calculation about Jacob and her serving women never once entered her mind. What did enter it was anger. "Lieutenant Commander Kimball, my brother just now came from the Western Kentucky front, suffering from chlorine in the lungs. I am not really in the best of positions to entertain visitors"—let him take that however he would—"at the present time."

"I'm very sorry to hear that, Miss Anne," the submariner said after a short silence. *Sorry to hear which?* Anne wondered. *That Jacob's been gassed, or that I won't let you lay me right now?* No sooner had the thought crossed her mind than Kimball continued, "That chlorine, that's filthy stuff, by everything I've heard tell about it. I hope your brother didn't get it too bad."

"It isn't good," Anne said, a larger admission than she would have made to someone with whom she was socially more intimate. The physical intimacy she'd known with Kimball was of different substance, somehow; despite it, the two of them remained near-strangers.

"I really do hope he gets better," Kimball said, and then, half to himself, "Nice to know there's *somethin'* in this war you don't have to worry about aboard a submersible." That brief bit of self-reflection done, he went on, "All right, I won't come up there right away—you'll be busy and all. Maybe in a few weeks, after I make a patrol or two."

His arrogance was breathtaking, so much so that Anne, instead of going from mere anger to fury, admired the quality of his nerve. He *had* been enjoyable, on the train and in New Orleans, a town made for enjoyment if ever there was one. Thinking about Jacob, she also thought she was liable to need relief from thinking about Jacob. She tapped a fingernail on the telephone case; indecision was unlike her. "All right, Roger, maybe in a few weeks," she said at last, but then warned, "Do telephone first."

"I promise, Miss Anne," he said. She didn't know what his promises were worth, but thought him likely to keep that one. He started whistling before he hung up the telephone. Anne wished she had any reason to be so happy.

George Enos set his gutting knife down on the deck of the steam trawler *Spray*, opened the ice-filled hold, and threw in the haddock and halibut he'd just finished cleaning. Then he went back to the latest load of fish the trawl had just scooped up from the bottom of Brown's Bank.

The seaman who was helping him clean the fish, a fellow named Harvey Kemmel who spoke with a harsh Midwestern accent utterly unlike Enos' New England dialect, wiped his face on his sleeve and said, "This here fishing for a living, it's damned hard work, you know?"

"I had noticed that, as a matter of fact," George answered dryly as he yanked another squirming halibut up off the deck, slit its belly open, and pulled out the guts. He tossed the fish into the hold and grabbed another one.

Patrick O'Donnell came aft, a mug of the Cookie's good coffee clamped in his right hand. With his left, he slapped the side of the hold. "Nice the boat's so much like the *Ripple*," he said. "Means I don't hardly have to think to know where things are at."

"Same with me, Skipper," George Enos agreed, "and I heard Charlie say the same thing about the galley. I like it that we're all still together—except poor Lucas, I mean."

"Me, too," O'Donnell agreed. He glanced down at the load of fish Enos and Kemmel were gutting. "We bring those into Boston, we'll make ourselves some pretty fair money off 'em." His gaze swung northward. Brown's Bank lay north and east of Georges Bank, where the *Ripple* had usually operated. In time of peace, that would have mattered only because it cost them more fuel to reach. Now, with the southern coast of Nova Scotia, some of it still unconquered, not so far away, other concerns also mattered. Under his breath, O'Donnell added, "If we get back to Boston."

Work went on. Work always went on, and there were never enough men to do it. Like Harvey Kemmel, several of the other sailors were working aboard a steam trawler for the first time. That meant O'Donnell and Enos and even Charlie White spent an inordinate amount of time explaining what needed doing, which in turn meant they didn't have as much time as they would have liked to do their own work.

One of the new men, a tall, skinny fellow named Schoonhoven who'd started life on a Dakota farm, was the first to spot the approaching boat. "Skipper," he called, his voice cracking with what might have been alarm or excitement or a blend of the two, "tell me that's not a submarine."

O'Donnell raised a telescope—just like the one he'd had aboard the *Ripple*—to his eye. "All right, Willem, I'll tell you that's not a submarine," he said, and then, after a perfectly timed pause, he added, "if you want me to lie to you."

Cleaning flatfish forgotten, Enos hurried to the rail and peered out across the Atlantic. It was indeed a submarine, traveling on the surface now because the *Spray* couldn't possibly hurt it. In case the fishermen hadn't noticed it was there, it fired its deck gun. A shell sent up a plume of seawater a couple of hundred yards in front of the trawler.

Patrick O'Donnell ducked into the cabin, then came out again in a hurry. "Run up the white flag!" he shouted. "Maybe they'll let us take to the boats before they sink the trawler." As the signal of surrender fluttered up below the U.S. flag the *Spray* was flying, O'Donnell peered once more through the telescope at the submersible. "That's a Confederate boat," he ground out. "The bastards cruise up to Canada and back, same as the Canucks do to their ports."

The submersible closed rapidly. Soon Enos could see the Stars and Bars flying above it, too. A sailor ran out onto the deck of the Confederate vessel and began working the signal lamp. "Abandon—ship." Along with the rest of the *Spray*'s crew, Enos read the Morse as it flashed across the water, letter by letter, word by word. "We—aim—to—sink—her."

"There's a surprise," Charlie White said with a grunt of laughter. "I figured they were going to buy our fish off us."

"Nova—Scotia—coast—100—miles—north," the signal lamp said. "Some—Yank-held—Good—luck—getting—there."

"Thanks a hell of a lot," Enos said. He helped Schoonhoven and Kemmel put the boat over the side. It looked very small, and a hundred miles of ocean enormously large. He glared toward the Rebel submersible, muttering, "And the horse you rode in on, too."

One after another, the crewmen from the *Spray* scrambled down into the boat. As captain, Patrick O'Donnell came last. "Let's get clear," he said. They worked the oars and moved away from the trawler. If no storm rose, you could row a hundred miles. The boat had food and water and a compass. All the same, Enos hoped they wouldn't have to try it.

Off to the other side of the *Spray*, he spotted what looked like a length of pipe sticking up out of the water and moving toward the Confederate submarine. He deliberately looked away from it. The Rebs on board the submersible paid it no heed. They were intent on coming right up to the *Spray* so they could sink her at point-blank range. If you didn't miss, you didn't waste shells.

Pay attention to the trawler, he thought at the Confederates. *Pay attention to the trawler a little longer.*

He'd just started to think that again when three men in the boat who hadn't made themselves not look at that moving length of pipe whooped at the top of their lungs. O'Donnell's whoop had words in it: "The fish is away!"

Everybody stopped rowing. Along with everybody else, George watched the torpedo's wake speed toward the Confederate submersible. He'd never seen anything move so fast in the water. "Run true," he breathed. "Come on—run true."

The torpedo did run true. It couldn't have had more than five hundred yards to travel: it was a point-blank shot, too. Three Rebs were standing with their heads and shoulders out of the conning tower. An instant before the torpedo slammed home, one of them spotted it. Enos saw him point. He might have yelled something, but that was lost in the dull *boom!* of the torpedo's slamming into the submarine a little before amidships.

Water and spray spurted up from the explosion, hiding the submersible for a moment. When it became visible again, it had broken in half. Bow and stern portions both sank amazingly fast. Diesel oil from the submarine spread over the water, flattening out the light chop. In the oil floated bits and pieces of debris and three splashing men—probably the ones in the conning tower, George thought. Most of the crew wouldn't have known they were in danger till the torpedo hit.

"Let's go pick 'em up," O'Donnell said, and they rowed toward the Confederates struggling in the Atlantic. As they did so, the U.S. submersible that had torpedoed the Rebel boat surfaced like a broaching whale. Men tumbled out of the conning tower and ran to the deck gun to cover the Confederate sailors.

Enos reached out a hand to one and helped drag him into the boat filled with the crew of the *Spray*. The Reb was filthy with fuel oil and, beneath that dark brown coating, looked stunned. "My name is Briggs, Ralph Briggs," he gasped in the accent George had learned to hate down in North Carolina. "Senior lieutenant, Confederate States Navy." He rattled off his pay number.

"Welcome aboard, Senior Lieutenant Briggs," O'Donnell said as sailors hauled the other two Rebel survivors into the boat. "You're a prisoner of the United States Navy."

Briggs looked over to the U.S. submarine, then glared at O'Donnell. "You're the luckiest damned fisherman in the history of the world, pal, having that damn boat show up just when we were about to blow you to hell and gone."

O'Donnell erupted in laughter. So did George Enos. So did all the other sailors from the *Spray*. "That wasn't luck, Reb," O'Donnell said, a huge grin on his face. "We were out hunting boats like you. We had the *Bluefin* there on tow behind us all the time. When you came up, I telephoned 'em, they slipped the line, and they put a fish in your boat while you were busy with us."

"We don't need to give you to the *Bluefin* to make you U.S. Navy prisoners, either," Enos added gleefully. "*We're* U.S. Navy, too, but I don't have to tell you my name, rank, and number."

More laughter roared out of the sailors and ex-fishermen who crewed the *Spray*. Charlie White said, "How many more Rebel submarines do you think we can sink before your boys catch on?"

Briggs and the other Confederates looked appalled to discover the trap into which they'd walked. The senior lieutenant had spunk, wet and stunned though he might be. Savagely, he ground out, "I hope you sons of bitches tow that damned boat right into a mine."

"You go to hell," Enos said, horrified at the notion. Several other sailors echoed him.

An officer from the *Bluefin* used a megaphone to shout across the water: "Shall we take your friends off your hands? We have more men aboard to keep an eye on them."

"Sounds good to me," Patrick O'Donnell yelled back. They rowed over to the submersible. Sailors there—sailors in Navy whites, not fishermen's dungarees—helped the Confederate survivors up onto the *Bluefin*'s deck and then marched them into the conning tower and down below. When they had disappeared, O'Donnell said, "All right, we can go home now."

They returned to the *Spray*, which bobbed in the chop. Once up on deck, Charlie White shook himself, as if awakening from a happy dream. "Lord, that was sweet," he said.

For the black man, jeering at the Rebels had to be doubly delightful. It was plenty sweet enough for George, too. "Didn't figure I'd just keep on doing a fisherman's job after I joined the Navy," he said. "It's worked out pretty well, though—couldn't have worked out better." He turned to Patrick O'Donnell. "This whole hunting scheme was your idea. Do you think they'll make you an officer now that it's worked?"

"I'm too old and too stubborn to make an officer out of me now," O'Donnell said. "CPO suits me fine." He waved to the Cookie. "Charlie, why don't you break out the medicinal rum? This may be the first submersible a fishing boat ever sank, but it isn't going to be the last."

"Yes, sir!" White said enthusiastically. You weren't supposed to call a chief petty officer *sir*, but O'Donnell didn't correct him.

Sam Carsten was walking along the wharf toward the *Dakota* when all the antiaircraft guns at Pearl Harbor started going off at once. Guided by the puffs of black smoke suddenly blossoming in the sky, he spotted an aeroplane flying so high, it seemed nothing more than a speck up in the sky, too high for him to catch the sound of its engine.

For a moment, he stood watching the spectacle, wondering if the guns could bring down the aeroplane. Then he realized that, if they were shooting at it, it had to be hostile. And a hostile aeroplane could not have come from anywhere on the Sandwich Islands, which were firmly under the control of the United States. It had to have been launched from an enemy ship, and an enemy ship not too far away.

"And an enemy ship means an enemy fleet," he said out loud. "And an enemy fleet means one hell of a big fight."

He started running back toward the *Dakota*. As he did so, klaxons and hooters began squalling out the alert the guns had first signaled. When he got to the battleship's deck, he looked around for the aeroplane again. There it was, streaking away to the southeast.

He pointed to it. "We follow that bearing and we'll find the limeys or the Japs."

One of the sailors near him said, "Yeah." Another one, though, said, "Thanks a lot, Admiral." Carsten shook his head. You said anything on a ship, somebody would give you a hard time about it.

"Battle stations!" shouted people who really were officers. "All hands to battle stations. Prepare to get under way."

Carsten sighed as he sprinted toward his own post. Inside the sponson, you couldn't see anything. All you ever got were orders and rumors, neither of which was apt to tell you what you most wanted to know.

As usual, Sam got to the five-inch gun after Hiram Kidde, but only moments after him, because no one else but the gunner's mate was there when he arrived. "Do you know what's up for sure, 'Cap'n'?" he asked.

Kidde shook his head. "Limeys or Japs, don't know which." That Carsten had figured out for himself. The gunner's mate went on, "Don't much care, either. They're out there, we'll smash 'em."

The rest of the crew was not far behind. Luke Hoskins said, "I heard it was the Japs." One of the other shell-jerkers, Pete Jonas, had heard it was the English. They argued about it, which struck Carsten as stupid. What point to getting yourself in an uproar about something you couldn't prove?

The deck vibrated under Carsten's feet as the engines built up power. Lieutenant Commander Grady, who was in charge of all the guns of the starboard secondary armament, stuck his head into the cramped sponson to make sure everything and everyone was ready, even though they were still in harbor. He didn't know to whom the aeroplane had belonged.

After Grady had hurried away, Carsten said, "There—you see? If the lieutenant commander doesn't know what's going on, anybody who says he does is just puffing smoke out his stack."

"We're moving," Kidde said a few minutes later, and then, after that, "I wonder how they—whoever *they* are; Sam's right about that—managed to sneak a fleet past our patrols and aeroplanes. However they did it, they're gonna regret it."

There wasn't much to see. There wasn't much to do, either, not until they'd caught up to whatever enemy ships had dared approach the Sandwich Islands. The gun crew took turns peering through their narrow view slits. Hoskins and Jonas quit arguing about who the enemy was and started arguing about how much of the fleet had sortied with the *Dakota*. Given how little they could see, that argument was about as useless as the other.

After he couldn't see Oahu any more, Carsten stopped looking out. He'd seen a lot of ocean since he joined the Navy, and one trackless stretch of it looked a hell of a lot like another. He didn't get bored easily, which was one of the reasons he made a good sailor.

Lieutenant Commander Grady came back, his thin face red with excitement for once. "It's the Japs," he said. "One of our aeroplanes has spotted them. Looks like a force of cruisers and destroyers—they must have figured they could sneak in for a raid, throw some shells at us, and then run home for the Philippines again. We get to show 'em they're wrong. Doesn't look like they know they've been seen, either." He rubbed his hands in anticipation.

"Told you it was the Japs," Hoskins said triumphantly.

"Ahh, go to hell," Jonas said: not much of a comeback, but the best he could do when his idea had struck a mine.

"Stupid slant-eyed bastards," Hiram Kidde said. "If they're raiding us, they don't want their damned aeroplane spotted. That pilot's going to join his honorable ancestors when they find out he dropped the ball like that."

"Cruisers and destroyers," Sam said dreamily. He patted the breech of the five-inch gun. "They'll be sorry they ever ran into us. The big guns up top'll pound 'em to bits at a lot longer range than they can hit back from."

"That's why we built 'em," Kidde said. He didn't sound dreamy. He sounded predatory.

By the sound, by the feel, of the engines, they were making better than twenty knots. An hour passed after they steamed out of Pearl Harbor, then another one. A colored steward came by with sandwiches and coffee from the galley. Pete Jonas got out a deck of cards. Kidde waved for him to put it back in his pocket. He made a sour face, but obeyed.

All of a sudden, the *Dakota* swung hard aport. The engine's roar picked up the flank speed. "What the deuce—" Luke Hoskins said, an instant before the torpedo slammed into the port side of the ship.

The deck jerked under Carsten's feet. If you got hit the right—or rather, the wrong—way, the shock wave from an explosion like that could break your ankles. That didn't happen, but Sam sat down, hard, on the steel plates of the deck. The electric lights in the sponson flickered. Then, for a dreadful second or two, they went out. "Oh, sweet Jesus," Jonas moaned, which was pretty much what Carsten was thinking, too.

He scrambled to his feet. He'd just regained them when the lights came back on. He glanced toward the door that led out of the sponson, out to the stairway to the top deck, out to the deck itself, out to the lifeboats. He didn't move toward the door, not a step. Nobody else did, either, in spite of bawling klaxons and shouts outside in the corridor. They were still at battle stations. Nobody had given any orders about abandoning ship.

Danger—hell, fear—made his mind work very quickly, very clearly. "We got sucker-punched," he exclaimed. "Nothing else but. The Japs put that little fleet out there where we had to spot it—Christ, they sent out that aeroplane to lead us right to it. And they posted submersibles right out here between it and Pearl, and just sat there waiting for us to come running out. And we did—and look what it got us."

"How come you're so goddamn much smarter than the admiral?" Kidde sounded half sardonic, half respectful.

"Not likely," Sam answered. "Now that we've been torpedoed, I bet he's figured out what's going on, too."

"If the engines quit, we're in trouble," Luke Hoskins said. "That'll mean the boilers are flooded." He stood quite still, a thoughtful look on his face. "We're listing to port, I think."

Carsten could feel it, too: the deck wasn't level, not any more. He glanced to the doorway again. If he left without orders, it was a court-martial. If he stayed and the battleship sank, a court-martial was the least of his worries. But the engines kept running, and the list wasn't getting worse in a hurry.

Lieutenant Commander Grady came in. "Looks like we're going to make it," he said. "Compartmenting's holding up, engines are safe, and the aft magazine didn't go up." He scratched his chin. "If it had, I think we would have known it."

"So what have we got, sir?" Kidde asked. "A couple thousand tons of water in us?"

"Something like that," Grady agreed. "We limp back to Pearl Harbor if we can, we go into drydock for six months or however long it takes to patch us up again, and then we go back to war." His features, lean, scholarly—more a professor's face than a naval officer's—went grim. "We got off lucky. They sank the *Denver*, and it doesn't look like many of her crew had time to get off before she went down. Not a better cruiser in the Pacific Fleet than the *Denver*."

"They were laying for us," Carsten said. "They showed the fleet and the aeroplane to bring us out, and then—"

"I'd say you're right," Grady replied. "The ships kept the submarines in fuel and supplies, too: not likely they'd have the range to go from Manila to here and back without stocking up along the way. I hope the rest of the fleet manages to punish them. We're out of the fight for now."

Out of the fight. The words seemed to echo in the sponson as Grady left to pass the news to the rest of the gun crews under his command. The *Dakota* swung through a long, slow turn, as awkward as a horse with a lame hind leg, and began limping back toward Pearl Harbor. They hadn't done anything wrong except pursue too eagerly, but they were, sure as hell, out of the fight.

"Fuck it. We're alive," Luke Hoskins said.

Sam looked back at the doorway one last time. He wouldn't have to run out through it, hoping he could make it up on deck before water or fire engulfed him. When you got down to it, that wasn't such a bad bargain. "We're alive," he repeated, and the words sounded very fine.

Mary McGregor bounced up and down on the seat of the wagon beside her father. "What are we going to get?" she said. She'd been saying that ever since they'd left the farm for the trip into Rosenfeld, Manitoba.

As he'd done every time she asked, Arthur McGregor answered, "I don't know. You're the one who's turning seven today. I've got fifty cents in my pocket, and you can spend it any way you please."

"I'll get a store doll, one with real glass eyes," Mary declared. Then she shook her head, making her auburn curls fly around her face. "No, I won't. I'll get candy. How much candy can I get for fifty cents, Pa?"

"Enough to make you sick for a week," McGregor answered, laughing. His youngest child was full of extravagant notions. He figured a few more years of living on the farm would cure her of most of them.

Off to the north, artillery rumbled. Mary took no notice of it, prattling on cheerfully about everything on which she might spend her half-dollar. If she got everything she wanted, it could easily have cost McGregor fifty times that. Moreover, her choice was liable to be severely limited: if Henry Gibbon didn't have it in his general store, she couldn't get it. Her father let her go on all the same. Dreams were free, even if presents weren't.

The artillery rumbled again. Arthur McGregor sighed. Though dreams were free, they didn't always come true. When the Anglo-Canadian offensive opened and pushed the Americans south from Winnipeg, he'd dreamt they would throw the Yankees out of Canada altogether. But Rosenfeld had never seen a single khaki uniform, not unless the Yanks had shipped prisoners through. The town and his farm hadn't even come within artillery range of the front. It was high summer now, and everything around these parts remained under the muscular thumb of the USA.

Coming into Rosenfeld, he saw just how muscular that thumb had become. Soldiers in green-gray crowded the streets, some no doubt going up toward the front, some coming back for relief. Their boots, and the tires of motorcars and great grunting White trucks, made dust swirl like fog all through the town.

They had soldiers serving as traffic policemen, now halting a stream of trucks so an officer in an automobile could cut across, now halting a column of men who looked fresh off the train so more trucks could get through, and now holding up McGregor to let another column of soldiers, these men veterans, go by. From the veterans, whose uniforms were sun-bleached and imperfectly clean, rose a smell that put him in mind of the farmhouse the morning before the bathtub got filled. He'd smelled it in barracks, too, and especially out on maneuvers—men on the front line had little incentive and less ability to keep clean.

"Get off the main road, Canuck," one of the soldiers called, pointing the wagon onto a little side street. There wasn't any particular animosity in the order. McGregor could even see the need for it. But—

"What's a Canuck, Pa?" Mary asked as he stopped disrupting traffic.

"You are," he answered, getting out of the wagon to tie the horse to a hitching post. "I am." He picked her up and put her down on the plank sidewalk. "It's what Americans call Canadians when they don't like us much."

"Oh." She thought about that, then nodded. "You mean the way we call them goddamn stinking Yanks?"

"Yes, just like that," he said, and coughed. "But we don't call them that where they can hear us. And, for that matter, who called them that where you could hear him?"

"It wasn't a him—it was Ma," Mary answered, which made McGregor cough all over again. He'd have to have a talk with Maude when he got home. Mary went on, "How come they get to call us names whenever they please and we don't get to call them names whenever we please? That's not fair."

"Because they have more guns than we do, and they drove our soldiers out of this part of the country," he told her. "If you have more guns in a war, you get to say what's fair."

She chewed on that. To his relief, she didn't argue with him about it. He took her hand and walked toward the general store. Several U.S. soldiers smiled at her along the way. A lot of them weren't far from McGregor's age: reservists called up for the war, probably with daughters as old as Mary or maybe even older. She took no notice of the Americans. She made a point of taking no notice of the Americans.

"Mornin', Arthur," Henry Gibbon said when they went into the general store. Gibbon beamed down at Mary. "And a good mornin' to you, little lady."

"Good morning, Mr. Gibbon," she answered, very politely: the storekeeper, being a Canadian, deserved not only notice but respect.

"Reason we're here," McGregor said, "is that somebody here just turned seven years old, and she's got half a dollar to spend however she pleases. She'll be wanting to look at your toys and dolls and candy, unless I miss my guess."

"We can probably do somethin' along those lines," Gibbon said. He beckoned Mary over to the jars of sweets on his counter. "Why don't you have a look at these here, little lady, and I'll see what I've got in the way of toys." He glanced up at Mary's father. "We're apt to be a bit picked over, things bein' like they is."

"I understand that," he answered. "But if anybody in Rosenfeld has anything good, you're the man."

"That I am," the storekeeper agreed solemnly. He had just turned around to see what a pasteboard box held when something exploded across the street. The plate-glass window at the front of the general store shattered, fragments flying inward. One glittering shard flicked McGregor's sleeve; another stuck out of the floor boards bare inches from his foot.

Mary screamed. He ran to her and scooped her up, afraid some of the shrapnel-like slivers of glass had cut or stabbed her. But she wasn't bleeding anywhere, though glass dust sparkled in her hair like diamonds. She trembled in his arms.

"Holy Jesus!" Henry Gibbon said. He looked at what had been his window and said "Holy Jesus!" again, louder. Then he looked out through what had been his window and said "Holy Jesus!" a third time, louder still. This time, he amplified it somewhat: "That's the *Register* office, blown to hell and gone."

McGregor had been too worried about his daughter even to think about what might have blown up out there. Now he looked, too. Sure enough, the wood-and-brick building that had housed Rosenfeld's weekly newspaper was nothing but a ruin now, and beginning to burn. If the fire engines didn't get here in a tearing hurry, that whole block was liable to go up in smoke, and maybe this one, too, if the wind blew sparks across the street.

In the street lay U.S. soldiers, some down and writhing, some down and still. A couple of horses were down, too, screaming like women in torment. An officer went up to them and quickly put them out of their torment with his pistol. McGregor thought well of him for that; he would have done the same.

In that spirit, he set Mary down and went out of the general store to see if he could do anything for the wounded U.S. soldiers. They were the enemy, yes, but watching anybody suffer wasn't easy. One of them had a leg bent at an unnatural angle. McGregor knew how to set broken bones.

He never got the chance. The officer who'd shot the two horses swung up his pistol and aimed it at McGregor's head. "Don't move, Canuck," he snapped. "You'll be hostage number one. We'll take twenty of you bastards, and if the bomber doesn't give himself up, we'll line you up against a wall and teach you a lesson you'll remember the rest of your life." He laughed.

McGregor froze. He'd known the Yankees did things like that, but he'd never imagined it could happen to him.

Mary came flying out of the general store. "Don't you point a gun at my pa!" she screamed at the officer. McGregor grabbed her before she could hurl herself against the American. He had to move to do that, but the man didn't fire.

Henry Gibbon came out of the store, too. "Have a heart, Crane," he said to the U.S. officer. "Arthur McGregor's no bomber, and he doesn't live in town, so he doesn't make much of a hostage, neither. Only reason he came in is that today's his little girl's seventh birthday." He pointed to Mary.

The U.S. officer—Crane—scowled—but after a moment he lowered the pistol. "All right," he said to McGregor. "Get the hell out of here."

McGregor's legs felt loose and light with fear and relief, so he seemed to be floating above the ground, not walking on it. He steered Mary toward the side street on which he'd left the wagon.

"But I didn't get my birthday presents!" she said, and started to cry.

"Oh, yes, you did," he told her.

"No, I didn't!" she said. "Not anything, not even one peppermint drop."

"Oh, yes, you did," he repeated, so emphatically that she looked up in puzzled curiosity. He pointed to himself. "Do you know what you got? You got to keep me."

She kept on crying. He wasn't a doll or a ball or a top or a peppermint drop. He didn't care. He was alive, and he was going to stay that way a while longer.

Jefferson Pinkard got to the foundry floor at the Sloss works a few minutes early, as he usually did. Vespasian and Agrippa, the two Negroes who'd taken over the night shift, nodded and said, "Mornin', Mistuh Pinkard," together.

"Mornin'," Pinkard said. Both blacks had proved themselves solid workers, worthy of being talked with almost as if they were white men. He looked around. "Where's Pericles at? He's usually in here before I am."

After a pause, Vespasian said, "He ain't comin' in today, Mistuh Pinkard."

"Oh?" Jeff said. "He sick?" Pericles and Vespasian were kin or in-laws or something of the sort; he couldn't quite remember what. Just because you talked with black men didn't mean you had to keep track of every little thing about them.

Vespasian shook his head. "No, suh, he ain't sick," he answered. He sounded tired unto death, not just because of the night's work but also from a lifetime's worth of weariness. A moment later, the words dragging out of him one by one, he went on, "No, suh, like I say, he ain't sick. He in de jailhouse."

"In the jailhouse? Pericles?" That caught Pinkard by surprise. "What the devil did he do? Get drunk and go after somebody with a busted bottle?" That didn't sound like Pericles, a sober-sided young buck if ever there was one.

And Vespasian shook his head again. "No, suh. He do somethin' like that, we can fix it. He in de jailhouse for—sedition." He whispered the word, pronouncing it with exaggerated care.

"Sedition?" Now Jefferson Pinkard frankly stared. Vespasian was right, he thought. You could fix a charge of brawling against a black man easily enough—provided he hadn't hit a white, of course. If he was a good worker, a couple of words from his boss to the police or the judge would get him off with a small fine, maybe just a lecture about keeping his nose clean. But sedition—that was another ball of wax.

Neither Vespasian nor Agrippa said much more about it. They waited till it was time for them to go off shift, then left in a hurry. Pinkard didn't suppose he could blame them. When one of your own got into trouble, you didn't spend a lot of time talking about that trouble with an outsider.

He had to start his shift by his lonesome, which left him too busy to think about anything else. About half an hour into the shift, a colored fellow who introduced himself as Leonidas joined him. Jeff hoped to high heaven Leonidas wouldn't take Pericles' place for good. He was strong enough, but he wasn't very smart, and he didn't remember from one minute to the next what Pinkard had told him. Jeff kept him from getting hurt or from messing up the job at least half a dozen times that morning. It was more nerve-racking than doing everything by himself would have been, because he never knew ahead of time when or how Leonidas would go wrong, and had to stay on his toes every second.

When the lunch whistle blew, Pinkard sighed with relief—half an hour when he wouldn't have to worry. "See you at one, suh," Leonidas said, taking his dinner bucket and heading off to eat with other Negroes.

"Yeah," Pinkard said. He wondered if Leonidas could find some way to kill himself when he wasn't anywhere near the foundry floor. He wouldn't have been a bit surprised: the Negro was an accident waiting to happen, and probably could happen any old place.

Pinkard opened his own dinner pail. He had a chunk of cornbread and a couple of pieces of roasted chicken in there: leftovers from the night before. He'd just started to eat when a couple of middle-aged fellows in gray police uniforms came up to him. "You Jefferson Davis Pinkard?" asked the one who wore a matching gray mustache.

"That's me," Jeff said with his mouth full. He chewed, swallowed, and then asked more clearly, "Who're you?"

"I'm Bob Mulcahy," the policeman with the mustache answered. He pointed to his clean-shaven partner. "This here's Bill Fitzcolville. We're looking into the matter of a nigger named Pericles. Hear tell he's been working alongside you a while."

"That's a fact," Pinkard agreed, and took another bite of chicken. They weren't going to hold things up on the floor because he was talking with police. If he didn't feed his face, he'd have to go hungry till suppertime.

"This Pericles, he been a troublemaker, uppity, anything like that?" Mulcahy asked.

"Not hardly." Pinkard shook his head. "Didn't cotton to the notion of workin' with a nigger, not even a little bit, I tell you. But it ain't worked out too bad. He does his job—did his job, I guess I oughta say. This nigger Leonidas, buck they gave me instead of him, he ain't fit to carry guts to a bear, doesn't look like. But Pericles, he pulled his weight."

Fitzcolville scribbled down his words in a notebook. Mulcahy shifted a good-sized chaw of tobacco from right cheek to left, then asked. "This nigger Pericles, he a smart fellow or a dumb one?"

"Nothin' dumb about him," Jeff answered. "You show him somethin' once, you tell him somethin' once, you don't need to do it twice, on account of he remembers it and does it right his own self."

"Uh-*huh*," Fitzcolville grunted, as if Pinkard had said something altogether damning.

Mulcahy kept on with his questions, steadily, imperturbably: "He ever talk about anything *political* while the two of you was working together?"

"Political?" Pinkard paused for a bite of cornbread. "What the hell kind of politics is a nigger supposed to have? It ain't like he can vote or nothin'."

"Oh, niggers have politics, all right," Mulcahy said. "*Red* politics, too damn many of 'em. This Pericles, he ever talk about how the war was going or how the war was changing things here back at home?"

Red politics. Emily had said something like that, and he hadn't taken it seriously. The Birmingham police did. Jeff said, "We was talkin' one time about how, after Herb Wallace got hisself killed in the war, the Sloss folks threw his widow out of factory housing here. Pericles didn't reckon that was fair."

"Uh-*huh*," Fitzcolville said again, and scrawled more notes.

"You gonna call him a Red for that?" Pinkard demanded. "You better call me a Red right at the same time, 'cause I think it stinks like shit, too, what they done to Daisy. Here her husband's gone and got killed for the sake of the fat cats up in Richmond, and they throw her out of her place like a dog. You call that the way things oughta be?"

He'd gone too far. He could see it by the way the two policemen stared at him—stared through him, really. "Maybe you *are* a Red," Mulcahy said, "but I doubt it. Most of the ones who are have too much sense to run off at the mouth like you do. 'Sides, white men can pretty much say what they please—it's a free country. Niggers, now, we gotta watch niggers."

"I been watchin' this crazy damnfool nigger Leonidas every goddamn minute of the mornin' shift," Pinkard said. "You give me a choice between him and Pericles, I'll take Pericles every goddamn time. When he's here, he does his job. I don't know what he does when he ain't here, and I don't care."

"That's not your job," Mulcahy said. "It is our job, and we've found this nigger tied up in all sorts of stuff niggers got no business sticking their noses into."

"Whatever else he is, he's a steel man," Jeff answered. "Steel he's helped make, I reckon it's done more to hurt the damnyankees than anything else he's done has hurt us."

The two policemen looked at each other. Maybe they hadn't thought of it like that. Maybe, too, they just didn't care for the idea of a white man speaking up for a black. That second maybe soon proved the true one, for Mulcahy said, "You like that nigger pretty well, don't you?"

Pinkard surged to his feet. "Get out of here," he said, his voice thick with anger and cornbread both. Both policemen gave back a step, too. The foundry floor was no place for anyone unused to it to feel comfortable, either. Jeff had an advantage, and he used it. "You got a lot o' damn nerve, you know that? Callin' me a nigger-lover like I ain't a proper white man. Go on, get the hell out."

"Didn't mean it like that, Pinkard," Bob Mulcahy said. "Just trying to get to the bottom of who all this damn nigger's been messing with."

"He ain't messed much with me, and he know what he's doin', too, not like this lamebrained halfwit they saddled me with now that you took him away," Pinkard said. "Pretty soon, way things look, they're gonna drag my ass off to war—hell of a lot o' white men gone already. You want to keep makin' steel, it's gonna be niggers doin' the work, mostly. Maybe you ought to think about stuff like that a little more often, 'fore you start haulin' hard-workin' bucks off to the jailhouse for no reason at all."

"We've *been* thinking about it," Bill Fitzcolville said, proving he did have more words in him than *uh-huh*. "Don't like the answers we get, neither."

"But this here Pericles, we got him dead to rights," Mulcahy said. "Found all kinds of subversive literature at his house: Marx and Engels and Lincoln and Haywood and I don't know who all else. Niggers ain't allowed to have that kind of stuff. He'll spend a while cooling off in jail, that's for damn sure. We're trying to track down how much damage he's done, is what we're doing here."

"Like I said, he ain't done me any damage I know of," Pinkard said. The policemen shrugged and left. But he didn't think that meant he was going to get Pericles back any time soon. He'd just have to go and see if he couldn't turn Leonidas into something a little bit like a steelworker. The odds were against him; he could see that much already. He sighed. Life could be a real pisser sometimes, no two ways about it.

Captain Elijah Franklin stuck out his hand. "We're going to miss you here, Moss," he said. The pilots and observers in Jonathan Moss' squadron all nodded. So did the mechanics. Moss knew why Lefty would miss him: no more easy pickings at the poker table.

"I'll miss you, too, sir, and everybody else here," he said. "But I've been sort of a fifth wheel ever since Percy got hurt, and when this chance to transfer came along, it looked too good to pass up."

"Fighting scouts? I should say so," Stanley McClintock said. He twiddled with one of the waxed spikes of his mustache. "You never did like the idea of company in your aeroplane, did you?"

"Why, darling, I didn't know you'd miss me *that* way," Moss said archly. The laugh he got let him slide over the fact that McClintock had a point. He'd been the one who'd complained longest and hardest about the introduction of the two-seater Wright 17s. In the old Super Hudsons, you had nobody but yourself to blame if you made a mistake up there. The new fighting scouts were like that, too. You did what you did and, if you did it right, you lived and you got to keep on doing it. If not, it was your own damn fault, no one else's.

People crowded round him, pressing chocolate and flasks of brandy and whiskey into his pockets. They slapped him on the back and wished him luck. McClintock wasn't the only one who looked jealous. If you did your job in a two-seater, your observer took his pictures and you came home and got them developed. If you did your job in a fighting scout, you shot down enemy aeroplanes, and soldiers in the trenches shouted their heads off for you. So did reporters. If you shot down enough enemy aeroplanes, people back home shouted their heads off for you.

"Come on, let's go," Lefty said. Moss shouldered his duffel bag and climbed into the Ford that did duty as squadron transport. Unlike models that came off the assembly line, this one had been modified to boast an electric starter button on the dashboard. Lefty mashed it with his thumb. The engine thundered to life. As they rolled away from the aerodrome, Lefty handed Moss a pair of dice. "You ever get in a hot crap game where you need some sevens in a hurry, these are the babies to have."

Moss stared down at the ivory cubes in the palm of his hand. Lefty doubtless meant them for a thoughtful going-away present. They made him thoughtful, all right. He thought about what a profitable time Lefty had had ever since the squadron went into Canada.

As if reading his mind, the mechanic said, "I never use 'em myself, and nobody'll ever be able to prove I do. Same goes for poker, Lieutenant, in case you're wondering. Know what you're doing and you'll never need to cheat."

By which, he was saying Moss didn't know what he was doing at cards or dice. He probably knew what he was talking about, too.

The Ford rattled along. The road was nothing to boast about, which made the motorcar's big wheels and high ground clearance all the more valuable. Nothing in American-held Ontario was anything to boast about, though. Every inch had been fought over, every inch wrecked. What had been little farms by the side of the road were now cratered ground and rubble, with hardly a house standing. Here and there, skinny people came out of ruins to glower at the automobile as it rolled past.

Lefty pulled off the road and onto a new track made by U.S. vehicles after the war had passed this stretch of Canada. The fighting scouts, having shorter range than the observation aeroplanes, were based closer to the front. The strip on which they took off and landed had so much fresh dirt on it, it had pretty obviously been shelled not long before, the land then releveled by tractors or more likely by lots of men working hard.

Alongside the strip sat the Martin single-deckers. Next to the bulky Wilburs he'd been flying, they looked little and low and fast. Next to the Curtiss Super Hudsons, pushers with more wires and struts than you could shake a stick at, they looked like something out of the 1930s, maybe the 1940s, not merely next year's model.

"You got to hand it to Kaiser Bill's boys," Lefty said, stamping on the none too effective brake to bring the Ford to a halt (when you needed to stop in a hurry, stamping on the reverse was a better idea). Puffy summer clouds drifted lazily across the sky. "They know how to make aeroplanes, no two ways about it."

"Yeah," Moss said with a small sigh. The Wright brothers might have flown the first aeroplane in 1904, but the machines had evolved faster in Europe than in the USA. The single-decker was a straight knockoff of the Fokker monoplanes now flying above France and Belgium. Also a knockoff was the machine gun mounted above the engine, almost the only bulge marring the smooth lines of the aeroplane. "Good to know somebody finally figured out how to build a decent interrupter gear. Even if it wasn't us, we get to borrow it."

"That's right, Lieutenant," Lefty said. "Chew the hell out of the Canucks and the limeys for me, you hear?" He stuck out his hand. Moss shook it, then grabbed his duffel bag and jumped down from the Ford. Lefty took his foot off the brake, gave the motorcar more throttle with the hand control, and *putt-putt*ed away.

Shouldering the bag, Moss made for the canvas tents that housed his new squadron. Such arrangements were all very well now, with the weather warm, but could you live in a tent in the middle of winter? Maybe the war would be over and he wouldn't have to find out. He clicked tongue between teeth. He'd believed nonsense like that the year before. He was a tougher sell now.

Somebody came out of the closest tent and spotted him. "Moss, isn't it?" the man called with a friendly wave. "Welcome to the monkey house."

"Thank you, Captain Pruitt," Moss said, letting the bag fall so he could salute. Shelby Pruitt lazily returned the gesture. Moss had already gathered he'd have to get used to a new style here; Captain Franklin, his CO since the start of the war, had been the sort who dotted every i and crossed every t. Pruitt didn't seem the sort to make much fuss over little things, as long as the big ones were all right.

Now he said, "Come along with me. We'll give you someplace or other where you can lay your weary head." He didn't particularly look like a flier—he was short and dark and on the dumpy side—and his southwestern accent made him sound almost like a Reb. When you watched him move, though, you got the idea he always knew exactly where every part of him was at every moment, and that was something a pilot certainly needed.

He led Moss along the row of green-gray canvas shelters till he flipped up one flap. "Ah, thought so," he said. "We've got room at the inn here."

Peering in, Moss saw the tent held four cots, the space around one of them conspicuously bare and empty. One airman sat on the edge of his bed, writing a letter. He looked up at Moss and said, "You're the new fish, are you? I'm Daniel Dudley—they mostly call me Dud." He shrugged resignedly. He had a pale, bony face and a grin that was engaging even if a little cadaverous.

"Jonathan Moss," Moss said, and shook hands. He set his gear down on the empty cot. Pruitt nodded to him, then went off on whatever other business he had. Moss understood his offhandedness: he wouldn't really be part of the squadron till he'd flown his first mission.

Dudley made a small production out of sticking the cap back onto his fountain pen. That let him effectively do nothing till Captain Pruitt was out of earshot. Then he asked, "What do you think of Hardshell so far?"

Moss needed a moment to grasp the nickname. "The captain, you mean?" he asked, to make sure he had it right. When Dudley didn't say no, he went on, "He seems all right to me. Friendlier than the fellow I'm leaving, that's clear. What do *you* think of him?"

"He'll do, no doubt about it." Dudley took a panatela out of a teakwood cigar case. He offered the case to Moss, who shook his head. The pilot bit off the end of his cigar, lighted it, and sighed with pleasure.

"Who else sleeps here?" Moss asked, pointing to the other two cots.

"Tom Innis and Luther Carlsen," the other pilot answered. "Good eggs, both of 'em. Luther's a big blond handsome guy, and thinks he's a wolf. If the girls thought so, too, he'd do pretty well for himself."

"That's true about a lot of guys who think they're wolves," Moss said, to which Dudley nodded. Moss turned serious in a hurry, though. "What can you tell me about the Martin that I won't have picked up from training on it?"

"Good question," Dudley said. A wide smile only made him look more skull-like than ever, but he couldn't help that. "We've just been flying Martins a month or so ourselves. They don't have a lot of vices that we've found: good speed, good view, good acrobatics." He paused. "Oh. There is one thing."

"What's that?" Moss leaned forward.

"Every once in a while, the interrupter gear will get a little bit out of alignment."

"How do you find out about that?"

"You shoot your own prop off and you shoot yourself down," Daniel Dudley answered. His face clouded. "That's what happened to Smitty, the guy who used to have that cot. If it does happen to you, the beast is nose-heavy. You have to watch it in your glide."

"Thanks. I'll remember." Moss started unpacking his bag. "When do you suppose they'll let me up in one?"

"Tomorrow, unless I'm all wet," Dudley answered. "Hardshell doesn't believe in letting people sit around and get rusty."

He was right. Captain Pruitt sent Moss up as tail-end Charlie on a flight of four Martins—himself and his tentmates—the very next morning. His scout aeroplane was factory-new, still stinking of the dope that made the fabric of wings and fuselage impenetrable to air. But the mechanics here had modified it as they had the other three Martins of the flight: by mounting on the left side of the wooden cockpit frame a rearview mirror like those on some of the newest model motorcars. Moss found that a very clever idea, one that would keep his neck from developing a swivel mount.

The rotary engine kicked over at once when a mechanic spun the prop. Castor-oil fumes from the exhaust blew in his face. The in-line engine in the Wright he had flown had been petroleum-lubricated, which had made his bowels happier than they were liable to be now.

One after another, the four single-deckers took off. Moss tried to get a handle on Innis and Carlsen by the way they flew their aeroplanes; he hadn't had much chance to talk with them the day before. Carlsen was always exactly where he was supposed to be in the flight, which Dud Dudley led. Captain Franklin would have approved of that precise, finicky approach. Innis, on the other hand, was all over the place. Whether that bespoke imagination or carelessness remained to be seen.

Up to the front they flew. Dudley swung the nose of his Martin so that he flew parallel to the front, on the American side of the line. The rest of the flight followed, Innis frisking a little, up and down, from side to side. They were under orders as strict as Captain Pruitt could make them not to cross over to enemy-held territory no matter what. Neither the Canadians nor the British yet had a working interrupter gear, and nobody in the USA wanted to hand them one on a platter.

Flying a combat patrol was nothing like being trained on a new aeroplane. Moss had discovered that when he'd made the transition from the Super Hudson to the Wright 17, and now found out all over again. When you were in training, you were concentrating on your aeroplane and learning its idiosyncrasies. When you were up here on patrol, all you cared about was the other fellow's aeroplane, with your own reduced in your thoughts to a tool you'd use to shoot him down.

He spotted the Avro in that newfangled rearview mirror. It had probably been flying a reconnaissance mission on the American side of the line, and was now heading back toward Canadian territory with its pictures or sketches or whatever it had. Moss peeled off from the flight and gave his Martin single-decker all the power it had as he raced toward the Avro.

Its pilot spotted him and tried to bank away, which also gave the observer a better shot at him. He dove and then climbed rapidly. All he had to do was point his aeroplane's nose at the enemy and squeeze the firing button on his machine gun. He'd practiced shooting during training, but having the bullets miss the prop still seemed half like black magic to him.

The Avro was still trying to maneuver into a position from which it could effectively defend itself. He kept firing, playing the stream of bullets as if they were water from a hose. All at once, the Avro stopped dodging and nosed toward the ground. As he had with his first kill, back when the war was young, he must have put the pilot out of action. The observer kept shooting long after he had any hope of scoring a hit. Martin respected his courage and wondered what he was thinking about during the long dive toward death.

He looked around to see if he could spot any more British or Canadian aeroplanes. He saw none, but all his flightmates were close by. He hadn't noticed them coming to his aid; he'd been thinking about the Avro, nothing else.

Dudley, Innis, and Carlsen were waving and blowing him kisses. He waved back. He might not have fully belonged in his new squadron the day before, but he did now.

The U.S. Army sergeant doing paymaster duty shoved a dollar and a half across the table at Cincinnatus and checked off his name on the list. "You get the bonus again today," he said. "That's twice now this week, ain't it? Don't usually see Lieutenant Kennan actin' so free and easy with the government's money."

Don't usually see him give a Negro anything close to an even break, was what he meant. Cincinnatus had no doubt that was true. But—for a white man, for a U.S. soldier—the paymaster seemed decent enough. Figuring he owed him an answer, Cincinnatus said, "Whatever you do, you got to do it as good as you can."

"Yeah, that ain't a bad way to look at things," the sergeant agreed. "But you made Kennan notice how good you're doin' it—you got a black hide and you manage that, you got to be doin' awful damn fine."

"My wife's gonna have a baby," Cincinnatus said. "Extra half-dollar now and then, it means a lot." He cut it short after that; no point to getting the laborers in line behind him angry.

He was about halfway home when it started to rain. Herodotus and a couple of the other Negroes with whom he was walking ducked under an awning for protection. The awning, conveniently for them, was in front of a saloon. They went on inside. Cincinnatus kept going. He took off his hat and turned his face up to the warm rain, letting it wash the sweat off him. That felt good. Sometimes, after a hot, muggy day, he felt as crusted in salt as a pretzel.

When he walked past Conroy's general store, he looked in through the window, as he often did. One lone white man was in there with the storekeeper. After a second glance, Cincinnatus stiffened. That white man was Tom Kennedy.

Kennedy saw him, too, and waved for him to come inside. He did, his heart full of foreboding. A U.S. Army patrol was walking down the other side of the street. One of the men paused to smear petroleum jelly on his bayonet to hold back the rain. All they had to do was look over and recognize Kennedy and everything went up in smoke. They didn't. They just kept walking, one of them making a lewd crack about what else you could do with a greasy hand.

"Hello, Cincinnatus," Kennedy said, about as cordially as if Cincinnatus had been white. He didn't know whether he liked that or not. It made him nervous; he did know that. He wished Kennedy had never come knocking at his door in the middle of the night.

But Kennedy had. "Evenin'," Cincinnatus answered reluctantly. "What kin I do for you today?"

"Glad you stopped in," Kennedy said, again sounding as if Cincinnatus were a favorite customer rather than a Negro laborer. "Would have had somebody by to pay you a visit tonight if you hadn't."

"Is that a fact?" Cincinnatus sounded dubious. The last thing he wanted was some white man coming around his house late at night. He'd been lucky none of the neighbors had said anything to the U.S. soldiers after Kennedy paid him a visit that first time. Lucky once didn't have anything to do with lucky twice, though. Half—probably more than half—the Negroes in Covington preferred the USA to the CSA, although *a plague on both their houses* had wide popularity among them, too. "Who wants to visit me, and how come?"

Kennedy and Conroy looked at each other: Kennedy kept doing the talking, which was smart, because Cincinnatus trusted him further than the storekeeper. He said, "We've got a delivery we need you to make." He grinned. "Sort of like old times, isn't it?"

"Not so you'd notice," Cincinnatus answered. "What did you have in mind? Drive a truck up in front of my house? Don't think I'd much fancy that." He'd been trained to be cautious and polite around whites, so as not to let them know everything that was going on in his head. That was the only thing that kept him from shouting, *Are you out of your skull, Mr. Kennedy, sir?*

"Nothing like that," Kennedy said, raising a soothing hand. "We'll have somebody bring by a wagon with a mule pulling it—nothing that would look out of place in your part of town." The unspoken assumption that that was the way things ought to be in the Negro district of Covington grated on Cincinnatus. Oblivious, Kennedy went on, "We'll have a colored fellow drivin' it, too, so you don't need to worry about that, either."

"You already got a wagon and a driver, you don't need me, Mr. Kennedy," Cincinnatus said. He put his hat back on and touched a forefinger to the brim. "See you another time. Evenin', Mr. Conroy."

"Get back here," Conroy snapped as Cincinnatus turned to go. "We know where you live, boy, remember that."

Cincinnatus had had all the threats he could stomach. Blackmail cut both ways. "I know where you're at, too, Mr. Conroy. Ain't never had reason to talk to the Yankee soldiers, but I know."

Impasse. Conroy glanced at Cincinnatus. He didn't glare back; in the Confederacy, even the occupied parts of it, blacks showed whites respect whether they deserved it or not. "We'd really rather you did this, Cincinnatus," Kennedy said. "We've got this other fellow, yeah, but we don't know how reliable he is. We can trust you."

"You can trust me?" Cincinnatus said. Kennedy's reasonable tones, in their own way, irked him more than the storekeeper's bluster. Bitterly, he asked, "How do I know I can trust you? Why should I? Suppose the Confederate States do win this here war. What kind of place are they gonna be for colored folks afterwards? Everything stay the same, it ain't worth livin' for us, not hardly."

Conroy looked as if he'd just taken a big bite out of a Florida lemon. Tom Kennedy sighed. "Reckon it's going to be some different," he said. "All the niggers working in factories these days, the CSA could hardly fight the war without 'em. You think they can send 'em all packing, send 'em back to picking cotton and growing rice and tobacco when the war is over? They can try, but you can't unring a bell. I don't think it'll work."

What he said made the storekeeper look even more unhappy. "Never should have set the niggers free in the first place," Conroy muttered.

"A little too late to worry about that now, wouldn't you say?" Kennedy scraped a match on his shoe and lighted a stogie. "Hell, I hear there's talk about putting Negroes in butternut and giving 'em rifles. You get in a war like this, you've got to fight with everything you have."

"Damn foolishness," Conroy said. He looked Cincinnatus straight in the eye. "And if you want to tell the Yankees I said so, go right ahead." He was, at least, honest in his likes and dislikes.

Tom Kennedy blew a smoke ring, then held his cigar in a placatory hand. "We don't want to get in a quarrel here, Joe," he said, from which Cincinnatus learned Conroy's Christian name. "But if a nigger fights for the CSA, how are you going to take his gun away and tell him he's got to go back to being a nigger once the fighting's done? He'd spit in your eye, and would you blame him?"

"Shit," Conroy said, "even the damnyankees got better sense than to go giving niggers guns."

"Mr. Conroy," Cincinnatus said quietly, "I ain't carryin' no Tredegar rifle, but ain't I fightin' for the CSA? The Yankees catch me, they won't give me no medal. All they do is put me up against a wall and shoot me, same as they'd do with you."

"He's right, Joe," Kennedy said. "Go ahead, tell him he isn't."

"He doesn't want to take the packages over to the Kentucky Smoke House, he ain't right at all—just a damn lyin' nigger," Conroy said.

"Kentucky Smoke House? Hell, you don't need me to take anything there," Cincinnatus said. "Y'all could go your own selves, an' nobody'd notice anything different." That was only the slightest of exaggerations. The Kentucky Smoke House did up the best barbecue anywhere between North Carolina and Texas. That was what the proprietor, an enormous colored fellow named Apicius, claimed, and by the hordes of Negroes and steady stream of whites who came to the tumbledown shack out of which he operated, he might well have been right.

"Easier sending somebody colored—safer, too," Kennedy said, which was probably true. "If you're making the delivery, people will think you're bringing him tomatoes or spices or something like that. Joe or me, we'd stick out too much hauling crates."

That was also probably true. Cincinnatus sighed. Sensing his weakening, Conroy said, "Got the wagon and mule out back in the alley, waiting to be loaded."

Cincinnatus sighed again, and nodded. "Good fellow," Kennedy said, and tossed him something he caught automatically. "This is for taking the risk." Cincinnatus looked down at the five-dollar Stonewall in his hand. A moment later, the goldpiece was in his pocket, along with the dollar and a half he'd made (bonus included) for eleven and a half hours of grueling labor on the docks.

Without another word, Conroy led him into the back room and pointed to a couple of crates and a tarp. He opened the door out onto the alley. Cincinnatus picked up the crates, which felt very full and were heavy for their size, then heaved the canvas sheet over them. The rain had stopped, but no guessing whether it might start up again. The weight of the crates and the need for the tarpaulin made Cincinnatus guess they held pamphlets or papers of some sort.

He hadn't driven a mule for a while; Kennedy had bought motor trucks three years before. But, he discovered, he still knew how. And the mule, a tired beast with drooping ears, didn't give him any trouble.

Kennedy and Conroy had done one thing right: no one, black or white, paid any attention to a Negro on a battered wagon pulled by a lazy mule. If they'd wanted him to leave a bomb in front of U.S. Army headquarters, he could have done that, too, he thought, and slipped away with no one the wiser.

His nose guided him to the Kentucky Smoke House. A lot of buggies and wagons were tied up nearby, along with a couple of motorcars. Again, he remained inconspicuous. The sweet smell of smoke and cooking meat made spit flood into his mouth when he went inside. There stood Apicius, splashing sauce on a spitted pig's carcass with a paintbrush.

"Got a couple boxes for you from Mistuh Conroy," Cincinnatus said, coming up close so nobody else could hear.

The fat cook nodded. "Felix!" he bawled. "Lucullus!" Two youths with his looks but without his bulk came hurrying up to him. He jerked a thumb at Cincinnatus. "He got the packages we been waitin' fo'."

His sons—for so Cincinnatus figured them to be—hurried outside and carried the boxes into a back room of the restaurant. One of them gave Cincinnatus a package wrapped in newspapers through which grease was starting to soak. "Best ribs in town," he said.

"I know that already," Cincinnatus said. "Obliged."

He drove Conroy's wagon back to the general store, then walked home.

The smell of the ribs tormented him all the way there. When he opened the door, Elizabeth started to yell at him for being late. That savory package started the job of calming her down. The five-dollar goldpiece finished it.

Because of the Yankee curfew, nights were usually quiet. The sound of banging—not gunfire, but something else—woke Cincinnatus a couple of times. When he headed for the docks the next morning, every other telegraph pole and fence post was adorned with a full-color poster of Teddy Roosevelt leading a detachment of U.S. soldiers, all of them wearing German-style spiked helmets, each one with a baby spitted on the bayonet of his rifle. PEACE, the poster said. FREEDOM.

In his mind's eye, Cincinnatus saw lots of Negro boys with hammers and nails running here and there, putting up posters in the dead of night. With his real eyes, he saw U.S. soldiers tearing them down. He didn't know for certain he'd had anything to do with that. Doing his best to take no notice of the angry U.S. troops, he kept on walking toward the docks.

Once upon a time, Provo, Utah, had probably been a pretty town. Mountains towered to the east and northeast; to the west lay Utah Lake. The streets were wide, and shade trees had lined them. This July, as far as Paul Mantarakis was concerned, the place was nothing but a bottleneck, corking the advance of U.S. forces toward Salt Lake City. The trees had either been blasted to bits by artillery fire or cut down to form barricades across the broad streets. Thanks to the mountains and the lake, you couldn't go around Provo. You had to go through it.

Mantarakis scratched his left sleeve. He was probably lousy again. The only notice he took of the third stripe on that sleeve was that the double thickness of cloth made scratching harder.

Captain Norman Hinshaw—a captain because of casualties, the same reason Mantarakis was a sergeant—squatted down in a foxhole beside him. He pointed ahead. "The big set of buildings—that big set of ruins, I should say—that's what's left of Brigham Young College. That's where the damned Mormons have all their machine guns, too. That's what keeps us from taking the whole town."

"Yes, sir," Mantarakis said. He knew where the Mormons had their machine guns, all right. They'd killed enough Americans with them. Deadpan, he went on, "Of course, it's just a few goddamn fanatics doing all the fighting. The rest of the Mormons all love the USA."

Hinshaw's narrow, sour face looked even narrower and more sour than usual. "They're still feeding that tripe to the people back home," he said. "Some of them may even still believe it. Only soldiers who still believe it are the ones who got shot right off the train."

"That's about the size of it, sir," Mantarakis agreed. As he spoke, he checked right, left, and to the rear. As in Price, the Mormons in Provo had the nasty habit of letting U.S. soldiers overrun their positions, then turning around and shooting them in the back. Paul summed it up as best he could: "If you're a Mormon in Utah, you hate the USA."

"Isn't that the sad and sorry truth?" Hinshaw said. "Only people who give us any sort of assistance at all are the ones the Mormons call gentiles—and they assassinate them whenever they get the chance." He snorted. "Even the sheenies in Utah are gentiles, if you can believe it."

"I'd believe anything about this damn place," Paul said. "Anybody who's seen what we've seen getting this far would believe anything."

Back of the line, back behind the train station, U.S. artillery opened up on Brigham Young College again. Up above, an aeroplane buzzed, spotting for the guns. The Mormons shot at it, but it was too high for their machine guns to reach.

Hinshaw looked up at the aeroplane. "Good for him," he said. "He'll find out where the bastards are at, and we'll blow 'em up. I like that. The more of 'em we kill, the less there are left to kill."

"You said it, sir," Paul agreed. "They *do* fight harder than the Rebs, every damn one of 'em."

"Amen to that," the captain said. "The Rebs, they're sons of bitches, but they're soldiers. When the war comes through, the civilians get the hell out of the way like they're supposed to. Here, though, anybody over the age of eight, boy or girl, is an even-money bet to be a *franc-tireur*. I heard tell they planted an explosive under a baby, and when one of our soldiers picked up the kid—*boom!*"

Mantarakis wondered if that was true, or something somebody had made up for the sake of the story, or something somebody had made up to keep the troops on their toes. No way to tell, not for certain. That it was even within the realm of possibility said everything that needed saying about the kind of fight the Mormons were putting up.

As if to remind him what kind of fight that was, the Mormons in the front-line foxholes and shelters in the rubble opened up again on the U.S. positions south of Center Street. Rifle fire picked up all along the line as government soldiers started shooting back. Machine guns began to bark and chatter. Here and there, wounded men shrieked.

"Be alert out there!" Paul shouted to his men as he got to his feet. "They're liable to rush us." The Mormons had done that to another regiment in the brigade, down near the town of Spanish Fork. Farmers and merchants in overalls and sack suits, a couple even wearing neckties, had thrown the U.S. soldiers back several hundred yards, and captured four machine guns to boot.

That regiment had had its colors retired in disgrace; it was off doing prisoner-guard duty somewhere these days, being reckoned unfit for anything better. Mantarakis didn't want the same ignominy to fall on his unit.

But the religious fanatics—*religious maniacs* was what Mantarakis thought of them, even if that did make him seem unpleasantly like Gordon McSweeney to himself—didn't charge. They weren't eager about battling their way through barbed wire, not any more. A few gruesome maulings at the hands of troops more alert than that one luckless regiment had pounded that lesson into them. Even if they didn't have uniforms, they were beginning to behave more like regular troops than they had: the effect, no doubt, of fighting the U.S. regulars for some weeks.

They still had more originality left in them than most regulars, though. Something flew through the air and crashed into the foxholes and trenches behind Mantarakis. He shook his head in bemusement. It had looked like a bottle. He wondered what was in it. Not whiskey, that was for sure—the poor stupid damn Mormons were even drier than the desert in which they lived.

Another bottle hurtled toward the U.S. lines. The Mormons had used some sort of outsized slingshot arrangement to fling makeshift grenades at the soldiers battling to crush their rebellion; Paul would have bet they were throwing their bottles the same way. But why?

A trail of smoke followed that second one. It smashed maybe twenty yards from Mantarakis, and splashed flame into the bottom of the trench. "Jesus!" he yelled, and crossed himself. "They've got kerosene in there, or something like it."

"That's a filthy way to fight," Captain Hinshaw said. Half walking, half waddling, he started down the trench line. "Let me get to a field telephone. We'll teach them to play with fire, God damn me to hell if we don't."

"Look out, Captain!" Paul shouted. The Mormons must have been saving up bottles, because they had a lot of them. Here came another one. Hinshaw ducked. That didn't help him. It hit him in the back and shattered, pouring burning kerosene up and down his body.

He screamed. He thrashed. He rolled on the ground, trying to put out that fire. It didn't want to go out. It wasn't just the kerosene burning any more, but also his uniform and his flesh. The harsh, acrid stink of scorched wool warred with a sweet odor a lot like that of roasting pork. Had Mantarakis smelled that odor under other circumstances, he might have been hungry. Now he just wanted to heave up his guts into the bottom of the trench.

He lacked the luxury of time in which to be sick. He jumped on top of Captain Hinshaw, smothering the flames with his body, beating at them with his hands, and then shoveling dirt onto them.

Hinshaw kept on screaming like a damned soul. Mantarakis remembered he'd asked God to damn him. Even as the Greek battled the fire burning his captain, he shivered. When you said something like that, you were asking for trouble.

A couple of other soldiers came running up and helped Mantarakis extinguish Hinshaw. More kerosene-filled bottles kept dropping all around. More men screamed those horrid screams, too.

Captain Hinshaw was still smoking, but he didn't seem to be burning anywhere, not any more. He sat up. That gave Mantarakis and the other two men the first look at his face they'd had since the bottle hit him. Mantarakis wanted to look away. "Jesus," one of the other soldiers said softly. It wasn't a live man's face any more, but a skull covered here and there with bits of charred meat.

In a voice eerily calm, Hinshaw said, "Will one of you please take your weapon and kill me? Believe me, you'd be doing me a favor."

"We can't do that, sir," Mantarakis answered through numb lips. He raised his voice to shout for stretcher-bearers. Trying to sound soothing, he went on, "They'll have morphia for you, sir."

"Morphia?" Hinshaw's laugh made Paul's hair stand on end. The officer groped for his own pistol, and got it out of the holster. Mantarakis knew he ought to stop him, but crouched, frozen. Neither of the other two soldiers moved. Hinshaw's hand was burned, too, but not too burned to pull the trigger. He fell over, mercifully dead.

A few minutes later, artillery stopped pounding Brigham Young College and started hammering the Mormons in the front-line positions. A couple of shells fell short, too, plowing up the ground too close to Paul for comfort.

Whistles shrilled. For once, Mantarakis was glad to go over the top, glad to struggle through paths in the wire that weren't paths enough—anything to get away from the roast-meat horror Captain Hinshaw had become. Beside that, the bullets cracking past him were nuisances, distractions, nothing more. By the way his men were shouting as they rushed the Mormon lines, they felt the same as he did.

He sprang down into a length of trench. The Mormons fought hard. They always fought hard. Hardly any of them threw down their rifles, even in the face of death. That didn't matter, not today it didn't. He hadn't planned on taking prisoners, anyhow.

From an upstairs bedroom came the insistent clanging of a bell. "I'll speak further to you later, Griselda," Scipio said. The servant, who'd given Anne Colleton rancid butter, looked suitably downcast, but he hadn't quite turned away before she stuck out her tongue at him.

She would have to go, he realized as he hurried up the staircase. Whether that meant another situation indoors somewhere else or work out in the fields, he didn't know, but such insubordination could not be tolerated. And then, around three steps higher, he remembered he was part of a revolutionary movement that, if it succeeded, would sweep away Negro servitude forever. Until it succeeded, though, the most he could do to help it was to make everything seem as normal as he could. Yes, Griselda would have to go.

"Coming, Captain Colleton," he called, for the bell went on and on and on. He had been too well-trained ever to look like someone in a hurry, but he was walking very fast by the time he got to Jacob Colleton's bedroom.

"Took you long enough," Colleton said in a slurring rasp. That didn't spring from the effects of the gas alone; he was drunk, as he was most of the time: a cut-glass whiskey decanter, nearly all the whiskey it had once held now decanted, sat on a table by the chair in which he perched.

"I am sorry to have inconvenienced you, sir," Scipio said. He had to fight to keep his air of servile detachment around Jacob Colleton. You knew people came back from war wounded, even maimed. You didn't think they could come back ruined this particular way, though, condemned to maybe a full life's worth of hell.

Chlorine gas . . . that was stuff more appalling than anyone had imagined back before the war. If the Confederates had thought of it, they wouldn't have used it against the USA, not at first they wouldn't. They'd have used it to keep their own blacks in line. He had a sudden, horrid vision of black men and women lined up and made to breathe the stuff. A lot more efficient than just shooting them . . .

In that choking wreck of a whisper, Jacob Colleton said, "I want to see Cherry. Bring her here to me. She can tell me a story, one of those Congaree yarns you niggers spin, take my mind off how wonderful the world is for me these days." He coughed. His face, already the color of parchment, went paler yet, to the shade milk had once you'd skimmed off the cream.

"You understand, sir, that she is in the fields at present," Scipio said. Colleton nodded impatiently. Face not showing any of what he was thinking, Scipio said, "I shall fetch her here directly."

Muggy heat smote him when he went outside. He felt himself starting to sweat. It was, for once, honest sweat, sweat having nothing—well, only a little—to do with fear. The kinds of stories Cherry told Jacob Colleton had nothing to do with words. Colleton, of course, had no notion Cherry was anything but one more Negro wench to distract him and keep his mind off his pain.

What she thought about him was harder for Scipio to unravel. She gave Colleton what he wanted from her; the butler was sure of that much. He wouldn't have kept asking for her if she didn't. Understanding why she did was harder. Come the revolution, Jacob Colleton, like every other white aristocrat in the CSA, was fair game.

Maybe he told her things, when they were in there together with the doors closed. Cassius might know about that; Scipio didn't. He didn't have the nerve to ask the hunter, either. Maybe Cherry reveled in making herself feel worse now so revenge would be all the sweeter when it came. And maybe, too, revolutionary sentiments or not, she also felt something akin to pity for Jacob Colleton. People weren't all of a piece, not whites, not blacks, not anybody. Scipio was sure of that.

He sent a little boy who wore nothing but a grin and a shirt that came halfway down to his knees out to find Cherry. That meant he'd have to give the little rascal a couple of pennies when he came back, but going out into the fields after a particular woman was beneath a butler's dignity.

While he waited for the boy to return with Cherry, he looked back at the Marshlands mansion. Halftone photographs in the newspapers showed what towns looked like after the rake of war dragged through them. He tried to imagine Marshlands as a burnt-out shell. Horror ran through him when he did. He loved and hated the place at the same time himself.

Here came Cherry, a plain cotton blouse over an equally plain cotton skirt, but a fiery red bandanna tied over her hair. Scipio gave the boy three pennies, which was plenty to send him capering off with glee. "Why fo' you wants me?" Cherry asked.

"Ain't me." Scipio shook his head in denial. "Marse Jacob, he want you. Say he want you to tell a story to he."

"He say dat?" Cherry asked. Scipio nodded. Now he was sweating from nerves. If Cherry told Jacob Colleton the wrong story, he himself was a dead man. He hoped she didn't truly care for Miss Anne's brother. If she did, she was liable to talk more than she should. That was the last thing Scipio wanted. She said, "Well, he gwine like de story he get."

Scipio wouldn't have doubted that. She was a fine-looking woman, with high cheekbones that said she had some Indian in her. You'd have never a dull moment between the sheets with her; of that much Scipio was sure. All the same, knowing what he knew, he would sooner have taken a cougar to bed.

Cherry walked on toward Marshlands. Scipio followed her with his eyes. Any man would have, the roll she put to her hips. She opened the door, closing it after her as she went inside. Something else occurred to Scipio, something he hadn't thought through before. Cherry was going up to that bedroom to do what Jacob Colleton wanted. Colleton probably didn't care much about whether it was what she wanted. If the uprising of which she dreamt ever came off, Scipio wouldn't have cared to be in the shoes Miss Anne's brother was—or, at the moment, most likely wasn't—wearing.

Well, that was Jacob Colleton's lookout, not Scipio's. The butler had enough to worry about, keeping Marshlands going with servants constantly leaving for better-paying jobs, and with the threat of revolt from the field hands growing worse every day.

And, he remembered, with insolence from the servants he did have. Dealing with Griselda came within the normal purview of his duties. That it was normal made it all the more attractive to him now. Straightening up until he looked as stiff and stern as the Confederate sergeant on the recruiting poster pasted to every other telegraph pole, he marched back to the mansion.

Griselda, predictably, screamed abuse at him when he told her she had to go. "That will be enough of that," he said, using his educated voice: he was speaking as Anne Colleton's agent now, not as himself. "If you comport yourself with dignity, I will prevail upon the mistress to write you a letter that will enable you to find a good situation elsewhere. Otherwise—"

But that was not so effective as it would have been a year earlier. "Fuck yo' letter, an' fuck you, too," Griselda shouted. "Don' need no letter, not these days I don't. Take myself to Columbia, git me work at one o' the factories they got there. Don' have to lissen to no nigger talkin' like white folks what needs to go take a shit, neither." She stormed out of Marshlands, slamming the door behind her.

Scipio stared out the window as she flounced down the path that led to the road. She hadn't even bothered going to her room and getting her belongings. Maybe she'd be back for them later, or maybe she'd have somebody send them on to her when she found a place in town. Wherever the truth lay there, she never would have behaved that way before the war made it possible for her to find a job without worrying about her passbook or a letter of recommendation or anything past a strong back and a pair of hands.

"The war," he muttered. It had dislocated everything, including, God only knew, his own life.

Anne Colleton came out of her office and looked down at him from the second floor. "What was that all about?" she asked. "Or don't I want to know?"

"One of the house staff has seen fit to resign her position, ma'am," Scipio answered tonelessly.

Miss Anne raised an eyebrow. "I didn't know an artillery accompaniment was required with resignations these days," she remarked, but didn't seem inclined to take it any further, for which Scipio was duly grateful.

The mistress of Marshlands was turning away from the railing when another door opened upstairs. Cherry walked by Anne Colleton, nodding to her almost, although not quite, as an equal. Miss Anne looked at her, looked back to the door from which she had emerged, and went back into her office, shaking her head as she went.

Cherry paused by Scipio. "I hear one of the house niggers up an' leave?"

she asked. When the butler nodded, she said, "How about you give de job she was doin' to me? I kin do it better dan she could, I bet you."

Scipio licked his lips. She might well have been right, but— "I gwine ask Cassius, see what he say." Using that dialect inside the mansion, even speaking quietly as he was now, made him nervous. Cassius would probably be glad to have an extra set of eyes and ears inside Marshlands, but if for some reason he wanted his followers to stay as inconspicuous as possible, Scipio didn't want to cross him. Scipio didn't want to cross Cassius for any reason. The hunter was altogether too good with a gun or a knife or any other piece of lethality that came into his hands.

Cherry tossed her head. "Cain't ask Cassius. He ain't here."

"What do you mean, he isn't here?" Scipio asked, returning to the form of English that seemed more natural—or at least safer—to him inside Marshlands. "Has he gone hunting in the swamps for a few days?"

"He gone, but not in de swamp," Cherry agreed. She too dropped her voice, to a throaty whisper. "Who know what kind o' good things he bring back wid he when he come home?"

What the devil was that supposed to mean? Scipio couldn't come right out and ask: too many ears around in a place like Marshlands, and not all of them—none of the white and too few of the black—to be trusted. He focused on what lay right before him. "Very well, Cherry," he said starchily. "We shall try you indoors for a time, and see how you shape in your new position. Have you anything more suitable for wear inside Marshlands?"

"Sho' do." Her eyes flashed deviltry. "Jus' axe Marse Jacob." She slipped outside, laughing, while Scipio was still in the middle of a coughing fit.

Chester Martin scratched his head. The gesture, for once, had nothing to do with the lice that were endemic in the front lines near the Roanoke—and everywhere else. "Sir, these are the craziest orders I ever heard," he said.

Captain Orville Wyatt said, "They're the craziest orders I ever heard, too, Sergeant. That hasn't got anything to do with the price of beer, though. We got 'em, so we're gonna obey 'em." But behind the wire-rimmed spectacles, his eyes were as puzzled as Martin's.

"Oh, yes, sir," Martin said. "But how are we supposed to pick out this one particular nigger? Those bastards do a lot of deserting." He scratched his head again. You had to want in the worst way to get out of your country if you were willing to crawl through barbed wire, willing to risk getting shot, to escape. And it wasn't as if the USA were any paradise for colored people, not even close. What did that say about the CSA? Nothing good, Martin figured.

Captain Wyatt said, "He'll let us know who he is. And when he does, we're supposed to treat him like he's whiter than the president." He spat down into the mud of the trench. That stuck in his craw, the same as it did for Martin.

The sergeant sighed. "Son of a bitch would have to pick our sector for whatever he's up to. I'll pass the word on to the men."

Specs Peterson, who was cleaning his eyeglasses on a rag that looked likelier to get them dirty, looked up, his gray eyes watery and unfocused. His voice was very clear, though: "What a lot of fuss over one damn nigger." The rest of the soldiers in the squad nodded.

So did Chester Martin, for that matter. But he answered, "When the order comes down from Philadelphia, you don't argue with it, not if you know what's good for you. Anybody who shoots that fellow when he's coming through the wire is gonna wish he'd shot himself instead."

"But, Sarge, what if this is all some kind of scheme the Rebs cooked up and they sneak a raiding party through? We won't shoot at them, neither, not till too late," Joe Hammerschmitt protested.

"You ought to be writing for *Scribner's* instead of what's-his-name, that Davis," Martin said. "Maybe you can make a gas attack sound exciting instead of nasty, too. But if the Rebels are that smart, they're probably going to overrun us. You ask me, though, they ain't that smart, or if they are, they sure haven't shown it."

With that the men—and Martin himself—had to be content. It turned out to be enough, too, for two nights later Hammerschmitt shook Martin awake. As he always did when he woke up, he grabbed for his Springfield, which lay beside him. "Don't need to do that, Sarge," the private said. "I think I got that nigger with me you were talking about the other day."

"Yeah?" Martin sat up, rubbing his eyes. It was dark in the trench; the Confederates had snipers watching for any light and anything it showed, same as the USA did. The man beside Hammerschmitt wasn't much more than a shadow. Martin peered toward him. "How you going to prove you're the one we've been waiting for?"

" 'Cause I de one gwine bring de uprisin' o' de proletariat to de white folks o' de CSA," the Negro answered. "Gwine end de feudal 'pression, gwine end de capitalis' 'pression, gwine end *all* 'pression. De dictatorship o' de proletariat gwine come, down in de CSA." His eyes glittered as he peered toward Martin. "An' de revolution gwine come in de USA, too, you wait an' see." His accent was thick as molasses, but if anything it added to the grim intensity of what he was saying.

"Jesus Christ, Sarge," Hammerschmitt burst out, "he's a fuckin' Red."

"He sure is," Martin answered. Plainly, the Negro wasn't just a Socialist. Martin voted Socialist as often as not, though he'd favored TR in the last election. The Negro was an out-and-out bomb-throwing Red, Red as a Russian Bolshevik, probably Redder than an IWW lead miner or fruit picker out West.

Martin scrambled to his feet. "I'll take you to the captain, uh— What's your name? They didn't tell us about that."

"I is Cassius," the Negro answered. "You sho' you got to waste time wid de captain? I got '*por*tant things to do up here in Yankeeland."

"Think a good bit of yourself, don't you, Cassius?" Martin said dryly. "Yes, you have to go see Captain Wyatt. You satisfy him, he'll pass you on up the line. And if you don't—" He didn't go on. Cassius sounded like a man with a head on his shoulders. He could work that out for himself.

Cassius picked his way over and around sleeping men and avoided holes in the bottom of the trench with an ease a cat would have had trouble matching and Martin couldn't approach. The Negro couldn't have acquired that sense of grace and balance chopping cotton all day. Martin wondered what he had done.

Captain Wyatt, as it happened, was awake, studying a map under the tiny light from a candle shielded by a tin can. He looked up when Martin and Cassius drew near. "This the man we're looking for, Sergeant?" he asked.

"I think so, sir," Martin answered. "His name's Cassius, and he's a Red." He wondered how the Negro would react to that. He just nodded, matter-of-factly, as if he'd been called tall or skinny. He *was* a Red.

Wyatt frowned. Martin knew he was a Democrat, and a conservative Democrat at that. But after a moment his face cleared. "If the Rebs have themselves a nice Red revolt in their own backyards, that won't make it any easier for them to fight us at the same time." He swung his eyes toward the black man. "Isn't that right, Mr. Cassius?" Martin had never heard anybody call a Negro *Mister* before.

Cassius nodded. "It's right, but we make dis revolution fo' our ownselves, not fo' you Yankees. Like I tol' you' sergeant here, one fine day you gits yo' own revolution."

"Yes, when pigs have wings," Wyatt said crisply. The two men glared at each other in the gloom, neither yielding in the least. Then the captain said, "But it's the CSA we're both worried about now, eh?" and Cassius nodded. Wyatt went on, "I still don't know if it was them or the Canucks who set Utah on its ear, but your people will do worse to them than Utah ever did to us." He pointed to Martin. "Take him back to the support trenches and tell them to pass him on to divisional headquarters. They'll see he gets what he needs."

"Yes, sir," Martin said. He headed for the closest communications trench, Cassius following. As they made their way back through the zigzag trench connecting the first line to the second, Martin remarked, "I sure as hell hope you give those Rebs a hard time."

"Oh, we do dat," Cassius said. With a dark skin, wearing a muddy Confederate laborer's uniform, he might almost have been an invisible voice in the night. "We do dat. We been waitin' fo' dis day a long time, pay they back fo' what dey do to we all dese years."

Chester Martin tried to think of it as an officer would, weighing everything he knew about the situation. "Even with the Rebs' having to fight us, too, you, uh, Negroes are going to have the devil's own time making the revolution stick. A lot more whites with a lot more guns than you've got."

"You Yankees gwine help wid de guns—I here fo' dat," Cassius said. "An' dis ain't no uprisin' o' jus de niggers o' de CSA. Dis an uprisin' o' de proletariat, like I done say befo'. De po' buckra—"

"The what?" Martin asked.

"White folks," Cassius said impatiently. "Like I say, de po' buckra, he 'pressed, too, workin' in de factory an' de mill fo' de boss wid de motorcar an' de diamond on he pinky an' de fancy *see*gar in he mouf. Come de revolution, *all* de proletariat rise up togedder." He walked on a couple of steps. "What you do 'fo' you go in de Army?"

"Worked in a steel mill back in Toledo," Martin answered. "That's where I'm from."

"You in de proletariat, too, den," Cassius said. "The boss you got, he throw you out in de street whenever he take a mind to do it. An' what kin you do about it? Cain't do nothin', on account of he kin hire ten men what kin do jus' de same job you was doin'. You call dat fair? You call dat right? Ought to point you' gun at dey fat-bellied parasites suckin' de blood from yo' labor."

"Telling a soldier to rise up against his own country is treason," Martin said. "Don't do that again."

Cassius laughed softly. "Tellin' de proletariat to rise up fo' dey class ain't no treason, Sergeant. De day come soon, you see dat fo' your own self."

A sergeant in the secondary trenches called a challenge that was more than half a yawn. Had Martin and Cassius been Confederate raiders, the fellow probably would have died before he finished. As things were, he woke up in a hurry when Martin identified his companion. "Oh, yes, Sergeant," he said. "We've been told to expect him."

Martin surrendered the Negro with more than a little relief and hurried back up toward the front line. Some of the things Cassius had said worried him more than a little, too. So did the Red's calm assumption that revolution *would* break out, come what may, not only in the Confederate States but in the United States as well.

Could it? Would it? Maybe it had tried to start in New York City on Remembrance Day, but it had been beaten down then. Would it stay beaten down? Capital and labor hadn't gotten on well in the years before the war. Plenty of strikes had turned bloody. If a wave of them came, all across the country . . .

After the war, something new would go into the mix, too. A lot of men who'd seen fighting far worse than strikers against goons would be coming back to the factories. If the bosses tried to ignore their demands—what then? The night was fine and mild, but Martin shivered.

Captain Stephen Ramsay remained convinced that his Creek Army rank badges were stupid and, with their gaudiness, were more likely to make him a sniper's target. He also remained convinced that entrenching in—or, more accurately, in front of—a town was a hell of a thing for a cavalryman to be doing.

Not that Nuyaka, Sequoyah, was much of a town—a sleepy hamlet a few miles west of Okmulgee. But, with the damnyankees shifting forces in this direction, it had to be defended to keep them from getting around behind Okmulgee and forcing the Confederates out of the Creek capital.

Where the blacks had run off, everybody had to do nigger work. Ramsay used an entrenching tool just as if he still was the sergeant he'd been not so long before. Alongside him, Moty Tiger also made the dirt fly. Pausing for a moment, the Creek noncom grinned at Ramsay and said, "Welcome to New York."

"Huh?" Ramsay answered. He paused, too; he was glad for a blow. The heat and humidity made it feel like Mobile. "What are you talking about?"

"New York," Moty Tiger repeated, pronouncing the name with exaggerated care, almost as if he came from the USA. Then he said it again, pronouncing it as a Creek normally would have. Sure as hell, it sounded a lot like *Nuyaka*.

"This . . . little town"—Ramsay picked his words with care, not wanting to offend the Creek sergeant—"is named after New York City?" Moty Tiger nodded. Ramsay asked, "How come?"

"Back in Washington's time, when the Creeks still lived in Alabama and Georgia, he invited our chiefs to New York to make a treaty with him," the sergeant told him. "They were impressed at how big and fine it was, and took the name home with them. We took it here, too, when the government of the USA made us leave our rightful homes and travel the Trail of Tears." His face clouded. "Richmond has been honest with us. The USA never was. Being at war with the USA feels right."

"Sure does," Ramsay said. But the Creeks had been fighting the USA back when his ancestors were U.S. citizens. That made him feel strange whenever he thought about it. The Confederate States had been part of the United States longer than they'd been free. If they'd lost the War of Secession the damnyankees had forced on them, they'd still be part of the USA. He scowled, thinking, *Christ, what an awful idea.*

Perhaps luckily, he didn't have time to do much in the way of pondering.

When you were digging like a gopher trying to get underground before a hawk swooped down and carried you away, worries about what might have been didn't clog your mind.

Colonel Lincoln, whose two-jewel insigne was twice as absurd as Ramsay's, came up to look over the progress the Creek regiment had made. He nodded his approval. "Good job," he told Ramsay. "You've got foxholes back toward town dug, so you can fall back if you need to, you've got the machine guns well sited, you've done everything I can think of that you should have."

"Thank you, sir," Ramsay said. "And this isn't any ordinary town, either." He told Lincoln the story of how Nuyaka had got its name.

"Is that a fact?" Lincoln said.

"Yes, sir," Moty Tiger answered when Ramsay glanced his way. Colonel Lincoln shook his head in bemusement. Like Ramsay, he was careful to do or say nothing that might offend the Indians he commanded. But Nuyaka, any way you looked at it, was pretty damn funny.

Lincoln peered back toward Okmulgee. Smoke and dust were rising up above the hills rimming the valley in which the town sat. The rumble of artillery carried across the miles. "They're pounding each other again," he said.

"Sure sounds that way, sir," Ramsay agreed. "I'm glad to be out of there, you want to know the truth. This here"—he waved at the Creeks preparing the position in front of Nuyaka—"it ain't cavalry fighting, but it's better than what it was back there. For now it's better, anyways."

"For now," Colonel Lincoln echoed. "The fight around Okmulgee has got itself all bogged down, the way things are in Kentucky and Virginia and Pennsylvania: a whole lot of men battling it out for a little patch of ground. But Sequoyah's got too much land and not enough men for most of it to be like that. And where men are thinner on the ground, you can get some movement."

"Not cavalry sweeps," Ramsay said mournfully. "Hell of a thing, training for years to be able to fight one kind of way, and then when the war comes, you find you can't do it."

"Machine guns," Lincoln said. By the way he said it, he couldn't have come up with a nastier curse if he'd tried for a week. He pointed to the ones the Creeks were setting up. "They'll mow down the Yankees if they try to come in this direction, but they mow down horses even better than they do men."

"Yes, sir, that's a fact," Ramsay said. He thought back to the days when the Confederates had been raiding up into Kansas rather than U.S. troops pressing down into Sequoyah. "If this war ever really gets moving again, it'll have to be with armored motorcars, not horses."

"Armored motorcars?" Moty Tiger said. "I read about those in the newspapers. Bad to run up against, are they?"

"You shoot a horse, it goes down," Ramsay said dryly. "You shoot one of those motorcars, the bullets mostly bounce off. It's got machine guns, too, and it keeps right on shooting at you. I'm just glad the damnyankees don't have a whole lot of them."

"More than we do." Captain Lincoln sounded grim. "Back before the war started, they were building a lot more automobiles than we were."

"They come this way, we'll deal with 'em, sir," the Creek sergeant said. Ramsay didn't want to discourage pluck like that. The Creeks had turned out to make far better, far steadier soldiers than he'd ever figured they would. One of the reasons was, they thought they could do anything. When you thought like that, you were halfway—maybe more than halfway—to being right.

They got the rest of that day, that night, and the first hour or so of daylight the next morning to dig in before the first U.S. patrols started probing their positions. Pickets in rifle pits well in front of the main Creek position traded gunfire with the Yankees.

Things had changed over the past year. When the war was new, infantry running up against opposition would mass and then hurl itself forward, aiming to overwhelm the foe by sheer weight of numbers. Sometimes they did overwhelm the foe, too, but at a gruesome cost in killed and wounded.

No more. The damnyankees coming down toward Nuyaka from the north must have been veteran troops. When they started taking fire, they went to earth themselves and fired back. Instead of swarming forward, they advanced in rushes, one group dashing up from one piece of cover to another while more soldiers supported them with rifle fire that made the Creeks keep their heads down, then reversing the roles.

In danger of being cut off from their comrades, the pickets retreated to the main line. When the U.S. troops drew a little closer, the machine guns opened up on them, spraying death all along the front. Again, the U.S. soldiers halted their advance where a year before they would have charged. It was as if they were pausing to think things over.

Not far from Ramsay, Moty Tiger peered out over the forward wall of the trench. "Uh-oh," he said. "I don't like it when they stop that way. Next thing that happens is, they start shooting cannon at us."

"You're learning," Ramsay told him. He looked back over his own shoulder. The Confederates had promised a battery of three-inch field pieces to help the Creek Nation Army hold Nuyaka. Ramsay hadn't seen any sign of those guns. Getting shelled when you couldn't shell back was one of the joys of the infantryman's life with which he'd become more intimately acquainted than he'd ever wanted.

Instead of rolling out the artillery, though, the damnyankees, as if to give Moty Tiger what he'd said he wanted, rolled out a couple of armored motorcars. The vehicles didn't come right up to the trench line. They cruised back and forth a couple of furlongs away, plastering the Creek position with machine-gun fire.

Ramsay threw himself flat as bullets stitched near. Dirt spattered close by, kicked up by the gunfire. Cautiously, he got to his feet again. "Shoot out their tires, if you can," he shouted to the Creek machine-gun crews. The tires weren't armored, although these motorcars, unlike the first ones Ramsay had encountered, carried metal shields covering part of the circumference of the wheels.

One of the armored motorcars slowed to a stop. The Creeks cheered. It was less of a victory than they thought, though, as they soon discovered. The motorcar, though stopped, kept right on shooting. "Where are those damn guns?" Ramsay growled. "A target you'd dream about—"

Sometimes dreams did come true. He'd just sent a runner back toward Okmulgee to demand artillery support when earth started fountaining up around the automobile. Its hatches flew open. The two-man crew fled for the nearest Yankee foxhole moments before the machine was hit and burst into flames. The other armored motorcar skedaddled, shells bursting around it. It hid itself behind bushes and trees before it got knocked out. The Creeks yelled themselves hoarse.

"The damnyankees already have one New York," Ramsay said to Moty Tiger, trying to pronounce the name as the Indian did. "What the hell do they need with two?" His sergeant grinned at him by way of reply.

XVII

Sylvia Enos finished tying George, Jr.'s, shoe. Her son had just turned five; pretty soon she or, better, George would teach him to tie shoes for himself, and that would be one less thing she'd have to worry about every morning. Quite enough would be left as things were.

She looked up. In the half minute during which she'd been dealing with those shoes, Mary Jane had disappeared. "Come here this instant," she called. "We're going to be late."

"No!" Mary Jane said from the bedroom she shared with her brother. *No* was her standard answer to everything these days; not long before, she'd answered *no* when asked if she wanted a piece of licorice. She'd realized that tragic error a moment too late, and burst into tears.

Sylvia didn't have much time or patience left. "Do you want me to whack you on the fanny?" she demanded, clapping her hands together.

"No!" Mary Jane answered, this time with alarm instead of defiance.

"Then come out here and behave yourself," Sylvia said. "I have to go to work, and you have to go to Mrs. Coneval's. Come out right now, or—"

Mary Jane appeared, both hands pressed over her bottom to protect it from the slings and arrows of an outraged mother. Sylvia knew she shouldn't laugh; that just encouraged her daughter's mischief, and a two-year-old needed no such encouragement. She couldn't help herself, though.

Virtuously, George, Jr., said, "*I'm* all ready, Mama."

"Good," Sylvia said. "And now Mary Jane is ready, too, so we'll go to Mrs. Coneval's." She held out her hands. George, Jr., took one and Mary Jane the other. They paraded down the hall to Brigid Coneval's flat.

At Sylvia's knock, Mrs. Coneval opened the door. "Ah, 'tis the hero's children," she said. "Come in, the two of ye." George, Jr., puffed out his little chest and looked impressive and important. It all went over Mary Jane's head.

"I'll see the two of you tonight," Sylvia said, bending down to kiss her children.

"Good-bye, Mama," George, Jr., said. "I'll be good."

"I'm sure you will, lamb." Sylvia turned to Mary Jane. "You'll be good, too, won't you?"

"No," Mary Jane said, which might have been prediction or warning or—Sylvia hoped—nothing more than the answer she gave to most questions these days.

"She's no trouble at all," Brigid Coneval assured Sylvia. "Good as gold, she is . . . most o' the time. But if I've coped with my own hellions so long, she'll have to go some to put me out of kilter." She cocked her head to one side. "And how does it feel to be after having your husband's picture in the papers and all?"

"It feels wonderful. We have a copy of the *Globe* framed in the kitchen," Sylvia answered, and then, "I wish they'd never done it."

Confusion spread across Mrs. Coneval's long, pale face. "Begging your pardon, but I don't follow that."

"Now that the papers have blabbed what that fishing boat did and how it did it, it'll be harder and more dangerous for them to do it again," Sylvia explained. "I wish the Rebs didn't have any idea what sort of trick they used."

"Ah, now I see," Mrs. Coneval breathed. "God bless you, Mrs. Enos, and may He keep your man safe." She crossed herself.

"Thank you," Sylvia said from the bottom of her heart. She did a lot of praying, too. It had brought George safe from the sea to North Carolina, and from North Carolina back to Boston.

Whatever God chose to do about that, He wouldn't let her stand around flapping her gums with Brigid Coneval. She hurried downstairs. The air was cooler and fresher outdoors than in the apartment building, but that wasn't saying much. It was going to be hot and sticky. It was usually hot and sticky in Boston in July, but she hadn't known what that meant, not really, till she'd put in a few shifts under a corrugated tin roof at the fish-canning plant.

She got onto the trolley. A man who looked like a factory worker stood up and gave her his seat. She sat down with a murmur of thanks. Men were more inclined to be gentlemanly in the morning, she'd found, than in the evening after a full day's work, when they were tired and wanted to get a load off their feet. Then it was everyone for himself. She'd heard women complain and shame men to their feet, but she never did that herself. She knew all about being tired.

Riding the streetcar gave her a few minutes to herself, even in a crowd of strangers. She spent half the time thinking of the pork chops she'd fry up for supper when she got home that night, the other half, inevitably, worrying about George. The *Spray* was out on patrol again. What she hoped most of all was that the boat would come back from the Banks with a hold full of hake and halibut, having seen no Confederate, Canadian, or British warships of any description. That had happened on one cruise already, and was probably the only thing the Navy was doing during the war to turn a profit.

Next best would be to sink an enemy submersible. George would have disagreed with those priorities, but what did he know? Going face to face with the Rebs and Canucks put him in even more danger than simply going out to sea, and so many men never came home in time of peace.

And, of course, the tables could turn. That was even more likely now, thanks to the enterprising reporters who'd published their stories about fishing boats that were so much more than they seemed. Making the foe wary might tempt him to shoot at long range or make him more watchful for the towed submarine or any number of other unpleasant possibilities.

On that cheerful note, she got off the trolley and walked to the factory. A couple of cats stared at her with green, green eyes. The smell of the fish-canning plant—and the scraps outside—drew them like a magnet. She wondered if they were jealous, watching her go into the dingy building. If they were, it was only because they didn't know what she did in there.

Her children's best efforts to the contrary notwithstanding, she got to work on time. "Has the machine been behaving itself?" she asked Elena Gomes, who worked the night shift.

"It did not jam much—not too much," the other woman answered. "Some nights, I think it has the Devil in it, but tonight it was not bad." She patted her lustrous black hair. Instead of cutting it short, as most of the women at the factory did, she wore it under a hairnet to keep it from getting caught in the machinery.

"That's something, anyway," Sylvia said, though what the label-gluing machine did on one shift was no guarantee of what it would do on the next. For the moment, as shifts changed all through the canning plant, the production line was quiet.

"Your husband, he is well?" Elena asked.

"As far as I know, yes," Sylvia said. "But his boat put to sea again three nights ago, so I won't know for certain till they come back from the trip." And if something did go wrong, she wouldn't know till days, maybe weeks, passed. Dead? Captured? She'd been through the agony of wondering once; she didn't know if she could stand to go through it again.

The Portuguese woman made the sign of the cross. "I pray for him, as I do for my own husband."

"Thank you," Sylvia said, as she had to Brigid Coneval. "How's your Pedro?" Elena Gomes' husband was in the Army, somewhere out in the Southwest. "Have you heard from him lately?"

"I got a letter yesterday, thank God," Elena said. "They are moving farther into Texas, to a town called—" She frowned. "Lummox? Is that right?"

"Lubbock, I think." Sylvia remembered seeing the name in the newspaper. "I'm glad he's all right."

"Oh, so am I," the other woman replied. "He says they are thinking of making him a corporal. He talks it down: he says it is only because—again, thank God—he has stayed alive. But I can tell he is proud of it. Still, it is nothing like what your George has done. To be one of the crew that sank a submarine—" Her eyes glowed.

What George had had to say about that was that the *Spray* had gone to sea with a big SINK ME! sign painted on the cabin, and that the Confederate submarine had thought it was part of the free-lunch spread at a saloon. He didn't think being a decoy was worth getting as excited over as the papers had gone and done.

Before Sylvia found a way to put any of that into words, the conveyor belt gave a couple of jerks. She knew what that meant—it would start up in earnest in a minute or two. Elena Gomes understood that, too. "I am going to go home and try to get some sleep," she said with a wan smile, "so I can come back tonight and do the same thing all over again. Such is life." She hurried away.

Such is life, Sylvia thought: drudgery, exhaustion, never enough money, never the time to lift up your head and look around. Wasn't it last week she'd had George, Jr., the day before yesterday she'd given birth to Mary Jane? If it wasn't, where had the time gone? How had it slipped past her? She hadn't even been working then—if, that is, you didn't call raising children work. People who didn't have to do it didn't think it was, which, as far as she was concerned, only showed how little they knew. Or maybe they thought it wasn't work because women didn't get paid for it. That was nothing but more foolishness.

With a clatter, the conveyor belt got rolling in earnest. Sylvia thought, *The trouble with this job is that I don't get paid . . . enough.* If she'd been a man, she would have made more money. Then again, if she'd been a man, she probably would have been in the armed forces by now. Soldiers and sailors didn't get paid much, either, and the things they did . . .

She remembered George talking about the torpedo that had slammed into the Confederate submersible. "It was there," he'd said, "and then it was in two pieces, sinking. Nobody had a chance to get out." He'd known some pride in being part of the ambush that sank it, but also a sailor's horror of watching any vessel go to the bottom.

She pulled the levers on her machine. As Elena had said, it was behaving pretty well. When the paste reservoir ran low, she poured more into it from a big bucket that sat by her feet. She had to keep an eye on the labels, too, to make sure the machine didn't run out of them. She'd let the feeder go empty once, and had the foreman screaming at her because unlabeled cans were going down the line. She never wanted that to happen again.

She ate dinner with Isabella Antonelli, whose husband had been a fisherman and these days was fighting somewhere up in Quebec. "He say they going to do something big," she told Sylvia. "What it is, I don' know. The—how you say?—the censor, he scratch out so much, I cannot tell what his big thing is gonna be."

"I hope he'll be all right," Sylvia answered, not knowing what else to say. Isabella nodded and then started complaining about her machine, which fastened strips of tinned steel into cylinders that would be soldered to make the bodies of cans. If half of what she said was true, it made the labeling machine a delight by comparison. But she liked to complain, so who could guess whether half was true?

When she finally slowed down about the machine, she said, "Your husband, he's a hero. You don't get no extra money for that, so you no have-a to work here?"

"I wish I did," Sylvia said. "But what I really wish is that we weren't at war at all, so he could just catch fish and make a living and we wouldn't have to worry about anything else. I wish we never had the war."

"So do I," Isabella Antonelli said. "But we have it. What can you do?"

"Nothing," Sylvia answered bleakly. "Nothing at all." She gulped her cold coffee and went back to work.

Behind Lucien Galtier, a motorized rumble and rattle and racket grew rapidly. He paid it no mind, clucking to his horse and saying, "In a little while, we shall be at Rivière-du-Loup. No point in hurrying on such a fine day—I am certain you agree." If the horse disagreed, it didn't tell him so.

Brakes squealed. Lucien did not look back over his shoulder. Then he heard the raucous squawk of a horn's rubber bulb as it was vigorously squeezed again and again. Through those squawks, an American bellowed at him: "Get out of the road, you goddamn stinking Canuck, or we'll run you down!"

Now Galtier did look back. Sure enough, he was holding up a convoy of big, snorting White trucks, all of them painted the green-gray of the U.S. uniform. "I am desolate," he said, dropping the reins so he could spread his hands in apology. "I did not know you were there."

The driver of the lead truck shook a fist at him through the dust-streaked windscreen. "Get the hell out of the road," he shouted again, "or we won't know you're there."

Lucien fumbled as he picked up the reins, which made the driver start squeezing that rubber bulb again. Lucien tipped his hat to show he did at last hear, then guided the wagon onto the verge to let the truck convoy pass. Delaying things any longer, he calculated, would be more dangerous than enjoyable.

Truck after truck roared past, gears clashing as drivers upshifted for better speed. The noise of the growling engines was appalling. So was the dust the trucks kicked up from the road. The horse snorted indignantly and twitched its ears, as if blaming Lucien for the gray, choking cloud that enveloped them. "I am sorry," Lucien told the animal. "We would have had the same trouble had we pulled off right away." The horse looked unconvinced. So did the chickens in the slotted crates in the back of the wagon; they squawked almost as loud as the truck horn and flapped their wings in a vain effort to escape. Galtier wasted little sympathy on them, not when they were bound for the stew pot or the roasting pan.

He counted the trucks that passed him, noting how many carried men and how many supplies. Having done that, he laughed at himself. The army stint he'd put in had trained him well: when in contact with the enemy, gather intelligence. The only problem with that was, he had nowhere to convey the intelligence he'd gathered. And even if he had known to whom to convey it, how much good would that have done him? Anyone on this side of the St. Lawrence would have needed a wireless set to pass the information on to where it might do some good. He knew no one with such exotic equipment.

Dust from the trucks hung in the air when he got back onto the road and headed up toward Rivière-du-Loup once more. Before he got to town, he had to pull off again to let another convoy pass him. As he had with the first one, he waited to the last possible moment and then a couple of moments more, forcing the whole convoy to slow down to a horse's walking speed before finally noticing the trucks were there and getting out of their way.

"How much good does this do, do you think?" he asked the horse when they started traveling again, after the curses of the U.S. drivers finished washing over him. "This getting them angry and giving them a couple of minutes' delay, is it worthwhile?"

Again, the horse did not answer. He got the distinct impression the horse did not care, although the animal had no great use for trucks whether delayed or rolling past. *Foolish beast,* he thought.

As he drew near Rivière-du-Loup, the wagon rolled through an enormous U.S. encampment: more tents than he had ever imagined, and he was familiar with tents. Soldiers bustled about, doing soldierly things. But for the color of their uniforms and the fact that their brand of soldiers' slang had no French in it, they might have been the sons of the men with whom he had served a generation before.

Up near the river, artillery pieces squatted like long-necked, dangerous beasts. Some of them were big, six- or eight-inchers, not just the three-inch popguns that had been here the year before. The Americans could answer warships in kind now. He still remembered the weight of metal the cruiser had been able to hurl at those popguns; thinking about it brought a smile to his lips.

Out in the river, guns boomed. For a moment, he hoped naval vessels were shelling the camp: it would be a target of the sort about which gunners dreamed. But then he realized it was the battery the Americans had placed on the Isle aux Lièvres, the Isle of Hares, out in the St. Lawrence. He wondered if the guns were shooting at ships on the river or at the Canadian and British positions on the north bank. Either way, they would miss if God was kind.

Those guns out on the Isle aux Lièvres had shelled the south bank once, after a couple of companies of picked men rowed over from St.-Siméon or somewhere nearby under cover of darkness and wiped out the American garrison. The locals had laughed about that for weeks, even though the soldiers of the British Empire hadn't been able to hold the island against a massive U.S. counterattack.

Into Rivière-du-Loup Lucien rode, enjoying such summer warmth as Quebec offered. Before he got to the market square, U.S. soldiers not once but twice inspected him, the horse, the wagon, and the chickens he hoped to sell. They didn't turn him back and they didn't demand payment in exchange for letting him go forward, so he supposed he had no real complaint. Maybe they thought he'd hidden a bomb in one of the capons. He thought about making a joke with them about that, but decided not to. They did not look as if they would be amused.

He found a place to hitch his wagon not far from the Loup-du-Nord. He thought about going in, too, but the place was bustling with soldiers. Neither the idea of good liquor nor that of leering at Angelique and the other barmaids was enough to counterbalance their presence.

As soon as he had his chickens on display, American soldiers came up and started buying them. The birds mostly went for a couple of dollars apiece; prices had shot up since the Americans came into Quebec, because there was little to buy here. Besides, most of the soldiers knew no more about haggling than they did about archery.

He soon found one exception to that rule, a small, swarthy man older than the latest class or two of conscripts. Where most of the U.S. soldiers looked like English-speaking Canadians, this one might have been a cousin of Lucien's. He also understood something of bargaining, to Galtier's disappointment. He had patience, which most of the Americans signally lacked. "Come on, Antonelli, you gonna stand there all day?" one of his comrades asked. "Buy the damn chicken, already."

"I'll buy it when this guy here quits trying to steal my money," Antonelli said. He turned back to Galtier. "Awright, you damn thief, I'll give you a dollar ten for the bird."

"*I* steal?" Galtier assumed an injured expression. "I? No, *monsieur*, you are the thief. Even at a dollar forty, it is for me no bargain."

He ended up selling Antonelli the hen for a dollar and a quarter. He could have done better by refusing to deal with the American at all and getting more from a less able haggler, but he enjoyed the bargaining enough to make the deal at that price simply for the sake of having met a worthy opponent. Marie, no doubt, would cluck at him when he got back to the farm, but money was not the only thing that brought satisfaction to life.

When the Americans had snapped up all the chickens he had for sale, he put the crates back in the wagon and then wandered over to the edge of the river. More boats were tied up at the quays below the town than he was used to seeing there. Not all of them were the usual sort of fishing boats and tramp steamers, either. He didn't think he'd ever seen so many barges at Rivière-du-Loup. A lot of them looked new, as if they'd just been put together from green timber and had engines bolted to them. They wouldn't go far or fast. For a moment, he had trouble figuring out why they were there.

Then he did, and crossed himself. As soon as he'd done that, he looked around to see whether anyone—especially Father Pascal—had noticed. But the priest was nowhere in sight, for which he thanked God. So many men around Rivière-du-Loup, so many barges and boats of all kinds assembled here, could mean only one thing: the Americans were making ready to cross the St. Lawrence and inflict on the rest of Quebec all the delights their rule had brought here.

"*Mauvais chance*—bad luck," he murmured under his breath. Too much of France already lay under the boots of the Americans' German allies—would all the French speakers in the world now be occupied and tyrannized? "Prevent it, God," he said quietly.

He wanted to run to the church, so his prayers would have more effect. But who presided over the church in Rivière-du-Loup? No one other than the odious Father Pascal. To the priest, his own advancement counted for more than the fate of his countrymen. When the day of reckoning came (if God was kind enough to grant such), Father Pascal would have much for which to answer.

Glumly, Lucien walked to the general store and bought his monthly ration of kerosene with some of the money he'd got from selling the hens. He was pleased by how little he paid for it; compared to other things, it hadn't risen so sharply. It would, he expected, but it hadn't yet. He understood military bureaucracies and how slowly they worked, having been part of one himself, but hadn't expected to be able to turn that to his advantage. With another half-dollar of hen money, he bought hair ribbons in several bright colors for his womenfolk.

He put the kerosene and the ribbons into the back of the wagon. He was just coming up onto the seat when Angelique came out of the Loup-du-Nord hand in hand with an American soldier. "Look at that little whore," one housewife said to another near Lucien.

The second woman's claws also came out: "Why doesn't she simply tie a mattress on her back? It would save so much time."

And then, as if to prove their own virtue and piety, the two of them turned their backs on the barmaid and, noses in the air, strode into the church: Father Pascal's church. Galtier sat scratching his head for a minute or two, then flicked the reins and got the wagon moving. Getting out of Rivière-du-Loup felt more like escape than it ever had before.

"It is a very strange thing," he told the horse when he was out in open country and could safely have such conversations, "how those women despise Angelique, who at most gives the Americans her body, and think nothing of going in to confess themselves to Father Pascal, who has assuredly sold the Americans his soul. Do you understand this, *mon cheval*?"

If the horse did understand, it kept its knowledge to itself.

"Well, I do not understand, either," Lucien said. "It is, to me, a complete and absolute mystery. Soon, though, I shall be home, and then, thank God, I shall have other things to worry about."

The horse kept walking.

Nellie Semphroch pasted a sign to the boards that still did duty for her shattered front window: YES, WE HAVE ICED COFFEE. She'd lettered it herself, along with the slogan just below: COME IN & TRY IT. IT'S GOOD. With summer's heat and humidity as they were, she would have lost half her business without iced coffee.

"Have to go to the bank," she muttered, and then laughed at herself. Banks in Washington, D.C., weren't safe these days. Anyone with any sense kept his money at home or in his store or buried in a tin can in a vacant lot. A robber might take it away from you, but the Army of Northern Virginia might take it away from the bank. The Confederates, from everything she'd seen of them, made the local robbers seem pikers by comparison.

Off in the distance, artillery rumbled. Nellie hadn't heard that sound since the early days of the war, for the Confederates' opening drive had pushed the front too far north for the gunfire to carry. It had returned with the U.S.

Army's spring offensive, the breakout from Baltimore. But the breakout, like so many breakouts in the war, had not turned into a breakthrough. The Rebs, though they'd drawn back from Pennsylvania, still held most of Maryland, and U.S. forces were nowhere near ready to regain poor Washington.

As if to underscore that, a couple of Confederate soldiers came out of Mr. Jacobs' shoemaker's shop across the street, one of them holding a pair of marching boots, the other shiny black cavalry boots. The fellow with the cavalry boots must have told a joke, for the other Reb laughed and made as if to throw half his own footgear at him.

Nellie ducked back inside the coffeehouse and said, "I'm going over to Mr. Jacobs' for a few minutes, Edna."

"All right, Ma," her daughter answered from behind the counter. The place was busy—too busy, Nellie hoped, for Edna to get into any mischief while she was gone. Nicholas Kincaid wasn't in there soaking up coffee and mooning over Edna, which Nellie took for a good sign.

She had to hurry across the street to keep a big truck from running her down. The colored man at the wheel of the truck laughed because he'd made her scramble. She glared at him till the truck turned a corner and went out of sight. She was a white woman. She deserved better treatment from a Negro. But, she reminded herself sadly, she was also a damnyankee, and so deserving of no respect from Confederates, even black ones.

The bell above the shoemaker's door jingled as Nellie went inside. She'd thought Jacobs was alone, but he was in there talking with another gray-haired, nondescript man. They both fell silent, quite abruptly. Then Mr. Jacobs smiled. "Hello, Widow Semphroch," he said smoothly. "Don't be shy—this is my friend, Mr. Pfeiffer. Lou, Widow Semphroch runs the coffeehouse across the street. She is one of the nicest ladies I know."

"Pleased to meet you, ma'am," Lou Pfeiffer said.

"And you, Mr. Pfeiffer, I'm sure." Nellie glanced over at the shoemaker. "Since you have your friend here, Mr. Jacobs, I'll come back another time."

"Don't hurry off," Jacobs said. "Mr. Pfeiffer—Lou—was telling me something very interesting. You might even want to hear it yourself. If you're not too busy, why don't you stay?"

"Well, all right," Nellie said, a little surprised. She'd intended giving Mr. Jacobs some of the dirt she'd gleaned from the coffeehouse, and he had to know that. He wouldn't have wanted her to do it while anyone else was around. So why keep her here when she couldn't speak of what really mattered? She shrugged. "Go ahead, Mr. Pfeiffer."

"I was just telling Hal here what a nuisance it is to try and keep pigeons in Washington these days," Pfeiffer said. *Hal*—Nellie raised an eyebrow. Years across the street from Mr. Jacobs, and she'd never known his first name. His friend went on, "The Rebs don't want anybody having birds these days. Pigeons aren't just pigeons, not to them. A pigeon can carry a message, too, so they've confiscated all the birds they could find."

"But they haven't found all of them, eh, Lou?" Jacobs said.

Pfeiffer shook his head. He had a sly look to him that had nothing to do with his rather doughy features—more the glint in his eye, the angle at which he cocked his head. "Not all of 'em, no. Not mine, for instance. Not some other people's, too. We've got an underground, you might say. We keep birds, but the Rebs don't know it. Makes life exciting, so to speak." He set a finger by the side of his nose and winked.

A few months before, Nellie would have taken his jaunty talk at face value and not even thought to look below the surface. Now— Now she was convinced everything had unplumbed depths. "That *is* interesting, Mr. Pfeiffer," she said. She looked at him, then at Mr. Jacobs: a silent question.

Ever so slightly, the shoemaker nodded. He turned to Pfeiffer and started to laugh. "You see, Lou? Not just a nice lady, but a clever one, too."

"I see," Pfeiffer said agreeably. "I've thought so, from what you've said about her every now and then."

That cleared up the last small doubt Nellie had had. "Can I tell you some interesting things I've heard in the coffeehouse, Mr. Pfeiffer, or would you rather have me wait and tell Mr. Jacobs so he can tell you?"

"She *is* a clever lady," Pfeiffer said, and then, to Nellie, "You can tell me—eliminate the middleman." He and Jacobs both wheezed laughter.

So Nellie, as if casually gossiping, told of the troop movements and other interesting bits of news she'd heard in the coffeehouse over the past couple of days. She got interrupted once, when a colored servant brought in a Confederate officer's boots for resoling. The Negro paid no attention to anything but his business, and was soon gone. Nellie finished her—*report* was the right word for it, she thought.

"Well, well," Lou Pfeiffer said. "Yes, I am glad I still keep pigeons, that I am. Thank you, Widow Semphroch."

"Nellie, isn't it?" Mr. Jacobs said suddenly.

"That's right—Hal," she answered, smiling at him. He smiled back. They'd knocked down a barrier, one they'd taken for granted but one that had been there for a long time. She smiled at Mr. Pfeiffer, too, partly for being what he was, partly for his help in making that barrier fall. "Gentlemen, if you'll excuse me, I have to go back across the street and keep the Rebs in order at the coffeehouse. A pleasure to have met you, Mr. Pfeiffer."

"And you, Widow Semphroch," Pfeiffer said as she went out the door.

When she got back into the coffeehouse, Edna discreetly beckoned her over. She went, curious to see what could make her daughter circumspect. In a low voice, Edna said, "There was a man came in here askin' after you, Ma, and I didn't fancy his looks even a little, if you know what I mean."

Fear leaped up and bit Nellie. The Rebs would have people hunting U.S. spies. "What did he look like?" she asked, forcing herself to speak quietly, too.

"Old and ugly," Edna answered with the callousness of youth. "Either he ought to shave or else he ought to let his whiskers grow, one way or the other. Said his name was Bill or Phil or Pill or something like that." She shrugged. It hadn't been important to her.

A chill ran through Nellie. That sounded altogether too much like Bill Reach to suit her. "If he ever comes back, tell him I don't want his business here. If he doesn't like that, throw him out. I'm sure some of our customers would be delighted to help you do anything you ask."

"Yeah, probably," Edna said; she enjoyed being attractive to the Rebs. Her gaze sharpened. "He's known you for a long time, this fellow, whoever he is, hasn't he?"

"Why do you say that?" Nellie asked, at the same time as she was thinking, *Longer than you've been alive.*

Edna gave back some of that thought: "He said I looked just like you did when you were my age, maybe even younger. Did he know you way back then, Ma? That's a long time ago now."

Don't I know it. Nellie made her shrug quiet, casual, easygoing. "I knew a lot of men when I was a young lady." *And even more when I wasn't being a lady.* "I don't remember anybody named Phil or Pill, though." She hoped her smile was disarming.

It wasn't disarming enough. "How about somebody named Bill?" Edna said.

"A lot of Bills back then." Nellie tried a small joke: "Always a lot of bills, never enough money to pay 'em."

"You're giving me the runaround, Ma." Edna didn't raise her voice, but sounded very certain. She had a right to sound that way; a lifetime with her mother had made Nellie transparent to her. "How well did you know this fellow, anyways? Did you . . . ?" She wouldn't say it, but she was thinking it.

"None of your business," Nellie hissed, and then, louder, "Go serve that man there, would you? He wants himself filled up again."

Edna glared at her, but went over to give the Confederate lieutenant another cup of coffee. "There you go, Toby," she said, smiling a smile very close to the ones Nellie had once had to paste onto her own face.

"Thank you, Miss Edna," Toby said. She put a little extra wiggle into her walk, too; the Reb's eyes followed her every inch of the way back behind the counter. Nellie wanted to grab her daughter and shake her or, better yet, pour a pitcher of iced coffee over her head.

And serving the Confederate hadn't distracted Edna or made her forget what she'd asked her mother. "C'mon, Ma," she said. "Don't tell me you actually had a *life* back then?"

"Whatever I had back then, it wasn't very good," Nellie said. "All I'm trying to do is keep you from going through the same things I did."

Edna shrugged. "You got through 'em, looks like, even if you're too goody-goody to talk about it now. You don't want me to have a good time, that's all. It ain't fair."

Nellie sighed. They'd had this fight before. Likely they were going to go right on having it, too. "You don't know what you're talking about," Nellie said. That was true. It was also the problem. Edna didn't know, and was wild to find out. *I won't let her,* Nellie told herself fiercely. *I won't.*

Bremen, Kentucky, had been a coal-mining town before the U.S. First Army drove the Confederates out of it. Abner Dowling had no doubt the place had been grimy and ugly and smelly back in peacetime. Now it was grimy, ugly, doubly smelly thanks to so many dead horses nearby, and wrecked to boot. Given a choice, it was not where Dowling would have made First Army headquarters. He had not been given a choice.

"Dowling!" George Armstrong Custer shouted. His rasping, old man's voice put his adjutant in mind of the braying of the donkey in the fairy tale about the musicians of Bremen. Dowling had done plenty of braying himself, reading his nieces the fairy tale. They'd giggled wildly, back ten years before. "Dowling!" Custer yelled again.

"Coming, sir," Dowling said. Listening to a real donkey bray wasn't nearly so much fun as impersonating one. The major squeezed his bulk through the narrow doorway of the house Custer had taken over. He came to attention; Custer was a stickler for courtesy—from subordinates. "What can I do for you, sir?"

"Bring me some coffee from the mess," Custer said. "Put some fuel in it before it gets here, too."

"Yes, sir," Dowling said resignedly. He turned to go. Custer didn't drink so much as some officers he'd known—but then, they hadn't been in command of whole Armies, either.

"Do you know," Custer said, "I hardly drank at all—no more than for medicinal purposes—till after we lost the Second Mexican War. No matter the renown I won in that last campaign, the thought of my beloved country having gone down to defeat at the hands of rebels and traitors and stabbed in the back by foreign foes twice in a generation's time was too much for me to bear. Since then, I have been known to indulge myself, as an anodyne if nothing else."

"Yes, sir," Dowling repeated. He didn't know whether the lieutenant general was telling the truth or not. He didn't much care, either. However Custer had first made the acquaintance of the brandy bottle, he'd since become quite intimate with it.

Getting the coffee and adulterating it was a matter of a few minutes. Dowling was carrying the steaming cup back to Custer when the general let out a great bellow, as if he'd been gored by a bull. *Oh, Lord, what now?* Dowling thought. It wasn't, he was sure, that the First Army drive on Morehead's Horse Mill had stalled: it had been obvious for days that U.S. forces weren't going to reach the road junction that had been their goal since they forced the Rebs out of Madisonville any time soon. It also wasn't the casualty figures coming from their efforts to reach the town. Custer viewed casualty figures with considerable equanimity, especially seeing how many of them his own headlong ferocity caused. What was rattling his cage, then?

"Is something wrong, sir?" the major said, advancing with the coffee cup. "Here, drink this and you'll feel better for it." *At least you won't be able to scream while you're drinking it.*

Custer seized the cup and poured its contents down his throat. His face, already red, got redder. He coughed a couple of times before coherent if highly irate speech emerged. "That son of a bitch! That no-good, lying, stinking scoundrel. That fiend in human shape. When I'm through with the bastard, he'll wish he was never born. I already wish he was never born."

"Uh—who, sir?" Dowling asked. If Custer was swearing at General Pershing or one of the other younger officers in the service, Dowling's job was to listen and calm him down and make sure he wouldn't do anything that would damage not only himself (something Dowling didn't mind at all) but also First Army (which would be regrettable).

"Who?" Custer thundered. "That blackguard Davis, that's who!" For a moment, Dowling remained confused, Davis being anything but an uncommon name. Then Custer pointed to the *Scribner's* magazine on his desk. It hadn't been there when Dowling went to get the general's coffee. A messenger must have delivered it to Custer and then disappeared in a hurry.

Dowling felt a certain amount of sympathy for that messenger. Unfortunately, he didn't have the option of disappearing in a hurry. Very cautiously, he asked, "You're disappointed in the coverage you got from Richard Harding Davis?"

"Disappointed? Great heavens, the man proves himself a pathological liar." Custer picked up the offending periodical and thrust it at his adjutant. "See for yourself, Major."

The title of Davis' article was innocuous enough: "The First Army Attacks: Part Two." Part One had run a couple of weeks before, and had been a paean of praise for First Army's courage. Custer had not complained about it at all. Dowling rapidly skimmed through Part Two. The more he read, the more he had to work to keep his face not merely straight but sympathetic. Richard Harding Davis, a manly man himself, had been imperfectly impressed with the person of George Armstrong Custer: "neck wattled like a turkey's," "squinting little pouchy eyes," and "hair that bought its color from a bottle in a vain attempt to hold back Father Time" were some of the choicer epithets.

Davis hadn't had much good to say about the generalship involved in the first gas attack, either. "Opportunity squandered" was a phrase he used several times. "Failure to achieve a breakthrough despite the advantages given by the preceding chlorine barrage" was also sure to raise Custer's hackles. To Dowling's way of thinking, though, the most telling bit of evidence that the war reporter did know what he was talking about was the comment that "up and down the front, troops were committed to battle in a deployment more aggressive than strategically sound." That was Custer's style, set out in black and white for all to see.

"I'm sorry, sir," Dowling said, handing the *Scribner's* back to the commanding general. "Those reporters, they're not to be trusted." Inside, he was chortling. Custer was drawn to publicity like iron filings to a magnet. He'd used it astutely, enabling himself to stay in the Army past what should have been retirement age. Now it had turned on him and bit him. There was a saying about he who lived by the sword, and another one about the pen's being mightier than that sword. Put those together and examine their implications . . .

Custer was not in a mood for logical examinations. "If I ever set eyes on that lying son of a whore again, I'll horsewhip him within an inch of his worthless life. I trusted him to tell the truth about me—"

I trusted him to paint me in glowing colors, the way too many reporters have done for too many years: Dowling had no trouble making his own translation of Custer's remarks.

The general was in full spate now: "—and my boys in the trenches, hearing about this—this tripe, will wonder whether I have the right stuff to lead them against the hereditary foe."

Reluctantly, Dowling admitted to himself that Custer had a point there. The men who did the actual fighting needed to think their general had their best interests at heart and was using them wisely. The loss of that feeling was what had made McClellan's Army of the Potomac fall to pieces after Camp Hill during the War of Secession: figuring they'd get licked no matter what they did, the rank and file gave up.

Back then, the feeling had been justified; studying McClellan's campaigns, Dowling had been struck by the way he was always a step and a half behind Lee. The trouble was, he didn't think Custer's men were justified in having confidence in their commander. Custer was brave and liked to go right at the enemy. Having said that, you exhausted his military virtues.

No—in military politics, at least, he had a solid Machiavellian streak in him. "Davis is TR's fair-haired boy, too," he muttered gloomily. "When the president sees this, I can kiss Canada good-bye forever—he's going to want my scalp."

That last was true only metaphorically, Custer being bereft of hair on the portion of his scalp Indians had customarily removed. "It will be all right, sir," Dowling said, sympathetically if not sincerely. "You and TR fought side by side against the limeys in the Second Mexican War. I'm sure he'll remember that."

Half to himself, Custer muttered, "Teddy always did say his troops outperformed my regulars."

Roosevelt's volunteer cavalry, a regiment of miners and farmers, had indeed done yeoman work in Montana, fighting their British opposite numbers to a standstill, and had led the pursuit after the British blundered straight into Custer's Gatling guns. In Dowling's view, TR had a point; only the armistice U.S. President Blaine had had to accept had kept the triumph from being bigger than it was.

"I'd have licked them anyway," Custer said, sounding as if he was trying to convince himself. Maybe he would have: nobody examined Chinese Gordon's campaigns alongside Napoleon's. Dowling's opinion remained that Custer had probably needed all the help Teddy Roosevelt gave him.

All of which was irrelevant. He pointed to the *Scribner's*. "What do we do about that, sir?"

"First, I shall write a memorial and send it to President Roosevelt, detailing the lies and calumnies and false accusations this Richard Harding Davis has leveled against me," Custer declared, using the correspondent's full name with equally full contempt. Dowling nodded. That was like Custer: if threatened, attack head-on, and never mind scouting the ground first. Sometimes you won that way; more often, you got your nose bloodied. Dowling would have bet TR would be imperfectly delighted to receive Custer's memorial, and that it would sharpen the president's focus on details he might otherwise have ignored. But that was Custer's lookout, not his. The general commanding First Army went on, "And after that is done and on its way, I am going to tear these lying pages out of the *Scribner's* and wipe my backside with them, which is precisely what they deserve, no more, no less. What do you think of *that*, Major Dowling?"

"Revenge is, uh, sweet, sir," Dowling said. He fled then, before his own big mouth got him into even bigger trouble.

Reggie Bartlett sighed with relief as he tramped away from the front line east of Big Lick, Virginia. He and his comrades were battered, worn, filthy, unshaven. Some of them had bandages on minor wounds; several were coughing from chlorine they'd sucked into their lungs during one gas attack or another. None of them would have been invited to serve as a model for a Confederate recruiting poster.

"Here come the rookies," Corporal Robert E. McCorkle said, pointing at the men marching up to replace Reggie's regiment. They were obviously raw troops, just out of one training camp or another. It wasn't so much that they wore clean uniforms; soldiers coming back to the line were often issued fresh clothes. It was more the look in their eyes, the way they stared at the veterans as if they'd never seen such spectral apparitions before.

"You think *we're* ugly," Reggie called to them, "you should see the fellows who aren't walking out."

That drew gales of laughter from his comrades. They'd seen everything war could do to the human body: bullets, shells, gas. If you didn't laugh about some of the things you'd seen, you'd go mad. A couple of men had gone mad, or so convincingly given the appearance of it as to fool their officers. They were out of the fight for good, not merely coming back for baths and delousing and a show or two from a charitable group. Reggie envied them intensely.

"You got to watch out for the front-line lice, boys," Jasper Jenkins said to the replacements. "Some of them babies is big enough so they have you 'stead of you havin' them." He scratched his crotch.

One of the men going up to the line, a tall, thin, pale fellow who looked so earnest that Bartlett pegged him for a preacher's son, went paler yet and visibly gulped. *Poor bastard,* Reggie thought with abstract, abraded sympathy. He'd been fairly fastidious himself, back in his civilian days. Anybody who couldn't stand living like a pig—right down to wallowing in the mud—had an even worse time at the front than everyone else.

He didn't like being in the zigzag communication trenches. They weren't deep enough, and they didn't have any shelters into which to dive if the damnyankees started throwing artillery around. The officers felt the same way he did. "Move along, boys, move along," Captain Wilcox said. "We don't want to camp here."

Major Colleton hustled up and down the line of marching—actually, more like shambling—men to deliver the same message: "Keep it moving there, fellows." His uniform was as spruce and neat as any of the ones the replacements were wearing. With Colleton, it was no more than part of his jaunty persona. He'd have been a plumed cavalryman back in the War of Secession. Cavalry these days wasn't what it had been, though.

And Major Colleton's jauntiness wasn't quite what it had been, either. "Shake a leg," he said. "Sooner we're back behind the secondary trenches, sooner the Yankees won't be able to reach us any more."

A lot of people—Colleton among them, and Reggie Bartlett, too—had gone into the war wanting nothing but the thrill of combat. Bartlett had seen plenty of combat. If he never had another thrill of that sort for the rest of his life, he'd be content.

And he, unlike Major Colleton, was the only man of his family in the Army. "Sir, how's your brother?" he asked when the major came near.

Colleton's face clouded. "He's back home now. From what my sister writes, he's never going to be able to do much for himself any more: a couple of more breaths of chlorine and they'd have put him under the ground. Likely that would have been a mercy." He remembered his manners; he had the virtues of the Southern gentleman. "Kind of you to ask, Bartlett."

Reggie nodded. Colleton went on his way, still urging the men to hurry. He knew just about everyone in the battalion by name. Of course, the battalion carried only about half of its establishment strength, which made learning names easier than it would have been when the war was young.

Machine guns poked their snouts over the parapets of the secondary trenches, ready to rake the ground ahead with fire if a U.S. attack should carry the front-line positions. In theory, Reggie approved of the precaution. In practice, a U.S. attack sufficient to bring those machine guns into action would likely have left him dead, wounded, or captured. He was happy they sat there quiet.

The men in the secondary trenches were veterans: grimy, worn men much like Bartlett and his comrades. A couple of them nodded toward the troops going out of the front line. One fellow touched his butternut slouch hat in what looked like half a salute. He'd likely been up there, and knew what the regiment coming back was escaping.

Behind the secondary trenches, Negro laborers, their uniforms dark with sweat rather than dirt, were digging positions for Confederate guns. "Nice to see those," Reggie said to Jasper Jenkins. "The Yanks have been throwing more shells at us than we've been able to give back."

"Ain't that the sad and sorry truth?" Jenkins looked back over his shoulder toward the front line. "One good thing about havin' to pull back to this side o' the river is, we don't have the damnyankees shellin' us like they was whenever we had to cross it."

"I've been places I liked more than some of those bridges," Bartlett agreed with a reminiscent shudder. His comrade's chuckle said Jenkins appreciated the understatement. Reggie went on, "It might not have been hell on earth, but if it wasn't, you could sure as blazes see it from there."

"You got a good way with words," Jenkins said. "You ever try your hand at writin' or anything like that?"

"Oh, all the time," Bartlett answered. Jasper Jenkins stared at him, maybe wondering whether he'd been serving alongside a famous author without knowing it. Jenkins could sign his name, but that was about as far as his reading and writing took him. Reggie explained: "I worked in a drugstore in Richmond. The pharmacist would make the pills and the syrups, and I'd write 'Take four times a day' or 'Take two before meals' or 'Do not take on an empty stomach' and glue the label to the bottle. It was a wild and exciting life, I tell you that."

"Sounds like it." Jenkins tramped on for another few paces, then said, "Bet you'd trade this for it in a red-hot minute."

"No takers," Reggie said with considerable feeling. Both men laughed as they marched back toward the base camp.

That was near the little town called Clearwater, a name it might once have lived up to but no longer deserved. No little town suddenly inundated by a great sea of butternut tents could hope to keep its water clear. The wonder was that it still had enough water for the men to drink. To men who had spent a turn in the trenches, the idea of sleep under canvas on veritable cots looked very attractive indeed.

But before they could approach the earthly paradise, they had to pass through purgatory. Purgatory was guarded by stern-looking military policemen, and bore the banner, DELOUSING STATION. "Peel off by squads," one of the military policemen shouted, and then, seeing how small the squads were (*What does he know about the front?* Reggie thought scornfully), corrected himself: "No—by sections."

The men had been through the drill before. They didn't need the military policeman, exultant in his petty authority, to tell them what to do. Along with the rest of the men in his section, Reggie went into one of the big delousing tents. He got out of his clothes and handed them to a Negro attendant, who threw his underwear into a pile that would go back to the corps laundry farther from the front and put his outer garments into a bake oven that went by the name of a Floden disinfector, after the genius who had invented the exercise in futility.

That done, Bartlett soaped himself at a footbath. The soap was strong and stinking. He rubbed it into his scalp, his half-grown beard, and the hair around his private parts anyhow, in the hope that it would get rid of the nits he was surely carrying. Then, along with the rest of the men in his section—and, he saw with amusement, with Major Colleton—he leaped with a splash into a great tub, almost a vat, of steaming-hot water.

Everyone was splashing and ducking everyone else. The major joined in the horseplay with no thought for his rank. He came up spluttering by Reggie after someone else pulled him under. Saluting, Reggie said, "It's a rare honor to share an officer's lice, sir."

"Don't know what's so damned rare about it," the battalion commander retorted. "You've been doing it in the trenches for the past year." And he ducked Reggie, holding him under till he thought he was going to drown.

The disinfector baked the soldiers' uniforms for fifteen or twenty minutes. When they were done, more colored attendants issued fresh underwear.

"Feels good—not itching, I mean," Reggie said, buttoning up his tunic. The laundrymen had ironed and brushed it, so he looked as smart as he was going to.

"Enjoy it while it lasts," Jasper Jenkins said.

They went with the rest of the unit to stake places in the tents assigned to them, and then had the rest of the afternoon to themselves. Before they even found the tents, they spotted a crowd of men listening to a tall, thin man in a black sack suit and a straw hat. Reggie's eyes widened. "That's the president!" he exclaimed.

"I'll be a son of a bitch if you're not right," Jenkins said. "Shall we find out what the devil he's got to say for himself?"

"Might as well," Reggie answered. "I was there in Capitol Square in Richmond when he declared war. Might as well find out how he likes it now that he's seen a year's worth." They hurried over and joined the crowd.

Woodrow Wilson was speaking earnestly, but without the changes in tone and volume and the dramatic gestures that were likeliest to win his audience over. He sounded more like a professor than the leader of a nation at war: "We must continue. We must dedicate our lives and fortunes, everything that we are and everything that we have, with the pride of those who know that the day has come when the Confederate States are privileged to spend their blood and their might for the principles that gave them birth and happiness and the peace they have treasured.

"The challenge, in fact, is to all mankind. The choice we make for ourselves must be made with a moderation of counsel and a temperament of judgment befitting our character and our motives as a nation. We must put excited feeling away. Our motive will not be revenge or the assertion of the physical might of the nation, but only the vindication of right, of which we are but a single champion in concert with our allies."

"That's pretty fancy," Reggie murmured to Jasper Jenkins.

"Too goddamn fancy for me," Jenkins whispered back. "What I want to do is, I want to smash those damnyankee bastards. If he'd tell me how we're going to do that, I'd be a sight happier."

"We must stay the course," Wilson said, though a few soldiers drifted away as others came to listen. "We must not swerve suddenly in the middle of the great conflict upon which we have embarked. Giving ourselves over to foolish radicalism at a time like this would only spell disaster for our nation and for all we hold dear."

A light dawned on Reggie. He'd wondered why Wilson had come to the base camp when speaking before soldiers was so obviously unnatural, even uncomfortable, to him. "Presidential election's less than three months off," he said. "He wants to make sure we don't go and elect the Radical Liberal."

"He don't have a hell of a lot to worry about," Jenkins said. "We've never sent one of those crazy bastards to Richmond yet, and I don't reckon we will this time, neither."

"Politicians take all sorts of crazy chances—don't suppose we'd be in this damn war if they didn't," Bartlett said. "But they sure as hell don't take chances about what happens to their party. Wilson can't run again himself, so he wants to make damn sure the vice president, whatever the devil his name is, gets the job."

"Sims? Sands? Something like that," Jenkins said. "Whoever the hell he is, I'm gonna vote for him."

"Me, too, I think," Reggie said, "but I've got better things to do than listen to speeches that tell me to do what I'm already going to do."

"Yeah," Jenkins agreed, and they both walked off. Signboards here and there in the base camp listed attractions. "Let's go watch a boxing match," Reggie suggested.

"White men or colored?" somebody asked.

Bartlett ran his finger down the list of matches to see who was fighting whom. "Our division's colored champion is taking on a fellow from the Confederate Marines who's touring base camps," he said. "That's gonna be the best fight today, no doubt about it."

Nobody argued with him. The crowd around the squared circle was already large by the time he got there. He and Jasper Jenkins so effectively used their elbows to get closer to the ring that they almost started a couple of fights of their own.

They cheered Commodus, the division champion, and lustily booed the Negro from the Confederate Marines, whose name was Lysis. "Which," shouted the soldier doing duty as announcer, "means *Destruction*." More boos.

Reggie bet another soldier two dollars that Commodus would win. He had to pay up depressingly soon: Lysis knocked Commodus cold in the third round. Attendants had to flip water into the fallen champion's face before he could get up and groggily stagger out of the ring.

"That's one tough nigger," Bartlett said as Lysis swaggered around with arms upraised in victory. He gave the fellow he'd bet a two-dollar bill. Then a strange thought struck him: "I wonder how he'd do against a white man his size."

"Bet he wonders, too," the fellow who'd won his money answered. "If he's a smart nigger, he won't let anybody know it, though. Wouldn't be much point if he did—nobody'd let a fight like that happen any which way."

"You're right, I expect," Reggie said. "Niggers start thinking they can fight white men, we got more trouble than we need. And seeing as how we've already got more trouble than we need—"

At that moment, as if on cue in a stage play, one leg started to itch in an all too familiar way. He scratched and swore and scratched again. The Floden disinfector was like an artillery barrage—it made the lice put their heads down, but it didn't get rid of all of them. Some nits always survived and hatched out after you'd had your clothes on for a while. He sighed and scratched still more. No matter what you did, you couldn't win.

Anne Colleton wrote a check, computed the balance remaining in the account, and made a nasty face. Everything cost more these days—niggers' wages, their food, the manure to keep the cotton fields fertile, the kerosene for the lamps in the nigger cottages—everything. She'd got more money than usual for the latest crop she'd brought in, but the rise in prices hadn't stopped since then. If anything, it had got steeper.

A discreet tap at the door to her office made her look up. There stood Scipio, starched, immaculate, stolid. In his deep, rumbling voice, he said, "Ma'am, as you ordered, I have brought the Negro Cassius here for your judgment at his recent abscondment."

She nodded. Disciplining the field hands was a job she undertook from a sense of duty and necessity, not because she enjoyed it. Disciplining a top-flight hand like Cassius was especially delicate. Being too lenient with him would provoke worse indiscipline from the field force. Being too harsh, though, would make another three or four or half a dozen Negroes up and leave the fields for factory work in Columbia or down in Charleston.

But disciplining him didn't look so repugnant as it usually did, not when the alternative was paying more of the bills that made her capital flow away like the waters of the Congaree—in fact, more swiftly than the lazy waters of the river. She nodded again. "Send him in."

"Yes, ma'am." Scipio turned and murmured to his companion in the hallway. Cassius showed himself for the first time. His shapeless cotton garments, brightened only by the blue bandanna he wore round his neck, made a sharp contrast to Scipio's formal livery.

Anne glared at Cassius for a few seconds without saying anything. Scipio silently slipped away, not wanting to hear—or to be known to hear—whatever punishment the mistress of Marshlands meted out. *He respects Cassius' position on the plantation, too,* Anne thought. Yes, she had to proceed with caution.

Cassius could not long bear up under her scrutiny. He cast his eyes down to the hardwood floor. Anne watched him intently. His gaze flicked to right and left, taking in the books that filled the office. She'd deliberately summoned him here, to add the intimidating alien environment to the moral effect of taking punishment from a white.

"What do you have to say for yourself?" she asked, her voice crisp and businesslike. "It had better be good."

He interlocked the fingers of his hands, a gesture almost prayerful in its supplication. "I is sorry, Miss Anne, I truly is," he said. "I couldn't he'p myself." The dialect of the Negroes of the Congaree district spilled thick as molasses from his lips. A white from Charleston would have had trouble understanding it; a white from, say, Birmingham would have been all at sea. So would a black from Birmingham, for that matter. Anne followed his speech as readily as she followed Scipio's formal, precise language. She'd grown up with the Negro dialect all around her. As a child, she'd spoken it half the time, till trained out of it by parents and teachers.

She didn't think of speaking it now. Using her own brand of English helped remind Cassius who was superior, who inferior. " 'Sorry' might be enough to make amends for being gone a day or two," she snapped. "You were gone for four mortal weeks. Where did you go? What did you do? Did you think you could just show up here again one day and go on about your business as if nothing had happened? Answer me!"

Cassius did some more hand-wringing. He was good at it—too good to be altogether convincing. He had a foxy gleam in his eye, too, one that never quite went away no matter how contrite and woebegone the rest of his face looked. "Whe' I was at? Miss Anne, I was up de country a ways. I was huntin'." He nodded in sudden assurance. "Dat's what I was doin'—huntin'."

"I don't believe a word of it," she answered. "If you wanted to go on a long hunting trip, you know you wouldn't have had any trouble arranging it with me. You've done that before—never for four weeks, but you've done it."

He hung his head again. Now she thought she recognized the expression on his face. If he'd been white, he would have blushed. After a long silence, he said, "Miss Anne, kin Ah talk to you like you was a man?"

Not *a white man*, she noted, just *a man*. A suspicion began forming in her mind. "Go ahead," she told him.

He twisted his hands once more, this time, she judged, in embarrassment. She wasn't a man; no one who was had any cause to doubt that. "Miss Anne," Cassius said, "what I huntin', she 'bout nineteen year ol', an' you kin put yo' han's roun' she waist"—he made a circle to show what he meant—"an' yo' fingers, dey touches theyselves. *Dat's* what I was huntin', fo' true."

Since he'd been gone that long, Anne reckoned he'd bagged her, too. He was a good deal more than nineteen—he was a good deal more than twice nineteen—but those things happened. She knew those things happened. She was still angry at the hunter, but not so angry as she had been. "What's her name?" she said. "Whereabouts exactly does she live? How did you meet her?"

"She name Drusilla, Miss Anne. She live on de Marberrys' plantation, over by Fo't Motte. She come into St. Matthews dis one time, I see she, I know I got to have she."

"And so you just went off after her." For all her effort, Anne couldn't make herself sound as severe as she would have liked. Men had their appetites, and whether they were white or black didn't seem to matter much there. A pretty face, a nice shape, and they were off like a shot. Sounding exasperated came easier: "I don't suppose anyone bothered checking your passbook?"

"No, ma'am." Cassius shook his head. But he might have said the same thing before the war. He was far and away the best hunter on the plantation; he was liable to make himself invisible to anyone who wanted to keep an eye on him.

Well, now that he'd come back, he wasn't invisible any more. Turning up the intensity of her glare, Anne said, "I am going to check on you. If I find out you are lying to me, you will regret it."

"I ain't lyin', Miss Anne. I is a truthful man."

"Scipio!" Anne called. When the butler came back, she said, "Take Cassius downstairs and have him wait there. We shall see what we shall see."

She picked up the telephone, rang Jubal Marberry's home, and put her questions to him. "What? Drusilla?" he said, shouting at her; he was old and deaf. "Yes, there's been some new buck nigger sniffing around Drusilla. There's always a buck or two sniffing around Drusilla, same as there's always flies buzzing around sugar water, heh, heh." The last was a wheezy chuckle. Anne wondered if Marberry was too old to go sniffing around Drusilla himself.

But that, whether or not it was his affair, was his concern. He'd told her what she needed to know. She summoned Cassius back to the office. "All right—it seems you were where you say you were. You could have gotten into worse mischief. Even so . . . Of course your pay for the time you were gone is gone, too." Cassius grimaced, but didn't say anything. Anne could have done worse. She did, in fact, do worse: "I'm also going to dock you every other week's pay for the next eight, to take out a matching sum. Losing both may remind you to stay here where you belong and not go chasing after every pretty woman you happen to see."

"Maybe, Miss Anne, but I doubts it." Cassius' grin was jaunty and very, very male. Anne wanted to throw something at him. Instead, she made a sharp gesture of dismissal. Grinning still, Cassius took his leave. *Just like a nigger,* she thought. *Too happy-go-lucky to care he's thrown away two months' pay, plus whatever he wasted on that Drusilla tart.* Anne hoped the Negro wench had soaked Cassius good.

She went back to her bill-paying. A few minutes later, the telephone rang. She was alert as she picked it up—maybe Jubal Marberry had done some more checking and found out that the Negro who'd been keeping Drusilla company wasn't Cassius after all. But the voice on the other end of the line wasn't old and rheumy, but young and vigorous: "Miss Anne? This here's Roger Kimball. I was just callin' to ask how your brother was doin'."

I was just calling to find out whether the coast is clear for me to go up there and sleep with you. Anne Colleton almost laughed in the submariner's face. She could have mortally offended him if she'd told him how much he reminded her of her black hunter. But, instead, she answered the question he'd asked: "I'm sorry, Roger; I'm afraid I have to tell you he's not much improved."

"Oh. I'm right sorry to hear that." *Sorry both ways, probably,* she thought; the wounded tone in his voice certainly suggested he was sorry she wasn't inviting him up despite poor Jacob's condition. And then he said, "Maybe you could come down to Charleston one day and pay me a visit, then."

Anne almost slammed down the earpiece of the telephone. The arrogance Kimball displayed infuriated her—but, as it had on the train to New Orleans, also attracted her. What with Jacob, what with the never-ending bills, what with escapades like Cassius', didn't she deserve a little amusement, a little escape, a little plain, old-fashioned physical relief? Life was about more things than simply running Marshlands. And so, instead of hanging up, she said, "Maybe I will, Roger. Maybe I will."

XVIII

Jefferson Pinkard shoveled a last forkful of ham and eggs into his mouth, then sprang to his feet. Emily, who'd already finished breakfast, was about to head out the door, and he didn't want to let her go without getting a kiss. Every time he took her in his arms, he felt like a brand new bridegroom. He knew how lucky he was, to have that feeling still after years of marriage.

All things considered, though, he'd had better kisses than the one he got this morning. "You all right, darlin'?" he asked his wife.

"I think so," she said. "Lately I'm just tired all the time. That's what it is, I reckon. They're workin' us hard. We got our quota kicked up again the other day—got to turn out more shells, make up for the ones the soldiers're shootin' at the damnyankees."

"Damnyankees," Pinkard muttered. The war had passed a year old now, no end in sight. "Who woulda thought they could fight like this here?" They stood in western Virginia, in Kentucky, in Sequoyah, in Texas, in Sonora. They were pushing Confederate forces out of Pennsylvania and Maryland, and giving the Canadians and British a hard time, too. "Ain't like it was in the last two wars."

Emily nodded, pecked him on the cheek, and hurried off to catch the trolley. Her step didn't have the bounce to it he'd once taken for granted. She wasn't pink and perky, either, the way she had been; maybe working to fill the increased quota was what made her seem so wrung out, so sallow.

"God damn the war," Jeff said sincerely. He grabbed his dinner pail and headed for the Sloss works.

As they did every morning, Agrippa and Vespasian greeted him with polite respect. He accepted that as nothing less than his due. "Leonidas ain't got here yet," Vespasian told him.

"Why ain't I surprised?" Pinkard said scornfully. "You ever hear anything about Pericles?"

"No, suh," Vespasian said. "He still in the jailhouse. I dunno if they ever gonna let him out."

"Hope to Jesus they do," Jeff said. "That Leonidas, he don't have the brains God gave a possum. Hell, the two of you do better'n I do with him, on account of I got to carry all my own weight and about three quarters of his. I been yellin' for a replacement—an' I don't care if he's black or white, long as he ain't stupid—but no luck so far."

Vespasian and Agrippa looked at each other. Pinkard wondered if he'd offended them, calling Leonidas stupid. So much landed on Negroes in the Confederacy, they stuck together and defended their own whether their own deserved it or not. But, God damn it to hell, Leonidas *was* stupid. He would have been stupid if he were white. Hell, he would have been stupid if he were green.

Slowly, cautiously, Vespasian said, "Mistuh Pinkard, suh, this here would be a different place if mo' people cared about gettin' the job done an' less of 'em cared about who was doin' it." When Jeff didn't blow up at that remark, the black steelworker made another, even more wary, comment: "Not jus' a different place. A better place."

"Get your ass out of here. Go on, go home," Pinkard said. "You don't want those policemen throwin' you in the jug for sedition."

Vespasian took off, Agrippa right behind him. Pinkard looked after them with something as close to approval as he was likely to give two Negroes. They did their job, they didn't complain—much, they didn't try to rock the boat. What more could you want from people?

He looked around. Still no sign of Leonidas. He didn't miss him. A lot of ways, he was better off without him. Handling his shift by himself would leave him dog-tired when the closing whistle blew, but the world wouldn't end on account of that. Jeff knew what he was doing.

Leonidas came in about half an hour late. The floor foreman reamed him out about it as he started to work. When the fellow finally let him be, he shook his head and said, "Lord, I wish that man would shut hisself up. Got me a hangover, make my po' head ring like a bell."

Pinkard grunted. He'd done that—once in a great while. When your head already felt as if somebody were forging steel in there, going to a place where they really were forging steel wasn't high on the list of enjoyable things. Leonidas had been working here for only a couple of months, and this was a long way from the first time he'd strolled in a good deal the worse for wear. *Stupid,* Jeff thought again. Some people belonged in the cotton fields.

Leonidas got through the day without maiming either himself or Pinkard.

He managed partly by not doing much, but that didn't matter, since he never seemed to do much. Pinkard minded less than he would have with a more capable partner. The more Leonidas did, the more he was liable to foul up.

The quitting whistle made the young Negro jerk as if he'd sat on a nail. "Thank God, I can get out of here," he said, and proceeded to do just that, moving faster than he had out on the floor.

Pinkard followed more slowly. He was just as tired as he would have been had Leonidas stayed home with an ice bag or whatever his preferred hangover cure was. He hadn't had to do quite so much as he would have had Leonidas stayed home, but being careful for two was hard work.

When he got back to his house, he built up the fire in the stove, sliced a few potatoes, and set them to frying in lard in a black iron skillet likely made from metal worked at the Sloss foundry. They'd go nicely with the pork roast Emily had put in the oven over a low fire before she went off to work. It wasn't really cooking, he told himself, only a way to save time and have supper ready sooner.

Emily came in about twenty minutes after he did. "Smelled those potatoes outside, comin' up the walk," she said. "They always smell so good like that, give me some of my appetite back."

"You haven't hardly been eating enough to keep a bird alive," Pinkard said. He took the potatoes off the stove so they wouldn't burn while he was kissing his wife. He wondered if she was finally in a family way, only not far along enough to be sure. She was tired all the time, she hadn't been eating well, and he'd noticed at breakfast how sallow she was.

He took another look at her in the evening sunlight pouring through the kitchen window. She wasn't just sallow—her skin was downright yellow. "Honey, what the dickens is the matter with you?" he demanded, and heard the alarm clanging in his voice.

"What do you mean, what's the matter with me?" Emily said.

He held her hand up in a sunbeam. It looked all the more yellow against his own rough, red, scarred skin. "I mean you're only a couple steps this way from bein' the color of a baby chick, that's what."

"Oh, that," his wife answered. "I didn't even hardly notice. It happens to a lot of the girls who work around the smokeless powder like me. It does somethin' to your liver, blamed if I know what, but it makes you yellow that way. Like I say, some of the girls are almost lemon color."

"Does it get better?" Jeff demanded.

"Oh, yeah, it does," Emily said casually. "When somebody gets sick—not just yellow, I mean, but really sick—they move her to another section of the plant for a while, till she gets over it. We haven't had but a couple of people come down that bad."

"Oh." Pinkard was about to shout at her, to demand that she quit her job and come back home where she belonged. The words died unspoken. People got killed every year at the Sloss works, and had been getting killed there long before the war pushed everybody up into a higher gear. He remembered poor Sid Williamson. Emily and her comrades were making munitions for the CSA. The country depended on them, hardly less than it did on the courage and tenacity of the Confederate soldiers.

"It'll be all right, darlin'," Emily said. "Now why don't you go sit down? I'll finish doin' up the potatoes and bring you your supper."

Jeff went and sat down. His wife had the right way of looking at things, and he couldn't very well complain about it. He had to hope her supervisors or foremen or whatever they called them there were paying attention to what they were doing. From what she'd said, it sounded as if they were.

When she came in with a full plate for him, he asked anxiously, "This color you're getting, it will go away if you stop doin' what you're doin', right?"

She nodded. "I've seen it happen with some of the other girls, the ones they had to move away from the powder. But this here, what I've got, it ain't hardly nothin'. And besides"—she cocked her head at a saucy angle and stuck out her hip—"ain't you got a yen for a high-yellow gal?"

He'd just taken his first mouthful, and almost choked on it. Men told smoking-car and after-supper stories about Negro women with a lot of white blood in them. They were supposed to provide some of the fanciest stock in the fanciest sporting houses all over the CSA. Jeff didn't know anything about fancy sporting houses, not from experience. Some of the stories about high-yellow women were pretty fancy all by themselves, though.

He tried to sound severe: "The way you do talk." He couldn't do it; he started laughing. So did Emily. He said, "Gal I got a yen for is you. An' if I say that after the day I put in, you better know it's the truth."

"I like that," Emily said. "I feel the same way about you." She'd always been a bold-talking woman. A lot of men, Pinkard supposed, wouldn't have liked that. He didn't understand why. As far as he was concerned, thinking about it and talking about it were almost as much fun as doing it.

After supper, he dried pots and dishes, as he'd been doing for a while. No sooner had he put the last plate back in the cupboard than Emily said, "You are the helpingest man. That's another reason I love you."

"Is that a fact?" He still didn't quite know himself how he felt about doing women's work. He never told anybody at the foundry he did it, for fear people would say he was henpecked. Emily usually didn't say much about it, either, maybe to keep him from worrying his own mind. Now that she had said it, he felt obliged to answer gruffly: "You know why I'm doin' this, don't you?"

"Why, dear, I haven't got the faintest idea." Her smile and her voice and the way she stood all conspired to make a liar out of her. "Why don't you tell me?"

Instead of telling her—or rather, instead of telling her with words—he picked her up and carried her into the bedroom. She squealed and beat at his shoulders, but she was laughing while she did it. Getting out of his own clothes was the work of a moment. Getting her out of hers required more complicated unbuttonings, unhookings, unlacings. His hands were big and clumsy, but he managed.

He scraped a match afire and lighted a kerosene lamp on the nightstand by the bed. The light it gave was ruddier than sunlight; by it, he could hardly tell Emily's skin had changed color. He didn't care. That wasn't why he'd lighted it. "You are one *fine*-lookin' woman," he told his wife. The words came thick from his throat.

"And what do you propose to do about that?" she asked. He reached out for her and showed her, again without words.

Afterwards, with her curled up, head on his shoulder, both of them drifting off toward sleep, he wondered if Fanny Cunningham had listened to the bedsprings creaking. He and Bedford had teased each other about that every now and again, heading off toward work of a morning. If Fanny heard it now, though, it had to remind her that her husband wasn't there. Pinkard hoped Bedford was all right. He hadn't heard anything different, but what did that prove? Not enough.

"Might be my turn next," he muttered; conscription had scooped more white men out of the Sloss works over the past couple of weeks.

"What's that, honey?" Emily asked drowsily. "You say somethin'?"

"No," he said, and she fell asleep. Eventually, he did, too.

Herman Bruck's face twisted in annoyance. "Why don't you want to go to the play with me tonight?" he asked in a low voice, doing his best not to draw the notice of anyone else at the Socialist Party office.

"I just don't, Herman," Flora Hamburger told him. "When I'm done with work, I'm tired. What I want to do is go home and rest, nothing else." That wasn't the entire reason, but it was polite and true, as far as it went.

Bruck, as usual, did not know how to take no for an answer. "But it's one of Gordin's best," he exclaimed. "It has the most powerful arguments against the war I've seen anywhere."

"I'm already against the war," she reminded him. "I don't need any fresh arguments to be against it. What educates the proletariat is liable to bore me."

"But it shows the effect of the war on the poor, on the working classes," he persisted. "You'll find things you can borrow and get use of here."

Flora exhaled. Bruck was drawn to her, and had trouble realizing she was not drawn to him in return. She'd done her best to avoid being rude; after all, whether she went out with him or not, they had to work together. Instead of sharply telling him to go away and stop bothering her, she answered, "I can see the effect on my own family, thank you very much. My sister married to a soldier, my brothers both turning into militarists and liable to go through conscription as soon as they get old enough . . . I was against this war before it was declared, remember."

"Do you have to keep throwing that in my face?" he said angrily. "Maybe you were even right. I don't know. But if the United States win this war and we're seen as opposing it, we won't win an election anywhere in the country for the next twenty years. People will vote for the Republicans before they vote for us."

"I don't know about that," Flora said. "I don't know about that at all. With so many dead, with so many maimed, even winning this war won't be enough to make anyone glad we fought it."

"Write that down!" Bruck exclaimed. "It's a good propaganda point, and I haven't seen it anywhere else." He swung from suitor to political animal like a weathervane in a shifting wind.

Flora preferred him as political animal. There his instincts were good, which she would not have said about him as a suitor. She did write down the idea. "We should let it come from someone who isn't operating out of New York City," she said. "The Roosevelt propaganda machine has made New York Socialists pariahs, as far as the rest of the country is concerned."

"That's not right," Bruck said. "It's not fair." He calmed down. "But it is real, no doubt about that. We'll manage. Roosevelt can't censor everything we do, no matter how much he wishes he could."

Figuring ways to do that kept Bruck happily occupied till quitting time. Indeed, Flora was able to slip out the door and down the stairs while he was still shouting into a telephone. When she could, she preferred to deal with annoying men peacefully and indirectly, rather than whipping out a hat pin. When peaceful, indirect means didn't work—

"Speak softly and carry a sharp pin," she murmured, laughing at the way she'd twisted TR's slogan. But the laughter did not last long. Roosevelt's stick had not been big enough to knock over either the Confederacy or Canada at the first onslaught, which meant casualties by the tens, by the hundreds of thousands over chunks of land hardly large enough to serve as burying grounds for the dead.

Soldiers' Circle men still prowled through the Lower East Side, but fewer of them than in the days just after the Remembrance Day riots. They weren't so likely to break heads as they had been then, either. She'd even heard a story that one of them had put aside his truncheon after falling in love with a pretty Jewish girl. She didn't know whether it was a true story; no one seemed to have details. That people were telling it was interesting, though. True or not, they wanted to believe it.

When she got back to her family's apartment, her sister Esther was helping their mother get supper ready. Her brother Isaac had his nose in a book. Her other brother, David, walked in a few minutes after she did, looking tired. He'd got a sewing job, and was putting in long hours at it.

Her father came in next. He'd worked the same hours as his son, more or less, but bore them better, or at least more easily: he'd been putting in a backbreaking day for many years, and was used—or resigned—to it. His pipe smoke, though harsher than it had been in the days before the war started, still blended nicely with the odor of the stewing chicken in the pot on the stove.

Sophie dragged herself in last of all. She was very close to her time of confinement, but that didn't keep her from putting in a full day's work. If you couldn't do the job, the boss would find someone who could. Once she'd recovered from having the baby, she'd have to find a new position, too; no one would hold the old one for her. It wasn't right, it wasn't just, but, as Herman Bruck had said, it was real.

"Did I get a letter from Yossel today?" she asked as soon as she walked into the apartment. A framed photograph of Yossel Reisen, looking stern in his U.S. Army uniform, stood on the table next to the divan-sofa where he'd slept so many nights.

"Not today, Sophie," Esther answered.

Sophie looked disappointed. "That's three days now with nothing," she said, setting both hands on her swollen belly as if to say the baby expected to hear from its father, too. Her fingers had got too swollen to let her wear the wedding band Yossel had bought for her, but she had worn it and, more to the point, had the right to wear it.

"He hasn't been writing every day," Flora said, and then quickly added, "But he has been very good about sending you letters." For one thing, that was true. For another, now that Yossel had made Sophie his wife, she defended him like a tigress defending its young. Flora didn't want her thinking she had to do that now.

"Supper's ready," their mother said, another way of defusing a situation that could get sticky.

Over chicken stew, Benjamin Hamburger said, "I saw in the papers today that we are making good progress in the Roanoke valley, that we are pushing the Confederates back there. Soon, *alevai,* we will clear them out of the land between the Blue Ridge and the Alleghenies."

"You sound like a general, Papa," David Hamburger said with a smile. "Did you know where these places were before we went to war?"

"I didn't know where these places were before I had a son-in-law fighting there," his father answered. He snapped his fingers. "And I didn't care that much, either. You care about what touches you. Everything else is not so important."

"That's shortsighted, Papa," Flora said, respectfully but firmly. "That's how the bosses keep the workers under their control: by mystifying them about what really is important to their well-being."

"Politics at the supper table we can do without," Benjamin Hamburger said. "I wasn't talking about politics. I was talking about this family."

"You can't separate them like that," Flora said. Her father started to raise a hand. She got in one last shot before he could: "If it weren't for politics, would Yossel be in Virginia now?"

"That's different," he said. A moment later, he looked sheepish. "If you ask me to explain exactly how it's different, I may have a little trouble." Flora smiled at him, liking him very much right then. Not many people had the intellectual honesty to admit something like that. Because he had admitted it, she didn't push him any further. The rest of the meal passed in peace.

Afterwards, Sophie sat and rested while her mother and Esther and Flora washed the dishes. The kitchen was crowded with the three of them in it, but they made short work of plates and glasses and pots and silverware.

Someone knocked on the door. Someone was always knocking on the door: neighbors wanting to borrow something, neighbors giving something back, young men coming to talk or play chess or cards with David and Isaac, young men coming to call on Esther, older men coming to talk and smoke with Benjamin, women coming to gossip, delivery boys . . .

Flora was closest to the door, so she opened it. The young man who stood in the hall was a few years too young for a military uniform, but the Western Union uniform he had on was of similar color and cut, even if its brass buttons were shinier and more aggressively visible than a soldier would have liked.

"Telegram for Mrs. Sophie, uh"—he looked down at the yellow envelope he was carrying—"Sophie Reisen."

"Sophie!" Flora called, and started to give him a nickel for delivering the wire. She was, for a moment, puzzled: who would send Sophie a telegram?

Then the Western Union boy said, "No, ma'am, I never take money for delivering these." He took off his hat when Sophie came to the door, handed her the envelope, and hurried away.

"Who is sending me a telegram?" Sophie asked: the same question Flora had put to herself. Suddenly, Flora knew a dreadful certainty. *God forbid,* she thought, and bit her tongue to keep from saying anything while Sophie opened the thin, flimsy envelope. "It's from Philadelphia," Sophie said, "from the Secretary of War." Her voice got weaker and more full of fear with every word she spoke. " 'It is my sorrowful duty to inform you that—' "

She didn't go on, not with words. Instead, she let out a great, full-throated wail of grief that had doors flying open up and down the hallway. Flora took the telegram from her limp fingers and read through it. Yossel had died in Virginia, "heroically defending the United States and the restoration of their proper place among the nations of the continent and of the world and the cause of liberty." Flora wanted to crumple up the telegram and throw it away, but didn't because she thought her sister might want to keep it. The only truth in it, she thought, was that Yossel was dead. Everything else was patriotic claptrap.

Sophie hugged her belly and moaned, "What am I going to do? What are we going to do? I'm a widow, and I never even had a husband!" That wasn't quite true, but it wasn't far wrong, either.

People came flooding into the apartment. The building had heard that kind of anguished cry more than once before. Everyone knew what it meant. Women began bringing food. Everyone who'd ever met Yossel Reisen had a good word for him, as did a good many people who hadn't.

In the midst of the gathering, Esther asked Flora, "Are we going to sit *shiva* for Yossel?"

"Sophie will," Flora answered, but that went almost without saying. Would the rest of the family sit in mourning with torn clothes and pray for a solid week? Everything American in Flora—and, evidently, in Esther, too—cried out against it, especially for a man who wouldn't yet have been part of the family if he hadn't impregnated their sister. But when death struck, new customs had a way of sloughing off and old ones reasserting themselves. Resignedly, Flora said, "If Mother tells us to do it, how can we say no?" Esther's mouth twisted, but in the end she nodded.

And Flora knew that, while she was rocking back and forth sitting *shiva* for Yossel, she would not be mourning him alone, but the country and the whole world thrown onto the fire of war.

"**S**alt Lake City!" Paul Mantarakis said with considerable satisfaction. "One more fight to go and then we've licked these Mormon bastards once and for all."

"Matter of fact, I hear tell there's one big town after Salt Lake City," Ben Carlton said. "Place called Ogden, north of here."

"Yeah, all right, I heard about Ogden, too," Mantarakis admitted. "But it stands to reason, once they lose their capital, they ain't gonna have a whole lot of fight left in 'em."

"Just like the USA and Washington, right?" the cook said with weary cynicism.

Mantarakis gave him a resentful look. "It's not the same," he said. "Salt

Lake's the only real city—city-type city—the Mormons have. Provo and Ogden, they're just towns. I'm from Philly, remember. I know the difference. Next to what I'm used to, even Salt Lake City isn't a big thing."

"Be a hell of a big fight, though," Carlton predicted gloomily. He stirred the cookpot. The smell that rose up from it was none too appetizing: he'd made some kind of horrible stew from bully beef and hardtack and whatever else he happened to have handy. Paul sighed. Since he'd started wearing stripes on his sleeves, he hadn't been able to see to the cooking nearly so often as he had before. That meant the whole company ate worse than they would have otherwise.

Gordon McSweeney, a man with a cast-iron stomach (or at least no sense of taste to speak of) came up, smelled the pot, looked into it, and scowled at Carlton. "If I were a Papist, I'd give that last rites," he said.

He was a sergeant these days, too, so the cook could only assume an expression of injured innocence. "It'll be ready pretty soon," he said, which, considering McSweeney's editorial comment, was apt to be something less than a consummation devoutly to be wished.

But McSweeney, luckily for him, was looking north, toward Salt Lake City. " 'Now also the axe is laid unto the root of the trees: there every tree which bringeth not forth good fruit is hewn down, and cast into the fire,' " he said. " 'Because they had no root, they withered away.' So it says in the Holy Scriptures, whose words shall be fulfilled."

Mantarakis looked north, too. Here and there, flames burned in the Mormons' capital. Artillery fire had blown the gilded angel off the east-center tower of the Temple and had knocked down two of the other towers, but the big building, the heart of Salt Lake City, still stood. Enormous beehive flags flapped defiantly from the towers that survived. "They read a different book there," Paul said.

"And they will burn in hell because of it," McSweeney answered, sounding as certain as he generally did when speaking of matters of religion. "The *Book of Mormon* is no more the word of God than is an advertising circular for stomach powders."

It wasn't so much that Mantarakis thought McSweeney wrong—he didn't figure the *Book of Mormon* was divinely inspired, either. But the way McSweeney said it, like the way McSweeney said anything, put his back up. "Lot of people up there think you're wrong, Gordon," he remarked.

"The more fools they," McSweeney said. "They suffer in this world for their arrogance and overweening pride, and in the next for their false and blasphemous faith." He wasn't simply armored in his faith, but also used it as a sword against the foe. Mantarakis supposed that helped make him a good soldier; it also made him a scary man.

An aeroplane flew in lazy circles above Salt Lake City, spotting targets for the U.S. artillery. All of a sudden, black puffs of smoke started dotting the otherwise clear summer sky around the aeroplane. What artillery the Mormons had was mostly here; they'd got their hands on it by overrunning Camp Douglas, east and north of town. They knew the aeroplane was the U.S. artillery's eye in the sky. If they brought it down, they could fight on more nearly even terms. And bring it down they did. The aeroplane seemed to stagger in the sky, then plunged earthward, trailing smoke and flame. It crashed just inside the Mormon lines. The cheer the religious rebels raised rang in Mantarakis' ears. *"Kyrie eleison,"* he muttered.

For once, Gordon McSweeney did not upbraid him for praying in Greek. "Damn them," McSweeney said, over and over again. "Damn them, damn them." It wasn't cursing; it was nothing like the casual way in which most soldiers would have brought out the words. It sounded more as if McSweeney was instructing God about what needed doing and how to go about it. Paul wanted to take a couple of steps away from the other sergeant, in case God got angry at him for using that tone of voice.

With their great factories, the United States had guns especially devoted to antiaircraft fire and others given nothing but ground targets. The Mormon insurgents did not enjoy the luxury of specialization. Having shot down the aeroplane, they began working over the front-line trenches in which Mantarakis and his companions sheltered. He crouched down in the dirt, hands clutching his head, his body folded up into a ball to make himself the smallest possible target.

He'd been through worse in Kentucky; the Confederates had far more guns to fire at U.S. forces than the Mormons did. But any barrage was a bowel-loosener. The ground shook and jumped. Shrapnel balls and fragments of shell casing filled the air. Whether he lived or died wasn't really in his hands, not for the time being. Either God's providence or random luck, depending on how the world worked, would decide his fate.

After about half an hour, the Mormon guns eased up. Men helped their wounded comrades back toward the rear. Mormon snipers took potshots at them. The Mormons were short of men, short of guns, short of munitions, but they not only held the high ground (they had their artillery on the mountain spur above Temple Square, not far from the wreckage of what had been the state capitol before the revolt), but they also knew the terrain well and squeezed from it all the advantages they could.

First Lieutenant Cecil Schneider made his way down the battered trench line seeing how his company had come through. He was a little weedy fellow who would have looked more at home in mechanic's coveralls than in his grimy U.S. uniform. He'd been leading the company since Captain Hinshaw died; a lot of companies had lieutenants commanding them these days, and more than one had no surviving officers left at all.

Schneider sniffed at Ben Carlton's stew pot, sighed, and crouched down by it. He took out his mess kit. "I'm hungry enough for this to smell good," he said. Paul Mantarakis didn't know if he could get that hungry, but he was aware he had higher standards than most people.

Carlton, as if vindicated, filled the lieutenant's tray with stew. Schneider dug in, sighed again, and kept on eating. That Mantarakis understood. You had to keep the machine fueled or it wouldn't run.

When Schneider was nearly done, Mantarakis asked, "Sir, is there any way of rooting out the Mormons without going straight at them?"

"General Staff doesn't seem to think so," Schneider answered. "They've got the Great Salt Lake on one side and the mountains on the other, after all. It's not going to be pretty, but it's what we've got to do."

Not going to be pretty was a euphemism for forward companies' getting melted down to nothing, like candles burning out. Paul knew that. So, no doubt, did Lieutenant Schneider. "Sir," Mantarakis said, "are the two divisions we've got here going to be enough to do the job?"

"I hear we have more troops on the way," Schneider answered. "This sort of fighting chews up men by carloads." He sighed one more time, now not about the vile stew. "We have the men to spend, and we're spending them. This narrow front makes the fighting as bad as it is in the Roanoke valley or in Maryland."

"Mormons don't help," Ben Carlton said. "The Rebs fought fair, anyways. Any civilian you see here—man, woman, boy, girl—is gonna cut your throat in a second if he catches you asleep."

"You got that right." Mantarakis turned to Lieutenant Schneider. "Sir, once we beat these Mormons flat, what the hell are we going to do with them? What the hell *can* we do with them?"

"Ubi solitudinem faciunt, pacem appellant," Schneider answered. That made Gordon McSweeney rumble, down deep in his chest. He obviously didn't know what it meant, but he knew it was Latin. Given how he felt about the Catholic Church, that was plenty to make him suspicious.

"Sir?" Paul said. He didn't know what it meant, either. He'd grown up speaking Greek, but you needed more in the way of education than he'd picked up to throw Latin around like that.

" 'Where they make a desert, they call it peace,' " Schneider said.

McSweeney rumbled again, this time in approval. "Just what the Mormons deserve," he said: "Solitude Lake City."

Mantarakis stared at him. McSweeney joking was about as likely as pigs with wings. He couldn't let it go by without trying to top it. "Yeah, we'll make a desert out of Deseret," he said.

Lieutenant Schneider laughed. Ben Carlton looked from one punster to the other, equally disgusted with both. "You birds don't shut up, I ain't gonna feed you."

"Promises, promises," Paul said, which made Schneider laugh louder than ever.

Irving Morrell studied the situation map of Utah with considerable dissatisfaction. If it had been up to him, he would have tried to push men through the Wasatch Mountains, and he would also have had a column coming down from Idaho to make the Mormons divide their forces and keep them from concentrating everything they had on the main U.S. attack.

But it wasn't up to him. He was new at General Staff headquarters, and only a major. He'd made suggestions. He'd sent memoranda. He might have been shouting into the void, for all the attention the higher-ups paid him. He hadn't expected much different. Sooner or later, they'd listen to him on something small. If it worked, they'd listen to him on something bigger.

A lieutenant came up to him, saluted, and said, "Major Morrell?" When Morrell admitted he was who he was, the lieutenant saluted and said, "General Wood's compliments, sir, and he'd like to see you immediately. If you'll please follow me, sir—"

"Yes, I'll follow you," Morrell said. Without another word, the lieutenant turned and hurried away. Walking along behind him, Morrell wondered what enormity he'd committed, to make the Chief of the U.S. General Staff land on him personally. He didn't think his memoranda on the Utah campaign had been as intemperate as all that. Maybe he was wrong. No—evidently he was wrong. He shrugged. If speaking his mind made them want to ship him out, odds were they'd send him back to one of the fighting fronts and let him command a battalion again. That wasn't so bad.

A captain in an outer office who was pounding away on a typewriter looked up when the lieutenant brought in Morrell. After he'd been identified, the captain—presumably Wood's adjutant—nodded and said, "Oh, yes, let me tell the general he's here." He vanished into the chief of staff's inner sanctum, then emerged once more. "Come right in, Major Morrell. He's expecting you."

He didn't sound overtly hostile, but the General Staff had an air of genteel politeness over and above the usual military courtesies, so that didn't signify anything. Wondering whether to ask for a blindfold, Morrell walked past the captain and into the office. He came to stiff attention and saluted. "Major Irving Morrell reporting as ordered, sir."

"At ease, Morrell," Leonard Wood said, returning the salute. He was a broad-shouldered man in his mid-fifties, with iron-gray hair and a Kaiser Bill mustache waxed to a pointed perfection that didn't quite go with his craggy, tired-looking features. Morrell eased his brace only a fraction. Wood said, "Relax, Major. You're not in trouble. The reverse, in fact."

"Sir?" Morrell said. He couldn't fathom why the general had summoned him, if not to call him on the carpet.

Instead of explaining, Wood went off on a tangent: "You may have heard that I earned a medical degree before I went into the Army."

"Yes, sir, I have heard that," Morrell agreed. He didn't know where General Wood was going, but he wasn't about to try to keep him from getting there.

"Good," the chief of staff said. "Then you'll have an easier time understanding why I was extremely interested when a memorandum from you and Dr. Wagner reached my desk earlier this year."

"Dr. Wagner?" In any setting less august, Morrell would have scratched his head. "I'm afraid I don't remember—"

"From Tucson," Wood broke in impatiently. "The memorandum where the two of you were discussing the potential advantages of protective headgear."

Light dawned on Morrell. "Oh. Yes, sir," he said. He'd utterly forgotten the physician's name, if he'd ever known it. He'd forgotten their conversation shortly before he was discharged, too. He'd figured the doctor had also forgotten it, but that looked to be wrong. Not only had Wagner remembered, but he'd remembered to give Morrell half the credit, too. Not just a doctor—that damn near made him a prince.

General Wood leaned over the side of his chair, picked something up, and set it on his desk: a steel helmet shaped like a bowl, with a projecting brim in front and an extension in the back to give the neck a little extra protection. "What do you think of your idea, Major?" he asked.

Morrell picked up the helmet. It weighed, he guessed, a couple of pounds. Leather webbing inside kept it from resting right on a man's head; a leather chin strap with an adjustable buckle would help it stay on. He rapped the green-gray painted metal with his knuckles. "Will it really stop bullets, sir?" he asked.

Wood shook his head. "Not square hits, no—it would probably have to be three times as heavy to do that. But it will deflect glancing rounds and a lot of shrapnel balls and shell fragments. Head wounds are so often fatal, anything we can do to diminish them works to our advantage."

"Sir, you're a hundred per cent right about that," Morrell said. He thought of the man in the bed next to him in Tucson, the man who'd been made into a vegetable in the blink of an eye. The memory made him want to shiver. Better to die straight out than to linger on like that without hope of ever having a working mind again.

"A commendation for this idea will go into your permanent file, Major," Wood said. "Our German allies, I understand, are going to copy the notion from us, and I've heard, though it's always hard to gauge how much truth comes from sources in enemy country, that the froggies are also working along similar lines. But we have the helmet first, and that's thanks in large part to you."

"Thank you very much, sir," Morrell said. Getting credit for the idea had never crossed his mind, not least because he'd never thought it would see the light of day. "I hope Doctor, uh, Wagner gets a commendation, too, sir. If it hadn't been for him, this never would have gotten off the ground."

"Yes, he has a commendation coming, too," General Wood assured him. "But such things count for rather more on a fighting soldier's *curriculum vitae*, eh?"

"Yes, sir." Morrell hefted the helmet. "Sir, may I keep this one? If I'm ever transferred back to the front, I'll need one, and I'd be honored to have it be the one you gave me yourself."

"My pleasure," Wood said, and Morrell tucked the helmet under his left arm. The chief of staff studied him. "So you want to get back to the front, do you? Why does that not surprise me? Fighting the war with map and wire isn't your chosen style, is it?"

Morrell had had very much the same thought himself. "Sir, I like the outdoors; I always have. I like hiking and fishing and hunting a lot better than filling out forms and such. I think I'm more useful to the country up at the front, if you want to know the truth."

General Wood steepled his fingers. "What you're saying, Major, is that you'd have a better time up at the front than you do here, which is not the same as being more useful to the country. We're going to teach you everything we can here, Major, and I suspect you'll teach us a few things, too. If you measure up, we'll change the color of the oak leaves on your shoulders, maybe give you eagles instead, and we'll send you back to the front in charge of a regiment. *Then* you'll be more useful to your country."

"Uh, thank you, sir," Morrell said again. He'd dared hope something like that might happen, but he hadn't taken the notion seriously. He made a mental note to write General Foulke a thank-you letter. Foulke must have seen something in him that he liked, and sent him on to the General Staff to find out if they saw it, too. That was how careers got made, if you were good—and lucky enough to be good when people were watching.

Wood said, "This isn't for your benefit, Major: it's for the benefit of the United States of America. We are surrounded by foes on all sides, as we have been since the days of the War of Secession: the Confederate States and the Empire of Mexico to the south, Canada to the north, England and France across an Atlantic none too wide, and the Japanese and the British Empire across the Pacific. Seizing the Sandwich Islands was a heavy blow against them; otherwise, they'd be menacing our western coast even now. But they are going to try to take those islands back, as a first step toward carrying the war to our shores. Surrounded, as I say, we can't afford to waste talent if we see it." He went from cordial to brisk in the space of a heartbeat. "Dismissed, Major."

Morrell saluted, did a smart about-face, and left the office of the Chief of the General Staff. The lieutenant was still in the antechamber with General Wood's adjutant. He bounced to his feet. "Do you need me to guide you back to your assigned area, sir?"

"I don't think so," Morrell answered. "I expect I can manage on my own, unless the birds have eaten the trail of crumbs I left behind." The lieutenant looked blank. The adjutant chuckled, recognizing the allusion.

Three different men stopped Morrell in the hallway, all of them exclaiming about the helmet he was carrying. Two of them, like him, were ecstatic. The third, a white-bearded brigadier general in his late sixties who might have first seen action in the War of Secession, shook his head in dismay. "It's a damned shame we have to resort to means like those to fill the men with the spirit of aggression," he growled, and walked on.

Being far outranked, Morrell didn't answer. He didn't see anything wrong with giving the common soldier some slightly better chance to do his job without getting killed or dreadfully wounded.

He set the helmet down beside the map of the Utah rebellion. Try as he would, he couldn't make himself believe the General Staff had come up with the best possible plan there was. His first efforts to convince his superiors otherwise had failed. If he was going to try again, he'd have to be more subtle.

He was poring over the map when someone behind him said, "Major Morrell?"

"Yes?" Morrell turned around. Before the turn was completed, he came to attention and revised his words: "Yes, Mr. President?"

Theodore Roosevelt pointed to the helmet. "General Wood tells me that's partly your idea. It's a bully one, I must say. We aim to win this war, but we aim to do it with the greatest possible efficiency and care for the men who fight it. Your notion goes a long way toward that end. Congratulations."

"Thank you, sir," Morrell said. He'd known Wood and TR were longtime friends. He hadn't imagined that might ever matter to him.

"What other useful ideas have you?" Roosevelt pointed to the map of Utah. "How would you cauterize that running sore, for instance?" He sighed. "My experience has been that, man for man, Mormons make excellent, even outstanding, citizens. In a mass, though, their religion gives them the ambition to be a nationality of their own rather than Americans. This, I realize, is in no small measure engendered by the treatment they have received at the hands of the United States since the 1850s. But fault is irrelevant. Revolt and secession from our country cannot be tolerated."

"Yes, sir," Morrell said. "What would I do in Utah, sir?" He took a deep breath and explained to the president what he would do in Utah.

Roosevelt listened with poker face till he was through, then said, "Have you presented these ideas to the General Staff with a view toward implementing them?"

"I have presented them, yes, sir," Morrell answered. "My superiors are of the opinion they're impractical."

"Fiddlesticks," TR burst out. "Your superiors are of the opinion that, since they didn't think of these things themselves, they can't be any good. That's what you get for your low rank, Major Morrell." He stood up straight and stuck out his chest. "*I* have not got a low rank, Major. When I see something worth doing, it has a way of getting done. I'm glad we had this little talk. A very good day to you." He hurried off.

Morrell stared after him, somewhere between horror and delight. If Roosevelt started shouting orders, the plan for operations in Utah *would* change. Morrell was confident enough that the results could not be worse than those now being obtained. Would they be better? Would they be perceived as being better? If they were perceived as being better, would he get the credit for that—or the blame?

Roosevelt slammed a door behind him. He was shouting already. Morrell glanced over to the helmet he'd brought from General Wood's office. He snorted. When he took it, he hadn't imagined he'd need to wear it inside General Staff headquarters. But TR might have taken care of that.

Achilles started crying. This was the third time he'd started crying since Cincinnatus and Elizabeth had gone to bed. Cincinnatus didn't think it was far past midnight. The baby might wake up a couple of more times before morning. When he woke up, Cincinnatus woke up. He'd be a shambling wreck on the Covington docks. He'd been a shambling wreck a lot of the days since Achilles was born.

With a small groan, Elizabeth staggered out of bed and over to the cradle where Achilles lay. She picked him up and carried him into the front room to nurse him. Nights were even harder on her than they were on Cincinnatus. She came back from her domestic's work ready to fall asleep over supper.

Cincinnatus twisted and turned, trying to get comfortable and get back to sleep. In the process, he wrapped sheet and blanket around himself till he might have been a mummy. When Elizabeth came back, she had to unroll him to give herself some bedclothes. That woke him up again.

When the cheap alarm clock on the nightstand jangled, he jerked upright, as horrified as if a Confederate aeroplane had dropped a bomb on the house next door. Then he had to shake Elizabeth out of slumber; she hadn't so much as heard the horrible racket the clock made.

They both dressed in a fog of fatigue. The smell of coffee drew Cincinnatus to the kitchen like a magnet, though the stuff for sale in Covington these days had more chicory in it than the genuine bean. Whatever it was made of, it pried his eyelids open. After bacon and eggs and cornbread, he was more nearly ready to face the day than he would have believed possible fifteen minutes earlier.

Someone knocked on the front door. Elizabeth opened it. "Hello, Mother Livia," she said.

"Hello, dear," Cincinnatus' mother answered. "How's my little grandbaby?" Without giving Elizabeth a chance to answer, she went on, "He must have been a terror in the night again—I kin see it in your face."

Cincinnatus grabbed his dinner pail and hurried out the door, pausing only to kiss his mother on the cheek. That damned Lieutenant Kennan timed things with a stopwatch; if you were half a minute late, you could kiss work for the day good-bye. Cincinnatus had seen it happen to too many other people to intend to let it happen to him.

"Get your black ass going," the U.S. lieutenant snarled at him when he got to the waterfront. From Kennan, that was almost an endearment. Barges full of crates of munitions had crossed the Ohio. Cincinnatus and his work crew unloaded the barges and loaded trucks and wagons. U.S. soldiers drove them off toward the front. Cincinnatus had given up asking to be a teamster. The Yankees wouldn't hear of it, even if it would have freed up more of their men for actual fighting at the front lines.

He disguised a shrug in a stretch as he walked back to unload another crate. Whites in the CSA had better sense. Black men in the Confederacy did everything but fight. They drove, they cooked, they washed, they dug trenches. Without them, white Confederate manpower would have been stretched too thin to have any hope of holding back the U.S. hordes.

When the long day was done, the paymaster gave Cincinnatus the fifty-cent hard-work bonus. "God damn!" said Herodotus, who stood behind him in line. "That there's gettin' to be your reg'lar rate."

"Got me a baby in the house now," Cincinnatus said, as if that explained everything—which, to him, it did.

Herodotus said, "Plenty fellers here got five, six, eight chillun in de house. Don't see them gettin' no bonus."

Cincinnatus shrugged again. That wasn't his lookout. An awful lot of people in this world wanted just to get by, no more. He'd always had his eye on doing better than that. Even now, in the middle of the war, he had his eye on the main chance. He didn't know what would come of it, but he did know he couldn't win if he didn't bet.

Herodotus made a point of not walking home with him, as if to say he disapproved of such effort. That meant Cincinnatus was by himself when he noticed a wonderful smell in the warm, wet, late summer air. A moment later, a delivery wagon with the words KENTUCKY SMOKE HOUSE painted in big red letters rounded the corner. He waved to the driver, Apicius' son Felix.

Felix slowed down and waved back. "My pa, he say for you to come in some time before too long," he called. "He got somethin' he want to talk over with you."

"Do it right now," Cincinnatus said. Felix nodded, flicked the reins, and got the wagon moving again.

When Cincinnatus got to the Kentucky Smoke House, the aroma there reminded him how hungry he was after a day hauling heavy crates. Apicius' other son, Lucullus, was basting the meat that turned on a spit over the firepit. Seeing Cincinnatus, he waved him into a little back room.

In there, Apicius was stirring spices into a bubbling pot, making up more of the wonderful sauce that went onto his barbecued beef and pork. "Ha!" he said when Cincinnatus came in. "Saw Felix, did you?"

"Sure did," Cincinnatus answered. "He said you wanted to see me 'bout somethin'. Somethin' to do with the underground, I reckon." He spoke quietly, after having closed the door behind him.

Apicius gave the mixture in the iron pot another stir. "Might say that," he replied after a moment. He gave Cincinnatus a thoughtful glance. "How'd you get mixed up with those underground folks, anyways?"

"Wish I hadn't, pretty much," Cincinnatus said, "but the white man I used to work for, he's one of 'em, and he was always pretty decent to me. 'Sides, from what I've seen, I ain't got much use for the USA, neither." He met and held Apicius' eyes. "How 'bout you?" Unless he got answers that satisfied him, he wasn't going to say anything more.

Apicius' massive shoulders went up and down in a shrug. "First time the Yankee soldiers come in here, they clean me out of everything I got, they say they shoot me if I squawk, an' they call me more kind o' names'n I ever hear before. They ain't done nothin' like that since, mind you, but it don't make me want to cheer for the Stars an' Stripes."

"Yeah, that's about right." Cincinnatus sighed. "I be go to hell, though, if I see us black folks gettin' any kind o' square deal after the war, an' it don't matter if the USA or the CSA win."

"Dat's the exact truth," Apicius said emphatically. "The exact truth, an' nothin' but the truth, so help me God." He held up a meaty hand, as if taking oath in court—not that blacks could testify against whites in court, not in the CSA. After stirring the barbecue sauce again, he went on, "On de odder hand, there's undergrounds and then there's undergrounds."

"Is that a fact?" Cincinnatus said. If Apicius was going to come to a point, he hoped the fat cook would do it soon.

And, in his own way, Apicius did. Offhandedly, he asked, "You ever hear tell about the *Manifesto*?"

He didn't say what kind of manifesto. If Cincinnatus hadn't heard of it, he probably would have slid the talk around to something innocuous, then sent him on his way none the wiser. But Cincinnatus did know what he was talking about. He stared, wide-eyed. "Be you one of the people who—" He didn't go on. He'd heard *about* Reds a good many times, always in the whispers that were the only safe way to mention such people. He hadn't really imagined he would meet such an exotic specimen.

"We git justice for ourselves," Apicius said in a voice that had nothing in it of the jolly-fat-man persona he affected, only steely determination. "Come the revolution, nobody treat a workin' man like dirt only on account of he be black."

That was a heady vision. Cincinnatus, however, had already met the heady visions of the Confederacy and the United States, and seen how neither reality lived up to those visions. He had no reason save hope blinder than he could justify to believe the Red vision would be different. And besides—"Even if the revolution come in the CSA, right now we be under the USA, and it don't look like they gonna give us up."

"Revolution comin' in the USA, too," Apicius replied with calm certainty. "Now we kin help the Red brothers in the CSA—we git stuff they kin use, ship it south, an'— What so funny?"

Between giggles, Cincinnatus got out, "We take stuff the white men in the Confederate States ship north, an' use it to drive the damnyankees crazy. Then we take stuff the damnyankees ship south, an' use it to drive the white men in the CSA crazy. If that ain't funny, what is?"

Apicius' smile was thin (the only thin thing about him), but it was a smile. "You wif us, then?"

When Elizabeth found out, she'd want to kill him. He had a baby now. He was supposed to be careful. That consideration made him hesitate a good half a second before he answered, "Yes."

Up in Pennsylvania, Jake Featherston had been acutely conscious that he'd come to a foreign country. Houses looked different; the winter weather had been harsher than he was used to; the local civilians, those who hadn't fled before the advancing Army of Northern Virginia, had looked and sounded different from their counterparts in the CSA; and they hadn't made any bones about despising the men in butternut who'd overrun their farms and towns.

Now the Army of Northern Virginia wasn't advancing any more. It wasn't in Pennsylvania any more, either. Hampstead, Maryland, where Jake's battery in the First Richmond Howitzers was stationed, looked a lot more like a corresponding small town in Virginia than had anything he'd seen in Pennsylvania. The Old Hampstead Store, for instance, wouldn't have been out of place in some rural county seat outside of Richmond: a two-story clapboard building, a hundred years old if it was a day, in the shape of an L, with a massive water pump shielded from the street by the longer side of the L.

Nero was working the pump. When he'd filled a bucket, Perseus lugged it over to the horse trough. The draft animals that had pulled the battery's cannons and ammunition limbers drank greedily. "Don't give 'em too much too fast," Jake said warningly. "They're liable to get the colic and peg out, and we can't afford that, not now."

"Yes, suh, Marse Jake, I knows," Perseus answered. "But they got to drink some. They been workin' hard."

"I know," Featherston said. "I don't think we'll do much more moving back, though." He paused to wipe his sweaty forehead. "We better not, or we'll be fighting this damn war back in Virginia."

Jeb Stuart III came round the corner in time to hear that. "It will not happen, Sergeant," he said crisply. "They will not get past us. They will not come any farther. All right: we couldn't take Philadelphia. That's too bad; it might have made the damnyankees roll over and show us their bellies like the cowardly curs they are. But Maryland we hold, Washington we hold, and we're going to keep them."

"Yes, sir," Jake said—you didn't get anywhere arguing with your captain. But he couldn't help adding, "If the damnyankees are such terrible cowards, how come they're moving forward and we're going back?"

"We aren't," Stuart said. "Not one more step back—I have that straight from the War Department in Richmond."

When Jeb Stuart III had something straight from the War Department in Richmond, he had it straight from his father, who'd worn the wreathed stars of a Confederate general for a good many years. That sort of information came straight from the horse's mouth, then. Featherston said, "It's good to hear, sir—if the Yankees cooperate."

For a moment, Stuart seemed more a tired modern soldier than the cavalier he tried to be. His shoulders sagged a little. "The trouble with the Yankees, Sergeant, is that God was having an off day when he made them, because he turned out altogether too many. They die by thousands, but more thousands keep coming—as you may perhaps have noticed."

"Who, me, sir?" All too well, Featherston remembered the U.S. barrage that had cost him his first gun crew, and remembered pouring shells into oncoming green-gray waves till they broke barely beyond rifle range of his piece. "There's a lot of weight behind them," he agreed.

"There certainly is—weight of metal and weight of men," Stuart said. "And they use that advantage of size in place of true courage, battering us down by stunning us with their big guns and then drowning us in those assaults that leave hillsides and meadows paved with broken bodies from one end to the other. You ask me, Sergeant, that has very little to do with real courage, real *élan*, as our gallant French allies call it. *Élan* consists of throwing yourself at the foe regardless of his size, and in going forward for the simple reason that you refuse to admit to yourself you might be beaten. Look what it did for us in the opening days of the war."

"Yes, sir," Jake said. "Took us all the way to the Susquehanna—but not quite to the Delaware."

"If we'd made it to the Delaware, we surely would have crossed it and broken into Philadelphia," Stuart agreed, "and Baltimore would have withered on the vine. But without *élan*, could we have stopped the Yankee breakout from Baltimore before it trapped all our forces up in Pennsylvania?"

"I guess not, sir," Featherston said, which, by the sour look Stuart gave him, was not a good enough answer. But he didn't know whether it had been *élan* or good field fortifications that had stopped the U.S. drive. For that matter, he didn't know for a fact it was stopped. The Yankees were still shipping men and matériel down into the bulge around Baltimore. Sooner or later, it would burst again, like any carbuncle. "But if they break past Poplar Springs toward Frederick, we may have to skedaddle out of here yet."

Now Stuart looked angry: he'd had his theory contradicted. He put a biting edge in his voice: "Sergeant, I've seen the trench lines we've constructed to make sure the Yankees don't break out. I am confident they will hold against any pressure brought to bear against them, just as I am confident the lines ahead of us will hold against any conceivable pressure from the north."

"Yes, sir," Featherston said woodenly. He was kicking himself for disagreeing with the captain after he'd told himself not to be so foolish. But, damn it, wasn't he a free white man, with the right to say anything he chose? The way the Army treated you, you had to act like a Negro to your superiors. He didn't see the justice in that.

Pompey came up and said, "Captain Stuart, suh, your supper will be ready in a couple minutes. We found us a nice wine to go with your lamb chops, suh. I'm sure you'll enjoy it."

"I don't doubt that," Stuart said. Pompey went on his way. Watching him, Stuart returned to the argument with Jake: "Without our niggers, the Yankees would squash us flat, no way around it. But with them to build the works we use, every white Confederate man is a fighting man. We use our resources more efficiently than the USA can."

"Yes, sir, that's a fact," Featherston agreed, now anxious for nothing so much as to get the battery commander out of his hair. He was watching Pompey, too, still wondering whether he'd been right to tell that major about Stuart's servant. He'd never find out now, not with the influence a Stuart had in Richmond just because he was a Stuart.

Happier now that the sergeant was agreeing with him, Captain Stuart headed off, presumably to enjoy his lamb chops. Featherston wasn't going to be eating lamb chops; he'd have whatever came out of the battery kettle, probably some horrible slumgullion whose sole virtue was filling his belly. He wouldn't have a nice wine with his slop, either. He clicked tongue between teeth. The First Richmond Howitzers had been an aristocratic regiment since the days of the War of Secession. He'd managed to get in because he was good at what he did. Everybody above the rank of sergeant had got in by being good at who he was. Some times the differences were more glaring than others.

To Nero, Perseus said, "Bet you that Pompey, he gwine eat hisself lamb chops tonight, too."

"I dunno," Nero answered. "Maybe he gwine wait till Cap'n Stuart done used 'em up, then go to the latrine to git 'em." Both black men laughed. So did Jake Featherston, down deep inside. Seeing the Army's Negroes distrusting one another made white men sleep better at night.

Actually, nothing could have made Featherston sleep well that night. U.S. aeroplanes buzzed over Hampstead, dropping bombs at random. None of them landed within a couple of hundred yards of the battery; none of them, so far as Jake could judge from the absence of screams and cries of alarm from Confederate soldiers, landed within a couple of hundred yards of any worthwhile target.

Even landing out of the range where they could do any damage, though, they made a hell of a racket. Antiaircraft guns hammered away at the U.S. bombers, adding to the din. They didn't hit anything—or, at least, the rhythm of the engines throbbing overhead didn't falter.

Eventually, the U.S. aeroplanes gave up and flew back to the north. Jake rolled himself tighter in his blanket—which was stiflingly hot but which had the virtue of shielding large areas of his anatomy from mosquitoes—and went back to sleep.

Some time in the wee small hours, another flight of bombing aeroplanes visited Hampstead. Again, they dropped their bombs with nothing more than the vaguest idea of where those bombs might land. And again, the bombs did no damage Featherston could discern. They did, however, wake him up and keep him awake when he would sooner have grabbed as much sleep as he could get.

The next morning, shambling around like a drunk, barely remembering his own name, he realized the bombers had done some damage after all.

XIX

A few miles outside of Boston harbor, Patrick O'Donnell stuck his head out of the cabin of the *Spray* and called to George Enos, "The submersible has cast off the tow and the telephone line. Haul 'em aboard."

"Aye aye, Skipper," Enos answered; the biggest difference between life aboard the *Spray* and the way things had gone aboard the *Ripple* was that commands got answered in Navy talk these days.

George wished he had a winch with which to haul in the thick line and the insulated telephone wire wrapped around it. But the *Spray* had no winches for its own trawls, and one would have looked decidedly out of place at the stern. The steam trawler wanted to look like an ordinary fishing boat, not arousing the suspicions of Entente warships till too late. And so he did the work by hand.

Harvey Kemmel said, "Talk about locking the barn door after the horse has been stolen."

Although he had been in the Navy for years, Kemmel still flavored his speech with Midwestern farm talk George Enos sometimes found incomprehensible and often amusing. Today, though, he could do nothing but nod. "We were a little on the excited side when we sank that Rebel submarine," he admitted. "Beginners' luck, you might say."

"One way to put it," Kemmel said. "Christ, our pictures in the paper and everything. Felt good while it lasted, but we haven't had a sniff from the Rebs or the Canucks since."

A nibble, Enos would have said. However you said it, though, the message was the same. Nobody could prove the enemy was wise to the trick the *Spray* and other boats like her were trying to play, but neither she nor any of those other boats had lured a cruiser or a submarine to destruction since, either. "Hey, we've got a good load of fish in the hold," George said, pausing for a moment to look back over his shoulder.

Kemmel rolled his eyes. "I don't think I'm ever going to look a fish in the face again, now that I know what a hell of a lot of work it is to try and catch the bastards. I thought I was tired on a destroyer, but I didn't know what tired was. I feel like somebody rode me hard and put me away wet."

That was another comparison Enos never would have come up with on his own; he had trouble remembering the last time he'd ridden a horse. Again, though, he understood what his comrade was driving at. He answered, "The smaller the boat, the more work it takes."

"You did this stuff for *years*, didn't you?" Kemmel said. "Each cat his own rat, but—" He shook his head in bemusement.

"I'd sooner fish than watch a horse's rear end all day," George answered, dirt farming being the only thing he could think of that might possibly have been harder work than fishing.

"Soon as I got old enough, though, I got off my pa's farm and as far away as I could go," Kemmel shot back. "War hadn't come along, you would have kept on doing this your whole blessed life."

George Enos shut up and went back to pulling in the heavy, wet rope and the telephone line, one tug after another, hand over hand. It was hard work, but easier than bringing in the trawl full of fish. There was, at the moment, nothing at the end of this rope.

He'd just brought in the dripping end and coiled the rope neatly in place when a tug steamed up alongside the *Spray* and demanded her papers: no ship got into the harbor these days without being stopped and inspected first. Since they were Navy, passing the inspection proved easy enough. A pilot came aboard to guide them through the mine fields protecting Boston from enemy raiders. Every time they came back from a trip out to one fishing bank or another, more mines had been sown. Every once in a while, the mines came loose from their moorings, too. Then, pilot or no pilot, a boat or even a ship was likely to go to the bottom in a hurry.

"Wonder where the submersible's gone," Enos said. As had become its custom, the submersible had remained under the sea after releasing the towline. Maybe it went into Boston, sneaking under the mines, or maybe to one of the other ports nearby.

Harvey Kemmel laughed. "I can tell you ain't been in the Navy long—you still ask questions. What they want you to know, they'll tell you. What they don't want you to know ain't your business anyhow." George would have argued with him, but he looked to be right.

The pilot brought them in to T Wharf as if the *Spray* were an ordinary fishing boat. Patrick O'Donnell disposed of the catch as if she were an ordinary trawler, too. Then the illusion that she was still a part of the civilian world took a beating: an officer with a lieutenant commander's two medium-width stripes surrounding a narrow one strolled up the wharf to the *Spray* and said, "Men, you'll come with me. We have some matters to discuss." By that, he meant he would tell them what to do and they would do it.

"What's going on, sir?" George asked him. Off to one side, Harvey Kemmel snickered. Enos' ears got hot. He *did* still ask questions. The United States were a free country, and most places you could do things like that. But when you were in the Navy, your freedom disappeared.

"I'm going to pretend I didn't hear that," the lieutenant commander said. The hell of it was, George understood the fellow was doing him a favor.

They all walked down T Wharf after the officer. Real fishermen and other people with business on the wharf gave them curious looks, those who didn't know they were Navy themselves. What the dickens did a spruce lieutenant commander want with a bunch of ragamuffins in dungarees and overalls and slickers and hats that had seen better days?

Most of the couple of blocks just back of T Wharf were full of tackle shops and saloons and boatbuilders' offices and whorehouses: businesses serving the fishing trade and the men who worked it. In one of the whorehouses, a girl stood naked behind a filmy curtain: a living advertisement. A cop across the street looked the other way. Actually, he looked right in at her, but he didn't do anything about her. George looked at her, too. He was happy being married to Sylvia, but he was a long way from blind.

He flicked a glance up toward the lieutenant commander. The man's head never moved. Maybe his eyes slid to the right, but George wouldn't have bet on it. He seemed as straight an arrow as Enos had come across in some time.

He led the crew from the *Spray* into a Navy recruiting station sandwiched between a saloon and a cheap diner. Charlie White said, " 'Scuse me, sir, but we already joined up." The ex-fishermen all laughed. The sailors who filled out the crew didn't.

A couple of young men sat in there, talking earnestly with a gray-haired petty officer. Enos had a pretty fair idea what they were doing: trying to convince him they ought to be allowed to put on whites before conscription made them don green-gray. From things he'd read about what life in the trenches was like, and from the black-bordered casualty lists the papers printed day in and day out, he had a hard time blaming them.

The lieutenant commander led the men from the *Spray* into a back room. "Be seated, men," he said, waving to the chairs around the big wooden table. There were just enough chairs for the ersatz fishermen and, at the head of the table, for the officer. As George Enos sat down, he wondered if that was a coincidence. He had his doubts. The Navy didn't run on coincidences.

He also wondered if Patrick O'Donnell would start asking questions. O'Donnell, after all, had commanded a naval vessel that had helped sink a

Confederate submarine, while the lieutenant commander had the look of a man who didn't go to sea much. But the former skipper of the *Ripple* sat silent. He had too much Navy in his blood to pressure an officer.

The lieutenant commander coughed. Maybe he was having trouble coming to the point. George didn't like that. If somebody didn't want to tell you something, odds were you didn't want to hear it, either. At last, the officer did speak: "Men, we are ending the program in which you have been engaged. Results have not shown themselves to be commensurate to the effort involved."

Kemmel and Schoonhoven and a couple of other regular Navy men aboard the *Spray* nodded. It didn't matter to them. One job, another job—so what? They were little rivets on a big machine. They'd fit wherever someone put them.

Now Patrick O'Donnell found his voice: "But, sir, we did sink a submarine."

"I know you did," the lieutenant commander said. "Another towing couple sank one off the western coast of the Empire of Mexico, too. Both, though, came in the very earliest days of the program, and both, unfortunately, received wide publicity. Now our enemies are suspicious of targets that look too tempting to be true, and towed submersibles are operating with a far smaller range than would be the case if they were cruising on their own. And so—" He spread his hands.

"What do we do now, sir, in that case?" O'Donnell asked.

"You'll be reassigned, of course," the lieutenant commander answered crisply. "Orders have already been cut for all of you, and transportation arranged for those being moved out of the area." He pushed back his chair; the legs scraped against the floor. "I have them in my office. I'll distribute them to you. Wait here."

He left the room, returning a moment later with a manila folder from which he drew envelopes with names typed on them. He handed O'Donnell his without hesitation, but had to ask who the other men were.

George Enos' fingers fumbled with the flap of the envelope, as if they didn't want to find out what lay inside. No, not *as if*: he had no desire whatever to learn that the faceless red-tape twisters in Philadelphia had sent him to New York or San Diego or San Francisco or—

Want to or not, he pulled out the papers folded into the fat envelope. The name leaped out at him at once: "St. Louis," he said, his voice a raw hiss of pain. *Report at once to the river monitor USS* Punishment, *St. Louis, Missouri*. A train ticket fell out of the mass of other papers. He stared at it in horrified dismay. "Sir, this says I'm supposed to leave this afternoon!"

"That's correct," the lieutenant commander agreed. "We expected the *Spray* in three or four days ago, and made arrangements accordingly. Your family will be notified, I assure you."

Your family will be notified. A bloodless way to say it, a gutless way to do it. Sylvia would be at the canning plant now; he couldn't reach her there. The children were at Mrs. Coneval's, but she had no telephone, any more than his own apartment did. Send a wire? He shook his head. That would make Sylvia think he'd been killed.

Charlie White said, "San Diego," in that same wounded, disbelieving voice. They looked at each other. Despite the difference in the color of their skins, they were, in that moment, very much alike.

Marshlands had two wheelchairs now, the old one for upstairs and a new one with bigger wheels, one also easier to maneuver outside, for downstairs. Anne Colleton had bought the second chair without a murmur after watching Scipio bump her brother down the stairway and escape losing control of the chair only by luck.

Getting Jacob Colleton downstairs without having to bring his chair along certainly made matters easier for Scipio. He wheeled the mistress' brother to the top of the staircase, helped him rise, draped one of Jacob's arms over his own shoulder, let the gassed man hang onto the banister with the other hand, and walked down more or less normally. Then he eased Jacob Colleton down into the other wheelchair. "My gun," Colleton rasped.

"Are you certain that is what you require, sir?" Scipio asked tonelessly. As usual, Jacob reeked of whiskey. He'd also given himself an injection of morphia not long before. The butler did not think well of a drunk, drugged man's prospects for straight shooting.

Jacob Colleton glared at him. His body was wrecked, his eyes red-tracked and blurry, but the hate and rage that poured out from them made Scipio back up half a step in alarm. They weren't aimed at him in particular, but at the world as a whole, the world that had done what it had done to Jacob. That made them more frightening, not less. "Bring me my gun," Colleton hissed. He paused to draw a painful breath, then added, "If you're lucky, I'll give you a running start."

Scipio's laugh was dutiful. He might have found that funnier if he hadn't been sure Miss Anne's brother at least half meant it. "I'll be back directly, sir," he said, and went upstairs again. Hung on brackets above the bed in which he could sleep only propped up by pillows, Jacob Colleton had a Tredegar military rifle. Scipio took it and a couple of ten-round clips of ammunition and carried them down to Colleton. Jacob laid the rifle across the arms of his wheelchair and stuck the ammunition in one of the deep pockets of his robe.

"Push me over by that stand of trees," he told Scipio. "You know, the one by the nigger cottages."

"Yes, sir," Scipio said.

"See what kind of varmints I can get," Colleton went on. What a .303

caliber bullet meant for knocking over men at five hundred yards did to a squirrel at fifty wasn't pretty, but Jacob Colleton didn't seem to care much about that. He was a good shot—a far better shot than he had been before he went off to war. He looked up at Scipio, those pale eyes blazing. "I keep wishing it was damnyankees in my sights. Do you have any idea what I'm telling you? No, you wouldn't. How could you?"

But Scipio did. As he opened the front door so he could push Jacob Colleton out of Marshlands, he thought of the Negro revolutionary cell to which he'd so unwillingly become attached, and of their endless, hungry murmurs of *Come de revolution*. Come the revolution, they'd take aim at Jacob Colleton with exactly the same loving hate he lavished on the men of the USA.

A couple of Negro children broke off their games to stare at Jacob and Scipio as they went by. Colleton made as if to lift his rifle. "You better run fast, you damn little pickaninnies," he croaked. Run the children did, squealing in delicious fear. Colleton laughed his ghastly, shattered laugh. He looked up at Scipio again. "If I don't have any luck in the woods, I'll bag 'em on the way back to Marshlands."

Scipio maintained a prudent silence. Again, he thought Colleton was making a joke. Again, he wasn't sure enough to be comfortable.

Some of the trees by the Negro cabins bore fruit or nuts. The plantation hands shared out what they got from them. Some of the trees and bushes were just there, and had been there since before the War of Secession, maybe before the American Revolution.

Colleton clicked a magazine into the Tredegar and chambered the first round. Scipio stood behind the wheelchair. He had other things he needed to be doing, plenty of them. Unless Miss Anne called him, they wouldn't get done for a while. Jacob wanted to be moved every so often if he didn't shoot anything. If Scipio wasn't there to move him, he really might use the butler for target practice on his reappearance.

A crow flapped by and landed in a pecan tree. Fast as a striking snake, Jacob Colleton slapped the rifle to his shoulder, aimed, and fired. The report, as always, made Scipio jump and his heart start to pound. He wondered what war sounded like. Every time he tried to imagine it, his imagination rebelled.

The crow lost its perch and fell to the ground with a plop. It lay, a black puddle, on the grass and moss and leaves below the tree. With a click, Jacob Colleton worked the bolt and brought a fresh cartridge into the chamber. The brass casing he'd ejected glittered by the wheelchair.

"Good shot, sir," Scipio said. "Shall I recover the bird?"

"Don't bother," Colleton wheezed. "Crow isn't worth eating. No kind of crow is worth eating."

You say that, to a Negro? Scipio wanted to snatch the rifle out of his hand

and smash in his skull. When whites came out with witless cracks like that, it did more than Cassius' Red rhetoric to make Scipio think the black revolution was not only needed but might succeed. No matter how sharp Jacob Colleton's eyes were, he was blind.

Colleton fired again, missed, and swore. His trainwrecked voice made ordinary words sound extraordinarily vile. Killing a foolish possum a few minutes later partially restored his spirits. "You can get that," he told Scipio. "Give it to one of those little niggers for the pot." Every once in a while, he remembered he was still supposed to be a gentleman.

Scipio carried the possum back by the tail. Jacob Colleton had put a bullet half an inch back of one eye. The ugly little beast couldn't have known what hit it. And possum, after some time in the pot or the bake oven, was tasty eating indeed. "Very good shooting, sir," Scipio said, laying the little body down beside the wheelchair.

Jacob Colleton started to say something, but coughed instead. He kept coughing, and finally started to turn blue. At last, as Scipio helplessly stood by, he mastered the spasm. "Lord God almighty," he whispered, "feels as if they're taking sandpaper and a blowtorch to my insides." Along with the clips of ammunition, he had a silver flask in one pocket of his robe. He gulped from it, swallowed, and gulped again. His color slowly improved. He looked down at the possum he had killed. "Good shooting, Scipio?" He shook his head. "This is nothing. It's not even proper sport. The possum can't shoot back."

"Sir?" Scipio knew he was supposed to say something in response to that, but for the life of him couldn't figure out what.

Colleton breathed whiskey up into his face. "Don't look at me like that. I wasn't joking, not even slightly. What better game to play, what more exciting game to play, than wagering your life that you're a better shot than the damnyankee on the far side of the barbed wire? But machine guns cheat, artillery cheats, gas cheats worst of all. It doesn't care how good a soldier you are. If you're in the wrong place, it kills you—and there's no sport at all about that."

Again, Scipio kept his mouth shut. A robin flew down toward a treetop. Jacob Colleton fired while it was still on the wing. It seemed to explode in midair. Feathers drifted to the ground. Scipio's eyes got wide. That wasn't just good shooting—it was outstanding shooting. And, since there wasn't much left of the poor songbird, Colleton hadn't done it for any reason but to show off . . . and maybe to savor the moment of killing something. Scipio shivered.

After he'd killed a squirrel and missed a couple of shots, Jacob said, "Enough of this. Take me back inside."

"Yes, sir," Scipio said, and he did. He helped Miss Anne's brother upstairs and back into the pillow-strewn bed in which he could not lie down. Scipio, whose mind took strange leaps these days, wondered how he did what he did with the women he summoned to his room. The Negro, who was very conventional in those matters, had trouble imagining alternatives.

He escaped from the bedroom with more than a little relief. But, try as he would, he could not escape Jacob Colleton. Down in the kitchen, he ran into Cassius; the hunter was bringing in a turkey he'd killed in the woods beyond the cotton fields. Cassius had been very quiet since his return from what he'd told Anne Colleton was Jubal Marberry's plantation. Now he signaled Scipio with his eyes. The two of them walked outside.

A stove had made the kitchen blazing hot. No stove burned outside, but it was blazing hot there, too, and so muggy Scipio expected rain. He and Cassius strolled along side by side. They made an incongruous pair because of their difference in dress, but nobody paid them any mind. Both the field hands and the white folks were used to seeing them together.

In a low, casual voice, Cassius said, "Kip, you got to keep Marse Jacob 'way from them trees." He pointed to the little wood into which Jacob Colleton had been shooting.

"How kin I do dat?" Scipio demanded. In a flash, he went from Congaree dialect to the English he used around Miss Anne and other whites. " 'I'm sorry, sir, but the huntsman-in-chief requires you to take your sport elsewhere'?" He fell back into dialect: "Ain't gwine happen, Cass."

Cassius guffawed and slapped his thigh. "Do Jesus, that funny." He grew serious again in a hurry, though. "Don' care how you do it, but you do it, hear?"

Scipio stared at him in something approaching agony. "Ah *cain't*, Cass. He say go dere, we gots to go dere. I tell he no, I dance me all round why fo' no, he jus' git mo' and mo' 'spicious. You hear what I say?"

"I don't got to hear you, Kip. You *got* to hear me," Cassius said, not loudly, but not in a way Scipio thought he could ignore, either. "Don' wan' no white folks traipsin' through they woods. Don' wan' no white folks nowheres *near* they woods, you hear?"

"Better shoot me now," Scipio said. He'd never tried standing up to Cassius till this moment. He'd never had any chance before; the hunter had effortlessly dominated him. But now he'd asked the impossible. If he was too stupid to recognize that, too bad—too bad for everyone, too bad for everything.

He stared at Scipio now; defiance was the last thing he'd expected. "You *got* to, Kip," he said at last. "Ain' no two ways 'bout it. You *got* to." But he wasn't ordering now; he sounded more like a man who was pleading.

"How come I got to?" Scipio demanded.

Cassius didn't want to tell him. He could see that, with no room for doubt. After a long, long pause, the hunter said, "On account of I got a whole raf' o' guns, whole raf' o' bullets back in there. White folks finds that, ain't gwine do nothin' but hang all the niggers on this here plantation."

"Reckoned it were sumpin' like dat," Scipio said, nodding; wherever Cassius had been when he was away, it wasn't in bed with a nineteen-year-old wench named Drusilla. Where had he got the weapons? How had he got them back here? Scipio didn't know, or want to know. He pointed toward the woods in question. "You worry too much, you know dat? Marse Jacob, he cain't git out o' that chair, not hardly. He shoot hisself a possum, *I* gits it an' brings it back. He ain't goin' in they woods. An' you wants me to ruin everything on account of you gits de vapors. Do Jesus!" He clapped a hand to his forehead.

Cassius soberly studied him. "All right, Kip, we does it yo' way," he said, and Scipio breathed again. "You better be right. You is wrong, you is dead. You is wrong, we all dead."

He walked off shaking his head, perhaps wondering if he'd done the right thing. Scipio stood where he was till he stopped trembling. He'd got away with it. Not only had he been right, he'd made Cassius recognize that he was right. As triumphs went, it was probably a small thing, but he felt as if he'd just won the War of Secession all by himself.

"Pa," Julia McGregor asked with the intent seriousness of which only eleven-year-old girls seem capable, "are you going to send me back to school when it opens again after harvest time?"

Arthur McGregor looked up from the newspaper he was reading. He rested while he could; harvest would be coming soon. The paper was shipped up from the USA, and full of lies; since the demise of the *Rosenfeld Register* (which had been only half full of lies), no local paper had been permitted. But even lies could be interesting if they were new lies: why else did people read so many books and magazines?

"I'd thought I would," he answered slowly. "The more you learn, the better off you'll be." He brought that last out like an article of faith, even if he couldn't see how he was all that much better off for his own schooling. He studied his elder daughter. "Why? Don't you want me to?"

"No!" she said, and shook her head so vigorously that auburn curls flipped into her face.

"I don't want to go, either," Mary exclaimed.

"Hush," he told her. "I'm talking to your big sister." Mary did hold her tongue, but looked mutinous. She had an imp in her that wouldn't placidly let her do as she was told. Her backside got warmed more often than Julia's or Alexander's ever had. But the imp also drove her to acts of real, even foolhardy, courage, as when she'd charged at the American officer who'd wanted to take McGregor hostage in Rosenfeld. Her father turned back toward Julia. "You used to like school. Why don't you want to go any more?"

"You remember how I went last spring, when the Yankees let the schools open up again?" Julia asked. Arthur McGregor nodded. His daughter went on, "The books they made the teachers use, they were *American* books." She couldn't have spoken with greater contempt had she called them Satan's books.

"Numbers are numbers, and you do have to learn to cipher," he said. Reluctantly, Julia nodded back at him. He added, "Words are words, too."

"No, they aren't," his daughter said. "Americans spell funny."

McGregor spelled funny himself. His spelling had probably got funnier in the years since he'd escaped the classroom. Julia, though, had always been clever in school. That must have come from Maude's side of the family; he knew it hadn't come from his. He said, "They don't spell all their words different—not even most." He thought that was true. He hoped it was.

At any rate, Julia didn't argue it. What she did say was, "It's not that stuff so much, Pa. It's the history lessons. I don't ever want to go to another one of those again." She looked and sounded on the edge of tears.

McGregor glanced down at the newspaper, which had come from a little town in the state of Dakota. He remembered what he'd thought about it moments before. "They telling you lies in the schoolroom, sweetheart?" he asked.

Julia's nod was as emphatic as her headshake had been. "They sure were, Pa," she answered. "All kinds of lies about how America was right to have the Revolution, and the king of England was a wicked tyrant, and the Loyalists were traitors, and they should have conquered us in 1812, and Canada was worse off for staying with England, and how England and France and the CSA kept stabbing the United States in the back. None of it's true, not even a little bit."

"Not even a little bit," Mary echoed happily.

"Hush," Arthur McGregor told her. He picked his words with care as he spoke to Julia: "It's what they have to teach to keep the schools open at all, same as the *Register* had to print what the Americans told it to a lot of the time."

"I understand *that*." Julia's voice was impatient. He'd underestimated her, and disappointed her because of it. She went on, "I know they're teaching us a pack of rubbish. I know what really happened, just like they taught me before when they were telling the truth. That isn't what bothers me, or not so much, anyway. But I don't think I can stand going back to school and listening to the teacher talk about all the lying things the Americans make him say and reading the books that say the same stupid things *and watching the other pupils at the schoolhouse listen to all the same lies and believe them.*"

"Do they?" McGregor wished he had enough tobacco to let himself light a pipe right now. It would have helped him think. He looked at the Dakota newspaper again. People all over American-occupied Manitoba were getting papers on the same order as this one. He didn't take seriously the propaganda with which it was laced, and had assumed nobody else did, either. But how true was that assumption? All at once, he wondered.

"They really do, Pa," Julia said seriously, making him wonder all the more. "It's like they never paid attention before, so when the teacher tells them American lies and the books say the same thing, they don't know any better. They just give it back like they were so many parrots."

"Awrk!" Mary squawked. "Polly want a cracker?"

"Polly want to go to bed right now?" McGregor asked, and his youngest got very quiet. He sat there thinking, his chin in his hand. He was a hard-nosed, rock-chinned Scotsman; he knew what was so and what wasn't. So did his wife. They'd brought up their children to do the same, and evidently succeeded.

But what about the people who weren't the same and who didn't do the same for their children? He hadn't thought much about them. Now, listening to Julia, he realized that was a mistake. What about the light-minded souls who believed the Germans were about to take Petrograd and Paris and the Americans Richmond and Toronto, for no better reason than that the newspapers said as much? What about their children, who believed when they got told the Confederacy had had no right to secede from the United States or that Custer's massacre of General Gordon's brave column had been a heroic victory, not a lucky ambush? What about all the people like that?

McGregor got an answer, far more quickly and with far more confidence in his accuracy than if he'd had to do arithmetic on paper. If you filled the heads of people like that with nonsense like that, and did it for a few years or maybe for a generation at most, what would you have? You'd have people who weren't empty-headed Canadians any more. You'd have people who were empty-headed Americans instead.

"Maybe we won't send you back to that school after all," he said slowly. Julia beamed at him, looking as much surprised as delighted. And Mary let out such a whoop of delight that her mother came out of the kitchen to see what had happened.

When Arthur McGregor explained what he said and why, Maude nodded. "Yes, I think you're right," she said. "If they're going to try to make us over, we can't very well let them, can we?"

"I aim to do everything I can to stop them, anyhow," he answered. "We have primers of one sort or another here around the house, anyway. You and I can give the girls some lessons, anyhow. That way, when this country is back in Canadian hands the way it's supposed to be, they won't have lost too much time with their schooling."

"Oh, thank you, Papa!" Julia breathed. "Thank you so much."

Mary was looking less pleased with the solution. "You mean we'll have to go to school *here*?" she said. "That's no good."

"I expect your mother and I can probably do a better job of riding herd on you than any schoolteacher ever born," McGregor said.

By the expression on Mary's face, she expected the same thing, and the expectation filled her with something other than delight. She turned on her big sister. "Now look what you've gone and done," she said shrilly.

"It's not my fault," Julia said. Before Mary could demand whose fault it was if not hers, as Mary was plainly about to do, she answered the not yet spoken question on her own: "It's the Americans' fault." That, for a wonder, satisfied her little sister. Mary believed the Americans capable of any enormity. Arthur McGregor was inclined to agree with her.

Later that night, after the children were asleep and he and Maude lying down in their bed, his wife said to him, "I wouldn't mind so much sending the children to the school, no matter what it taught about history and such, if . . ." Her voice trailed away.

McGregor understood what she meant. He didn't want to say it, either, but say it he did: "If you thought they'd only have to listen to American lies for another year, or two at the most."

Beside him, Maude nodded. The night was warm, but she shivered. "I'm afraid we're going to lose the war, and I'm afraid we won't have a country we can call our own any more."

I'm afraid we're going to lose the war. Neither of them had come out and said that before now. "I think we'll beat them in the end," McGregor answered, trying to keep up his spirits as well as hers. "They haven't licked us yet, and the mother country is helping all she can. Everything will turn out right. You wait and see."

"I hope so," she said. But then she sighed and fell asleep. Arthur McGregor hoped so, too, but he'd long since discovered the difference between what he hoped and what came true. Now that Maude had named the fear, he could feel it nibbling at his soul, too. *I'm afraid we're going to lose the war.* No matter how tired he was, sleep took a long time catching up with him.

Sam Carsten peered out of the barracks at Pearl Harbor toward the drydock where the damaged *Dakota* was being repaired. Other buildings hid the drydock from sight, but he knew exactly where it was. He thought he could have been dropped anywhere in or near Honolulu and pointed accurately toward it, just as a compass reliably pointed north. His affinity for the ship was hardly less than the instrument's for the North Magnetic Pole.

Knowing the *Dakota* was wounded ate at him, so much so that he burst out, "I'm afraid we're going to lose the goddamn war."

Hiram Kidde understood him perfectly. "Fleet's not gonna go to the devil on account of we're one battleship light," the gunner's mate said reassuringly. He got a sly look in his eye. " 'Sides, Sam, I know what's really eating you."

"What's that?" Carsten said.

"Now that we're stuck here on the beach, we have to make like soldiers instead of sailors," Kidde answered.

"That's not all bad." Carsten pointed to the row on row of iron cots. "Nice to be able to get some sack time without Crosetti farting in my face from the top bunk. Chow's better, too, same as it always is when we're in port instead of steaming. But . . . yeah. I haven't been out of a ship for such a long stretch since I joined up. I don't much like it."

"Me, neither," Kidde said, "on both counts, and I been in the Navy damn near as long as you've been alive. Other thing is, when you're on a ship you aren't just spinning your wheels. You keep things clean, you keep things neat, on account of it makes the ship work better. Doing it on dry land . . . Why bother?"

"Orders," Carsten said, making it a dirty word. "Somebody says you got to do it, you got to do it, never mind whether it makes sense."

"I'm damn glad you understand how that is, Sam, damn glad," Kidde said in a tone of voice that made Carsten realize he'd been betrayed—worse, that he'd just gone and betrayed himself. Smiling at how nicely the trap had worked, Kidde went on, "Got a lot of walks out there that need policing. Get yourself a broom and get to it."

"Have a heart, 'Cap'n,' " Sam said piteously. "You send me out in the sun for a couple hours here and they can stick an apple in my mouth and serve me up at the officers' mess tonight. I'll be cooked meat." He ran a hand along his arm, showing off his fair, fair skin.

"Grab a broom," Kidde said, all at once sounding much more like a chief petty officer than a buddy.

"I hope you screw Maggie Stevenson," Carsten said, and then, while Kidde was still blinking (any male human being who didn't want to screw Maggie Stevenson had to have a screw loose himself), he added, "Right after the guy with the chancre."

There were people who, when they said things like that, started fights. When Carsten said things like that, he got laughs. "You're a funny guy—funny like a crutch," Kidde said, but, if he was trying not to chuckle, it was a losing effort. "Go on, funny guy, get moving."

Sam smeared his arms and his nose and the back of his neck with zinc oxide ointment. He was unhappily aware that the stuff didn't do much good, but it was, or at least it might have been, better than nothing. He supposed that made up for the medicinal stink of the goop.

Resigning himself to baking, he went out, broom and dustpan in hand. The dustpan wasn't standard military issue; some ingenious soul had mounted it on the end of a broomstick, too, so Sam didn't have to bend down every time he swept something into it. He approved of that. He approved of anything that made work easier, especially when it was work he had to do.

The walks were pretty clean. Even ashore, sailors were most of them neat people, carrying over the habits they'd picked up at sea. Whenever he came across a cigar butt or a crumpled-up empty pack of cigarettes or a scrap of paper, he swept it into the dustpan with a muttered, "God damn the Marines."

He muttered his curses for two reasons. First, he didn't know whether Marines were actually responsible for the trash, though he would have bet on it: they weren't trained to neatness the way ordinary Navy men were. The other reason was that, even if he'd been right, some Marines walking by might have heard him, and they'd have beaten the stuffing out of him just as enthusiastically as if he'd been wrong.

Marines strolled through Pearl Harbor as if they owned the world. Marines acted that way even aboard ship. It drove Navy men crazy—but you had to be worse than crazy to want to mess with one of the hard-faced men in forest green. Even if you were a tough guy and you beat him, all of his buddies would come after you then, and they hung together a lot tighter than sailors did. Marines put Sam in mind of mean hunting dogs. You took them to where the game was, you pointed them at it, and you stood back and let them kill it. If you got in the way, they'd chew you up, too.

And so, when, after an hour or so of Sam's being out in the sun, a Marine walking past turned to his friend and said, "You smell something scorched?" Carsten kept on pushing his broom. Both Marines, themselves bronzed and fit-looking, laughed. He sighed. He couldn't do anything about the kind of skin he had except wish he were back in San Francisco, or maybe up in Seattle. Seattle was a good town if you were fair. The sun hardly ever came out, and when it did it was a lot paler than the lusty fire in the sky above Pearl Harbor.

Thinking of things in the sky above Pearl Harbor, Sam scanned it for aeroplanes. He didn't see any, either American or belonging to the enemies of the USA. He wished he hadn't seen the last aeroplane, that one from Japan. If it hadn't come buzzing around, the *Dakota* wouldn't have been in drydock with a large hole blown in her flank.

A couple of Navy men came by. They weren't off the *Dakota*; Carsten hadn't seen them before. He picked up snatches of their conversation—place names, mostly: "Kodiak . . . Prince Rupert . . . Victoria . . . Seattle."

Since he'd just been thinking wistfully of a cooler clime, he called after them: "What about Seattle?"

The two men stopped. "Nothing good," one of them answered. "The goddamn Japs have reinforced the limey fleet off British Columbia."

"You're right—that isn't good," Sam agreed. The places they'd mentioned made sense to him now. "They sailed up by way of Russian Alaska and then down along the west coast of Canada, did they?"

"That's what they did, all right, the bastards," the other sailor agreed unhappily. "On account of it, the North Pacific Squadron can't hardly stick its nose out of Puget Sound."

"You don't have to tell me about the Japs," Carsten said. "I was on the *Dakota* after they suckered us out of Pearl." The two strangers nodded sympathetically, for once at a predicament other than his sunburn. He went on, "You ask me, everybody in the whole damn Pacific had better watch out on account of the Japs. They're making like they're buddy-buddy with England, but if the limeys ever turn their backs on 'em, they'll get cornholed faster'n you'd believe. Us, too. I already seen that happen."

"We weren't out here yet when the Japs suckered you guys," one of the strangers said. He stuck out his hand. "Homer Bradley, off the *Jarvis*." He was sandy-haired but, to Carsten's annoyance, suntanned.

"Dino Dascoli, same ship," his companion added. The Honolulu sun wouldn't faze him; he was as swarthy as Vic Crosetti.

Carsten shook hands with both of them and introduced himself. Then he explained how the Americans' dash after the fleet that had launched the aeroplane had gone wrong, finishing, "As soon as we got torpedoed, it was easy to figure out what the hell we hadn't thought about. Next time, I hope we don't stick our dicks in the meat grinder that particular way."

"That's the truth," Bradley agreed. He studied Carsten's uniform. "You talk like a Seaman First, Sam, but you sort of sound like you think like an officer, you know what I mean?"

"Too damn much time on my hands, that's what it is, just like everybody else on the *Dakota* who isn't fixing her up," Sam said. "Nothin' to do but stuff like this or else sit around and play cards and shoot the breeze and think about things." He grinned. "Catch me at my battle station and I'm as stupid as anybody could want."

His new acquaintances grinned. "You got a good way of lookin' at things, Sam," Dino Dascoli said. He lowered his voice. "And since you got a good way of lookin' at things, maybe you got a good way of lookin' for things, too. A guy wants to have a good time around here, where's the best place at?"

"A good, good time?" Sam asked. Dascoli nodded. "You don't mind spending some money?" Dascoli nodded again. Sam smiled till his sunburned face hurt. "All right. What you do, then, is you hop on the trolley into Honolulu and you get off at the Kapalama stop. There's this gal named Maggie Stevenson . . ." Dascoli and Bradley leaned closer.

Down below Jonathan Moss, the town of Guelph, Ontario, was dying a slow, horrible death. Incessant artillery fell on the Canadians and Englishmen still holding out in the provincial town built of gray stone. The guns had been hammering at the Church of Our Lady Cathedral for days; the Canucks weren't shy about putting artillery observers up in the spires, and so the spires had to come down. Come down they had. Only smoke rose above the cathedral now. It rose high enough to make Moss cough and choke some thousands of feet above the ruined house of God.

In a way, he wished the order loosing the one-deckers to fly above enemy-held territory had not come. It would have spared him the sight of towns given over to pounding from the big guns. He'd seen plenty of that while piloting observation aeroplanes, and would not have minded missing it in his flying scout.

In another way, though, it mattered little. Although he might not have seen them as they were being wrecked, he'd flown over plenty of towns after the United States took them away from Canada, and they made a pretty appalling spectacle then, too.

And, thrusting ahead like this, he felt he was doing more to help the American soldiers on the ground push forward against the unceasing and often insanely stubborn opposition of the Canadian and British troops struggling to hold them back.

"More than a year," he said through the buzz of the engine. "More than a year, and we still aren't in Toronto." He shook his goggled head. Back in August 1914, no one would have believed that. The Americans weren't in Montreal. As long as Canada still hung on to the land between the one big city and the other, she was still a going concern.

Moss knew better than to let such gloomy reflections keep him from doing what he needed to do to stay alive. He kept an eye on his position in the flight of four Martins. Without consciously thinking about it, he checked above, below, and to both sides; his head was never still. He used the rearview mirror the mechanics had installed on his aeroplane, but did not rely on it alone. Every minute or so, he'd half turn and look back over his shoulder.

He hoped that was all wasted precaution, but his hope didn't keep him from being careful. The Canucks hadn't been sending many aeroplanes up lately to oppose the U.S. machines, but the British were shipping over more and more aeroplanes and pilots to make up for the shrinking pool of Canadian men and aircraft. He and his comrades had found out about that the hard way.

If the prospect of running into more British airmen bothered Dud Dudley, he didn't let on. The flight leader waggled his wings to make sure his comrades were paying attention to him, then dove down toward the ground. Moss spotted the target he had in mind: a column of men in butternut—no, he reminded himself, up here they called that color khaki, limey fashion—moving up toward the front.

The first time he'd machine-gunned men on the ground, he'd felt queasy and uncertain about it for days afterwards. He'd heard robbers were the same way: the first job they pulled was often almost impossibly hard. After that, things got easier, till they didn't really think about what they were doing, except the way any laborer might on the way to work.

He didn't know about robbers, not for sure. He did know that the only things going through his mind as he swooped on the marching soldiers like a hawk on a chipmunk were considerations of speed and altitude and angle, all the little practical matters that would help him do the foe as much damage as he could.

He swore when the men on the ground spotted him and his flightmates a few seconds faster than he'd hoped they would. The infantrymen began to scatter, and had good cover in which to shelter, for the road along which they were marching ran through what had been a built-up area that American artillery had rather drastically built down.

Little flashes from the ground said the soldiers down there were shooting at him. He didn't think much of it: after antiaircraft fire from cannon dedicated to the job, what were a few rifle bullets? Then one of them cracked past his head, almost close enough to be the crack of doom.

"Jesus!" he shouted, and stabbed his thumb down on the firing button of his machine gun. Bullets streamed out between the spinning blades of his propeller. He wished Dudley had never told him what happened when an interrupter gear got out of adjustment. If he shot himself down now, flying so low and fast, he'd surely crash. And even if, by some miracle, he did manage to glide to a landing, no insurance salesman would give him a dime's worth over coverage if he landed anywhere near the men he'd been shooting up. In their shoes, he would have settled his own hash, too.

There was a knot of them, running for the shelter of rubble that might once have been a row of shops. As long as he didn't shoot himself down, he held the whip hand. He fired another long burst and saw some of the men in khaki fall before he zoomed by.

Those are people, he thought with a small part of his mind as he gained altitude for another firing run. He had no trouble ignoring that small part. Those fleeing shapes in uniforms of the wrong color? They were just targets.

And if they weren't targets, they were the enemy. He'd just been thinking about what they'd do if they caught him. They hadn't caught him. He'd caught them instead.

He turned and shot them up again. They put a lot of lead in the air, trying to shoot down his aeroplane and those of his flightmates. After the second pass, Dud Dudley waved for the flight to pull up and head back toward the American lines. Moss had no trouble obeying the flight leader. Neither did Tom Innis. But smoke was pouring out of Luther Carlsen's engine. The careful pilot hadn't been careful enough.

After the smoke came fire. It caught on the fabric of the one-decker's fuselage and licked backwards with hideous speed; the doping that made the fabric resist the wind was highly inflammable, and the slipstream pushed the flames along ahead of it.

Carlsen did everything he could. He beat at the flames with the hand he didn't keep on the controls. He brought the aeroplane's nose up into a stall, to reduce the force of the wind. But when he recovered from the stall—and he did that as precisely and capably as he did everything else—the fire engulfed the aeroplane. He crashed into what might once have been a pleasant block of houses in Guelph.

Numbly, Moss, Innis, and Dudley flew back to their aerodrome, which, with the forward movement of the front, had advanced to near the city of Woodstock. Woodstock, before the war, had been famous for its tree-lined avenues. When the front passed through it, the famous trees were reduced to kindling, in which sad state they remained. Woodstock had also been prominent for its munitions plants. Nothing was left of them but enormous craters: the retreating Canadians had exploded them to deny them to the USA.

The three survivors landed without any trouble. Groundcrew men asked what had happened to Carlsen. The pilots explained, in a couple of short sentences. The mechanics didn't push them. Those things had happened before. They would happen again, all too often.

Captain Shelby Pruitt took their report. "Nothing to be done," he said when they were through. "Go where there are bullets and they're liable to hit you." He shook his head. "It's too damn bad. He knew what he was doing up there." Pointing to a big tent not far from the one in which he made his office, he added, "Go on over to the officers' club. I'm not going to send you up tomorrow."

That was the polite way of saying, *Go get drunk and then sleep it off.* The pilots gratefully took him up on it. Staring down into a glass of whiskey, Tom Innis said, "I always figured I would be the one to go. Luther did everything right all the time. Now he's dead. God damn it to hell, anyway." He knocked back the drink and signaled for another.

"Don't talk about who's going to go," Moss said, earnestly if a little blurrily—the tip of his nose was getting numb, and so was his tongue. "Bad luck."

"Bad luck," Innis repeated. He gulped down the new drink, too. "How many pilots who started the war will still be alive at the end of it, do you think?"

Moss didn't answer that. He didn't want to think about it, not at all. To keep from thinking about it, he got as drunk as he could as fast as he could. He and Innis and Dud Dudley were all staggering when they made their way back to their tent. By the time they got there, somebody had cleaned out Luther Carlsen's personal effects, to send back to his next of kin. Seeing the bare, neat, empty cot made Moss shiver. He'd taken over a cot like that. Who, one of these days, would take over the one over which he now sprawled at an angle no sober man would have chosen?

He was lucky. He fell asleep—or passed out—before he could dwell on that one for long. When he woke up the next morning, the whiskey had taken its revenge, and he hurt too bad to dwell on anything.

But that afternoon, after gallons of coffee and the hair of the dog that bit him, he felt almost human, in an elderly, melancholy way. He was writing a letter to a cousin in Cleveland when the tent flap opened. Captain Pruitt led in a gawky young man with a green-gray duffel slung over his shoulder. "Gentlemen," he said, "this is Zach Whitby. Lieutenant Whitby, we have here Dan Dudley, Tom Innis, and Jonathan Moss."

Whitby threw the duffel down on the cot that had been Luther Carlsen's. He stuck out his hand. "Pleased to meet you all."

"You all?" Moss ran the words together. "Look out, boys, we've got a Reb flying with us." If you laughed, you didn't have to think about it . . . not so much, anyhow.

"Why, Major, why did you pick *my* farm?" Lucien Galtier demanded. As he knew perfectly well what the answer to that question was, he was not so much seeking information as plumbing the depths of Major Jedediah Quigley's hypocrisy.

"I have several excellent reasons, *Monsieur* Galtier," Quigley answered. As he spoke, he ticked them off on his fingers, which, with his elegant Parisian accent and his incisive logic, made him seem more a lawyer than a soldier to Galtier: an invidious comparison if ever there was one. "First, *monsieur*, your farm is sufficiently far back from the banks of the St. Lawrence as to be beyond artillery range even from the gunboats that try to harass our operations on the river and our crossings. This is an important matter in the placement of a hospital, as I am sure you must agree." Without waiting to learn whether

Galtier agreed or not, he went on, "Second, the road is already paved to within a couple of miles of your farm. Extending it this much farther is a work of no great trouble."

"I would not put you to any trouble whatever," Galtier said, knowing he was fighting a losing battle.

"As I say, it is a small matter," Quigley replied. "It will even work to your advantage: an all-weather road passing by your farm will enable you to sell your produce ever so much more readily than you do now."

"I shall have ever so much less produce to sell, however, as you are taking so much of my patrimony for the purpose of building this hospital," Lucien told him. "And you appear to be taking the best land I have, that given over to wheat."

"Only the most convenient," Major Quigley assured him. "And you will be compensated for the use."

"Compensated as I was for my produce last winter?" Galtier shot back. Quigley shrugged, a fine French gesture to go with his fine French tongue. Yes, his hypocrisy was deep indeed. He never once mentioned Lucien's refusal to give names to Father Pascal or to collaborate with the Americans in any other way. But the farmer was as sure as he was of his own name that, had he chosen to collaborate, the hospital would have gone up on someone else's land.

Quigley said, "Do not think of this hospital as a permanent structure, *Monsieur* Galtier. It will serve its purpose for the time being and then pass away and be forgotten. As we establish and enlarge our foothold north of the St. Lawrence, no doubt it will become practical for us to build hospitals in secure areas there."

"No doubt," Lucien agreed tonelessly. Thinking he ought to learn all he could about the American incursion on the far side of the river, he asked, "And how is the war faring for you there?"

Major Quigley spread his hands. Though not a real Frenchman, he played the role well enough to take it on the stage. "Not so well as we would like, not so poorly that the enemy will be able to throw us back into the river."

By *the enemy*, of course, he meant the forces of Galtier's rightful government and those of Great Britain, which was proving a loyal ally to France. Lucien did not reply. What could he say? He was just an ordinary farmer. He supposed he should have been grateful that the American's revenge was no worse than this. From what he had heard, people who crossed the U.S. military government sometimes disappeared off the face of the earth. He had a wife and half a dozen children who needed him. He could not afford to let his tongue run as free as he might have liked.

When he didn't say anything, Jedediah Quigley shrugged again. "There you are, *Monsieur* Galtier. We should start construction in the next few days.

If you have any objections to the plan as currently constituted, you can offer them to the occupation authorities in Rivière-du-Loup."

"Thank you so much, Major Quigley," Galtier said, so smoothly that the American did not notice he was being sardonic. Oh, yes, you could make a trip up to Rivière-du-Loup for the privilege of complaining to the authorities about what they were doing to you. But, since they'd already decided to do it, how much was that likely to accomplish? The short answer was, *not much*. The longer answer was that it might do harm, because daring to complain would get his name underlined on the list the occupation authorities surely kept of those they did not trust.

"Now that I have given you the news, *Monsieur*, I must return to town," Quigley said. He climbed onto an utterly prosaic bicycle and pedaled away.

Off to the north, across the river, artillery rumbled. Galtier wondered whether it belonged to the American invaders or to those who tried to defend Quebec against them. The defenders, he hoped. He glanced up to the sky. The weather was still fine and mild. How much longer it would remain fine and mild, with September heading toward October, remained to be seen. Long enough for him to finish getting in the harvest—that long, certainly, if God was merciful even to the least degree. But the day after the harvest was done . . .

"Let the snow come then," he said, half prayer, half threat. The Americans would not have an easy time keeping an army on the far side of the wide river supplied if the winter was harsh. The defenders would not have an easy time, either, but they would not be cut off from their heartland as the invaders would. How well did Americans, used to warm weather, deal with weather that was anything but? Before long, the world would find out.

Marie came out of the farmhouse and looked down the road toward Rivière-du-Loup. Major Quigley, a rapidly disappearing speck, was still visible. Lucien wished Quigley would disappear for good. His wife asked, "What did the *Boche américain* want of you?"

"He was generous enough to inform me"—Lucien rolled his eyes—"the Americans are taking some of our land for the purpose of building a hospital on it. It is a safe place to do so, Major Quigley says."

Marie stamped her foot. "If he wants to build it in a safe place, why does he not put it in Father Pascal's church? No one would bring war to holy ground, is it not so?"

"That is an excellent thought," Galtier said. "Even the pious father could not disagree with it, good and Christian man that he is." He shook his head. The war was making him more cynical than he'd ever dreamt of being before it began.

"But no," Marie went on. "It must be on our good cropland. Well, I have a hope for this hospital of theirs."

"I have the same hope, I think," Lucien said. His wife looked a question his way. "I hope it is very full of Americans," he told her. She nodded, satisfied. They'd been married a long time, and thought a lot alike.

Stephen Ramsay used a makeshift periscope to look up over the parapet at the Yankee lines between Nuyaka and Beggs. If he'd stuck his head up to have a look around, some damnyankee sniper would have blown off the top of it. The Creek regiment in which Ramsay was a captain had pushed U.S. troops a few miles back from Nuyaka, but then the lines had set like concrete.

He turned the periscope this way and that. What he saw remained pretty much the same, regardless of the angle: barbed wire, some shiny and new, some rusting; firing pits for Yankee scouts; and then another trench line just like his.

Lowering the periscope—a couple of little hand mirrors mounted at the proper angles on a board—he turned to Moty Tiger and said, "Far as I can see, those damnyankee sons of bitches are here to stay."

"That's not good, sir," the Creek sergeant answered seriously. "This is our land, Creek land. If we can, we have to throw them off here. You Confederates have the right to be here. You are our friends. You are our allies. But we have been enemies of the United States for many generations. The Yankees do not belong here."

"I'm not going to argue with you, Sergeant," Ramsay said. "All I'm going to do is give you this here periscope and let you take a look for yourself. If that looks like a position we can rush, you tell me straight out. Go on—take a look."

Moty Tiger looked. He looked carefully—or as carefully as he could, given the limitations of the instrument. As Ramsay had before him, he lowered it. His coppery face was glum. "Doesn't look easy, Captain," he admitted.

"I didn't think so, either," Ramsay said, with more than a little relief. He'd been afraid Moty Tiger would think like a Creek before he thought like a soldier, and would feel duty-bound to try to recover every scrap of Creek territory regardless of the cost. He outranked his sergeant, of course, but Moty Tiger was a Creek and he wasn't. In a contest for the hearts and minds of the soldiers in the Creek Nation Army, that counted more than rank did. For that matter, Moty Tiger didn't just influence the opinions of his fellow Indians: he also reflected those opinions.

There the matter rested till late that afternoon, when Colonel Lincoln came up to the front-line trench. When Ramsay saw the regimental C.O.'s face, his heart sank. Lincoln looked thoroughly grim. He didn't say anything. Ramsay got the idea that wasn't because he didn't know anything—more likely because he knew too much, and didn't like any of it.

When Lincoln stayed quiet for more than five minutes, Ramsay, who favored the direct approach, asked him, "What's gone wrong now, sir?"

Colonel Lincoln gestured for Ramsay to walk with him. Once they got out of earshot of the men, Lincoln said, "I'll tell you what's gone wrong. Charlie Fixico's up and decided he's a goddamn general, that's what."

"Uh-oh," Ramsay said, without any great eloquence but most sincerely. "What sort of stupid, impossible thing does he have in mind for us to do?" He still thought like a sergeant, not an officer: what were generals for but ordering troops to try to do stupid, impossible things?

Lincoln was a longtime officer, but he looked to feel the same way. Pointing northeast, he answered, "He wants us to break through that Yankee line and retake Beggs."

"Jesus," Ramsay said. He'd talked Moty Tiger out of that. Talking the chief of the Creek Nation out of it wasn't going to be easy. "Why does he want to do that? Isn't he grateful we saved Okmulgee for him?"

"Not any more, he's not. That was a while ago, and politicians aren't what you'd call good at remembering," Lincoln answered. "Why? Two reasons, far as I can make out. First one is, he wants to get back the oil fields around Beggs. Second one is, it's Creek territory, it's got damnyankees on it, and he wants 'em gone. That's about what it boils down to."

"Jesus," Ramsay said again. "Doesn't he know that if we try to take those Yankee positions, we're gonna get ourselves slaughtered, nothing else but?"

"If he doesn't, it's not because I didn't tell him till I was blue in the face," Lincoln answered. "He ordered the attack to go in anyhow."

"I hope you got the Confederate corps commander to overrule him, sir," Ramsay said. "It'd be suicide, like I said."

"I went to corps headquarters, yes," Lincoln said. "They told me that if Chief Fixico wants an attack, Chief Fixico gets an attack. Two reasons, again. One is, his own men—us—are in it, so he's not asking the CSA to do all his work for him. Two is, near as I can tell, they don't want to make the Indians angry, so they go along with any requests they get. Bombardment begins tomorrow morning at 0300—supposed to chew up the barbed wire between us and them and make reaching their trenches easier. We go over the top at 0600."

"Yes, sir," Ramsay said. He couldn't think of anything else to say. He knew what was liable to happen shortly after 0600. He wasn't afraid—or not very much afraid, at any rate. What he felt was more like numbness, as if he'd been told out of the blue he'd need a surgical operation.

He went up and down the trench line, letting the men know what they'd be doing at dawn tomorrow. Some of the Creeks, especially the younger ones and the replacements who hadn't seen much action, looked excited. A couple of them let out happy yowls: war cries. Moty Tiger just glanced up at Ramsay and nodded. What was going on behind those black eyes, that impassive face? Ramsay couldn't tell.

He made sure his rifle was clean and that he had plenty of ammunition, then wrapped himself in his blanket and tried to sleep. He didn't think he would, but he did. The beginning of the barrage at 0300 woke him. He got up and made sure the men would be ready to move forward when the shelling stopped. "With luck," he said, "the damnyankees'll be too battered to do any shooting back till we're in amongst 'em. Good luck, boys."

At 0600 on the dot, the bombardment ended. Colonel Lincoln blew a whistle. "Let's go!" he shouted.

Out of the trenches swarmed the Creek Nation Army, along with Confederate troops proper to either side of them. They went forward as fast as they could, knowing their best hope for safety was getting to the enemy front line before U.S. troopers could recover from the barrage they'd taken and reach the firing steps—and the machine guns they surely had all along the line.

The shelling had knocked aside or wrecked some of the barbed wire, but not all, or even most. First one Creek, then another, then another, got hung up in it. "Don't try and cut 'em loose," Ramsay called. "Keep moving. That's the best thing we can do." It wasn't easy. The stuff grabbed and clung and bit, so you felt as if you were moving underwater with sharks nipping you, or through a nightmare, trying without much luck to run from a monster you dared not turn around and see.

But the monster was in front. Here and there along the Yankee line, muzzle flashes showed men who, despite the artillery barrage, knew they had to kill the attackers now or die themselves in moments. Then a couple of machine guns, one right in front of Ramsay, came to hammering life.

Men of the Creek Nation Army fell before that hateful patter like wheat before a reaper. There went Moty Tiger, clutching at his belly. There went Colonel Lincoln, down with boneless finality.

My regiment now, Ramsay thought. He waved the survivors forward. "Come on!" he shouted. "We can still—"

One moment, he was advancing. The next, without warning, he found himself lying in a shell hole, staring in confusion at dirt and a couple of bits of rusty barbed wire. He had trouble breathing. He couldn't figure out why till he tasted blood in his mouth. *How did that happen?* he wondered vaguely. He looked up at the sky. It was going black. *That's not right,* he thought. *It's morning, not*

XX

Sylvia Enos collected the mail from the box in the front hall of her apartment building. She crumpled up a patent-medicine circular. The allotment check from the Navy she kept.

Her lips twisted in a bitter smile. She had the money, drawn from George's pay, as he'd said she would before he enlisted. The only trouble was, she didn't care about the money. She would sooner have had her husband back. When he'd stayed in Boston after joining the Navy, when he'd, in essence, gone back to being a fisherman, she'd been overjoyed. Her life had returned to one not far different from what she'd known before the war started, even if she had kept her job at the canning plant. Considering all the dislocations that had come since 1914, she'd counted herself lucky.

"So much for luck," she said as she started upstairs. Now George was gone, and gone farther and more irrevocably than when he'd languished in Confederate imprisonment. All she had by which to remember him were the monthly allotment checks and an occasional letter. There could have been more letters, she supposed, but George had never been much of a writer.

The hallway and the stairwell were not so warm as they had been a few weeks before: Boston's summer, hot while it lasted, couldn't be counted on to last far into September. For the moment, cutting the heat only made days and nights more pleasant. Pretty soon, though, she wouldn't be wrangling with the Coal Board over fuel enough to cook her food. She'd be wrangling with its inflexible clerks and stubborn supervisors over fuel enough to keep her from freezing during the winter.

She left the stairwell and trudged wearily down the hall to Mrs. Coneval's apartment. She stood there in front of the doorway for a moment before she knocked. It sounded as if the children were fighting a battle of their own inside, a battle about the size of some of the big ones on the Kentucky front. She wondered how Brigid Coneval put up with the noise.

When she did knock, she needed to hammer on the door to get anyone within to notice she was there. After a while, Brigid Coneval opened the door. The racket, without wood between it and Sylvia, grew from alarming to appalling. "A bit rowdy they are today," Mrs. Coneval said with a smile that could only be described as wan.

"So it would seem," Sylvia agreed. She knew she would have gone crazy, cooped up in there the day around with a horde of screaming children. Given the choice between that and the factory job she had, she would have chosen factory work a hundred times out of a hundred. Her own two children were plenty to try to keep under control.

"I'll get your wee ones," Brigid Coneval said, and disappeared back into chaos. A toddler smaller than Mary Jane started to howl. Sylvia thanked heaven she hadn't got pregnant again after George came back from the CSA. Trying to take care of a new baby by herself, along with two small children, was nothing to anticipate with glee.

Mrs. Coneval came back holding Mary Jane by one hand and George, Jr., by the other. George, Jr., twisted in her grasp and fired an imaginary rifle at one of the other children. "I got you, Joey, you dirty Reb!"

"No, you didn't—you missed me," Joey shouted back—the next small boy who admitted himself slain in imaginary conflict would be the first. "And I'm not the Reb—you are!"

"Liar, liar, pants on fire," George, Jr., yelled at him, which made Mary Jane giggle. George, Jr., said, "Hello, Mama. Joey cheats."

"I don't either!" Joey exclaimed.

"It doesn't matter now, one way or the other," Sylvia said. By the look on his face, her son was prepared to disagree with that as eloquently as he could. She didn't give him the chance. "See you tomorrow morning," she said to Mrs. Coneval, and took her children back to their apartment.

It seemed empty without her husband there. She was used to having him gone for days at a time; she'd even had to grow used to having him gone for much longer than that while he was a Confederate detainee. Now, though, with him in St. Louis, she had the strong sense she wouldn't see him again till the war ended, and it didn't look as if it was going to end any time soon.

She had some good scrod in the icebox. She hadn't lost the connections she'd made down on T Wharf; as a fisherman's wife (even if her husband wasn't actually fishing right now), she could find better fish than the ordinary shopper and pay less for it. She breaded the scrod, pan-fried it in lard on top of the stove, and served it up with mashed potatoes.

George, Jr., ate everything up and demanded more. He ate almost as much as a man, or so it seemed. She was probably wrong about that, she admitted to herself as she gave him more potatoes, but she wasn't wrong about his outgrowing all his clothes. She patted her purse. The allotment check would come in handy the next time she went shopping at Filene's.

Mary Jane, by contrast, had to be cajoled into eating much of anything. Sylvia produced a gumdrop from a bowl on a shelf too high for the children to reach. She set it on the table. "Do you want it?" she asked her daughter.

Eyes wide with longing, Mary Jane nodded. Having once made the dreadful error of saying no to candy, she wasn't about to repeat it.

"All right," Sylvia said. "Eat up your supper and you can have it." Sometimes that got results, sometimes a tantrum. Today it worked. Mary Jane cleaned her plate and stretched out a hand that needed washing. "Good girl," Sylvia told her, handing her the sweet.

After she'd scrubbed the dishes, she settled the children down on the couch, one on either side of her, and read to them from *Queen Zixi of Ix*. Mary Jane's attention sometimes wandered. When she got off the couch, went over to get a doll, and then came back to play with it, Sylvia didn't mind. The story held George, Jr., rapt for most of an hour. By then, it was time for Sylvia to get the children into bed. Morning came all too early.

Then she had the apartment to herself, before she also had to go to bed. When George was home, they'd sit and talk while he smoked a pipe or cigar. When he was out fishing, she'd look forward to his return. Now . . . now he was gone, and the place seemed large and empty and quiet as the tomb.

She walked around for a while with a feather duster, flicking specks from tables and gewgaws. What with the dirt and soot always in the air, things got dusty faster than they had any proper business doing. That would worsen in winter, when everyone burned more coal—always assuming the Coal Board didn't decide to let people turn to blocks of ice instead.

She realized she was dusting a china dog for the third time. Shaking her head, she put the feather duster away. Time hung heavy when she was alone, but not that heavy. She went into the bedroom, changed into a nainsook cotton nightgown with lace at the neck and sleeves, and set out the drawers and skirt and shirtwaist she'd wear the next morning. Then she went into the bathroom, where she cleaned her teeth and gave her hair a hundred strokes with the brush in front of the mirror over the sink. Evening ritual done, she went back into the bedroom, turned off the gas lamp, and lay down.

She sat up with a start. "Lord have mercy, I'd forget my head if it wasn't sewed on tight!" she exclaimed. Not wanting to get up and light the lamp again, she fumbled in the darkness with the alarm clock on the nightstand. Had she forgotten to set it, she would surely have been late to work, which would have got her docked at best and fired at worst. "Can't have that," she said, as if someone lying beside her was trying to talk her into sleeping as long as she wanted.

But no one was lying beside her. The bed felt large and empty. Some nights, she was so tired she hardly noticed George was gone and would be gone God only knew how long. Others, she missed him to the point where tears ran down her face. They did no good. She knew that. Knowing didn't help.

She lay on her back, staring at the ceiling and trying without much luck to go to sleep. She closed her eyes, which didn't seem to make the room much darker. But with her eyes closed, as they usually were when she and George made love, it was easier to imagine him on top of her, imagine his familiar weight pressing her down on the mattress, imagine his breath warming the hollow of her shoulder in quick gasps.

Imagination, now, was all she had. She shifted restlessly on the bed. If George were there now, she'd be able to sleep pretty soon. She shifted again. The hem of her nightgown rode up past her knees. She reached down. Instead of straightening it, she hiked it up to her waist.

A few minutes later, she rolled over onto her side. She would sleep now. She knew it. She bit her lip, not caring to remember what she'd just done. But when your man was away for months, maybe for years, what were you supposed to do? It wasn't as good as the real thing with George (actually, that wasn't quite true—it felt as good, or maybe even better, but it was lonely at the end), but it was better than nothing.

"Better than nothing," she muttered drowsily. With the war on, wasn't that as much as anybody had any business expecting? Her eyelids slid down over her eyes, of themselves this time. She started to say something else, but only a soft snore passed her lips.

"Masks and goggles!" Captain Orville Wyatt ordered as the bombardment of the Confederate positions east of the Roanoke began. Chester Martin quickly tied the hyposulfite-impregnated mask over his mouth and nose. He breathed in chemical dampness. That was unpleasant, but much less so than breathing in the poison gas that shells were spreading up and down the Rebel lines. He took off his newly issued helmet to strap the goggles over his eyes. He didn't know whether to curse the weight of the thing or bless it for making his brains less likely to be splattered over the landscape.

Beside Martin, Specs Peterson swore. "They've been usin' this damn gas more since they started loading it into shells than they did when they shot it out of those projector things, and I fucking hate it," he said. "I can leave my glasses on and have the chlorine eat my eyes up, or I can take 'em off and fall on my damn face half a dozen times before I get to where the Rebs are at. Hell of a deal, ain't it?"

"I'm in the same boat, Peterson," Captain Wyatt said, touching the earpiece to his own spectacles. "I've been leaving my glasses on. My eyes get better after a couple of days, seems like."

"Yeah, but you want to be a hero," Peterson muttered under his breath. "Me, I just want to get out of this in one piece."

"Amen," Chester Martin said. "All I want to do is live through this damn war and go home and make steel. I used to complain about that job like nobody's business. It was hot and it was dirty and it was hard and it was dangerous. And it's still every damn one of those things. And you know what else? Next to what we're doin' now, it's so fine, I'll never grouse again."

"Nothin' worse than farm work—I always used to say that," Corporal Paul Andersen put in. "Only goes to show I didn't know what the hell I was talking about. You do your two years as a conscript and that's not so bad. You figure real soldiering works out the same way. Ha!" His wave took in the trenches, the filth, the vermin, the fear, the foe.

Captain Wyatt said, "Once upon a time, Virginia used to belong to the USA. Now we're working to take it back. It's not the kind of job anybody wants to do, but it needs doing. If everything goes right, we keep their front trenches. No matter what happens, we bring some prisoners back for interrogation." He went up and down the trench line, checking to make sure his soldiers' masks and goggles were on securely. He was a long way from being the most good-natured of men, but he fussed over the soldiers in his company like a mother cat with a litter of kittens. As far as Martin was concerned, that made him a good officer.

The bombardment went on and on. Every so often, the Confederates would lob a few shells back at the U.S. lines, but they were taking it a lot harder than they were dishing it out. That suited Martin fine. He'd been on the receiving end of too many barrages to suit him. Giving was better—an un-Christian thought but a true one nonetheless.

Sharp as an axe coming down, the shelling ended. Up and down the trench line, whistles sounded. Martin scrambled up the steps made of sandbags, over the parapet, and toward the Rebel lines.

Pioneers had cut some paths through the barbed wire between the U.S. and Confederate lines, marking them with strips of cloth tied to the wire. Martin liked that and hated it at the same time. It gave him an easier way toward the enemy trenches, but also gave the Rebel machine gunners a notion of what the way was. If they'd zeroed their weapons on it . . . He tried not to think about that, as he tried not to think of any of the disasters that might befall him.

Here and there, the bombardment had knocked down the posts that supported the barbed wire, leaving it sprawled in snaky coils on the rubble-strewn ground of what had probably been a suburb of Big Lick, Virginia.

When Chester Martin saw relatively clear stretches of that sort, he used them to move forward. The Rebs wouldn't have so many guns pointed there as they would at the paths.

He blew out through the thick, wet gauze pad he wore over his mouth. The first couple of gas attacks had let U.S. forces gain and consolidate their positions east of the Roanoke River. Now, though, the Rebs had learned how to defend themselves against the new American weapon, and pushing them back had turned into another hard job.

He wasn't more than halfway toward their trenches, and already the Rebels were shooting back at him and his men, the muzzle flashes of their rifles seeming bright as the sun. Machine guns started up a moment later. Somewhere not far away, he heard the wet smack of a bullet striking flesh. Whoever was hurt there, he hoped it wasn't too bad and he hoped they'd be able to get the fellow to a doctor before he bled to death. That also made him hope nobody would get hurt picking up the wounded man. Nobody was supposed to shoot at people wearing Red Cross armbands, but bullets, as he'd learned too well, weren't fussy about whom they hit.

One of the machine guns, traversed by what their crews matter-of-factly called a two-inch tap, sent bullets kicking up dirt not far from his feet. He dove headlong into a shell hole in front of him. A horrid stench rose. Part of it came from the pool of noisome, stagnant water at the bottom of the hole. More was from the body, or rather fragments of body, entombed under dirt and shattered bricks. U.S. forces were advancing, so the dead man was presumably a Confederate. But he would have smelled just as bad had he been born in Michigan.

Martin wished the gauze mask he wore were as good at neutralizing stenches as it was at keeping chlorine from searing his lungs. That, though, wasn't why it had been designed. He tried to keep his unruly stomach under control. If he took off the mask to puke, who could guess how much poison gas he'd breathe in after every retch?

The hail of machine-gun bullets passed on beyond the shell hole. Crawling through muck of a sort he didn't care to contemplate, Martin peered out over the forward lip of the hole. Whatever else he did he couldn't stay there. Grunting under the weight of his pack, he heaved himself upright again and ran on.

Here came the trenches. He could see murky spots up and down their length, spots where chlorine gas still lingered. The Confederate defenders wore masks like his. A lot of them had goggles, too. They were either bareheaded or in caps, though: no one had yet issued them helmets.

One of the Rebs raised a rifle to shoot at Martin. He shot first, though, on the run and from the hip. As much by luck as anything else, the Confederate howled and dropped his weapon to clutch at his chest.

Yelling, Martin leaped down into the trench. He used his bayonet to make sure the Confederate wasn't going anywhere, then pulled a grenade improvised from nails and a half-pound block of explosive out of one of his equipment pouches and flung it into the next trench back. Somebody screamed a moment after it exploded, so he supposed he'd done that right.

He looked around, collected a couple of his soldiers by eye, and headed down the trench toward the next traverse. Like U.S. forces, the Confederates sensibly did not dig their trenches as long, straight gashes in the earth. Had they been so foolish, any foes who got into them could have delivered a deadly enfilading fire. Unfortunately, the game was harder than that.

Firebays like the one he and his companions were in led to other firebays advanced or recessed from them by a short stretch of perpendicular trench, a traverse, so that the line, if viewed from an aeroplane, took on the look of a postage stamp perforated with insane regularity. Just because your side held a firebay didn't mean the enemy wasn't still lurking in the next traverse.

Finding out who was in the next traverse—or the next firebay, if you were in a traverse—was not a job for the faint of heart. Neither was getting rid of those people, if they happened to be wearing butternut while you were in green-gray. One way was to go up out of the trenches and crawl along the ground between them. Doing that, though, was a lot like a snail's jumping out of its shell to run faster: the poor creature was all too likely to get squashed.

Charging round a corner was not recommended, either. The other fellow had had too much time to prepare nasty surprises for you. Nearing a corner of the firebay, Martin called, "Give up, you Rebs!"

The only answer he got back was a grenade flying through the air. It was thrown too far, and detonated on the level ground beyond the firebay. His own men knew how to reply to it. Several grenades, tossed with better effect, rained down on the Confederates. Grenades, Martin reflected, were handy things: they gave an infantryman a little artillery of his own. And, like artillery, they didn't have to wound to be effective. Even a near miss could leave a soldier shaken and stunned.

Martin bet his life the grenades had stunned the Rebs in the traverse for a couple of vital seconds. He charged round the corner of the trench. One Reb had been stationed there to deal with any such unwelcome newcomers, but he was down and thrashing, blood pouring from his belly out between his fingers. Followed by the men he'd gathered, Martin ran past him and around the next bend. Another Confederate was down there, and still others on their feet. "Hands up, you Rebs!" he screamed.

Reggie Bartlett could barely hear the screamed order to surrender. One of the grenades the damnyankees had thrown had gone off only a few feet away from him. He looked down at his trouser leg. He was bleeding. Neither the pain nor the flow of blood was too bad, though, so he guessed whatever fragment or nail had hit him had drilled straight through muscle without getting stuck there or slamming into bone.

"Hands up!" the Yankee sergeant yelled again. Reggie let his rifle fall to the mud of the trench floor and raised his hands over his head. He knew he and his companions were lucky to get a chance to surrender after they'd tried to fight back. A lot of times, in situations like that, the side winning the fight in the trenches left only the losers' corpses.

The U.S. soldiers swarmed over him, Jasper Jenkins, and the other privates who hadn't been hurt—or not badly hurt, anyway, as a couple of them bore minor wounds not much different from Bartlett's. Corporal McCorkle lay on the ground, moaning. The U.S. soldier shook his head. "Poor bastard must have taken most of a grenade's worth, right in the gut," he said.

"He had a lot of gut to take it in," the sergeant answered, truthfully but unkindly. He frisked Reggie with thorough haste, depriving him of his pocket watch, his wallet, and whatever loose change he had in his pockets. Bartlett made no move to stop him, understanding it would be the last move he ever made if he did. Confederate troops plundered Yankee prisoners just as enthusiastically when they got the chance.

Off toward either side and back deeper in the Confederate position, the sound of fighting was picking up. The U.S. sergeant peered ever so cautiously over the parados at the rear of the trench, treating it as if it were the parapet at the front, which, from his point of view, it was.

He fired a couple of rounds at whatever he saw back there, then shook his head. The iron kettles he and his men wore gave them a look as if out of another time, old and fierce and sullen. What with helmet, goggles, and mask, hardly any of his face was actually visible. One of his men, who wore ordinary glasses instead of goggles and whose eyes were red and teary, said, "We ain't gonna be able to hold these trenches, Sarge."

"Yeah, I think you're right," the sergeant answered regretfully after gauging the noise again. "We're bringing back prisoners, so the brass can't grouse too bad." He turned to Bartlett and the other captured Confederates. "All right, you lugs, up over the top and back to the American lines. Don't try anything cute or you'll find out how cute dead is."

Reggie had gone over the top a good many times, but never before without a rifle in his hands. He felt very naked, very much exposed as he awkwardly got up into no-man's-land and scrambled back through the barbed wire toward the forwardmost U.S. trenches. A few of the damnyankees in those trenches shot at him and his comrades. He was glad they quit when they saw the Yankee soldiers coming along behind the men in butternut.

He'd hoped he'd have a chance to jump in a shell hole and have the sergeant and the rest of the Yankees go on by so he could sneak back to his own lines. It didn't happen. One reason it didn't was that the Confederates whose positions hadn't been overrun were shooting at the damnyankees, who bunched up close to their prisoners to discourage that. How were you supposed to escape a man who kept stepping on your bootheels?

The unhappy answer was, you couldn't. Bartlett had jumped down into U.S. trenches, too, but this time the Yankees had rifles and he didn't. "Well done, Sergeant," said one of them—an officer, by his demeanor.

"Thank you, Captain Wyatt," the sergeant answered. "Long as you're back here, I don't suppose I'm in trouble for not holding onto that stretch of Rebel entrenchment."

"No, nothing to worry about there, Martin," the officer—Wyatt—said. "Sometimes we manage to advance a few yards, sometimes we don't. They're more ready to face gas than they used to be." He pointed to the mask on Reggie's face.

"Yes, sir." Sergeant Martin shed his own mask and goggles. He rounded on Bartlett. "All right, Reb, let's have it."

"Reginald Bartlett, private, Confederate States Army," Reggie answered, and recited his pay number.

"What unit, Bartlett?" Sergeant Martin asked.

"I don't have to tell you that," Bartlett said.

The sergeant glanced over to his captain. Like one of Martin's soldiers, Captain Wyatt wore spectacles. Behind them, his eyes were not only reddened by chlorine but thoroughly grim. "I'm only going to tell you this once, Bartlett, so you'd better listen hard—the rest of you Rebs, too. Do you know how many thousand miles this godforsaken chunk of Virginia is from the Hague?"

It wasn't a geography question, although, from the way Jasper Jenkins frowned and scowled, he thought it was. Reggie knew better. What Wyatt had just given him was a warning: no matter what the formal laws of war said about forcing information out of prisoners, he was going to ask whatever he was going to ask, and he expected answers.

"Let's try again, Bartlett," Martin said, proving Reggie had been right. "What unit?"

If he didn't talk, he knew exactly what would happen to him. He didn't want to die in a Yankee trench, without even a chance to hit back at the enemy. He wished the U.S. sergeant had picked someone else on whom to start the questioning. He wouldn't have been so ashamed had he been the second or third man to open up rather than the first.

"Seventh Virginia Infantry," he said rapidly. There. It was done.

Captain Wyatt turned to the rest of the Confederates. "How about you boys?" The other men fairly fell over themselves agreeing. Reggie wondered if Wyatt had called them *boys* to stress that they were as much his inferiors as Negroes were whites' inferiors in the CSA. If so, the captain was one devious fellow. Bartlett covertly studied him. That seemed likely.

"Who's your battalion commander?" Wyatt demanded.

"Major Colleton." Jasper Jenkins got it out a split second ahead of Reggie. As if to make up for that, Reggie added, "I don't think he was there when you all raided us—he was back at Division HQ."

"Was he?" Wyatt said in an interested voice. "What was he doing there?"

"Don't know, sir," Bartlett answered truthfully. He didn't like the expression on the Yankee captain's face. It spoke of bodies forgotten in shell holes. He touched his sleeve and said, "I'm just a private, sir. The only time officers tell me anything is when they tell me what to do." A chorus of agreement rose from his fellow prisoners.

"It could be." Wyatt's face went from grim to thoughtful. "It might even be true with us—and you Rebs, your officers are a pack of damned aristocrats, aren't they?" Somehow, he contrived to look languid and effete for a moment before turning to Sergeant Martin. "Next time we hit them, we have to catch some bigger fish than privates. These boys don't know anything."

"Raids like this, sir, you take what you can grab," Martin said, which matched Bartlett's experience in the trenches.

"Maybe." From the way Wyatt acted, that seemed to mean he was yielding the point. Sure enough, he jerked his head toward the opening to a communication trench. "All right, Sergeant, take 'em back. We'll let the chaps from Intelligence see if they have any—intelligence, I mean."

"Yes, sir," Martin said. He picked out a couple of his own men with quick hand gestures. "Specs, Joe, come on along with me. These desperate characters'd probably knock me over the head and run off to assassinate TR in a red-hot minute if I was with 'em all by my lonesome." His grin said he was not to be taken seriously.

Reggie Bartlett felt like a desperate character, but not in the way the Yankee sergeant meant. If you were a prisoner of war, you were supposed to try to escape. That much he knew. How you were supposed to try was another question. He didn't have time to think about it. Martin gestured with his bayonet-tipped rifle. The Confederate prisoners got moving.

"Keep those hands high," warned the damnyankee with the glasses—Specs. Guys with glasses were supposed to be mild-mannered. He wasn't, not even close.

Confederate shells—a belated response to the gas barrage and trench raid—fell not far away as they went out of the front line. Reggie swore. He'd almost been killed a couple of times by short artillery rounds. What irony, though, to end his days on the receiving end of a perfectly aimed Confederate shell.

Martin and his comrades turned the Confederate prisoners over to other men farther back, then returned to their position. The grilling Reggie got from U.S. Intelligence seemed perfunctory—occupation before the war, name, rank, pay number, unit, a few questions about what they'd been doing and what they might do, and a few more questions, just as casual, about the state of morale of the Negro laborers attached to their units.

"Who pays attention to niggers?" Jasper Jenkins said. "You tell 'em what to do, they do it, and that's that." The man recording the answers, a wizened little fellow who looked like a born clerk, wrote down the words without comment.

When he was through with the interrogation, the wizened fellow said, "All right. You're going back to a holding camp now. Don't forget your pay number. We'll keep track of you with it. I expect you'll be bored. Can't help that." He nodded to a couple of guards in green-gray.

Almost, it was like going out of the line. Almost. The prisoners were marched back toward a railhead out of artillery range of Confederate guns. That felt familiar, even if nobody boasted about the havoc he aimed to wreak in saloons or brothels. Waiting for a train was familiar, too. Getting into a stinking boxcar that had once held horses was less so, although not unknown.

The train fought its way up over the Blue Ridge Mountains. That line hadn't existed before the war started. The Yankees had built it to haul supplies to the Roanoke front. It was a two-track line; several eastbound trains growled past the one on which Bartlett unhappily rode. "Damnyankees do a lot of haulin', don't they?" Jasper Jenkins said, his voice mournful.

Somewhere on the downhill grade—or rather, one of the downhill grades—they passed out of Virginia and into its breakaway cousin, West Virginia. When the train hissed to a stop, armed guards threw open the doors and shouted, "Everybody out! Move, move, move, you damn Rebs!"

Again, Bartlett might almost have been back in a rest camp. He went through the same surely useless delousing process he had then. He also had his hair clipped down to his scalp. The uniform he drew on completion of all that, though, was not his own. The tunic was tight, the trousers and boots too large. He complained about it. The fellow handing out clothes looked at him as if he were insane. "Shut up," he said flatly. Reggie shut up.

Prisoner barracks were of rough, unpainted wood, with spaces showing between boards. Reggie didn't look forward to that in winter. Bunks were similarly rough, and stacked on top of one another not double, not triple, but quadruple. He found a third-level one to call his own and climbed into it. "Home," he said sadly.

* * *

Evening was coming to Hampstead, Maryland. As far as Jake Featherston was concerned, it looked like a pretty good evening. The Yankees out in front of the Confederate lines had been quiet, and the battery had needed to fire only a few rounds at them. Some of those had been gas shells, too.

"About time," Featherston muttered to himself. The United States had been using gas against the Confederacy for months. Being able to respond in kind felt good. "Let those bastards worry about masks and goggles when we want 'em to, not the other way round."

He got his mess kit and went over to the stew pot Perseus had bubbling. Some damnyankee farmer was short a chicken. Jake found himself imperfectly sympathetic, especially when the Negro ladled a drumstick into his mess tin. He smacked his lips. Sure as hell, things were looking up.

He sat around shooting the breeze with his gun crew. It wasn't the same as it had been back in the old days, with the veterans who'd served beside him before the shooting started. But the new fish weren't virgins any more, either. "We've got us a pretty good gun here," Featherston said, looking back at the howitzer.

"The best," Michael Scott said. The loader was probably right, at least as far as the battery went. By their smug grins, the rest of the gun crew agreed with him. "We got us the best niggers in the battery, too," he added in the fond tones a man might use about a child of whom he is proud: the typical tones of a Confederate white talking about the achievements of a Confederate Negro. He patronized so automatically, he had no idea he was doing it.

"That they are," Jake Featherston said. His tone of voice was a little different: he'd used Nero and Perseus as men, however uncomfortable that had made both him and them. He shook his head. He neither particularly liked nor particularly trusted Negroes, and the principal reason for that was his certainty that they had more capacity than they showed. As an overseer's son, that worried him. The surprise you got if you kept thinking a man a boy was apt to be dreadful.

He didn't mention that the two Negroes had helped him fight the gun. The crew he had now knew it, but they seemed intent on pretending they didn't. He understood that; he tried to pretend it hadn't happened, too. Doing anything else tore a hole in the fabric of the Confederate way of life. He was glad Nero and Perseus hadn't turned uppity on account of their exploit. They would have been sorry for that, and some of the blame would have stuck to him, too.

He wandered over to see if anything was left in the stew pot, and came back with a couple of potatoes. The rest of the chicken seemed to have walked with the Lord, or more likely with the cooks. He shrugged. You had to expect that. Who ever heard of a cook's going hungry?

After he'd disposed of the potatoes, he washed his mess tin in a bucket of water and scrubbed it with a rag till the metal took on a dull gleam. He made sure the rest of the gun crew did the same. Nothing gave you food poisoning faster than eating out of a dirty mess tin.

Scott broke out a deck of cards. Jake declined to get into a poker game, saying, "My luck's been lousy lately." That was, if anything, an understatement; he'd lost most of a month's pay a week before, betting a full house against four artfully concealed nines.

He walked out onto Hampstead's main street and peered north. The fall air was cool against his cheek. He couldn't see anything much in the deepening twilight, and told himself that was just as well. If he had seen something, it would have been Yankee artillery flashes lighting up the horizon, which would have meant Yankee shells paying the battery a visit. This past year, he'd had all the glory and drama and excitement of combat he'd needed to prove to him that the best thing to hope for in the middle of a war was a nice, quiet day—or two or three of them in a row.

Since he didn't feel like sleeping, he went back to check on the horses. Perseus and Nero had done their usual capable job of taking care of the animals. He patted the gray gelding on the nose, then headed out of the barn where the animals were resting.

A cricket chirped. Somewhere off in the middle distance, an owl let loose with a mournful hoot. From the front came the occasional crack of rifle fire. It was only occasional, though, not the continuous, almost surflike roar it became when the action heated up. He looked up to the rather cloudy heavens and thanked God he wasn't an infantryman.

Captain Stuart's tent was pitched not far from Jake's gun. A lot of officers, instead of living under canvas, would have commandeered a house and made themselves comfortable there. That would have been all right with Featherston; what point to being an officer if you couldn't take advantage of it? But Stuart, despite his fancy dinners and such, still affected a pose as just another artilleryman—except when he needed something from his father. The hypocrisy irked Jake.

He heard a low murmur of voices from beyond the battery commander's tent. He frowned. What was going on back there? The voices grew quiet as he approached. He found Nero and Perseus, along with the Negro laborers from the rest of the guns in the battery and even with Captain Stuart's servant Pompey, gathered in a circle around a tiny fire. Walls all around made it impossible for any Yankee to spot from the ground; they could smother it in an instant if aeroplanes came over.

Near the fire lay a pair of dice and some money. "Evenin', Sergeant," Pompey said in his mincing voice when he recognized Jake. "We is just spreadin' the wealth around, you might say." He grinned. His teeth were very white in his dark face.

"Yeah, well, I done spread my wealth around lately," Featherston said. Perseus and Nero laughed. They'd heard him grouse about losing his shirt with that full house. When Pompey reached for the dice, Jake shrugged and left.

His own gun crew had their poker game going strong. He watched for a while, then pulled out what money he had left and sat in with them. He won a couple of little hands, lost a couple, then lost with a flush to a full house. That cost him a big piece of the anemic bankroll he'd brought to the game. He quit in disgust and went off to wrap himself in his blanket.

Some time in the middle of the night, somebody gently shook him awake. He looked up to find Perseus squatting beside his bedroll. In a voice not much above a whisper, the laborer said, "We ain't actin' like niggers no more, Marse Jake. Figured I'd tell you, on account of you know we don't got to. You want to be careful fo' a while, is all I got to say." He slipped away.

Featherston looked around, not altogether sure he hadn't been dreaming. He didn't see Perseus. He didn't hear anything. He rolled over and went back to sleep.

A little before dawn, Captain Stuart's angry voice woke him: "Pompey? Where the hell are you, Pompey? I call you, you bring your black ass over here and find out what I want, do you hear me? Pompey!"

Stuart's shouts went on and on. Wherever Pompey was, he wasn't coming when called. And then Michael Scott hurried up to Jake, a worried look on his face. "Sarge, you seen Nero or Perseus? Don't know where they're at, but they sure as hell ain't where they're supposed to be."

"Jesus," Featherston said, bouncing to his feet. "It wasn't a dream. Sure as hell it wasn't." Scott stared at him, having no idea what he meant. He wasn't altogether sure himself. One thing seemed clear: trouble was brewing.

The policeman at the corner of Beaufain and Meeting Street—a pudgy, white-mustached fellow who might have fought in the War of Secession—threw up his right hand, halting north-south traffic on Meeting so trucks and wagons on Beaufain could continue making their way to and from the Charleston railroad lines and harbor.

Anne Colleton snarled something distinctly unladylike and stomped on the brakes of her Vauxhall Prince Henry. The motorcar groaned and squeaked to a stop, its radiator grill projecting slightly out onto Beaufain. She'd bought the Vauxhall because it could go fast, not for its ability to stop in a hurry. The brakes were a good deal weaker than the sixty-horsepower engine.

A man in a battered Ford was stopped alongside her. He gave her a look halfway between curious and rude. She'd long since grown used, if not resigned, to that look. Even in the USA, lady automobilists were a small minority. In the more conservative Confederacy, they were rare. She smiled back at the man. He might have thought it a sweet smile . . . if he were an imbecile.

Rather nervously, he tipped his straw hat. "Sure you know what you're doing in the car"—he proved himself a Charleston native by pronouncing it *cyar*—"little lady? Wouldn't you rather have a chauffeur drive you around?"

Anne smiled again, even more savagely than before. "I had to fire my last two chauffeurs," she answered. "They went too slow to suit me."

The policeman halted traffic on Beaufain and let the waiting vehicles on Meeting Street move. Anne put the potent Vauxhall—with three times the power of the Ford next to it—through its paces. She left the Ford's driver choking on her exhaust.

She was almost sorry the Charleston Hotel lay only a couple of blocks south of Beaufain. The sensation of speed in the Vauxhall exhilarated her far more than the same speed would have in a train. Here she was the engineer, her foot on the throttle. *Freedom,* she thought.

A pair of Negro servants came dashing out from under the columned portico of the hotel. One of them handed her down to the sidewalk. Then both of them grabbed her suitcases and followed her inside. The doorman, a fat colored fellow in a getup that made him look like a Revolutionary soldier, threw wide the door to allow the procession to enter.

Electric fans mounted on the ceiling stirred the air without cooling it. Anne strode up to the desk clerk, gave her name, and said, "I believe you have the Presidential Suite reserved for me."

"Uh, Miss Colleton, I'm uh, very sorry, ma'am," the clerk said, plainly alarmed at having to give her bad news, "but we've, uh, had to move you to the Beauregard Suite on the third floor."

She froze him with a glance. "Oh? And why is that?" Her voice was low, calm, reasonable . . . dangerous.

"Because, ma'am, President Wilson's in the Presidential Suite," he blurted.

"Oh," she said again. Her laugh, much to the unhappy clerk's relief, held acquiescence. "Nothing you can do about that, I suppose. I didn't know he was going to be in Charleston."

"Yes, ma'am," the clerk said. "He's come down to launch the *Fort Sumter*—you know, the new cruiser that just got built. That's tomorrow. Tonight there's a reception and dance here. In fact . . ." He turned back to the rectangular array of message slots behind the registration desk and pulled out a cream-colored envelope. "You have an invitation here. When Mr. Wilson's private secretary learned who had been booked into the Presidential Suite before him, he made sure to give you one."

"I should hope so," Anne said, conscious of her position in South Carolina. Then she turned the warmth up on her smile. "That *was* thoughtful. The Beauregard Suite, you say. It will do."

After she'd ridden upstairs in the lift and tipped the servants carrying her bags, she sat down on the bed and laughed till tears rolled down her cheeks. The Charleston Hotel was modern enough to boast telephones in its fancy suites, the Beauregard among them. She made a call. "Roger?" she said when the connection was established. "I'm afraid I won't be able to see you tonight after all . . . Yes, I'm seeing someone else . . . Who? . . . Why should I tell you? . . . Oh, all right, I will—it's President Wilson."

That produced a good fifteen-second silence on the other end of the line. Then Roger Kimball said, "I hope you're not going to see as much of him as you were going to see of me."

Though the submariner couldn't see her, she nodded approvingly. He had gall. She admired that. "How can I be sure?" she said. "He hasn't asked me." That made Kimball sputter, as she'd hoped. She went on, "I will see you tomorrow—unless the president sweeps me off my feet."

Kimball chuckled. "Or you sweep him off his. But he's a long ways from young. Two nights running'd probably be tough for him. Tomorrow, then."

"He *does* have gall," Anne murmured after she'd hung up. She pondered her luggage. She'd brought clothes for going out with a young, none-too-wealthy naval officer, as well as some frilly, silky things for more private moments with him. What did she have that was suitable for dinner with the President of the Confederate States of America?

She went through the dresses she had with her. When she came to the summer-weight rose floral voile, she smiled. The full, pleated skirt would flow nicely around her legs as she moved, and the laced bodice over the white voile chemisette might draw the eye even of a president no longer young. The dress was wrinkled from its time in the suitcase. She grabbed for the bell pull by the bed. A maid knocked at the door less than a minute later. She gave the colored woman the dress for pressing.

As she'd been sure it would, it came back in plenty of time for the dinner, which, the invitation said, was to begin at eight o'clock. She had expected to have dined earlier and to be engaged in other things by then, but what you expected and what you got weren't always the same.

Like the Presidential Suite, the Beauregard Suite had not only cold but also hot running water. Anne ran the bathtub full and washed away the dust and grime of the trip from Marshlands down to Charleston. She knew she would start perspiring again as soon as she stepped out of the tub, but no one could do anything about that, not in South Carolina. She was glad she wore her hair short and straight, so the bath did not badly disarrange it.

She went downstairs about half past seven. As she'd expected, a crowd of rich and prominent South Carolinians had already gathered outside the doors of the banquet hall; a couple of Negro attendants with almost the presence of Scipio made sure those doors did not open prematurely.

Being a rich and prominent South Carolinian herself, Anne Colleton knew a good many of the people there. Being younger, more attractive, and more female than most of them, she had as much company as she wanted, and perhaps rather more. She saw a couple of wives whose husbands had abandoned them to talk to her sending imperfectly friendly looks in her direction. She sent back the same sort of carnivorous smiles she'd given the fool in the Ford.

They pride themselves on being useless, she thought. *They don't know anything, and they don't want to know anything. If you asked one of them to drive a motorcar, she'd tell you how unladylike it was, and how she had a chauffeur to take her everywhere she wanted to go. Old-fashioned, boring frumps.* She wondered what they would have made of the exhibition of modern art she'd organized. Her lips pulled back in even more contempt. As if any of them could have brought off a show like that!

The women's stares turned even more poisonous when, after opening the doors, the attendants began escorting people to their seats. Not only was she placed at the president's table, but right across from him. "We were told to put you here, ma'am," her Negro guide said, "to make amends for Mr. Wilson taking your room away from you." He pulled out her chair so she could sit down.

Woodrow Wilson strode in, long and lean, at exactly eight o'clock. Everyone stood to honor him. He had something less than the almost demoniac energy of Theodore Roosevelt; you could not imagine him leading a charge across no-man's-land, as you would with the Yankee Kaiser. His appeal was more to the intellect, and he gave the impression of having that and to spare.

Which was not to say he could not be charming in his own way. Smiling across the table at Anne, he said, "I do hope you will forgive me for so rudely dispossessing you this afternoon, Miss Colleton."

"Quite all right. I feel I'm doing my patriotic duty by moving, Your Excellency," Anne answered. Out of the corner of her eye, she saw she was getting more looks from people who didn't know exactly who she was. Down deep where it didn't show, she grinned. President Wilson had known who she was long before he'd taken the suite away from her. He'd visited Marshlands, after all. And Anne would have been astonished if more than half a dozen men in the banquet hall had contributed more money to Wilson's election campaign back in 1909 than she had. Her brothers had laughed at her then, but she thought the investment had paid off well.

No sooner had the thought of Tom and Jacob crossed her mind than Wilson said, "I understand one of your gallant brothers was wounded this summer in a U.S. attack."

"He was gassed, yes," Anne said shortly. Having Jacob back at Marshlands in such a state would have been hard enough. Having him back at Marshlands in such a state and drugged on morphia and drunk when he wasn't drugged (and sometimes when he was) and fornicating his way through the colored wenches was ten times worse. That Cherry was getting so stuck up, it was as if she thought herself the rightful mistress of Marshlands.

At her anger, Wilson's narrow, deeply lined face hardened. "It is because the United States, like the Huns across the sea with whom they are allied, employ such vile and unrestrained means of waging war that they and their arrogant pretensions must be checked."

Down the table, a plump man with a red face that had grown redder with each glass of wine he'd poured down said loudly, "The damnyankees need whipping on account of they're damnyankees. Once you've gone and said that, what more needs saying?"

Anne nodded emphatic agreement. But Woodrow Wilson shook his head. "I would share this continent with them if I could," he said. "If tomorrow they would agree to a peace based on the *status quo ante bellum* with us and our brave Canadian comrades, I would accept on the instant. Then this half of the world would be at peace, and we could work toward peace as well between our allies on the one hand and Germany and Austria-Hungary on the other."

"They won't agree to any such thing, though," Anne said. "They tried to keep us from becoming a nation in the first place and they still think we belong to them by rights. If they can snuff us out, they will. We can't let them."

"Unfortunately, Miss Colleton, I fear you are correct," the president said sadly. "And so we have no choice but to continue the struggle, confident that God and justice are on our side. I came down to South Carolina to celebrate our production of another tool toward our ultimate triumph." He still seemed unhappy about such duty, and paused, shifting from the political to the personal: "But you undoubtedly know why I am here. What brings *you* to Charleston? Business or pleasure?"

He did not say that slightingly, as many a man might have: he knew she was a businesswoman in her own right. "Pleasure," she answered. It was, at the moment, pleasure she was forgoing for the sake of the dinner, but President Wilson did not need to know about that.

Colored waiters cleared away dishes. Wilson got up and made a brief speech, one line of which stuck in Anne's memory: "There is one choice we cannot make, we are incapable of making: we will not choose the path of submission and suffer the most sacred rights of our nation and our people to be ignored or violated." It got, she thought, less applause than it deserved.

Colored musicians began playing a sprightly waltz. Couples drifted out onto the dance floor. Anne succeeded in dismaying the old frumps once more, for President Wilson asked her for the first dance. He had been a widower for more than twenty years, but must have had a good deal of practice at affairs like this, for he was strong and sure; Anne enjoyed dancing with him. She thought he took pleasure in it, too, and wondered if he was interested in something more than dancing.

Whether he was or not, she wasn't, despite the way she'd teased Roger Kimball. If you slept with a man of such power, he might want to go to bed with you again. Anne flattered herself that, if she slept with Woodrow Wilson, he *would* want to go to bed with her again. But if she slept with him, he would never take her seriously again. To her, that was more important.

When the music ended, she said, "Win the war, Your Excellency. Whatever it takes, win it."

"I have done my utmost, Miss Colleton, and shall go on doing my utmost till next March," he answered. "After that, God willing, it will be in the capable hands of Vice President Semmes."

"God willing," Anne agreed. She suspected Gabriel Semmes might prosecute the war with more vigor than Wilson had done. For that matter, Semmes' principal opponent in the November elections, Doroteo Arango, would probably prosecute the war with more vigor than Wilson had done: Arango was a young fire-eater if ever there was one. But Arango, she thought, had almost no chance of winning; the Radical Liberals, who had nominated him, would sweep Sonora, Chihuahua, and Cuba, and might take Texas, too, but she doubted they'd have much luck farther north and east.

Wilson said, "Will you be at the launching tomorrow, Miss Colleton? If you would like to come, see my secretary for an invitation in the morning."

"I may do that. Thank you, Your Excellency," Anne said. Going down to the harbor would make meeting Roger Kimball all the more convenient.

The music started up again. Three gray-haired men with the look of financiers almost got into a football scrimmage with one another, inviting her to dance. They'd dutifully waltzed the first round with their gray-haired wives, and now, obviously, had decided they were entitled to some fun.

Anne danced with each of them in turn. She stayed on the floor till a little past eleven, then went to bed. When she checked with the front desk the next morning, she discovered Wilson's secretary had given her an invitation to the launching ceremony even without her asking for it. She put it into her handbag, then went back to her room, telephoned Roger Kimball, and arranged to meet him at the Firemark on State Street, not far from the harbor.

The launch of the *Fort Sumter* disappointed her for a couple of reasons. For one, even with the pass, she couldn't get close enough for a good view of President Wilson smashing a bottle of champagne against the cruiser's bow. And, for another, Wilson, a staunch temperance man, made it plain in his speech that the champagne hadn't really been champagne, but soda water instead. Anne heartily approved of overturning some traditions, but that wasn't one of them.

Roger Kimball was waiting under the Firemark—a seal dating back to the seventeenth century showing that the building on which it was affixed carried fire insurance—when Anne drove up in her Vauxhall. The submariner looked avidly at her, and even more so at her motorcar. "May I drive it?" he asked.

She judged he would sulk and pout unless she indulged him, so she said yes and slid over into the passenger seat. Kimball bounded into the automobile and roared up and down the streets of Charleston with a panache that sometimes bordered on the suicidal. Anne prided herself as a bold driver, but after a few hairsbreadth escapes realized she had to yield the palm to her companion.

"Try not to put both of us through the windscreen," she said with some asperity as Kimball screeched to a stop bare inches from a Negro fisherman selling shrimp out of a basket. The Negro jumped back from the Vauxhall, but spilled no seafood.

After a moment, he realized he wouldn't be crushed after all. Smiling at the Navy man in his dashing whites and at his pretty companion, the fisherman held out the basket and gave forth with his sales call:

"Ro-ro swimp!
Ro-ro swimp!
Roro-ro-ro-ro swimp!
Coma and git yo' ro-ro swimp!"

Kimball took him at his word, jumping out of the automobile and buying a couple of pounds of them. The motorcar rested on a slight downgrade; Anne had to reach out a leg and stamp on the none-too-potent brake to keep the Vauxhall from getting the fisherman after all, and Kimball with him.

"What *are* you doing?" she demanded when the submariner, his hands full of crustaceans, got back into the motorcar.

Nothing fazed him. He dropped the shrimp, a couple of them still feebly flailing little legs, on the seat between them. "I know a little place where they'll cook the shrimp or the fish if you bring it in. Can't be beat." He smacked his lips, then added, "And it's only a couple of blocks from a hotel that never heard of house detectives."

"And how do you know that?" she asked.

"How many girls have I brought there before you, do you mean?" he returned. "Does it matter? If we aren't doing this for fun, why are we doing it?"

To that, she had no answer. Kimball had never claimed to offer more than amusement, or to want more than that from her. Under those circumstances, wondering about others before her was foolish. She hadn't been a virgin there in the Pullman car on the way to New Orleans, either. She nodded and said, "Let's go."

The restaurant was in the far northwest of Charleston, well away from the fancy part of the city. It was, in fact, much closer to one of the Negro districts, which began only a few blocks away. The proprietor, who looked as if he might have been a quadroon passing for white, greeted Roger Kimball as an old friend. If he was used to seeing the submariner in variegated company, he gave no sign of it.

What he did with those little shrimp made the visit worthwhile. Cooked with rice and okra and chopped bacon and some spices he coyly refused to name, they made a better meal than Anne had had with President Wilson the night before. She didn't tell him that, assuming he wouldn't have believed her. She did give him as much praise as she thought he could accept. He bowed low when she left on Kimball's arm. The Navy man looked bemused, remarking, "He's never done that before."

He handed Anne into the Vauxhall, then drove to the hotel, which was even closer to the Negro section of town than the restaurant had been. As if to impress on her that it was a tough district, he took the key out of the ignition and gave it to her, a precaution with which she seldom bothered.

As he'd predicted, the desk clerk placidly nodded when Kimball signed the registry, *Mr. and Mrs. Jefferson Davis*. A night's rent was a night's rent. The second-story room was small but surprisingly clean. Kimball locked the door behind him, lighted the kerosene lamp, and then turned to Anne with a grin. "What are we waiting for?"

"Not a thing." She smiled back. From a lot of men—from most men—such brashness would have put her off, but it was what drew her to Roger Kimball. She stepped forward into his arms. He squeezed her to him, tilted her chin up, and delivered an authoritative kiss.

For him to get out of his uniform, a little later, was the work of a few moments. Once naked, he saluted her without using his hands. He took his time about undressing her, pausing to kiss and caress each new bit of flesh revealed. She sighed with relief when, after detaching her stockings from their garters and sliding them down her legs, he finally peeled her out of her steel-stiffened corset.

"You men are so lucky not to have to wear those things," she said, "especially in weather like this."

He set his hand on her sweaty belly, then let it stray lower. Suddenly impatient, she caught his shoulders and pulled him onto her. He rode her hard, which was just what she wanted. When they were through, he rubbed at his back. "You clawed me good there," he said, sitting up.

"I hope it was good," Anne answered, sated and greedy at the same time. The room had no sink, but did have a pitcher and a bowl. She used some water to wash him off, then took him in her mouth. She wanted him hard again. As soon as he was, she straddled him and rode him as ferociously as he'd taken her, until she quivered again and again and he groaned beneath her as if in pain rather than ecstasy.

Afterwards, they lay side by side on the bed, too spent to move, neither of them much wanting to get back into stifling clothes when being naked felt so much better. Roger Kimball fell asleep first. Anne was going to tease him about it, but discovered she was yawning, too. She dozed off a few minutes later.

Sometime in the middle of the night—the lamp had burned out, leaving the hotel room very dark—she woke up, needing to use the chamber pot. Her motion woke Kimball, and they made love again, lazily this time, she on her side facing away from him, barely touching save at one sweet place in the warm, muggy night.

When Anne woke again, dawn was beginning to leak through the venetian blinds over the window. But the light was not what roused her. From out in the street came a terrific racket of shouts and crashes and, after a moment, gunshots.

Roger Kimball sat bolt upright. Unclothed though he remained, he was suddenly and obviously a military man, not a lover. "What the devil . . . ?" he said, his voice sharp as a cracking whip.

Right under the window, a black man, without intending to, gave him his answer: "To de barricades!" the fellow yelled. "De revolution comin'!"

Anne and Kimball stared at each other. "Oh, Lord," they said together.

Below them, the cry grew louder and came from more and more throats, till it seemed to fill the whole world: "De revolution! De revolution comin'!"

Scipio was talking with one of the cooks in the Marshlands kitchen when the woman's scream came from upstairs. "Good God in heaven, what can that be?" the butler exclaimed. Since he was talking as an extension of the estate rather than in his own person, he used the elegant formal English he would have employed when addressing Anne Colleton or some white guest at the mansion.

"Dunno, but I gwine find out," the cook said, and, ignoring the fine points of the pecan-and-sweet-potato pie about which Scipio had been trying to instruct him, ran up toward the front of the house.

Scipio followed. He had no sooner reached the foot of the stairs than another scream rang out, this one louder than before. "No! Godalmighty, no!" the woman up there wailed.

"Who dat?" the cook demanded.

"I believe that is Cherry," Scipio replied. Had it not been undignified to do so in front of the cook, he would have scratched his head. The second scream and the wail had both come from Jacob Colleton's room—so, presumably, had the first. But that made no sense. Cherry had gone up to Jacob's room a great many times. Scipio didn't know exactly what she and the mistress' gassed brother did behind that closed door, but he did know she'd always kept quiet about it till now.

The closed door opened, then slammed shut. Cherry came running out. Now the cook said "Godalmighty!" in a tone half shock, half admiration: she was naked and, though she clutched her dress to her, quite a lot of her remained on display.

She dashed down the stairs, moaning, "Dat debbil! Dat horrible debbil! What he try an' make me do!" She ran past Scipio and the cook, both of whom stared even more, for she was not covered at all from behind. She opened the front door and ran outside, out toward the fields if the direction from which her cries came was any indication.

"Damn white folks," the cook muttered, glaring up toward the closed door from which Cherry had emerged.

A moment later, the door opened again. Jacob Colleton wheeled himself out to the banister. "Come up here, Scipio," he croaked.

Scipio obeyed, as he had obeyed white men and women every day of his life. "How may I help you, sir?" he asked, his voice the polite, attentive, meaningless counterpart to the mask of service stretched across his face.

Instead of answering at once, Jacob Colleton wheeled back into his room, motioning for Scipio to follow him. Once they were inside, Colleton demanded, "What's the matter with that wench? Has she gone mad?"

"Sir, I would not have the faintest idea," Scipio answered stiffly.

"Oh, don't act stupid with me," Colleton said, anger bubbling in his hoarse whisper. "You know we don't play caroms up here. We were about to screw, not to put too fine a point on it, the same way we've screwed two dozen times before this, when all of a sudden she went tearing out of here as if—I don't know as if what. I haven't found anything she doesn't do—and like doing, too, by God."

He panted, trying to catch his breath after such a long speech. To Scipio's own surprise, he believed Colleton. He knew bewilderment when he saw and heard it. What was wrong with Cherry, then? *Had* she gone round the bend?

Scipio glanced out the window toward the fields. Sure enough, there stood Cherry, still holding the dress in front of her, haranguing a swelling group of field hands. Scipio couldn't hear what she was saying, but he recognized the pose from meetings of the Reds in Cassius' cottage.

And— Scipio stiffened. Here came a good many Negroes with rifles in their hands. All at once, everything came clear. This was the moment Cassius and Island and Cherry and the rest had been talking about for so long. Jacob

Colleton hadn't done anything out of the ordinary with or to Cherry . . . but she was saying he had, to bring doubters over to the cause.

Whatever Colleton had or hadn't done with Cherry, he had seen Scipio's attention focus on what was happening outside. Coughing and swearing in rasping gasps, he had a look for himself. And then, most abruptly, he reminded Scipio he had been a soldier, and a good one: he had the Tredegar down off the wall and a clip in it before the butler could blink. He pointed it straight at Scipio's head.

Scipio stared down the barrel. It was black as midnight in there, and looked about a foot wide to his frightened gaze. He could smell gun oil. "Get out of here, boy," Colleton said, his bubbling whisper making the words all the more deadly cold. "You niggers want to play games, I'll show you how it's done up at the front." He was smiling. Scipio hadn't seen him so happy since he'd been gassed. The rifle barrel twitched toward the doorway. "Git!"

Scipio fled, not just out the door but down the stairs. Jacob Colleton slammed the door behind him, and locked it. The first shot from upstairs rang out when Scipio got to the front door, which Cherry hadn't closed after her.

He reached the doorway just in time to watch Island's head explode into red mist. The revolutionary took half a step, then fell on what was left of his face. The rifle he'd been carrying bounced on the ground beside him.

"Git *down*!" Cassius yelled as another rifle shot barked and another Red went down, probably for good. Some of the armed Negroes listened to the hunter. Some just started banging away at Jacob Colleton's window. The racket was like the end of the world. Then Colleton fired again, and another black man sprawled twitching in the grass. By then, Cassius had taken cover behind a buggy. A *bang!* from upstairs and yet another Red went down. Scipio remembered what Colleton had said about the game of war. He was getting another chance to play, sure enough, and he still remembered how.

"Rush de house!" Cassius shouted. "I cover you." His men—and there could be no possible doubt they were *his* men—did as he ordered. Colleton knocked down another of them, but Cassius was shooting at him, and Cassius was no mean shot, either. Three barefoot Negroes in gray homespun dashed past Scipio up the stairs.

They pounded on the door to Jacob Colleton's room with their rifle butts. One fell back with a groan, shot from inside the room. But the door flew open. More shots rang out, and then a black man's whoop of triumph: "Dat white debbil, he done fo'!"

Cassius came walking up to Marshlands, rifle in his hand. He shouted for everyone to get out, waited half a minute, shouted again, and then went inside. "Wish dat damn Frenchman still have he ugly paintings here," he remarked to Scipio. "I do dis wid dey." He struck a match and touched it to a gauzy curtain. Flames raced up it, reached the wall above the window, and caught there. Grinning, Cassius hurried back outside, catching Scipio by the arm and hustling him along.

Scipio stared in through the window at the growing fire, feeling a pang for beauty destroyed no matter upon how much suffering it rested. *The bourgeois in you,* Cassius would have said. "You got to do dat, Cass?" he asked.

"Got to," Cassius said firmly. "Gwine burn it all, Kip. De revolution *here*."

About the Author

Harry Turtledove was born in Los Angeles in 1949. After flunking out of Caltech, he earned a Ph.D. in Byzantine history from UCLA. He has taught ancient and medieval history at UCLA, Cal State Fullerton, and Cal State L.A., and he has published a translation of a ninth-century Byzantine chronicle, as well as several scholarly articles. He is also a Hugo Award–winning and critically acclaimed full-time writer of science fiction and fantasy. His alternate history works have included several short stories and the novels *A World of Difference*, *The Guns of the South* (a speculative novel of the Civil War), and the *Worldwar* tetralogy that began in 1994 with *Worldwar: In the Balance*. Following on the heels of *How Few Remain*, *The Great War: American Front* is the first volume of Turtledove's alternate-history tetralogy of the Great War.

He is married to fellow novelist Laura Frankos. They have three daughters: Alison, Rachel, and Rebecca.